First Person Stories

First Person Stories

Jay Dubya

www.bookstandpublishing.com

Published by
Bookstand Publishing
Pasadena, CA 91101
4353_6

ISBN 978-1-63498-248-1

Other Books by Jay Dubya

Adult Fiction

Black Leather and Blue Denim, A '50s Novel
Frat' Brats, A '60s Novel
Ron Coyote, Man of La Mangia
So Ya' Wanna' Be A Teacher
Pieces of Eight
Pieces of Eight, Part II
Pieces of Eight, Part III
Pieces of Eight, Part IV
The Wholly Book of Genesis
The Wholly Book of Exodus
The Wholly Book of Doo-Doo-Rot-on-Me
Thirteen Sick Tasteless Classics
Thirteen Sick Tasteless Classics, Part II
Thirteen Sick Tasteless Classics, Part III
Thirteen Sick Tasteless Classics, Part IV
Thirteen Sick Tasteless Classics, Part V
Nine New Novellas
Nine New Novellas, Part II
Nine New Novellas, Part III
Nine New Novellas, Part IV
Mauled Maimed Mangled Mutilated Mythology
Fractured Frazzled Folk Fables and Fairy Farces
FFFF & FF, Part II
One Baker's Dozen
Two Baker's Dozen
RAM: Random Articles and Manuscripts
Snake Eyes and Boxcars
Snake Eyes and Boxcars, Part II
Shakespeare: Slammed, Smeared, Savaged and Slaughtered
Shakespeare: S, S, S and S, Part II
O. Henry: Obscenely and Outrageously Obliterated
Twain: Tattered, Trounced, Tortured and Traumatized
London: Lashed, Lacerated, Lampooned and Lambasted
Poe: Pelted, Pounded, Pummeled and Pulverized
Suite 16
Time Travel Tales
UFO: Utterly Fantastic Occurrences

Young Adult Fantasy Novels

CONTENTS

Introduction

First Person Stories is a collection of forty-one writings, twenty-four being fictional tales and seventeen being of the non-fiction variety. Some of the works are writings taken from other already published Jay Dubya fiction and non-fiction books.

The First-Person writing technique is particularly difficult in literary expression, especially when writing fiction, because the author must continually use the pronouns "I, me, my and mine" over and over, and there's always a danger of communicating a sense of monotony and boredom to the reader. This is why most fiction is written in the third person, the author utilizing the more functional pronouns "he, she, you, they and we."

Three types of non-fiction writing represented in *First Person Stories* are autobiography, humor and the essay point of view structure, which is often used in newspaper journalism and always found on the publication's editorial page.

In Memory of William "Billy" Burns, (1967-2009)

FICTION

"Growing Young"

December 7th, 2014 had become my own personal self-inflicted *Pearl Harbor Day*. I recollect that *that* particular Sunday morning started-out quite routine and nondescript. After waking-up early, shaving, dressing, and then hastily drinking a tall glass of orange juice, I promptly left my Hammonton, New Jersey Pratt Street humble ranch home, entered my green *2012 Subaru Outback* and mechanically drove four blocks to St. Mary of Mt. Carmel Church on Third and French Street to attend 9 a.m. Mass, where each and every Sunday I predictably sit isolated and self-exiled in the next-to-last right-side pew nearest the center aisle.

After the perfunctory religious service was finished, I silently departed the all-too-familiar building, re-entered my *Outback* in the church parking lot and drove my dependable automobile twelve miles west on Route 30 toward Berlin to peacefully enjoy a delicious breakfast in complete anonymity. Being introverted as is my shy demeanor, I impatiently sat alone among the singular patrons at the Berlin Diner's counter and soon ordered a Belgian waffle topped with bananas, walnuts and an abundance of whipped cream.

"Where ya' from Stranger?" the middle-aged brunette waitress asked, cheerfully initiating a casual conversation. "You're new in here! Ya' don't live in Berlin, I do believe."

"You're right about *that* observation!" I politely answered. "I'm from Hammonton."

"What's wrong with the Silver Coin Diner?" the chatty waitress quickly asked. "They have great food there too, ya' know. My sister-in-law is a hostess at that diner and says the tips are terrific."

"Well," I uncomfortably replied, shifting my level position upon my elevated seat, "I felt I needed a change in venue this morning so I'm exploring a little bit out of my regular territory. Confidentially, I have to buy some heater filters over at the local *Home Depot*. I change the buggers twice a year, once in April for my summer air-conditioning and then once again in October for the heating system as our nemesis Old Man Winter approaches South Jersey on the yearly calendar. It's quite an annual ritual for me!"

"That's right!" the attractive waitress verified with a forced smile. "You don't have a *Home Depot* over in Hammonton. Your town only has a smaller-type *Wal*Mart* store. The huge Berlin box-store you're gonna' patronize certainly has a much better selection of hardware and home products! But be careful Mr.! It's December 7th, *Pearl Harbor Day*. Don't be jinxed and have your own private 'Day of Infamy'!"

"I promise not to buy any Japanese heater filters!" I quipped.

The nosy customer seated two stools down had been eavesdropping on *our* courteous, non-flirtatious dialogue. Hearing the flash-point words "Pearl Harbor," the old geezer felt obligated to contribute what he valued as being somewhat significant to the general diner verbal exchange.

"After Pearl Harbor," the codger awkwardly interrupted, "my pop was drafted into the Army at age thirty-six, since there was a basic shortage of manpower to go up against Hitler and his evil minions. Pop served in France, Germany, Luxembourg, Holland and Belgium before returning back to the States. My ears got me interested in *your* discussion when you had mentioned Belgian waffle. It made me think of my pop stationed in Belgium."

"Did your dad bring home any special trophies or interesting souvenirs from *World War II?*" I inquired, attempting to exhibit a degree of social decorum. "A French or Dutch wife perhaps! Maybe some Brussels sprouts!" I innocently joked, contrary to my usual introspective nature.

"Yes," the elderly fellow remarked, ignoring my feeble attempt at humor before taking another sip of hot coffee. "Pop found a nifty bombshell casing and had it engraved with the names of all the cities, towns, villages and countries he had visited on his three-year European tour of duty. The finished mortar shell was a beautiful metallic piece that Mom used as a flower vase in the family den."

After consuming my delectable Belgian waffle, side-of-bacon and coffee breakfast, I deposited a three-dollar tip on the diner's front serving counter, quietly said "Goodbye" to both the 'affable waitress' and the garrulous 'old curmudgeon', paid my breakfast bill at the cashier and then exited the then semi-crowded Berlin Diner. I ambled to the back lot, climbed into my green *Subaru*, fired-up the engine and headed west on *Route 30* in the direction of the Berlin Shopping Center and the popular *Home Depot* store.

'This superficial task should only take about fifteen minutes,' I reckoned as my left foot stepped upon and released the car's emergency brake. 'In another hour I'll be replacing the 16 inches x 25 inch x 1 inch gas heater filter down in my cellar. But I gotta' remember to buy a large *Snickers* candy bar on my way out!'

After locking the doors of my *Outback*, I sauntered into the Berlin *Home Depot*, quickly located the appropriate exact-size air filters in a side aisle, and when I bent-down to grab the two sought-after items, a

4

heavy cardboard merchandise box fell from the top overhead shelf. The dangerous object grazed the right side of my scalp and ears and then violently crashed into my right arm and chest, the simultaneous impacts immediately knocking me to the tiled floor in an unconscious state.

In retrospect, it was *that* specific event that placed my long-kept longevity secret in jeopardy of having public disclosure and scrutiny. The next thing I remember, I was lying in a hospital bed experiencing heightened agony and discomfort, and next a pleasant blonde-haired nurse was informing me that the actual date was Monday, December 29th and then disclosing that I had been surviving in a deep coma for over a three-week period. But truthfully, at that moment I was absolutely glad to be alive!

* * * * * * * * * * * *

That late December Monday afternoon I had fully awoken from my three-week-long unconscious state and my drowsy pupils immediately noticed the distinguishable presence of a vertical IV stand and a side catheter/urine bag. Instantly I was aware that I had been occupying a hospital bed.

"Where am I? Who are you? What the heck happened" I neurotically asked the nurse and doctor peering-down at me while standing next to my bed.

"I'm Dr. Stephen Arena and this is Nurse Linda Rizzotte," the physician professionally introduced himself and his assistant. "I'm the surgeon who had operated on you. You had quite a near-death experience at the Berlin *Home Depot,* I must admit. If that enormous box had hit you squarely on the head, I don't think we'd be having this informal conversation right now!"

"What hospital is this?" I requested knowing. "It looks pretty modern and new."

"You're in Room 311 at Virtua Hospital, Route 73 in Voorhees," Nurse Rizzotte related with a somber expression exhibited upon her face. "The Berlin Rescue Squad transported you here soon after your near-tragic *Home Depot* accident."

Everything seemed fuzzy and nebulous at that exact moment, so my new medical companions decided to prattle about the harsh weather, about the *Philadelphia Eagles* football team and about the impending winter snowstorm before returning to their review of my identity and my improving condition. The pair suggested that they were happy to note that I apparently was not suffering from either amnesia or any severe memory loss.

"You were fairly easy to identify from your New Jersey driver's license and from your wallet's credit cards," stern-faced Dr. Arena indicated. "But one aspect of the entire matter seriously concerns me. Your license amazingly shows that your birthdate was July 2nd, 1899. Is that a misprint that needs to be changed and rectified? The date seems to defy basic reality!"

"That would make you approximately 115 years old!" Nurse Linda Rizzotte exclaimed and then disbelievingly shook her head from side-to-side. "The oldest man still living in the United States is...."

"Reportedly 112 years old," Dr. Stephen Arena finished and objectively reported, "and that aged fellow happens to be residing in New York. As a matter of fact, I had read a fascinating magazine article about him last week. The guy was born in Spain and then later emigrated to the U.S."

"And not that it's so important, but we've also noticed that you've never donated blood to the American Red Cross," Nurse Rizzotte stated. "Is there something especially wrong with your blood? For example, do you have Hepatitis C antibodies or any other irregularity like that?"

Those startling perceptive commentaries had made me become rather anxious and nervous. I feared that my coveted long-held secret might be harmfully revealed and exposed. I worried that my former orderly human existence was suddenly becoming unraveled and disheveled, all because of the unfortunate *Home Depot* incident I had experienced. Momentarily I had become lost for words. Then after careful neurotic deliberation, I uttered what constituted a boldface lie which I orally conveyed in a depressed state of mind. "I've always had a fear of needles. Yes, fear of needles has kept me from giving blood over the years!"

"As you probably know," the medical doctor diplomatically explained, sensing that I had been clumsily prevaricating, "your blood type is O Positive. O negative is often referred to as 'the Universal Donor'. Because of the complicated operations we had to perform on you," Dr. Arena hesitated and then resumed his incisive narrative, "we had to administer four units of RH O Positive blood during the lengthy six-hour O.R. procedures, all due to your critical loss of plasma."

"Over the years," I shakily declared from my sitting semi-erect hospital bed position, "I've become an unrecognized authority on blood," I almost guiltily confessed. "I probably know more about the composition and properties of blood than anyone working in your sophisticated hospital labs."

I continued delivering my comprehensive explanation by citing that blood is manufactured in a person's bone marrow and that the vital body substance can be broken-down into erythrocytes, or red blood cells, leukocytes, or white blood cells, platelets, which allow for clotting and coagulating, plasma, hemoglobin and finally, into essential proteins. "Too many leukocytes, which are part of the body's immune system, could lead to leukemia, and having not enough platelets could drastically mean developing hemophilia. A healthy human body depends on just the right ratio of these indispensable and fantastically interrelated blood elements."

"Granted, you do understand plenty about the chemistry and functionality of blood," Dr. Arena complimented my conceited expertise. "Whatever caused you to be so academically enamored and intrigued about *that* highly specialized subject?"

"I suppose it all started with me seeing the 1931 black and white movie *Dracula* at the Hippodrome Theater in downtown Baltimore," I recalled and declared to my astonished listeners. "It was an impressive vampire movie, and over the decades I too have evolved into a sort of contemporary vampire myself," I im*patient*ly mentioned, obviously confusing the wits of my two-member audience. "In the original classic film starring Bela Lugosi, Dr. Van Helsing had performed blood transfusions on a patient named Lucy Weston, and that's precisely when I had organized my eccentric blood immortality theory."

"Yes, I've read Bram Stoker's novel at least a half-dozen times since high school," Nurse Linda Rizzotte contributed, "but your Lucy Weston appearing in the film version was really named Lucy Westenra in the famous *Dracula* novel."

"Wait a minute now!" a slightly irritated Dr. Arena insisted. "You're losing me by your weird account, evidently leaving-out some pertinent details. We've conducted a meticulous background check on you and I must acknowledge that we've discovered that your unique driver's license is incredibly accurate. You were indeed born in Posen, Michigan just outside of Alpena on July 2nd, 1899. Your family then moved to Baltimore around 1907. And so, remarkably," Dr. Arena cleared his throat and continued his precisely on-target commentary, "your claim about seeing the movie *Dracula* at the Hippodrome Theater in 1931 seems to jibe with our intensive background research done on you. Now for the sake of logic and sanity," the skilled surgeon suavely qualified, "please reveal how you've managed to age to a ripe 115 and still look like a rejuvenated man of fifty years. You don't have any dark age marks on your hands or any expected wrinkles on your neck and face!"

"That's totally correct!" Nurse Rizzotte concurred with her immediate superior. "Have you discovered the Fountain of Youth that Ponce de Leon had been futilely seeking?"

"Well," I reluctantly said in response, "the New Jersey Department of Motor Vehicles has for a long time been mighty suspicious about my recorded chronological age," I verbally shared. "I have to take a new written test every two years along with a thorough-and-redundant behind-the-wheel test, too. The Motor Vehicle inspectors are flabbergasted about my phenomenal mental acumen along with my extraordinary physical dexterity. As you've both learned," I deliberately hesitated and paused to gauge the doctor and the nurse's overt reactions to my seemingly peculiar statements, "I'm now probably the oldest man currently living in the United States!"

"This is one oddball story that most definitely must be published in the American Medical Association Journal," Dr. Arena instinctively determined. "Sir, you must reveal how you've managed to achieve the age of 115 without ever exhibiting any signs of being affected by the common and debilitating aging process!"

At that most critical juncture of our rather unorthodox hospital room conference, my mind and body suddenly felt weak and fatigued. Much to the frustration and consternation of Dr. Arena and Nurse Rizzotte, my weary eyes slowly shut, and next my encumbered consciousness was soon drifting-off into a rather disturbed-and-stressful dream slumber.

* * * * * * * * * * * *

On Tuesday morning at 9:30 Dr. Stephen Arena and Nurse Linda Rizzotte escorted two black-business-suit and tie gentlemen into Virtua Hospital Room 311. Earlier that morning I had been disconnected from the bothersome catheter and accompanying urine bag and my regenerated spirit possessed a degree more energy because I had finally eaten solid food for breakfast two hours before.

"These two federal government men have a distinct interest in *investigating,* or should I more discreetly say 'interviewing' you about your rather bizarre age situation," Dr. Arena candidly greeted. "May I now introduce Mr. Frank Mitchell of the Social Service Agency and Mr. Lawrence Delaney representing the Internal Revenue Service."

"Have I committed any major felony while I was hibernating in the coma?" I defensively replied. "I hope I'm not being interrogated without any lawyer being present to protect my First Amendment civil rights!"

"We promise that we won't prosecute you in any way," Mr. Mitchell pledged with a grin. "Mr. Delaney and I are only interested in ascertaining how you've successfully defeated the aging process. We hope that you'll be cooperative in answering our basic questions. Just be a little patriotic, that's all we ask. Uncle Sam is relying on your honesty, you know!"

"Well Gentlemen," I skeptically declared to my newfound federal acquaintances, "the Social Security System was set-up to compensate workers that paid into it upon reaching their retirements. But obviously," I boldly and bravely clarified, "people back in the 1940s had a life expectancy of around fifty-six years. The government was betting that few public and private sector employees would ever reach age 62 to collect their monthly entitlement checks."

"Very sagacious observation," Inspector Delaney answered. "Our Washington records reveal that in *your* working lifetime you were once a prosperous grocery store owner, a prominent fruit and produce broker and distributor, and also a partner for sixteen years in various boardwalk businesses in New Jersey, Delaware and Maryland. Isn't *that* information all true?"

"Yes," I suspiciously affirmed. "Now please tell me what your relevant concerns are in relation to me."

"Mr. Mitchell and Mr. Delaney would like to learn how you've conquered aging in order to live to be 115," Nurse Rizzotte expressed, hoping to ease the general tension that quite ostensibly dominated the room's cold atmosphere. "They've already stated with Dr. Arena and me as their witnesses that you'll suffer no federal consequences from truthfully conferring with us."

"Yes," piped-up Dr. Arena. "From the government's perspective, if all citizens lived to be 115, the Social Security Trust System along with the entire U.S. Treasury would go bankrupt within the next fifty years. I truly hope that you now fathom the government's curious examination of your incomparable longevity from 1899 up to the present."

"Why don't you begin where you had left off yesterday," constructively recommended Nurse Rizzotte. "You can start with your captivation with the 1931 movie *Dracula* and with your strange interest in blood transfusions."

"This ought to prove to be a rather 'sanguine' story," jested Mr. Frank Mitchell in an effort to allay my apprehension. "Already Sir, Mr. Delaney and I feel like we're your blood brothers."

I inhaled several deep breaths and cautiously collected my random memories and thoughts. I then steadfastly stated that from the movie *Dracula* I had considered all facets of the art and science of blood transfusions. I had conjectured the prospect of 'What if I were to have a doctor remove my blood at certain intervals over the span of a month and then give me back my younger drained blood five years later so that the technique could be repeated every half decade?' I then concluded my sensational exposition by saying, "I hypothesized that the fresh old blood from my body would favorably replenish my vital organs like my lungs, liver, pancreas and spleen and therefore, the younger five-year-old injected blood would allow me to effectively stifle the dreaded aging process?" I directly divulged.

"Astounding to say the least!" evaluated and articulated Dr. Arena. "In certain Transylvanian legends, vampires live by acquiring blood samples to drink from selected victims. In *your* particular case, you are kind of imitating a vampire by inserting your younger blood back into your body and substituting it for your tired blood every five years or so. And that's probably why you still look like you're a young and fit sixty-year-old male specimen, even though, quite obviously, you are way beyond being a deteriorating centenarian!"

"Brilliant idea!" agreed Nurse Rizzotte while addressing me as I was sitting almost vertical in my elevated hospital bed. "But you could only have adopted *this* exceptional self-transfusion practice of yours forty or forty-five years ago!"

"Why is that?" curiously asked the now-bewildered Social Security official. "Why is it only forty or forty-five years ago?"

"Because Mr. Mitchell," Dr. Arena plausibly explained, "blood can only be preserved over time by freezing it at a very low temperature, and *that* complex technology has only been recently perfected within the past half century. The blood must be stored at a minus 85 degrees after being initially frozen at a minus 122 degrees."

"How many pints' of precious blood does the average human have in his body?" wondered and asked Mr. Lawrence Delaney. "I think I remember from a high school science class that it's about six quarts, which I presume is equivalent to around…"

"Twelve pints," I estimated and voluntarily offered. "Each pint is called a 'unit', and the average male has around twelve pints constantly flowing inside his arteries, veins and capillaries, with each separate pint or unit weighing precisely 16.7 ounces."

Dr. Arena then pontificated about how donated blood is normally distributed for hospital use and next the veteran surgeon emphasized that the dark red fluid is usually broken-down into plasma, hemoglobin, red blood cells, white blood cells, proteins and platelets for necessary individual medical and O.R. requirements.

"So, *you* say that over the course of the past fifty years you've gotten blood specialists to administer your own whole blood that had been drained from your veins five years prior, and now you' maintain that this frozen older blood stimulates your immune system and revitalizes your principal vital organs too!" assessed and marveled Mr. Delaney. "That's so preposterously simple! Why hadn't anyone in the scientific or medical communities ever considered that sort of revolutionary-yet-elementary experiment? I mean, why is blood ordinarily only donated to give to other people?"

"Yes Sir," I frankly confided to the perplexed IRS Treasury Man. "I have to pay a blood expert ten thousand dollars to remove my twelve pints of blood over a month's time and then provide another ten thousand bucks to replace my blood with the new/old blood five years later. But truthfully, most of my life's savings have been spent on the very costly and illicit underground economy frozen blood storage fees. The entire enterprise can be quite expensive as you can well-imagine, but in stark reality, 'virtual immortality' does have its price! That's why this former multimillionaire must now live in a modest ranch home over in Hammonton. I've traded my wealth for longevity!"

"This whole confidential matter is entirely preposterous!" claimed and exclaimed Social Security Inspector Frank Mitchell. "Yet conversely, it's not a colossal hoax at all! Your prodigious 115 years upon this Earth verify your seemingly ludicrous assertions! According to indisputable government records, you actually *were* born in 1899! Government documents also show that *you* had been married in 1942 in Elkton, Maryland and that your wife had died in 1974. Yes, you *were* born in Michigan in 1899!" florid-faced Mr. Mitchell uncharacteristically bellowed. "That's totally unbelievable! Why that's even before Queen Victoria had died over in England! Historically speaking, it's remarkably eighteen whole years before America's involvement in World War I!"

"Exactly Mr. Mitchell!" I enthusiastically acceded, automatically nodding my still-aching head up and down. "Now I hope that you two eminent Gentlemen will accept and appreciate the legitimacy of my former blood-transfusion secret. But I can't guarantee that the explicit method I've just described will satisfactorily work for all other human beings! In summary, older blood cells get tired and worn-out, eventually not being able to perfectly duplicate themselves as thawed-out five-year younger cells can more easily do."

"And to my knowledge," Dr. Stephen Arena pertinently stressed, "no others except *you* had ever imaginatively had twelve pints of their own *whole blood* frozen and sinisterly held in the underground black market, and then systematically transfused back into their own bodies every five years or so."

"Have you had any fears living all these years guarding this miraculous knowledge you've just shared with us?" sincerely asked exasperated Treasury Department Man Mr. Lawrence Delaney. "The emotional pressure must've been quite extreme!"

"Yes," I soberly replied. "Even though I could retain my youthful vitality and appearance, I always worried about how I could avoid any accidental death in, let's say for example, an auto' collision or perhaps drowning. In fact, I haven't gone swimming in the ocean, in a lake or in a pool ever since I began receiving my essential blood transfusions back around 1968. And that's the honest-to-God truth!"

"And you almost were permanently eliminated at the Berlin *Home Depot* with that heavy large box descending upon you," astutely noted Nurse Linda Rizzotte. "That near-disaster was a close call which almost sent you directly to the cemetery."

I had little opportunity to express my deepest gratitude to Dr. Arena, to Nurse Rizzotte and to the absent Berlin Rescue Squad paramedics.

"Sir, you don't have to worry about going to a federal penitentiary for committing any red-blooded felony," Inspector Frank Mitchell told me. "And we won't implicate and investigate any of your co-conspirators either! The main reason for Mr. Delaney and me being here today is to save our country's fragile Social Security System from imminent insolvency," the very high-ranking Washington agent austerely announced. "Now here's my proposal agreement. For obvious reasons, it's both mandatory and imperative for the five of us to take an official oath to never divulge the essence of the esoteric blood-rejuvenating secret that has been discussed and described today in this New Jersey hospital room. Is this matter perfectly clear?"

"Yes!" we all chanted in unison before ever repeating and reciting our dutiful allegiance to the United States of America. "Yes!" we all coincidentally reiterated.

"Excellent then!" exclaimed a very relieved Mr. Frank Mitchell. "Now please raise your right hands and repeat after me, "I hereby solemnly swear that...."

"The Inimitable Dr. Spencer"

Dr. Spencer quickly took a keen interest in me. I first talked with the man twenty-five years ago while I was selling patron ads for my high school senior yearbook. I mustered enough courage to rap on his door. The distinguished gentleman invited me inside. Soon I became fond of his intellect and visited his modest abode every Thursday evening at precisely eight p.m.

Over the years the gentle scientist gave me many valuable insights into various aspects of academic endeavor. I discovered that "the shy professor" possessed an extensive treasury of knowledge. Dr. Spencer was an expert in biology, chemistry, physics, law, genetics, medicine and economics. In recollection I believe I was more drawn to his wisdom than to his impressive academic expertise. I learned that the one thing my new mentor passionately despised was "government bureaucracy." Once I had finally won his confidence, I found the scientist to be very normal with me but extremely paranoid of the troubling outside world.

I soon discovered that Dr. Spencer deplored festivity. The man had no time for celebration. The experimenter had a serious demeanor that had little regard for trite everyday social conventions. He abhorred picayune street-corner conversation like a devout Amish man shuns blatant public indiscretions. I audaciously asked Dr. Spencer about his bashful nature on my second 1975 visit to 3132 Foster Avenue.

"Are you afraid of society?" I boldly asked. "There are many brutal people roaming around on the streets."

"I, like you, have little time to waste on trifles," Dr. Spencer stated. "We sleep one third of our lives away. If I live to be seventy-five, that means I have lived only fifty conscious years. I must accomplish my important research before I expire. As you can imagine my work is very important to me. I only have a few productive years of life left, you know."

"Exactly, but what is your work?" I impetuously inquired.

"You shall fully learn of its significance at an appropriate later date," the scientist solemnly and confidentially promised, "and I will see that you'll benefit from my work's application," he cryptically elaborated.

At the time I could easily comprehend why so much petty community conjecture flourished around Dr. Spencer's "secret experiments." The man did not manufacture any product in his back-room laboratory. He did not sell items from his door. Delivery trucks never arrived to drop-off or pick-up parcels. The postman never stopped at his address. These things I thought and evaluated that night as I wondered how I would reap the harvest of his labor.

Once a week Dr. Spencer trekked to a post office seven blocks west from 3132 Foster Avenue. After the retired professor visited his postal box, the secretive man did his banking and made his pharmacy purchases at businesses near the distant post office. Then Dr. Spencer would predictably return to his lonely residence. I would deliver meats and groceries to him every Thursday night before we had our "weekly symposium sessions." After several months we became trusting friends.

Dr. Spencer's secluded lifestyle baffled his nosy Foster Avenue neighbors. His reclusive habits contributed to his public mis-perception. I often wondered if Dr. Spencer cared about the neighborhood's abundant prejudices. I advanced that question to him during the summer between my high school graduation and my freshman year of college.

"Do you care what people think of you?" I inquisitively queried.

"I care about my work and about *your* future," Dr. Spencer remarkably declared. "People should spend their time thinking and inventing instead of engaging in idle chattering and in fruitless supposing. They all have the capacity to do so, you know, if they ever learned how to realize their potential."

"But why do you talk with me and not to anyone else?" I curiously inquired.

"Because you're the only one in the neighborhood that has taken an interest *in* me and not simply a curious interest *about* me," the Dr. emphatically answered. "I see in *you* great aspiration and opportunity for success. Everyone else seems content to waste their lives away engaging in what constitutes frivolous unproductive conversation."

The sole resident of 3132 Foster Avenue had no immediate family. No distant relatives ever paid him visits. Local scuttlebutt maintained that Dr. Spencer had inherited a considerable fortune, which benevolently sustained him as a lucky member of the "gainfully unemployed." People wondered why the gentleman had to walk to that distant bank, pharmacy and post office and bypass seven nearer financial institutions, six drugstores and two post offices situated closer to his home.

On a particular August '75 visit to 3132 Foster Avenue, I directly confronted Dr. Spencer with the outside world's distorted perception of him. "The neighborhood people think you're eccentric and involved in some illegal practices. How do you pay your bills?" I insisted on knowing.

"My neighbors erroneously think that life is a witch-hunt," Dr. Spencer replied. "It was because of people of their ilk that it took modern democracy two full millennia to be born from the seeds of barbarian dynasties. Those people around this section of Baltimore presently practice the peasant mentality quite prevalent in medieval times."

In late August of '75 I again ascended his marble front steps and rang the doorbell. I was immediately welcomed inside. The good doctor offered me a comfortable green-felt chair in which to sit down. First, we enjoyed a cheerful exchange of ideas about academics in general. Then we intensively discussed the plight of public-school education in particular.

"I endorse and advocate the European system of learning," Dr. Spencer maintained and insisted. "American schools try to educate everyone in the grand accomplishments of *Western Civilization*. This practice is actually dangerous and ineffective. Not everyone is ready to learn or wants to learn. Those derelict students who don't care about their' studies ought to be put in factories or vocational schools until the apathetic lazy dawdlers show they really do care about themselves and their world."

I was about to enter the *University of Maryland* the following fall semester. I swiftly took offense to Dr. Spencer's critical remarks. I felt alienated by his fervor concerning the need for "student academic discipline."

"One must first master self-discipline before he can ever expect to have academic discipline," my host firmly stated. Dr. Spencer cynically viewed the American public school educational system as being "shallow and ineffective" as long as it futilely devoted the bulk of its energy to the masses.

"Don't you think your attitude is elitist?" I keenly asked. "Aren't you being undemocratic? Education should be open and available to everyone!" I defensively challenged.

"Only three percent of the population creates knowledge," Dr. Spencer lectured. "Twenty percent, or the teachers, transmit the information to the masses what the three-percent creators of knowledge have developed. The remaining seventy-seven percent of the population are what we liberally call *students*," the professor concluded and opined. "American education treats the seventy-seven percent receivers of information almost as highly as it treats the three percent discoverers of knowledge and just as highly as the twenty percent that valiantly transmit the fundamentals of civilization to the general populace."

"I never really thought of it that way," I reluctantly admitted.

"You have admirable conviction and idealism," Dr. Spencer observed and commended. "I highly value those traits. They remind me of my youth when I was carefree, naive and believed I was immortal and virtually invincible, just like you presently do."

"Thank you for your compliments," I gratefully acknowledged.

Throughout that mild and friendly debate, I had the impression that my character was being tested and that my mind was being perceptibly analyzed. I believe that my audacity had won the professor's respect and loyalty. Dr. Spencer invited me back for other more comprehensive dialogues. My return visits led to a succession of Thursday evenings that I had faithfully honored for the next twenty-four years.

The following year, a rather strange incident occurred involving my dear mentor. I was an ambitious freshman on spring break from the *University of Maryland* when I again visited 3132 Foster Avenue on a mild April 1976 Thursday night.

Dr. Spencer surprised my sense of awareness and insisted on hypnotizing me. I would have refused his suggestion under normal circumstances but I had adapted to his unique personality and anxiously wanted to please him. I implicitly trusted his judgment. I did not desire to jeopardize our compatibility by doubting his motives or by appearing grossly uncooperative.

"Why do you intend to do this?" I sincerely wanted to know.

"You will not regret it one iota," he answered in a riddle. "You know, of course, that hypnosis is both healthy and therapeutic to the subconscious mind, don't you?"

"Yes," I hesitantly replied. "I do remember reading that somewhere."

"Good, there should be more young men in this cruel world that demonstrate your high integrity," he generously praised. "I guarantee you that you'll ultimately benefit from this little experiment."

I self-consciously reclined on the couch in his dimly lit laboratory. My pupils stared at a gold watch the professor dangled from a fob chain. My eyes watched the familiar object swing back and forth like a pendulum. My ears heard his command to relax. Soon I was under *his* spell.

I later woke up drowsy. I rubbed my eyes. My memory remembers refusing a cup of coffee. Dr. Spencer then escorted me to his front door.

"I presume you'll come again next Thursday evening," he persuasively suggested.

"Certainly," I replied, still in a stupor.

I left his modest place, realizing I had been under his special influence from seven to ten p.m. My mind was upset that there had been a three-hour void missing from my consciousness. I knew that vicious lies had been circulating around the "Hollandtown" (Highlandtown) section of East Baltimore that Dr. Spencer and I had been engaged in a questionable relationship, which the perpetrators maintained went well beyond a mere platonic companionship.

Although I doubted that I had been physically tampered with, naturally my sensibilities had become slightly out of kilter. I did not savor the notion that my mind had been temporarily arrested in "suspended animation" for three hours while *he* was in control. I was indeed somewhat distraught. Dr. Spencer might have taken liberties beyond the parameters of propriety defined by contemporary civilization. It took me an entire day to fully recover from my nebulous participation in the strange experience. Despite my myriad suspicions, I still valued Dr. Spencer's noble research aspirations and I intuitively trusted his character.

My reputation around East Baltimore had extensively suffered over the years because of my innocent connection with the inimitable Dr. Spencer. Residents had become less conversant with me than they had been in the past. Even my family began shying away from personal contact with me. Local businessmen now instinctively perceived me as a sinister person.

In the fall of 1982, I became a literature professor at a local college. I bought a small house on Eastern Avenue not far from Linwood. I married in 1990, hoping that a devoted woman would bring stability into my life. Even my wife, ordinarily a very tolerant civil woman, had asked me to limit my affiliation with the bland gentleman I had learned to revere over the years.

"Why do you keep visiting that hermit?" my new spouse challenged one morning. "You know what everybody else is saying about him!"

"Joanne, I see more-good in Dr. Spencer than in all of East Baltimore put together!" I exclaimed and objected.

"I think you should consult a team of psychiatrists," my wife rudely criticized. "You're married to me and not to *him!*"

I must honestly confess I was partially to blame for the abundant local skepticism about Dr. Spencer and his very reclusive private life. In 1997 I was in a corner barbershop getting a haircut. The neighborhood barber asked me about Dr. Spencer's "surreptitious activities." I revealed that my benefactor had once been a prominent university professor.

"Where did he teach?" the curious hair cutter asked as six waiting patrons suddenly became silent and pricked up their ears. "Was he at *Johns Hopkins?*"

"Dr. Spencer graduated from *Harvard University*, class of '48," I proudly said. "He taught at the same *Ivy League* college until his retirement in 1973."

"How do you know this?" the barber asked.

"I read the diploma hanging on his parlor wall," I informatively replied. "Then I asked him where he had worked before moving to Baltimore."

"Do you know the man personally?" inquired a waiting customer sitting in a hard wooden chair. "His behavior is quite puzzling, you know."

"No, not really," I denied, feeling a trace of guilt at succumbing to palpable social pressure. I paused a second, waiting to hear a distant rooster crow three times. "He's simply a casual acquaintance, that's all."

My stubborn nature compelled me to seek out Dr. Spencer's company the following Thursday night. I stubbornly ignored the orchestration of protest being generated by my spouse, her friends and the garrulous gossiping East Baltimore citizens. I was certain that discernible "peer pressure" was also affecting my wife's better judgment. I found a degree of solace making that assumption. "It's *them* and not her," I expressed one morning to the bathroom medicine cabinet mirror.

On a cold and windy Thursday evening in late October of '99, Dr. Spencer made a peculiar promise to me in his parlor. I was amazed by his shocking announcement. His profound words vividly echoed through my very unsettled mind.

"You are my sole support from the outside world," he diplomatically began, "and you have steadfastly demonstrated your friendship and support. My last testament will honor your steadfast allegiance," the good doctor articulated.

Then the proud man told me that he was without family. "I never married," he confided and revealed. Dr. Spencer then disclosed that his only brother had been killed in Germany during *World War II*. "There are no blood relatives to share my good fortune," he lamented. "You're the closest person on this earth that I have to leave the bulk of my estate."

"I don't know what to say!" I awkwardly reacted.

"Don't say anything. Just receive and relish my blessing," Dr. Spencer plainly insisted. "I've grown quite fond of you this past quarter century. You'll greatly profit from my estate, I assure you. To put matters succinctly, I want you to be the executor of my will and also my principal heir."

18

I was dumbfounded at being named the dear professor's chief beneficiary. My heart was wildly vacillating between humility and greed. Dr. Spencer sensed the extreme struggles going on inside my consciousness.

"Nonsense," he tersely uttered, "I'll entertain no more silly folly from your lips. You need not be grateful for my promise. I have pondered this bequest for many years. I insist you respect my firm decision."

"Thank you for your kind consideration," I acceded. "I'm still staggered by your extraordinary announcement."

The professor's demeanor then returned to his ordinary subdued tranquil state. He talked about the imminent danger of atmospheric pollution caused by worldwide industrial neglect. I listened rather inattentively to his monologue. I was still trying to evaluate the significance of being chosen Dr. Spencer's exclusive legal custodian and heir. 'I wonder how wealthy he might be?' I imagined. 'He doesn't seem to be too materialistic!'

When Dr. Spencer had announced his surprise, I received the impression that the matter was all of the utmost importance to him. I believed him to be a genuinely sincere man. I knew he was consecrated to pursuing truth in science. That exploit was his sole passion. I consented to implementing his explained wishes. I left his home with a mind burdened with awe and suspense. I briskly walked the three blocks to my Eastern Avenue row home. My face was numb to the hard cold raindrops pelting under my umbrella against my cheeks and forehead.

Last July I became disturbed by the proliferation of more malicious neighborhood lies. My wife said that people claimed I had been visiting Dr. Spencer more often than I actually had. Many eyewitness accounts credited me in the vicinity of 3132 Foster Avenue when I had actually been out of town or at the suburban college teaching my American Literature courses. My wife had overheard the idle chatter at her hairdresser's salon while the talebearers were unaware of her being present sitting under a domed hairdryer.

"That's completely absurd!" I yelled at Joanne over my morning breakfast of bacon and eggs. "It's absolutely preposterous! I was at the college teaching my classes! Callous hypocrites! They're spreading a rash of savage vicious lies!" I shouted in a rage.

Over the next two weeks similar erroneous stories supplemented the earlier ugly testimonies. I tried dismissing the wicked damaging gossip. But it came to pass that the local East Baltimore babble was having a severe impact upon my mental health. I was cracking under the great neighborhood scrutiny and teeming criticism.

My mind had difficulty dispelling the multitude of "evil" rumors that were being perpetuated. I endeavored eliminating their annoying effect from my concentration. I reassured myself with one of my favorite maxims, "Consider the source. Then you can better assess the merits, or should I say demerits of the misinformation," I kept repeating to myself while gazing into the bathroom's medicine chest mirror. "Even my wife is turning against me," I woefully regretted.

Last November 14th, I called upon my beloved Dr. Spencer. We enjoyed a wonderful discourse about American literature, a subject I regarded as my forte. I was amazed that Dr. Spencer's vast knowledge in my specialty exceeded my expertise.

"Were you ever a professor of literature?" I automatically inquired.

"No, but I'm an avid student on that subject," he answered.

Then, much to my captivation and fascination, Dr. Spencer recited verbatim E.A. Poe's "The Raven," all from rote memory. His powerful interpretation and flawless presentation amounted to a magnificent "Liberal Arts achievement" for a retired "professor of science."

I sat stunned and mute, listening intently to Dr. Spencer's fantastic romance with death. He envisioned the termination of earthly existence as a welcomed escape from what he considered a bitter bleak human reality. Finally, he eloquently concluded his astonishing recitation of the lengthy poem.

"That was undeniably terrific!" I excitedly complimented. "Aren't you afraid of the Grim Reaper's approach?" I jested.

"He's the one phantom I am anxious to meet," Dr. Spencer eerily concluded and claimed.

My eccentric benefactor was not laden with dread. The funereal elements of Poe's morose rhythmic language did not vex me. Instead, I was deeply depressed by Dr. Spencer's suave acceptance of death's proximity and the nonchalance evident in his deportment. "Charon robotically rows his barge in my direction," he said, "and I can hear his eerie oar splashing through Styx's macabre waters."

The very thought of the "good doctor" anticipating death's encroachment numbed my heart. I became emotionally disoriented that night while sitting stationary in his parlor, and the only event that I can accurately compare it with was the Thursday evening I had been hypnotized for three hours on his laboratory's hard brown couch.

Much to my dismay my inscrutable host then recited an impeccable rendition of William Cullen Bryant's "Thanatopsis." I had a queer sensation that the two-haunting death-theme poems were omens of some sinister forthcoming phenomenon. Dr. Spencer's resonant voice made my already nervous body shiver and then tremble. I was becoming more paranoid as he continued his oration.

My eyes scanned the dark shadows of his library/parlor. The cold chill I felt meandering throughout my being only accentuated my sense of morbidity. My spirit lacked the courage to request an explanation of his choice of narratives. I simply sat there reticently, spellbound by his powerful eloquence. I remember praying that his awesome entrancing enunciation would cease.

I felt my rapid pulse. I also perceived that my breathing had become accelerated. My hands were clammy and I could feel sweat beads cascading down my chest and arms. My heart was very much relieved when Dr. Spencer terminated his inspiring rendition of "Thanatopsis." My mind was completely unprepared for the surprise that followed.

Dr. Spencer finalized our meeting by presenting me with a small package, "a token gift" as he termed it. I hesitated before unwrapping the unexpected item. Inside a gift shop box was a key, a very ordinary-looking key that could easily be duplicated at any hardware store. "Keep this object in your possession at all times," my mentor advised. "Don't share it with anyone. This key is a symbol of future good fortune you will certainly enjoy. I implore you, keep its existence in strictest confidence until the appropriate moment for its use arrives."

"When will that be?" I stammered.

"The situation will make you aware of its need and implementation," the professor obtusely answered. "This very mundane key will afford you access to rewards beyond your greatest expectations," Dr. Spencer guaranteed with sparkling eyes.

"Thank you," I responded in a weak tone of voice. I momentarily felt very groggy and giddy. I hastily shook his hand to politely express my gratitude. I left 3132 Foster Avenue a bit dizzy and light-headed as I started my five-block amble back to my Eastern Avenue residence.

As I approached the all-too-familiar white marble steps, my soul was still drenched in uncertainty. I repeated *his* arcane words about the key over and over, but I could not comprehend their relevance. "What compensation could a commonplace key bring me?" I asked my front door's heavy metal knocker.

The following Thursday afternoon, I was heading to the corner drugstore to purchase a bottle of cough syrup. A speeding caravan of flashing lights and screaming sirens originating from two police cars and an ambulance interrupted my concentration while on my errand. The high-speed vehicles halted directly in front of 3132 Foster Avenue and that event immediately had my undivided attention. Hordes of curiosity-seekers flocked out of neighboring houses like disturbed hornets leaving their nests.

My legs and feet frantically dashed to the scene of commotion. I was hoping that "the emergency" would turn out to be a false alarm or a case of mistaken identity. I felt my heart wildly beating inside my chest as I sprinted toward Dr. Spencer's row house. My body maneuvered without caution between the still running motors of the police cars and the line of parked automobiles.

My shoulders recklessly bumped into several spectators craning their necks for a better view. My arms pushed their way through two rows of bystanders and then my feet ascended the spotless white marble steps leading into 3132 Foster Avenue.

I stepped inside and witnessed two grim paramedics carrying a covered figure on a stretcher. They hastened from the parlor into the hallway, nearly knocking me off balance as they mechanically rushed by. I was spellbound by the activity, which seemed surreal, as if it all had been occurring in another obscure dimension. I moved swiftly to the front door and observed the attendants depositing the stretcher into the rear of the ambulance. I heard the agitated crowd murmuring, sounding like a volatile gaggle of excited geese. "Irreverent imbeciles!" I said to myself. "Shut up you craven inconsiderate fools!" I yelled in their direction.

I then stepped to the rear of the row house. In Dr. Spencer's laboratory I recognized Dr. Morse, my dedicated family physician. The medical man was nervously putting his stethoscope back into his standard black carrying bag.

"Excuse me Dr. Morse," I interrupted. "I'm a close friend of Dr. Spencer. What has happened here?"

The medical man momentarily stared at me with an odd blank expression on his countenance. He seemed temporarily taken back by my innocent inquiry. "My dear young man," he prefaced, "this has to be the strangest death I have ever been called to verify. I can't equate another incident with it!"

"Could you tell me more?" I prompted. "I can't seem to fathom what has happened!"

"This man, your Dr. Spencer, who, I might add, has never been my patient, called my office an hour ago," Dr. Morse stated with a befuddled look on his face. I watched the doctor methodically wipe the perspiration off his forehead. "He said over the phone that there was a very sick person at this address. He added he would leave the front door open to allow for my entrance."

I detected a degree of concern in Dr. Morse's voice. "Then what happened?" I demanded, not giving the bearded physician sufficient time to catch his' breath.

"He begged me over the phone to rush over here. I left a waiting room full of patients," Dr. Morse stated from recollection. "When I arrived at this home it didn't take me long to realize that the caller was also the victim, for lack of a better descriptive term. I tell you young man, my hands are still shaking from this most bizarre experience."

After exhaling those words, Dr. Morse quickly reopened his black bag, removed a small whiskey flask, and gulped down a throat full of bourbon. "For medicinal purposes only," he indicated as an excuse.

"Do you suspect foul play?" I asked like a detective.

"I'll level with you, young man," the doctor elaborated, "before I sign any death certificate, I'll demand that a complete and comprehensive autopsy be performed by the coroner's office."

"Why?" I persisted.

"This man Spencer was some kind of lone-wolf scientist. He was despondent, a loner," Dr. Morse observed and argued. "He knew plenty about chemicals. I don't want to alarm or badger you with theory, but the possibility of suicide is very real here."

I left the gloomy premises with my soul imprisoned in a cell of desolation and my heart swimming in a sea of sorrow. I slowly waded through the pitiful, pitiless, gossiping throng. Their drivel was an irksome harsh anthem to my sensitive ears. I quickly turned and vociferously hollered, "Vile lunatics!"

My mind had to escape their irritating gibberish. I could feel hostility surging within me. I believed I would soon become violent and injure a few people if I did not immediately abandon the scene. I knew that "the gossip mongers" had been flagrantly discussing my innocent association with my revered and now deceased Dr. Spencer.

As I trudged home with my head crestfallen, I reached into my right pants' pocket and removed the dull inexpensive silver-colored key. I gazed upon it, looking for meaning and clarity to explain the horrible event I had just witnessed. My memory of the benign professor made me squeeze the object tightly in the palm of my hand. At the time I felt very frail, vulnerable, and dazed. I stumbled home to Eastern Avenue in a disheveled state of mind.

My always-busy wife was away attending her weekly Civics Club meeting. I had no one with whom I could share my tremendous loss. I slumped deeply into my living room's softest lounge chair. My right hand reached over and poured a hearty draft of brandy from the decanter situated on a nearby table. I sipped the rich blackberry flavor, meditating about Dr. Spencer's peculiar death. My introspection was suddenly disrupted. I heard a heavy rapping upon my front door. I instinctively resented that my somber meditation had been so rudely interrupted. I angrily arose to answer the irritating knock.

My eyes were startled to see Mr. Blake, the stern-looking neighborhood mortician. I welcomed the undertaker inside. My eyes begged for an explanation of his unanticipated sudden appearance at my door.

"I was specifically directed to come and see you," Mr. Blake began rather impetuously.

"By whom?" I reflexively asked.

"Unlucky as it might seem, just yesterday I was visited by a certain Dr. Spencer," the emotionless funeral director continued. "I had never personally known the man, but much to my astonishment he began outlining his funeral arrangements in great detail. He seemed to know as much if not more about the funeral business than I did," Mr. Blake panted.

"Then what?" I asked. "What happened next?"

"I never encountered anyone who had such an intrepid attitude about death than did this strange man Dr. Spencer," Mr. Blake solemnly intimated. "I had learned about your Dr. Spencer's demise only minutes ago. In our chat inside my office, Dr. Spencer said that *you* would gladly take care of the burial arrangements. He even paid me ten thousand dollars, cash in advance. How did this man know he was about to die? He seemed in very good health and in sound spirits just yesterday!"

"I don't know, I just don't know!" I stuttered as my words mixed grief with wonder.

The austere-looking mortician grimly peered at me, shook his head in confusion and then continued. "At any rate, I want you to know I pride myself on being an honest reputable businessman. Mr. Spencer paid me to deliver first class services, and I vow that he'll receive first class services. Your friend divulged he didn't have any living relatives."

"That's true," I confirmed. "He has no family or descendants."

"Therefore," Mr. Blake proceeded with somber alacrity, "barring any obstacles from the medical examiner's department or any complications from the city police, I have tentatively scheduled Dr. Spencer's viewing for next Tuesday evening at seven."

I nodded my head in agreement, bade the rigid custodian of the dead a morbid "good night," and then returned to my pathetic inconsolable mood. I sank down into my soft green-clothed chair and gulped down the remaining quantity of pacifying blackberry brandy.

My wife arrived home an hour later from her Civics Club meeting. News of Dr. Spencer's passing had spread throughout Highlandtown like a wild forest fire. "I'm sorry to hear about Dr. Spencer," Joanne casually said after entering our abode.

I detected that her remote demonstration of sympathy was done out of love for me and not because of any immediate remorse for Dr. Spencer's soul.

"Will you come with me to his wake?" I courteously requested.

"When is it?" she asked.

"Tuesday night," I replied.

"I'm sorry," she expressed with a lack of conviction, "but I've already committed to chair a club fund-raising activity Tuesday evening."

I reluctantly accepted her excuse as a valid reason. I detested that my wife's esteem for the dearly departed was but a fraction of the high regard I had had for the deceased. Joanne seemed quietly relieved that my Thursday night schedule would no longer be cluttered with my loyally visiting Dr. Spencer. I found her apathy for his death very disquieting. I loathed her very apparent disinterest and her overall superficiality.

Tuesday morning my sadness reached its low point. After a sleepless night I was very exhausted and melancholy. Too many aspects about Dr. Spencer's isolated existence remained a mystery and required clarification. I had known the man for two and a half decades, yet I really didn't know him outside his home. He never solicited my companionship. I then regretted really never extensively speaking to him outside the safety and comfort of 3132 Foster Avenue.

Despite ugly public opinion, which coincided with my wife's particular attitude, I still regarded the former *Harvard* professor as a distinguished scholar. I regretted that I was the only Highlandtown native who had been exposed to his brilliance and who had learned to cherish his unpretentious personality. Throughout that very arduous Tuesday, I thought about how benign and how helpful Dr. Spencer had always been to me.

A relentless storm settled over Baltimore that late November Tuesday evening. As I left my Eastern Avenue row house and trekked under my black umbrella to Blake's Funeral Home, the wet cold air, the cheerless damp pavement and an inhospitable howling wind collaborated to create a very morose atmosphere. The gloom of the dark cloudy hostile sky made me hesitate at the foot of the mortuary's flagstone steps.

'Wakes are traditionally regarded as social events in East Baltimore,' I thought. 'Where are all of the curiosity seekers tonight? They ran to his death, yet they ignore his funeral,' I surmised.

I slowly made my entrance inside the bleak edifice. I was appalled at realizing I was the sole mourner. It felt most awkward inspecting the vast vacant viewing room. The world preferred treating Dr. Spencer exactly as he had *viewed* it, from afar. "Dr. Spencer once told me that urban society was an evil influence from which a sane human being should seek exile," I nervously mumbled to myself. "His interpretation was absolutely right."

I cautiously approached his expensive bronze casket. No pictures of him rested against easels. No flower displays distracted my attention. No dreary organ music droned to drown out my cadence. My eyes focused upon the inanimate form that rested in peace before me. I mentally prayed the "Our Father" in memory of *his* former self.

I respectfully knelt at a small altar stationed before his corpse. My eyes meticulously scanned his horizontal embalmed remains. I begged for his soul's salvation; a soul truly worthy of any heaven. 'Before me rests the mere shell of a great man,' I humbly prayed. 'Your wonderful mind was too good to share the horrible demise of your mortal flesh,' I silently concluded.

My body carefully rose and then I turned my head. My eyes gazed upon the empty first row sofa. I recalled seeing it filled on many occasions with solemn mourners during past wakes. 'No man is an island, but this man was a continent unto himself,' I presumptuously thought.

My pupils panned the silent hollow chamber. My mind cursed the horde of cowardly neighbors. They lacked the decency to pass through those ominous purple-draped portals into this gruesome room. 'Fools!' I angrily thought. 'You should have come out of respect for the dead, even if you deplored this wonderful man! And if not for Dr. Spencer, you should have at least come here out of respect for me!' I concluded.

I considered how my status in East Baltimore had suffered because of my link with Dr. Spencer. The local residents perceived me as a sorcerer's apprentice. It was guilt by association based on lies, biases and superstitions. Presumption and ignorance, education's prime adversaries, had prevailed. 'Dr. Spencer's assessment had been right,' I thought. 'The neighborhood's fear was indeed primitive in nature, and its venomous resentment was borderline medieval.' I soon felt several very salty tears rolling downward under my glasses to the sides of my mouth.

I foolishly began wishing for a miracle. I wanted so desperately for that magnificent man to resurrect in triumph from what I consciously knew to be his unalterable eternal sleep. 'Such naive hopes of supernatural intervention are futile and childish,' I finally decided.

Mr. Blake entered the expansive deserted room to console me. I told the mortician several interesting anecdotes about Dr. Spencer. The curator of the dead nodded his head in appreciation of my revelations. A spooky silence then reigned supreme throughout the vacant chamber. I was temporarily at a loss for words. The undertaker attempted filling the void with several commentaries of his own. I failed to find any humor in his mediocre remarks. I again talked about Dr. Spencer.

"He was a splendid man," I neurotically recalled. "So fastidious and detailed in his methods. He was the most intellectually versatile person I have ever known."

"I understand," Blake replied in a low bass voice. "I understand!" he reiterated.

The first hour and a half of my gruesome vigil had passed by very slowly. At eight-thirty a minister stopped in at the mortuary, read several appropriate psalms, gave a brief sermon on the mystery of death, and then offered his condolences before hastily departing. Reverend Brady felt very uncomfortable lecturing before such a small audience. Mr. Blake informed me that Dr. Spencer had paid for Reverend Brady's standard oration in the funeral fees, so thorough was my mentor's preparations.

Dr. Spencer's burial was performed on Wednesday morning. I felt like Scrooge probably had at Marley's funeral, the sole mourner and the sole friend. I was my confidant's sole legal administrator. First I observed the eerie black hearse enter the graveyard's rusty metal gates. Then Reverend Brady drove into the big city cemetery in a black Ford automobile.

Six burly pallbearers hired by Mr. Blake carried Dr. Spencer's casket to his final resting place. During Reverend Brady's short speech, the minister seemed very fidgety, slurring many words. As my mentor's bronze casket was lowered into its vault, I recalled how I had pleaded with my wife to attend the interment, but she was adamant that she had had a scheduled dental appointment. I was certain that community opinion had dissuaded Joanne from appearing at Dr. Spencer's grave-site.

And so, I very sadly honored my valued friend's end, alone. I felt a large tear trickle down my right cheek as his cold metal coffin was lowered into its cold concrete vault. 'God rest your marvelous soul!' I quietly begged.

After the unusual burial, my spirit was miserable and my body depleted from the overall duress I had suffered. I had to endure the entire perplexity without the mercy and support of other human beings. Because of my intense anguish, I took the next day off from work. The stressful event had sapped my zeal and had diminished my energy. Rest was the only cure that could allay my fatigued mental condition.

The next morning, I was awakened from a deep slumber by the telephone's annoying ring. I glanced up at the wall clock. 'Eight-thirty,' I thought. My hand gingerly lifted the phone from its cradle. An official from the state inheritance tax bureau was on the other end. He requested that I meet him at Dr. Spencer's bank to assist in the opening of the deceased man's safety deposit box. The state auditor's office had been in communication with Dr. Morse and Mr. Blake, and the distinguished gentlemen had informed the government investigators that I had been delegated sole executor of the scientist's estate. The date of opening the safety deposit box was scheduled for the following Friday.

The following Friday, I put on a warm black leather jacket. My wife gave me a cursory kiss on the cheek, thinking that Dr. Spencer had possibly left me a small inheritance. I drove to the designated bank, making sure I had brought along the small key with which I had been entrusted. I knew the key was not the type that would give access to a bank safety deposit box. I think that I had taken "the token gift" along as a much-needed security symbol and as a special remembrance of Dr. Spencer.

I met Mr. Jacobs, a state auditor, in the bank's impressive marble-walled foyer. Mr. Thompson from the *Internal Revenue Service* had accompanied the state tax agent. The highly motivated government officials seemed quite anxious about opening Dr. Spencer's mammoth safety deposit box.

"Your friend's bank account had amassed the handsome sum of eight-hundred-fifty-thousand-dollars," Mr. Jacobs pompously and cunningly revealed.

"We suspect his safety deposit box might contain a similar amount," Agent Thompson professionally added. "If it does, we'll then have to see if taxes had been paid on all earned and unearned income. Any remaining funds or certificates will belong to Dr. Spencer's estate."

My blue eyes were set upon Box #100, the largest safety deposit container in the huge bank vault. I recalled Dr. Spencer's intense dislike for government bureaucracy. I smirked as I coyly glimpsed at the obvious anticipation noticeable in Thompson and in Jacobs' eyes.

I immediately shared the other men's ostensible apprehension. I felt a peculiar sensation that Dr. Spencer's ghost was in our midst, laughing incessantly at the government agents' eagerness to proceed. Soon, bank executives arrived inside the vault and produced two keys that could readily open the giant metal container in question.

The three of us carefully removed the huge metal box from its brass enclosure. The tax investigators quickly unfastened the latch. We prudently pushed back the lid on its squeaky hinges.

'What an incredibly remarkable sight!' I thought. The enormous safety deposit box was devoid of contents. I saw the looks of frustration and disbelief on the other men's faces. Ten seconds later, their disappointment converted into pure anger. They regarded the innocent event as a ruse, "a deceitful trick."

"I plan to challenge your Dr. Spencer's financial records anywhere in the continental United States," Mr. Jacobs ranted showing unbridled bravado. "Every transaction, every bill, every detail will be conscientiously audited. I want all of his financial records and property impounded immediately."

"I too will initiate a full-scale examination of your friend's tax and bona fide money records," Mr. Thompson predicted. "If there's a paper trail, it will be uncovered. No one accumulates eight-hundred-fifty-thousand-dollars nowadays without having funds hidden elsewhere. I suspect your Dr. Spencer was involved in some illicit activities. No taxpayer," Thompson elucidated, "dead or alive, is gonna' make a horse's rear end outa' me," threatened the totally peeved federal government official.

I stood still and mute as a statue, not uttering a syllable. I hated their presumption. I deplored the *IRS* agent's malicious intent. I quietly chuckled, contemplating *their* general impotency. 'Now I thoroughly understand why Dr. Spencer despised government bureaucracy,' I concluded.

Despite my emotional ecstasy I secretively pledged my conscience I would not make any untimely comment that would further antagonize the already hostile government representatives. 'Play dumb,' my mind thought. 'Don't jeopardize your inheritance.' I reasoned that little would remain of Dr. Spencer's fortune if vindictive government vultures like Jacobs and Thompson were allowed to conduct their ravenous confiscation.

"I'll cooperate with you gentlemen in all matters," I calmly but facetiously stated.

"All right for now," Thompson mumbled grumbled. "Show us his house."

The antagonized authorities did not explicitly communicate it, but I felt they seemed determined to implicate me as Dr. Spencer's accomplice in illegally withholding cash and taxable income from government scrutiny. After arriving at 3132 Foster Avenue, I used a spare house key that Dr. Spencer had given me to enter his former residence.

I shrewdly showed the tax officials every room in the entire place. Then I honestly answered their every question with poise and confidence. I relaxed and competently reflected suavity. 'My self-control will be a noble silent protest to their invasive speculations,' I cleverly thought. All the while, I marveled at Dr. Spencer's admirable cunning. His schemes were functioning quite well a full week after his death.

The on-a-mission tax authorities rummaged like desperate men through every desk and bureau drawer. I stealthily descended the cellar steps during their preoccupation. An inexplicable impulse brought me to the house's old furnace. Inside I saw the ashes of numerous copybooks and notepads. The archaic heater had incinerated all the professor's confidential records. The books had deteriorated to the point where the objects disintegrated into dust upon touch. All documentation of the furtive scientist's experimental work was lost forever.

My legs ambitiously clambered up the rickety wooden cellar steps. I relished the thought of the now-livid government officials pursuing their fruitless folly. Jacobs and Thompson had (in my absence) frantically strewn mounds of debris all over the previously immaculate rooms. Embarrassment and rage further facilitated their frenzy. Their paramount concern was to discover one small trace of convicting evidence. But the two men were no competition for my benefactor's wonderful sagacity.

The crazy frenetic hunt persisted for two additional hours. Finally, Jacobs and Thompson were exhausted from conducting their futile labor. The government predators gave me superficial apologies to excuse their unsavory desperate ransacking. The tax agents left in a huff, still vowing to continue deep probes into Dr. Spencer's private financial affairs.

Three days later, I received a Registered Letter from Marvin L. Webster, Esquire. Dr. Spencer had designated Attorney Webster as the legal counsel for the distribution of his estate. The letter indicated that the professor's "Last Will and Testament" would be probated in Baltimore City Court on January 24th, 2000. The letter also instructed me to appear at the lawyer's office on December 24th, at two in the afternoon. Finally, the communication advised me to take along the small silver-colored key that Dr. Spencer had given me.

My spirits vacillated between exhilaration and depression over the late autumn span between *Thanksgiving* and *Christmas Eve*. The surging excitement was owing to the secret disclosure of the doctor's will, and my sadness was attributable to the loss of my very close friend. At last, the afternoon of December 24th arrived.

Priding myself on punctuality, I was a full half-hour early for my legal appointment. I walked with swagger into Attorney Webster's handsomely decorated reception room. I discreetly conversed with two pretty blonde secretaries while the industrious lawyer attended to another client's needs. Then, Attorney Webster opened a side entrance to his office. He cordially introduced himself and welcomed me inside.

"You're here for Dr. Spencer I presume?" he asked.

"Why yes!" I enthusiastically replied.

"Please come this way and have a seat while I get Dr. Spencer's folder," Webster directed.

The very efficient lawyer and I engaged in several minutes of small talk, which came rather easily upon both of us learning that we had attended the same university. Soon the conversation switched to the business at hand. The short bespectacled bushy-haired barrister started reading the stipulations and covenants of Dr. Spencer's will. Webster spoke with a smooth and steady Virginia accent.

The generous professor had left the enormous sum of eight-hundred-fifty-thousand-dollars, on deposit at the prescribed Baltimore bank, to the *Harvard University* Department of Scientific Research. I figured that Dr. Spencer still possessed an avid love for his beloved alma mater into his later years. 'The fact that his gift is given to an educational institution makes it mostly tax-free, and that bestowment will naturally further aggravate Mr. Jacobs and Mr. Thompson,' I conjectured.

Marvin L. Webster read that the house at 3132 Foster Avenue, along with all of its contents ranging from furniture to test tubes, was to be sold at public auction. The proceeds derived from the sales were to be donated to a scholarship fund for deserving "at need science students" attending *Harvard*.

"I must advise," the gregarious Attorney Webster' cautioned, "that the conditions of this will cannot be satisfied until the *IRS* and the state inheritance tax office conduct their independent reviews. Litigation or unforeseen challenges may result in considerable legal expenses to the estate."

My lips formed a broad smile and my head nodded in full concurrence with Webster's statement. I was certain that Dr. Spencer had deliberately arranged the *Christmas Eve* date for the reading of his Will to be more than a mere coincidence. I was confident that the dear Dr. Spencer had planned my special inheritance to simultaneously dovetail with the Yuletide tradition of gift giving. I speculated what my generous award might be.

'I probably won't receive my inheritance until after Jacobs and Thompson complete their' laborious investigations,' I realistically reckoned.

"I am elated with Dr. Spencer's stellar intentions," I said, "and you must agree, Mr. Webster, he proved to be quite a fabulous philanthropist. Better the money be used for scientific progress than to be butchered up by wasteful government bureaucracies," I boldly stated to the affable probate lawyer.

Marvin L. Webster keenly peered at me through his thick bifocals. My opinion about the mammoth government tax bureaucracy had apparently struck a sensitive nerve hidden somewhere in his psyche. I anxiously anticipated the moment when Webster would ultimately convey the good news of my just rewards.

"I hope you haven't spoken too prematurely," the attorney chastised. The legal consultant then paused, gulped down the remainder of his tall glass of water, poured some more from a pitcher, and then rested his elbows upon his solid dark oak desk. Finally, he continued with our conference.

"My dear sir," Webster continued, "eight weeks ago I had the pleasure of visiting your Dr. Spencer. He then enumerated the various provisions of his Will."

"Yes," I amiably agreed, "I must admit that he was so organized and so analytical."

The attorney cleared his throat to gain my full attention. "I assented to write down the terms Dr. Spencer had specified. I wholeheartedly concur with your assessment that the man was very knowledgeable about all the legalities regarding the disposal of his estate. I next drove him to my office, had my administrative assistant type up the document, and then had my two secretaries sign it as witnesses. Then we notarized it." Webster downed his second glass of water before he returned to my involvement with Dr. Spencer's extraordinary Will.

I glanced around the office, studying the array of diplomas and certificates displayed on the mahogany-paneled walls. I thought I had sensed Dr. Spencer's spiritual presence. I looked around to catch some image or shadow of him laughing at the lawyer's incompetence, but I saw no wandering apparition.

Attorney Marvin L. Webster rose up from his soft black leather swivel chair, ambled over to a side coat closet, removed a beautiful jewelry chest from the top shelf and then sauntered back to his dark oak desk. The box resembled a small pirate's chest. It was made of ebony, encircled by heavy silver buckles and hinges. The object looked like a valuable heirloom that had been passed down from antiquity.

Webster plopped down into his comfortable swivel chair and directly looked into my eyes. "I was rather stunned when Dr. Spencer brought this fascinating article to my office the next day after I had written his Will," Webster shared. "Your unique professor friend must have had a premonition of his own death. Never before have I had a client so emphatic about the disposition of his affairs. He told me *you* would have the key to open this exquisite chest. He told me you were the only individual on this earth deserving of its contents."

I sat there restlessly, ecstatically anticipating my *Christmas* present. I could tangibly feel the blood pulsating in the veins and arteries behind my ears.

"I must say," Webster genially summarized, "my mounting curiosity is now as great as yours. Open the case. Its contents are your entire inheritance."

My zeal was so great that I could not hold back another second. I fumbled in my pants' pocket to locate the coveted key. I hastily inserted it into the lock. A slight twist to the right soon freed the hinge. I removed the lock and then gradually raised the lid. Inside was a small standard black index book and after examining it, I discovered that the reference contained fifty addresses scribbled on fifty separate pages. The first designation was that of my Eastern Avenue residence. The forty-nine remaining ones were each located in a different state of the union.

Marvin L. Webster and I stared at each other in total disbelief. The lawyer then broke out in a very unprofessional lusty roar of laughter.

"Excuse my excessive rudeness, kind sir," he apologized, "but this phenomenon has to be the most ludicrous prank I have ever seen. It looks like you've been made the recipient of some bizarre posthumous practical joke. This treasure chest ploy amounts to nothing more than a colossal death hoax. Please pardon me sir, but I don't quite know how to harness my emotions."

"It was all very imaginative, quite nifty in the final analysis," I admitted in a tone of voice indicating my shock.

"I should really be more sympathetic with your predicament," Attorney Webster confessed. "I know you were expecting much more than a simple black address book. I'm afraid you're more of a poor victim instead of a wealthy heir. I've never seen the likes of this in over twenty-five years practicing law. In your hands lies your complete and total inheritance."

I left Attorney Webster's mahogany-paneled office in a very pensive mood. I needed solitude to precisely weigh the odd weird event that had just transpired. I was not quite as dejected as Marvin L. Webster might have guessed. I drove my black Chevy Blazer back to Eastern Avenue. I needed the quiet sanctuary of my kitchen nook to clear away the disarray cluttering my vulnerable mind. A hot cup of coffee would help me contemplate the significance of Dr. Spencer's most unusual gift.

Joanne was out grocery shopping so I had a full hour of solitude to ponder the professor's very intriguing puzzle. I was determined to decipher his cryptic riddle. I knew that Dr. Spencer would never deceive me as Attorney Webster had erroneously theorized.

I carefully rehashed the entire sequence of events over and over. I still placed trust in my mentor's promise. I adroitly fended off doubt's persistent challenges. In the end my admiration for Dr. Spencer's integrity eclipsed my mind's tendency to practice cynicism.

My body rose from the chair and I hurriedly wrote a note to my wife. Soon I scurried out the front door and then jumped into my Blazer. I journeyed north on *Interstate 95* through Delaware, took the *New Jersey Turnpike* non-stop to Exit 11, the *Garden State Parkway*, which eventually led me to the *New York Thruway* straight to Albany, a six and a half-hour drive from Baltimore. I knew I'd never be able to sleep until I had cracked the mysterious code of Dr. Spencer's black address book.

"He had the intelligence to beat the system," I repeatedly said to my image in the rearview mirror. "He's smart enough to beat any system, especially the inflexible tax bureaucracy that he so strongly abhorred."

I finally reached my destination Albany later that *Christmas Eve*. I asked directions at three service stations, and soon I found the second address listed in Dr. Spencer's incomparable black book. I walked up the asphalt driveway and knocked loudly upon the chocolate brown wooden front door. My rap was quickly answered. I was completely flabbergasted. My troubled mind was in such a shattered-shambles that I could hardly utter a common salutation. The figure that stood before me was a facsimile of myself.

My cooperative replica explained it all to me. "I have been instructed by Dr. Spencer, my creator, to forward his 'tithe,' one tenth of my earned salary, to a Baltimore, Maryland literature professor, you I surmise."

My likeness said that he had previously sent the monthly sum to his master, the inimitable Dr. Spencer, and upon the noble professor's death, the four-hundred-dollar contribution would then go directly to me. Since I was "the original," my forty-nine clones would now help me build my own financial independence. My Albany "ditto" provided me with a "duplicate key" to Dr. Spencer's Baltimore post office box, which I later made my own. All moneys forwarded by my "loyal carbon copies" are now sent directly to that address.

I have been richly reimbursed for my faith in Dr. Spencer. Webster, Blake, and Morse all believe that I had been duped by a series of imaginative ruses. Mr. Jacobs and Mr. Thompson still think that I had been dramatically used and snubbed by my closest friend.

Let those skeptics all believe what they think. I knew and believed all along that Dr. Spencer would prove to be an honorable and virtuous man. I had faith all along that his wisdom would transcend the banality and ineptitude of typical government bureaucracy.

After the very rewarding summer hiatus, I took a much-deserved sabbatical from my monotonous college teaching career. I never shared my vast inheritance with my wife. She had sarcastically rejected Dr. Spencer's veracity. Joanne still thinks I am touring the country, gleaning much needed material to organize my *Ph.D.* I am euphorically spending the autumn of Y2K traversing the continent, seeking out my forty-nine marvelous reproductions. Next year I plan to visit Hawaii. I am eternally indebted to Dr. Spencer's noteworthy foresight and benevolence. Upon his large tombstone I had the epitaph engraved, "Here lies the inimitable Dr. Spencer." Until now, only I knew the true meaning of those memorable words.

"Doing Bristol"

Prior to last summer, my personal value system had never placed much faith or credence in what my previous beliefs had regarded as preposterous conjectures in matters like the theory of the time/space continuum, like *Twilight Zone* parallel universes, or like the prospect of actual time travel. So being a born pragmatist, I've either always been rather suspect of such 'wild speculation', or I have been somewhat wary of such 'impractical science fiction fantasy'. But because of my experiencing certain extraordinary events having their genesis on Monday, August 11th, 2014, I've recently learned to respect the powers of certain arcane forces that inexplicably transcend everyday objective scientific investigation and logic.

At 4 p.m. on that sultry afternoon I had dropped-off my wife at the Delta Airlines Terminal of Philadelphia International Airport. Joanne was scheduled to fly to Orlando, Florida to visit her sister Eileen, who would be driving over from her condo' in Vero Beach to greet her. My spouse would be away for an entire week's hiatus, with her flight back to Philly' being scheduled for Monday, August 18th.

After leaving the congested airport vicinity, I drove my silver Nissan Maxima north on I-95 through standard center city expressway traffic, through bustling North Philadelphia industrial zones and soon my vehicle exited the high-density busy thoroughfare at the Levittown/Bristol interchange. Now I have a certain nostalgic memory for *that* particular Bucks County area, for in the 1950s, me being between the ages of eleven and sixteen, my family had lived at 50 Daffodil Lane in Levittown's Dogwood Hollow section.

'I've made arrangements to spend the night at the *Comfort Inn* on Route 13, between Levittown and Bristol,' I neurotically reminded myself. 'I'm glad I've confirmed my reservation this morning before leaving Hammonton and driving Joanne out of Jersey to Philly'. Before motoring to the *Comfort Inn* on Bristol Pike, I think I'll perform a little sentimental tour of Levittown and nearby Bristol.'

I switched on Sirius XM Radio and listened to Chuck Berry's all-too-stellar "Sweet Little Sixteen" and then heard Bill Haley and the Comets' sensational rendition of "Rock Around the Clock," and those most terrific early rock and roll songs immediately resurrected fond recollections from my youth while then living in Levittown. Next I pressed my radio's second button to reminisce 60s' tunes and my ears quickly discerned the Dovells fast harmony lyrics belting-out "The Bristol Stomp", which actually had been a new teen dance that had originated in 1961 at the Bristol Fire and Hose Department Hall, a nifty place where I had attended lively "bobby socks and poodle skirt dances" in 1958 and 1959.

My improvised itinerary around Levittown was quite sentimental-but-melancholy in both scope and sequence. As my Maxima exited left from Route 13 onto Levittown Parkway, my pupils immediately recognized that my revered Catholic high school, Bishop Egan, had been demolished and that a weed-laden, empty lot now occupied the landscape where the four-story building had formerly stood.

Then as I carefully made a left-turn into what used to be the Levittown Shoparama Outdoor Mall, I was saddened to witness that the former shopping center had been razed and has since been replaced with several large modern-day box stores.

'Wow!' I instantly regretted. 'Even the Towne Movie Theater has been eliminated from existence.' In the mid-fifties my friends and I would frequent the establishment in July and August because *that* then-new structure was about the only special place that featured the amazing revolutionary technology known as air-conditioning, which to us was actually 'a scarce-but-welcomed novelty.'

I next drove through the community's Kenwood section, where all the streets began with a K. I gently turned right into Stonybrook with all its S streets and a half mile ahead stopped my automobile outside where the Brook Pool used to be, but now that former popular recreational facility was also gone from existence along with the side Little League baseball field where I had played for the Meenan Oil team in 1954-'55.

'Holy cow!' I sadly lamented. 'Even the pool's rear basketball court is gone.' I had enjoyed so many teen Friday night outdoor dances there during the mid-'50s Golden Age of Rock and Roll. Kids from Stonybrook, Farmbrook and Greenbrook would frequent the Brook Pool that had been by design sandwiched between those three 'Letter Sections', and they mingled with clean-cut kids but deliberately avoided the tough greasers from Junewood, Kenwood and Dogwood Hollow.

More dejection entered my heart when I piloted my Maxima into Dogwood Hollow and observed how the homes had generally deteriorated over the course of the last sixty years. My former residence at 50 Daffodil Lane looked almost-alien to my eyes with different dull siding and faded roof shingles being viewed. And much to my utter dismay, a ruinous-looking lawn and accompanying inferior-looking shrubbery were evident throughout the now-aged shabby property.

My final Levittown excursion was me venturing into Junewood, where for two years I had worked a newspaper route delivering the now-defunct *Philadelphia Bulletin*. 'I was making ten dollars a week profit, which today would be equivalent to a hundred dollars,' I recalled and then smiled.

Driving around Junewood, I stopped in front of my old pal Bob Jalonec's home on Jonquil Lane, and I especially remembered him and his boss green and cream '57 Chevy, and then my cluttered mind mentally reviewed the countless hours "Jokes" and I would spend "cruisin'" the region and listening to disc jockey Joe Niagara, the "Rockin' Bird", playing the latest hits on WIBG Radio 99.

My final connection with my '50s Levittown past was heading east on Haines Road past the now-empty Delaware Canal and after crossing Route 13, I judiciously applied the brakes and halted in the center of a strip mall, my eyes staring at the Eagle Nest Tavern, which has replaced Hal's Delicatessen where I had diligently worked inside the business's backroom kitchen on Saturday and Sunday afternoons to earn additional steak sandwich and pinball money.

My final Bristol Pike visitation was to park my Nissan at the adjacent Dairy DeLite custard stand and actively enjoy devouring a medium-size vanilla cone, my appetite habitually repeating a tasty treat my mouth had savored so often back in the 1950s. As I munched on the soft cone, my eyes glanced next door at a seafood restaurant presently named 'Under the Pier', which in the '50s used to be the fabulous Feed Bag, which was a popular eatery and teenage hangout where Bob Jalonec and I had encountered a myriad of romantic and culinary adventures.

* * * * * * * * * * * *

Continuing on my casual Bucks County jaunt through Bristol, Pennsylvania, population fourteen thousand, I temporarily parked my car in front of the Bristol Fire and Hose Department and soon a mental newsreel of past favorable escapades promptly switched on inside my brain. From Mifflin Street I traveled south to Mill, and at the 'L right angle corner' of Mill and Radcliffe Street my silver Maxima slowly descended a short-but-steep ramp, and I quickly maneuvered my comfortable leather-seated Nissan to a parking lot situated next to a Lions Club Park and also conveniently located near the town boat pier, which Bob Jalonec and I had often utilized as our private *Delaware River* fishing destination.

I departed my vehicle and my elderly feet ambled into the historic King George II Inn, 102 Radcliffe St., which is a landmark Bristol establishment that had originally been constructed in the 17th Century. I nonchalantly sat-down at the bar, ordered a Coor's Light draft and a medium-well-done sirloin steak with mashed potatoes, and since I was the only patron seated upon a stool, the affable bartender (who identified himself as "Bill") decided to initiate a friendly conversation.

"Where ya' from Stranger?"

"Hammonton, over in South Jersey," I quietly answered. "It's halfway between Philly' and Atlantic City."

"I know the town well," Bill replied with a smile. "It's called the Blueberry Capital of the World. My wife and I attend the annual festival each late June over at your high school. Quite an event, I must say! We were just there two months ago!"

"The town's farmers grow over ten thousand acres of the luscious blue fruit," I informed the inn's very efficient employee. "In the 1950s, Hammonton farm acreage was half peaches and half blueberries, but in the end, the blueberry guys won-out and the former peach growers have admitted defeat. Now *they* almost exclusively harvest the eight-week-long summer blue crop!"

I soon learned that Bill was an avid history and geography enthusiast. "Bristol was named after a city in England," I remarked. "The Pilgrims sailed from Bristol to Massachusetts on the *Mayflower* in 1620," I proudly-but-erroneously stated.

"Not exactly!" the congenial bartender laughed. "The Pilgrims sailed from Plymouth, England and landed near Cape Cod. That's where we get Plymouth Rock! Lots of places in the New World were named after towns and cities in England. For example: New York, New London, New Hampshire, New Jersey and New Castle Delaware. Your own New Jersey was named after the Isle of Jersey in the English Channel."

"Well then, didn't Sir Francis Drake voyage out of Bristol?" I asked, attempting to redeem my very evident knowledge deficiency in the British maritime history category.

"No Sir!" Bill chuckled and then reflexively coughed. "Like the Pilgrims, Drake also embarked from Plymouth. But Sir, Bristol was the home base of John Cabot, the famous North American explorer who led several important expeditions out of the port in 1496!"

Just then, coincidentally, the familiar 'Bristol Stomp' rhythm was heard emanating from the tavern's overhead speakers. I related to my new beer and alcohol acquaintance what represented the true inspiration for the 60s' hit song.

"One of the singing group's members had stayed at the Deauville Hotel in Miami Beach, and that's how the Philly' group got its name the Dovells," I authoritatively informed, again endeavoring to compensate for my obvious lacking in Bristol, England nautical history. "Another band member had heard of a new teen dance started right here in town at the Fire and Hose Hall over on Mifflin, so the song's lyrics were expeditiously composed and the hit number was soon recorded and went national in a hurry."

Bill nodded his head in appreciation of my sage rock and roll commentary, swiftly stepped into the kitchen and soon returned to serve my plate of sirloin and mashed potatoes, and then the ambitious young man attended to the thirst needs of another guest sitting four stools to my left. When the pleasant young fellow again arrived to where I had been eating, we mutually resumed our cheerful dialogue.

"Ya' know," I prefaced, "back in the '50s a good buddy and I used to fish off of that pier out there. Of course, we always wanted to come inside for a beer or two but were too young to be served."

"Yeah, *that* landing dock date's back in 1681 when goods and supplies began arriving up the Delaware from Philly' to Bristol," the encyclopedic bartender deftly explained. "Those Pre-Revolutionary War colonial days must've been something else!"

I glanced-up at the inn's liquor shelf and noticed bottles of Jack Daniels, Jim Beam, Southern Comfort, and Seagram's Seven displayed among other whiskey favorites, all lined-up and ready for public consumption. "Say Bill, since I'm here in good old Bristol, why don't you give me a glass of that Harvey's Bristol Cream up there on the liquor rack?"

"Good choice!" the bartender commended my selection judgment. "It's a dessert sherry nicely blended ever since the year 1880, but the famous distillery was first begun by Mr. John Harvey and Sons in Bristol, England in 1796."

"Your impeccable and impressive knowledge of British history is absolutely amazing!" I generously praised. "I guess you know plenty about the blue bottle too?"

"It's referred to in the trade as Bristol blue glass," Bill related as the garrulous guy poured the tempting dessert liquor into my glass. "Not too many customers order it. Most prefer chugging-down hard whiskey shots instead!"

"I'm staying the night at the *Comfort Inn* over on Route 13," I revealed, desiring to continue our rather courteous conversation. "Say Bill, when was the last time someone else came in here and drank a glass of this Harvey's Bristol Cream?"

"It was a whole week ago today," the bartender reflected and then uttered. "Yes, in fact the fellow swallowed-down two glasses. Apparently, he really liked the smooth flavor."

"Well, in that case," I insisted, "give me a refill. That stuff was positively delicious!"

"Just like yourself'," Bill calmly stated as he recharged my empty glass, "this guy I'm mentioning also lived in Levittown in the 1950s. Junewood section I believe. Said his name was 'Bob' something or other. Was from Florence, South Carolina and was visiting relatives in New York before taking a detour and touring the area before entering the King George. But for the life of me, I can't remember the fella's last name. It began with a J., I think."

My eyes widened and my mouth was then totally agape. "Jalonec?" I asked with subtle surprise.

"Yeah, that's it!" Bill eagerly verified in a semi-excited tone of voice. "Jalonec! Said he' was also staying at the *Comfort Inn* up on Bristol Pike."

"Know the highway well!" I remarked without divulging that gregarious Bob Jalonec was once my closest Levittown friend. "It's below Edgely Road and near Green Lane. When I was sixteen, I was a junior fireman for the Edgely Fire Company and there was a big blaze at Delhaas High School over near the small plane airport on Green Lane. Levittown was really something else back then. Could you imagine? Seventeen thousand brand new homes erected on open land in a mere five-year period!"

"Maybe I shouldn't tell you about *this* incident, Mister," Bill indicated, getting back to our main topic of discussion, "but this guy Bob Jalonec was back in here just an hour or so ago before you entered. Said he' was anxiously heading south to Dixie."

"Did he have another two glasses of Harvey Bristol Cream?" I wondered and inquired. "The stuff is delectable! I think I'll buy some at the local liquor store and sample it at home! The flavor could be addictive!"

"No Sir!" Bill mildly exclaimed. "The guy instead asked for a double shot of Jack Daniels on the rocks. He drank it down in three seconds as if he had just crossed the Sahara Desert on foot and needed to quench his parched tongue and throat!"

"Did this fella' Bob J. say anything to you about his seven-day activities between his two visits?" I deliberately asked. "Why was he so thirsty?"

"I reckon the gentleman wasn't nearly as thirsty as he was scared," Bill communicated with a serious expression suddenly appearing upon his florid face. "Ironically, that same 'Bristol Stomp' song began playing and the music seemed to drastically affect the man's behavior. At least that's my impression!" the grim-faced bartender qualified. "He slammed a twenty dollar-bill on the counter, mumbled some barely discernible words about some weird time and space travel incident, and then the perturbed fella' rapidly scurried out the door and off the premises, bolting straight to his car like a frightened jackrabbit!"

* * * * * * * * * * * *

My emotions were a trifle addled on the brief drive from the King George II Inn on Radcliffe Street to the *Comfort Inn* on Route 13. Many random thoughts meandered about inside my head. 'What a remarkable coincidence!' I evaluated. 'I haven't seen nor heard of Bob Jalonec in over a half century and now I just missed him by a matter of an hour. Swell; at least I now know he lives in Florence, South Carolina. Maybe I'll look him up in a telephone directory and get on the horn to have a much-needed talk about our memorable past friendship in 50s' Levittown.'

Being fatigued from the day's various travails, I gathered my wits and checked into the 'cookie cutter lodge', made my way up a flight of steps to Room 201 and slowly unpacked my suitcase. After showering and watching Fox News on cable TV, at eight p.m. I called Joanne on my cell phone to determine how her flight from Philly' to Orlando had gone. My wife reported that everything was "copacetic" and that the daytime climate in sunny Florida was hot and nearly sweltering.

After hanging-up my portable phone, I brushed my teeth and retired to bed early, all the while anticipating my pleasurable ride across the *Delaware* on the Burlington-Bristol Bridge back into New Jersey and then enjoying the scenic forty-mile trip south on Route 206 to agricultural Hammonton. For some remote reason, feeling highly exhausted, I fell asleep upon the bed wearing my designer jeans, a light blue cotton shirt, and contrary to my sleeping habits, I was still wearing my white socks and brown penny loafers.

The following morning, I awoke at daybreak, but incredulously, the entire room, wallpaper, furniture and decorations were all now quite different in appearance. I hastily opened the drapes, peered out the window and much to my astonishment, Route 13 was nowhere in sight, but instead, a heretofore unknown massive edifice with the designation Wellmont Hospital somehow existed across what was now identified by a street sign as 'West State Street'. A nearby red, white and blue sign surprisingly read I-81. Being fully confused, I hastily dressed, left

Room 201 with my plastic key in hand and nervously roamed downstairs to obtain necessary, plausible clarification of my exact whereabouts.

A local tour-guide pamphlet and brochure rack of area sightseeing attractions described such foreign venues as 'Bristol Speedway just off Exit 5 of I-95', 'King College Walking Tours', 'Marvelous Bristol Caverns' and 'Beautiful Skyline Drive Bus Tours'. I turned my head, glanced at the wall logo situated above the main registration desk and then my bewildered eyes noticed that the newfound emblem mysteriously read: 'Holiday Inn, 3299 West State Street, Bristol, Tennessee'.

'I guess I'm no longer in Bristol, Pennsylvania!' my puzzled brain surmised and shockingly realized. 'I'll peruse this pamphlet section and try acting inconspicuous while doing so. Then I'll sit-down in the side room and sort things out over a Continental breakfast!'

One particular brochure showed the colorful photographs of the nearby Comfort Inn, 2368 Lee Highway, Bristol, Virginia. Then my thought processes finally comprehended that Bristol, Tennessee and Bristol, Virginia were sister cities that physically bordered each other in two separate states. For mental security, my hands quickly honored my instinctive reaction. I frantically reached into my back and side pockets and my furious searches, much to my relief, simultaneously confirmed that my wallet and my cell phone were still in my possession.

After consuming my early meal in a rare, perplexed state of mind, I walked-up a flight of steps to Room 201 and after entering, plopped-down on the bed and contemplated my extremely bizarre circumstances. 'I dare not leave the property if I'm under some obscure evil spell or curse. I don't want to be jinxed or be punished by mystical supernatural forces I can't right now clearly fathom,' I dreadfully assessed. 'If I boldly step out of the Holiday Inn, then who knows what my' resultant fate might be?'

I stayed secluded in my room that entire day and later, after regaining my composure, I ordered from room service a hamburger and French fries for supper. My troubled mind was now singularly worried about my arcane time and space travel misadventure. 'Perhaps this 'Bristol visitation phenomenon' is what had caused Bob Jalonec to panic into a frenzy and swallow-down his Jack Daniels double-shot after hearing the Dovells singing 'Bristol Stomp' at the King George II bar?' my mind wondered and conjectured.

At nine that evening I sufficiently calmed-down, called Joanne in Vero Beach and was happy making contact with her and hearing her wonderful, comforting voice over my cell phone. My suspicious-minded wife articulated that she could not reach me during the afternoon and that she was becoming somewhat concerned.

"Maybe *my* cell phone is only transmitting and had trouble receiving incoming calls," I cleverly theorized and communicated to my better half. "From now on this week, I'll call you until I have Verizon correct my cell phone's malfunction."

"Okay Honey!" Joanne aptly agreed. "Miss you! Can't wait to be arriving back home in Hammonton next Sunday! Don't forget! Meet me at eight at the Delta baggage carousel! Love ya' Babe! See you then!" Click.

That evening, I watched the late-night CNN and local newscasts and finally managed to doze-off around midnight. But after a restless night of tossing and turning, I climbed-out of my queen-size bed at dawn, hustled to the window, but amazingly, my vision saw no Wellmont Hospital across the highway. Instead, I noticed three distinct arrowed road signs, the first one reading I-93 and the second indicating, "Bristol, New Hampshire." I clumsily turned-on the side wall light to further investigate the apparent visual aberration. The third arrowed sign in the far distance read: "Wellington State Forest near Newfound Lake."

'Oh my God!' I imagined in awe. 'I've been vacationing in these parts before. This is no doubt New Hampshire out there. Joanne and I had taken a senior citizen bus trip up here three falls ago to enjoy the splendor of the autumn foliage. The White Mountains are just north of here and Wolfeboro and Lake Winnipesaukee located just southeast. If I accurately recall, Squam Lake is geographically near Lake Winny. That's where the popular 70s' movie *On Golden Pond* had been filmed! In fact,' I remembered, 'friends of ours had moved up here from Jersey and now live not too far away in Meredith. If I had the courage, I'd intrepidly walk out of this *Comfort Inn* and pay Steve and Nancy a visit in an effort to escape this terrible ongoing Bristol nightmare!'

The following three nights the same type of reprehensible time/space travel pattern had been experienced and again repeated in Hilton Double Tree Hotel and Comfort Inns in Bristol, Rhode Island, in Bristol Virginia, and in Bristol, Connecticut. All the while, fortunately I was able to successfully recharge my cell phone, call Joanne and pretentiously assure her that out of sheer boredom, I had been staying the week in New York City attending 'a spectacular merchandise show' being featured inside a huge exhibit hall near Columbus Circle.

The sixth night I was fretfully staying in Room 201 of the Bristol, Connecticut Double Tree Hotel on 42 Century Drive. Again, I dared not leave the building out of fear of some unintended supernatural repercussions being surreptitiously administered upon me by alien invisible powers. My whole beleaguered psyche was now overwhelmed with abundant dread and apprehension. My spirit and audacity were both indeed being mercilessly challenged.

After I almost-mechanically ate an ordinarily excellent crab cake dinner inside the exclusive Willow Restaurant, I strolled across the Double Tree's lobby and then curiously trekked around the entire downstairs, impatiently examining without any specific purpose the facility's exercise room and large indoor swimming pool, both accommodating amenities enclosed inside the high-end boutique hotel's glass-paneled atrium.

A tall, thin gentleman standing in the main lounge innocently asked me if I had attended the recent Newport Jazz Festival just across the state line in Rhode Island. I quickly answered a little too curtly, "No Sir. I prefer the mid-June Monterey Pop Festival out in California!" I then briskly sauntered away to again be alone in my misery.

'Gee! Now I know why Bob Jalonec was acting so petrified and so psychotic last Sunday afternoon at the King George II Inn!' I genuinely-but-erratically thought. 'And no one at any of the hotels has been charging any fees or expenses to my credit card. All I do is sign my name and show the waiters and employees my 201 Room key! If I ever get back to Hammonton,' I decided, 'I'm never going to risk my reputation and disclose this hellish tale to anyone, including Joanne! The only person on the face of the Earth whom I might ever consider telling is Bob Jalonec!' I rationally concluded. 'If I ever get back to Jersey with some remaining sanity, I think I'll spend several weeks rehabilitating in Ancora State Mental Hospital in order to recover from this incredibly outlandish and wholly enigmatic Bristol six-state astral journey!'

* * * * * * * * * * * *

Much to my emotional alleviation, on Sunday, August 18th I awoke, hopped out of my bed, bolted to the window, opened the drapes and immediately, thankfully perceived that Bristol Pike, Route 13 constituted the wonderfully ordinary outside physical and commercial environment. I quickly turned on a table lamp, examined my wristwatch and was elated to note that the time was 6:15 a.m. and that the timepiece's calendar element indeed indicated August 18th.

I next ecstatically paced to the bathroom, removed my harshly wrinkled designer jeans, blue cotton shirt, brown penny loafers and white socks. Next, I showered, shaved my week-long beard (for my

46

small traveling bag had still been kept inside my suitcase), and then I merrily donned my much-needed change in underwear, summer weight black pants, green tee-shirt and new white socks.

'This Bristol Comfort Inn already has my credit card,' I reasoned. 'I'll just leave a twenty-dollar maid's tip on the bureau along with the room key and furtively exit the lodge. I'll skip the monotonous free Continental breakfast and later eat at a New Jersey diner on the drive back to Hammonton.'

Then I again rushed to the window to confirm that my 2013 silver Nissan Maxima was still there in the lodge's asphalt parking lot. 'Oh yes!' I gladly thought upon performing additional searching. 'My car keys are still in the top bureau drawer, right where I had deposited them last Sunday night!'

I was never so happy to be back in Jersey again after crossing the two-lane Burlington-Bristol Bridge into Burlington City, which like Bristol, was an old Delaware River town dating back to the American colonial era. Somewhere between Mt. Holly and Medford on Route 541, my disheveled mind awkwardly rehashed the exceptionally strange developments that I had inadvertently survived during the past incomparable seven days.

'I refuse to turn on Sirius XM radio and accidentally hear the Dovells singing Bristol Stomp,' I firmly resolved. 'And I'm never going back to the King George II Inn like Bob Jalonec had unfortunately done. And I'm never again going to stay at the Route 13 Comfort Inn either. And I'm never ever again going to drink two or more glasses of Harvey Bristol Cream. And absolutely,' I further rationalized, 'I'll never ever do any combination of those four Bristol-related things on the exact same day!'

After having a pancakes, coffee and bacon breakfast at the Red Barn Restaurant on Route 206, I called Joanne in Vero Beach to see if any time changes had been made for her return flight from Orlando to Philly' International. Truthfully, I was never so glad to hear her soft, feminine voice chatting about simple, nondescript, mundane, every day matters.

On my final drive home to Hammonton, my mind still futilely tried understanding how I had consecutively time/space voyaged from Bristol, Pennsylvania to Bristol, Tennessee, to Bristol, New Hampshire, to Bristol, Rhode Island, to Bristol, Virginia, to Bristol, Connecticut, and then miraculously arriving full-circle back to the Comfort Inn, Bristol, Pennsylvania.

After gingerly pulling into my all-too-familiar driveway and stopping to obtain my week-long mail, I coyly decided while sitting behind the steering wheel, 'The next time Joanne flies down to Florida to visit her sister in Vero Beach, I'm going to merrily drive down to Florence, South Carolina and have a lengthy chat with Jalonec about our dual week-long Levittown and Bristol adventures. Bob and I will definitely have a plethora of items to converse about. And then,' I imaginatively considered, 'I'll secretly motor down to Vero and pay a surprise visit to my wife and sister-in-law.'

"The Evil Force"

I, Colonel Cliff Dawson am accurately recording this incredible account into my personal electronic journal and not into the official ship's log for reasons that will obviously be self-explanatory later on in this narrative. Captain Jeremy Parker and I have been on a courageous ten-year space mission exploring outer space and methodically charting our landmark discoveries for the International World Coalition. Our well-publicized mission was described in the world's media as "an awesome enterprise" and quite basically, I've always been attracted to the prospect of being one of the first 'daring humans' to find intelligent human-like life thriving elsewhere in the nearby Milky Way Galaxy.

Our lengthy expedition started out from Earth in the year 2534 A.D. and it is now, according to our ship's reliable instrument panel May 5th of 2542. The Newton III is now ready to lift off and leave the planet that Captain Parker and I have labeled EL-741, which is an *Earth-Like* sphere rotating around a Sun-Like star that my cohort and I have named Mater Seven.

But plenty of exceptionally weird and eerie phenomena have happened since our momentous landing on EL-741 approximately forty-eight hours ago, and thus, my guilty conscience would not allow the Newton III to take off until all of the pertinent details have been accurately documented into my personal diary and not into the ship's authentic log.

Captain Parker and I have been close friends ever since our dual graduations from the American Space Force Academy in Cape Canaveral, Florida in June of 2520. Jeremy happened to be a veritable wizard at understanding and repairing complex matter and anti-matter equipment and my 'space partner' was very adept at proficiently fixing warp drives whereas I am highly regarded back on Earth as being an academic expert at comprehending the intricacies of astrophysics and biochemistry.

Throughout our glorious odyssey trek across this sector of the Milky Way our general relationship on the Einstein III had been both cordial and compatible and my comrade and I satisfactorily shared navigation responsibilities and Captain Jeremy Parker and I had cooperatively alternated slumbering inside the spaceship's one and only Deep Sleep Hibernation Compartment, which over the course of our decade-long expedition efficiently slowed down our mutual biological aging process by five years, thus effectively halfing our breathing and our heartbeats.

Captain Parker and I had quite different motivations in volunteering for this very vital space mission. Jeremy had experienced marital difficulties and was divorced without any children and my co-pilot possessed a zealous spirit for adventure and challenge and also, my ambitious comrade always wanted to become historically famous. Jeremy's core aspirations were always goal-oriented and it would be an understatement for me to suggest that throughout his career Captain Parker possessed both the dream and the drive to achieve his valued objective.

As for myself, I am happily married to the former Carol Anderson and we have two wonderful kids, Tom, now age seventeen and Denise, now age thirteen. I had applied to participate on this historic journey because first and foremost, I consider myself an American Union patriot and quite truthfully, I despise all of the mundane conflict existing back on Earth like war, famine, pestilence, political wrangling, drought, disease and human envy, jealousy, greed and abundant spite too, which I assess to be the fundamental roots of all human evil.

Tending to have an introverted nature, I have always preferred to be a loner and as I now recollect, my personality was never very gregarious and convivial at military social events and at gala receptions. And besides, I had reckoned that *our* significant space voyage would be only five years in duration and not ten because of our body-preservation time spent in suspended animation inside the very essential Bio-Chemical Deceleration Chambers. Indeed, I have greatly missed my family during this extensive space voyage.

Although Jeremy and I have visited, explored and thoroughly documented fifty-three unique planets during our current expedition, more importantly, we have successfully located and ambitiously catalogued three special planets very similar to Earth on our interstellar maps, but the only evidence of life prior to our recent comprehensive investigation into EL-741 had merely been primitive microorganisms, new strains of bacteria and various types of peculiar protozoa. Generally speaking, everything seemed rather normal on our galactic 'Interstellar Study' until we had eventually entered the most remote solar system of the Constellation Pegasus.

Upon approaching Mater Seven and eventually orbiting EL-741, Captain Parker was uncharacteristically excited to report that the Earth-like sphere had an atmosphere very similar to that of our native planet, seventy-five percent nitrogen, twenty-two percent oxygen and three percent hydrogen, along with minute quantities of other rare gases. My eminent co-pilot had always been quite eloquent in expressing himself.

"And Colonel Dawson, there's an excellent ozone screen filtering out traces of ultra-violet and infra-red rays so *that* important condition means that the possibility of plant and animal life existing on EL-741 is dramatically heightened," Captain Parker observed and communicated. "This is pretty thrilling Cliff both in scope and in sequence! A good chance exists that over the eons life has migrated from the planet's rivers and lakes onto land just like it had done back on Earth hundreds of millions of years ago," Captain Parker euphorically articulated to me. "Just imagine what kind of fantastic evolution might have occurred over the ages here on EL-741! Just the contemplation of such an evolutionary miracle is absolutely mind-boggling!" my friend indicated. "This extraordinary planetary encounter might be the first genuine human contact with alien life forms in outer space," Jeremy enthusiastically gushed and giggled. "Neil Armstrong should've been as lucky as *we* are right now! That ancient astronaut's biggest accomplishment as an audacious space pioneer was to set foot on the lifeless crater-pocked Moon. We have a terrific opportunity to become internationally renowned back home on good old Mother Earth!"

"Yes Jeremy," I passively answered, trying my utmost to contain my emotions from running rampant, "but I recommend that you now carefully study the topography of EL-741's surface. There aren't any oceans or seas as far as I can determine; just evidence of various irregular coastlines forming one enormous circular-shaped continent, if you like."

"But look Colonel!" Captain Parker ecstatically yelled to justify his total fascination. "There's an abundance of beautiful rivers and lakes on that one vast global continent that you've just so aptly described. And there're bountiful forests and trees and vegetation and deserts and mountains too, all fairly similar to those features existing on Earth!" Captain Parker anxiously vociferated. "The entire planet reminds me of depictions I've read of the American west before the invasion of the Conestoga wagons that traversed through Colorado, Utah and sunny California."

"Well Jeremy, it's always better to be safe than being either sorry or dead!" I objectively and rationally replied. "I'm not setting foot upon the surface down there until we perform a complete and comprehensive atmospheric analysis and finish a general land elements' probe. But Jeremy, I must admit that the present daylight surface temperature of seventy-five degrees and polar readings of twenty below zero are indeed favorable and possibly conducive to supporting advanced life forms."

"Okay Dr. Caution!" Parker promptly jested. "Let's look before we leap. *That* expression ought to be our new motto!"

"It would be nice if we could investigate without having to don our cumbersome space suits," I casually noted, trying to impress my colleague with my calm self-discipline. "But after landing, let's be patient and wait a few hours before we initiate our examination of the physical elements of EL-741. Who knows? We might be able to add a few more chemical items to the standard Periodic Table and become scientifically famous in addition to historically famous!"

Most of the minerals that we had identified on EL-741 were similar to those prevalent on Earth and on other foreign planets that we had recently explored and surveyed: iron, phosphorus, potassium, sulfur, sodium, aluminum, potash, quartz, silicon and gold were in good supply. More remarkably though, certain chemical compounds were commonly detectable in the forms of carbon dioxide and sodium chloride, along with measurable complex sugar molecules.

The evidence of carbon dioxide strongly suggested to us that plant life could exist and thrive, and *that* fortuitous factor could consequently support natural food growth through photosynthesis, specifically provided by radiant orange-glowing Mater Seven, which incidentally happened to be a very favorable hundred and twenty million miles away. That intriguing coincidence of satisfactory conditions promoting the possibility of EL-741 surface life represented a distinct and encouraging prospect, and both Captain Parker and I were highly motivated to commence our essential quest, searching for indigenous plant and animal life.

Twenty-four hours after landing on EL-741 (which incidentally rotated on its axis every twenty-six Earth hours), and after determining that the planet's atmosphere was indeed conducive to breathing and walking without the use of space suits and the need for any artificial aid apparatus, Captain Parker and I next intrepidly exited the Newton III's air lock chamber and then bravely stepped down the access ramp, eventually audaciously setting foot onto what later was defined as the "Planet of Evil Force."

* * * * * * * * * * * *

I am not a particularly religious man but I have always viewed my conscience's value system as being one founded on strong moral convictions and upon discreet ethical principles. Throughout my adult life I've generally assessed organized formal religion as being something analogous to superstitious and primitive prehistoric thinking, that is, until I had made certain incidental interactions with the mysterious "Evil Force" that I soon learned dominates EL-741. Now as the Almighty is my witness, I am convinced that some diabolical omnipotent power pervades and controls this God-forsaken planet that Captain Parker and myself' had randomly-but-intentionally encroached upon.

Please allow me to articulate the astute recounting of my experiences, all of which I maintain will adequately justify and defend my seemingly implausible and fictitious testimony, for I now believe that any goodness that exists in the Infinite Universe is conversely counterbalanced with a diametrically opposed Evil Equivalent, a contemptible Evil Equivalent that has wretchedly pushed my mind to the threshold of insanity. I shall now be more specific in my elaboration.

After intensively analyzing the remarkable planet's atmosphere and thereby determining that the air was consistently safe enough to breathe, Captain Parker and I boldly exited the Newton III and steadfastly ambled out into what appeared to be a pristine New England environment abounding with late springtime forest deciduous and pine trees, the overall physical landscape exhibiting assorted strange-looking green leaves, branches, pinecones and accompanying needles.

About a half-mile distant from the Newton III, we soon encountered a swift-running brook and the two of us followed its rocky meandering path until we eventually arrived at a gorgeous grove comprised of what appeared to be wild peach and apple trees interspersed with random bushes laden with red berries that seemed to be a combination of a raspberry and a blackberry, that is, in their physical three-dimensional appearance.

"This is what I truly love about EL-741," Captain Parker opined and declared. "It's pristine and astronomically remote and now there's definite evidence of delicious-looking luscious fruit growing here. Perhaps there're some human-like inhabitants residing nearby in this desolate vicinity too! Colonel Dawson, I don't want to sound too optimistic but right this minute *this* observation could be the all-too-elusive cosmic missing link that we've been desperately searching for, the crucial connection that decisively proves once and for all that Homo sapiens are not the only cerebral creatures populating our enormous galaxy."

"Jeremy, I want to do a complete property molecular inspection of this alluring fruit before we ever attempt devouring it," I suspiciously answered my best friend. "Ah yes!" I exclaimed as I gazed at the gauge reading being registered on my bio-chemical spectrometer compound-measuring mechanism. "Elements of fructose, glucose, chlorophyll and carbon-related compounds are quite prevalent inside the odd-shaped lavender peach and also inside the purple apple and inside the distorted-looking red and black berries too. I confidently deduct that they're all devoid of harmful toxins or poisons and I'm convinced that the fruit is edible and nutritious as well as being digestive tract friendly."

"This is truly wonderful because I'm sick of all the monotonous processed food meals, artificially flavored juices and all of the tasteless energy tablets we've been swallowing-down for breakfast, lunch and supper," my dependable companion eagerly stated. "I just can't resist the temptation any longer. With your permission, I desire sampling the berries and the apple facsimile right away. But honestly, I've never liked the taste of peaches ever since I was a youngster, thinking the fuzzy produce to be too sweet for my sophisticated palate. I think I'll pass on eating the peach."

"Okay Jeremy," I amenably acknowledged. "I'm going to try the lavender peach and the purple apple while your fussy taste buds can enjoy the apple and the red berries. According to the spectrometer's readings," I observed and plainly stated to my companion, "the three kinds of fruit growing here in this valley seem to be of chain store quality."

The edible fresh fruit we consumed was positively mouth-watering and I made a mental note of the grove's location and considered it 'a must responsibility' that I should visit the wonderful wild fruit orchard again simply to satisfy my voracious appetite. After simultaneously synchronizing *our* solar-powered watches, Jeremy and I decided to separate and explore north and south respectively and we agreed that we would rendezvous at the aforementioned orchard in an Earth hour. Hence, I wandered south while my conscientious partner conducted his separate exploration north along the brook.

After trekking for twenty minutes, my wandering arrived me' at a double ridge that was divided by a deep valley. Realizing that my forward progress was impossible, I stubbornly trudged my way back to the vicinity of the exotic peach and apple tree grove.

'I know what I'll do,' I deviously imagined. 'I'll proceed north and meet-up with Jeremy' as he's returning south along the fast-flowing stream. My adventurous co-pilot will be surprised to see me prematurely trespassing on *his* turf!'

As I exited a nondescript patch of pine trees, I noticed my friend stooping down and collecting what appeared to be some sparkling gold nuggets from the brook's bank. 'I'll see if Jeremy is honest enough to tell me about his treasure trove find,' I wisely thought. 'It'll be like a little character test! Surely the gold bonanza will have no special value to either of us until we return back to Earth. Precious metals and paper money are absolutely meaningless up here on EL-741.'

After filling his deep white collection sack with the precious mineral, Jeremy oddly headed west along a dirt trail and then paced through a small-woods, and much to my astonishment and bewilderment, he entered a house that was an exact facsimile to mine back in Vero Beach, Florida, inadvertently or deliberately leaving the stucco rancher's front door open.

My palpitating heart became filled with anxiety and curiosity. I surreptitiously ascended the three brick steps and next distrustfully ducked-down on the front porch. Not detecting Jeremy's presence inside, I stealthily entered the foyer, turned right past the living room and then nervously hesitated before entering the master bedroom. Furtively sticking my head through the portal, my disbelieving eyes caught a glimpse of Captain Parker making love to my formerly faithful wife Carol.

'How could this possibly be reality?' I skeptically speculated. 'It must be some perverted illusion or inexplicable hallucination, or perhaps some ugly mental manifestation! Anger is raging inside me! Could the same repulsive scenario have happened in the past on Earth without my knowledge?'

My mind was incensed. I furiously left the area of the familiar looking house and headed directly for the peach and apple orchard. An innocent-looking Captain Parker showed-up fifteen minutes later than the designated grove rendezvous time and Jeremy had the unmitigated audacity to offer the lame excuse that his attention had been diverted when he had perceived a giant human-sized frog catching a huge flying insect with its sticky tongue.

I pretended to accept his exaggerated tale as being truthful, but on our long hike back to the Newton III, not once did my avaricious and baneful companion mention to me either the white linen collection sack full of gold nuggets or his sinful adulterous love affair with Carol.

'Ever since our academic days at the Space Academy, my rival Jeremy's always been exceedingly jealous and especially envious of my numerous accomplishments and awards,' I selfishly conjectured in defense of my faltering ego. 'He's without a doubt greedy, arrogant and spiteful and will do anything malicious to pilfer my pride and ruin my good public reputation! My moral standards have been impugned by that conscience-less maniac!' I lividly concluded. 'Captain Parker is going to pay dearly for violating my wife's fidelity to me and he'll suffer dire consequences for not demonstrating military honesty and integrity in regard to his recent gold discovery! I swear I'll get my just revenge on that unscrupulous traitor and marriage-wrecker! I've never loathed anyone as much as I now wholly abhor detestable Captain Jeremy Walter Parker right this very minute!'

* * * * * * * * * * * *

My disheveled mind had difficulty fathoming how my transplanted Vero Beach home and how my cheating wife happened to realistically appear on Planet EL-741, which logically was over ten light years away from Earth in the constellation Pegasus and furthermore, where were the remainder of the homes in my Florida neighborhood?

On our arduous amble back to the Newton III, Captain Parker and I exchanged few words but midway during our three-mile ramble, I did remove from my jacket's pocket and then munch on a lavender peach that I had previously pulled from the strange-looking orchard tree. The entire way trekking back to our spacecraft I had felt both resentment and hatred toward my betraying co-pilot.

That evening, after exiting the ship's shower compartment and then drying my body off with a soft towel, I dressed into clean clothes and silently stepped into *our* sleeping quarters. Intense acrimony filled my spirit when my alert eyes detected Captain Parker assiduously searching through my wallet and at that point in time, I instinctively suspected that the sneaky thief was brazenly attempting to pilfer my identity.

Never before had I ever felt such antagonism towards another human being. Feeling grievously violated and deceived, I quietly retreated to the galley's pantry to sit at the table and drink down a cup of ice-cold water, but all the while my offended mind was strategically contemplating my next move.

'Why is Parker rummaging through my personal belongings?' I asked my confused self. 'I know! He's jealous of me, desires to steal my wife and probably also covets my expensive vacation hacienda in Andalusia, Spain! But money and gold have no particular value out here on this desolate end of the celestial zodiac! Property and wealth are irrelevant here on EL-741 too! According to the astronaut's manual,' I continued thinking and evaluating, 'with the exception of military rank, all basic relationships between Parker and me away from Earth are supposed to be egalitarian in nature! Now everything's changed for the worse!'

My poisoned mind actually believed that I possessed the uncanny capacity to fully perceive every aspect of Parker's sinister intent. 'The greedy scoundrel envies my rank, despises my ability, resents my integrity, loathes my fame and curses my success,' I irrationally concluded. 'He's now my one and only adversary who is wickedly planning to either harm or kill me! That's why I must plot to destroy the demonic wretch first!'

My ears heard Captain Parker's feet casually shuffling into the ship's library and then five minutes later they discerned 'my nemesis' striding into our sleeping quarters' chamber. 'Parker must be eliminated because I fear he's secretly preparing to execute me in cold blood! I'll wait here in the craft's library for a half hour pretending to be chewing on a snack and then when he's later slumbering in his bunk,' I cunningly planned, 'I'll swiftly perform my wicked deed!' I deviously schemed and determined.

An hour later. I rose from my soft chair and very quietly walked to our small bedroom. 'Forget about implementing the paralyzing stun mode!' I shrewdly decided. 'My avowed enemy must be instantaneously eradicated from mortal existence! Parker's soul is defective and the villain must be eliminated!'

I slowly and meticulously removed my trusty ray gun from my waist holster and while Captain Parker was soundly sleeping under the blanket inside his lower bunk, I mercilessly pulled the trigger and zapped him with the weapon's potent laser beam.

The following dawn I dragged Parker's limp lifeless body into the heavy equipment room and next clumsily lifted his corpse into the 'All Purpose Digger's' passenger seat. After pressing a button on the sidewall control panel, thus opening the ship's exit portal, I started the machine's engine and then fanatically drove the versatile vehicle down the Newton III's back ramp.

Not far from the now familiar peach and apple grove I used the machine to dig a six-foot-deep hole, deposited my vanquished foe's remains into the hollow and then skillfully manipulating the device's levers, I competently covered the makeshift grave with ample dirt. Before departing the vicinity, and exhibiting no sign of remorse, I hopped off the All-Purpose Digger and forcefully plucked a ripe lavender peach from the nearest fruit tree. Appeasing my sudden hunger, I ravenously ate the juicy fruit.

On my short excursion back to the Newton III, I was confronted with several inexplicable threatening situations. First a ferocious lion-like creature crossed my path but I managed to adroitly maneuver my All-Purpose Digger and scare the awesome fierce beast away with several laser volleys from my handy ray gun.

I next encountered a giant hungry anaconda-like snake and honoring my need for self-preservation, I deftly escaped its imminent danger by adroitly speeding away in my swift reliable contraption. But then a seven-foot-tall squirrel accompanied by a ten-foot-high rat accosted me, and in a flash, I shot at and chased away both apparent existential threats during the height of the emergency.

Soon a bizarre idea registered inside my addled brain. 'Parker said that he had witnessed a huge frog eating a very large insect,' I neurotically recalled. 'Perhaps he wasn't lying or hallucinating after all! Or maybe he was simply fabricating a tall tale to conceal his guilt for having an adulterous affair with Carol? There must be some lucid logical explanation to account for all of these abnormal crazy things that are occurring on this hellish planet! What is causing these very disturbing evil aberrations to happen?'

When I eventually returned the vehicle to the Newton III, I raised the segmented entrance ramp and next systematically closed and locked all exit portals. I was happy to note that the ship was still there at the landing site and that it had not somehow been stolen or damaged, but when I curiously looked inside Captain Parker's white linen collection sack, it was totally empty and much to my amazement, no glittering gold nuggets were hidden inside.

* * * * * * * * * * * *

As I impatiently sit here in the Commander's Chair ready to take off from EL-741 in always reliable Newton III, I am pensively reflecting on what exactly had provoked me to act like a savage felon and callously and maliciously murder Captain Jeremy Parker.

My co-pilot had eaten the apple and the red berries and I had consumed the apple and three peaches and had avoided sampling the berries. These relevant factors should be germane for me to better comprehend the true moral dimension of the Evil Force that capriciously governs the myriad strange events transpiring here on EL-741.

'The lavender peaches caused me to see certain illusions and delusions,' I keenly realized and hypothesized. 'The peaches were more of a hallucinogenic drug than were the purple apples and the red berries. And Parker had tasted the purple apple and the red berries while I had eaten one apple and three peaches. Therefore,' I pondered, 'I had imagined that the incident I had witnessed involving Jeremy and the gold nuggets at the stream, his affair with Carol and his scrutiny of my wallet in our bed chamber all were illusions generated as a result of the effect of the combination peaches and apples I had digested. Parker only ate the apple, so that singular action caused him to envision a mammoth frog feasting on an oversized bug.'

I next theorized that a chemical synthesis of the ingredients that constituted the peaches and the apple had influenced me to behave like an evil person temporarily possessing a criminal mindset. Somehow the accidental chemical compound mixture in my body had a similar effect to that of the Lotus Plants in Odysseus's extraordinary adventure in the Land of the Lotus Eaters where *his* recalcitrant crew ate of the potent flowers and soon refused to obey their king's incessant commands to leave the idyllic paradise. Because of *this* noteworthy analogy between my zany adventure on this evil planet and the weird Lotus Flower episode described in Homer's *Odyssey*, I have decided to rename EL-741 'Lotus 1.'

'Those golden nuggets, along with the deceitful love affair and also the oversized lion, the immense squirrel and the huge snake were all distracting illusions that my fertile mind had projected into my physical surroundings,' I considered. 'This postulation of mine must be true because the Evil Force on this planet does not know that a lion is many times the size of a squirrel and that a frog is not the same size as a human being. That formerly perverted scenario that I had imagined all makes perfect sense now,' I finally comprehended. 'But the stark reality is that I have murdered Jeremy and now my conscience deeply regrets my grotesque and misguided misdeed. His death was no mental manifestation! It was truly real! I am now a bona fide wanton criminal; all because I could not readily distinguish Lotus I fantasy from, Lotus I reality.'

After I had started the atomic thrust engines and lifted off the remarkable planet's surface, according to my ship's compass and gyroscope, my course was heading due west. My sensitive pupils then observed a squadron of UFOs flying and then hovering over a gleaming city having enormous skyscrapers and spectacular obelisks along with stunning round and pyramid-shaped majestic edifices. Also, quite conspicuous were a plethora of lustrous mass transportation tubes connecting the various outstanding vertical glistening structures.

'My scanners have determined and verified that those distant objects do not in reality exist!' I perceptively realized. 'The vivid visions are only products of my active subconscious imagination being diabolically projected into that distant illusionary environment, all somehow caused (I believe) by the tempting fruit or fruits that I had eaten on Captain Parker's EL-741. Naturally I'll have to mimic what most dishonest businessmen do when they keep two sets of books: one for the government agents' scrutiny and the other documentation exclusively for themselves. There's no way that this visual rendition that I'm presently observing is going to be entered into the ship's official log. In my' own defense, the aberrant and outlandish story of the Evil Force that exists on 'Planet Lotus I' will forever remain a closely guarded secret solely preserved in my personal journal.

As the mythical Satan is my witness, according to *this* Devil's Advocate, Captain Jeremy Parker had died from a lethal unknown virus on Planet Lotus I and out of traditional human sympathy and my' sense of duty, I had respectfully buried his remains somewhere on the alien planet.

"Inspiration for All"

Peace and serenity: What really are those evasive words? I haven't experienced either abstraction since *he* had totally ruined my life! How could I have been so damned gullible? I've lost all self-esteem. I am disconsolate. I am confused. I am livid. Yes, I'm living an eternal Hell on Earth. I now closely identify with the unbearable travails suffered by the *Bible*'s Job, but *his Old Testament* anguish lasted for only one miserable lifetime. Mine will last possibly forever. Allow me to fully explain my dilemma.

I once envisioned damnation as a mere illusion, a vicious religious threat that had been preached and warned mostly by fire and brimstone evangelists. I had naively thought that damnation was nothing more than authoritarian church dogma exploiting my hopes, my fears and my dreams. But now I fully comprehend that actually being accursed can be a very devastating daily implacable living nightmare. Being accursed is beyond a doubt a living unsympathetic death that I often find too torturous to imagine or endure. Ironically, I am both cursed and blessed because of the terrible phenomenon I've achieved, and all because of *him*.

It was natural greed and vanity that had caused my swift plummet into the great decadent abyss. I've been justly punished for my iniquity. And indeed, excessive pride had been the genesis of my swift plunge from social acceptance. Hubris had triggered my rapid ostracism from my family, from my church and from my community. I'm now a social freak, a pariah, and I've nothing to blame but my curiosity and no one to blame except my avaricious selfish self. Please let me explain the whole *damned* thing in detail.

Now the recollection of *our* last meeting seems almost like an insane encounter, an encounter that escapes logic and believability. But despite all reality, my stubborn *will* still desires to endure and persevere. My astute memory will now reconstruct for you the exact scenario as it had developed. I know it will, and *you* will then fully understand the magnitude of my suffering and fathom my burden.

In truth, my greatest fear is awakening in a torrential thunderstorm anywhere along the Holland coast. You think me insane? Many so-called experts believe I am indeed demented. My medical doctor thinks I'm over-fatigued. My minister thinks I need spiritual renewal. My psychiatrist (I insist I don't need his ineffective services) claims I'm psychotic and neurotic. His incompetent associate claims I'm schizophrenic. All of those buffoons and charlatans consider my veracious testimony a fantastic voracious hoax.

I know I tell the truth. I haven't sipped an ounce of water in three months because of it and because of *him*. I'll not allow any excess of fluid to enter my body and kill me. And I know my soul is spiraling-down to hell even though my body still lives. The Devil already has claimed and mortgaged my restive spirit. I must keep it away from *his* wretched foreclosure for as long as I possibly can.

Besides the horrible prospect of drowning, I also fear being swept away in a great deluge. I'm paranoid about tumbling over Niagara Falls either inside or without a barrel. I often wake-up from a horrendous nightmare in a cold sweat while I'm falling midway down a very deep water-well. Another nightmare that perpetually haunts my psyche has my arm caught in a coral rock crevice while I'm snorkeling near the base of an ocean reef. I fear I will soon die by drowning and then I thank the Almighty that I've woken-up from near tragedy.

My parents have disowned me. I loathe being disinherited. My former mother-in-law insists I'm possessed by at least several different demons. My wife has cruelly divorced me. I've been unemployed for over a year. My heart feels an overwhelming degree of emotional agony. I've been cruelly subjected to personal ridicule and to public scorn and rejection. All of these very egregious consequences have happened to me because of *him*.

Thank God I still have the gift of communication. *You* will soon learn that I am civil, that I am righteous, that I am compassionate, that I am still genuinely rational. Insensitive ignorant impostors masquerading as medical professionals have maliciously derided and mocked me. Those pathetic cynics are all intoxicated with their own distorted ambitions while the dolts ignore the blatant and obvious truth that I currently profess. You will soon discover that I am intelligent and that I am honest and that *you* too are vulnerable.

I swear on my ancestors' graves that I am of sound mind and of good conscience. My closest critics have placed me in a sanitarium where I've been furtively compiling this very accurate chronicle. I will not allow my immortal soul to be condemned by the stupidity of social sciences' many fallacies. Public prejudice will never be the yardstick to measure my benign character. Institutions will never crush my indomitable spirit with their myriad discrepancies. Conventional wisdom has labeled me crazy. How can I be insane when I can communicate my ideas so concisely, so lucidly?

* * * * * * * * * * * *

My mania all started several years ago at that *harmless* high school class reunion. That seemingly innocent event proved to be a travesty that would sabotage my entire future life, and maybe even *yours*. That innocuous class reunion was the origin of my present extreme alienation from mainstream civilization.

It might all seem like frivolity to a skeptical stranger, but *you*, the discerning interpreter will, once *you* have evaluated the full nature and scope of my dire situation, then *you*, the objective third party will instantly detect my story's singular veracity. So be it. I shall tell it from the beginning, for the love of Heaven and for the hate of *him*. Beware of my very intriguing tale, all of you audacious doubters and abundant cynics. I once was exactly like you. You will regret ever reading these damned words I've secretly scribbled on paper for your literary perusal.

I hereby pledge that my testament is valid. I will wager my soul on the *Wheel of Truth and Lie* that my words are honest and sincere. I hope to gain more than your empathy. I shall convert you into a warrior in my determined relentless crusade against *him*.

As I have already stated and alluded, this disastrous misadventure all horrendously began at my last high school class reunion. Thirty-five wonderful years had elapsed since graduation. The anniversary of the notable event is faithfully celebrated by my former classmates and by me every half-decade.

I had learned from *him* at my last reunion one major axiom. Three primal forces drive the behavior of human beings. Those undeniable compelling factors are biology, curiosity and fear. Those three "powers" control our every instinct, even our natural urge to love. Combined together those three entities are evil, ruthless, incessant, obsessive and absolutely invincible.

* * * * * * * * * * * *

My wife and I had faithfully attended my Edgewood Regional High School class of '60 reunion every five years. I had only been a student at Edgewood my senior year. At Levittown, Pennsylvania's Bishop Egan High I had been a class officer, a baseball player and had been very popular with my classmates. I still revere Bishop Egan as my true Alma Mater. When I had transferred into Atco, New Jersey's Edgewood High, that' transition was precisely when I had unfortunately met *him*. *He* does not masquerade in cloven hooves and feature a jagged red tail, and *he* doesn't carry a sharp-pronged pitchfork, but *his* sadistic wickedness is definitely an extension of hell itself.

I lacked sufficient time to forge meaningful friendships at Edgewood High. Few celebrants even remember me at the class reunions. If only *he* had the decency to boycott that last fatal class of '60 get-together, I would still be leading a "normal" happy gullible life. But I foolishly sought-out *his* company and I instantly became a victim of *his* vile treachery.

My soul finds some solace in making these self-serving rationalizations. You wonder what particular grudge I hold against *him*. You will be horrified to know why I feel a need for vengeance, a need that you too might share toward both *him* and *me* when you completely comprehend the fantastic magnitude of *his* nefarious scheme. Be prepared to hate two strangers.

"My Edgewood peers who do remember me recall a skinny bashful newcomer," I reminded my wife Joanne just before the thirty-fifth high school class reunion in October of 1995. "And Honey, that's exactly how I remember myself, too," I added.

"That's the same way I also remember *you*," my St. Joseph High School (of Hammonton, New Jersey) spouse answered as she gracefully entered her green chiffon dress. "Here, zip me up."

"But it's like I never had gone to school there," I complained. "It's like I don't belong. I mean, I graduated from *Glassboro State College*, but now it's changed its name to *Rowan University*. And now I hear that Edgewood High is going to switch its name to Winslow Regional. I'm totally baffled and bewildered. It's like my whole educational past is being egregiously erased right before my doubting, incredulous eyes!"

"You should go to your Bishop Egan reunions instead," my wife intelligently suggested. "I'll bet you'd have more fun connecting with those old Pennsylvania friends. You always say you were very popular there in the late '50s."

"That's over forty miles away," I negatively replied, "and besides, I never get invited because I had never graduated from Egan. And you'll never guess what? The old Pennsylvania high school is now boarded-up and the name has been switched to Conwell-Egan and the campus is now located two miles away from Levittown in Fairless Hills."

"The only kid you really talk to at the Edgewood reunion is that weird joker who would always get you in trouble with the teachers," Joanne remembered from past reunions. "And I must admit *he* gives me the creeps too!"

"*He* never would get caught misbehaving but I was always punished for whatever chaos he had mischievously instigated," I told

64

my wife. "*He* almost made me into a juvenile delinquent, but I never once suspected that *he* was so totally *malicious.*

Then my mind rehashed my relationship with *him*. 'I don't know why I ever befriended *him*,' I thought as I formed the standard Windsor knot on my tie. 'Everyone else shunned *him* as if *he* had an advanced case of small pox. I should've been as intelligent as they were,' I mentally concluded my sad recollection.

"Five years from now I want you to take me out to supper and to a decent stage show in Atlantic City," Joanne demanded. "Your Edgewood reunion is a real dud. It's for the birds. Make that for the ravenous 'buzzards'."

"Five years from now I might be dead," I joked without realizing the possible bizarre gravity of my foolish remark.

On the twelve-mile drive west from Hammonton to the prestigious Old Tavern Restaurant in Berlin, Joanne asked me the names of some people that might be at the Edgewood reunion. "The only reason people go to these things is to brag about their past and present achievements," my opinionated wife claimed. "Even my St. Joseph High reunions seem like the *I* and *Me* Arrogant Club."

"Well now, I'll bet that Frank Daniels will be there," I answered with relative certainty. "He was all state fullback in football his senior year. Now Frank's a venerable New Jersey State legislator. He'll have plenty of success to brag about."

"Wasn't there a Jerry somebody?" Joanne remembered and asked. "That first name seems to ring a bell."

"You must mean Jerry Kaiser, captain of the basketball team," I recollected and replied. "I used to copy his objective test answers in Chemistry Class. Jerry's now an important researcher at *MIT*. He married Susie Fischer, head cheerleader. She's now a prominent children's doctor up in Massachusetts."

"Will Carol Sooy, Jean Liberto, Phyllis Celia, Anita Hoffman or Marian O'Neill be there?" Joanne asked. "They're the only girls I had known that had gone to Edgewood High and who had hung-out around Hammonton."

"No Dear. I've already seen the printed list of paid attendees," I explained, "and those names you've just mentioned were not on it. You're right Ginger. This reunion looks like it's goin' to be a real boring redundant bummer!"

I pulled my merlot-colored *Nissan Maxima* up to the Old Tavern Restaurant and parked in the rear of the fine banquet hall to avoid the money-grabbing valets. As Joanne and I entered the classy establishment's main dining room, my eyes noticed numerous middle-aged people, none of whom I immediately recognized from the wear and tear that *time* had inflicted on each Edgewood graduate from the class of '60.

Then I unfortunately observed *him* sitting near an end-stool at the left side of the bar. My inner voice cautioned me to avoid any and all interaction with *him*. I should've honored my conscience's instinctive wisdom. I had always long-suspected that *he* was fundamentally and blatantly evil, right down to the tiniest electron in *his* smallest atom.

My keen scrutiny of *him* was temporarily distracted when I quickly identified Esau Washington, a six-foot-ten black basketball player who had sat in front of me in homeroom. Immediately Esau and I struck up a conversation.

"Hey Esau, do you remember me?" I boldly asked. "Don't I look vaguely familiar?"

"Yeah, you're the dude who sat right behind me in homeroom. Mr. Curly would always mark you absent because he could never see ya' sittin' behind me," Esau gleefully remembered and nostalgically verbalized.

"This is my wife Joanne," I introduced to the human giant.

"Hi, glad to meet you again at a reunion," Washington pleasantly acknowledged. "Say J.W., did ya' hear about Bill Atkins and Tommy Bevins?"

"No," I politely answered as I turned to the bar to see if *he* had observed my presence yet. "If I recall Esau, Bill Atkins was high school quarterback and Tommy Bevins was class president. I hope my failing memory still recalls reality as it was."

"That's right, Cat," Esau said and then sipped-down a heavy gulp of his *Southern Comfort* on the rocks. "Well, J.W., Bill's now the night janitor at Winslow School # 3 and Tommy's now doing rehab' for alcohol abuse," Washington related with a mild laugh at the apparent dual ironies. "Pretty hairy crap, eh?"

"Guess those preoccupied fellas' aren't here braggin' about their myriad accomplishments," I laughed and stated as Esau smiled and nodded his head in tacit agreement. "Time has a way of twisting and mangling reality around. We're all either victims or masters of fate. Esau, what about you?" I asked as I quickly glanced again over at the left end of the crowded Old Tavern bar. "What I mean is, are you retired yet from the Harlem Globetrotters?"

"Good one J.W.," Washington giggled and commended. "I've been an investigator with the Camden County Sheriff's Department ever since I graduated Trenton State College," my old very tall homeroom comrade proudly communicated. "Fact is I plan to retire from the grueling job next year."

"Well, good to see you again Essau," I sincerely replied. "Enjoy your drink and I'll perhaps talk to you again later on."

Joanne noticed a former St. Joseph High classmate that had married an Edgewood graduate of the class of '60. My wife dismissed herself from my company to go and converse with Judy Watson. I knew Judy's husband Mark from several real estate business deals I had made back in Hammonton. The bank lender was nowhere in sight, so I figured I would meander through the prattling crowd of cocktail and wine drinkers and search-out another familiar face to exchange pleasantries and sentimental anecdotes with.

I milled around the vast chamber like a jittery child, trying to evade the inevitable eye contact with *him*. I then bumped into Bob Garguilo, who had sat and often clowned around with me at *our* fifth period cafeteria table.

After I introduced myself, Bob vaguely remembered my identity from the distant past. We conversed about certain shared school experiences and finally, "Bob the mob" recalled my name and my personality by my distinct mannerisms and by my lateral-lisp minor speech impediment.

"Remember bobby-socks, D.A. haircuts and poodle skirts," I reminisced. "What about the jitterbug, the twist and *American Bandstand*?" I merrily reminded my former impish lunch period acquaintance.

"Things sure aren't quite as innocent as they used to be back in 1960," Bob momentarily frowned and grimly noted. "With all' of this rap crap J.W.," my old cafeteria companion maintained, "what ever happened to true teenage romance and to real music? I mean good old-time rock and roll Daddy-o!"

After five minutes of perfunctory small talk, I dismissed myself from Bob's illustrious company. My body wove through a cluster of synthetic palm trees overlooking circular tables heaped with tropical fruit piled inside huge colorful bowls. I passed by human-sized statues of Aphrodite, Athena and Hera, each one being sculpted and then expertly having splendid diadems gilded with gold leaf on their heads. Life-sized representations of Cupid and Diana had also been creatively carved out of real marble. 'So much for atmosphere, decor and decorum,' I peevishly and pessimistically thought. "Do I dare approach the bar and order a drink?'

My eyes detected a vacant spot at the left side of the long bar where I could get the bartender's attention fairly easily and quickly order a couple of potent Manhattans.

I confidently sauntered to my intended location with desire to leave as soon as the drinks had been obtained. I did not plan to initiate any extended conversation with one Harold J. Danforth, class egghead, intellectual maverick, resident sophist, oddball recluse, unpredictable lone wolf, and most of all, detestable abhorrent snob.

'There he is now, the lousy freakish rogue,' my mind regretted and thought. '*He* could never elevate himself above being deplorably obnoxious,' I mentally reminded myself. Joanne once told me, "He gives me the creeps!" Then she added, "He *is* the creeps"!' I lucidly remembered and then grinned.

Danforth turned in my direction and immediately recognized me. I began our perfunctory dialogue all-too-courteously. I should have stabbed the repugnant beast to death with a long sharp butcher's knife right there and then.

"How are ya' doin' Harold old boy?" I began, feigning sincerity. "Long time, no see. It's been exactly five years ago I believe," I deceitfully stated.

"Oh, J.W., it's only you again, coming around to annoy me with your annoying drivel," Danforth sadly acknowledged. "Every five years you have to bore me to sleep with your all-too-abundant petty prattle. What kind of stupid things ya' been up to now? Still living your mediocre lackluster existence in Jersey?"

"Yes, over in Hammonton," I smiled and answered, "and I'm only sitting next to you because it's the only damned empty seat available," I specifically clarified. "Nobody else wants to get anywhere near you or close to your offensive insensitive diatribe."

"You might as well be living your indolent existence in limbo or purgatory," Harold brutally criticized. "You aren't too damned popular right here and now either with anybody, except maybe your beautiful wife!"

My squinting eyes slowly glanced around the huge room and witnessed everyone else talking amiably and sharing genuine camaraderie. I wondered why I had chosen to even make eye contact with the disgusting egomaniac sitting beside me. My apprehensions and suspicions were indeed well-founded and wholly justified.

A quintet of elderly-looking gray-haired musicians climbed-up on the stage, the fellows clad in flamboyant-looking Hawaiian shirts with purple leis draped around their wrinkle-skinned fat necks. The band began playing a medley of songs from the nifty '50s', melodies and lyrics that brought back fond memories of a gentler, more civil decade than *those* that have since followed in that era's path.

My eyes casually took another glimpse around the immense chamber and I again perceived everyone still gossiping about old times, about their children, about their careers, about their exotic vacations and about their expensive summer seashore homes in Avalon, Margate, Ventnor, Brigantine, Cape May and Stone Harbor.

But Danforth was far different from the rest of the attendees. *He* was apathetic to the common interests that the other alumni were so excited about. *He* was bizarre, unorthodox, uncouth, and yet I had always found *him* totally novel, unique and different from the crowd, or better yet, from the masses. I believe that *that* drastic distinction is what had always fascinated me about *him*: his most peculiar individuality stood out like a swollen sore thumb.

"Now Danforth old buddy," I proceeded with my suave rhetoric, "let me buy you a few drinks to show you my humane civility. Then you can bombard me with your devious views of Vietnam, about test tube babies, about *AIDS*, about politics, the Middle East or about whatever else floats your boat or drafts your raft."

How utterly stupid I was! I actually thought that my casual comments would aggravate him, but the spiteful scoundrel was not one bit ruffled or perturbed by my intended nasty insults.

Danforth rather politely ordered a scotch on the rocks. I was unprepared for his next rather strange reaction. "J.W., do you realize that millions of paramecia swim around in a simple drop of ordinary water?" the dangerous apostate seriously asked. "Pollution, germs, bacteria, viruses, contamination, traces of human and animal waste, even undiscovered varieties of micro-organisms all thrive in each toxic drop of water," Harold Danforth calmly related without ever blinking an eyelash.

My better judgment figured that my stay at the bar might just be an extended one, so I generously instructed the bartender to bring us two more Manhattans and two additional scotches before the Old Tavern employee became too busy down the line to attend to *our* particular drinking needs. Then most regrettably, we resumed *our* rather awkward discussion.

* * * * * * * * * * * *

"So, we're all still alive in spite of all that filthy water contamination!" I laughed, not realizing the actual stupidity and ignorance of my ludicrous statement. "Harold, I know you've always valued trivia, but why is an insignificant irrelevant drop of water so important to an intelligent dynamic guy like you? Why can't we simply talk about something a little bigger like the origin of the Universe for instance?"

Harold J. Danforth ignored my fairly constructive suggestion and persisted in his desire to frivolously discuss the composition and the chemical structure of water. "I shudder when I think that the Earth is over four-fifths water," Danforth diabolically declared. "Water could easily kill me', and J.W., you don't yet realize it, but some day it just as easily might even destroy you."

He was so callously shrewd, adroitly enticing me into his precarious lethal corral as if I was a targeted steer being skillfully guided to the first stage of its prospective slaughter. "Water will eventually be the death of humanity," Danforth peculiarly predicted. "It's much more deadly than earthquakes or raging infernos."

"Noah escaped the great flood," I countered, "and you must admit that modern man is equipped with much better tools than those that had existed in *Biblical* times during the primitive *Bronze Age*."

"Water will certainly eliminate me and it might even eradicate you along with the remainder of our vulnerable species, too," Harold sternly and irrationally insisted, "and if you tell others all that I might tell you about water tonight, it will certainly obliterate them also, even before the relentless Grim Reaper shows his' ugly gaunt face in their neighborhoods."

The efficient bartender finally delivered the two scotches on the rocks along with the two additional Manhattans that I had ordered. Harold gulped-down his first-served mixed drink as if it were *water* and then the absurd intellectual fraud pedantically began elaborating about the Earth's microscopic place in the vast Universe in general and its small existence inside the *Milky Way* galaxy in particular.

After Harold quaffed-down his next potent scotch, the academic impostor told me that the Earth's relationship to the Universe was comparable to a microorganism's importance in relation to the *Pacific Ocean*. "And remember J.W., everyone in this room and on this insignificant miniature planet is just like an infinitesimal sub-atomic part of an amoeba," Danforth inanely pontificated before the charlatan commenced imbibing his third scotch that I had then so foolishly purchased.

"So," I dumbly replied without intelligently departing the scene, "bigger is better is only true with military power and with female breasts and hips. So, what Harold if you and I are like grains of sand on a damned beach! That's all totally silly college Philosophy 101 stuff you're trying to use to impress me!" I challenged.

My ringing ears patiently listened again to Harold's monotonous perception of man's inconsequential place in the gigantic Universe. If Danforth had lived in ancient Greece, he would have made Diogenes look like a flamboyant optimist.

"J.W., the entire population of the United States is nothing more than two-hundred and ninety million or so naked 'time slaves' all trying to scale a gargantuan wall," Harold maintained, utilizing a rather queer analogy. "And *that* numerical figure is not counting all of the unregistered illegal aliens. But each person is licking above and defecating below, wallowing amidst tons of human waste in one colossal human pyramid. That's *their* perception of a normal life. Just look at *them* standing around and sharing useless bits of negligible information," Harold suggested as the maniac pointed to the other alumni assembled inside the massive banquet room.

"Bartender, give this man two more scotches," I directed. If only I knew what type of grotesque monster my generosity was hatching. I closely studied Danforth's vernal-looking face. I finally mustered the nerve to ask him a seemingly pertinent question my mind had been pondering ever since I had arrived at the bar and seated myself next to *him*. My rather innocent inquiry would later change my life for the worse. My curiosity was about to give birth to a heinous pernicious vile mendacious grotesque abomination.

"I think twice before I turn on a faucet," Danforth continued as the contemporary sophist stared blankly at his empty glass of scotch. "Do you realize J.W. that simple every-day faucets are very dangerous and also are potentially lethal objects?"

I evaluated Harold's latest jargon as mere academic gibberish coming from a drunken idiot's mouth, but I couldn't be more wrong in assessing the basic truths of his strange revolutionary theory as I would inadvertently discover five years later.

"J.W., if everyone on this freakin' planet was a plumber, the colossal problem could never be adequately addressed let alone solved," Danforth cryptically disclosed. "It's quite a rather futile situation I'm describing!"

My mind figured that I had better change the subject from such imbecilic rambling about hazardous water molecules to something more acceptably sensible. "Harold, you just have to tell me a truthful answer," my curious mind and mouth insisted. "Be careful, because St. Peter will hold you responsible for your deeds and misdeeds at the Pearly Gates, especially if you dare lie."

"Exactly what do ya' want to know J.W.?" Danforth asked as he reached and fumbled for his next drink that had just been delivered.

"It's been thirty-five grueling years since we graduated from Edgewood," I indicated. "Yet you don't have a wrinkle on your face and not one gray hair on your head. You look exactly as you did back in high school. Remarkably, you apparently haven't aged a day since graduation."

Harold took a sip from his new glass of scotch and smiled to signify his general satisfaction with my sage perceptive observation. I figured I should proceed with my flattery.

"Your impeccable teeth Harold; they still look like polished ivory, and your physique is slender and exactly as I remember it being when we went gallivantin' all over DC on the senior class Washington trip," I foolishly praised the fake savant. "Have you discovered what Ponce de Leon never found? Tell me straight; how have you eluded the formidable ravages of time?"

Harold Danforth's cheeks turned rosy. His eyebrows slanted downward and the poor excuse for a human being stared at me with fixed beady eyes. I awaited his presumed exaggerated reply with feigned cordiality.

My former friend imbibed another mouthful of scotch and then hunched his shoulders forward. Then Danforth's goose-like neck retreated into his tie-less white shirt like a tortoise's head does going into its protective shell. I imagined him wearing a sign that read "Warning: Danger Area: Keep Your Distance!" My vigilance was finally rewarded with a succinct terse response, a totally amazing response which I now wish I had never solicited or elicited.

"J.W., you ought to mind your own damned business. Your bloodhound nose should be sniffing around somewhere in safer territory," the royal prevaricator uttered in a freakish arcane manner. "You might suffer drastic consequences if this private conversation continues any further. Do you understand?"

"I always said I wanted to be reincarnated as a revered hunting dog," I whimsically joked, symbolically referring to me being a sleuth. "Now's my chance!"

"This serious business I'm presently discussing with you is no laughing matter," Danforth persisted with his grand lunacy. "I have no time for sleuths or for reckless impetuous dreamers like you J.W., and frankly, I totally detest your prying into my personal treasure chest of esoteric cosmic secrets. My youthful appearance is *my* own personal business and only *mine*! Is that simplistic minor detail perfectly clear?"

How incredibly naive I was! *He* was luring me into his kill zone like a shark fisherman's smelly bloody chum attracts a Great White. I should have known that Danforth was only faking his ill will, that in fact *he* was *baiting* me as if I had been a targeted blue marlin or a common sea bass. His sharp brown eyes were cold, cunning and calculating. Harold's staccato voice seemed prehistoric, atavistic, distant and preternatural. It sounded as if it were originating from another dimension, from another bleak much darker world.

I sensed that Danforth's evil sinister-side was about to betray my all-too-honest curiosity. I should have terminated our discussion right then and there because the detestable predator was merely parrying with me, testing my mettle, assessing my weak resolve. His words were not theatrical or contrived. They were powerful and antediluvian, seemingly not of this time or place.

Now I promise I shall not wander any further from the essence of my extraordinary tale. Heed my sage advice! Be very alert and cautious! *You too* might be voraciously consumed into this wild madness, just as I had been. You too might be swiftly relegated to your animal nature and proceed to define all reality from *that* wicked perspective. *You* will soon learn why I abhor every baneful molecule of protoplasm within *him*. Soon your exposed mind and your victimized soul, like mine, will become *his* doomed hostage.

"But Harold, everyone else in this room looked about the same as they had back in high school at our' tenth class reunion," I observed and pragmatically reviewed. "Some of us had minutely changed and aged at our twentieth get-together. Thirty-years later everyone had dramatically become altered by age except you. After thirty-five years," I commented and marveled, "you are the only class member that has successfully managed to escape the wrath of Father Time."

Harold J. Danforth re-actively bit his tongue. His bar stool posture became more stilted and less erect than before. I was not asking him for last night's trigonometry homework or for extra cafeteria lunch money as I had frequently done thirty-five years before. I had regrettably hit a very sensitive nerve in his heinously evil psyche.

From observing his skittish body language, I worried that Harold was about to enter an epileptic seizure. If only I knew better, I would have gotten up from my rickety bar stool and immediately left his devious company. Danforth simply sat there in a half-drunken stupor, meditating whether or not to divulge the essence of his great paradigm. I naively listened attentively to *his* rather outrageous and outlandish rhetoric.

"Through my diligent research, I have learned how to out-race the Grim Reaper," the human enigma vaguely answered my solicitous inquiry. Harold then wiggled his nose as if he were a hyperactive rabbit. Danforth was about to release the essence of what I then believed was merely a "perverted perplexing joke-type riddle." All he needed was a little more coaxing and the untrustworthy villain would cease being so nebulous and then spill forth his highly coveted secret like *Mt. Etna* spewing-out lava. I didn't know that *his* "arcane knowledge" could be more lethal and more destructive than any natural disaster, or any powerful volcano, or any other cataclysmic calamity could ever inflict upon the Earth.

Danforth scrutinized me with his large brown eyes that seemed magnified three times their normal size by his super-thick bifocals.

"Now Harold," I persisted and urged, "it's almost as if you've been preserved in a germ-free environment, a benign time capsule, or a nurturing protective bubble so to speak. Tell me, do you bathe in formaldehyde?" I jokingly asked my mentor/tormentor. "You can share your fabulous secret with me. I solemnly pledge never to tell a living or dead soul!" I quixotically laughed as I tried defrosting his historical glacial-like coldness toward civilization.

"I strongly feel I cannot expose my study of immortality to you at this moment," Danforth stubbornly insisted. "If I do, I fear I would jeopardize my immunity to aging. There are supreme powerful forces acting here that I don't fully comprehend. I just can't trust anyone with my fantastic discovery. Do you fathom my words?"

"I don't understand what's so dangerous," I jested. "Do you drink nectar and eat ambrosia in imitation of the Olympian gods? Have you signed a strategic non-trade contract with the Prince of Darkness?" I indulgently laughed before swallowing-down more delicious liquor.

"I'm extremely fearful of the dreaded unknown consequences that could result," Harold divulged. "You can't imagine how afraid I am. I really and truly shrink away from the retribution of the awesome *Hidden World.* It is quite omnipotent and vindictive, much more so than you could ever imagine J.W., despite the salient fact that *it's* entirely invisible to us. I fear that I'll be violently crushed like a bothersome floor insect under a giant's shoe if I insolently disobey the *Invisible World's* inflexible set laws. I don't wish to be smashed out of existence like a damned disgusting cockroach J.W."

"Are you telling me that some kind of supernatural force will exterminate you like a pathetic cockroach if you share your fabulous discovery with me?" I questioned, adroitly employing the Socratic

Method of thinking. "What kind of ruthless demons inhabit this remarkable ubiquitous *Hidden World* of yours?"

"J.W., although I do not age," Danforth uttered in a shaky tone of voice that seemed virtually believable, "I can still die by disease, by being run over by a *Mack* truck, by being shot, or by perishing in a fire or tsunami. Accidents can still terminate my existence even though I'm now quite immortal as long as I can avoid potential accidents or natural disasters."

I was completely astonished. My curiosity was peaking. I stupidly begged my former classmate for more defining details. What an absolute irresponsible incompetent dunce I was! I couldn't say anything clever or erudite at that culminating phase of our dialogue; I had become both spellbound and speechless.

* * * * * * * * * * * *

"J.W., true, I *am* generally sheltered from the avaricious aging process," Danforth euphorically confirmed. "My very life depends on all the practical discretion I can muster. I must continually exercise restraint in every move or decision that I make. I want to enjoy living without the ever-present prospect of death. If I tell you what I've learned and know, I might be jeopardizing all of that meticulous precaution by recklessly throwing caution to the wind!"

Harold J. Danforth was then at that moment in a virtual self-induced trance. My comprehension recognized his words, yet I could not grasp their full meaning until the diabolical paragon finally told me certain additional particulars that instantly changed my perception of life and of living. I suspected that *he* must have read some medieval book on sorcery or black magic to be presently thinking so erratically and so fearfully the way that he was.

"J.W., you understand that I must keep my great knowledge sacrosanct," Harold Danforth surreptitiously emphasized and maintained. "I am a partner with omnipotent astral energies that your limited mind cannot even begin to imagine. I must never violate *that* already assumed-but-established harmonious alliance which I've made with the Omnipotent Universe. If I reveal *my* amazing secret to you now, I shudder to think that quick and devastating punishment might instantly follow my disclosure."

I had never before in my entire life heard such unmitigated nonsense emanating from anyone's lips. I was totally puzzled. Was Harold enacting some sort of mystical pretense? A charade perhaps? Were my ears hearing sagacity or was it simply absurdity being articulated from his lying lips? Had Harold actually made an evil pact with the formidable *Powers That Be*? Perhaps the pseudo-intellectual fanatic had signed a Plutonian covenant with Hades?

At that particular moment while we were seated at the noisy bar, it all seemed like ethereal poppycock, an incomprehensible crock of nonsensical bull. That falsity, I had thought, and *that* erroneous notion I had wrongfully believed, but my suspicious and reliable sixth sense certainly perceived otherwise.

Harold's face was now very serious and stern-looking, reflecting a sincere, grim expression. His demeanor at the bar reminded me of a pregnant woman an hour before she is about to deliver her child. Whatever unbearable burden was troubling *him*, he had to eventually *deliver it* out and share the terrible wisdom with someone that possessed sympathetic ears.

My petty pedantic colleague Harold J. Danforth sensed and felt he needed to finally communicate his excessive burden to me, but conversely, the inebriated fellow also knew that he really shouldn't-risk the consequences of revealing it to anyone. I saw intense pain beaming from his eyes and seemingly reflected in his melancholy now-pallid face. My Old Tavern bar stool companion required just a degree more of convincing.

"Stop repeating yourself about that *Powers of the Universe* crap!" I belligerently exclaimed into his vernal-looking face. "I promise you Harold, I'll talk to no one about your sublime truths, not even my wife," I candidly pledged. "Quite obviously, this law, this principle or whatever you want to call it has had its heavy toll on your mental health. It seems like some sort of great sacrifice you're making, a tremendous burden you feel that you must unload. You know you can't live with it all by yourself any longer. Exactly what have you traded or given-up to get what you have?" I anxiously implored. "Remember Mr. Jenkins telling his Chemistry Class that everything must always balance out on both sides of the equation."

I discreetly made my persuasive remarks very judiciously, very prudently. I had attempted to win over Harold's confidence, and the perverted phantom dwelling deep within him did not seem too enamored with my continuous interrogation. I sincerely desired to alleviate Danforth's very apparent apprehension along with his observable escalating depression. Harold raised his hands to his face and covered his eyes in anguish. Harold's cerebrum, his heart, his hidden subconscious mind and his soul were all swirling-around in a massive internal quandary. I felt a degree of sorrow for the great duress that his beleaguered conscience was undergoing.

Felt sorrow! I should have castrated and decapitated *him'* right there on the spot. I should have slain the dreadful monster before he could ever pronounce another sentence. The miserable knave methodically lowered his hands from his thick-rimmed Buddy Holly eyeglasses. His formerly lithe fingers began quivering. His lips puckered. His eyelids rapidly blinked.

My attentive pupils searched around the mammoth hall to see if anyone else had noticed Harold's severe psychological struggle, which had impressed me as being half-dramatic, half-awe-inspiring, and wholly and traumatically frightening.

Shafts of glimmering light refracted through the lenses of various rotating colored ceiling disks situated at all four quadrants of the spacious banquet room. The many-colored light beams converged and magically converted the room into a kaleidoscopic, surrealistic, almost supernatural atmosphere.

Dense cigarette smoke billowed-up into low clouds that acted like a giant spectrum without an appropriate prism as the puffs wafted-around and then eerily joined forces with the artificial shafts of light. I saw former classmates mingling around hors d'oeuvres trays, while others were glibly exchanging their trivial anecdotes and eating shrimp and crab meat from their tiny plates while standing around the three, long, linen-covered appetizer tables. All of those occurrences I acutely observed through the hypnotic revolving rainbows inside the amazingly enchanting banquet room.

"Truly Harold, two pillars are stronger than one," I claimed and argued. "Let me share the weight of your great burden."

"I hate to sound too metaphysical since it's contrary to my general cynical nature," Danforth confessed. "I don't want to see you so wickedly eternally cursed as I presently am."

"Will you' please get on with your damned narrative!" I yelled, losing my tolerance with the instigator's ongoing evasive tactics. "I'm quickly losing my patience and my self-control, and also, I'm about to get physically violent with you any second now!"

Harold reluctantly told me how he had been fascinated with mythology in high school and how Zeus and the other Olympian gods had discovered immortality but then kept the fabulous secret from humans. "I enjoy keeping my discovery to myself," Harold related as if he were a contemporary Zeus. "I derive a certain pleasure watching *you* and those other proletarian idiots out there progress steadily along the, as H.G. Wells so aptly put it in the *Time Machine* novel,' along the definite time line called history."

My eyes again glanced around the very large banquet hall and my 20/30 imperfect vision focused on Joanne, who was casually trading pleasantries with Bob Bauers, Nichole DeSordi and Nancy Ranger, three Hammonton people she knew from our church. 'I don't know what is worse,' I thought, 'listening to meaningless gossip or listening to Danforth's meaningless craziness.'

"Harold, stop being so vague and downright nebulous," I neurotically complained and accused. "*Mt. Olympus* doesn't explain a blessed thing about your obscure *Fountain of Youth* knowledge. Get on with it!"

Danforth again leaned forward, and for confidentiality's sake, the 'irascible rascal' whispered so that not even the bartender standing three feet away could hear his distressing words. "I warn you for the last time J.W., I'm endangering myself and *you* by telling this eternal secret. If I die soon, *you* will be held accountable for my' demise, do you understand the gravity of my statement?" Danforth softly uttered with an element of heightened alarm very evident in his hoarse stammering voice.

I again gazed around the impressive hall and perceived people loudly talking and boisterously laughing, people completely apathetic toward the lunatic Danforth's continuous inexplicable youth and presently quite ignorant of Danforth's terrible emotional meltdown. At that moment my mind was quite dizzy from the many potent Manhattans I had consumed, and I felt a bit feverish and nauseous too. I mechanically bobbed my head to indicate feigned agreement with Harold's litany of preposterous declarations. His excessive procrastination was truly frustrating my composure and also gradually eroding my all-too-susceptible emotional stability.

Harold explained that he had always been fond of biology in addition to favoring ancient mythology. The avid reader divulged that many remarkable inventions are mere imitations of simple things we take for granted in nature. "J.W., the camera is modeled after the human eye," Harold anxiously explained, "and the telephone is merely a crude adaptation of the human ear. And also J.W., the computer files and classifies information away just like the human brain does."

"So!" I loudly exclaimed in my standard obnoxious voice when not impressed by someone's flimsy comment. "Everybody is aware of *those* very simple elementary school associations. Harold, at best you're speaking ninth grade science crap now. Stop beating around the proverbial bush."

"So J.W., all human activities like seeing, hearing, thinking, and even aging can be modified to conform with the needs of the experimenter. The *ends* can be arranged to justify the *means*. And, besides *that* rather functional, fundamental truism," Danforth nervously added, "scientific principles can work in reverse, but nobody seems to ever care about *that actuality!* Those idiotic scientists in all major disciplines just want to go forward, not backwards."

I was growing weary of Danforth's deliberate attempt at being facetious and evasive. I urgently insisted that he be more exact, more specific or else I would leave him alone at the noisy bar to commit a dramatic public suicide all on his own.

Harold J. Danforth next related that the human body has all three states of matter that need to co-exist in order to support life. "Our flesh and bones are *solids* J.W., our blood and fluids are obviously *liquids*, and our noble minds and souls are abstractly ethereal, or should I say *gas*-like."

"Big deal!" I defiantly challenged the psychopathic liar. "You should teach eighth grade science for a damned living."

"J.W., the trick to immortality is to keep *your* spiritual gas confined inside the perimeter of *your* solid and liquid composition. Do you understand?" Harold rhetorically asked. "I'm not speaking eighth grade science to you now!"

"Not exactly," I answered while still philosophically disagreeing with his fraudulent premise. "It all sounds too unrealistic to either appreciate or mentally digest! I have enough trouble controlling my own intestinal gas," I giddily laughed as I inadvertently spilled some of my Manhattan on the bar counter.

Although the existence of *inverted* physical laws seemed remotely plausible, I still skeptically thought that Danforth was being too characteristically coy, too inscrutable for his own good. I should have known that my persistent tenacity would soon doom me to eternal depression. "You're being too obscure and indirect!" I boisterously accused my nefarious comrade above the surrounding din. "Give me something tangible to logically consider!" I demanded. "I think I've wasted the last half hour conversing with a garrulous dunce!"

"I urge you J.W., heed my wise advice," Harold neurotically warned, his anatomy shaking as if he was suddenly experiencing severe flu symptoms. "Go talk to your wife and her harmless small-minded friends right now. You'll regret hearing all that I have to tell you. Believe me, you'll despise me and my name forever!"

"Tell me now or else I *will* definitely go over and join my wife and her small-minded friends right this very minute!" I yelled like a stark-raving maniac. "You my drunken friend sound like you're the epitome of stupidity!"

"Very well then!" the lonely recluse acceded. Danforth very deliberately revealed that he had been investigating his theory of "breathing backwards" while a graduate student at the *University of Pennsylvania*. "I was taking a night course on Eastern Religions and I soon became a devout student of yoga breathing exercises," Harold indicated. "I developed a rather simple theory that was a miraculous marriage of ancient Oriental philosophy and modern Occidental scientific pragmatism."

I smiled at Harold, thinking that his half-baked idea belonged in the "Recycle Bin" displayed on my desktop computer screen. I had been gaffed like a prized game fish and now I couldn't shake the sharp hook out of my mouth. I felt like *I was his* personal game fish being reeled in as a trophy after swallowing his *chum* bait

"Suddenly J.W., it all came together for me," Harold excitedly related. "Everyone including Socrates, Plato, Aristotle, Newton, Galileo, Einstein, Shakespeare, and even the great gurus of classical history, they all breathed the exact same way. All humans first inhale and then they exhale. We all regard the rudimentary method as being perfectly normal. We all perform a subliminal counting in our subconscious minds as we engage in respiration: one-two, one-two, one-two, and we subconsciously recite those words as a common breathing mantra. The number one represents inhaling, and the number two is when we exhale. Do you read me?"

"So!" I fatuously argued. "That's so elementary in scope and sequence that even a kindergarten kid has mastered all there is to know about basic animal and human respiration."

"Remember this J.W., Isaac Newton purported that for every action, there is an opposite and equal reaction," Harold Danforth reminded me from Mr. Jenkins high school Physics Seminar. "If *you reverse* the subconscious message and exhale first and then inhale second, establishing a rhythm of two-one, two-one, two-one," Harold crazily related, "then you stop aging by simply successfully breathing backwards. By first exhaling and then inhaling, you've reversed the aging process in all of your cells because you have in effect reversed the breathing process."

"You've fallen too far from your tree!" I laughed. "You're completely out of your gourd! You need psychiatric help immediately," I negligently and ignorantly chuckled.

"J.W, breathing backwards will invert the biological signals from the brain. The reversed breathing will reverse the body's biochemistry and the aging process will also be subsequently reversed. The new rhythm will soon be reprogramming your genes, your chromosomes, your hormones, well, your' everything!"

"What an absolutely mind-boggling *inspiration*!" I inanely exclaimed, unaware of my unintended dumb pun. "How do you stop from regressing into an infant if you're constantly getting younger?" I disrespectfully mocked.

"I breathe the two-one pattern one day and then I breathe the one-two pattern the next," Harold confidentially disclosed. "That way, once I got back to looking like I'm eighteen again, I have stayed the same age every single day."

The entire matter all seemed so ridiculously elementary that Harold's bizarre theory positively bordered on the preposterous. "How could that be?" I ranted in his ear. "What you said is logical but it sounds pretty damned illogical too! It's like saying and arguing that a spider is a mammal. It's grammatically correct, but in fact, it's also simultaneously quite scientifically irrational."

"Are you a totally inept moron?" Harold condescendingly wanted to know. "When a tape recorder rewinds, it will go back and play the same music it had played earlier. If a car goes backwards, it will occupy the same space it had moments before. If you become adept at breathing backwards, then you're essentially reversing the *aging mantra* that Mother Nature had surreptitiously programmed into your tiny brain at birth," Harold insisted. "Humans are nothing more than nature's computers, J.W. We just follow genetic programs instilled inside us. I've now gone against my conscience and given you the essential knowledge you need to know in order to effectively reprogram yourself against both aging and so-called natural death."

I swallowed the rest of my final potent mixed drink, hoping that Harold would start talking about the *Phillies* or about deer hunting or about the high price of gasoline. I noticed that I had exhausted thirty-five dollars of the Ulysses S. Grant I had plunked-down on the bar counter. I awkwardly picked-up the ten-spot, leaving the bartender a modest five-dollar tip.

"J.W., by breathing in reverse order," Danforth very distinctly enunciated and summarized, "*you* are really rewinding the mainspring of your biological clock!"

"It all sounds too good and too easy to be true," I commented like a disgusted renegade Judas Iscariot. "If you' really think about it, the whole pretentious notion approaches sheer lunacy!"

"Remember what esteemed Lord Byron had stated about the relationship of truth to fiction," Danforth reminded me. "If *you* simply practice the basic method that I've told you about, then you will stop aging. Truer words were never spoken."

My aching head turned and looked at my reunion class's fellow members and their talkative spouses sounding like an all-too-close indiscernible *Tower of Babel*. I saw for the first time an assemblage of fickle fools jabbering gibberish amidst the eddying spirals of multi-colored thick smoke. I then viewed *them* exactly as Harold Danforth perceived the remainder of humanity, an aggregation of self-centered dolts, ignorantly growing older by the second, all of them moronic blue marlins and Great White sharks splashing-around in a phony ocean of flattery, praise, egotism and foolish fawning; all of them just preparing to surrender their minds, hearts, bodies, souls and wills to ever-stalking Death.

My haggard brain imagined Joanne, Bob Bauers, Nancy Ranger and the rest of my' simpleton peers all wearing outrageously high dunce caps on their pointed heads as the gaggle babbled and cackled on about anything and everything that was not in any way, shape or form relevant to immortality.

I thanked Harold J. Danforth for his unique and singular company. My conversation with the loner had eclipsed everything else I remembered from my thirty-fifth Edgewood High School class of '60 reunion. 'No doubt Danforth is still questioning whether he should have divulged his great postulate to me after I had deliberately isolated his intoxicated presence at the crowded bar and then interrogated his vulnerable psyche as if I was a determined county prosecutor,' I thought as I groggily ambled over to finally speak a few pleasantries with Joanne, Bob and Nancy.

* * * * * * * * * * * *

I did not dare discuss the nature of my extended bar conversation with Joanne on the ride home from the Old Tavern back to Hammonton. My wife would have viewed "the eternal life reverse breathing law" as nothing more than a silly juvenile fairy tale.

From *that* "Road to Damascus" "Epiphany Moment" night on, I have quite faithfully and secretly practiced Harold Danforth's indispensable reverse breathing method. At first it was very difficult to abandon the familiar routine "one-two" cadence I had used since birth, but after hours of assiduous discipline, I had finally mastered the new rhythmic technique in a mere several months.

'What a truly delightful change this reverse respiration is!' I appreciatively thought. 'I'm getting and feeling younger with each passing day. 'Oxygen is a gas', Danforth had reminded me, 'and my soul and my conscience are both basically abstract intangible gases. It all now makes perfect indisputable sense. Gases must balance out liquids and solids inside the human body. Breathing backwards magically makes *that* wonderful phenomenon happen more efficiently.'

Four years had rapidly passed by and I was definitely feeling much healthier and stronger. Quietly I became arrogantly belittling of all those unfortunate loyal adherents of the traditional aging process, all of whom were also advocates of the inhaling/exhaling style of regular "one-two" breathing. After my first year actively experimenting with Danforth's flawless reverse breathing methodology, I then knew in my heart that I had been satisfactorily and gradually conquering that repulsive debilitating adversary known as "death by aging."

Joanne casually dismissed my increased daily energy and my greater stamina, but my spouse had trouble dealing with my lust for carnal gratification. "You must think you're a teenager again!" my wife often quipped. "You're frantically searching for a second childhood as you pass through the trauma of middle-age! Get a grip, grow-up and act your age!"

Let my former beautiful Italian wife speculate all she wants. I realize I have experienced a glorious Renaissance in body strength and also in my now-confident ego. I always feel vibrant and virile in anything I attempt or pursue. I no longer get the flu or common colds or seasonal allergies. 'Joanne would certainly berate me with a litany of stinging verbal barbs if I ever dared share my specific knowledge with her,' I smiled and thought as I gazed intently into the bathroom mirror and admired my physical prowess. 'Thank you, Harold Danforth for gloriously changing my life for the better.'

I no longer feel that Danforth's extraordinary "discovery" is a cute vignette or some insular inadequate fictional allegory. But I soon learned the true meaning of "cosmic terror" and instantly became awed by its transcendent overwhelming power.

Nearly five years had then elapsed since Danforth had educated me about his fantastic reverse breathing knowledge. Locks of curly brown hair began replacing the bald spots on the top of my head. My general health and strength were measurably improving day by day. Mr. Loomis, my employer at the real estate agency, appreciated my new sales success and so my grateful boss wholeheartedly granted me a substantial "annual bonus."

All along my marvelous return to youth, I was very aware that someday my "secret" might somehow turn on me, haunt me, backfire and ultimately, possibly destroy me. I had often pondered the inherent risks associated with being both immortal and perishable simultaneously.

"Honey, next week is my fortieth Edgewood reunion," I reminded Joanne in early October of *Y2K*.

"Do we have to go to that giant bore?" my disappointed wife objected. "Can't you take me to *Bally's Casino* or to the *Taj* instead? Anything in Atlantic City is better than that grueling event."

"I'll take you to the boardwalk venues next week, I promise," I sincerely answered. "We'll go down to A.C. seven days after the reunion and spend several nights there. What do ya' say?"

"Now I'm a little more interested in attending your dull drab reunion," Joanne euphorically replied. "This year it's going to be at Kerri-Brooke, right here in town. I'll try my very best to endure the monotony!"

My eyes again inspected my magnificent appearance in the master bathroom mirror. 'I'm going to live longer than Methuselah ever imagined he could,' I cheerfully thought. 'I'm going to tell my good pal Danforth all about my new stamina and genuinely thank him for my terrific new lease on life.'

I was certain that I had thwarted and reversed the cruel aging process. I knew I had become deft at exhaling and then inhaling because Joanne had said that she often heard me counting backwards in my sound sleep. 'I'll vanquish and thoroughly trounce the Washington bureaucracy,' I contemplated. 'I'll be on *Social Security* forever. I'll happily collect what I've contributed a hundred times over and completely beat the whole lousy government system.'

But like most fools, I was completely ignorant of my folly. I have already stated in the beginning of this narrative how much biology, fear and curiosity combine to influence daily human existence on this planet. Danforth's reverse breathing *mantra* touched upon the *biology* aspect, my *curiosity* led to my mastery of reverse breathing and now, I was to learn the third applicable facet, *fear.* My false sense of eternal welfare suddenly collapsed just before my next Edgewood Regional High Class of '60 reunion. It was then that I soon knew both horror and penance all-too-well.

While Joanne was in the bathroom taking her shower the night before my fortieth reunion, I peered at the morning copy of the *Atlantic City Press*. I incidentally opened the paper to the "Obituary Page" and then scanned through the names to see if any remote acquaintances had passed away. I automatically became shocked when I read that Harold J. Danforth of Atco, New Jersey had accidentally drowned in a neighbor's swimming pool.

I then quickly and nervously turned to the "Local News Section" to see if I could glean more associated details from a regular article. A brief column described the unexpected tragedy. A paramedic called to the drowning scene was quoted as saying, "Our desperate attempts at artificial respiration failed to revive the victim. I've never before seen so much fluid come out of a man's lungs. It was as if the gentleman were trying to breathe underwater. He must have been so panic-stricken that he *inhaled* underwater when obviously he should have been exhaling."

Harold J. Danforth's strange death struck a sad note deep inside my soul. I told my wife that we were not going to attend the fortieth reunion at Kerri-Brooke Caterers. Instead, I escorted Joanne to the boardwalk's glittering casinos, but throughout the entire evening, I was very withdrawn, reticent and rather miserable all night long.

I now have nightmares of sphinxes, chimeras, cyclops, minotaurs and gorgons trying to drown and trample me in all different depths of water. I told Joanne that my horrific nightmares were an extension of acute insomnia.

"You need immediate psychological and theological help," my opinionated, devoted spouse sternly recommended. "I think an exorcist would probably prove most beneficial."

"I need anything but a glass of water," I emphatically answered. "I never want to drink another glass of water for as long as I live."

"You're becoming stir-crazy," Ginger logically criticized. "You make no sense at all."

"The whole world is crazy, but I'm certainly not," I replied, defending my valued integrity and my esoteric reverse breathing knowledge to the hilt.

"Why did you sell our waterbed?" my spouse demanded to know. "It was so comfortable and relaxing! That thing was one of our most cherished luxuries."

"Because I was afraid of dying by drowning in it," I softly and unconvincingly answered, a trifle too candidly.

Six months later my wife filed for divorce. If only she' knew my anguish, my guilt, my penitence, and my excruciating emotional suffering. Joanne will live to regret her drastic legal actions against me, and in the future, she will ultimately pay with her life for her commonplace agnostic views about my sanity, about human death and about human immortality.

Now *you* too share *my* incredible secret knowledge. *We* don't require psychiatrists, doctors, clergymen or counselors, now do we? *We* really require an army of highly proficient exorcists as Joanne had suggested. Am *I* mad? Are *you* mad? Are *we* mad? If only *we* had gills. It wouldn't really matter then.

You are now my privileged accomplice in this great evolving catastrophe. I truly pity you. You will soon know that the powers of the *Invisible World* are mind-boggling and extremely overwhelming. Fantasy and stark reality have consolidated into one lethal puzzle, a strange conundrum whose specifics lack definition and clarity until *you* begin evaluating the confounded mystery of "water."

My pathetic aqua-phobia is now *yours* to share and to endure. Soon *you* will feel the pressures of this sick mania enveloping your spirit. I recently read a plausible account in a science magazine where an adult could drown in a bathtub containing only two inches of water. Three times I have accidentally fallen out of bed dreaming that I had been a bewildered *Titanic* cruise passenger without any accessible lifeboat to enter.

My psychiatrist reports that my erratic thought patterns "lack clarity, coherency, unity and organization." What does *he* know about immortality? What does *he* know about the multiple dangers associated with everyday mundane water?

Our life drives have been equipped with two imperatives: to survive by eating and drinking and the need to reproduce. But I still adhere to the central truth of Danforth's phenomenal disclosure. My living cells are in perfect harmony with all the lifeless matter present all around me. I am now just as permanent, just as durable and just as eternal as the Earth itself. Water is *our* chief ally and also our chief nemesis.

Now is *your* opportunity to revisit the innocence of *your* wondrous youth. Two-one, two-one, two-one: that reverse *mantra* pattern will grant *you* the chance of becoming immortal. Exhale and inhale with deliberate awareness. It will only take you several months of conscientious discipline to develop and perfect the skill.

Live in defiance of certain supernatural predators that persistently stalk human beings every earthly day. Learn to live precariously as I do but stay away from accidental death, and by all means, heed *our* vital need to fear water.

Do *you* now regard *me* as being a wanton devil for democratizing Danforth's great discovery? My Edgewood Regional High School classmates had regarded Harold as if he were a contagious leper. And *their* narrow-minded prejudice kept them safe and at a distance from *his* great malice. But conversely, their gross ignorance *makes* them extremely vulnerable to the stalking Grim Reaper's relentless steady advance.

You must adapt and live with your new-found "gift" and your new-found "curse." Harold Danforth was right when the inimitable sage told me that *academics* have nothing to do with *wisdom*. All those souls who are currently deceased should be revered as great benefactors to civilization. But my hero, the illustrious Harold Danforth, should have museums, schools, highways and stadiums named in his honor. His impeccable knowledge that *we* now share had abruptly killed him. The vindictive forces of the *Invisible World* might next decide by fate's decree to dispose of both *you* and *me.*

And now I have sadly lost my real estate career. Mr. Loomis soon joined ranks with my wife, my parents, my mother-in-law, my minister, my counselor and my psychiatrist. My new enemies have all waged a concerted campaign to discredit me and to dismantle my remaining dignity. Why should I care *what they* think? I plan to be around centuries after *those sanctimonious dolts* are deceased.

We will all laugh exceedingly while witnessing *their* mortal departures into the hereafter. *We* will relish seeing all other non-believers disappear into oblivion, their tarnished souls escaped from decaying bodies, bodies which will be deposited beneath cemetery epitaphs engraved in cold gray granite. Yes, and a century later those apathetic deceased souls will have become fully forgotten memories.

All *we* have to do is stay away from personal disaster. I shudder whenever I see tidal waves and hurricanes being reported on the television screen. I suddenly become claustrophobic whenever I see fish swimming about in enormous aquariums. Sometimes at the mere sight of a pond or lake my body twitches as if I suffer from palsy. St. Vitus, please have mercy on me! Please have mercy on *us!*

My delirium and my misery are now also *your* crosses to bear daily. My' elevated anxiety, along with my inconsolable depression, are now *yours* to tolerate also. My special breathing gift to you is also a very wretched curse in disguise.

Harold Danforth had had a short cameo role appearance on my life's stage as I have now played a small but now-significant part on *yours.* I must warn *you*: keep a safe distance from pools, ponds, lakes, brooks, lagoons, creeks, inlets, streams, swamps, rivers, marshes, channels, straits, canals, everglades, bays, gulfs, seas and oceans. Be wary! Our frail mortal bodies are almost ninety-five percent water. *We* could possibly drown from within! *We* humans are basically nothing more than intelligent water.

Hell knows no amnesty. Lucifer be damned! Pluto be damned! Poseidon be damned! Damnation be damned! And yes, Harold J. Danforth be damned too!

If morbid Charon steers his macabre barge in my direction, I will laugh directly into his skeletal face and boldly steal his coveted toll coins of passage. Then I shall spit into his hideous bony hand's palm. I shall brazenly throw the Grim Rower from his ghastly boat and make death's ferryman swim back to Hades black foreboding shores. I shall prevail. I assure *you*, in the end w*e* shall prevail.

Water is the most dangerous and lethal threat to *our* earthly survival and happiness. Two atoms of oxygen plus one atom of hydrogen form one molecule of water. Remember what tiny atoms had done to Hiroshima and to Nagasaki and to Chernobyl. Guard *your* accursed retrieved youth with *your* every precious breath.

I have become Harold's only true apostle. Now *you* are my devoted disciple. Let's be positive about *our* dilemma! Danforth's reversed breathing *mantra* is most definitely inspiration for all.

"Dual Events"

My wife and I had never been to Bermuda. Joanne and I had always previously vacationed at resorts on popular islands in the *Caribbean*. We had enjoyed week-long hiatuses on exotic isles like Barbados, Puerto Rico, Aruba and St. Thomas. We once took a *Cunard* cruise from San Juan to Venezuela, which featured scenic stops in Grenada, St. Lucia, St. Marten, St. John and St. Croix.

Joanne and I have always been warm-weather people. We prefer sunbathing and snorkeling to winter lodges, snowmobiles and skiing. Our travel agent had recommended Bermuda anytime from May to October to experience the best weather. My wife and I looked over some literature about the famous *Atlantic* paradise before boarding Flight #98 out of *Philadelphia International Airport*.

The takeoff from Philly' was smooth and easy. When the "Unfasten Your Seatbelts" light flashed on, Joanne and I became engaged in a casual conversation. It felt good getting away from the mayhem and the myriad demanding routines of American mass society.

"It says in this excellent brochure that Bermuda is a British territory and only a mere two-hour flight from Philly'," my wife read out loud. "It takes us longer to drive from our South Jersey home to New York than to fly from the *Quaker City* to Bermuda."

"We'll probably spend more time going through customs in the *Bermuda International Airport* than we will on the plane," I cynically answered. "Let me take a gander at the map on the back of that pamphlet when you're through with it. I need to know exactly where everything is located in our new environment."

I immediately observed that Bermuda was not an island but actually a chain of about three hundred islands. I learned from my reading that nine of the coral masses are populated and they are connected by a series of well-designed drawbridges and causeways.

"Claire said at the travel agency that the island's capital Hamilton is a tourist's paradise," I recalled and shared. "It's remarkable that a cluster of tiny specks could be populated and yet so isolated in the *Atlantic* six hundred miles off the coast of North Carolina."

"I don't think the Wright Brothers would have made it from Kitty Hawk to Hamilton," my clever wife, a veteran middle school geography, English and history teacher laughed. "If I remember correctly their initial flight was just over a hundred feet."

"I read that the *Princess Hotel* has perhaps the finest accommodations on the main island," I added, "and just by coincidence that's our exotic destination. Actually, I can't wait until we land and get situated."

"It's pink, my favorite color," Joanne observed and related with a smile and a wink. "Just like my bikini and my nightgown."

The entire *Boeing 727* flight out of Philly' was as smooth as satin. My wife was perusing some more pertinent literature about Bermuda's various sites of interest while I was examining a small booklet that described in detail our choice of lodging. At that moment the entire Universe seemed tranquil and harmonious.

"Joanne, I gotta' admit the *Princess Hotel* is really gorgeous, in this advertising photo'," I said before taking another sip of my *Seagram's Seven* on the rocks. "It's situated on a scenic harbor, has both a salt-water and a fresh-water swimming pool, and the facility has four splendid gourmet dining facilities. It even has fishing charters and glass bottom tour boats docked right on the harbor."

"And we also have beach privileges at the *Southampton Princess* on the other side of the harbor," my wife informed. "They have a ferry shuttle that transports guests between the sister hotels. I'm definitely going to check out the *Southampton* the first chance I get."

"Honey, that sounds really great," I amiably agreed, "and I just know that this hiatus is going to be a memorable vacation, I just know it. I'm glad we chose this hotel and this island. This is goin' to be an unforgettable pleasure adventure."

"Look here at this article describing our hotel," Joanne pointed out. "It states that Mark Twain used to stay at the *Hamilton Princess*. It says it was the author's favorite place on the island. If it's good enough for Samuel Langhorne Clemens," the social studies/language arts teacher told me, "then it oughta' be good enough for us."

It all seemed like a wonderful fantasy. There we were, escaping hectic work responsibilities and flying thirty-five thousand feet above the gleaming *Atlantic*, leaving the doldrums of jobs and home chores back in New Jersey. And Bermuda guaranteed us floral splendor and radiant sunshine. I looked at my watch to confirm reality. It was Monday, July 8. We were on a jet heading towards tropical leisure and elegance. I was at peace with the Universe.

I again glanced at my wristwatch that I had received as a college graduation present and noticed that the trade name was *Hamilton*. Then I realized a small coincidence, Hamilton, Bermuda and Hamilton wristwatch. My name is Hamilton Alexander, and remarkably, I did bear a strong resemblance to Alexander Hamilton's singular portrait engraved on the ten-dollar bill, but I refused to acknowledge *that* similarity when someone would insist that I looked like someone else.

90

I chuckled at the cute parallelism that my mind had coordinated. 'Life is full of such unique associations,' I mused and thought. It came to mind that my birthday was July 27, or 7/27, and we were flying southeast on a *Boeing 727*. I conveyed those subtle vignettes to Joanne, who indulgently laughed at my "absurd superstitious imagination."

I glimpsed across the jet's aisle in the midst of our general merriment. My eyes scrupulously observed a dark-complexioned gentleman seemingly staring at Joanne and me. I suspiciously thought I had caught him peering at us several times before during the flight since we had left Philly'. At first, I mentally wrote the matter off as 'someone who disliked others that were a little loud and having a good time.' Instinctively though, I almost automatically loathed the stranger.

At that moment, bad vibrations pulsated down to the marrow in my bones. I turned and sipped the last ounce from my delicious rye whiskey on the rocks. My sixth sense perceived a bad chemistry existing between *him* and me. I whispered my secret feeling to my wife. Joanne casually dismissed my intuition as "an acute case of badly jangled nerves" and as "possessing a too-distrusting nature."

"Maybe you're right about my imagination and my twisted nerves," I answered as politely as I could. "I'm gonna' hit the lavatory and wash my face. That *Seagram's Seven* was supposed to tranquilize me, not activate my defense mechanisms along with my kidneys. Maybe I'll be a better evaluator of character when I return," I softly said to my wife, "but my sixth sense is seldom wrong when it comes to sensing another man's motives and his malicious intent."

I freshened-up in the small bathroom cubicle and then returned to my seat five minutes later. I was deeply disturbed seeing the sinister gentleman now sitting across the aisle engaged in polite conversation with my all-too-garrulous lovely wife. The new acquaintances were jovially exchanging anecdotes about freak accidents each had experienced on past vacations. Joanne introduced me to our fellow passenger, but I must confess that I felt very uncomfortable and self-conscious in Nolan Phillips' presence.

'Nolan Phillips, where had I heard that name before?' I pondered as I briefly peered into the man's cold gray eyes. The name had a definite familiar ring. 'Something to do with history or literature,' I guessed. 'It has to be another bizarre coincidence like Hamilton and 727,' I surmised. 'Nolan Phillips seems to register some academic association but I can't exactly identity what it is.'

My natural audacity was tempted to ask Nolan and Joanne what person in history or literature shared Phillips' vaguely familiar name but I did not want to impress the stranger as being academically deficient in common cultural knowledge. As a rule, I generally try avoiding public embarrassment or awkward situations at all costs.

'My mind must be really fatigued,' I determined in my defense. 'I need this *Princess Hotel* escape from the pressures of everyday reality,' I concluded. 'Joanne's right. I'm probably overacting to something that doesn't even warrant a second thought.'

Our new acquaintance tried his best to be affable. I was certain that the appellation Nolan Phillips my distrustful mind was considering was not a contemporary name but was somehow connected with the past, the remote past. As I intensely studied the man's very distinct facial features, I believed his name might have been that of a former high school classmate or perhaps someone from twenty years ago from an old *Rutgers* college seminar. His name was like one of those trivial facts my high school teachers made me memorize only to be forgotten a week after the final exam' had been administered. It was there in my memory, yet it wasn't.

As Joanne and Nolan Phillips amused each other with broken elbow and sprained ankle stories, I promised myself that I would research the gentleman's name when I could find quiet sanctuary and sufficient time to fully analyze the situation in a Hamilton public library. There I could fully investigate the matter, if indeed it were a matter at all.

"Hamilton, Nolan would like to buy us drinks," Joanne informed me. I acceded to the stranger's friendly request simply to be cordial, but I did not relish my wife socializing with Phillips. I was puzzled that she hadn't sensed the danger in him that my instincts had felt. Maybe it was my strict neo-Puritan childhood resurfacing. Joanne had always called me "a prude." 'Could it all be jealousy in disguise?' I wondered. 'I don't even know this man,' I further thought. 'Why should every cell in my being instinctively hate him? He doesn't look like a criminal after all!'

After a pleasant blonde stewardess served us our particular drinks, much to my displeasure Nolan Phillips disclosed that he would also be staying at the *Hamilton Princess Hotel*. The impertinent fellow then told me that I looked exactly like someone he had known in the past but he couldn't pin it down exactly who that anonymous person was. His observation rattled my consciousness. I felt that Phillips possessed the sixth sense, too.

"Nolan, everybody says that to me," I deceivingly answered, "and I do have a pretty standard-looking face. Today the *American Airlines* receptionist back in Philly' mentioned the exact same thing. But Nolan, unfortunately nobody seems to be able to tell me who my facsimile is," I responded as courteously as I could feign.

I conjectured what Nolan Phillips might have looked like wearing a white colonial wig or a tilted confederate hat. He too looked vaguely familiar but my rampant imagination couldn't pinpoint his identity if at that moment my life immediately depended on it.

"Well then, who do you think I look like?" I candidly challenged. "The President, the British Prime Minister, the Pope, Bill Gates?"

"I don't know," Nolan replied with an element of regret in his voice. "I can't seem to associate it right this minute. I've seen a portrait of you somewhere, perhaps in the *Guggenheim*, the *Metropolitan Museum of Art*, the *Louvre*, or maybe in the *Smithsonian*. But the mystery gentleman I have in mind has a long nose curved up at the end, just like yours!"

Joanne was amused with Nolan Phillips' insulting description but I was deeply mortified. 'Is he trying to harass and ridicule me in front of my wife? Does he have malicious intentions?' I reflected and fumed. 'If we had lived in olden days, I would probably be motivated to challenge him to a duel with swords or pistols,' I thought.

Much to my chagrin Joanne had not detected any malevolence in Nolan Phillips' disposition or in his graphic language. She considered his vile comment about my nose as being "cute and on-target."

'Maybe it's your strict upbringing that makes you skeptical of anyone that appears too convivial upon first contact,' I rationalized. 'It must be my *WASP*ish childhood, my jangled nerves and my fertile imagination,' I speculated. 'Learn to just get along!'

The *727* gently landed at *Bermuda International Airport* and the passengers eagerly disembarked. Inside the terminal courteous Customs Officials dressed in khaki Bermuda shorts thoroughly inspected the anxious tourists' luggage. The three long arrival lines moved forward at a fairly rapid pace.

My wife was talking up a storm with two lady passengers she had met before boarding the *727* in Philly', and Joanne was vividly relating her excitement about being there "in paradise." My nervous mind ignored her prattling and focused on getting our traveling credentials together for inspection. And to add to my quandary my brain was preoccupied with fears, doubts and suspicions concerning Nolan Phillips, and those turbulent thoughts were all rotating simultaneously in my mind like strange patterns inside a mental kaleidoscope turning in many directions.

Contrary to my ordinarily calm disposition I angrily admonished Joanne about her apparent friendliness with Nolan Phillips. My wife indicated that she was tired of being embarrassed by my unwarranted "public hostility toward *friendly strangers*."

"Now that's an oxymoron if I ever heard one," I criticized, "and I think your false observation about me is downright *pretty ugly*."

"Sometimes you don't realize how cruel and offensive you can be," my wife flippantly snapped back, "and you must learn to control your nasty temper or seek psychiatric help. Did you hear me Hamilton?"

"You're possibly right," I guiltily acknowledged. "I'm sorry for overreacting like that. I'll be better tomorrow once I get acclimated to this new environment. You know Joanne, I have trouble adjusting to new places. I promise to treat you like a lady for the rest of our glorious stay here."

My spouse applied a big hug around my neck right in the center of the waiting line. Several other travelers smiled in recognition of her affectionate gesture. I looked behind me and saw Nolan Phillips snidely gazing in our direction, his evil eyes hidden behind thick dark sunglasses. I immediately felt antagonism toward his deliberate visual intrusion into our brief romantic interlude.

I felt compelled to go over and shatter his big protruding mandible into a dozen or more fragments. Fortunately, I resisted that very strong impulse and reason prevailed over reckless inclination. An attack of that nature would confirm to my wife that I was indeed paranoid and that I indeed lacked maturity and self-esteem.

Finally, much to my relief, *Ginger* and I proceeded through Customs without incident or difficulty. A representative from the *Hamilton Princess Hotel* was holding a sign over his head to attract the resort's prospective guests around him. Soon the employee assembled an entourage of thirteen people. 'Thirteen is an unlucky number,' I automatically thought. 'If it weren't for the presence of Nolan Phillips, who was traveling alone, the number of people being transported would be a more acceptable dozen,' I reckoned. The hotel driver very efficiently loaded everyone's luggage inside the rear compartment of the large pink van, and the excited tourists all found comfortable seats after clambering inside.

The trip from the airport on St. George's Island to downtown Hamilton on Bermuda Island was about six scenic miles. The vehicle passed merry tourists riding on mopeds, the basic means of transportation for the more courageous and independent-minded island visitors.

The driver courteously pointed-out various places of interest on our splendid route. The hotel van traveled over a picturesque bridge and then it motored through the village of Flatts. Stately boats gently rocked back and forth in a majestic canal of crystal-clear aqua-green water. The driver stopped and told us to scan the canal for varicolored tropical fish flitting about in the shallows, and we all claimed to have seen at least five apiece, even though I never saw even one during the "mass hallucination."

Fifteen minutes later the large pink van pulled into the main entrance to the elegant *Hamilton Princess Hotel*. The edifice was truly worthy of its dignified royal name. It was a pastel pink castle enveloped in and abounding with lush green semi-tropical landscaping. The extremely beautiful palace regally lorded over placid *Hamilton Harbor*.

I sauntered up to the mahogany registration counter, showed my reservation voucher to the desk attendant and then presented my *MasterCard*. I received prompt polite service from an attractive brunette hotel clerk who possessed a distinct British accent.

"Here are some terrific pamphlets on sites of interest you might want to visit or itineraries you might desire taking during your stay," the pretty young lady communicated. "Be sure not to miss the colorful military band parade on Front Street on Wednesday night at eight. It's a must. Be sure to take your camera."

"I understand you have a ferry that goes over to the *Southampton Princess*," I inquired. "That's quite a convenience for your guests."

"Yes, and they leave every two hours," the registration clerk said, "and don't forget the glass bottom boats that take you out to some really wonderful coral reefs," the young lady reminded me. "People often tell me they come back here just to see the beauty of it all over again."

I thanked the well-mannered obliging young woman for her assistance and then turned toward Joanne and was troubled to see Nolan Phillips standing several yards behind us in a parallel long registration line. I tried ignoring his presence but then my wife gave the ubiquitous annoyance a half-hearted wave. My concentration was interrupted by the voice of the charming brunette female clerk. "By the way Sir, I must tell you that you do have a very familiar face," she stated. "Have you ever been told about that resemblance before?"

I felt like screaming-out, 'Just look on a U.S. ten-dollar-bill, remove the guy's wig by placing your thumb over *his* head, and see if you could figure out the great mystery, you fool!' but I miraculously controlled myself along with my notorious volatile temper.

The young lady's question really pestered me because its timing coincided with the disquieting appearance of Nolan Phillips at the registration counter. I knew that the young lady's inquiry was purely innocent but nevertheless at the time, its utterance irritated me.

"I only wish I knew who my anonymous twin is," I answered the clerk's commentary. "You can't imagine how many people ask me that same question. I think I'm getting some sort of phobia over it," I added, "but somehow, I've managed to live with the vexing riddle."

A cheerful bellhop brought our four luggage pieces down the magnificent mahogany-paneled lobby that featured an exquisite pink marble floor. Expensive vases, paintings, wall tapestries and statues ornamented the stately corridor on both sides. Our room guide next conducted Joanne and me through several smaller hallways and then into the oldest section of the well-constructed palace. We were swiftly led across a verdant garden that featured hibiscus bushes and tall royal palm trees, which could have rivaled any that might have flourished in Eden. We finally arrived at our well-appointed suite situated in the newest section of the inimitable hotel.

Our luxurious accommodations overlooked the salt-water pool in the forefront and also the calm waters of aqua-blue *Hamilton Harbor* in the serene background.

"This is no doubt the same view that Mark Twain enjoyed here at the *Princess*," I theorized and reported to Joanne while feigning enthusiasm. "The guy had good taste and good eyesight too."

"We gotta' commend my favorite literary genius on his terrific selection of accommodations," my wife replied. "I'll have my Advanced English class read a selection of chapters from *Tom Sawyer* when I'm assigned my new teaching schedule in September."

Being in a blithe spirit, I gave a five-dollar tip to the appreciative bellboy. Joanne and I unpacked our suitcases and she put away her cosmetics in the bathroom vanity while I stored away our toiletries inside two matching bureaus. After getting the remainder of our things situated, we donned our bathing suits and scampered out to the salt-water pool as if we were a couple of carefree school kids.

A friendly employee advised me that beach towels could be obtained near the fresh water pool on the opposite side of the hotel's central promenade. Upon returning from my errand with the towels, I became angered when I noticed Nolan Phillips, in a tight-fitting French bathing suit, casually talking with my wife. Sensing that I was distraught with his presence, the bothersome fellow dismissed himself from *our* company before certain confrontation would ensue.

"I'm going to try a rum-swizzle at the hotel's Flamingo Bar," Phillips announced just before departing. "Care to join me for a few libations?"

"Maybe tomorrow Nolan," I rankled, "because we're just getting used to the place. And besides, Joanne and I are still a little exhausted from the flight and from the long waiting lines in the airport and in the hotel."

When Nolan Phillips left our presence, I jealously interrogated my wife. "What did he talk to you about?" I demanded to Joanne. "And what was so amusing between you two? He must think our relationship is weak and vulnerable."

"Just wait a minute," my wife warned. "You're overreacting a bit, don't you' think?"

"Before this week's up that obnoxious creep's gonna' swallow his teeth!" I threatened. "All twelve of them," I sarcastically added.

"Please stop being so nasty Hamilton," Joanne insisted. "Nolan seems like a very lonely man. He's just trying to be friendly. I can't understand for the life of me why *you* despise him so. You must have had an unhappy childhood and very few close friends!"

I had difficulty concealing the extreme animosity my total being felt for Nolan Phillips. "Maybe you're right but I have my doubts about him having any honorable motives," I lectured Joanne like a modern-day Diogenes. "I just don't like how he boldly approaches you when I'm in the airplane's lavatory, or when I'm off for forty seconds to pick-up a pair of beach towels. I really trust you Honey," I confided, "but I don't trust Phillips as far as I can throw him. I guess I'm basically a very possessive husband."

That Monday evening Joanne and I had supper on the American Dinner Plan in the regal *Three Crowns Restaurant*. My emotions had finally adjusted back to an even keel from the afternoon's brief encounter with rather aggravating Nolan Phillips. From a small nearby lounge my wife and I heard a band playing a nostalgic medley of Frank Sinatra hit tunes.

After sumptuous dinners of shrimp and crab-meat delicacies, Joanne and I stepped to the romantic musical lounge where we were enjoying tropical rum-based cocktails. We intimately danced and romanced to the familiar powerful lyrics of "My Way."

"Ginger, I didn't mean to explode like I did at the pool today," I confessed and apologized. "I'm a little edgy being in a foreign place with so many strangers surrounding me."

"You always do things *your way* regardless of the circumstances," my spouse declared while alluding to the Sinatra song we were dancing to. "Give Nolan a chance to prove himself," Joanne objectively suggested. "He seems lonelier than you are, as hard as that is to believe. At least you have me to lean on."

The six-piece band took an intermission break. My wife and I made peace and strolled like two newly-weds hand-in-hand back to our secluded table. I glanced across the almost empty room and saw Nolan

Phillips sitting all by his lonesome. Joanne followed a whim and suggested that I invite him over for a drink. I stubbornly refused.

Much to my astonishment, my wife signaled for the reprehensible acquaintance to join our company. I was deeply distressed by Joanne's gesture of sympathy. Nolan Phillips casually strolled over to our cozy table. We ordered a round of tropical drinks and then randomly talked about college fraternities, pro' football and also the Venus and Mars natures of men and women. After we consumed a few more rounds of drinks Phillips didn't seem like such a bad fellow after all.

"Where did you go to college?" I inquired. "You have a North Jersey accent. I'll bet you attended either *Seton Hall* or *Fairleigh Dickinson*."

"*New York University*," Phillips corrected. "I'm a prosecutor assigned to the Manhattan *DA's* office. What fraternity did you belong to?"

"Lambda Phi Sigma at *Glassboro State College*," I said, "and then I transferred to *Rutgers University* in New Brunswick and became a Kappa Phi, studied architecture and am now a builder. I also loyally serve as a Hammonton town councilman back in Jersey."

I volunteered to amble over to the bar and get a third round of tropical cocktails, since our waiter was nowhere in sight. The beleaguered bartender had trouble hearing my order because the band had returned from its break and started playing again and I had to loudly scream my requests above the catchy melody of "New York, New York."

As I turned around my soul became infected with grief and inflamed with hate. I detected Nolan Phillips jitterbugging with Joanne. My next reaction was thinking that I did not want to cause a wild scene. 'Could this creep be so insanely stupid that he can't read my absolute contempt of him?' I wondered. 'When the time and place are right, I'll gladly read him the riot act for sure,' I thought.

When the two nimble dancers returned to our table, I told Joanne that I was experiencing a very vicious headache. I insisted that *we* should return to our luxury suite so that I could relax. Nolan noticed my sudden discomfort and sensing my enmity toward him, the deceitful jerk diplomatically asked to be excused from our presence for the evening. As he nonchalantly walked away, I glared menacingly at his back like a mongoose scrutinizing a cobra.

On the return to our suite, Joanne and I stopped to converse at Adams Lounge, a large colonial hall of great grandeur inside the hotel. Our conversation, which centered upon Nolan Phillips, became a little too raucous for our fellow pedestrians to hear in *our* sophisticated public environment. The argument continued as we stepped briskly down the corridor to the privacy of our quarters. Inside I had to control myself from angrily slapping Joanne across her face. I recalled wishing that we had gone to the Bahamas instead.

"I never want to see you dancing with that lousy creep again, do you hear?" I wildly demanded. "He's up to no good! Can't you sense that in him?"

"You're a very vain, shallow and jealous man!" my wife shouted back. "You're an ingrate!"

"Maybe so, but I'm really going to hurt that idiot if he doesn't figure-out which women he can't become aggressive with! He needs a good pulverizing!"

Tuesday morning Joanne and I rented mopeds to further explore the city of Hamilton and its vicinity. It was great fun sightseeing the island and leisurely stopping at various unscheduled destinations. The warmth in our fragile relationship seemed to be rekindled.

At noon we took a lunch break at a side-street fast food stand several miles outside Hamilton. A blue and white striped canopy covered a rear garden area where customers could eat in American picnic style, insulated from distracting highway noise. Joanne and I had hamburgers, French fries *Cokes* and some frank conversation.

After consuming the "American cuisine", we decided to ride our motorbikes over to Flatts Village to again enjoy the fantastic view the place provided. But then Joanne's moped refused to start. I was never mechanically inclined and my futile attempts at correcting the malfunction proved it. Then a very suspicious and repugnant thing happened.

Nolan Phillips climbed out of a nearby rented car and offered to transport Joanne's incapacitated bike in his trunk back to the *Princess Hotel* Rental Agency. I reluctantly agreed to *his* cavalier show of friendship. I didn't trust his intentions or his sincerity. I wondered how he had managed to show-up right in the height of the motorbike crisis. Nolan Phillips was the last person in the world I wanted to owe a favor.

I hypothesized that Phillips had surreptitiously tampered with Joanne's motorbike, rendering it immobile so that the devious fellow could arrive on the scene and role-play "Mr. Messiah." I did not relish the notion that the obnoxious man had been keeping *our* private movements on the islands under close surveillance.

I drove Joanne to the *Hamilton Princess Hotel* with her riding on the back of my moped with her arms wrapped around my waist. I told her en route to Hamilton that it had been more than coincidental that

Phillips showed-up at the exact same time as when the moped suddenly became inoperable. My wife saw matters differently.

"The guy's doing us a really big favor by taking my rented moped back to the hotel and now you're being totally vindictive and ungrateful for him helping us out," my wife chided. "You wouldn't be happy if you had a hundred-dollar bill and were the only kid in a candy store."

Nolan Phillips had dropped Joanne's moped off at the Princess Rental Agency before Ginger and I got back to the Hamilton resort. I observed him standing next to the outdoor business counter smoking a cigarette and glancing nervously every now and then at his *Rolex* wristwatch.

At the counter, the rentals' manager gave my wife and me a twenty-dollar rebate for our "unfortunate inconvenience." The amiable man then said that I looked exactly like someone else. I became a little peeved and told him to mind his "own moped business."

"Sir, I didn't mean to offend or quarrel with you," the gentleman qualified, "and believe me when I say I don't want to pry into your personal life."

"You've been on Bermuda for too long and are suffering from a warm-climate version of cabin fever," I retorted to the congenial fellow living six hundred miles away from the nearest continent. "You probably also think that my wife looks like Miss Universe!"

"Now that you've mentioned it," the British gentleman responded. The moped manager then indulgently laughed while Joanne gave me a Medusa-like stare that should have turned me into stone.

I slowly walked over to Nolan Phillips and reluctantly thanked him for his unexpected assistance. He very deliberately winked at Joanne and me and then said, "It was the least I could do Hamilton." I wondered what "the most" Phillips could do really might be.

That night my wife and I again dined at the *Three Crowns*. I had filet mignon and Joanne raved throughout the meal about her "fantastic" shrimp, clams and mussels' combo'. I was happy to see that Nolan Phillips was not around to torment my sanity. "Thank God *he's* nowhere in sight to further instigate me," I mentioned to my favorite traveling mate.

"You're just envious because Nolan is acting like Superman or the Lone Ranger," my wife very effectively needled. "He always comes to the rescue right when we need him. He's a Johnny with spots everywhere to be standing on."

"I need him like I need three broken ribs and two massive malignant brain tumors," I sneered like a true chauvinist pig. "That guy's trouble with a capital T!"

Wednesday morning my wife and I had continental breakfast in our well-appointed suite. We donned our swim suits and took the early morning ferry across Hamilton Harbor to the *Southampton Princess*. We improved our rapport by frolicking in the surf, snorkeling and sleeping for an hour on the pink-sanded beach.

At noon, my pretty Italian wife and I enjoyed a sumptuous seafood buffet at the resort's Whaler Inn and then we rode the ferry back to the more conservative *Hamilton Princess Hotel*. Joanne and I took turns showering and decided to have room service deliver our dinners.

Just before dusk Ginger and I dressed in typical tourist attire and strolled six blocks to downtown Hamilton for the Wednesday night military parade that the girl at the hotel's reception counter had strongly recommended for us to see. The colorful event celebrated the *British Empire's* glory days during the late-colonial Victorian era. I sensed Nolan Phillips' presence in the crowd of spectators, but thankfully I did not see him anywhere in the throng throughout the hour-long elaborate military march spectacle.

"Will you please learn to relax and become a cooperative tourist," my wife reprimanded me towards the end of the parade pomp and pageantry. "You're obsessed over nothing! Why do you keep turning around? You're going to need a chiropractor before this trip is done. You should only rubberneck back in the states where reality is more informal."

"He's here, I know he's here scrutinizing our every move," I sullenly replied. "I know he's spying on us, that uncouth uncivil intruder."

"I think you're developing agoraphobia, claustrophobia and Nolan Phillips' phobia all at the same time," Ginger smartly and spontaneously answered my paranoia. "You need to lie down on a psychiatrist's couch and tell the mind doctor everything you know about your mother!"

On Thursday morning I ambled down to the lobby's Registration Desk and purchased two glass bottom boat tickets for a late morning coral reef expedition. When the genteel male clerk handed me the tickets, I instinctively checked the immediate vicinity to ascertain that Nolan Phillips was not stealthily observing my personal activity at the main desk.

Later that morning, Joanne and I boarded the ominous-sounding *Perils of Fate* and were standing near the stern of the glass bottom boat. I gritted my teeth when my keen eyes perceived Nolan Phillips sauntering down the long narrow dock ramp heading in the direction of the sightseeing boat. The sinister rogue was the last passenger to board the *Perils of Fate*, which soon eased from its mooring and cruised into *Hamilton Harbor*, hardly leaving a wake.

The genial captain was knowledgeable and pointed-out various places of interest to his captivated all-tourist audience. Joanne gave Nolan Phillips a tentative wave. I gave him the absolute cold-shoulder treatment. I sensed that conflict was imminent but tried appearing generally civil and benign.

The *Perils of Fate* passed through an open drawbridge that connected two parts of Somerset Island, the last major link in the eastern Bermuda chain. The captain navigated his vessel to a rendezvous point about a quarter of a mile out to sea where *we* joined-up with four other glass-bottom boats originating from other hotels and marinas, forming what my erratic mind synthesized as a "sightseeing armada." The ship's pilot explained over the intercom speakers that the five boats would motor out to the coral reef and view the spectacle one ship at a time in a "caravan on water" so that the sea animals below would not be disturbed in their natural habitat.

While the jovial captain was busy addressing his alert enchanted passengers over the intercom, I overheard Ginger chatting with the same ladies that had been on our flight from Philly'. The gossipers were exchanging ideas about different merchandise and clothing bargains available on Front Street. In the meantime, I was involved in deeply thinking about how to resolve certain negotiations of my own.

I decided to define some basic terms with my assumed adversary. I figured it was time to let Nolan Phillips know my exact sentiments about his constant intrusions. I approached the agitator's position on the other side of the glass bottom boat. The scoundrel leech was looking-down at the colorful coral reef, admiring its beauty.

"I'll level with you Phillips," I diplomatically began. "I would like to be on friendly terms with you for the remainder of my vacation here. I'm a very jealous man," I strongly maintained, "and I would appreciate it if you would stay away from my wife. That means keeping your eyes and hands off of her, is that perfectly clear?"

"Look here Hamilton, I'm not trying to make time with your wife if that's what you're implying!" Phillips defensively stated with a florid face. "Your wife reminds me of an attractive girl I used to date in Manhattan. Joanne brings back pleasant memories of Cindy."

"That's a very unimaginative and completely lackluster excuse," I curtly answered, "but I'm warning you Nolan; lay off or there's going to be big trouble in paradise. Stop stalking my wife like you're some kind of predator!"

The captain's voice came over the intercom's speakers and he instructed all passengers to report to the "below deck." He then maneuvered the *Perils of Fate* to a favorable position directly above a marvelous array of tropical fish, thick vegetation and coral resplendence. Soon everyone was below and partaking of the real-life visual fantasy, that is, everyone except Nolan Phillips and me. I wanted to continue our disagreement in private.

"Look Phillips, it's not my fault Joanne looks like an old flame of yours," I emphasized. "Just remember pal, she's still *my* wife regardless of how your warped mind associates her with your past! I'm not going to allow *your* past to interfere with *my* present!"

"Ya' know Hamilton, your mind contrives situations that don't really exist. You're always trying to reinvent reality and then define it in your own neurotic terms," Phillips assertively accused, "and I seriously do believe, if I may add, that you need professional psychological help!"

"Tell me the truth," I adamantly insisted, "did you follow us to the luncheonette outside Hamilton the other day and tamper with Joanne's moped while we were eating? Did you stoop to committing that kind of vile sabotage?"

"You've really gone off the deep end!" Phillips hollered while losing his temper. "You're crazy! Neurotic! Psychotic! You need the services of a competent shrink quick!"

I roughly grabbed Nolan's arm to indicate my seriousness. He attempted escaping my tight grasp. We violently wrestled against the railing above the boat's stern. Phillips frantically swung his clenched right fist twice at my jaw. I blocked his first punch but his third blow caught me solidly in the chest. We fiercely grappled some more as the captain monotonously continued his loud lecture into his microphone, his voice being amplified over the boat's speakers.

I managed to get my right hand free from my tormentor's grasp and savagely smashed Phillips with an uppercut to his chin. It was a lucky clean shot I had delivered that stunned him in his tracks. The lummox staggered backwards from my blow's force. We had degenerated into two desperate animals, primitively struggling for survival. Danger was not a concern. The laws of civilization had been abandoned. We were strenuously battling for dominance in a two-man jungle.

I wrapped my hands around Phillips' throat and squeezed firmly with all my might. My heart and wrists wanted to strangle the obnoxious jerk in the worst possible way in order for me to achieve my ultimate victory. We were both desperately gasping for air, panting like two lung cancer patients. Adrenaline liberally rushed through my arteries and veins, giving me extra strength. I twisted all my weight to the left and maniacally shoved Nolan Phillips over the boat's stern. My ears heard a loud splash. Thirty seconds went by on my *Hamilton* wristwatch. Nolan Phillips did not surface.

My obstinate ego defensively justified to my conscience that my extreme violence had been performed in self-defense. I considered leaping into the *Atlantic,* but I instantly thought that the salvaging of *his* life wasn't sufficient motivation to convert me into a Good Samaritan exercising self-sacrifice. '*He* wouldn't do the same for me if our roles were reversed,' I selfishly speculated. 'I will live to enjoy the rest of my life at Nolan Phillips' expense,' I decided.

My pupils again intensely scanned the azure-emerald water below, searching for some evidence of the despicable brute, but there was no sign of his body. 'He's drowned and good riddance,' I thought. 'He's hit his head against the coral rock, went unconscious and drowned,' my stubborn mind concluded.

My lungs inhaled and exhaled ten deep breaths to help me regain my composure and my sanity. I tucked my light blue cotton shirt inside my blue denim jeans and then pretending that everything was normal, I furtively descended the black metal steps to listen to the captain's drab narration. Everyone standing in a circle below deck was preoccupied, visually appreciating the magnificent coral reef. No one ever noticed my stealthy arrival.

Joanne was still intermittently gossiping with her lady tourist friends and did not observe my quiet return below deck. My conscience was now saturated with guilt but my heart felt little sorrow for Nolan Phillips' demise. My mind truly believed that I had vanquished a terrible foe. Phillips had been bent on wooing my wife and then destroying me in the process. I observed that the other more docile tourists were content staring-down at the fabulous reef through the boat's glass bottom, so I pretended to do likewise in order to cunningly conceal the atrocious felony I had recently committed.

"If you'll all direct your attention to the direction of the bow," the captain suggested, "you'll see some really splendid tropical fish. Those two yellow ones are known as long-nosed butterflies. Those multicolored ones are queen angelfish. Look at those lobsters crawling near the center of the reef next to that impressive white brain coral."

The other tourists' eyes keenly focused on the underwater enchantment. I still was breathing heavily and perspiring from my traumatic ordeal that incidentally had exhausted most of my energy. My mind was spinning in a quandary as the captain continued his boring monologue.

"Have you ever seen such beauty anywhere before?" the boat's official lecturer rhetorically asked. "There's a spotted goat fish to your right and that mean-looking critter over there is called a Nassau grouper."

The captain's glib presentation was rudely interrupted by an elderly woman's horrendous shriek. The startled lady pointed her forefinger to the right side of the glass bottom's underwater coral reef view. Everyone reflexively turned to witness the source of her terror. Soon there were numerous cries of shock and loud exclamations of disbelief.

Nolan Phillips' rigid body was seen floating beneath the boat, face down, slowly drifting toward the ridge of coral rock. His forehead then roughly banged into the coral reef and everyone aboard the vessel cringed except me. The impact turned his corpse sideways, facing the boat's bottom. Nolan's eyeballs were bulging out of their sockets. Screams of terror echoed throughout the cluster of shock-stricken passengers. The captain pleaded with the crowd to "quiet down, please don't panic!" But much to his dismay, the mass hysteria continued.

Everyone else observing the gruesome phenomenon gasped as Phillips' remains continued drifting with the current underneath the *Perils of Fate*, eventually wedging between the boat's hull and the immovable coral formation. Blood seeped out of the corpse's forehead and traces floated upwards from his mouth. The red water plume then filtered outward in the direction of the boat's glass bottomed pane. The stressed-out captain ineffectively commanded for his now-delirious passengers to climb up to the main deck.

The Harbor Police were notified of the tragedy. They sent an expert *SCUBA* team down and soon located and successfully removed Nolan Phillips' body from the sea, and the victim was immediately taken to the Hamilton Hospital Morgue.

That afternoon I was visited in my hotel suite by a team of very intelligent detectives conducting a "routine investigation." The chief inspector believed Nolan's death "an apparent suicide" rather than a homicide. "Nolan Phillips had confided to me that he had been despondent, lonely and depressed," I divulged to the investigators. "He was in a total state of anxiety, sort of bipolar if you know what I mean," I clarified and continued. "I believe he was psychotic or perhaps even paranoid. When the fellow was finally alone, I suspect that Nolan surrendered to his death wish and decided to abandon this cruel world once and for all."

Joanne related to the authorities that Nolan Phillips was "a lonely sort of man." Our corroborative statements were accepted as depositions to be presented during the coroner's inquest. The team of officers thanked us for our "cooperative, helpful observations and comments."

"His body does have a broken jaw," the chief inspector noted. "We know *that* fact even before any autopsy has been performed. Do you know anything about how that injury might have happened?"

"I saw his chin hit up against the coral reef as his head drifted below the glass bottom boat," I calmly testified under duress. The policemen conscientiously jotted-down my testimony on their report pads. I wisely hid the sore knuckles of my right hand behind my back while I was providing the examiners with the false information.

"Unless there's some radical change in venue," the chief inspector said, "you won't be detained on Bermuda for further questioning. I think you've both satisfied all our immediate concerns."

Friday was our last scheduled day on the heavenly main isle. Joanne wanted to purchase some souvenirs for our two nephews and niece. We agreed to separate and then meet again an hour later in front of the *Atlantic,* a huge tourist ship out of New York docked along Front Street.

I casually walked the pavement, strolling past a strip of shop window displays colorfully designed to lure American and European tourists inside. I glanced into a novelty photography store that took old time black and white pictures of vacationers dressed in "authentic historical period costumes." I stepped inside the cheerfully decorated establishment out of sheer curiosity. I must honestly confess that some mysterious psychic force seemed to attract my attention and then magnetically draw me into the store.

My eyes perceptively surveyed the wide variety of outfits on exhibit from different periods in history, and I observed that the apparel was hanging on long display racks. I decided to try on a colonial costume along with an accompanying white wig. My fancy thought that Joanne would be delighted with a photo' of me attired in eighteenth century garb. 'She desperately needs me to show her something amusing so that she'll think I still possess a sense of humor,' I reckoned. My hands eagerly put on my chosen ensemble. A sprite British sales clerk assisted me with maneuvering into my complementing silk long-tailed coat. My blue eyes examined and appreciated my stellar appearance in a full-length mirror.

"Sir, if I may say so, you look just like that chap on the American ten-dollar bill," the salesman alertly observed and stated. "Hamilton, I believe the man's name was. Never made it to President, did he?"

"No," I said; "he was assassinated before he could ever attain that high office."

The genial salesman was elated when I ordered ten reproductions of the original photo' he had taken of me dressed in the colonial haberdashery. I paid the affable gent in fifty and twenty-dollar denominations. I did not want to give him a ten-dollar bill and have him meticulously compare the portrait to my profile, and I certainly didn't wish to give him my *MasterCard* with my name "Hamilton Alexander" on it standing out in bold relief.

At that odd moment, I was grateful that I didn't have to explain those particular details to the cheerful clerk, who was delightedly preoccupied making arrangements to send the ten duplicate photos' to my New Jersey residence. I then asked for and received directions from the blithe salesman to the Hamilton Library. I told him I was a visiting college professor who needed to study an "important academic matter."

At the library I located *Encyclopedia Britannica* H. I avidly read the biographical account of Alexander Hamilton. My mind's interest was impressed that Alexander Hamilton had been the first U.S. Secretary of the Treasury and that he and Benjamin Franklin were the only two "non-presidents" honored by having their portraits engraved on American paper currency. The informative article further stated that Hamilton had been killed in a pistol duel with Aaron Burr in Weehawken, New Jersey on July 11, 1804. 'July 11!' I thought in amazement. 'That was yesterday, the same day that Nolan Phillips had met his demise! What a weird coincidence!'

I rushed to grab *Encyclopedia Britannica* N. I thumbed-through the pages and found the information for Philip Nolan, the coincidental name reversal of my deceased former enemy. Next to the listing was the instruction "See Edward Everett Hale." I directed my attention back to Encyclopedia H and anxiously leafed through the pages with great anticipation. My comprehensive research yielded some satisfactorily staggering results.

Edward Everett Hale (1822-1909) was a distinguished clergyman, editor, humanitarian and noteworthy author. He is most remembered for his popular novella *Man without a Country*. The tale, the encyclopedia explained, was about a young officer named Philip Nolan, who had exclaimed during a court martial hearing, "I never want to hear of the United States again." As punishment for his lack of patriotism, Nolan was then placed on a warship and his commanding officers were instructed that no one would be permitted to provide the prisoner with any relevant news about the United States until *his* death. Philip Nolan was the notorious *Man without a Country*.

The informative article further indicated that Nolan had been court-martialed by the Army because the defiant young soldier had been suspected of being a disciple of Aaron Burr, a former maverick United States Vice President under Thomas Jefferson. The encyclopedia description detailed that according to Edward Everett Hale's story, Burr desired to carve-out a new independent territory for aristocrats and Federalists in the American frontier. The article finished by clarifying that Philip Nolan was actually a fictitious character but that the story *Man without a Country* had been written in the style of a factual account and the famous tale was especially designed to muster Northern patriotism during the *Civil War*.

'Philip Nolan, a fictional character,' I pensively thought. My inquisitiveness had reached its ultimate peak. I found *Britannica Encyclopedia* B and frantically flipped through its pages until I located "Aaron Burr." I felt a trifle dizzy and giddy when I examined his portrait. The dimensions of the library room seemed to expand and contract several times during my intense scrutiny. Aaron Burr's documented portrait looked identical to the Nolan Phillips that I had briefly known on my Bermuda vacation.

Burr had murdered Alexander Hamilton in a gun duel on July 11, 1804. I looked very much like Hamilton. Nolan Phillips looked almost identical to Aaron Burr. I had been responsible for Nolan Phillips' death on July 11. The incredible 'dual events' were really 'duel events'.

'I've gotten revenge for a spectacular pistol duel that had occurred back in 1804,' I thought and considered while sitting inside the stone silent library. But quite confidentially, I felt no particular guilt or remorse for performing my evil deed aboard the ironically named *Perils of Fate*. After all, according to the infallible *Encyclopedia Britannica's* text, Philip Nolan was a fictitious character. Nolan Phillips had to be a reincarnation of that same fictitious character. I've objectively concluded that I did not murder Nolan Phillips. Let me be completely rational about this entire matter. It is absolutely impossible to kill a recycled imaginary fictional character from American literature. I must be genuinely specific in my astute analysis. 'Only a crazy person would think otherwise,' I intelligently evaluated and concluded.

"Obadiah Bush, Gene Alter & Branche Sawyer"

I was driving my metallic blue *Buick LeSabre* towards Atlantic City, New Jersey on congested *Route 30* on a Saturday morning in March 2000. My destination was *Harrah's Casino* to try my luck at blackjack and to play an additional hundred dollars' worth of video poker. On the way driving east on the *White Horse Pike* I figured I would stop in at Hammonton's Silver Coin Diner to eat a hearty breakfast. I remember thinking, 'I have all day to lose my hard-earned money at the casino so what's the rush?'

After entering the bustling establishment, which was packed with mostly town patrons, I noticed that there was an end seat vacant at the busy counter. I sat down to the left of an acne-faced teenager, who seemed disinterested in my arrival while he concentrated his attention on devouring his breakfast of toast, ham and eggs.

I had learned in my college sociology class back in the mid-'60s that it is wrong to judge anyone by his or her appearance even though the personal stereotype is probably correct ninety percent of the time. Civilized people know that it is improper and downright discourteous to be presumptuous. "Prejudice is when you *pre-judge* someone," I remembered a discriminating professor had once lectured.

So, what if the kid had four fake silver chains and a bronze medallion dangling down from his dirty neck! So, what if he wore baggy pants and sported an unkempt long shaggy hairstyle that looked like it could feed a colony of lice! 'I should not do the unthinkable and stereotype the young fellow,' I perceptively thought. I reckoned I would show some basic decency and strike up a casual conversation with the young man just to demonstrate that I was a friendly sort of guy. I wanted to show my young fellow-breakfast diner that I was an open-minded civil American citizen that respected everyone's sacred *Constitutional* rights.

"How ya' doin' amigo," I said in very contrived friendly salutation. "I used to teach at the local high school, that is, before I intelligently retired two years ago. But I don't seem to remember you as being a student there. Are you from out of town?"

"Sort of," the kid succinctly mumbled with a gross amount of food and saliva spilling out from the corners of his enormous mouth. "I'm just passin' through the area and heading for Philly' for some recreation. I come around these parts once or twice a year."

"Where ya' from?" I persisted with my amiable interrogation. I figured the lad would say something like Berlin, Atco, Pleasantville, Folsom, Egg Harbor, Medford or Atlantic City.

"I'm actually a time traveler from the year 2085," the teenager calmly answered. "I don't really stay in one place all too long."

"Sure, and I'm the nefarious Sheriff of Nottingham and I'm here in this diner looking for Robin Hood, Friar Tuck and Little John," I laughed. "I must say young man, you' have quite an active imagination. You wouldn't have any idea where Maid Marian is, would you? I live just around the corner in the center of Sherwood Forest."

The thin teenager stared at me with a nasty scowl that seemed to exaggerate his strange-looking facial features. "All right, don't believe me when I tell you I'm from the future, the future you'll never live to see!" the kid testily challenged. "See if I really care!"

I didn't desire to appear as rude as I had really been so I humbly apologized for what *he* had perceived as a rather sarcastic remark. Strangers often misinterpret that I am anti-social but actually, I am usually very shy and reserved upon first contact. 'I oughta' humor this spoiled super-sensitive kid,' I thought. 'Then I can go home and look him up on the Sci-fi cable channel.'

"Tell me young man," I suavely stated to deftly disguise my very abundant skepticism, "is your great-grandmother Chelsey Clinton?"

"Who in *Andromeda* is she?" he replied. "Does she live up on the space station? I remember a Dorothy Clinton from my third-grade astronomy class, but no Chelsey Clinton. Who is Chelsey Clinton anyway?"

"Former President Bill Clinton's daughter," I clarified. "Never mind about her," I declared, believing that my new acquaintance was probably not a conscientious student of current events. "Well, who is the President of the United States in 2085?"

"Obadiah Bush," the kid casually responded quite matter-of-factly while munching away on his slightly burnt toast. "Obadiah Bush is President of the United States," he repeated with his mouth completely full. "And I didn't vote for the guy in my high school's mock election, either!"

"Is Obadiah Bush George W. Bush's grandson?" I innocently asked.

"Naw," the kid muttered as he chewed another disgusting mouthful of his slightly burnt toast. "I think I read in a telebook somewhere that he's some long-gone politician named Jeb Bush's great-grandson."

A polite waitress exited the diner's swinging kitchen doors and approached the busy counter. She applied her pencil to her check pad and jotted down my simple order of pancakes, coffee, orange juice bacon and eggs. After the waitress rushed back through the swinging doors into the Silver Coin Diner's busy kitchen, I realized that I had become rather intrigued by the laconic teenager's overall nonchalance regarding my questions about the future president. I decided to extend our conversation to the vital domestic and international issue arenas. I asked the lad what types of social problems plagued the USA in the year 2085.

"None," the kid tersely replied. "There aren't any major problems like there are in your time. President Obadiah Bush took care of all that stuff. Many people regard him as a born genius."

"How is that possible?" I insisted on knowing. "You must be gravely mistaken. There will always be wars and recessions. Everyone with half a brain knows that."

The enigmatic kid explained that President Obadiah Bush had used his great influence to pass a very critical bill through Congress during his initial term as the nation's "CEO." All high school students were expected to graduate with honors and after age eighteen, a law mandated that every student was required to either serve four years in the military or an equivalent number of years performing vital social service. Then after demonstrating their dedication the young men and women of the future had earned *the right* to attend college. The twenty-two-year-olds then would have a greater sense of maturity and responsibility upon entering universities. They would not goof off, would not frivolously join fraternities and sororities, would not party all the time, would not make having sex and orgies their avocations, and finally would not waste their parents' hard-earned money drinking beer and vodka. Everything seemed plausible.

"Wow!" I exclaimed. "That's a terrific idea you just described. Going into the military or doing four years' community service work delays adulthood," I marveled. I paused for a second to capture my next fleeting thought. "Then students will not graduate *Princeton* or *Michigan* until they're around twenty-six. College grads will finally be mature enough to enter the competitive job market place. That plan you mentioned sounds very practical."

I proceeded to ask the kid about hot-button social problems such as teen pregnancies and abortions. The young man informed me that Dr. Gene Alter, a renowned *Nobel Prize* recipient from *Harvard*, had perfected a formula that effectively delays the onset of puberty until age thirty. Congress had passed a law in 2082 mandating that every infant had to be inoculated with the secret chemical solution right after his or her first birthday. The program was an important part of their required vaccination schedules.

"No teenage girls get pregnant anymore because of that amazing formula," I stated, "and stupid sexual urges are put on hold until well-after high school, and the onset of puberty is delayed well-after military training or mandatory social service and subsequent college attendance are under students' belts. Without destructive hormones interfering with essential brain functions," I continued, "college students could engage in very serious career pursuits. They could for the first time in history actually be bona fide college *students*. This creative story of yours is absolutely phenomenal!"

"Unfortunately," the kid said, "I'm still a virgin because of Dr. Alter's stupid research. That's one reason I often come back to your wonderful immoral time period so that I can be with non-virgins. Nine out of ten kids that live in your time are non-virgins, did you know that?"

"Don't feel badly and take it to heart," I sympathized with elementary compassion, "but I really like the idea that science is actively involved in prevention and in intervention. In the future kids' minds and instincts are no longer controlled by dumb biological impulses and temptations," I said to the adolescent above the din inside the diner.

I was wondering how the United States Congress managed to pass such controversial bills with the great philosophical divide separating Republicans and Democrats. "How did the Republicans ever push through such strong laws with the likes of the *ACLU*, the *NAACP* and *NOW* activists out there?" I curiously asked.

"There are no longer any robotic-like Republicans or Democrats," the young man indicated before burping loudly. "Only Republicrats and Demlicans exist in the future. President Obadiah Bush shrewdly made both parties learn to agree so much on all things. That's why there's little or no difference between them."

'This kid sitting next to me is either Nostradamus reincarnated or an absolute fraud possessing a very rampant imagination,' I thought. I wondered what had been done in 2085 in the area of ecology, so I requested clarification from the vernal guru, who incidentally appeared too knowledgeable to be believed. I wanted to know exactly what the time voyager had to say about the future world's environment now that Obadiah Bush had solved the country's fundamental educational and teenage delinquency crises and Dr. Gene Alter had effectively remedied the very formidable teenage pregnancy and abortion dilemmas. I was becoming more and more interested in the kid's past, which would naturally be my grandson's future. My inquisitive mind needed more explanations.

"What has the government done about preserving and conserving the environment?" I instinctively asked. "Has air pollution been controlled? Have all the world's forests been restored?"

The unkempt-looking boy's response was very enlightening. He described in detail the remarkable sage Professor Branche Sawyer, who taught "Science and Forest Destruction" at *Waterloo University*. The remarkable genius was instrumental in developing two dynamic special waste-conversion machines. The first apparatus ingeniously manufactured oxygen and nitrogen from garbage, and the second amazing device produced carbon dioxide from raw sewage. According to my new acquaintance President Obadiah Bush signed a law that every American household's residents must have their garbage disposal units and toilets and sinks hooked up to the two wondrous inventions or ten more years of military or social service was required of the wasteful non-law-abiding violators.

"That's great!" I observed and praised. "No more trash collection and expensive recycling of paper, metals and plastic rubbish. Those machines Professor Branche Sawyer invented can easily recycle nature without any need to have trees, rain forests and plants doing the job. You don't need any more 'Save the environment' campaigns or slogans," I declared. "You don't need people and animals exchanging oxygen and carbon dioxide with plants and bushes any more to keep the complicated life cycles going."

"That's correct," the young man readily agreed, "and all the trees on the earth have just about been chopped down and it really doesn't matter too much whether we have them or not. I mean, who really cares about toothpicks or splinters?" the lad rhetorically asked. "But when ya' need toothpicks or sawdust, ya' gotta' have a few of those stupid forests around to knock down."

I began to place some credence in the young man's insistent claim that he was indeed a time traveler. I suddenly converted into my greed-mode and thought that I might materially profit from *our* chance encounter. "How about some good stock tips?" I pleaded. "And please tell me, who's gonna' win the next *World Series* and the next *Super Bowl*? If you just tell me those things, you can stop here at this diner every Saturday morning and I promise I'll buy you breakfast."

"Forget it you self-centered moocher," the youthful Silver Coin Diner customer criticized. "Spend all your dough while it's still worth something. The *Greater Second Stock Market Crash* will happen on December 23, 2010. You have just a few more years to lose all you've got before you *will* definitely lose all you've got."

"Wow! The winter solstice," I acknowledged. "And two years later on December 21, 2012 the world's supposed to end! Just like the ancient Mayan calendar predicted. Disaster and doom are scheduled to happen on those dangerous dates. Those Mayan priests really knew every Aztec aspect of their astrology!" I wholeheartedly joked.

The future boy wonder was not at all impressed with any aspect of the Aztec or Mayan calendars. He switched subjects and related that he was on his merry way to an *N*Sync* concert at Philadelphia's *First Union Center*. "If I drop out of high school," the kid explained, "the law states that I'd have to be trained by the government to work in a factory or do boiler-room telemarketing to recruit more people into the Army or Navy. What a horrible punishment! I'd much rather be here sittin' and talkin' with you!"

"Well then," I said, "if you're under so much pressure to succeed in the year 2085, why are you sitting here in this diner eating breakfast right now? Shouldn't you be home studying your subjects? If you' flunk out of high school, you'll then qualify for the government's cruel and unusual rehab' punishment programs."

"I need some recreation time real bad," the boy declared. "My high school curriculum is really intense. I like going to *N*Sync* concerts because Oldies music tends to calm my nerves. Once in a while I also check out the *Back Street Boys* too."

I dared not ask the youth what the music of the year 2085 sounded like when today's rap and hip-hop songs sound so much like maniacal urban dissonance. Before I could proceed with our extraordinary discussion the unpredictable kid pulled out a shiny metallic object from his jacket's left pocket. I mentally examined the queer-looking item as he held it in his hand as he generally described the instrument's very unique functions.

Four designations were on the metallic object's top segment: a Pound Key, a Star Key, and buttons P (Place) and T (Time). The rest of the exquisite "Time Calculator's" surface contained red-colored buttons labeled zero through nine. The boy continued showing me his fantastic "Space/Time Pocket Coordinator" device as he identified its various fascinating features. To tell the truth, the casing looked authentic and it appeared that it very possibly could perform all the capabilities that the kid claimed it could.

"This sophisticated transporter is my own personal molecular atomic space/time/matter compressor and re-materializer," he casually explained, "and it can transport me to any place in any specific time period."

"Sort of like Scotty doing his thing on *Star Trek*," I smartly added.

"Who the heck is Scotty?" my fellow customer asked. "Is he your dog?"

My eyes glanced down at the young man's notepad that had been placed between us on the diner's front counter. On it were scribbled nine numbers, which I attempted to memorize. Without any warning or clue, the young fellow said "See ya'!" He grabbed his notepad, pressed a sequence of buttons on his magical calculator and then instantly disappeared in a flash into thin air.

I looked around the crowded diner and all of the other patrons were preoccupied chattering and kibitzing, completely oblivious to the futuristic *N*Sync* fan's hasty, impressive departure. My next instinct was to search under the counter. I was still in a stupor about the boy's incredible testimonies regarding his future world when the harried waitress approached carrying my breakfast order.

I volunteered to pay for the boy's meal and politely instructed the diner employee to simply add his $4.98 tab to my bill. 'His company was worth the small additional expense,' I thought. 'If he was a fraud, he was indeed a very intriguing fraud.'

The next morning, I awoke at 8 a.m. with an inspiration. I would call the eight-digit number the kid had scribbled at the diner on his notepad's front cover. I anxiously lifted a pen and jotted down the numbers I had recalled from the Silver Coin. I wanted to know if the kid was a terrible hoax and I also wanted to know exactly where he lived. I slowly and carefully dialed the number and I was happy to hear the voice of the youthful *N*Sync* fan on the other end of the line.

At first, he was not too thrilled to be hearing from me because where he was, it was five o'clock in the morning. Gradually I got the kid to come to his senses and he stopped being so grumpy and defiant over the telephone.

After I apologized for my waking him up, we amiably talked for over an hour. I didn't learn too much more about the year 2085 because all the kid really wanted to talk about was N*Sync, Britney Spears, Madonna, Fleetwood Mac and the Back Street Boys.

Yesterday, I stepped out to my mailbox and picked up my long-distance phone bill. After re-entering the house, I opened the envelope and then inspected the list of long distance calls I was being charged for. One particular number had been billed for the incredible sum of $987.52. I angrily lifted my living room phone from its cradle and promptly dialed my long-distance company.

"Hello," a pleasant female voice greeted, "how may I help you?"

"Look, I just received my monthly phone statement," I hollered like a maniac, "and one call is erroneously listed here for the amount of

$987.52! There's gotta' be some gross error here! I'm not paying for your company's negligence in keeping accurate records."

The well-trained operator suavely told me to wait on the line while she did her due diligence and professionally conducted her investigation into my inquiry. In the meantime, I was able to harness my emotions and simmer down a bit.

The woman's soothing cordial voice returned. She skillfully read the appropriate relevant information off of her computer's screen. "Sir, you had spoken for one hour after calling San Diego," she aptly stated.

"That's right," I admitted, "and I did speak with someone in San Diego, a teenager I believe."

"The San Diego call was a 900 number. The cost of the service was over sixteen dollars a minute. Wow sir, that's a pretty expensive 900 number you were calling!"

"What!" I nastily shouted. "You must be joking! That's impossible! The first numbers on the billing are 1-999 and not 1-900! I had called a 999 number and not a 900 number."

"Sir," the operator eloquently interrupted, "apparently they have run out of 900 numbers out in California just like they had run out of 1-800 numbers all over the country. You could easily solve this kind of problem by not making any *future 900* or 999 phone calls."

I slammed my green living room telephone down into its cradle. I grabbed the sheet of paper upon which I had scribbled the young man's San Diego phone number. I hastily ripped the paper to shreds and then promptly threw the tiny flakes into my kitchen garbage compactor. I cared less that in the year 2085 oxygen would be efficiently made out of common household rubbish.

"The Hotel Delaware"

Superstitious people believe and attest that strange incidents often occur on February 29 of every *Leap Year*. I had never placed too much credence in that unscientific claim until Tuesday, February 29, 2004, which unfortunately is a date I will certainly remember forever. Let me fully explain my accursed dilemma so that all will comprehend the true nature of my misery. The courtesy of another person's sympathy and understanding will be greatly appreciated. I realize that my tale will seem both illogical and incredible to anyone interpreting it, yet I believe I must share its veracity.

A *Leap Year* has three hundred and sixty-six days on the annual calendar, one more twenty-four-hour interval than that which exists in a normal year. Greenwich, England scientists and concerned astronomers have adjusted the mechanics of the moon and months to interface with the Earth's revolution around the sun because a quarter of a day is lost each normal year when coordinating those particular solar system relationships. To accurately adjust for the quarter-day time discrepancy in the Earth's elliptical orbit around the sun, February 29 was created on the post medieval *Gregorian Calendar* (developed in the 1580s by Pope Gregory), which we still honor today after the old Julian Calendar (developed in 46 B.C. under the reign of Julius Caesar) had been discarded.

Some *Leap Years* are unluckier than others. Every year divisible by the number four (lets' say the year 2004 or 2008) is generally regarded in common knowledge as a legitimate bona fide *Leap Year*. No problem! So far so good! But every "century year" divisible by a hundred is *not* a *Leap Year* unless that particular year is also divisible by four hundred; then it is still defined as a legitimate, bona fide *Leap Year*. For example, the years 1800, 1900, 2100 and 2200 AD are *not Leap Years* because they can't be divided by four hundred. Conversely, the Year 2000 *was* recognized as a legitimate, bona fide *Leap Year* because it *was* divisible by four hundred.

A person born on this planet Earth has a one in 1,506 chance of being born on February 29 of a *Leap Year,* but nevertheless 4.1 million individuals living around the globe have made their official grand appearance on that weird day and of that large number, 188,000 of them live in the United States. Before February 29, 2004, I had always felt sorry for people born on February 29 because their birthdays arrive only once every four years. Now I feel sorry for myself' for not staying at home on that ill-starred date. Allow me to fully explain my dilemma.

Some humans residing on this remarkable planet have attempted to conceal the bad omens that are associated with *Leap Year*. For example, *Sadie Hawkins Day* is celebrated on February 29 when single women once every four years are permitted to abandon traditional courting practice and chase after or propose marriage to men, thus attempting to make the "unlucky aspects" of that ominous day appear less threatening and more tolerable to the human race. But I can earnestly assert from my own personal experience that February 29, 2004 is a day I feel compelled to remember for all eternity. Soon you'll learn why.

I had made an appointment for Tuesday, February 29, 2004 to meet the book editor of a small publishing company at eleven a.m. at the *Regal Restaurant*, Baltimore Avenue, at the southern end of Ocean City, Maryland. I had been an arcade owner and operator of *Dealers Choice Games* at 410 South Boardwalk, Ocean City, Maryland, from 1967-'81. So naturally I was quite familiar with the city and with the reputable *Regal Restaurant*, which was one of my favorite breakfast and lunch haunts when I had been an industrious summer boardwalk businessman in that popular resort city. From a nostalgia point of view, I was really looking forward to making the business/pleasure trip down to the Maryland shore.

The editor's publishing firm was located in Annapolis, Maryland, and so Ocean City was a convenient halfway destination for us to rendezvous to discuss my book submission that had attracted David Evans' attention. A contract had been signed by me and mailed to the publishing company. All I had to do was drive seventy miles from my Hammonton, New Jersey home to Cape May, catch the 7:30 a.m. ferry across *Delaware Bay* to Lewes, Delaware and then drive another hour down the Atlantic Coast to Ocean City, Maryland. My only regret at the time was that the very busy editor had scheduled our "brunch engagement" at 11 a.m. on the very inauspicious date, February 29, 2004.

My wife wanted to borrow my merlot-colored *Nissan Maxima* to impress some of her friends with *our* new driving machine, so I had to settle driving her light brown *Nissan Altima* from Hammonton seventy miles south down to Cape May, New Jersey. I left my home at six a.m., figuring I had more than sufficient time to make my easy connection with the *Cape May-Lewes Ferry* since I had conducted similar trips hundreds of times before from 1967-1981.

Driving down Bellevue Avenue in Hammonton, I accidentally ran over a board lying in the street that had nails protruding face-up. I felt the *Altima's* steering wheel wobble when I drove another three miles to the *Atlantic City Expressway* entrance. Five miles in the direction of

Atlantic City I frantically veered my wife's brown automobile into the *Frank Farley Rest Area* and quickly inflated the hissing tire with air.

Speeding down the *Expressway* at eighty-miles an hour, I thought I had had a hallucination of sorts. I had an uncanny sensation that I had skidded off the right shoulder of the highly traveled highway and that the light brown *Nissan Altima* had entered a pine barrens' forest and had then slammed into a tree, knocking me unconscious. 'I really didn't get a good night's sleep!' I remember thinking after surviving the rather surreal manifestation that seemingly featured a very real impact. 'I must get to the ferry before this confounded front tire goes flat. Then I will have really *missed the boat*!' my mind mused. 'I mustn't disappoint the editor by having a real collision. That accident was merely a wild figment of my imagination!'

In my wandering mind, the same "air injection" of the affected tire was duplicated fifteen miles down the *Expressway* when I exited the toll thoroughfare at Pleasantville and then I again anxiously repeated the nerve-racking inflation procedure. After taking the *Expressway* to the *Garden State Parkway* I had to again stop at a *Parkway Service Area* and fill the tire with air and then desperately continue my extremely harrowing journey south. At Cape May I anxiously drove into a gas station and repeated the left front tire inflation a fourth time until I finally and gratefully made it to the ferry dock at 7:20. My mind was in a very paranoid state from all of the duress that had converted a supposedly pleasant ride into a living nightmare.

When I pulled-up to the *Cape May-Lewes Ferry* tollbooth, I turned up the volume on the *Altima's* stereo radio and then paid the unwary grim-faced female collector the exact amount for crossing the bay. She never heard the air hissing and sizzling out of my left front tire. I was too arrogant and proud to understand that the tire traumas were seemingly attempting to warn me not to cross the *Delaware Bay.*

I drove the light brown *Altima* forward and boarded the ferry and at the time I felt haughty and confident that I had cleverly outsmarted a major obstacle (by fooling the apathetic toll collector) caused by unlucky February 29, 2004. The ferry's entrance ramp was raised, the ship's loud horns sounded, and next I perceived that the huge one-hundred-twenty-vehicle capacity boat had gently slid out of its daily mooring.

I smugly sat in my wife's car, speculating that I would exit it a half-hour later and report my flat tire predicament to the captain when the ferry was halfway across *Delaware Bay.* 'The captain will get several of his crew-members to go down with a can of air-sealant and inflate my front tire so that I can safely make it down to Ocean City without further incident,' I cleverly imagined. 'I've outsmarted the ferry personnel by making my tire problem *their* tire problem to solve! I can always buy a brand-new tire and have it mounted at a service station in Ocean City.'

A half-hour finally elapsed on my watch. I casually got out of the *Altima*, inspected the front tire and immediately ascertained that it had indeed gone flat. 'Tires are only flat on the bottom!' I recollect humoring myself' with a familiar overused joke.

My eyes glanced around and extraordinarily observed that the light brown *Altima* was the only car on the ferry, which (as I have mentioned) could easily carry and transport over a hundred similar-sized vehicles across the bay. Furthermore, after ascending the white metal steps to the top-deck, I detected that the ferry was enveloped in a very dense fog. I could barely see the landmark partially sunken concrete ship situated in the distance off of Cape May Point, but the famous *Cape May Lighthouse* was completely shrouded by the heavy veil of dense atmospheric haze that had descended on *Delaware Bay*.

Looking ahead south in the direction of the Delaware shoreline, I couldn't see any signs of land or of man-made structures. 'The fog's as thick as pasta sauce!' I evaluated. 'It's a good thing this ship has an adequate radar system!' I thankfully considered in an effort to allay my heightened anxiety.

Upon entering the main concession area I immediately recognized that something was very abnormal. 'Where are all the other passengers? I'm the only one in the entire room! Where are the waitresses and the food attendants? Nobody's on this cursed ship except me!' I quickly realized.

I wildly clambered up metal stairs to the captain's deck and attempted to open the door to his control room but the doorknob would not turn and the windowless white metal object would not budge. 'This is stranger than peculiar!' I nervously thought. 'This popular ferry has transformed into a mysterious ghost ship of some kind! Damned February 29!' I neurotically blamed that date. "Damned February 29, 2004!" I lustily screamed out into the apathetic dense *Delaware Bay* fog.

I investigated the entire ship and found no evidence of any other human being aboard. I anxiously searched in the Men's Room, in the lounge area, in the engine rooms, and even had the audacity to enter the forbidden "Ladies Room" but much to my' disappointment and dismay, apparently I was the only person making the 'supernatural passage.' I recall wishing 'Please Lord, if only I could locate just one petrified passenger to provide me some semblance of comfort from my overwhelming apprehension.   Then I'll feel a whole lot better,' I solemnly prayed.

My feet stepped to the ship's bow and I futilely held my left-hand up to my sweaty forehead, endeavoring to get a glimpse of some remote familiar landmark or perhaps hear a *Delaware Bay* oil tanker's horns. 'I've taken this ferry ride at least seven hundred times between 1967 and '81 transporting merchandise from family boardwalk stores in Ocean City, Maryland, Rehoboth Beach, Delaware and Atlantic City, New Jersey,' I remember thinking and analyzing. 'But this misadventure has got to be the most frightening seventeen-mile crossing above and beyond any nightmare or seasickness I could ever have experienced!' I concluded as my body trembled and my knees knocked together. 'There just has to be some feasible explanation!'

The ferry's eerie foghorn blasted three times and as I stared off into the distance, my eyes finally were able to identify a nebulous-looking familiar object, the first of two parallel jetties that had been constructed about a mile into the *Delaware Bay* on the Lewes, Delaware side. 'At last, something I know and recognize in this crazy horrifying mental jigsaw puzzle! Now I have some hope! Those jetties had been built to prevent beach erosion,' I recalled.

The captain-less ship then strangely deviated from its normal course (that I had memorized in my head) and slowly cutting through the very palpable fog, it turned left and then entered the channel between the two jetties instead of continuing straight ahead past them to the Lewes, Delaware dock. The vessel was now nearer to Cape Henlopen than to its appointed destination, the Lewes, Delaware terminal.

I felt an intense chill circulating throughout my stunned body. The combination of an overall sinister atmosphere and an accompanying damp mist was comparable in my mind to imagining *me* traveling to a close friend's funeral aboard a mysterious lost ghost ship adrift at sea. At least that was the odd-type of sensation or perception that my consciousness had been rationalizing.

The ferry sounded its loud foghorn one final time and then effortlessly glided and slowly eased into a berth (that was unfamiliar to me) on the Delaware shore. I was quite perturbed and distraught with my heart filled with distinct trepidation, not knowing whether my crazy misadventure was an actual experience or a fantastic arcane delusion. Overhead gears threaded with thick chains suddenly began rotating and next the exit ramp for cars and passengers squeakily descended. 'We've landed near Cape Henlopen and not near Lewes, the ferry's destination,' I recollect thinking. 'This is definitely not where *we're* supposed to be! Something's certainly amiss here!'

My pupils steadfastly gazed through the persistent dense fog and saw a vague illumination directly ahead. A dim light shone from a hand-held lantern and a shadowy figure was silhouetted behind the weak glow. As if my body and spirit had suddenly been magnetized, my legs reflexively began walking in the direction of the obscure figure holding the morbid lantern.

My mind was still aware of the light brown *Nissan Altima* parked near the ferry's bow but my heart and body could not resist the inexplicable potent force that was deliberately pulling and dragging me like an invisible tractor-beam to the ominous figure holding the ancient-looking lantern.

"Welcome to the *Hotel Delaware!*" the old white-bearded man greeted. "Do not be afraid. I'm your host and your guide who will supervise your tenure here. I suppose you have many questions to ask me as most guests initially do."

"Who are you?" I tentatively inquired. "Why am I here? What's going on?"

"I am Diogenes," the ghostly character revealed, "and *you* are here dear visitor obviously because you're dead and your prodigious spirit desperately requires rest, rehabilitation and requiem. Come with me inside your new lodging," the grayish apparition dressed in ancient Greek garb communicated.

"And if I refuse?" I defiantly challenged. "What will be the consequences? What will be my punishment?"

"You have no say in the matter whatsoever," Diogenes grimly uttered. "You had surrendered your free will when your spirit escaped its confinement from inside your body. You have no choice as a dead entity other than to cooperate with my mandates. I can force you to perform any act that I want you to execute so don't resist my standard commands!" my pallid-faced guide explained. "Insolence will not be tolerated. I repeat. You surrendered your free will when your spirit evacuated your body! Do you now comprehend that basic simple truth?"

My emotions were dominated by shock and awe. I remember thinking, '*You've* spent thirty-five years of your life teaching public school kids English grammar, vocabulary, writing and literature, have finally reached retirement age, have begun a promising writing career and have sabotaged it all by suddenly becoming deceased on February 29th!'

My body reluctantly followed Diogenes away from the spooky ferry mooring and then we meandered through the thick fog in the direction of a dilapidated structure situated on a high sand dune directly ahead.

My restless spirit (or that element of it which still remained in my consciousness) demanded some plausible explanations from the hoary-looking guide dressed in a wretched-looking ancient mendicant's dull gray robe.

"I must have died in the automobile accident on the *Expressway!*" I gasped in horror. "Diogenes, did I die in an automobile accident? I just have to know *that* detail to alleviate my general nervousness!"

"What is an automobile?" the twenty-four-century old man asked. "It really doesn't matter what that item is," he continued speaking like a verbal cadaver. "You're dead as a doormat and now charged to my professional custody, automobile or no automobile. Do you fathom my words? The ideas and objects of your former world, of *my* former world, no longer interest me. They're both irrelevant and obsolete here!"

We slowly paced forward in the direction of the ominous-looking *Hotel Delaware*, which was now visibly outlined in the very thick mist with a rickety-looking shingle hanging on one hinge indicating my whereabouts. I found my eerie-sounding guide's answer very incomprehensible (let alone reprehensible) but nevertheless quite intriguing. "Diogenes," I boldly said, "are you the ancient Greek known to history as the *Cynic?*"

"You're quite a knowledgeable fellow because not too many souls make that particular association," my spooky host articulated, "and yes Stranger, you are correct in astutely making that connection. You must read books to be aware of that academic fact!"

"But how have you gotten from ancient civilization to the United States in the year 2004, and where did you learn to speak perfect English?" I stammered.

"Please Sir, one annoying question at a time," my new guardian insisted with a stern grimace featured on his ghostly and macabre-looking pale face. "I really don't know or care how I've arrived at *your* distant country. I can only tell you that once every three hundred and eighty-four years I'm moved and re-stationed by the unpredictable *Powers That Be* to a new drab and monotonous assignment in a new odd land. And finally," Diogenes proceeded with his fascinating monologue, "I've learned and conquered your language from conversing with other guests that have stayed or are staying at the *Hotel Delaware*. Does that answer satisfy your rather simplistic primitive curiosity?"

"Well, somewhat!" I marveled and replied. "I had read about you in a college philosophy class," I nervously stated, "and you were notorious for diligently walking the streets with a lantern looking for the face of an honest man. Is that legend actually true? Is that why you're still carrying your lantern?"

"You're most perceptive and appear to be highly educated," my alert guide observed and reluctantly complimented. "Yes, it is true, but historical truths are meaningless now, both to you and to me. The only significant fact that really matters is that we're both dead and that *you* must reside by Heaven's decree at the very serene *Hotel Delaware.* That is why the ferryboat delivered you to these obscure premises in that rather intense fog. Each and every time the mist settles, I know I'll be hearing the ship's horns," the old withered specter lethargically related, "and then that ominous blast is my signal to come out from the hotel and cordially escort our latest guest inside. After that task is done my next responsibility is to make my most recent ward as comfortable as possible."

As my famous deceased mentor and I paced up thirteen flimsy steps and gradually arrived at the *Hotel Delaware's* main entrance, the creaky door with un-oiled hinges slowly opened and Diogenes led me inside the musty building, which immediately reminded me of a dingy and despicable murky funeral parlor. Cobwebs, broken windows, bleak-looking dirty chandeliers and layers of dust everywhere suggested that the ramshackle hotel for death-transients was truly a ruinous unkempt *deathtrap.*

"Diogenes, is it true what I've read in encyclopedias that you believed that wealth and honor are of little value because they do not help men lead just and moral lives?" I instinctively asked my laconic host. "I recollect that principle as being the cornerstone to your philosophy."

"All of those seemingly important old ideas are quite immaterial and irrelevant now," Diogenes glumly answered. "Virtue, honor, wealth and morality are no longer essential elements of behavior. If I were you," Diogenes imperatively cautioned, "I would ask fewer questions and then pay strict attention and learn the fundamental elements of *your* new environment. Just remember Sir, you're now dead, and nothing else really matters. Please leave the myriad minuscule problems of the world to the living."

"But didn't you once visit and meet *Alexander the Great,* and he insisted on granting you any wish you wanted," I almost hysterically ranted, "and then you absurdly replied, 'Please move out of my sunlight,' and then *Alexander the Great…*"

"Silence Fool!" Diogenes angrily exclaimed as he held his spectral lantern up, fully exposing his hideous skeletal face. "Any more outbursts from you will surely result in dire consequences for your captured soul. Heed my simple basic commands Stranger, or else you'll certainly be doomed to a far worse eternal fate than mere death! I trust now that I've concisely communicated that stark cause-effect relationship to you."

'*I'm* very much like Diogenes, an avowed cynic and a devout skeptic,' I rationally thought. 'Perhaps that is why I'm assigned here and *he* is here too. The poor Greek scholar has been commanded to teach *me* what I need to know and what years of doubt could not make me realize,' I conjectured.

My heart felt tempted to mentally ask (for *we* were transmitting thoughts and words through a fantastic telepathy and not by using our mouths and voice-boxes) my distinguished escort if he had ever heard of an Athenian named Socrates, but since I didn't desire to antagonize the melancholy morose apparition and subsequently suffer his wrath, I refrained from making the inquiry, for I fathomed that presently *he* had absolute dominion over my weak (and maybe absent) will.

Diogenes led me through the dingy foyer of the shabby antiquated edifice to a gloomy dusty poorly lit lobby and we passed empty chairs with torn upholstery and several sofas neglected by time and quite apparently in dire need of repair. At the *Hotel Delaware's* front desk my escort solemnly asked me to sign both my real name "John Wiessner" and my pen name "Jay Dubya" in the ledger, which I cooperatively complied while coincidentally and obediently enacting his baneful command.

"How did you know my real name and how did you know I had a pen name?" I requested knowing. "You must be omniscient," I mentally transmitted.

"Knowledge in this afterlife is transparent and not opaque as it is in *our* former world," Diogenes telepathically related, "and it is not exclusively confined to a person's form or body. I simply read your vulnerable mind as if I was reading an elementary book or a tablet. It's quite easy once you learn the knack!"

"Well," I commented in sheer amazement, "what about heaven and hell and purgatory and what about everybody else that's dead and *Jesus* and…"

"Look!" my upset teacher said in an admonishing tone of voice, "the information you're requesting is not available or known on *this* lowly death level. Once you leave this holding area and move on into the greater transcendent after-world," Diogenes carefully enunciated, "then those typical questions that presently riddle your limited comprehension might be satisfactorily answered at the next higher phantom station. Now do you fully evaluate your lowly status on the eternal ladder?"

"But if I died when my car had veered into the woods," I mentally rebutted, "how could I have lived to put air into my front tire several more times before arriving at the ferry terminal?" I desperately argued. "And Diogenes, if my' car was wrecked up and if I was dead on impact, how did I manage to drive it all the way to Cape May to take the ferry across the bay to this horrible *Hotel Delaware?*"

"It probably takes about an Earth hour for true death to finally set in," Diogenes theorized and objectively communicated, "and you were still mentally carrying out your trip to the ferry during that delicate hour of transition from your former life to this one. So spiritually, mentally and emotionally," the ancient pessimistic sage cleverly observed and concluded, "you had completed that part of your trip even though your body had perished in the accident you had previously so vividly described."

"Who else is registered here as a guest?" I inquisitively asked. "How many rooms does this place have for occupancy? It looks pre-Victorian in architecture!"

"Please Sir, one appropriate question at a time," Diogenes aggressively chastised. "You have all eternity to learn and decipher what you feel you need to know. You'll soon discover that the *Hotel Delaware* has thirteen guest rooms. And I don't know if that mediocre number is symbolic of anything or not."

I glanced outside a window and the only thing I could discern in the dense fog was the aforementioned unhinged black shutter hanging down from the wooden outside wall that quite evidently needed several serious heavy coats of paint. "Oh," I thought and communicated, "that' numerical symbolism makes a lot of sense, having thirteen rooms. Delaware was the first state, and there were thirteen original colonies that had united in the war of independence against England. One room for each colony is a wonderful coincidence! Wouldn't you agree Diogenes?"

I learned from my orientation guide that the other spirit guests residing at the hotel were distinguished personages Benjamin Franklin, George Washington, Thomas Jefferson, Edgar Allan Poe, Abraham Lincoln, Ulysses S. Grant, Mark Twain, Henry Ford, Albert Einstein, Franklin D. Roosevelt, George Herman "Babe" Ruth and Marilyn Monroe.

"But those people are all famous?" I challenged my honorable guide. "What's the meaning of all this? Where do I fit in, a common public school English teacher?"

"You mean they all *were* famous," Diogenes cunningly corrected and clarified.

"But tell me, why am I here with all of these deceased celebrities, inventors and presidents if I'm just an unfortunate ordinary dead person?" I demanded knowing. "Honestly, I certainly lack their accomplishments and their credentials!"

"Maybe you'll become famous after your death just like Herman Melville or William Shakespeare," my ancient Greek ghost page speculated and mentally conveyed. "My senses perceive that you had always wanted to communicate with the dead. Now here's your big chance."

I soon learned several bizarre things from Diogenes. When Babe Ruth had registered as a guest Christopher Columbus had simultaneously checked out and had been moved to another higher plateau in the afterlife. And when Marilyn Monroe's shade was accepted as an official resident, Henry Hudson's apparition was allowed to move on to loftier post mortem pursuits.

"At the rate of new guests and old ones coming and going," I commented to the stone-faced and generally apathetic Diogenes, "I won't get out of this lackluster *death trap* for another two hundred years judging by how long George Washington has been a prisoner, er, I mean a visitor here."

"That logical assessment seems about right," my ghastly-looking skeptical companion agreed. "But you must remember," Diogenes ruefully clarified, "time as you knew it is meaningless at this place. There is little difference between a minute, a day, a century and a millennium at this splendid and unique hotel. Time here can either expand or it can contract. As that fellow Einstein in Room 1955 once told me, everything including time is relative!" my host mentally related with a very weak-but-irritating smile vaguely reflecting from his countenance.

"Oh," I mentally answered, "now that explanation of yours makes perfectly good sense. When one person moves in, the lucky spirit that has been here the longest is finally eligible to move out. It's sort of like a predictable rotating lottery of sorts!"

"Right you are, Sir," Diogenes aptly concurred with my brilliant deduction. "When you moved in, Ben Franklin, according to the established rotation, must step onto the ferry and be taken to the next higher station, wherever that is!"

Just then the ferry horns blasted three times, suggesting that Ben Franklin was obediently ambling up the ramp and happily departing the dismal dreary grounds and sinister vicinity of the *Hotel Delaware* to embark to some new destination in the very bewildering indefinable death realm.

"But why have I been summoned to this morbid death holding station if I'm not famous?" I stubbornly asked my pale pathetic transparent partner. "I think I really don't deserve to be here! The accomplishments of your other guests certainly eclipse and dwarf mine!"

"Maybe you'll finally have become famous when it's time for your departure on yonder ferry," my gruesome-looking ghoulish host imaginatively suggested. "Don't short-change yourself, even after you're certifiably dead!"

"I would rather have led a full normal life as a no-body than to sacrifice twenty-five golden years of retirement for fame after my ill-fated automobile accident!" I strenuously objected. "Life is unfair and now I know that death is too!"

My addled mind (or what was left of it) was in a complete quandary. I asked to be led to my assigned room, which was the only one situated on the hotel's second floor, ironically Number 2004. Then a certain parallel relationship connected inside my confused, befuddled and disoriented mind. The hotel's room numbers corresponded with the exact year each person had perished. I had died in 2004 and I knew from biographical accounts I had read that Dr. Albert Einstein had died in the year 1955.

"Thank you for showing me my living quarters, or should I say my death quarters!" I mentally said to normally reticent Diogenes. "Are you the only employee here?"

"Why yes," the now guide-turned-butler cerebrally transmitted, still holding his trademark dimly lit lantern. "You'd better keep that exquisite sense of humor of yours," the notorious cynic smartly advised, "because it's guaranteed to raise everyone's *spirits* around here! Ha, ha, ha," he shockingly cackled like an obsessed maniac.

"Why do we have to enter and exit via doors if we're spirits?" I seriously asked. "Why don't we just filter through the walls like ghost vapors?"

"We could, but that would be impolite and too annoying to our other prominent guests," Diogenes reprimanded. "It obviously would infringe on their privacy. You wouldn't want that ferry to *barge* into your room would you? Ha, ha, ha," the ancient Greek wildly cackled. "So, George W., Abe L. or Marilyn M. wouldn't enjoy *you* interrupting *their* privacy or their meditation by *your'* intrusively whisking your way through the outer wall, would they? I doubt it!" the now-spirited ghost convincingly argued.

I asked Diogenes to provide me with an abundant supply of pens and writing paper, and to accommodate my requests the specter later rummaged through closets and through desk drawers and eventually located the prescribed requested items. I thanked my new acquaintance, prudently sat at the dusty desk and assiduously began re-writing my manuscript that I had recently sent to my supportive Annapolis publisher. And after meticulously completing that project, which I thoroughly believed far surpassed the original version in quality, I commenced authoring the first of four prodigious novel-length manuscripts that I had felt inspired to write. 'I have two hundred years to write at my leisure,' I intrepidly surmised, 'and this is one labor of love that I feel compelled to perform. I must organize my novels and novellas as carefully as possible and make each page of superior quality. I'll be my own ghostwriter!'

Diogenes had told me that I could export (without penalty) one package into the "physical world" so I was elated when I was able to fill a storage chest with eight thick manuscripts, novels and novella collections. The old chest, loaded to capacity, was then addressed and sent to my publisher in Annapolis, who would be shocked to receive the unanticipated documents authored by a dead writer and surprisingly delivered via conventional parcel post. The details of exactly how this *novel* transaction was done or negotiated had never been disclosed to me, but I had placed implicit faith and trust in the integrity of the sad-faced Diogenes, who incidentally had expertly and expeditiously handled that special favor for me.

It has been a very strange existence for me in this morbid-but-placid afterlife, having no need for either eating or drinking. The desire for biological satisfaction (or for its accompanying pleasures) was totally absent from the *two-dimensional* death world to which I was confined, but I was happy to note that mental pleasure could still be experienced after I had finished the task of writing those assorted "perfect manuscripts."

Feeling exceptionally lonely, I finally summoned sufficient courage to exit my drab and uninspiring room and visit the eldest guest spirit at the *Hotel Delaware*, so I politely knocked on the door of Room 1799. George Washington graciously answered my knocks, and the tall pale specter asked me to enter and review post-colonial history events for him.

"It's indeed a distinct honor to meet my country's first President," I anxiously began, "and you look identical to your famous portrait that appears on the one-dollar bill."

"Sir," the eminent Founding Father and renowned military general telepathically stated with his sagacious mind, "confidentially, I've never visited anyone else in this confounded hotel. I was afraid that there might be some sort of supernatural reprisal associated with me leaving my humble quarters. Apparently, Sir," white-wigged George Washington continued, "you possess great daring to act independently without knowledge of rules and death customs, or without fear of dire consequence."

Then George Washington's specter stated that I too must be a famous person to be confined to the obscure sanctuary of the creepy *Hotel Delaware* even though I was totally unaware of my fame or reputation by virtue of my untimely and premature departure from mortal existence.

I thanked the venerable American for his unsolicited praise and encouragement and then I learned that all of the books in General Washington's room had been printed *before* 1800. The poor fellow thirsted for knowledge about America after his unfortunate death on December 14, 1799.

'Shades of yesteryear,' I automatically thought.

"Tell me, Sir," the tall powder-wigged giant of history mentally said, "has the *Constitution* and the nation adequately survived the past several hundred years?"

I cogently explained to President Washington all that had transpired from his colonial and *Revolutionary War* era up to the year 2004 including the sensational changes associated with the *Industrial Revolution,* the *Civil War*, the invention of the train and the automobile, the *Great Depression*, the two world wars and the atomic and computer ages. I also divulged that the *Constitution* had been *amended* many times, and we discussed those particular modifications in great length.

"Do you mean to tell me that you own a device you call a car that can go up to sixty miles per hour in just six seconds and you have a special gauge you call a speedometer that registers one hundred and forty miles an hour?" Washington marveled and mentally conveyed. "I guess the stagecoach and the horse and wagon are obsolete. These commentaries of yours are quite astounding! Oh! I get it!" Washington exclaimed. "The word automobile means that a coach could move all by itself without any horse pulling it! Quite in-genius terminology if I may add!"

"Well, not exactly," I respectfully clarified. "People still go to race tracks and bet on horse races. A big one each May is called the *Kentucky Derby. "*

George Washington was fascinated by all that I told him, for we must have exchanged uninterrupted conversation for at least a full Earth month without the need of sleep, food or drink. I never thought that I could be so vociferous as I had been in *his* inimitable company. And when Washington discovered from our lengthy discourse that there were now fifty states instead of thirteen, his pale face produced a proud broad smile.

President Washington became rather disconsolate upon hearing about the notion of "separation of church and state" and how "the establishment clause" had been "misinterpreted" by a sequence of "unfortunate" *Supreme Court* decisions. "National morality cannot last in exclusion of religious principles," our first chief executive lamented and expressed, "and your public schools should not be devoid of teaching morality based on religious principles either," he mentally elaborated. "Your institutions of learning are therefore producing a vile generation of bratty dolts who might have knowledge in subject matter but who lack discipline, resolve and wisdom that come from the practice of simple basic religious morality. The first *Ten Amendments* to the *Constitution* should be predicated upon the *Ten Commandments* handed down to Moses and embodied in the *Bible,*" George Washington adamantly insisted and emphasized.

I meekly informed my perceptive listener about abortion rights, about homosexual marriage and about criminal and animal rights. He nearly blew a fuse arguing, "It's a travesty to believe that such ungodly things have been resulting from the misguided interpretation of a Godly-inspired document such as the sacred *United States Constitution.* And when you tell me that God has been taken out of your public schools," Washington continued in an emotional state that bordered rage, "then I believe that I had fought the entire *Revolutionary War* in vain. Our nation is doomed to decay from within. Civil rights will ultimately destroy individual morality, which will produce the decadence that will weaken and then eventually erode away the foundational values of *our* great nation. There is no doubt in my mind that *that* catastrophic end will be inevitable!"

On the optimistic side, the first President was elated to know that the country had survived over two centuries of critical challenges since his death in 1799. The great statesman and military strategist found hope in the prospect that a national crisis similar to the *Civil War* or the *Great Depression* might once again shake the country out of apathy after the year 2004. George Washington's spirit explicitly indicated to me that there possibly would emerge a noble crusade to return to the great moral roots and the powerful American traditions strongly embodied in the *Declaration of Independence* and in the *Bill of Rights*. He referred to this phenomenon as "the Phoenix resurrection."

Upon leaving the General's "solitary confinement sanctuary," George Washington's ghost thanked me for my informative visit while regretting that I had conveyed some "distasteful news" about future events and changes in the "established moral codes" that have been over the years erroneously affected by judicial and legislative adaptations in the "legal codes."

I left George Washington's shoddy modest accommodations at the singular *Hotel Delaware* and returned to my own morgue-like second floor room. It again occurred to me that since I had died in the year 2004, I had the only *death quarters* on the second tier. Then an interesting thought flashed through my transparent brain. When additional renowned people would die, more second-floor rooms would have to be added on to the ancient hotel so that the new restless spirits could peacefully dwell until they were allowed to ascend to the next dreadful echelon in the afterlife. 'Or perhaps there are many other death holding stations similar to this *Hotel Delaware* to allow for the other decedents,' I hypothesized.

I stayed dormant in my room for an unspecified interval of time, which to my comprehension remained quite anonymous and mysterious because there were no clocks or wristwatches or views of the sun and the moon from anywhere inside the dreary deplorable hotel. Then I attempted to prepare the outline to a new manuscript but ideas and words eluded me, so I temporarily abandoned that ambitious enterprise.

My mind decided that I would pay a visit to another extraordinary personage trapped in the archaic weather-worn domicile, so I elected to interact with a particular idol of mine from nineteenth century American literature. I had to choose between Edgar Allan Poe and Mark Twain. I chose the former hoping to have an opportunity to speak with Samuel Langhorne Clemens at a future date (even though calendars and dates did not exist anywhere inside the very weird and mystical hotel).

My knuckles rapped on the door of Room 1849 and mused that Edgar Allan Poe would assume that I was an itinerant raven determined to annoy and pester him, all relaxed and pensive in *his* tranquil solitude.

"Hello," I hesitantly greeted the literary master. "May I come in to chat for a while?"

"Certainly," Poe cooperatively-but-cheerlessly replied. "You look harmless although I must laugh at the strange apparel ornamenting your body. I presume you are from a future age? You appear too casual to be dead. Is that how you were buried? Has formality been abandoned entirely?"

"No Sir, er I mean, I don't think I was ever buried and have no knowledge of being buried," I stammered. "This is what I was wearing when I died."

"Well then," my illustrious academic erudite host persisted, "are you from *my* future?"

"Yes Sir," I keenly answered the much-revered genius. "You happen to be a favorite author of mine and I immensely enjoyed teaching my students many of your excellent stories," I sincerely elaborated. "I was a school teacher during most of my life," I clarified, "and your tales of horror and your classic adventure stories were among the best I ever read or analyzed. I especially liked teaching my students your tales 'The Cask of Amontillado' and 'The Fall of the House of Usher'."

Poe was quite flattered by my complimentary remarks and asked me to sit down even though I no longer possessed a body that required rest from its weight or from its exertion. I respectfully honored my literary benefactor's request out of force of habit and out of reverence for past human courtesy customs.

"Well kind Sir," E.A. began, "you must know about my dear Virginia?"

"Your wife Virginia died of tuberculosis in 1847, so in all due deference," I acknowledged, "you' know more about her last moments on Earth than I do since you had passed away in 1849."

"I apologize, kind Sir," Edgar Allan Poe mentally transmitted while momentarily exhibiting a rare smile, "but I originally meant the state of Virginia where I grew up and whose memory I have always held dearly inside my miserable heart."

And after I had educated Edgar Allan that there were now forty-nine states in the Union besides his precious Virginia, the cheeks upon the pale ghost's countenance almost turned from ashen to pink. He had accurately speculated that a bloody forthcoming *Civil War* was imminent after 1849, but a tear seemed to form in his right eye when I explained the tragedy and the widespread suffering in both the American North and the Dixie South. Many painful wounds had to be healed after the devastating conflict between the *Union* and the *Confederacy.* "A period of *Reconstruction* had to be initiated," I very patiently revealed and explained. My listener was just as glad as George Washington had been about the acquisition of additional states to the *Union.*

I immediately identified with the dead man's unique sense of patriotism and with his skeptical outlook on death and its eternal idleness. Much to my surprise, Edgar Allan Poe was amazed that he would become a famous giant in American literature after his untimely death in 1849. The master of the macabre had been found lying outside a Baltimore voting place on October 3 of that year, and he had died in a city hospital four days later without ever regaining consciousness.

"Do you mean to say that my work is read in virtually every high school and college English class in the country?" Poe incredulously mentally asked and marveled. "I knew I would die in poverty and disgrace," he bluntly continued with remorse and disenchantment, "but I never reckoned I would achieve national and international acclaim. You Sir, pardon my aggressive nomenclature," E.A. paused to measure my reaction, "are a most welcomed time courier. In you I see much of me, and I mean this with sincerity when I say that it is most grievously calamitous that you too are deceased and doomed to incarceration in this especially decrepit hotel. Have you attained notoriety during your lifetime?"

"No," I bluntly lamented, "and I really don't know why I've been assigned to and incarcerated here inside the *Hotel Delaware* with such a distinguished group of literary, famous and historical souls occupying the other rooms."

"Perhaps you too will be visited by a messenger rapping on your door several hundred years from now and told of your great contributions to civilization," Poe theorized and suggested. "Then *you* will know the pure pristine genuine delight I'm presently feeling at learning that my life's work has achieved honor and prestige in the literary community, a community that vehemently abhorred me and my endeavors and one that I absolutely despised and loathed during my brief tenure on the all-too-mundane Earth."

Then I had the pleasure of discussing with the master most of his outstanding literary gems including "The Cask of Amontillado," "Murders in the Rue Morgue," "The Fall of the House of Usher," "The Tell-Tale Heart," "The Black Cat," "The Pit and the Pendulum" and the "Masque of the Red Death." I was *literally* held spellbound and was thoroughly captivated by Poe's vivid animated descriptions and by his graphic explanations in regard to what critics consider his classic works.

In the Purloined Letter," I curiously stated, "you had essentially invented the entire theory and methodology of the detective story," I praised the great short story author, "and thousands of writers since your time have imitated the superior model that you've so effectively pioneered. I believe," I respectfully continued, "that you Sir, and I sincerely mean this, have been perhaps the greatest influence on the course of American literature over the past two centuries."

"I always believed that the ideal critic should be objective while slightly leaning toward the negative side," Poe declared while alluding to his own literary reputation at being a premiere reviewer of essays and short stories. "So that's why I get along so well with Diogenes," he humorously added. "But above all else, an author must possess originality, courage of heart and the grammatical skill to efficiently convey *his* intended message to his readers. Otherwise," the disconsolate and totally bored fellow decided, "the author is not an author at all but merely a very ambitious *writer* aspiring to great accomplishments but doomed to failure or in the final analysis, be destined to produce volumes of mediocrity."

I had fathomed and found much merit in Edgar Allan Poe's enlightening commentaries and I only wished at that moment that I could return to my human form and pursue my literary aspirations with the superb knowledge I had absorbed during our most intriguing dialogue. When neither of us had anything additional to relate or to discuss, I bid the prolific genius (possessing a burgeoning vocabulary) "adieu" and next shuffled down the dank dim corridor and then climbed up the rickety wooden steps, ascending back to my non-inspirational room.

My consciousness was gratified by the keen insights that the eminent editorial authority had to share with one of *his* less-talented admirers. Poe's final words remained in my mind and after the comprehensive interview, my energized brain tended to review them incessantly. "Always remember kind Sir," the literary master had imperatively transmitted, "a combination of truth, soul, passion, beauty and creativity is what elevates literature to a higher shelf than the one occupied by traditional newspaper journalism and by ridiculously written political propaganda."

Throughout my humble life I, like Edgar Allan Poe, tended to be reclusive, shy and moody. I never really liked gossip, small talk or was fascinated by glib and garrulous people. 'An introverted nature was also an introspective advantage that both Poe and I cherished and exercised during *our* separate writing sessions,' I realized. "We both like to be alone to ponder and to explore our inner souls and to investigate the deepest secrets lying within our secluded hearts,' I then understood. 'We both quietly loathed obnoxious and ultra-gregarious people.'

And soon a much more enlightening theory entered my troubled mind. I was in one way or another much like all of the inhabitants of the deteriorating un-maintained *Hotel Delaware*. I was diplomatic and gentlemanly like Washington, introverted and emotionally tormented like Poe, and inventive with an *Alpha* (aggressive and determined) personality like Thomas Alva Edison, whom I had selected to be my next hotel resident to interview.

I had by then willfully accepted my possible two-hundred-year confinement in the gloomy *Hotel Delaware* in a rather stoical manner, and frankly, I finally became cognizant of another interesting facet of the complex bizarre puzzle. I was also very much like Diogenes, priding myself on being a skeptic and a cynic about most everything and most anything.

I confidently descended the decrepit staircase to the ground-level corridor and floated (without walking a single step) down to Room 1931 where Thomas Alva Edison's spirit was quietly kept to ruminate. The man's *shade* was a little hard of hearing but after I had introduced myself in a loud clear voice, Edison welcomed me into his disheveled room that had so many cobwebs that it reminded me of a monstrous cocoon. That graphic notion immediately made me contemplate that *we* were indeed trapped in some sort of indefinable chrysalis, waiting to be released into a new existence just as an ugly caterpillar transforms into a beautiful butterfly inside a second *natural* womb.

"I must say I admire your very evident audacity," Edison's ghost remarked as it eagerly greeted me at *his* door. "You demonstrate the daring of an old friend of mine, Henry Ford," he generously praised. "Make yourself comfortable if that's at all possible in this bizarre rudimentary plateau in the afterlife."

"Why Henry Ford!" I exclaimed in a very un-ghostly-like manner. "He's staying in this same hotel in Room 1947. I remember his name and room number from the registry ledger that's kept down in the main lobby."

"Why I'll be giraffe's grandfather!" Thomas A. Edison bellowed in an uncharacteristic and excessive display of emotion. "I've been staying here at this repugnant run-down hotel right down the hall from one of my favorite contemporaries and have been completely ignorant of that fact until *you* came along and informed me. I'll have to garner up enough gumption to mimic your fine example and pay the old coot a belated surprise visit!"

Edison was very anxious to know what had transpired in the world after 1931, and upon hearing about *Bose* sound systems, computer floppy and compact disks, video cassettes, color television, cell phones and the *Internet*, the great inventor, who possessed over a thousand United States' patents, heartily and exuberantly laughed out loud.

136

"You know," the incomparable genius Thomas Edison responded, "I only wish that I could've lived to see in full operation all that you've so admirably described. I'm so glad and proud that my years of research and experimentation had led to the discovery of these phenomenal creations that you've so wonderfully related," the ingenious fellow mentally said and savored. "Your good news has brought joy to my heart and peace to my restless soul!"

"Yes," I matter-of-factly added, "and Sir, there are high schools, towns and townships named after you all over the United States," I congratulated, "and believe it or not you're still affectionately referred to as the *Wizard of Menlo Park*. And your famous statement 'A genius is one tenth inspiration and nine tenths perspiration' is widely quoted all the time all over the modern world," I sincerely complimented.

"Allow me to modify that if I may," Edison insisted. "It ought to be 'A genius is one-third inspiration, one-third perspiration and one- third desperation!" the great contributor to science and technology aptly joked. "If only I could return to my laboratory in Menlo Park for just one earthly minute! That would be a terrific moment I would definitely cherish for all eternity!"

Thomas Alva Edison and I conversed for the longest time and reviewed just about everything from stereo radios to space satellite communications. Throughout our extended dialogue, the wrinkle-faced man was again a human dynamo exhibiting a great *spirit* and a youthful enthusiasm for all subjects our imaginations touched upon. And when the accomplished inventor heard that his New Jersey research laboratory had been proclaimed a treasured national monument by President Dwight D. Eisenhower in 1956, Edison's sunken eyes seemed to illuminate and his mental articulation became most jubilant.

"You are indeed a Godsend," the creative guru triumphantly declared in appreciation of the intellectual stimulation our conference had provided. "I'm deeply indebted to you for verifying that my life's work has been worthwhile. I now feel that I had laid the foundations for the discovery of more intricate and sophisticated appliances and devices that'll most certainly be beneficial to mankind," the gray-faced spirit gleefully announced. "You have definitely *made my century*!"

Edison and I must have talked for at least several more Earth months without any trace of exhaustion evident in the rhetoric of either of us. Finally, after informing my prestigious host all about the capabilities of the *Hubble Space Telescope* and all about exploratory interplanetary probes to Mars and Jupiter, I left the highly esteemed inventor's company and returned to the quiet sanctuary of my shadowy second floor room.

Several more months must have elapsed before I decided to exit my "dying quarters," slowly amble down to the dark and dreary lobby and initiate a conversation with the sometimes' talkative-but-moody sage Diogenes.

"Well Diogenes," I cunningly began, "I have had the pleasure of meeting the ghosts of George Washington, Edgar Allan Poe and Thomas Edison. Now I can't wait to mingle with Thomas Jefferson, Abraham Lincoln, Mark Twain, Ulysses S. Grant, Albert Einstein, Henry Ford and Marilyn Monroe, if I accurately recall all of the other hotel's spectral guests."

"Kind Sir," Diogenes answered, "please examine the new names listed in the register. I believe almost two centuries have expired in the outside world since your arrival, and now I suspect that *you* are now the senior resident of the *Hotel Delaware*."

I gazed down at the ledger situated on the dusty registration desk and noticed that all of the honorable names I had just enumerated were gone from the list. Instead, were unfamiliar appellations such as Sir Hiram Applebee, Salvatore Giovanni, Mildred Carson, Thomas Attanasi, Roseann Celia, Gerald Gares, Arthur Orsi and William Burns.

"Who are these people?" I uttered in sheer protest. "I never heard of any of them! They must all be pedestrian commoners!"

"They are inventors, presidents and entertainers that have become famous during *your* relaxing two-century stay at the *Hotel Delaware!*" Diogenes academically lectured quite nonchalantly. "However, they will certainly recognize your name since your glorious fame has certainly preceded theirs!"

"Do you mean it's already time for me to be transferred to a more enlightening holding area somewhere else in the afterlife?" I sadly asked my aged and withered friend. "I thought I heard the ferry's foghorns several times but I was so engrossed in meditating in my room that I never looked out the window into the dense mist or stepped downstairs to investigate its arrival," I reported to Diogenes in a melancholy tone of voice.

Just then the ferry's whistle blasted three times and I instinctively knew that a new hotel occupant was about to come ashore. Diogenes left me standing in the dingy lobby, and several minutes later the scary-looking apparition reappeared alongside a middle-age spirit still attempting to decipher and define his new gloomy surroundings.

"Hello," I said to the new *Hotel Delaware* guest standing next to me in the dark and dreary lobby. "My name is John Wiessner and I'm glad to meet you!"

"John Wiessner!" the fellow gasped in astonishment. "You mean John Wiessner, alias Jay Dubya! Why you're my favorite author! I've read all of your short stories, *Hammonton Gazette* opinion columns, all of your novellas and all of your novels. This is indeed the highlight of my death experience!"

"And who might you be?" I curiously inquired. "Certainly, you must be famous to be invited as a welcomed guest at this temporary holding platform."

"My humble name is Jason Parsons," the dead fellow's ghost mentally stated, "and I perfected and invented the *Babel Universal Communicator* in 2154. That's indeed my biggest accomplishment."

"What does it do?" I insisted on knowing. "Does it communicate with other planets in the *Milky Way*?"

"*The Babel Universal Communicator* is a hand-held computer device that enables people of different languages to communicate the brain pulses of their thought patterns in *their* language into the words and sentences of a person speaking another language, no matter what it is," Jason Parsons eagerly explained. "A voice simulator I had developed and patented translates the words through a powerful micro-speaker into the second language so that two people of different nationalities or cultures could easily hold an intelligent extensive conversation upon first contact."

"Wow!" I exclaimed with great admiration. "Babel then refers to the *Biblical Tower of Babel* where everyone in the Babylon area suddenly spoke different languages. Jason Parsons, I'm very glad to make your acquaintance," I genuinely expressed, "and don't worry about a thing. Your stay at the *Hotel Delaware* will be both rewarding and soon completed before you know it if you know how to use your time constructively and wisely. Now tell me, how did you happen to die?"

"I think my envious wife poisoned me when she found out I was having an affair with a beautiful and voluptuous *Hollywood* movie star," Jason Parsons disclosed. "But I'm not sure if jealousy was her real motive or whether she simply wanted to inherit my fortune because she was having extra-curricular affairs with the gardener and also with the chauffeur. At any rate," Jason finished with a degree of anguish and distress, "I'm damned dead now and I don't give a Marley's or a Great Caesar's Ghost about it. I just feel extremely betrayed, that's all."

"Women led to *your* demise," Diogenes concluded and insisted as he held *his* dimly lit lantern up to Jason Parsons' honest-looking face. "Both the woman that you desired and the woman that you had, namely your spouse, have each contributed to your eternal fate!"

Then I heard the ferry horn blast three additional times, signaling its intent of disembarking from its mooring and venturing out into the thick *Delaware Bay* fog en route to the second level of enlightenment and emotional growth in the peculiar-but-fascinating vertical death tier hierarchy.

"Maybe now I'll find out about heaven, hell and Jesus and everything else," I mentioned to Diogenes and to Jason Parsons. "I'm now fully prepared to deal with the attendant duties and responsibilities of the next level of spiritual growth, whatever those specific details might entail!"

Diogenes adroitly escorted me to the *Hotel Delaware's* lobby door. I warmly shook his cold numb hand, stepped out of the macabre dilapidated structure, descended the thirteen rickety steps and hastened through the dense fog to the awaiting ferry. I enthusiastically ascended the entrance ramp with all the vigor that a veteran ghost could muster. I had no apprehension about or fear of my next surreal destination.

My inspired mind then understood that I was mentally equipped and emotionally mature to sufficiently deal with the elements that would confront me on death's enigmatic second stage of existence. I intuitively also now fully understand that Diogenes had successfully shipped the wooden chest of manuscripts into the past via some wonderful alien method of time compression. The following revelation is now quite lucid in my mind. I now thoroughly comprehend and appreciate a third significant truth, a germane inspiration that currently is quite obvious in its essence. Quite remarkably, I had indeed become Jay Dubya's anonymous *ghostwriter* during my most memorable two-century hiatus at the singular *Hotel Delaware.*

I'm presently placing *this manuscript* describing my death experiences in an empty five-gallon plastic spring water bottle that I've fortunately found inside a remote storage compartment on the deserted ferry. And after inserting the cork tightly into the bottle's neck, I'll carefully toss the container overboard hoping that some lucky mortal will someday discover it and have a brief glimpse of the mystical spirit world awaiting him or her.

"My Ubiquitous Acquaintance"

I've been an acquaintance of Ray Canfield since January of 1968. Ray had married a Hammonton, New Jersey girl Phyllis Amedio, who at St Joseph High School happened to be one of my wife Joanne's best friends, and in retrospect, I recollect that the four of us had attended a memorable New Year's Eve party at a popular local bar/restaurant down near Vineland. Upon first impression, I found Ray Canfield to be a rather easy-going amiable fellow.

"You're not from Hammonton," I remember politely asking my new friend. "Where did you go to high school?"

"Actually, West Catholic over in Philly'," Ray promptly answered. "It was an all-boys school back then, but even without girls, we still drove the Christian Brothers crazy."

"No kidding," I pleasantly remarked. "When I had lived in Levittown, Pennsylvania back in 1958 and '59, I had a good buddy named Bob Jalonec who also had been a student at West Catholic. And if my fuzzy memory serves me correctly, Bob had attended *that* high school before moving to Levittown and my pal wanted to continue his education back in Philly' because the newly constructed Bishop Egan High only had academic accommodations for freshmen and sophomores in its first several years of existence."

"Did this guy you're describing have blond hair slicked back in a really cool D.A.? Was he good-looking and a real ladies' man?" Canfield innocently inquired, showing more than a mild interest.

"You got *that* depiction right!" I quickly verified. "Bob's dad had a fantastic cream and green '57 Chevy, which as you know was perhaps the neatest cruisin' automobile around in the late '50s. But that's quite remarkable Ray!" I exclaimed. "You once knew my best Levittown teenage friend Bob Jalonec. Fact is, I haven't seen or heard from the incredible stud for a half-century now!"

"And believe it or not," Canfield coyly added and then paused for dramatic effect. "I too had ridden in that same boss '57 Chevy when good old Bob would occasionally visit West Philly' and deliberately show-off his hypnotic mean machine! We had no trouble picking-up hot-looking chicks!" Ray inadvertently emphasized as Phyllis and Joanne simultaneously frowned in his direction at our small crowded New Year's Eve table.

At that same raucous New Year's Eve affair, precisely ten minutes before the traditional exuberant celebration time, Ray Canfield had slightly moved his rickety chair several inches backward from the table and had accidentally nudged his shoulder against a not-too-sociable highly-tattooed motorcycle gang member, whose volatile burly, surly amigos immediately wanted to initiate a barroom brawl with Canfield and me, so *we* quickly grabbed our wives by the arm, spontaneously meandered through the throng of jubilant revelers and next hastily escorted the ladies out of the rollicking restaurant mere moments before any of us could be brutally mauled, maimed, mangled or mutilated.

In March of 1976 I had been invited to join the Hammonton Lions Club by Arthur Orsi, who was then the charitable organization's president. Much to my curiosity and momentary surprise, that evening Art had also invited Ray Canfield as a guest for *him* to consider becoming a prospective member. As destiny turned-out, Ray Canfield (whom I had often jokingly called "Ray Cranfield" just to aggravate his ego) had later become club president in 1979-80 and I had eventually assumed that extensive responsibility in 1982-83.

Ray had a friend named Jim Thomas who had recently moved from Wallkill, New York to *our* somnolent New Jersey town, and after joining the Hammonton Lions Club, our newest member convinced seven prank-loving individuals from his former Wallkill Lions Club to pay a South Jersey visitation to Frog Rock Country Club, where *we* predictably met every first and third Thursday of each month. Lion Jim Thomas had introduced to the Hammonton Club a new creative fundraiser that he had chaired up in Wallkill, selling giant coloring books to the grateful parents of enthusiastic young kids throughout the community.

The un-magnificent seven New York Lions traveled around 150 miles down to Hammonton and just when a group of the on-a-mission instigators were cleverly distracting *our* club officers, two other mischievous Wallkill Lions nefariously pilfered our club bell and accompanying gavel. According to standard Lions' custom, the Hammonton Club then had to journey all the way up to Wallkill to humbly retrieve our' very necessary lost inventory, *that* very common practice essentially designed to promote genuine fellowship along with subsequent visitations to other Lions Clubs.

On the way up to Wallkill I was diligently driving a huge rented RV on the Jersey Turnpike with all-too-garrulous Ray Canfield riding shotgun and with twenty other opinionated Hammonton Lions ambitiously drinking and eating at various tables and seats situated directly behind us. The New York metropolitan-area traffic was bumper-to-bumper in the vicinity of the Newark Airport. Upon Canfield's ridiculous unsolicited advice, I elected to change lanes during all of the intense congestion and turn the gigantic steering wheel to the right amidst all of the distraction and boisterous male confusion being enacted behind. While executing the rather difficult maneuver, to my chagrin, my initiative had partially ripped-off the expensive RV's rear bumper when a stubborn tractor trailer driver took offense to me aggressively switching lanes in front of him.

The alluded-to minor accident had occurred in the late '70s during the Jimmy Carter Administration, and there happened to be long gas lines (along with frustrating fuel rationing) everywhere. Later at the scheduled meeting our club had successfully reclaimed our treasured bell and gavel up in Wallkill, and on the return trip south we (out of absolute necessity) stopped at the north end of the Garden State Parkway for the explicit purpose of replenishing our gasoline supply. At that terrible time in American history, if your vehicle's license plate ended in an odd number and your intended refill was attempted on an even-numbered day of the month, then the service station attendants would refuse filling-up your tank. But the Hammonton Lions were not to be denied

On board the RV were four half-inebriated feeling-no-pain New Jersey State Troopers, who fortunately were also Hammonton Lions Club members. Several of the more daring cops flashed their badges and then nonchalantly opened their jackets, thus exposing guns inside their shoulder holsters.

"Look Pal!" one of our more distinguished and loquacious state policemen imperatively addressed the now-alarmed and incidentally petrified gas center attendant. "We're on a really serious drug-bust mission and if you don't cooperate with us as expected, you'll be accused of obstructing justice in a court of law! Do you now fully understand the potential consequences of your intransigence?"

"Yes Sir! Right away Sir!" the intimidated and exasperated pump-worker hollered-up to the open window. "I'm law-abiding! I didn't mean to cause you important fellas' any trouble!"

Now the affected Lions aboard the RV would have never had to go through all of that hard-core melodramatic delay if irascible Ray Canfield hadn't invited Jim Thomas to voluntarily join our close-knit fraternity. One of our more dynamic club members, Nick Perone, owned a large automobile repair shop up on Route 30, Hammonton's White Horse Pike. Upon arriving back into town at midnight, Nick audaciously hopped into the RV's driver seat and then sternly demanded that we all exit the mammoth-but-convenient mode of transportation. Perone then put the transmission's gearshift into reverse and the ingenious mechanic proceeded to violently slam the oversized RV smack-dab into the side cinder-block wall of his commercial garage, and miraculously, upon impact, the formerly dangling back bumper had become pressed back into its proper position without any particular notice of ever being mangled on even somewhat tampered with.

Throughout the last five decades, Ray Canfield had tried his hand at many different challenging occupations and businesses, among the most prominent endeavors being: boldly buying the Town House Restaurant on North Third Street and soon changing the establishment into The Bull's Horn Bistro; being a highly skilled bartender at three often-frequented South Jersey taverns; driving a utilitarian "prescription drug van" and competently delivering vital medical supplies to ailing patients' homes; playing bass guitar in a '50s rock and roll band; being a reliable bus driver, and finally, once owning and operating a viable driving school with his wife Phyllis.

Naturally, Joanne and I would run-into Ray Canfield at various regional places when we least expected it. Once we had met "the itinerant one" thirty miles away from town at the March Philadelphia Flower Show at the downtown Convention Center, and another time Ray and Phyllis suddenly appeared by surprise, their familiar faces landing in line just behind my wife and me outside 5th Avenue's Radio City Music Hall with *them* showing-up only minutes prior to *our* admission into the annual Rockettes Christmas Show extravaganza. And on still another occasion, Joanne and I were standing in a boring buffet line at the elegant Las Vegas Bilaggio and who magically materializes right next to us but an animated Ray Canfield, who incidentally had been attending a New Products and Franchising Convention being given in Sin City, the eager entrepreneur/attendee apparently seeking a new profitable method of earning a comfortable living.

Around Thanksgiving of 1979, Joanne and I were at a dinner engagement at the historic Smithville Inn over on *Route 9* near Atlantic City, and who do you imagine was the extremely cordial bartender? None other than the ubiquitous Ray Canfield.

"Hey Ray, I thought you were tending bar at either Frog Rock Country Club or over at Joe's Maplewood?" I casually interrogated, obviously anticipating basic clarification.

"The tips are much better here at Smithville!" Ray loudly commented above the obnoxious human voices saturating the surrounding atmosphere. "There's definitely more customer volume! And you know me! Always searching for something better and never satisfied with where I am! And besides this gig," the talkative omnipresent fellow continued his splendid narrative, "starting next

144

week I'll be playing bass guitar every Friday and Saturday nights over on Pacific Avenue in Atlantic City. Maybe you and Joanne could stop in and hear my group perform some fine night."

Much to my heartfelt regret, I had never visited the recommended Pacific Avenue bar establishment but in later years, Joanne and I were stunned wedding guests down at the Avalon Yacht Club when we suddenly witnessed Ray Canfield standing upon the elevated stage, fretting away on his cherished electric bass guitar, his newly organized band being the posh affair's principal source of entertainment. And as a related addendum, I was not astonished upon discovering that "Cranfield" later that year turned-out to be my son Joe's Little League baseball coach and also that autumn, my youngest son Steve's youth soccer coach.

In July 1981, Ray Canfield had secretly driven a contingent of Hammonton Lions down to Ocean City, Maryland, where I had owned the Dealers Choice Amusement Arcade at 410 South Boardwalk. Naturally I felt obligated to leave my thriving summer business in the charge of my two experienced store managers while I reluctantly entertained the six rather-jovial New Jersey gentlemen to a fairly expensive beer, spicy steamed shrimp and Maryland crab supper up in my small Apartment #10, which was located directly above the country's oldest operating merry-go-round, the unique colorful carousel constantly playing loud calliope music emanating from inside Trimpers Amusement Center situated near the south end of the famous Ocean City, Maryland boardwalk.

Then in late August of 1981, I was busy working behind the cash register inside my boardwalk tee-shirt store (which I only visited one night a week), the retail business located under the Star of the Sea Condominiums at the south end of the Rehoboth Beach, Delaware boardwalk. Much to my prodigious shock, who strolls inside the front portals to buy a decal-emblazoned piece of summer heather-material apparel but the inimitable Ray Canfield.

"Hey, I didn't know you had a tee-shirt store!" Canfield typically bellowed and laughed. "I knew all about your Ocean City, Maryland gaming arcade but nothing at all about this pretty nifty place! In all our previous conversations, you never told me about this certain enterprise of yours! Say now, how would you like investing in a terrific new project I have in mind? I plan on buying the Town House over on North Third Street right across the road from Marinella's Funeral Home! In the early '60s Joanne and Phyllis would often walk over there to the old Town House for a late lunch after attending their afternoon St. Joe classes."

"No thanks Ray!" I skeptically and suspiciously replied to his partnership proposal. "I'm trying to save enough money for my three sons' college educations. And besides *that* big problem, I still have a sizable mortgage on my house and also quite frankly, I need to purchase a new station wagon to transport tee-shirts and stuffed animals from my garage up in Hammonton onto the Cape May-Lewes Ferry to travel across Delaware Bay and then motor down to my two separate boardwalk stores, which of course, as you now know, are a full thirty miles apart."

In 1986, I had been teaching English at the Hammonton Middle School, and over the week-long Christmas holiday vacation, Gordon Strycula, a faculty colleague (and an avid amateur taxidermist) asked me to accompany him on a "shooting expedition" at a Gettysburg, Pennsylvania hunting preserve.

"Who else is going?" I characteristically asked.

"Oh, you', me', John Maglieri and another fella' from town named Ray Canfield," Strycula informed. "Ray says he knows you."

"Yeah Gordy. Ray and I go way back. We're both past presidents of the town Lions Club."

At the aforementioned hunting preserve, I had proudly bagged a beautiful white ram with enormous curved horns that I intended to display above my den's fireplace mantel. While the majestic-looking animal was being gutted back at the camp, Spanish instructor John Maglieri and I were walking up a ridge to see if we could spot Gordon Strycula and Ray Canfield scouting-out targeted animals they desired bagging for both meat and prospective trophy mounting. Suddenly our sensitive ears perceived two loud rifle blasts and then discerned excited shouting originating from the opposite side of the grassy incline.

"Run for your lives!" I recognized Ray Canfield's apprehensive voice vigorously commanding. "Run for your lives!" the neurotic hunter wildly reiterated.

Near the top of the ridge, my then-frightened eyes witnessed an enormous wounded wild boar speedily descending the incline and rapidly hustling towards John and me. The angry beast, possessing razor-sharp tusks, was vociferously snorting with an ample amount of rancid-looking blood and saliva ominously dangling from its very ferocious jaws. The distressed monster had selected Maglieri and me for its new-found 'revenge victims', whom the vicious brute would savagely take its elevated agony and animosity out upon.

John and I swiftly dropped our rifles and desperately scampered to a nearby thin oak tree. We managed to shinny-up to the first pair of limbs, around ten feet off the ground, when the incensed fierce boar smashed its thick skull hard into the tree base, its action being a hostile exhibition of primal rage. The dangerous creature repeated its mania twice again with the skinny oak tree wildly shaking, and then the agitated black boar amazingly darted around the tree three consecutive times before Ray Canfield and Gordon Strycula finally approached and fired two shots each into the ugly bleeding lice-infested pig, effectively sending the crazed beast's out-of-control soul directly to hog heaven.

That evening back in Hammonton the four of us reminisced about the day's sensational events and then shared other extraordinary stories from our separate pasts. I suavely related to the other three amateur hunters how in my youth I had often taken a public service bus with a few friends from downtown Hammonton to the world-renowned Steel Pier on the Atlantic City boardwalk. The bus would invariably stop at a small cafeteria on Route 30 called Burdicks, and ironically, three of my distant cousins, Johnny, Phil and Tommy Fallucca, whom I had never known, (but had known of from random family drivel), worked summer days at Burdicks, and each cousin had probably waited on me at one time or another from behind the counter without me ever being aware of their true identities.

"You gotta' be kidding me!" a dumbfounded Ray Canfield piped-up with an element of wonder quite evident in his tone of voice. "You mean Burdicks, which was located in Devonshire on the White Horse Pike right across from the old Circus Drive-in Movie! I can't believe it!"

I hesitated a few seconds before resuming our conversation. I organized my scruples and again communicated to Canfield inside the Route 30 Silver Coin Diner, not entirely realizing the general significance of my initial statement. "What's the big deal about *that* rather ordinary bus stop activity from my teen past?"

"When I was a struggling student at Trenton State College," Canfield seriously revealed, almost choking on the hamburger meat still lodged inside his mouth, "to earn some money for school tuition I drove a public service bus on my all-too-familiar route from Camden through Hammonton, a total of sixty mundane miles east all the way to Atlantic City. I probably had...."

"Picked *me* up as a passenger and now, a half century later, the weird jigsaw puzzle pieces are astoundingly and coincidentally connected!" I marveled and uttered. "This is almost too hard to believe Ray. You drove a summer bus and then later owned a driving school with Phyllis, who had done your basic accounting and had kept all your books. I recall hearing a fascinating story with you teaching driving to that Indian woman that works at the Atlantic County Library over on Egg Harbor Road, I think her name is...."

"Pridy Mody," Ray chuckled and disclosed for the benefit of *our* two captivated listeners, John Maglieri and Gordon Strycula seated beside us at the diner's serving counter. "I had dropped off Mrs. Mody, who incidentally was attractively dressed in her fancy silk New Delhi apparel, at the Hammonton Post Office, where she had to mail some personal letters. Upon her return to the car, the very formal well-mannered Indian lady entered the passenger side and immediately observed a black cat staring at her on the sidewalk. This woman Pridy Mody anxiously told me to step on the gas because the wicked cat had an especially evil nature and would soon attempt attacking my dual-control driver training car. I scoffed at the lady's seemingly absurd idea when...."

"When the black cat jumped onto the car's hood with raised fur on its back and fanatically hissed and screeched, scaring the living daylights out of both you and Pridy Mody," I finished Ray Canfield's fascinating story. "Your abundant adventures often seem more like misadventures," I accurately concluded, much to the total amusement of both Gordon and John.

On December 28, 2012 I had called my plumber Joe Hiltwine to come over to my residence to replace an old bathtub valve and also to install a brand new environmentally-friendly low-water-usage toilet in my downstairs powder room. Joe passively explained to me that he had just paid a visit to Ray Canfield's house on Fourth Street to snake-out a clogged septic pipe all the way from the basement out to the street sewage connection.

"Do you know Ray Canfield?" Joe Hiltwine wondered and asked. "In such a small town like Hammonton, everyone knows or probably has heard of everyone else."

"A remote acquaintance," I fibbed, trying to satisfactorily reconcile in my mind the monotonous redundant recurring Canfield appearance pattern. "Ray was once in the local Lions Club with me and I had been his public relations chairman, constantly feeding club activity news and a stream of publicity pictures to the area press."

Thirty minutes later, I suddenly became involved in a classic slapstick *Three Stooges'* episode with Joe Hiltwine playing Larry and me starring in the victim's role of Curly. Thinking about the latest Ray Canfield coincidence, I had opened the white wooden door and stepped from my laundry room down onto my garage's cement floor, and immediately after undertaking my first step with my left foot, my right foot then made painful contact with my recently removed downstairs toilet, which Joe had unintentionally placed behind the door while going to his van to obtain the new toilet for appropriate installation.

I lurched forward, my right leg making initial excruciating contact with the object's dense hard rim, and next, my in-flight vulnerable torso then forcefully crashing (with noteworthy authority) directly into the empty toilet tank, immediately knocking the heavy white object over onto its side. My abused body roughly bounced off of the overturned ceramic obstacle with me fortunately landing upon my outstretched hands, being somewhat grateful that the toilet had somehow cushioned my clumsy fall.

Instantly I rose to my feet, vaguely comprehending that a pretty decent chunk of flesh had been torn from my right shin as a result of me not noticing the misplaced toilet hidden behind the closed mudroom door.

"Did you just yell something?" Hiltwine hollered from inside his parked van. "What did you yell?"

Feeling fully embarrassed and under extreme duress, I boomed back in agony while examining my ugly leg damage, "No Joe! I just wanted to see how you were progressing with the toilet exchange. I'll talk to you later about it."

The next morning Joanne didn't like the way that my' leg wound was healing so being concerned, she drove me a mile down the White Horse Pike to the AlantiCare Emergency Hospital Clinic. I endured the terrible throbbing discomfort pulsating from my right shin simply because two good-looking medical babes washed and cleansed the deep cut, gave me a preventative tetanus shot, wheeled me down to the X-ray department for an obligatory injury photo' shoot (to ascertain that there was no fracture or bone chip), and then the pair of pretty nurses dressed the bloody area, and since the shin could not be easily stitched, the two merciful dolls finally released me from their most benevolent custody.

On December 30th friends from Burlington, Jerry and Irene Gares gave me a call and announced that they would be coming to Hammonton for a surprise 70th birthday party for a high school friend. The party was to be held at Frog Rock Country Club, since their honored female high school classmate was now living in Egg Harbor City, only twelve miles east of my ordinarily quiet hometown. Jerry alerted me that he and Irene would be stopping by the house after five pm to share some recent gossip and to drink (with Joanne and me) a fresh bottle of vintage Cabernet Sauvignon.

Before I could ever tell Jerry and Irene about my severe toilet-caused shin injury, the Gares related to me something that sounded virtually phenomenal in scope and sequence.

"At Frog Rock we were sitting with an area friend of our ex-Burlington classmate," Jerry confidentially related. "The really nice guy lives in Hammonton and his name is Ray Canfield."

"Did this fella' Ray Canfield tell you that he remotely knows me," I asked. "Ray and I had joined the local Lions Club together way back in March of 1976, the nation's Bicentennial Year!"

"No, your name never came-up in *our* lengthy conversation," Jerry sadly divulged. "I gotta' apologize. I'd neglected to mention to Ray that you were a Hammonton friend of mine. If you remember, you and I had been introduced to each other back in 1996 by Professor Bill Burns when all of us were partying at his beach home down in Stone Harbor."

"Yes!" I automatically confirmed, my frazzled cerebrum still focused on the most current Ray Canfield coincidence over at Frog Rock. "Bill Burns is friendly with Earnie, a guy who owns seven pharmacies in various South Jersey towns. In fact, here's another outstanding coincidence for you to consider Jerry. In addition to a home in Stone Harbor, Earnie also has a home in Florida and a third one over in Medford too. My good friend Jim Amari, who had taught with me at Hammonton High School for nine years before becoming a guidance counselor in Glassboro and later an elementary school principal in Marlton, well anyway Jerry," I awkwardly proceeded, "Jim has a home in Medford that's only a block away from Earnie's."

"That's mighty odd and it's relatively unbelievable!" Jerry Gares acknowledged and stated. "My older brother Will had once worked in Earnie's pharmacy in Beverley, just outside Burlington City. And as you very well know," Dr. Gares pontificated before imbibing more delicious red wine, "I'm also acquainted with your good buddy Jim Amari. When I was the Assistant Superintendent of schools over in Burlington Township, I had met your pal Jim at several regional administrative conferences!"

The very next afternoon I received a common phone call from my younger brother Skip, who was returning from visiting friends out in Michigan. My brother had stopped his long excursion to spend the night at a motel in Ohio.

"Just to let you know I'm safe and sound and still breathing oxygen," Skip pessimistically began our sibling dialogue. "To tell you the honest truth, I had a great time touring the Ford Museum and Greenfield Village in Dearborn, just outside Detroit. The museum was fabulous and my old New Jersey friends Frank and Mike enjoyed it all too! The Ford Museum even had the original Oscar Mayer Weinermobile on display!"

"Excellent Skip!" I diplomatically commended. "Now I suppose you're about seven hours away from Jersey, still having to drive through all of the Keystone State from Pittsburgh to Philly' on the very long Pennsy' Turnpike. What city are you near? Cleveland? Columbus?"

"Actually, Big Brother, I turned off of *Interstate 76* ten miles south of Youngstown and I'm now camping-out for the night at the Colonial Inn Motel in a remote town called Canfield, which is, I estimate, around the same size as Hammonton."

There was a momentary pause in the bland discussion as my confused brain gathered and then crudely synthesized its totally disheveled wits. I then alertly and ingeniously perceived that Canfield, Ohio symbolically represented yet another peculiar arcane omen or cryptic cosmic sign.

"Okay Skip, call me when ya' get back to Hammonton," I insisted. "I've been taking care of your cats, feeding them in your cellar every day and also disposing of their litter. Sometimes I'm pretty big on logically practicing home hygiene."

"Thanks a lot Bro. See ya' when I get back to town," Skip closed. Click.

On New Year's Eve Joanne and I had just returned from a merry party at her cousin Chick Sceia's Fernwood Drive place when the kitchen land-line phone rang with the caller being euphoric Professor Bill Burns on the horn. Bill and wife Fran were celebrating January 1st at their friend Earnie's plush Stone Harbor residence.

"Guess what!" Burns prefaced his genial comments, attempting to arouse a degree of suspense in me. "Fran and I are at Earnie's place and your Medford friends you talk about all the time, Jim and Loretta Amari, well, they're here too. We just met them. Earnie introduced us! And I gotta' admit, they're both funny people, just like you had always described them!"

"That's truly supreme!" I reflexively praised the former Political Science prof'. "Happy New Year to you and Fran and kindly give Jim and Loretta my best regards!"

"And there's someone else here at Earnie's who claims to know you, a talkative Hammonton guy by the name of Ray Canfield."

"Tell Ray 'Happy New Year' for me," I requested, my addled brain then swimming in a deep quandary, my fragile mind being curious as to how Canfield had been acquainted with the notoriously prosperous pharmacist mogul Earnie. "Joanne and I will see you, Fran along with

Jerry and Irene at Maggiano's Restaurant at noon right after your next January eye appointment in Cherry Hill," I reminded my retired professor pal. "Don't forget to check your calendar! See ya' on January 15th Bill! Happy New Year!" Click.

Last night I received a phone call from Pete Santilli, a former middle school teacher colleague who is now retired and presently organizing an upcoming two-week Italy/Sicily trip this coming April.

"Hi Pete, say hello to Barbara for me," I cheerfully greeted. "Let me see if I correctly remember our itinerary. We fly from Philly' to Rome, with three days touring the Eternal City. Then we' motor-bus to Florence. Two days in Florence and next we bus north over to Venice. Two days in Venice and then we jet to Messina, Sicily, where we'll tour for two days. Finally, it's on to Taormina for three days at a luxurious resort before flying back to Rome. Then it's a nine-hour flight to Philly' to complete our grueling European vacation!"

"Do you know who's all going?" Pete slowly quizzed me.

"Yes, there's Joanne and me of course, and you and Barbara, and your sister Mimi and Benny, and there's Carl and Dottie Mortillite, and Franco and Nancy Scianni, and their son John and his cute wife Michelle, and let's not forget the couple from the Atlantic City."

"There's been one more couple added," Pete methodically mentioned. "The guy says he knows you. It's..."

"Let me guess!" I quickly interrupted. "I theorize that the latest trip couple happens to be Ray Canfield and his wife Phyllis!"

"How did you ever know *that* information?" Pete questioned, with an iota of awe evident in his voice tone. "Canfield and I just closed the deal ten minutes ago!"

"Let's just say Pete that I have a super-bad case of advanced ESP!" I emphatically complained, futilely feigning emotional irritation. "Being psychic does have its radical downside though! In fact," I clearly maintained, "being clairvoyant can at times be a real bummer, that is, once you've fully mastered the rather humdrum talent!"

"The ING Problem in English"

I've always found the *I-N-G* words in English grammar rather annoying and bothersome. Of course, Gerunds are I-N-G words that look like verbs but act like nouns in sentences. For example the sentences "Skat*ing* is fun," "My favorite sport is skat*ing*," "I like skat*ing*" and "There are many moves in ice skat*ing*" show the Gerund skat*ing* acting as a subject, as a predicate nominative following a linking verb, as a direct object following an action verb and as an object of the preposition "in." Gerunds only occasionally give me a hard time as in the cases of me not wanting to own a lightn*ing* rod out of fear of being electrocuted or me wondering in which direction a newspaper head*ing* is actually head*ing*.

The I-N-G ending (or Present Participle) words that behave like verbs occasionally give me a hassle. I sometimes speculate that "mow*ing* lawns" could cut me up pretty good and that "pet groom*ing*" advertised on a sign makes me think, "I don't want any pet groom*ing* me!" I mean "paint*ing* houses" could change your skin color in a hurry' and "hear*ing* aids" sounds plenty more dangerous than H-I-V. Revolv*ing* charge accounts can make you dizzy if you watch one long enough, and I often wonder if fenc*ing* companies sometimes abandon using sabers and instead fight with swords? If an idea' is swimm*ing* around in my head, would I then be a candidate for contracting water on the brain? Incidentally, I believe that eat*ing* crow is for the birds, particularly the buzzards, but I prefer tell*ing* the truth while stand*ing* up rather than ly*ing* on the ground. And how could a person ever be caught throw*ing* a tantrum unless the spectator knows exactly what a tantrum looks like and how much it weighs. And once at a circus sideshow I was gullible and paid a dollar to see "the man-eat*ing* crabs" only to walk into a back room and see a man sitting at a table eat*ing* crabs.

Sure, stupid jokes can be made by inter-playing *ing* verbs but it's when the Present Participle is used as a Participial Adjective that my patience and tolerance are absolutely tested to their limits. I mean how would you like to go into a large contingent of stores and have to compete with a shopp*ing* mall. And why don't hunt*ing* lodges walk around in the middle of the forest with loaded shotguns? Astronauts have to worry about being wounded by shoot*ing* stars and museum visitors often must duck down when entering a shoot*ing* gallery. And baseball umpires occasionally have to call a slid*ing* board or a slid*ing* door "Out" at second base and heaven forbid if you intrude on and embarrass a dress*ing* room. And in my home's kitchen I always keep my head away from the chopp*ing* block and I often question why smok*ing* chimneys never get cancer or emphysema.

And to really aggravate me about Participial Adjectives, park*ing* lots make it difficult for me to find a place to put my automobile and I don't desire to be maimed, mutilated or injured during TV break*ing* news. And I feel extra tall when in the presence of a shrink*ing* violet and I wish I had a local plann*ing* board on my wall so that I wouldn't have to think about what I had to do next. And quite confidentially one of my biggest apprehensions is to be consumed and incinerated by a burn*ing* desire.

These very troublesome commonplace Participial Adjectives are both abominable and horrendous! How come swimm*ing* pools are never seen doing the breaststroke out in the Atlantic? And if a person is in a swimm*ing* pool then that individual must be careful not being injured by a div*ing* board. Naturally I fear being gulped down by drink*ing* water and I don't want to be threatened or molested by drink*ing* cups. And besides that remote possibility, driv*ing* rain doesn't even have any steering wheels and speaking of driv*ing* (a Gerund here), I make it a habit to stay out of the pass*ing* lane (Participial Adjective) because I don't want to get run-over by part of the highway. And despite how intelligent they may sound, writ*ing* tablets still require the use of pens and pencils and in addition they should never be swallowed.

And how come runn*ing* water has no feet let alone no legs? And how come the school cafeteria ladies are never serv*ing* tennis balls? And why does my liv*ing* room make the other parts of my house seem dead? And how come I've never been cleaned by a wash*ing* machine or physically defeated by a winn*ing* lottery ticket? And how does a student start finish*ing* school? My mother once authoritatively told me, "You have to look quickly or else you'll miss seeing the vanish*ing* cream!" and I remember my sister once saying, "This gust*ing* (Participial Adjective) wind is totally disgust*ing*!" (Participial Predicate Adjective).

Other relevant questions often confound my cerebral function*ing* (Gerund). Do print*ing* specialists also know how to write in cursive? Why do citizens participate in elections if we already have vot*ing* booths to do the job for them? And why do hospitals need surgeons when they already have operat*ing* rooms and operat*ing* tables? And did you ever cower away from the idea that a hang*ing* basket might actually strangle you? And just think about the poor innocent Mesopotamians that were lynched in the Hang*ing* Gardens of Babylon even without the essential services of hang*ing* judges, who might have also been suspended from ropes in the Hang*ing* Gardens! And why

154

don't fly*ing* insects require pilot licenses when fly*ing* humans do? Can fish*ing* boats really catch tuna all by themselves and can Mexican jump*ing* beans pole vault too? I wonder!

These very frustrating I-N-G Participial Adjectives can easily drive an emotionally disturbed person (like myself) to the brink of insanity. A paranoid college student might never take a test next to a copy*ing* machine out of fear of getting caught in a scandalous cheating incident and I never show my novels to employees at bookkeep*ing* companies because I'll never get my hard covers or paperbacks back. And I can tolerate my telephone answer*ing* machine until it begins to challenge my statements and then defiantly answers me back. And I definitely avoid tann*ing* salons because when I was young, I once threw a football and broke a window, and my father tanned my hide pretty good. Once I had eavesdropped on a private conversation between two meet*ing* rooms and whenever I go to Atlantic City casinos, I pick up bad habits from gambl*ing* devices that coincidentally have had one of their arms amputated. And mov*ing* vans are still called mov*ing* vans even when they are parked or when they are stationary at a red traffic light!

Over the years I have learned to stay away from practic*ing* physicians and dentists because I don't like any rank amateurs experimenting on me and recently, I have mastered the art of runn*ing* (verb) away from walk*ing* (Participial Adjective) pneumonia. And I was recently shocked when I drove by a local manufactur*ing* company because I had formerly believed that only people made and assembled things. But my biggest concern is not gett*ing* (Verb) my legs mangled when ambl*ing* (Verb) by the area bowl*ing* (Participial Adjective) lanes. Quite frankly, that kind of bowl*ing* (Gerund-Object of Preposition) is not up my alley!

"Stairway to Heaven"

I had suddenly died in my home's master bedroom's bathroom while I had been staring into the vanity mirror after finishing shaving. A sudden pain spread from my left arm to my chest and the last thing I remembered as a human being was collapsing upon the brown-tiled floor. There is no doubt in my mind that my body had ceased functioning and that my awareness had slowly exited my form and then transferred into a strange energy-spirit state. I don't remember any spectacular catharsis when my soul had been ejected from its human shell.

Next, I was somehow cognizant of hovering over my lifeless corpse and a moment later my senses were aware of my wife's delirious screams as she frightfully bent over to touch my neck feeling for a pulse. 'So much for her being a veteran R.N.,' my still intact consciousness sarcastically thought. 'She does really love me after all!'

To my fallible knowledge I never traveled through any dark tunnel to any ethereal bright light destination. I believe *that* scenario is what some minds fearfully manufacture when brain cells are rapidly deteriorating and nerve endings are desperately transmitting the wrong information because of severe oxygen deficiency. So I firmly believe that after the spirit evacuates the body at the moment of the heart's cessation, the actual process of dying has just begun, for every cell in the human form must then soon die off one by one after breathing has permanently stopped. But still, conscience, mind and spirit survive the momentarily painful ordeal quite satisfactorily outside *the host* that had once sheltered *those* entities. I steadfastly maintain that death can be best described as a combination spiritual/biological process that has occurred.

The next event I remember was that my weightless atom-less spirit vertically floated through the ceiling and then right through the house's roof as if both physical objects were porous intangible imaginary masses. At that moment I felt as if I had been a scintilla of light penetrating through two transparent thermo-glass window panes. I recollect drifting around fifty feet above the ground and my *new* keener senses detected a crowd of curious neighbors dashing out of their homes. Soon an ambulance with red flashing lights entered and screeched to a halt atop my former dwelling's driveway.

As a scene of mayhem developed both in and around my Hammonton, New Jersey ranch-home, my ghostly consciousness began gliding slowly downward in the direction of a gray limousine parked at the curb across the street from my residence. I passed through the density of a tall tulip tree like water rushing through a teabag. While my *intelligent spirit* was descending, the limousine driver, a facsimile of the Grim Reaper (wearing a dull brown robe), opened the back door.

My soul easily entered the vehicle, and my three-hundred and sixty-degree consciousness was acutely aware that all participants and eyewitnesses involved in the pandemonium in front of my Valley Avenue home were totally oblivious to my ghostly departure. However, many spectators grieved, sobbed and gasped when *they* observed two strong paramedics carrying my listless form out of the house on a Hammonton Rescue Squad stretcher. All attempts at reviving my body with special electric shock equipment inside the ambulance had failed.

My awareness felt no grief, remorse, shock, pain or anxiety from my sudden death. My mind remained calm, curious and alert as the gray limousine gradually moved forward and passed right through four people standing on Valley Avenue without them one bit knowledgeable about the 'spiritual hearse' or the phenomenon that was occurring.

"I suppose the afterlife is not governed by the laws of physics," my *spiritual intelligence* said to the macabre driver, who passively ignored my attempt at initiating a telepathic conversation. All the Grim Reaper duplicate did was stare menacing at me' in the rear-view mirror. My chauffeur's face featured giant voids in the hollowed-out bony cavities where its eyeballs should have been. A hood covered the forehead part of the driver's skull above his grotesque-looking skinless face. The chauffeur's super-white teeth appeared twice as large as the average human's would be. I remember how futile and stupid it seemed contemplating escape from my alien captivity.

I dared not speak to my eerie escort again but instead my cognizance used my *intelligent spirit* to scrutinize the passing environment I remember perceiving while somehow looking out of dark-tinted windows without possessing any functioning human eyes. 'I must remain rational and try to make some sense out of this new world I've entered,' I nervously thought. 'After all, everyone is going to eventually die and go through the whole same experience too.' I did find some comfort in making that conjecture, even though I had believed that the process of dying was quite singular to the individual that was doing the perishing. 'Death seems to be much more morbid and harrowing to the survivors of the dearly departed than it does to the deceased,' I concluded while prematurely evaluating the nature of my own recent demise.

As my reticent driver's non-palpable gray luxury sedan zoomed down the White Horse Pike my perceptive spiritual intelligence suddenly made a rather stark observation. All of the automobiles on the highway in my new dimension were limousines and they were of three colors, black, gray and white in their order of frequency. Instantly my astute mind-spirit concluded that the black ones were on their way to hell, the gray ones heading to purgatory and the few white ones en route to heaven.

Then I became a little more sober about my fascinating excursion because I was certain that my destination was going to be purgatory. 'It's logical that the bulk of people are heading for hell, a small percentage to purgatory and only a select few to heaven,' my mind-spirit surmised. 'I could have and should have led a better life,' I shallowly lamented without any evidence of heavy guilt, remorse or regret. It was more as if I was being disappointed rather than being angry with myself', and my soul was now resigned to accepting whatever fate awaited me without objection or without endeavoring to rationalize fanciful excuses in defense of my past actions and misdeeds. I felt as if my entire free will had been sacrificed and surrendered.

My foreboding chauffeur stopped at the traffic signal at Fairview Avenue and the White Horse Pike. I remember thinking that he really didn't have to stop, so he must have halted for a specific purpose designed to enlighten me about some aspect of the afterlife. A black 'hearse/sedan was visible approaching on Fairview directly behind us, and as *our* limo' turned left on green, I noticed the black hearse turn right in the general direction of Woodlawn Avenue, apparently heading to Valley to make a pick-up at my former home. 'Fools,' I mentally criticized *their* human enterprise. 'That's only my limp body lying in the ambulance over on Valley Avenue. I'm now in this immaterial non-visible gray limousine, you hapless money-hungry incompetent morticians!'

I then saw the facsimile Grim Reaper driver nastily stare at me in the rear-view mirror and my spirit became quite uneasy when I realized that *he* could read my innermost thoughts that, in the conundrum-like dimension I had entered were now public knowledge (at least to him) and were no longer secret notions exclusive to myself.

'We're coming to Old Forks Road, and there's the new Hammonton High School up on the left abounding with vibrant adolescent life,' I genuinely thought. Soon the gray limousine made a left-hand turn into Oak Grove Cemetery and the unearthly vehicle first stopped at a recently dug grave with *my name* inscribed on the granite headstone. 'I'm now glad I had the foresight to buy grave plots and an en*graved* headstone,' my awareness concluded. 'But I'm sitting without any sensation of sitting in this sleek gray vehicle and only an expensive bronze casket (as specified in my will) containing my embalmed remains will be deposited into that lurid one-fathom-deep hollow.'

Then I realized that time-warping was a unique characteristic of the afterlife I had entered since I had just died what seemed moments before and I now recognized that my grave-site had already been excavated and a vault had been snugly placed inside. I stared at the vault's gilded golden lid as the gray limousine next moved slowly forward on the cemetery's narrow leave-strewn asphalt lane. I recalled I had died in early autumn, October 15th to be exact. 'One always knows the month he or she is born but the individual seldom if ever considers which month he or she will die,' I philosophically pondered.

As the Grim Reaper (or his replica) drove me around the various twisting roads of all-too-familiar Oak Grove Cemetery, I soon realized that at age sixty I knew more people that had already died than individuals who were still alive. But I still could not accept the notion that *I* had made any dramatic transition at all and had *crossed over* to anywhere except to Oak Grove Cemetery as a translucent passenger now dressed as a two-dimensional ghost in a now white-shaded black suit and tie I would be buried in.

My eerie-looking escort stopped at a particular grave-site and then an ominous newsreel flashed onto the video screen located above the limo's back seat. Mark DiMeo was a good friend of my son Steve. Mark had been killed in a tragic automobile accident. The teenager's parents had also been killed in an automobile accident twelve years earlier while crossing *Route 30* in a jeep. The young man had to be raised and mentored by his grandfather and I would often take Mark home after school events or when he had visited my abode on Valley Avenue. I say *my* abode? How absurd of me! When a person dies, he or she has absolutely nothing: no home, no money, no possessions, no capital gains' assets and certainly no material comforts. The richest man in the world isn't worth a mere brown penny once he succumbs to death.

The gray-shaded limousine driver very deliberately maneuvered the vehicle down and around a tree-lined oval lane and halted at the headstone of a former business associate. Our partnership had not been an amiable one, and I had outsmarted Jack Merlino in our one-sided business settlement. Merlino had bought me out and then went bankrupt ten years later. The sequence of events did not have to be reminisced because the incidents involving Jack and me had all been captured on tape and then mercilessly shown to me upon the back-seat video screen. But being cleverer than Jack Merlino now seemed quite irrelevant and meaningless.

160

Apparently, the visual representations on the television screen were not being presented in chronological order. A vision of me taking a final college exam' flashed upon the unique video monitor. I had needed an A on the difficult final to pass the "Educational Psychology" course and graduate, mostly because I had squandered valuable time absent from class relaxing in the student lounge playing poker and pinochle. A fraternity brother had stealthily and illicitly acquired the professor's final exam', and he and I spent two entire nights figuring out the seemingly enigmatic answers to the instructor's stolen "objective questions." I easily aced the final by cheating, but now I was specifically being supernaturally reminded of my unethical transgression that had somehow been mysteriously captured on some inexplicable arcane videotape.

Then it finally occurred to me that this uncanny itinerary through the cemetery was really a brief review of the good and the bad that I had contributed to civilization during my short lackluster tenure upon the Earth. An unsettling feeling drenched my spirit as the apparition of a female suddenly appeared sitting next to me. The woman's stone-cold face was horribly ashen and as she turned her head to stare at me, her distinct image was that of Persephone, daughter of Zeus. I recalled from a myth I had read in college that she had been abducted to the Greek underworld to be the companion of its heartless ruler/tyrant, Hades.

Persephone's grim and ghastly facial features then transformed into the countenance of Connie Morgan, a beauty queen I had dated in college, but then I had cruelly dumped her in favor of my present wife. I did not feel any guilt about my past un-meritorious deed. 'My comprehension of our college relationship is rational, objective and coldly analytical, just as my judgment by the *Powers That Be* will probably be conducted,' I hastily hypothesized, instinctively accepting the uncertain fate that awaited me.

Connie Morgan's image then magically transformed back into Persephone's face and form, which gradually crystallized, vaporized and soon vanished into thin air. 'My entire past has been systematically recorded on tape to be used against me on Judgment Day,' I logically concluded.

The next cemetery stop was at my younger brother's grave-site. My grandmother had left me an inheritance and I neglected to share it with Tony, who had a not-so-easy life struggling to make ends meet. Then scenes of me' enjoying myself at Atlantic City casinos, going on expensive Caribbean vacations and cruises with my wife and children and next buying new house furniture with stock market earnings appeared in my brief visual biography. I rationally concluded that every good and bad behavior of my preempted life had been systematically recorded and documented by invisible camera crews using indiscernible equipment. 'If excessive pride and hubris were convicting criteria for eternal condemnation, then I'm definitely a prime candidate for such a deserving sentence,' I uncomfortably generalized.

'But these are only venial-type sins I've been witnessing!' my consciousness rationalized. 'Certainly, any type of after-world justice would have to weigh all of the good against all of the bad,' my spiritual existence determined and justified, 'and undoubtedly I have performed much more of the former in my earthly existence than the latter. These are *not* serious mortal sins I'm observing here!' my uncomfortable *spirit-intelligence* mentally editorialized.

The hideous-looking driver moved ahead and passed by the grave-sites of my father, mother and my maternal grandparents. I was surprised that the limousine operator did not stop to haunt my mind with videotaped episodes of the insolence and defiance I had exhibited toward any of my dearly departed ancestors during my wild rebellious adolescence.

Then the gray limo' stopped at a Catholic priest's (who had willed to be buried with his' family) tombstone. I recollected the name Father Thomas Randazzo, who had officiated at marrying my wife and me' in St. Joseph's Church on Third Street. Upon the now-familiar video screen appeared the image of my wife and three young sons sitting in a church pew without their father during a Sunday service. I quickly understood how futile and flimsy my argument had been that I hadn't been shown on the video screen any mortal sins I had committed. 'My six-decade life was not without deviation from expected behavior. In many respects, a model father I was not,' I too late recollected and decided.

Another tableau appeared on the monitor and depicted me indulging in food and drink at a local restaurant. Gluttony had been practiced by myself' on numerous occasions, and according to inflexible church teachings, *that* bad habit was not exactly a stellar virtue. Now I immensely missed food and drink and I no longer have a body that requires biological sustenance. 'Physical pleasures and sensations now have to be sacrificed to allow for spiritual growth to occur,' I reckoned.

Ever since graduating high school, I believed that sin had merely been an invention of religion designed to instill in worshipers a promise of eternal reward that functioned as a cultural mechanism capitalizing on making churchgoers dread the possibility of eternal damnation. I had always thought that organized religion exploited one's hopes and fears to make individuals conform to certain austere and rigid codes of deportment. Now I was being graphically confronted with the strong chance that I had been erroneous in my assumptions and that the church's prescribed teachings (that I had liberally violated) had been infallibly right.

My mind was preoccupied pondering the nature and the structure of the overall afterlife my spiritual intelligence had been gauging. 'Humans live in a parallel dimension, an alternate illusion to the fantastic actual mysterious reality I have entered. This *is* the real world that the material world wrongfully thinks is an illusion,' I theorized, 'and the real world is truly the fantasy experience and the after-world venue is really the actuality of existence.'

My back-seat limousine imagining was interrupted by my awareness that *my* gray 'hearse/sedan was finally leaving Oak Grove Cemetery. In the distance I observed a westbound funeral procession heading toward Oak Grove from downtown Hammonton, and then it dawned on my powerless soul that the automobiles in line were filled with family and friends assembled to pay their final respects to *me*. 'I always thought that there would be more than just twenty-two cars,' my restless spirit protested as I counted the automobiles entering the graveyard. 'I suppose I wasn't as influential on others as I had wrongly imagined!'

Evidently, time in the after-world had the ability to expand and contract, for it had seemed like only fifteen earthly minutes or so since I had suffered a fatal cardiac arrest to the moment when my mortal remains were about to be buried in Oak Grove Cemetery. Obviously, my corpse had been taken to the mortuary, been embalmed, had a viewing and a funeral mass while my underdeveloped soul was being given preliminary exposure to phase one of the afterlife. This knowledge led me to suspect *too late* that the body and its attendant pleasures were but irrelevant distractions in both corporal life and to temporal death. I finally realized *too late* that one's soul, one's spirit and one's conscience were the only important factors in all human activities.

My morbid gray limousine turned west (left) on the *White Horse Pike* just as *my* slow-moving funeral procession entered the main gate into the century-old cemetery. The grim chauffeur's creepy mouth seemed to sullenly smile in *his* rear-view mirror reflection, but I imagined that the ridicule was simply a manifestation that my addled mind had conjured.

The Grim Reaper's duplicate sped without detection through a police radar trap in Chesilhurst. My escort zipped through a traffic light in Atco while simultaneously filtering through a bus, two cars, a dump truck and a tractor-trailer stopped at the congested intersection. He then passed through the towns of Berlin and Clementon with the speedometer registering a hundred and ten. Under ordinary conditions, I would have been petrified and panic-stricken at the dangerous speed but since I was already deceased, my faculties had evolved beyond normal fear and I no longer was awed by anyone human or anything that had been produced by humans. My ride was all rather surreal but in retrospect, quite humdrum because all along I knew I was already dead.

The gray limousine then turned right onto Linden Avenue beyond Clementon, and I was just meditating about how much fun I had had as a teenager at Clementon Lake Amusement Park when my frightening-looking skeleton operator abruptly pulled into the *Lindenwold High-Speed Line's* huge parking lot. The train service conveniently connected southern New Jersey to Philadelphia and it carries over forty thousand commuters daily to the *City of Brotherly Love* and then in the late afternoon transports them back home to suburban towns situated east of the *Delaware River*.

The robotic-like wretched chauffeur stopped the limo' in front of the main terminal entrance and as I curiously glanced around, I noticed that the entire parking lot was filled with other nondescript empty gray limousines rather than the usual standard array of domestic and foreign cars and trucks.

Two celestial-looking gentlemen converged on *my* vehicle and the taller specter opened the back door. I obediently stepped out, and then after the door was slammed shut, remarkably without any accompanying thud, the Grim Reaper casually stepped on the gas pedal, evidently dispatched to journey and pick up his next assigned unfortunate trans-migratory spiritual passenger.

'Hello!' my consciousness greeted, for I no longer possessed a functional tongue, throat or voice box.

'Welcome to a higher echelon!' the first figure returned in a weird sort of mental telepathy. 'I'm Gabe, and my companion's name is Mike.'

Immediately, I felt inclined to query whether my new after-world acquaintances were the archangels Gabriel and Michael but I did not have the audacity to pursue that particular presumption upon initial introduction. I did not perceive any fluffy white wings on their shoulders, any flowing radiant gowns around their forms or any dazzling halos around their dual transparent heads, so I did not wish to appear facetious or foolish during that initial encounter even though the two immortal beings ostensibly knew exactly what I had been thinking and evaluating.

I glanced up at the sky and perceived that it was overcast, and *that* impression instantly suggested to me a general mediocre dull atmosphere that appropriately corresponded to the thousand or so stationary empty gray limousines in the giant parking lot, and my casual observation reinforced the notion that *they* had been symbolizing purgatory. When my spirit endeavored to initiate a mental exchange of ideas, I quickly fathomed that Gabe and Mike could understand me completely, but I could not comprehend or decipher their inter-angelic communications. The phenomenon was analogous to high-pitched sound frequencies dogs could hear and identify that happen to be out of the limited range of human auditory perception.

'Is this still the Lindenwold Station?' I mentally transmitted. 'I used to ride the High-Speed Line from this terminal into Philly' to take my wife shopping downtown, to attend plays at the *Walnut Street Theatre* or to visit *Thomas Jefferson University Hospital* for physical checkups.' The mere thought of my devoted wife made a trace of sentimentality surface from my *subconscious spirit*, which I suddenly fathomed was an important extension of (or a substitution for) my *subconscious mind* in the afterlife.

'You no longer have a free will to do whatever your hedonistic mind pleases or desires,' Gabe mentally informed, 'and your undernourished soul must now undergo massive cleansing and purging until you're ready to be reborn and live a better life than the uninspired lame one you've just left.'

'Do you mean that I haven't been resurrected?' I mildly balked. 'Now *you* are telling me I have to be reincarnated after I am somehow sanctified by penance and anguish. Don't you have any good news to report?'

'We don't like that obscene word reincarnation!' Mike corrected. 'Be careful of your nomenclature! Let's just use the terminology *regenerated.* It's much more accurate, discreet and appropriate. There are entirely too many esoteric facts that an un-evolved dolt such as yourself' must master. I advise you to learn to pay attention and to ignore your own limited mental impulses!'

After mentally trading several additional curious comments, I finally understood that this first phase of the afterlife was comparable to what humans do to *refuse* like paper, plastic and metal cans; they recycle them. That creative supposition was significantly consistent with what was happening to me and to all other passengers arriving in gray limousines under very dull and gloomy cloudy skies. *We* were in the sorting-out phase of being recycled before being washed and treated, but much to my bewilderment, the applicable acceptable vernacular was 'regenerated' and not 'reincarnated.'

'Well then,' I cautiously persisted in my inquiry, 'where is God the Father, Jesus and the Holy Ghost? Will I get to meet Them'?' I innocuously and presumptuously desired to know.

'You ask too many impertinent questions for a lowly neophyte,' Mike mentally reprimanded, 'but if you really want to know, you're not evolved enough to have *that* kind of special audience. Don't try running when you haven't yet conquered the art of crawling! Sorry, but I had to relate the advanced concept to you in mental language you could readily grasp.'

'Are we going to board the next train?' I rambunctiously asked. 'I've never been an advocate or a practitioner of *mass* transportation. Are we going to a Catholic Church or to a religious tribunal?' I awkwardly mentally joked.

'You must learn to temper your curiosity, your impudent sense of humor along with your rash opinions,' Gabe admonished with grim features showing on his angelic face. 'If you keep your soul open and receive knowledge and wisdom rather than send out wild flurries of cynical questions, then you'll finally comprehend the abstract nature of your new environment. That kind of discipline must be fully realized by you before you can ever evolve to a higher rank,' Gabe telepathically elucidated. 'Don't expect *us* to volunteer information on demand. You'll soon be on your own and have to journey through the emotionally grueling ordeal of final atonement all by yourself.'

The two enigmatic angels then grabbed me by the arms. The three of us effortlessly floated across the parking lot above the gray limos' to the High-Speed Line's eastern terminal entrance ramp. I looked up above the concrete platform's pavilion and read the designation: "HA" where the lettered appellation "Lindenwold Station" should have appeared on the overhanging shingle.

'What *on Earth* does HA indicate?' I mentally asked Gabe, who in truth seemed rather bored and annoyed with my perpetual inane inquiries.

'Why you really aren't too imaginative now, are you!' he thought-transmitted. 'HA is an abbreviation or more specifically, an acronym for Heart Attack Station. All New Jersey humans that have died of heart attacks and who must be purged of past misdemeanors and indiscretions must ingress to the next stage of their eternal existence from *this* particular platform.'

166

'Let's get on board or else *our* supervisors will warrant more menial jobs for us to complete,' Mike mentally declared to Gabe. 'I don't want to be demoted from management to labor! Not with all of my accumulated on-the-job experience!'

'There's just as much stupid bureaucracy in the afterlife as there is in real life,' I thought to myself, forgetting that my mind was being eavesdropped upon. 'I hope there isn't any work, or any prying government, or any abominable *IRS* to contend with!'

'I warned you to keep your grandiose pin-headed opinions to yourself!' Gabe chastised. 'Try to impress us that you're more than the imbecile you boastfully appear to be!'

The three of us stepped into the nearest car, and within what must have been thirty earth-seconds, the doors closed and the train rapidly advanced on its rails in the direction of what used to be Philadelphia. I surveyed my surroundings and quickly discovered that I had been the only heart attack victim to get onto the death train at the former Lindenwold Station terminal.

'This' is a pretty inefficient system,' I critically evaluated, again neglecting to remember that my private thoughts were now public. 'This entire train is operating just to transport one passenger to some obscure destination. This confounded world is even worse than the one I had just escaped!'

'You'll never adequately comprehend your new dimension until you abandon your propensity for fabricating ludicrous and inconsequential impressions!' Mike mentally chided. 'I strongly advise you, try respectfully learning your new environment rather than merely engaging in all of this boring childish critiquing!'

Three miles down the track the train jerked to a stop in front of what used to be the Ashland Station, which now bore the identification 'C,' meaning Cancer Station. Four unfortunate doomed passengers were escorted onto the train by well-dressed supernatural beings that coincidentally looked like mass-produced carbon copies of Mike and Gabe.

'Well, I think the authorities oughta' have a crab up there on the sign to symbolize Cancer,' I mused while forgetting that my two companions and the eight new archangels could easily intercept and interpret my caustic ruminations. 'Perhaps the next heavenly station will be Libra or Aquarius.'

'Show more compassion and sensitivity, you blundering ingrate egomaniac!' one of the new angels who looked similar to Gabe mentally rebuked. 'No wonder why you have to be regenerated, you repulsive self-centered conceited cretin!' the very intimidating form pontificated.

It didn't take me long to ascertain that each new station had as its name a new disease or a particular cause of death. Those passengers that boarded with their angels at the next 'SD' platform (formerly Woodcrest Station) had suffered from strokes and had perished from drowning, Haddonfield was now renamed 'DMD' (The Drugs and Murder Death Station), and what was previously Collingswood now had the ominous title 'AND' (Accidents and Natural Disasters Station).

I glanced around the half-full car and counted a total of twenty-nine newcomers escorted by fifty-eight very competent-but-bored angel guides. The next stop on the unorthodox train route was ordinarily Ferry Avenue Station. I wondered if the stop's name would remain the same with boating accident and ship sinking victims entering through the train's ominous portals. Mike again criticized me for being too arrogant and too immersed into my own thoughts rather than empathizing with the new admissions to 'the Purgatory Local.'

The new Ferry Avenue pick-up destination had the appellation 'GDW' (General Diseases and War Station). A horde of misery-faced victims and their divine escorts patiently waited on the cement platform and when the doors opened, at least a hundred ghoulish-looking new riders were promptly escorted aboard.

'Why don't *they* simply pass through the doors rather than just stupidly standing there and be waiting for the portals to open?' I skeptically thought. I noticed infants that had died from birth defects being pushed in baby carriages by somber-faced guardian angels, and many of the deceased appeared to have been terminated by chronic neurological maladies like multiple sclerosis and Lou Gehrig's Disease. The specters of six fatally wounded soldiers also entered accompanied by *their* twelve nonchalant and apathetic angel hosts.

'Why must death come to innocent babies and patriotic warriors?' I considered. 'It all seems so wicked and unfair!'

'Your reckless words border on heresy,' Gabe very deliberately transmitted and pointed out, 'and if you persist in continuing your abusive absurd remarks, you'll soon discover that you're only extending your stay on this perpetual elevated train ride.'

'It all seems like random arbitrary selection,' I imagined and inadvertently communicated. 'It's like we were all put into a worldwide lottery and each unlucky recipient happened to wind-up a victimized duck in a giant shooting gallery. I wonder who's been taking the rifle shots that are eliminating each of us from our happy, earthly status?'

'You definitely are going to be made an example out of!' Mike mentally predicted and accused. 'Moral justice in *this* dimension is much more decisive and conclusive than political justice was in your former world. There are no appeals' courts in this afterlife you've entered after the sand in your *life-glass* had expired. You'll soon discover the profound significance of my statement. Now stop being so *damned* opinionated!'

I must confess I always had a proclivity for being frivolous during crucial situations. For example, I had a tendency to always want to crack a joke at a funeral or at a viewing and had to exercise self-discipline not to do so, my spirit recalled. 'At least half of the people on the General Diseases and War platform must have succumbed to debilitating *terminal illnesses.*' Then Gabe adroitly intercepted my most recent ludicrous brainstorm.

'If you persist in attempting to be an obnoxious comedian,' my ethereal companion's flawless superior mind conveyed, 'then Mike and I will be required by forces greater than ourselves to put you on a southbound *black* train at the next station. And believe me! You don't want to go there! Lucifer Prince of Darkness absolutely and positively loves tormenting and torturing pretentious morons such as you happen to be'.'

'I'm sorry,' my suddenly guilty consciousness automatically apologized. 'It was just my sanguine disposition surfacing from my subconscious mind, er, I mean from my subconscious spirit,' I mentally answered. 'I know I tend to be facetious and sometimes playfully sarcastic, but in this new dynamic mental environment, I must admit, I'm definitely at a disadvantage.'

'Control yourself! Harness your frivolous impulses, you pathetic excuse for a human being,' Mike critically cautioned, 'and just absorb everything that your spiritual eyes witness. Otherwise, your actions will not only have severe consequences. They'll also be the genesis of diabolical results you'll long regret.'

Gabe informed me that he had to attend to another assignment and was scheduled to get off the phantom train at the next designated station. I did not possess sufficient courage to ask him to describe his next mission, so my two-dimensional form sat solemnly in my seat and contemplated the general morbidity of the other deceased and melancholy purgatory-bound passengers. The speeding train entered the familiar tunnel just before what used to be the Camden City Hall exit and before Gabe departed my company, he handed me a gray pen to be utilized soon in 'your next major post mortem enterprise.'

I politely bade 'farewell' to my radiant angelic chum, who then casually sauntered onto the former Camden City Hall platform, which now bore the reference 'ND' (Natural Death Station). Depressing apparitions with wrinkled elderly faces cluttered the subterranean platform, and many of the new arrivals crowded aboard the thirteen unlucky cars that constituted the 'Purgatory Express' as I had now preposterously labeled it. I imagined that the phantom express could hold over a million ghosts if it had to, since all of us lacked anatomies or forms to occupy real physical space, and *we* could have easily been stacked on top of one another like sheets of construction composition board or otherwise simply crammed inside.

'Does this underground tunnel we're now in represent some sort of a birth canal in reverse?' I mentally asked Mike. 'Am I' reentering the womb, so to speak, er, I mean so to think!'

'You are undoubtedly and indisputably a completely annoying dunce!' my all-too-perturbed escort reproached. 'It isn't like *that* at all. It's more like when light travels from air into water. It sort of gets warped or bent going from one predictable medium into another. That's exactly what's happening to you right now. You're going from one medium to the other.'

'What happened to what used to be the Broadway Station in Camden?' my curious spirit inquired to my austere host.

'Oh now, you must be referring to the Limbo Station,' my illustrious guide matter-of-factly replied. 'LS is temporarily out of commission because it's under repair and having drastic renovations being done to accommodate all of the horrible abortions being performed and all of the unfortunate stillborns being delivered back on Earth. Just look at all of the unnecessary work you daft former humans are causing the already-overtaxed eternal staff!'

The high-speed train surfaced from its subterranean cavity and next crossed what used to be the *Ben Franklin Bridge* into what used to be center-city Philadelphia, but now the connection had the designation *Crossing Over Bridge.* I looked at the traffic on the span's seven lanes and readily determined that it consisted exclusively of white, black and gray limousines conducting novice ghosts to their more permanent destinations. A second more-deliberate analysis determined that there were only a few white limousines traveling on the mile-long span, suggesting that Heaven was indeed under-populated.

The first underground Pennsylvania stop, which should have been Philadelphia's Eighth and Market Street platform, was now listed as 'CN' (Celebrity Notoriety Station). Transparent images of deceased rock and roll singers, movie stars and political and historical figures were standing around and idly conversing on the concrete walkway. I observed Elvis Presley interacting with John Lennon, John Wayne exchanging thoughts with Marilyn Monroe, Franklin Delano Roosevelt mentally mingling with Harry S. Truman and Dwight D. Eisenhower and Edward G. Robinson sharing ideas with Abraham Lincoln and J. Edgar Hoover. Many other famous specters were visible on the dismal platform including Daniel Boone, Charlie Chaplin, Thomas Edison and Edgar Allan Poe, but I had insufficient time to recognize the identities of all the distinguished phantasms.

'I have to get off at the next stop,' Mike imperatively stated. 'Here's a small gray notepad that you can write some of your impressions upon. I'll allow one written communication with a past acquaintance so that you can then successfully forget about your former world and concentrate on being processed into your new *medium*. Do you have any final relevant questions? This is your last opportunity to ask them!'

'Er yes,' my spirit telepathically stammered. 'How do I mail this document after I have authored it?'

'Oh, pardon me for the silly oversight,' Mike courteously responded. 'I'm usually much more thorough and dependable. I suppose I'm suffering from chronic mental fatigue! Use the gray pen Gabe had given you and jot down your thoughts and reactions inside the gray notebook. Here's an official gray envelope. Address it to whomever you wish and then drop the correspondence into the gray *Inter-Dimensional Mailbox* you'll occasionally see at selected underground train platforms.'

'But I won't have enough time to write down all I want to describe!' my adamant spirit hastily communicated in a frustrated mood. 'Are you deliberately trying to aggravate me?'

'On second thought, seal and drop the envelope into the postal box's slot at the next station when the subway train again gets there sometime in your eternal future,' my guide suavely and convincingly advised. 'You must remember that you have all the time in the world to randomly scribble-down your notes in this book, so you don't have to foolishly rush. Practice good penmanship if you wish. Notice that adequate postage has already been attached to the standard gray mailing envelope.'

I was sage enough not to doubt the angel's veracity. 'My only alternative is to trust *his* instructions,' I logically decided. Then the train slowed to another subterranean halt.

Mike exited the perfectly noiseless and quiet train at the vacant 'SH' (Stairway to Heaven) platform. I attempted to rise from my seat to take an instant shortcut to paradise, but some supernatural force field prevented me from accomplishing my selfish pursuit. I again tried standing up. I experienced a sensation akin to a sleep paralysis I had once undergone while my mind was emerging from a strange dream. I could not move a muscle, feeling as if I was being subjected to a potent enchantment that completely enslaved my will and easily manipulated my spirit. 'Oh well,' I surmised. 'I have the entire future to be introspective and objective. I'll take my time in organizing this important narrative.'

The eternal high-speed train pulled-out from the rather fascinating brightly lit' empty Stairway to Heaven Station, which in my prior life was known as 10th and Locust. The next stop of the High-Speed Line Express, which ordinarily was the last one, was 15th and Locust. I again tried to rise from my seat but was thwarted by that same indomitable spiritual force's resistance. I glanced around the filled-to-capacity train and confirmed that all of the other more compliant passengers were assiduously writing down notes into *their* small gray tablets. I figured it was time for me to abandon my intractable disposition and finally conform to Gabe and Mike's expectations and obediently imitate my fellow passengers' appropriate example.

I then peered-out onto the platform from the window above my seat and read the name of the last station, which was peculiarly labeled 'FJ' (First Judgment Station). Standing on the platform were twelve individuals wearing long gray robes with accompanying gray-haired wigs positioned above their ashen-colored foreheads. The dozen jurors were all dead persons that I had wronged when they and I were living our independent lives back in Hammonton, New Jersey.

I objectively speculated that the twelve Solons would be judging my candidacy for probation from my dull uninspiring subterranean purgatory. I theorized that if I eventually passed *their* verdict, I would be assimilated into Heaven's lowest denomination once I had finished filling the small notepad and mailing it whenever the train were to again stop at a platform that had a convenient *Inter-Dimensional Mailbox*. Then, I assumed, my contributions and transgressions would finally be re-judged by a Superior Intelligence on *Judgment Day*.

'My arrogance and my defiance must be discarded in favor of humility and modesty,' I sincerely vowed. 'I will eventually escape this wicked underground punishment and hopefully qualify to ascend the *Stairway to Heaven* and be able to finally appreciate and 'see the light.' That is now my utmost aspiration in this mystical but monotonous and tedious underworld train afterlife. I feel like a groping lost charlatan in quest of admission to a world belonging to sage wizards.

'I will not send this manuscript to my wife,' I judiciously decided. 'I'll mail the package from an *Inter-Dimensional Mailbox* to Marilyn Jenkins, my editor and publisher at cyberread.com. She'll know precisely what to do with this vague glimpse of eternity so that in the future others can benefit from its content.'

"Signals"

Wednesday, April 2, 2003 started-out as an ordinary day. I rose from the king-size electric bed, put on my slippers, fed and walked the family Chihuahua, had breakfast with my moody wife and then sauntered out of the house in my bathrobe. I waved to a neighbor and ambled down my long asphalt driveway to retrieve the morning newspaper. The *Atlantic City Press* was not in the paper box situated next to my highway mailbox as expected. Instead, at the mouth of the driveway was a folded-up newspaper with unique letter fonts. I inspected the date on the front page and it was indeed Wednesday, April 2, 2003.

'*The Weekly Chronicle!*' I dubiously read. 'Never heard of the idiotic publication.' My curiosity compelled me to further examine the main headline. 'Deadly Snakes Invade Area' was read in large print right under the masthead, which coincidentally disclosed 'Published in Hammonton, New Jersey.' I was very intrigued by the strange feature article so I further perused the unsolicited edition of the *Weekly Chronicle* as early morning traffic whizzed by on busy *Route 30*, the White Horse Pike.

My fancy scrutinized other front-page articles and they too all dealt with snakes, lizards, amphibians and reptiles. I had my misgivings. 'This must be some kind of very sophisticated practical joke,' I impetuously speculated. 'The only newspapers published locally are the *Hammonton News* and the *Hammonton Gazette,* and they are both printed on Wednesday but are delivered by the mailman's white Jeep on Thursday.'

My interest being thoroughly stimulated, I thumbed through the front section to find the mysterious edition's editorial page. Anonymous authors had written twelve opinion columns on lizard and snake conservation and there were no standard "Letters to the Editor" on the page nor was there any customary address listed for the publisher. My next inclination I immediately honored and that intention was to toss the 'practical joke' into the garage's blue Atlantic County Recycling Trashcan. 'Who would go to such extremes to play an expensive prank like this one on me?' I wondered with great curiosity. 'This must be some sort of belated *April Fool's* ploy,' I reckoned as I checked the day's date on my trusty wristwatch.

On Wednesday, April 9th I stepped out to my *Atlantic City Press* newspaper box, waited for the speeding traffic to pass and reached into the object's interior. I was more than a little surprised when I discovered that another undesired edition of the *Weekly Chronicle* had been stuffed inside in substitution for my regular daily *Press* subscription. The main headline read, "Dangerous Snakes Terrorize Hammonton."

I intensively scanned all the pages and every single article and advertisement again had to do with lizards, snakes, amphibians and reptiles. 'Well, at least alligators, crocodiles and Gila monsters are not trespassing into this part of New Jersey. We've always had snakes living in the nearby pine-barrens and in the local deciduous mixed forests,' I considered with deep reflection. 'Someone is going to great lengths trying to rattle my confidence.' I demonstratively threw the 'trick item' into the blue Atlantic County Recycling receptacle and thought, 'I won't even give the sender any satisfaction and won't even keep the *Weekly Chronicle* as a silly souvenir. Is my *Press* news-paper man part of a perverted prank conspiracy?'

But a week later my aggravating quandary became ever more stressful. On Wednesday, April 16th I ventured out from my property in my merlot-colored *Nissan Maxima* to the Fairview Avenue *Wawa* convenience store to purchase a loaf of square-cornered sandwich bread, a half-gallon of milk and a chocolate candy bar. I saw a headline in the morning *Philadelphia Inquirer* that instantly caught my attention: "Three Hammonton Town Officials Indicted For Mafia Ties." My hands picked up the reputable Philly' paper and the portly genial clerk tabulated my bill on his computerized cash register that sounded like slot machine bells and featured clanging sounds whenever the drawer opened. The accommodating attendant neatly placed my four new acquisitions into a white *Wawa* plastic tote bag and thanked me for my loyal patronage.

Upon arriving home, I entered my two-story white colonial house and methodically removed the purchased items from the plastic bag. The milk was placed inside the refrigerator and the bread was laid in the top pantry cupboard. The candy bar I left on a counter to consume at my leisure. My irritable wife was upstairs taking a shower so I figured that I would read the juicy town article in the *Inquirer.* To my astonishment the all-too-familiar and very perplexing *Weekly Chronicle* was between my hands instead of the anticipated Philadelphia newspaper. The main headline shockingly read: "Hammonton Infested with Black Snakes".

I disgustedly ripped up "the tabloid" and chucked the fragments into the kitchen garbage disposal, turned the plastic dial and crushed the *Weekly Chronicle* into the other trash that already was inside the waste container. 'That paper isn't even good enough for the Atlantic

County Recycling Trashcan!' I angrily discriminated. 'How could the newspapers be switched? Perhaps the *Wawa* cashier is in on the practical joke too just like the *Atlantic City Press* newspaper man?' I suspected and theorized. 'On the other hand I don't even know either *their* first or last names!'

At 4:37 p.m. on Wednesday, April 23rd I was viewing a cable newscast when I heard a gentle rapping at my residence's front door. An amiable *UPS* deliveryman handed me a small brown cardboard package. "Working late today huh!" I greeted the nameless familiar face. "Take it easy! Looks like rain out to the west towards 'Philly!"

"Have a good one!" the regular driver answered. "I still have fifteen more stops before I can call it a day! It's my wife's birthday and I still have to buy her a gift and then take her out to dinner!" the driver informed, indicating to me his propensity for procrastination.

After the exchange of pleasantries with the harried driver, I stood for a moment and watched him maneuver his big brown truck out of my U-shaped driveway and then zip west on *Route 30*. 'I don't remember ordering any product from Amazon.com!' I suddenly thought. And after I tore open the rectangular cardboard box with the Amazon logo on it, I was very alarmed to discover another reprehensible edition of the *Weekly Chronicle*. The main headline ominously read: "Venomous Vipers Plague Isolated South Jersey Community." I was determined to ascertain exactly who was responsible for initiating the very elaborate-but-frustrating 'roguish newspaper mischief.'

The advent of May proved to be even more confounding and haunting than April had been. My annual horoscope personality profile suggests that I am very superstitious by nature and that I strongly believe in signs, omens and the sensational powers associated with *ESP* as an extension of a primeval human early warning system. Joanne was at the hairdressers on that late Thursday May 1st afternoon, when the telephone annoyingly rang. I was writing checks for due utility bills and looked at my portable phone's *Caller ID* readout. 'No name or number!' I immediately realized. 'Why should I pay the phone company money for an extra service I'm not receiving. This better not be one of those irksome telemarketers!' I effortlessly picked-up the portable land-line phone and said "Hello!"

A rather weird-sounding dial tone was followed by a very undeniably familiar voice from the past. "Giovanni, you had better do the right thing," the recognizable baritone with the Italian accent cautioned. "Your grandmother and I want you to make sure no one gets hurt, injured or killed. Please listen to my wise advice!"

"Who is this?" I wildly demanded with my head swimming in awe. "This is a very cruel and vile prank you're playing, whoever you are!" I yelled into the bottom of the telecommunication device. "Don't call me again or else I'll have the phone company trace your number and then I won't hesitate to prosecute you!"

"I'm warning you Giovanni," the eerie deep hollow voice remarked as if it were originating from another entirely different dimension. "Pay attention to everything that you do!" Click.

I was too perturbed and too exasperated to later tell Joanne of the 'peculiar disturbing and most obnoxious crank phone call. I could not think of any unscrupulous enemy that would be so diabolical as to pretend to be my deceased grandfather's ghost. 'Grand-pop died in 1973,' I recalled. 'And whoever has committed this atrocious outlandish deed should burn in hell for all eternity! That couldn't be my maternal grandfather beckoning me from the hereafter! No way!' I rationally concluded.

On Thursday May 8th Joanne was visiting a half-mile down the highway over to her sister's home when I had another inexplicable arcane experience. I was checking my e-mail when an unanticipated letter flashed-up on my computer monitor. "My Dear Nephew," it strangely and ominously began. "Uncle Leo and I wish only the best for you. Be on the lookout for any unexpected treachery or danger looming on the horizon. Love always, Aunt Vera." The message then slowly faded off the computer screen before I could print it.

I was in an absolute state of mental disarray as ideas and emotions collided and deflected all throughout my head. I could not satisfactorily account for the wretched phenomenon. Aunt Vera and Uncle Leo were both killed in an automobile accident in September of 1972 while traveling to Uncle Al and Aunt Elsie's summer place in Virginia on the Potomac River. 'And besides that,' I worried, 'my father's sister is buried alongside Uncle Leo in a Baltimore cemetery a hundred and twenty miles away. I know because I had attended *their* very sorrowful dual funerals.'

Then my muddled mind considered a few other ideas. 'How come these friendly spirits aren't using direct and specific references when they're benignly contacting me?' I pondered. 'Why must they always communicate in general language that sounds more like a series of riddles than like lucid comprehensible communication?'

I felt myself languishing in emotional torment. My spirit needed rejuvenation. My mind decided to relax, contriving that my imagination was causing me to become "stupidly paranoid." I inserted an easy listening CD into my computer room's stereo system and believed that the inspiring music would liberate me from my mental dilemma. 'I'm depressed and simultaneously suffering from mild anxiety,' I decided. 'Joanne's probably right when she cutely diagnosed me last week as being bipolar!'

My perplexed mind had an instantaneous premonition that the stereo would betray me and soon I discovered the validity of my suspicion. A very distinct voice with a Baltimore accent was discernible and it was coming from the unit's twin wall speakers. "Cousin John, this is your late Cousin Joan," the distinct-but-hollow voice vociferated. "Listen Babe, even though I am drifting about in the after-world, I am still fond of you and must look out for your earthly welfare. Heed the previous signs that have been intentionally beamed towards you. We'll meet again when your time has finally come. Take care, John. The finite sand in the hourglass is gradually falling."

I was so flustered and so neurotic that I hurried to the downstairs liquor cabinet, opened the doors, removed a quart of *Southern Comfort* and swallowed the remaining contents in less than an hour. When Joanne returned from her visitation at her sister's home, she blasted me for being intoxicated.

"What's wrong with you!" my wife sarcastically hollered. "I leave you home alone for three hours and then I have to come back to a drunken fool!"

"I'm sorry," I genuinely apologized in a very disconsolate mood, "but I'll never be able to explain the situation to you in a million years, and if I could Joanne, you would immediately have me tested for admission into an insane asylum."

"Well, at least you realize you do have serious mental problems, even while you're drunker than a fish swimming in vodka!" my mate sharply criticized. "Go up to the bedroom and sleep it off while I prepare a late supper. I hope that you're somewhat sober by seven-thirty!" Joanne sarcastically finished.

On Thursday May 22nd the voice of my maternal grandmother (who had passed away in 1987) contacted me on my private cell phone number and on Thursday May 29th I had heard my deceased father's singular raspy voice warning me of perilous future events over my *Maxima's* stereo radio. 'I only wanted to push a button and hear some seventies music,' I nervously thought. But my heart sank almost into my abdomen since I realized I had missed my father so very much. 'Dad died of a heart attack on September 10th, 1974!' I sentimentally recalled. 'I can't figure out how or why these bizarre events are happening. If I tell Joanne, she'll want to divorce me and live with her aged mother. I'm really going to have to carry this heavy almost-unbearable burden all by myself!'

Early Friday morning, June 13th I exited my home's white laundry room door and proceeded into the two-car garage to drive to the local *Dunkin' Donuts* and then buy several morning treats. I had noticed that my wife had not sufficiently pulled her green *Nissan Altima* inside the night before because the *Altima's* garage door had not fully descended and had stopped against my spouse's back bumper. 'She probably had pressed the electronic garage button, entered the house, closed the mudroom door without becoming aware that the electronic garage door had never touched the cement,' I concluded.

I entered the thirty-three-year-old house and vehemently scolded my companion for her "gross oversight." Joanne became antagonistic upon being "disciplined like a child" and defended her ego by firing back wild accusations in what resulted in a rather major boisterous disagreement between us. We both were livid and stubborn.

"A vagrant-turned-criminal could have rolled his body under the raised door, entered the house and suddenly become greedy while we were sleeping," I imprudently argued. "Or maybe an itinerant band of Mexican farm workers might have walked by on the highway, have seen the partially open garage door, got an idea of grabbing some easy money and then would storm into our bedroom at midnight wielding knives and threatening our lives," my accusative lips loudly indicted.

"You're always hypercritical and too quick to blame others, you chauvinistic hypocrite," my wife acrimoniously snapped back. "Nothing really happened because of the garage door, did it John? I made an honest inadvertent mistake and then *you* try to arraign me in your arrogant court of perverted justice. I'm sorry Husband, but I'm not quite as perfect as *you* are!"

"And besides that, the garage door made a dent mark on the back bumper-area of your new green *Altima*," I caustically blamed my spouse. "You don't respect property enough to be more careful when you haphazardly do things. You should pay more attention to what you are doing, especially when you drive your new green *Nissan*," I nastily rankled. "Money doesn't grow on trees ya' know!" I yelled. "Try to be more careful next time!"

"Just for that I'm going grocery shopping with *your* new red *Maxima*," my wife angrily volleyed back. "Maybe I can dent *that* car up too!"

"Now wait a minute!" I countered. "I'm not going to have you go to the chain store in *my* mint-condition *Maxima*. You always park too close to the front of *ShopRite's* or *Wal-Mart's* main entrance because you're too lazy to walk another hundred feet and get some needed exercise. Some person in a rush is liable to slam their shopping cart into the *Maxima* and cause a needless dent without *you* doing it yourself!" I bellowed. "And besides that, my car's color is merlot and not red!"

"What if I park *your* precious vehicle further away from the store and then some punk idle kids with nothing better to do savagely key the paint on both sides?" my wife loudly returned. "You can't spend the rest of your life worrying about every possible little thing that might happen or might go wrong!"

"Just like in the winter two years ago!" I argued back, showing a very nasty temper. "You came into the driveway, approached the house too fast and then skidded into the left garage door. There are still two big dents on the door showing exactly where you had impacted the automobile. Sometimes Joanne, your absent-mind both acts and looks like you're on drugs or something! You must learn to always be more alert!"

My resolute high-strung Italian wife was not-too-enamored with my critique of her lackluster driving ability. "That was just a minor accident you're alluding to and you have the very bad habit of magnifying every little deviation into a major catastrophe," she very effectively maintained.

"And what about the time last year when *you* anxiously hopped into your last car and started up the engine without realizing that the garage door had not been raised," I reminded Joanne. "You backed up your old gray *Sentra* into the closed door and caused considerable damage. We had to purchase two new automatic doors and then *you* insisted on buying a new vehicle and that's why we acquired your *Altima* because the gray *Sentra* had two gigantic dents in the trunk bumper area from the unnecessary accident. Remember Joanne," I scoffed, "accidents just don't happen; they are caused by human error, and in this case it was *your* human error!"

"I'm leaving right now to go shopping!" my wife shouted in frustration at my continual faultfinding. "I hope you're more sensitive and objective when I return. Be ready to carry all of the grocery and shopping bags inside when I pull into the driveway. And don't go to that silly doughnut place," she tyrannically barked. "You're getting entirely too fat! You're beginning to look like a huge inflated sausage!" the woman venomously assessed while effectively getting in the last word in her typical flight retreat mode.

No sooner had Joanne exited the laundry room door and entered the adjacent garage that she let out a most hideous and spine-chilling scream. I rushed into that section of the house to determine the cause of her hysteria. "Ahhhh!" she shrieked in extreme alarm. "There's a long black snake that just slithered into that corner behind those empty boxes and metal cans."

"Great!" I exclaimed in a true moment of awe. "How long was the reptile?"

"Around three feet!" Joanne yelled back as she was too petrified to move an inch either left or right. "But it was skinny and not that big around!"

I honored my sense of self-preservation, reverted into my survival mode and instinctively picked-up a long flat-bottom shovel. I apprehensively moved several stacked boxes from the corner and scared the already frightened creature from its place of hiding. The black snake slithered out in a flash, lashed out at me and I was skillful and lucky enough to lower the long shovel's flat blade directly behind the snake's head. It lifted its mouth in agony and then began hissing through its opened fangs as my shovel applied more weight and downward pressure. The garden tool had eventually punctured the reptile's skin and blood squirted out its back.

"Hurry John! I can't stand watching this happening! Please hurry and kill it!" my terrorized wife implored in a delirious state of total pandemonium.

Like a crazed barbarian I raised and lowered the shovel a half dozen times and finally severed the creature's scaly neck from its still wriggling body. In another moment I ceased my mania, realizing that I had successfully decapitated the innocent animal and that it was now dead.

"It's probably only a non-venomous snake," I said to Joanne as I felt my heart wildly palpitating inside my chest. "I wish I was as courageous and as trained as one of those Australian animal capturers I see on the *Discovery Channel*. Steve Irwin would have simply stooped down, picked the snake up by the neck and then safely deposited it into the field next door."

"I'm glad you killed it!" my wife commended me in a rare display of appreciation. "I hope it doesn't have a lair inside one of our walls. This horrible event was traumatic enough!"

"No Joanne, it probably got in here because *you* failed to observe that *your* garage door was not closed last night!" I accused. "The cold-blooded snake was obviously seeking warm shelter and a pleasant place to spend the night and you had absent-mindedly provided it to him!"

Joanne seemed relieved and paused for a moment to regain her sensibilities. After taking a deep breath she amazingly asked a rather plausible question. "Where did you get the idea of using the shovel as a killing tool? That was pretty inventive on your part. You do have a practical imagination after all!"

"Last May a few hours before your father died a large black snake appeared in your mother's driveway," I answered while still breathing heavily. "Your Uncle Dick bolted into your mother's tool shed and obtained two blunt-ended shovels. He handed me one and instructed that I should keep the huge snake's head down against the asphalt while he repeatedly sliced the thing's back and spinal cord to shreds with his shovel's flat edge!"

"You never ever show good discretion!" my spouse quickly admonished. "You're so insensitive! You didn't have to remind me of Dad's passing. You're just too honest for your own good! Maybe you could have been a little less graphic and used a trifle more good judgment by keeping *that* particular information to yourself'! That's why you've made so many enemies in your life!" Joanne alleged. "You don't think of the other person's feelings before you impulsively say something that they consider offensive!"

"Why don't you just drive over to the shopping center while I scoop the remains of this snake up and then bury the pitiful black creature in back of the house near the woods?" I answered as pragmatically as I could. "Sometimes absence makes the heart grow fonder!" I finished.

After disposing of the long skinny snake, I drove the green *Altima* a quarter of a mile east on *Route 30* to the wonderfully quiet and serene Oak Grove Cemetery. The new Hammonton High School had recently been constructed across Old Forks Road on the east edge of the old graveyard and the modern-looking contemporary architecture represented a stark contrast to the cemetery's tall oak trees and general soothing tranquility.

I usually trek all of the cemetery's asphalt lanes, which amounts to a little more than a mile of beneficial cardio-vascular exercise. The daily early morning ritual always proved to be good healthy therapy for both my body and my mind. My brain cells are then energized, my emotions become stabilized, and I could once again bravely face my wife with a cordial disposition and deal more diplomatically with her mercurial snide rancor.

'I'll just ease my tensions with this satisfying daily trek,' I imagined. 'Soon the notion of evil black snakes will dissipate and fade from being important. It was too bad Joanne's father died several hours after her uncle and I had killed the larger black snake in her parents' driveway. Ever since *that* event happened, I have always regarded the horrible occurrence as a precursor of his death!'

Nothing irregular occurred during my morning hike around all of the various loops and bends of beautiful Oak Grove. Natural beauty and things that are placid tend to feed, to positively charge and to pacify my psyche. The cemetery's stately oak, elm, tulip and pine trees have a definite beneficial remedial effect upon my mental state of being. 'I always seek asylum here to avoid being institutionalized in a state asylum,' I mused. 'And I enjoy periodically stopping and reading inscriptions etched on tombstones dating back to the nation's *Civil War* era when the graveyard had been established. Many of the original headstone epitaphs have almost eroded and are hardly legible.'

My spirit reconstructed, I felt compelled to return home and attempt to peacefully coexist with my flamboyant and sometimes nasty wife. I am a *CPA* by profession and prefer the company of numbers and statistics on a sheet of paper in a quiet room rather than be exposed to the nuisance of bothersome human beings prattling their shallow commands, complaints and trivial grievances in my face. That is why I prefer having an office downtown on Bellevue Avenue rather than be pestered by continual marital interruptions and quarrels at home while trying to concentrate on my work. I basically abhor harsh verbal conflict and endeavor to avoid it whenever I can. A docile moderate life has always been the ideal pursuit that my heart has striven to attain.

Invigorated by my "morning constitutional," I rested for a half-hour on a cemetery bench and contemplated the meaning of life and the significance of my lackluster existence. Then I drove the green *Altima* back to 699 North White Horse Pike to reunite and bond with Joanne. 'It's now Saturday, June 14th and nothing sinister or malicious had occurred the day before,' I gratefully thought. 'I've safely made it through another unlucky Friday the thirteenth,' I imagined. 'I see that Joanne is home from doing her light shopping.'

When I stepped through the garage portal into the tan tile-floored laundry room, I found my wife to be in an extremely aggressive and prosecutorial mood. Regretfully I did not honor my first impression and abandon her rancorous diatribe before she made her vicious scathing incrimination.

"Look John, I'm not a witch so stop thinking that I am!" she instantaneously reprimanded.

"I am not insinuating that you are one, although sometimes that particular thought does enter my mind!" I cautiously replied to camouflage the true belligerence I was feeling toward my spouse at that moment. I tried getting by her nagging mouth into the main part of the house when "my significant other" felt motivated to lambaste me some more.

184

"And stop thinking that I am bossy, spoiled and arrogant," my wife imperatively squawked. And as if she were accurately reading my tender mind, she next bellowed, "And yes John, you must trim the bushes, mow the lawn and weed-spray before you decide to watch television, drink your *Southern Comfort* or take your predictable afternoon nap."

'She's undeniably reading my mind!' I quickly concluded. 'She *is* a damned witch after all and I don't even live anywhere near Salem, Massachusetts!' I defensively decided but kept to myself. 'I'll remain quiet and see what caustic rhetoric she'll verbalize next!'

"And besides," my incensed wife adamantly uttered in a ridiculing tone of voice, "you can't go to Atlantic City and gamble your hard-earned money away while drinking more *Southern Comforts* at the poker tables. Do as I say or else, I'll live with my mother and you'll soon be hearing plenty from my lawyer!" the crazed lady yelled with bulging brown eyes.

'Joanne's apparently become psychic and possibly even clairvoyant!' I strongly suspected. 'She was actually reading my mind word for word and idea for idea in the exact sequences I had thought them, or was it just a series of coincidences dealing with known circumstances in my daily household responsibilities and in my predictable personal amusement interests?'

I obediently changed into my work clothes, put on my orange work gloves and conscientiously trimmed the bushes, mowed the lawn and weed-sprayed around the property's flowerbeds and trees. I am not henpecked, but my wife could definitely be a miserable shrew so my compromising disposition often judges that it is better to get along rather than to perpetually do battle, for I pride myself on being judicious and civil-minded. My zodiac sign is Libra and I naturally am constantly in quest of balance, truth and beauty in all life experiences.

On Sunday morning, June 15th I was perusing the thick *Philadelphia Inquirer* I had purchased at *Wawa* and my horoscope read: "Dear Libra, today's your lucky day. Don't be afraid to take some risks you ordinarily wouldn't attempt. Whatever you endeavor today will certainly have a fortunate conclusion."

I eagerly exited the house without consulting my wife, skipped my morning cemetery jaunt, had a quick high-calorie snack breakfast and coffee at *Dunkin' Donuts* and then anxiously drove thirty miles east on *Route 30* toward Atlantic City. I parked my immaculate merlot *Maxima* in a casino concrete high-rise garage, took the elevator to the appropriate second floor and then meandered my path through the crowded gaming hall.

My first inclination was to play poker or roulette, but some mysterious *ESP* sensation led me in the direction of the five-dollar slot machines. 'I never play slots because the odds are highly against me and they are the casino industry's greatest revenue producers,' I remember generalizing. 'And five-dollar slots are usually out of the question,' my conscious mind determined. Despite my cynicism concerning high-stakes slot machines, I inserted three crisp one hundred dollar bills into the conversion slot and sixty five-dollar-tokens were automatically registered on the mechanism's impressive read-out display.

I experienced little initial luck but some remote force persuaded my will to persevere. 'There are only three tokens left!' I soon realized. 'Oh well, here's to Donald Trump!'

The reels rotated and halted and before I knew whatever was happening three handsome red sevens appeared in the triple windows with accompanying bells clanging and bright lights flashing. When I finally fathomed that I had hit the super progressive jackpot, my heart started pounding fiercely and I felt a rush of blood surging-up to my head, making me somewhat dizzy and giddy.

A casino cameraman rushed over to obtain pertinent newspaper publicity and the employee snapped my photograph standing next to the three majestic magic red sevens. Momentarily, I was in ecstasy at winning a cool million dollars. I am a very bashful person, felt grossly uncomfortable being in the center of a gaudy circus environment and almost fully resented all of the excessive adulation and exaggerated ballyhoo.

The casino's floor manager and three attendants then checked my driver's license, casino card and several credit cards to verify my identity. I was briskly escorted to a special room where in half an hour a wonderful check for $650,000.00 was graciously handed to me amidst flashing cameras and multiple questions from several shouting reporters. "The federal and state income tax money has been withheld and will be paid in your name to Uncle Sam and to the Governor," the barrel-chested casino head official professionally and sanctimoniously revealed. "The rest is yours to keep and spend at your own volition."

My heart was wildly throbbing and I was in fear of having a major coronary right there on the spot. I refused an offer to notify my wife by phone, explaining to the casino managers that I preferred to surprise Joanne with the extraordinary bonanza. "I'll certainly buy her a mink coat and a new diamond ring," I prevaricated to my captive audience. "And then she's always wanted a white *Lexus* and a three-week Hawaiian vacation. Maybe she'll get those special rewards if she learns how to play the marriage game by *my* rules," I shrewdly announced. Everyone there in that well-guarded vaulted room laughed in response to my "unique sense of humor."

I drove from Atlantic City thirty miles west back to Hammonton in a state of wild exultation. Never before had I ever felt so exhilarating. Some impulsive internal force compelled me to pull into the Oak Grove Cemetery and to triumphantly walk the mile of twisting and looping asphalt lanes, something I had neglected to perform that morning in deference to my most fortuitous excursion to the bustling Atlantic City casino. 'I'll dedicate this happy victory stroll to Joanne's legendary temper!' I contemplated.

I found the venerable graveyard devoid of other living humans. My soul sought solitude and quietude to sufficiently evaluate and adequately appreciate my recent good fortune. 'Gambling is usually regarded as a self-defeating sin but today it ironically proved to be a marvelous blessing,' I conjectured as I parked my merlot *Maxima* under a tall shade tree. 'Ah, only a few gray squirrels darting around looking for last fall's remaining nuts!'

The casino check had been gently placed in my *Maxima's* glove compartment and then I carefully closed and locked the small door. I pressed an overhead button and closed the roof's sky-hatch, fearing that some wayward itinerant would enter the graveyard and dastardly climb into my automobile while I was strolling a half mile away. I then locked all doors with my electronic key device and distrustfully checked all four of them twice to make certain that the sedan was absolutely secure.

About a quarter mile into my trek I stopped at my father's grave-site and stared blankly at the headstone. I closed my eyes and quietly recited a brief prayer, thinking that my deceased Dad's intercession had something to do with my fantastic Atlantic City windfall. When I opened my lids, at least fifty brown acorns rained down from various oak trees in the vicinity and that sudden surprise instantly made me feel extremely nervous. 'That's awfully strange!' I thought. 'It's late spring and acorns have yet matured to their brown state where they could *fall* to the ground. That happens in autumn.'

My mind thought about my previous day's Libra horoscope advising that I identify and honor all signals for the next forty-eight hours. 'The casino payoff was the result of the newspaper signal I had intuitively obeyed, and now this Oak Grove Cemetery acorn aberration must be a definite harbinger of another event about to occur,' I restlessly hypothesized.

Next, my pupils stared at my maternal grandmother's grave-site situated directly in front of my father's final resting place and the name and the dates of birth and death mystically vanished and then supernaturally reappeared three consecutive times at separate five-second intervals. I rubbed my eyes to ascertain that I was not imagining the implausible anomaly I had just witnessed. 'I suppose nothing is really carved in stone, not even granite headstones,' I remember rationalizing. My brain was in a state of flux and my jangled emotions were in a near state of panic.

My eyes then focused on my maternal grandfather's grave and the flowers all amazingly wilted, died and then came back to life in a most remarkable sequence of botanical resurrections. 'Even the plastic artificial flowers perished and then rejuvenated,' I marveled at what I considered a series of inexplicable 'miracles.' I resolved to abandon my deceased relatives' burial places and finish my mile-long haunting hike through the normally peaceful cemetery. 'My head must be so enthralled at winning the jackpot that it's playing devious tricks on my five senses,' I evaluated in a disguised vain effort at allaying my overall trepidation.

A half-mile further into my daily pilgrimage I stopped at my father-in-law's mausoleum on the Old Forks Road side of the hallowed cemetery. I glanced over at the modern high school building and felt some comfort while considering the notion that other living human beings were in close proximity.

Before I could finish my reverie, I was alarmed and staggered when my eyes perceived a long thick black snake emerge from behind my father-in-law's two-tier mausoleum and then slither across the grass into a thick tangle of tall yew bushes. 'My God!' I thought as my body trembled. 'That's another signal from the afterlife. I didn't heed the acorns falling, the tombstone acting like a classroom blackboard and the flowers dying and then self-resuscitating.'

My legs and knees felt rubbery, but without buckling, they somehow managed to sprint and carry my anatomy as quickly as they could back to my merlot-colored *Nissan*. Hastily I re-entered the car, turned on the ignition and then stepped heavily on the accelerator. The responsive vehicle's back wheels squealed as my tires made traction against the asphalt and the performance-oriented *Maxima* quickly responded to the transmission and drive train's synergy.

I abruptly turned left onto *Route 30* and then a quarter of a mile down the congested thoroughfare adroitly maneuvered the car into my driveway without the courtesy of using my right turn signal. The overhead automatic garage door button was pressed and the portal on the right ascended. I found Joanne lying unconscious on the cold cement but her pallid face, even with closed eyes, still showed an expression of ghastly horror.

I hurriedly exited my car. My eyes scanned the garage's shadowy interior and they immediately identified a black snake sliding its way towards a wall crevice where the clothes dryer vent's metal tube led from the laundry room to the exterior outside wall. My animosity towards the slinking sliding reptile enraged me and I instinctively picked-up the "death shovel" leaning against a stack of four cardboard boxes and then I crazily and mercilessly smashed and thrashed the creature's head and body with the improvised weapon. In fifteen seconds, I had killed the vile-looking animal with a series of maniacal thrusts.

My unsettled mind still possessed a degree of rational problem solving-ability. My first impulse was to call *911* and have the Hammonton Rescue Squad's paramedics administer first aid and then transport my unconscious wife to Kessler Memorial Hospital. I next demonstrated good mental self-discipline and honored my second strategy. 'I can be at the hospital in just about the same time it takes the ambulance to get *here*,' I decided.

My arms lifted my wife's limp body from the cold cement and I frantically hustled her over to the *Maxima,* which was parked in the driveway. I managed to open the door and after placing Joanne inside, I harnessed her with the front passenger's seat-belt. I felt her pulse, which was weak and almost non-existent. Being in a virtual state of delirium, I pressed the electronic button that lowered the garage door and without any regard for traffic laws, I squealed my back wheels in reverse, halted, placed the gearshift in 'Drive' and soon sped out of my driveway onto busy *Route 30.* The four-mile nightmarish hospital drive seemed to take an hour as I discourteously wove in and out of intense highway congestion and luckily zipped past one yellow and four green traffic lights at seventy-to-eighty miles an hour.

The *Maxima* was steered into Kessler Hospital's back ambulance entrance and *that* split-second decision actually wound-up saving my wife's precious life, for if I had carried her into the emergency ward the apathetic by-the-book admissions' desk clerks would have insisted that I fill-out bureaucratic paperwork before Joanne could have been treated. The only thing I told the emergency room doctor and two nurses was that I believed that a poisonous snake had possibly bitten my wife.

As I impatiently waited for word of Joanne's condition in the small visitors' lounge, my disorganized mind reviewed the past two-month's highly-irregular events in a rather vivid mental newsreel. 'An excess of money is evil and leads to decadence,' I morally surmised and concluded. 'I was much happier *before* I became a filthy rich egomaniac!'

I then quietly prayed as I sat in the lounge and next vowed to donate the entire six-hundred-and-fifty-thousand-dollars to charity if Joanne were to survive her snakebite trauma. A half-hour later the physician in charge of the emergency room exited the suite and met me on the other side of the huge swinging doors. "Your wife was indeed bitten by a snake but I'm happy to report that it was non-poisonous," the surgeon calmly explained. "Your better half went into shock and fell unconscious from her terrible ordeal. She's now fully awake. You'll be able to speak to her privately in about ten minutes."

I never told Joanne about the lost Atlantic City treasure-trove. I did donate the spectacular sum to various community charities and churches. 'My peace of mind and Joanne's life are worth far more than a mere six-hundred and-fifty-thousand dollars!' I intelligently concluded.

"The Power of Suggestion"

Personal Record

Monday, October 6, 2003

I, Peter Simon, Dr. of Psychiatry have been assigned to study and hypnotize a certain Martin Quade, an inmate at the United States Federal Penitentiary, Lewisburg, Pennsylvania. The subject has been convicted of using a butcher knife to brutally murder Richard Anderson, *his* dormitory roommate at the *University of Pennsylvania*, Philadelphia.

The felony had occurred on the evening of Friday, September 13th, 2002 near the Memorial Tower Archway, not far from the prestigious *Ivy League* campus's famous *Ben Franklin Statue*. Dr. Eugene Fischer, a prominent psychiatrist and colleague, desired to have an independent study undertaken so he had requested for me to psychoanalyze Martin Quade while the prisoner would be under hypnosis. My inquiry's purpose is to determine if the subject had indeed been sufficiently criminally insane when he had committed the heinous murder. Execution by lethal injection is scheduled for Monday, November 17, 2003. All defense appeals have been exhausted and the prison authorities strongly believe that a reprieve from the state governor will not be forthcoming unless new relevant information can be obtained.

This afternoon I had the opportunity to interview the Death Row convict under hypnosis to assess if any negative event from Martin Quade's past had contributed to the perpetrator's motivation to kill his former friend and roommate, Richard Anderson. I must confess that I'm a staunch advocate of the Penitentiary System and I endorse the principle that murderers should become remorseful and subsequently pursue "self-reformation" after admitting guilt to a major felony involving human death. However, I am not in any way a supporter of the death penalty. I think that only the Almighty should have *that* divine privilege, and I have always maintained that incarceration in the form of a life sentence constitutes far more punishment than execution would subsequently effect. Indeed, etymologically speaking, the word "penitentiary" derives its origin from the adjective *penitent.*

After I had placed Martin Quade under the influence of my verbal suggestion, my design was to keep the experiment confidential so I gestured with my hand and immediately dismissed *his* two guards to an adjoining area outside his cell. I had effectively put the subject (who was lying in his prison cell on his bed) under hypnosis and then I comprehensively interrogated him. I found Martin Quade to be cooperative in both his conscious and subconscious existence, but most of the convict's answers were delusional and his psyche appeared plagued with paranoia and also with denial of guilt. I took accurate notes during the entire analysis, and here is the essence of *our* spontaneous question and answer session.

"Martin, please state your full name, age, hometown address and place of birth," I prudently commenced with my interview.

"My name is Martin Quade. I am twenty-two years old. My family and I live at 423 Park Drive, Willow Grove, Pennsylvania," the subject very clearly stated. "I have lived at that residence all my life prior to attending college."

"What prompted you to viciously attack and murder your college' roommate, Richard Anderson on the night of Friday, September 13th, 2002?" I bluntly proceeded. "The police report indicates that Richard had been savagely stabbed forty-seven times in the chest, abdomen, arms and shoulders."

"Richard was always making unnecessary demands upon me, forcing me to write his term papers and to help him study for *his* tests and for his first semester courses' final exams," Martin explained. "He would borrow money from me every week, usually a hundred dollars at a clip and then never pay me back. Richard would constantly intimidate me and push me around because the brute was nearly twice my size. I saw the butcher's knife as a great equalizer the next time he would badger me and shove me around. The relentless bully took me to the brink."

"I see, but your court trial defense was that you had *only* claimed you were being *verbally* and not physically abused," I indicated, "but the jury was not convinced since you had maliciously stabbed the victim forty-seven times."

"I admit I do have a fairly nasty temper at certain times," Quade conceded. "But when I learned that Richard was having a love affair with my girlfriend Lori, I lost it and went off the deep end! And besides that rather horrible situation, my strange roommate had ambitions of becoming a sadistic Fascist dictator!"

"Why didn't you tell the story about the love triangle to the jury?" I curiously asked while completely ignoring the ridiculous Fascist comment. "Your legal defense could have been that you had murdered Richard Anderson out of sheer jealousy!"

"I didn't want the jury to know I was jealous," Martin revealed. "I have always felt inferior to other more aggressive men because of my short height and my light weight. I've always tried to consciously conceal that fact from the public's view and that's why I have a sort of *Napoleon Complex*, acting cocky and arrogant, obviously to compensate for my diminutive size."

"Had you ever committed a major crime before you had savagely assaulted Richard Anderson on Friday night, September 13th, 2002?" I asked as I feverishly jotted down notations.

"Yes Sir, in another life, in a previous life," Quade surprisingly replied without any trace of emotion. "I certainly had committed another murder in a previous life!"

"And exactly what did you do? On what date did you perform the previous crime and where did it occur?" I curiously inquired.

"Forty years ago, at 12:30 in the afternoon, I had assassinated President John F. Kennedy. The date was November 22, 1963. The crime had been done in Dallas, Texas," the patient/inmate incredibly disclosed in a monotone voice. "I was an expert marksman and had shot bullets from an Italian scoped-rifle. My position was a sixth- floor window of the Texas School Book Depository. I especially aimed at Kennedy, who was in a motorcade on its way to the Dallas Trade Mart. John F. Kennedy died a half hour later at Parkland Hospital."

"How could you have done such a deed as Martin Quade, a 2002 senior at the *University of Pennsylvania* in Philadelphia? You weren't even born yet in 1963!" I further interrogated.

"I was not Martin Quade on November 22, 1963," the interviewee under hypnosis calmly emphasized. "My identity at the time was Lee Harvey Oswald. After I had assassinated the President, forty-five minutes later I then shot a Dallas policeman that had attempted to arrest me. I was finally apprehended by the cops in a movie theater that same eventful afternoon."

"What was the name of the Dallas policeman you had also shot?" I anxiously asked, for I myself' was well-versed on *that* particular historic assassination detail and *this* astute researcher was quite cognizant of the answer.

"I heard other cops at the scene yell out the name Tidbit or Tippit or something like that," Quade recalled and said, "but I was more concerned about the news of the President's death than learning that the life of a mere Dallas cop had been snuffed out!"

'This young man is definitely suffering from an advanced latent and suppressed case of schizophrenia,' I suspected. 'He has a most complex multiple-personality-syndrome and Quade probably psychologically identifies with Lee Harvey Oswald, also a short man that wanted to make a sensational impact statement on the world.'

I was fascinated with Martin Quade's confident answers, which appeared to be genuine along with being both distorted and unrealistic. My fundamental intent at that moment was to delve deeper into the controversial Lee Harvey Oswald relationship. I felt compelled to ask Martin Quade about Lee Harvey Oswald's widely publicized Marxist ties, about the political dissident's connection with Fidel Castro and about a possible assassination conspiracy (organized with Oswald principally involved, or government-inspired with Oswald as the designated scapegoat) but then I observed that the subject was beginning to squirm under duress so I immediately terminated the trance.

"Martin, you may wake up now!" I sternly instructed. "I'm going to count backwards from ten down to one, and when you hear the number *two* you may passively wake up and return to Monday, October 6, 2003."

Personal Record

Monday, October 13, 2003

Only Hindus, quacks and charlatans profess a belief in reincarnation, and I presently contend that Martin Quade falls within the second and third more ignoble categories. He has subconsciously experienced "delusions of grandeur" in a most nefarious way, gaining satisfaction and a sense of accomplishment in enacting negative villainous deeds both in reality and in fantasy. This I suspected was the truth but I required additional information to verify my hypothesis. The fanciful reincarnation manifestation had been invented by the subject's imagination to camouflage his basic feelings of inadequacy about his puny body's size and strength.

I am a cynic by nature and generally regard skepticism as an excellent counterbalance to a patient's euphoria or to his or her emotional despair. I am certain of one axiom of modern-day psychology and that one indisputable truth is that individuals are *driven* to perform an act (whether it be murder or societal achievement) to satisfy an emotional need (gratification, honor, recognition, infamy). In Martin Quade's case the subject feels a need to alleviate his myriad shortcomings and insecurities. Consequently, Martin's subconscious mind imaginatively fabricated the Lee Harvey Oswald story to mesh and identify with John F. Kennedy's assassin's confused and somewhat neurotic personality. At least this is what my' professional opinion and impression happen to be this bright Monday morning, October 13th at *Lewisburg Federal Penitentiary.*

After I again put Martin Quade into a relaxed mental state and thus rendered him harmless, I again signaled for his jailers to depart the examination sector, which doubled as *his* prison cell. I had had a bout with insomnia the entire past week and was quite anxious to hypnotize my newest patient and then enthusiastically initiate the second meeting with the convicted killer.

"Martin, do you still believe that you are Lee Harvey Oswald?" I asked after I had ascertained that the subject was ready for his new series of questions. To my amazement Quade insisted that he was someone else other than Oswald, a person named Johann Georg Elser, and then the subject mysteriously continued answering my interrogatives in a distinct German dialect. I was absolutely dumbfounded by the whole bizarre phenomenon.

"Martin, excuse me Johann, I am not that proficient in German so please speak English if you possibly could," I had the wherewithal to formally request while my reasoning was temporarily trapped in a mild state of shock. "Now allow me to rephrase my question," I persisted. "Do you think that justice has been served with the jury finding you guilty of murdering your dormitory roommate Richard Anderson? Was justice served?" I reiterated.

"Who is Richard Anderson?" my state-assigned client inquired from his deep trance. "Richard Anderson sounds like a Swede. Where in Germany does *he* live? English is such a barbaric language. Please speak in German."

"Aren't you Martin Quade?" I incredulously asked. "Everyone knows you as Martin Quade!"

"No Sir, my name is Johann Georg Elser. That filthy Nazi Heinrich Himmler has ordered the Gestapo to execute me in one hour," Quade informed.

"What is today's date?" I neurotically questioned with my mind in an advanced state of bewilderment. "Try to be as specific as you can."

"It is the morning of April 9, 1945," Quade remarkably described. "I will soon be executed as scheduled at *their* whim and volition! It's supposed to be a Nazi secret order, but I have heard of it from other prisoners. Hitler, Himmler, Goering, Rommel and the rest of their putrid ilk are avowed human butchers. To call them cannibals would be too great a compliment!"

"Why have you been sentenced to death?" I nervously prompted. "Specifically, what have you done that warrants that extreme punishment?"

"I am accused of attempting to assassinate Adolph Hitler on November 8, 1939," Quade said from his deep trance. "My elaborate plot fell short of its goal!"

"Then this failed attempt you allude to was not the famous conspiracy organized by Hitler's generals to dispose of him in 1944 when a time-bomb had exploded in the Fuehrer's headquarters!" I proceeded.

"No, that was another separate incident altogether!" Quade maintained. "I had *his* explosives attached to a timing devise behind the rostrum at the Buergerbraeukeller on November 8, 1939. Hitler was about to address some of his most dedicated veteran fighters in the enormous Munich beer hall."

"For my records, let's go back a page or two!" I recommended while under intensified emotional duress. "Johann Georg Elser, where were you born?" I awkwardly flipped back pages in my notebook.

"In the village of Hermaringen in 1903," Quade disclosed. "In 1917 I was apprenticed as a lathe operator in an iron works. I later became a skilled cabinet builder."

"Why had you attempted to kill Adolph Hitler?" I probed. "What was your motive?"

"I strongly despised the dictator's political philosophy and his cruel methods of obtaining and keeping power," Martin Quade logically replied. "I had belonged to the Rotfrontkaemferbund, a communist organization opposed to Nazi right-wing militancy. I wholeheartedly believed that the people should have governmental power and coincidentally share the country's wealth."

I was captivated by Quade's mammoth claim. I conjectured that the subject I had been interrogating under hypnosis couldn't be all that evil if he had planned to eliminate the epitome of twentieth century brutality, Adolph Hitler. But how Quade knew so many obscure details about this hardly known man Johann Georg Elser's life presented itself to me as a distinct mystery. Lee Harvey Oswald's biography is well-documented and could have been easily studied in high school or at *Penn'*, but how could the subject be knowledgeable about a remote insignificant historical figure such as Elser? I then carefully resumed my comprehensive psychological investigation.

"Tell me more about this socialist, or should I say communist organization that you had joined?" I asked. "What did it aspire to achieve?"

"The underground Rotfrontkaemferbund stood for the *Red Fighters' Association*, but I was not a leader and was content taking a subordinate role by playing a trumpet in the organization's brass band," Quade, now

196

alias Johann Georg Elser elaborated. "As an impressionable youth I had seen the devastation and the havoc that *World War I* had had on both Germany and on Europe," my extraordinary subject answered. "I did not wish to have the civilized world experience a second atrocious war where armies were equipped with sophisticated weapons produced by advancements in science and technology! And the Nazis, as despicable as they were, had developed missiles and military equipment that could potentially bring massive death and destruction to all cultures on all continents," Quade added. "I felt that I had to act and terminate a demented madman bent on dismantling western civilization and then diabolically rewriting it in *his* vile name!"

I promptly ended Quade's second session and must indicate that my opinion of this complicated man has been drastically altered. Quade is amazingly retreating further back into history going from October 6, 2003 to September 13th, 2002 to November 22, 1963 to November 8, 1939. I am certain that the subject is sincere in his declarations and that he is incapable of deliberately deceiving me while in his controlled hypnotic condition.

I have gone home and have thoroughly researched Johann Georg Elser on the *Internet* and have discovered substantial documentation on *his* here-to-fore unknown life. I am eagerly anticipating my next engagement with Martin Quade's exceptional and somewhat addled psyche. What has intrigued me the most is the fact that Martin Quade claims to be several different people from the past that had opposing political ideologies to the men that happened to be in political power at the time. But Quade seems incapable of distinguishing between the act of assassinating good men and the art of assassinating evil men. I find this distinction (or lack of it on Quade's part) to be most fascinating.

Personal Record

Monday, October 20, 2003

I honestly think that when Martin Quade had been under hypnosis, he actually believed that he had been in previous lives Lee Harvey Oswald and the less notorious Johann Georg Elser. I wondered if indeed my subject would again regress further into the past and take responsibility for committing a third act that had gained national notoriety or had had significant international impact. During my third visit I found Martin to be in a very genial mood in spite of the fact that his court ordered execution was to be less than a month away. Upon getting the subject comfortably relaxed into *his* hypnotic state, I then endeavored to have the unconscious convict connect with his true identity as Martin Quade.

"Martin, would you care to describe how Richard Anderson showed evidence of Fascist objectives?" I tersely inquired. "Was your college roommate a neo-Nazi, a Ku Klux Klan leader or right-wing militia sympathizer, or was he a white supremacist pushing for Master Race world domination? Possibly Richard Anderson was a combination of several of these factors."

"My name is not Martin and I cannot fathom why *you* refer to me as such!" Quade adamantly declared. "Why do you speak to me in English? I am Gavrilo Princip, assassin of Archduke Francis Ferdinand, heir to the Austro-Hungary throne. Is that fact perfectly clear to you?"

"Where and when did the surprise assault of the Archduke take place?" I excitedly and emotionally urged.

"In the Serbian city of Sarajevo, in 1914," Quade blandly responded. "I jumped onto the automobile's running board and fired the shots that killed the Archduke. It was incredibly easy and required more audacity than actual skill!"

"Now I remember the event you are describing from high school sophomore history," I purposely interrupted. "Tell me Gavrilo, why did you want to trigger off *World War I?* Upon first impression you look very much like a peace-loving pacifist!"

The subject paused to fully fathom the substance of my inquiry and then he gave a weak flinch. I had trouble understanding how Martin Quade was so well-versed in history, particularly in European history. I knew that an assassination had sparked the *First World War* but the exact circumstances surrounding the incident were not stored in my brain's information file cabinet. "What caused you to shoot the Archduke? Why did you do it?" I persisted in asking.

"A patriotic group of Bosnian Serbs had formed a secret society we called 'Union or Death'," the reclined patient recollected and then slowly communicated. "The Serbs wanted Bosnia and Hercegovina liberated from Austro-Hungarian control and then fully reunited with Serbia, whose history and traditions were more aligned with *our* cultural heritage. Since Francis Ferdinand was the favorite nephew of Austrian Emperor Francis Joseph and since *we* had learned through *our* reliable intelligence sources that the Archduke was to be riding in an automobile through Sarajevo," the patient sedately uttered, "he became a prime assassination candidate for the noble Union or Death' Society."

"Do you regret what you had done?" I questioned. "Do you feel any guilt?"

"Not at all," the patient firmly returned in his unconscious state. "My people had to be reunited and I wanted to send a strong message to the Emperor that his forced reign would not be tolerated! Serbia had to be emancipated from the pompous Emperor's control! That's why the society strategically targeted *his* nephew, the Archduke."

"Did you ever think that your action would instigate *World War I?*" I volleyed. "*That* was really a horrendous and merciless conflict!"

"No, I thought that the act was simply an isolated incident to demonstrate Serbian contempt for Austro-Hungarian tyranny," the man lying on his jail cell's bed slowly and methodically uttered. "I would not in good conscience hesitate doing it a second time. In fact I know I would do the exact same thing again if given the command and the opportunity!"

"One final question for today," I slyly announced. "Do you' know any of the following men: Lee Harvey Oswald, Johann Georg Elser or Richard Anderson?"

"I am not acquainted or familiar with any of those persons," Martin Quade (a.k.a. Gavrilo Princip) articulated. "The name Elser sounds German in origin and the other two individuals sound as if they are foreigners."

My mind was in flux as if contemplating a great conundrum, for I felt as if I was being exposed to and was being administered a tremendous hoax that I myself' had ironically generated. My instincts tell me not to divulge the essence of my studies to my honorable mentor Dr. Eugene Fischer or to any other distinguished consultant in the elite psychiatric world out of fear of being ridiculed in academic circles and then being labeled a hypocrite or a pretender.

I am conscientiously keeping this personal record as valid and reliable documentation of my research and plan to create a fictional account of my professional interactions with the inimitable Martin Quade to later present the fabrication to Dr. Fischer. Nevertheless, I must confess that I am so engrossed and so immersed in this most intriguing case that the project has indeed transcended all other appointments and interests in my already busy life. I can hardly wait until next Monday to hear whose identity the inimitable Martin Quade will assume next.

My career and my professional learning at first made me consider discarding Martin Quade's testimonies as rubbish, but I still remained quite introspective and receptive to *his* outlandish commentaries concerning his litany of past lives. Chronologically the young man's meshing of murder stories made sense ranging backwards from 2002-to-1962-to-1938-to-1914. But Johann Georg Elser and Gavrilo Princip had to be both living in Europe at the same time, which would negate any validity to the lame invalid reincarnation theory.

The subconscious mind is quite frightening because scientists know so little about its function or about its dysfunction. The conscious mind (what psychology refers to as the superego) is a combination of learned and socially expected behavior patterns that are predictable and acceptable by public standards. The converse holds true for what lurks and lies below the conscious surface, and that direction was precisely where my intensive probing of Martin Quade's heart and soul was heading.

Personal Record

Monday, October 27, 2003

After I had again gotten Martin Quade into his relaxed hypnotic state, I motioned for the cooperative guards to exit the penitentiary cell. I was ready to hear additional attestations from the convicted criminal's lips. Today his disposition seemed to be both pleasant and candid. I then commenced with my inquiry.

"To whom am I speaking?" I diplomatically began. "Please give your name and occupation."

"I am Aaron Burr, former United States Vice-President under Thomas Jefferson from 1801 to 1805," Quade firmly and dispassionately claimed. "My political career became endangered when I violently and intentionally shot Alexander Hamilton in a pistol duel on July 11, 1804 at Weehawken, New Jersey."

"What did you have against Hamilton?" I cautiously queried. "Why was he your adversary?"

"Hamilton and I had our basic political differences," the subject vicariously and almost persuasively stated. "Hamilton threw his support to Jefferson at the end of the presidential election debate and that action on *his* part betrayed my trust. Alexander Hamilton abandoned me so I had to settle for the Vice-Presidency and had to play second fiddle to that devious scoundrel Jefferson. Those four inglorious years of my life as Vice-President were rather humiliating for a man of my great pride to endure!"

"I recall reading a magazine article about you Aaron Burr being tried for treason," I added. "What was that controversy all about?" I probed since I wanted to test Quade's knowledge foundation on whom he claimed to be.

"I was set up by the frivolous political establishment, all of whom were allies and friends of that devious rogue Hamilton. My patriotism was as solid as a rock but I was ruined by ruthless power-hungry lie-perpetrators in *Congress,*" Quade elucidated. "Many political opponents alleged that I wanted to make Mexico into a U.S. Territory and other enemies accused me of trying to get the western territories to secede from the Federal Union. Politics is the most formidable game on this damned planet," the prone horizontally-lying patient editorialized. "The stakes are high and the avaricious vipers are just waiting to condemn a good man's aspirations and sully his reputation. I found that I was surrounded by countless envious political vultures!"

"Have you ever heard of Franklin Delano Roosevelt, Thomas Edison, Henry Ford or Sigmund Freud?" I asked, for I wanted to determine some definite time-line consistency to either support or refute the man's most recent assertion of being the notorious rogue Aaron Burr.

"No, those names are alien to me," Martin answered. "They do not connect anywhere in my memory."

"Did you ever hear of a famous literary story titled 'The Man without a Country' by Edward Everett Hale?" I advanced. "Your name Aaron Burr is mentioned in the work several times."

"No, both the story and the author are unfamiliar to me," Quade confidently replied from his trance. "I have always viewed literature and fiction as the politics of ludicrous fools! Literature is not pragmatic and that is why I loathe it and abhor its dreaming creators!"

"What about a person named Philip Nolan?" I pressed on. "Have you ever heard that name before?"

"He sounds like a fictitious person or an author or a worthless whimsical philosopher to me," Quade aptly declared. "Surely I would remember a queer name like that one if I had ever been introduced to the gentleman!"

I was at wit's end. The entire sequence of interviews made perfect historical sense but yet lacked plausibility and credibility when scrutinized by scientific analysis. I rejected the absurd reincarnation explanation in favor of the more feasible multiple-personality-disorder hypothesis. But if Martin Quade was not a serious student at *Penn'*, how could he ever have formulated such an intricate-yet-flawless string of murderers' lives without possessing an adequate knowledge base?

Personal Record

Monday, November 3, 2003

Today I became very disenchanted with Martin Quade. He was moody and more dramatic than he had demonstrated in past sessions. My hunch is that the subject is undergoing internal turmoil as a result of his rapidly approaching execution date (Monday, November 17). Quade meticulously keeps a calendar on his cell wall and marks a large X for each successive day that has expired.

Martin today professed to be Jonathan Small, an unimportant pirate lost somewhere in early 1700s' micro-history oblivion. According to Quade, Jonathan Small was conspiring to kill the ruthless Blackbeard and was betrayed and reported for his treachery. Small was brutally tortured and then horribly decapitated by the heartless seafaring swashbuckling monster.

And then Quade began speaking in what sounded like some archaic Oriental language, and after I directed him to converse in English, the subject insisted that in 1225 A.D. he was a constant companion of the infamous Genghis Khan and that he later double-crossed the Asian conqueror and was ultimately punished for his insubordination with a death sentence that had been carried-out by the chief Mongol himself'.

I am not looking forward to next week's visitation. Both Martin and I are lapsing into melancholy and show symptoms of depression as *his* measured time on this Earth is reaching an end. I will have to really motivate myself to be able to finish what has evolved into a most preposterous project in terms of psychological justification. I feel as if my personal journal simply contains an offbeat bizarre fictional story of questionable merit, even by recognized contemporary liberal literary standards.

Personal Record

Monday, November 10, 2003

I am now feeling and showing symptoms of despondency. I presently and unprofessionally feel genuine compassion for Martin Quade. I realize that a sea of erratic turbulence is eddying around and swirling about inside his hyperactive subconscious mind. I am presently organizing and falsifying a second "more professional study," which I intend to submit to Dr. Eugene Fischer. Even though I have learned to care greatly for the subject, I must still protect my untarnished psychiatry reputation among my judgmental peers. The principal aspect that greatly disturbs me about Quade is that (in his mind) he indiscriminately betrays those individuals that trust him and feels no obvious guilt or compunction about his very evident lack of loyalty. He seems much more loyal to *causes* than to people, and this might explain his very evident guilt deficiency. Thank God I only have today's final session to record, for next week my focus of study (Martin Quade) will be cruelly eradicated from earthly existence.

As I entered the man's solitary confinement penitentiary cell, I expected to find a fellow with a dismal and negative perspective regarding his absolute fate. Instead, Martin was in a jovial and almost buoyant frame of mind and he couldn't waste any valuable time and requested that *this* researcher immediately place him under hypnosis, which quite frankly was beginning to also mesmerize *my* sanity.

The inmate lay in his bed and I dangled the usual fob chain and gold watch before his eyes and spoke the monotonous soothing words and phrases that gradually dulled his eager senses. Then upon counting backwards Quade was finally under the dominion of my suggestion and had compromised all external features of his mercurial conscious demeanor. I then motioned for the vigilant guards to again depart the cell.

Under deep hypnosis Quade was more rational but also quite ambivalent in terms of his identity. However, the subject's volition was not weakened and he was now a prime candidate for my next (for me) unorthodox interrogation.

One thing was for sure: I had to find out if Quade was going to continue his reverse chronology regression from the age of abominable Mongol conquests that paralleled the European Medieval Period, or would he retreat into the *Dark Ages* or even take an ambiguous mental journey into ancient history?

"What is your name and where do you live?" I objectively asked, while thinking that *this* would be an extended session in that it was to be *our* last encounter.

"My name is John Wilkes Booth and I used to reside in Washington, the nation's capital," my extremely unique subject mechanically stated.

I felt I knew plenty from reading magazine articles about the Lincoln assassination so that I was sufficiently qualified to find a weak point in Quade's responses and then be enabled to exploit that vulnerability. I was so enthused about Quade's new identity that I had overlooked the essential fact that *he* was no longer journeying further into the past but had accelerated from the Age of Genghis Khan to the *Civil War* era, a more than six century leap. "Who is your father? Why did you assassinate President Abraham Lincoln? What was the date and hour of the assassination?" I verbally fired back in rapid succession.

"My father's full name was Junius Brutus Booth," Quade very soberly replied. "My sympathies during the *War between the States* were with *the South* so naturally I detested Lincoln and his traitorous ideas on changing a traditional set way of life in *Dixie*. The assassination took place at just past 10 p.m. on the evening of April, 14, 1865."

'Remarkable!' I thought and concluded. 'Every detail is accurate and all of *his* facts are valid.' I needed to compose myself to further quiz the young man, who must have exclusively read and studied the *Encyclopedia Britannica* for the past several years while pretending to be an authentic student at the *University of Pennsylvania*. But during that final fascinating interview I felt an urgent compulsion to disprove *his* up-to-that-time very audacious and ostensibly intimidating historically accurate knowledge.

"At what Washington theater did you perform the deed and what play was in progress?" I demanded from the imposter pretending to be a very iniquitous *Civil War* era actor/murderer.

"I enacted the noble accomplishment at Ford's Theatre while the play 'Our American Cousin' was in progress," the subject appropriately answered. "I knew the theater well because I myself had often performed as an accomplished actor there. I surreptitiously entered Lincoln's private box and then wounded the traitor in the head. Next I leapt from the box and landed poorly on the stage, breaking my leg in the process."

I recalled something salient from past textbook and magazine readings that only a true-blue history buff would remember or know. "What Latin phrase did *you* proclaim to the shocked Ford's Theatre audience and what does it mean when translated into English?" I zealously insisted on finding out from *my* patient.

"I shouted 'Sic semper tyrannis!' which means in English 'Thus always to tyrants'!" the subject astoundingly conveyed. "Sic semper tyrannis!" he hauntingly repeated.

"What happened when you fled the theater?" I queried. "Were you immediately pursued?"

"Despite my broken leg I rode a swift horse and fled the city and after a series of misadventures, at night I secretly crossed the *Potomac* by boat from Maryland into Virginia," Martin Quade mentally masquerading as John Wilkes Booth communicated. "I was soon captured at a barn outside the town of Port Royal where I was hunted down and shot."

I was so exasperated and so spooked upon hearing his remarkably accurate testament that I inadvertently abandoned my next question and repeated, "Who was your father?"

"Junius Brutus Booth," he stated for the second time. And with the utterance of that name from his lips, Quade began to shake and quake upon his cell bed as if afflicted with a sudden palsy attack. I grabbed his trembling hands and folded his arms over his chest as best as I could. Fortunately, the subject gradually evolved out of his frightening and quite turbulent self-destruct mode. Three minutes later the patient's breathing and pulse rate returned to medically acceptable levels. "I must kill Gaius Julius Caesar! I must kill Gaius Julius Caesar!" Quade eerily exclaimed and reiterated. "He plans to declare himself a god! His dictatorship is a threat to the Republic! Caesar must die!"

Obviously, the aforementioned pronouncement of John Wilkes Booth's father's middle name *Brutus* had sent the subject's subconscious mental dynamics back into the rudimentary days of the Roman Republic. I couldn't think of anything pertinent to say so I mentioned the first vague idea that flashed across my mind. "What day is it? What year is it?" I ranted like a raving maniac.

"It's the *Ides*, which is celebrated according to Roman tradition on March 15th on the Julian calendar," the Brutus impersonator almost magically imparted. "The year is what you now know of on the Gregorian calendar as 44 B.C."

"Who were some of your accomplices?" I prodded. "What were their names?"

"Gaius Cassius Longinus and Marcus Lucinius Crassus were my principal conspirators," Quade (alias Brutus) divulged, "and other noblemen from the Senate assisted us in meticulously carrying out *our* foolproof plot! Death to tyrants I say! Sic semper tyrannis!"

Then Martin Quade commenced shivering and radically tossing about on his jail cell bed. Soon he was going into wild convulsions and foaming at the mouth while still remaining in his unpredictable unconscious state. I panicked and summoned the assigned guards, who immediately returned with several very alarmed prison physicians. The spectacle had chills running up and down my spine for I frightfully thought that Quade's spirit was at that precise place and time in actual communion with the Devil (if such a beast exists). His final incongruous words during his erratic frenzy on the bed were, "I am the betrayer Judas! I am the betrayer Judas!"

'He'll be dead next week so why has everyone including myself tried to save *his* life?' I questioned my heart in a very perplexing self-examination of conscience. 'The doctors, the guards and I are all hypocrites living totally fake quack lives!' I further critically evaluated. 'A human death now, next week or next year has miniscule significance in relation to the complex operations of an infinite and eternal universe!'

Personal Report

Friday, November 21, 2003

Martin Quade was finally executed by lethal injection at 9 a.m., Monday, November 17, 2003. He showed no repentance for murdering his college roommate Richard Anderson, who the now-deceased subject thought was a future dangerous Nazi tyrant. 'Since man loves and values freedom, Quade was no exception,' I theorized. In each case, right or wrong, whether he believed he was Johann Georg Elser, John Wilkes Booth or Marcus Junius Brutus, Martin Quade shared one common denominator with those historical characters he had pretended to be: he deeply felt that *his* personal freedom was being diminished or was being jeopardized. Consciously Martin Quade was a stalking spotted leopard and his bullying adversary Richard Anderson became *his* unfortunate prey. But subconsciously the subject was an amoral guiltless human chameleon.

As for my humble self, I have become quite unstable and jittery ever since I read graphic accounts of Martin Quade's execution in the Tuesday morning newspapers. I had developed a certain endearing attachment to the young man, and I firmly believe that the *University of Pennsylvania* student in *his* heart felt that he had assassinated a ferocious future dictator (Richard Anderson) that represented a great potential threat to the world's prominent civilization.

The Friday after the *Thanksgiving* holiday (November 28th) I presented my thick falsified report in a portfolio to Dr. Eugene Fischer. Visiting at the eminent doctor's Philadelphia office at the time was Dr. Charles Garrison, an internationally acclaimed foremost authority on hypnosis. Dr. Fischer noticed my nervous deportment and suggested that Dr. Garrison be permitted to place me under hypnosis to alleviate my apparent stress. I was suffering from such acute anxiety that I foolishly consented to *his* rather irregular request. My subconscious had been penetrated for a full two hours when I finally became aware that Dr. Garrison's experiment had finally been completed.

Dr. Fischer's revelations about my "inner sunken mind" both staggered and dismayed me. My ears and brain wanted to instantly reject his and Dr. Garrison's insistence that I had indeed vociferated the peculiar claims I purportedly had made.

"Peter, you had said the most incredible things while under hypnosis," Dr. Fischer began. "For instance, you first maintained that you were a young German named Gunther Schmidt who had failed in assassinating Adolph Hitler in Munich in 1938. Next Peter, you stubbornly argued that you were Jack Rubinstein, who the public knows as Jack Ruby," my mentor lectured. "You then said you had been selected by the *Almighty* to exterminate John F. Kennedy's assassin. I don't quite know how *you* managed to trick Dr. Garrison and me with your facetious statements but you had done a very competent and undeniably enviable job at doing so! You appeared to have been completely independent of the power of suggestion!"

"And Peter," Dr. Garrison injected, "you then jumped two thousand years into the past. You insisted that you were Simon Peter, the frugal-minded apostle that bought the food and provisions for the *Last Supper*. You even went as far as elaborating that the word par*simon*ious comes from *your* name, because you Simon Peter were a very shrewd and stingy shopper and a clever trader for Jesus Christ's traveling entourage. Ha, ha, ha," my fellow distinguished and world-renowned hypnotist cackled. "And furthermore, dear Peter Simon, you insist you have felt extremely guilty for not killing your despised enemy Judas Iscariot when *you* had the opportunity! And as you well know Peter, a very innocent Jew died on a cross outside Jerusalem because of *your* failure to act! Ha, ha, ha! Peter Simon, Simon Peter, what a marvelous play on words! Ha, ha, ha!"

Monday, December 8, 2003

After my ears had heard Dr. Fischer and Dr. Garrison's startling summary presentations, my knees buckled and I soon staggered and then collapsed to the office's floor. An ambulance was summoned and the dispatched paramedics hastily transported me to the *University of Pennsylvania Hospital* where I was immediately admitted to the facility's Intensive Care Unit.

I am encouraged to positively report that I have almost completely recuperated from what Dr. Eugene Fischer and Dr. Charles Garrison have authoritatively described as "a minor nervous breakdown." Two days ago I had been transferred to a semi-private hospital room. I was released from the acclaimed Philadelphia medical institution on Friday because my *HMO* hospital-stay insurance coverage had expired.

Despite the overall adversity I have endured and suffered, I, Peter Simon hope to still have a wonderful and joyous *Christmas*.

Dr. Peter Simon
Licensed Psychiatrist

"The Yard Sale Mirror"

Journal Entry

Saturday, September 6, 2003

The state's psychiatric team working on my case study had determined that I'm criminally insane. The very conservative judge that presided at my biased trial ordered me incarcerated in a high security ward of Ancora State Mental Hospital. I had become so angry at the outset of my "legal evaluation" because of incompetent defense representation that I had soundly punched my state-appointed attorney in the jaw, knocking the New Jersey lawyer unconscious right inside the crowded courtroom. That chaotic incident meant that I had to endure the remainder of my court appearance shackled in handcuffs.

The psychiatrists assigned to my case maintain that my thought patterns are both erratic and inconsistent. My psyche frequently craves chocolate sweets and I positively love eating *Snickers* bars. I'm allowed one candy bar a day and chew it ravenously every time the hospital attendants hand it to me, usually just after supper. In fact, come to think about it, *Snickers'* candy bars and some other delectable chocolate treats are the only things I really love in life.

I despise other people who are all-too-secure in their "authority professions," especially lawyers, politicians, judges, psychiatrists, doctors and priests. Those charlatans have abusively used their influence and their public power to have me wrongly declared criminally insane. The ruthless diabolical parasites! How could I possibly be daft if I can communicate my thoughts so lucidly? I absolutely loathe people that manipulate laws and hurt the helpless victims of *their* suspect whims! Sometimes I even hate myself!

Saturday. September 13, 2003

Every Saturday I'm encouraged by the nosy hospital employees to make a new entry into "my journal." I don't trust the curious mental hospital doctors or their nefarious nosy staff members. How could I have mental health problems? I know I'm very intelligent without them incessantly studying me, only to eventually tell me *that* obvious truth later! *They* actually mean 'emotional problems' when they say "mental problems," but like everyone else in standard American society, the psychiatrists and psychologists disguise what they really mean by using tricky semantics.

Mental refers to the ability to think and to reason. That process has always come easily to me. But I resent to the point of absolutely despising the particular nomenclature *emotional*. I truly detest anything emotional. Reason triumphantly transcends emotion in my adult mind. And so I value principles and methods like cause and effect, interpretation, analysis, synthesis and explanation over the raw feeling of or expression of *emotion*. I believe that I do like people, but I certainly do *not* love them. To me the word *love* means sustaining security and its various functions, all done as a need to keep others along with myself' safe. Love to me also *used* to mean sharing a spouse's companionship, even if the general relationship had been or is riddled with animosity.

The hospital doctors are bold-faced liars and their shallow theories are borderline foolish. During my cursory interrogations of the resident charlatans, I soon learned they know little about *Hamlet, Macbeth, King Lear*, Hemingway, Steinbeck or even about the famous literary genius Edgar Allan Poe. Just because I've claimed that I'm Poe reincarnated into a new dynamic personality, the narrow-minded hospital quacks eschew my expressed veracity and totally doubt my credibility. But indeed, my vast knowledge of literature far supersedes their limited mastery of the marvelous subject.

Yet the people in power adamantly claim that I'm 'mentally and criminally crazy' when *they* habitually and chronically lie and really mean that I'm simply 'emotionally unstable'. Is there no truth existent in this whole damned world*? They* don't care one iota about my mental welfare! The all-too-powerful decision-makers only care about perpetuating their own careers, their own bank accounts and their own professional reputations!

My greatest fear at present is that the in-house doctors plan to use *this* accurate diary as evidence against me for the ulterior purpose of keeping me corralled inside the perimeter of their despotic custody. The incompetent witchdoctors desire to keep me imprisoned inside *this* dreadful hellhole for the remainder of my days on this God-forsaken Earth. I don't care one ounce of horse manure about their myriad malicious intentions. In the end the truth must prevail. *My* truth must prevail!

Saturday, September 20, 2003

Now it all makes perfectly legitimate sense. A circular mirror is hanging on my Ancora State Hospital room's wall, the ornament having a gilded golden frame. My keen instincts confirm that this mirror I view daily is evil. I realize I'm supposed to believe that only people are evil and that objects are not or cannot be, but my intuitive perception immediately had discerned and determined the hanging mirror as being diabolical both in nature and in origin.

Each day I cover the evil wall mirror with my pillowcase and at night before I slumber, I use a towel to camouflage the wretched reflecting device in an effort to isolate it from my daily scrutiny. The hospital's main psychiatrists have falsely described this behavior as being "delusional, paranoid and neurotic."

But I assure you, I have good reason to exhibit such "aberrant deportment." That evil mirror has the ability to induce me into a state of uncontrollable rage. It possesses the uncanny ability to motivate me to become both hostile and violent. I fully realize that I must definitely curb my silly emotional weakness. I'm cognizant that I must practice sane rationality at all times. Thank God it's now time to devour another *Snickers* bar. Last week I was given a *Milky Way* bar instead during my nocturnal snack time sugar rush. It was delicious, but not nearly as scrumptious as a fabulous *Snickers* bar is.

It's my unbiased contention that the untrustworthy hospital staff is experimenting and immorally toying with my fragile mind. I suspect that the idiots are assiduously documenting false evidence while erroneously purporting that I possess an irreversible obsessive-compulsive personality. I'm completely and scrupulously well-aware of *their* surreptitious devious motives.

The cynical lot should all be committed to *this* despicable pitiless institution and not me. I now keep two journals, *this* valid secret documentation and a substitute one, which contains all contrived happy thoughts and observations that the psychiatrists and psychologists want to hear and read. I plan to submit to the hospital the imaginary fictional record and conversely, keep *this* other accurate diary for my own perusal. After all, that's all *they* really are interested in: a fake society in a fantasized artificially contrived world! But now I'm shrewdly wise to their vile cruel antics. Who do *they* think they're fooling?

Saturday, September 27, 2003

I've always been regarded by former acquaintances as a maverick and as an iconoclast. Today I saw a mother visiting the hospital kiss her son goodbye. Affection has always greatly disturbed me. It's an unnecessary behavior that chimpanzees, gorillas, dogs and other lower animal forms often feel compelled to display. The ability to think and to solve problems is emblematic of human existence and exists on a much loftier plane than mere asinine affection does.

I mean, I'm affectionate in what my ambiguous doctors consider "a strange sort of way." I like to tease, tempt and taunt, showing my intellectual interest in other people as my sole expression of affection. I can't understand why others persist in having to fawn, dote-on and grope each other in public. Don't they know how to think or solve problems in a rational manner? The kissers and the huggers are essentially inferior creatures always requiring instant and constant gratification on demand. Affection ought to be intellectual and understood among curious people and not overtly physical and needlessly demonstrable. Those lacking individuals that frequently engage in affectionate behavior are really only seeking emotional security, and those same weak-minded buffoons don't have adequate confidence in their own abilities to ever finish a major task all on their own.

My psychiatrist believes that my thoughts are incoherent and lack both transition and connection. He moronically calls the essential thought development phenomenon that I espouse "fragmentation." What does *he* know outside of the suspect theories cramming his archaic textbooks and also his limited thoroughly-corrupted mind? The misguided dolt should be better acquainted with Maslow's pyramid where the ultimate goal of human existence is successfully attaining self-actualization.

Affection tends to stifle and interfere with people achieving their own individual supreme attainment. Affection harbors dependency and creates strong restrictive 'giving and receiving bonds' between people. It therefore quite egregiously discourages introspection, imagination, creativity and self-determination. That's why I become infuriated when I witness public affection! It's thwarting someone's mental growth and his or her exploration of self-actualization! Ralph Waldo Emerson had it dead wrong! Empiricism *is* honestly worthy of pursuit. I'm an avowed advocate of "reverse transcendentalism." Reason should continuously triumph over emotion, and pure logic should relentlessly guide *our* every action.

Haven't we humans evolved beyond the primitive monkey state of existence twenty or so millennia ago? Let's leave the Simian affection behavior to Darwin and Freud. Why do people revel in slobbering all over each other while perpetuating germs and disease and then persist in acting like non-evolved orangutans, chimpanzees and gibbons? Now I fully comprehend what I'm attempting to explain. That's precisely what New Jersey is, along with its politicians, mental hospitals and damned psychiatrists: a damned out-of-control monkey state!

And just meditate a moment on what a kiss meant to the *King of the Jews*! Judas's kiss was symbolic of betrayal and ultimately led to a most heinous crucifixion. That's the principal reason why I distrust another person who is so eager to kiss me! I view that person as a jungle gorilla or as a primitive mother chimpanzee, or as a prospective Judas Iscariot.

It's now time to remove the pillowcase covering the mirror and replace it with the towel. I find that the red towel works just as effectively as the blue towel does. You can't imagine how relieved I am when I safely make the important transition from pillowcase to towel each night or from towel to pillowcase every morning. Thank God that towels and pillowcases are not transparent! That ominous circumstance of the pillowcase or the towel being transparent and exposed to my scrutiny would be a worst-case scenario that could produce repercussions that would be absolutely catastrophic!

Oh well, it's now time to abandon this accurate notebook and again author false entries into my pathetic phony journal. I feel like a smart businessman keeping a second set of records exclusively for *IRS* inspection. It's now 6:30 p.m. and my *Snickers* bar has not yet been delivered. Where the hell is it? The world is full of gross injustices and unfair practices! Where's my sole reason for living? Where's my damned *Snickers* bar?

Saturday, October 4, 2003

My formerly nebulous memory is becoming keener as I contemplate my present predicament in relation to my past. Epilepsy runs in my family, but epilepsy is certainly not insanity. I've had several frightening seizures while vegetating in this troubling forsaken institution. I remember the faces of the interns as the imbecilic novices endeavored to control my gyrating and thrusting on the floor during those periodic "episodes." The bozos definitely appeared scared and overwhelmed. *My mental power* has made *them* feel subordinate, impotent and inferior. My divine dominance over *them* has been both deliberately and methodically inspired, this undeniable truth I am certain.

And history teaches that Julius Caesar and Alexander the Great were both reputed to be epileptics, so as any objective analyst can readily determine, I'm in very glorious company each time I have what the staff here at the hospital describes as "a fit." Just like the two great aforementioned conquerors of ancient history, I believe I'm in communication with the gods or with heaven whenever my mind and body enter into *that* incomparable state of mental and physical ecstasy. I can then fully identify with the great and noble epileptics of antiquity. I share Caesar and Alexander's passion for living an abundant, productive and satisfying life. But why can't I enjoy halcyon days of wonderful victory like my historic epileptic counterparts had experienced? Why must fate be so despicably and so redundantly cruel? Why am I denied fundamental victory over my vile antagonists? Why does the State of New Jersey have dictatorial dominion over me? Whoever gave those bungling, bureaucratic ignoramuses jurisdiction over my fate?

And thanks to the benevolence of the equally bureaucratic American justice system, I've been callously committed to a mental hospital instead of being *humanely* executed or given a life sentence in an apathetic state prison environment. In fact, *this* forced hospital confinement is analogous to life imprisonment in a state or federal penitentiary. What an ironic coincidence!

And no one else except me knows the fiendish character of that evil wall mirror I wisely keep covered all the time with either a pillowcase or a towel. The hellish mirror has nothing to do with *Snickers* bars, intellectual affection, writing an honest journal or the ecstatic joys associated with epilepsy. Those hypocrites that are in control of my destiny have no faith in the supernatural or in the hereafter whatsoever. The hospital sophists are agnostics, atheists and sinners, yet the dunderheads maintain positions of authority within the hospital and within the government's judicial system. I promise and pledge that they will be adequately punished in the Afterlife for their widespread heresy! This I can guarantee with absolute (and not relative) certainty from the Governor on down to the lowest town official!

It's now again time to conceal the face of that demonic wall mirror with another covering! I'm so glad that I can use a red towel today. I mostly prefer it to the blue towel, which I imaginatively alternate with the crimson one daily. But I must confess that I value the green pillowcase over either the red or the blue towel; however, I favor the

214

light blue pillowcase over the dark green one. The hospital attendants change the pillowcases every week, and I suspect that their obscure motive is to intentionally switch from blue to green to radically aggravate and disturb my irrelevant emotional stability. My astute mind plausibly fathoms exactly what *they* are attempting to accomplish by indiscreetly and unethically using their lame power and their weak persuasion to deliberately subvert my sensibilities through the fools' tacit defiance of my basic sincere proclivities, or in other words, *them* maliciously attempting to control and change my inner core concepts of what actually constitutes right and what actually constitutes wrong.

The ignorant facetious world ignores my clever subterfuge. I seem to only impact what is going on *inside my mind,* and that's exactly the way my quack doctors want it to be. Why didn't the judge and jury ever place credence in my foolproof testimony? Even my court-appointed attorney tried preventing me from squawking out, "I only was revolting against female domination while being under the jurisdictional fiat of *that* damned evil mirror!" That's when I triumphantly battered the politically correct defense lawyer squarely in the face until the bailiff and two armed policemen finally managed to physically restrain me.

Where's my confounded *Snickers* bar? I now require physical pleasure and mental gratification to wholly compensate for the detestable emotional duress I'm presently suffering.

Saturday, October 11, 2003

Now I am seeing things in reality perfectly crystal clear. Besides my repugnance of affection and my wonderful epilepsy "affliction," I also am a genetic product of incest and so are my fortunate children. The hospital doctors capriciously discriminate by also holding *that* particular noble heritage against me.

My maternal grandmother's father and my maternal grandfather's father were brothers. That means that my mother's parents (my grandparents) were cousins. The merits and difficulties associated with *that* specific genetic background have been carried-on and are now shared by my three sons.

But I insist that "Incest" does have its splendid benefits. It is believed that Cleopatra and the Egyptian Ptolemy rulers were the offspring of close incestuous relationships. And incest either usually breeds genius or insanity, and who can legitimately define the fine and almost indiscernible line between the parallel behaviors? I tend to think that I'm more of the former than of the latter variety. Indeed, I am neither retarded nor insane!

And I maintain that I have no obvious genetic defects. I don't have six fingers, three necks, thirteen toes or two navels. That's why my psychiatrists cannot fully assess my mental capacity and why the knuckleheads stubbornly adhere to the pretentious notion that I'm 'mentally insane.' The hospital clowns lack the mental capacity to validly fathom the true benign nature of "Incest."

Now my wife's maternal grandmother was *my mother's* maternal grandfather's sister and also simultaneously, *my mother's* fraternal grandfather's sister. So consequently, my three sons have inherited common genes from both sides of the incestuous family. Are my sons' geniuses, or are they each in need of a bed in a bogus State asylum too? Still the three young men all seem to function in a so-called normal existence in what is innocently termed "mainstream American society."

And I must pertinently mention that my great-grandparents were continually annoyed by my wife's surreptitious great grandmother, who constantly tormented *them* and caused conflict whenever *she* could. My great-grandfather would get drunk from his sister's (my wife's great-grandmother's) incessant abuse and then angrily beat-up his innocent wife in his drunken stupor.

And my garrulous dominant wife inherited that busybody trouble-making characteristic from her obnoxious great-grandmother, from her petulant grandmother and also from her mercurial mother, and I believe that *that's* what eventually led to *our* perpetual arguing. My louse of a spouse would harangue and harass me to no end and then we would verbally wrangle for hours.

Who says that behavior is learned? Phony psychology? Behavior is often genetically transmitted from one generation to the next and it's influentially present in our *DNA* and abundantly evident in our chromosome transmission from one generation to the next.

My wife's maternal grandfather was an excellent swimmer, in fact, reputed to be the best in the entire town. He inexplicably drowned one summer morning in 1934 in the town lake. Many residents suspected that his demise was a desperate suicide and that the dominated fellow had not been suffering from "severe muscle cramps" as the contrived police report had fallaciously indicated. I've always viewed the man's probable suicide as a courageous act of escapism from the curse of relentless and brutal henpecking at home. Bless you Rip Van Winkle for abandoning your shrew of a wife and bravely going up into the Catskill Mountains with your dog Wolf to randomly hunt squirrels while enjoying your freedom from constant petticoat tyranny!

216

You would think that my inane mental health doctors would be cognizant of *that* salient fact about the merits of incest and other arguments I've already adroitly identified. All that the totally ludicrous hospital shrinks' care about is tormenting my already tortured spirit by denying me recognition of my often-expressed principles, or the mentally deficient charlatans derive sadistic pleasure by wickedly tantalizing me by mischievously delaying my daily *Snickers* bar delivery!

Saturday, October 18, 2003

My wife's mother's family was mostly matriarchal in character. Females ruled and dominated their deliberately chosen more recessive timid spouses. The women on my wife's side were and are all bossy, arrogant, conceited and ruthless brow-beaters. I strongly believe that the nasty attitude and the vile practice originated at least four generations ago back in Sicily in the late 1800s.

My father's family was an entirely different but no less of a pathetic dysfunctional brood. My father's father in the early 1900s was a logger who leased government timberland in the upper Michigan peninsula. A roaring forest fire surged through the camp and destroyed all of my victimized grandfather's material assets. With the absence of any insurance policy to reimburse his tremendous losses caused by the devastating inferno, my grandfather (who I never knew) died a year later, a bankrupt broken man. Soon his wife (my grandmother that I never knew) died of pneumonia.

The remainder of my father's family moved east from Alpena, Michigan to Baltimore to start a new life. Dad was the youngest child and had to live under the jurisdiction of Aunt Marie, an austere straightlaced martinet that tolerated no tomfoolery from her younger siblings. And Dad also had four other elder sisters in addition to Aunt Marie supervising and superimposing *their* collective feminine wills on him. So Dad too was henpecked under female domination just as I had been.

It's no wonder that Dad married to get out of *his* family female exploitation. Mom also was a product of a matriarchal family that believed men should provide for the financial welfare but also keep their mouths shut and shy away from all-important family decision-making and money matters. It's no secret that Dad died at an early age to escape the overwhelming tyranny of applied female dictatorship at home.

And now I understand too late why I had married a dominant female originating from a matriarchal family, an Alpha female who stalked, targeted and then lured me into her encumbering treacherous spider's web. But unlike Dad, I rebelled and battled against being daily suppressed and oppressed. That's precisely what got me admitted into Ancora State Hospital.

But I'm clever enough to know the doctors' stealthy ploys along with their furtive motives. I've conscientiously read most of Shakespeare's works and am well-versed in the art of assessing human character or lack thereof. And if it weren't for my self-esteem and for my delightful daily *Snickers* bars, then suicide would be a viable option for me to seriously consider, even if it involved drowning as a viable escape mechanism.

In the past, whenever my wife would vindictively dictate "Go jump in the lake!" I had felt persecuted because I knew that *her* exploited grandfather had drowned doing *that* exact same thing. And so I often mentally escaped my dire female domination dilemma by imaginatively fantasizing an alternate reality. My spirit and psyche both demanded it: male independence and male liberty. Otherwise, I would've taken an alternate less acceptable route by escaping this world by means of my desperate soul prematurely departing my body just like my wife's grandfather had done while swimming in the town lake back in 1934.

Do you now know why I crave and value *Snickers* bars? The scrumptious candy represents my only compensation for wanting to continue living on this wretched God-forsaken planet.

Saturday, October 25, 2003

I think my present anguish had originated with the birth of my eldest son in 1967. I had planned that the boy should be named after me, but after several heated debates with my argumentative spouse and her' dominant mother, I reluctantly acceded and consented to naming him after my ill-tempered father-in-law. I should've never surrendered *that* vital stance to my wife and to her inflexible nasty mother. My spouse ever since then has favored *him* over me, and she also values her dominant mother's opinion over mine. I had been reduced in influence to being the family subsidizer of all of this accumulative despotic matriarchal female-dominated chicanery. I refused to permit *them* to wheedle-down my already fragile ego any further, and I've successfully resisted their avaricious female attempts at dominating my spirit ever since.

My obsessive-compulsive father-in-law owned a prosperous car dealership in the community. I had been coerced by family pressure to quit my boring accounting job and agreed to work for him, and that terrible decision constituted the greatest mistake of my entire life, that is, besides getting married. My new boss and I bickered verbally and fought incessantly, even coming to blows on two occasions. His personality thrived on having continuous conflict and that was the long and short of his simplistic-but-mean nature. And his high rank in the company was always pulled on *me,* his entrapped victimized subordinate son-in-law whom he could easily manipulate.

I wanted to sell cars and be the organization's Sales Manager. My wife's father and mother relegated me to meagerly washing new and used cars and being a lowly delivery boy, always driving around the area obtaining automotive parts from other dealerships and from local distributors. I endured that massive unbearable humiliation for over twenty years, but my wife would always ally with her wealthy parents whenever push came to shove.

And when my eldest son graduated college, the young man was automatically elevated over me in the family businesses' "blood-over-water pecking order." I had to take instructions and commands from *him,* the favored chosen male in my matriarchal-oriented family. I wouldn't mind taking orders from *him* if it were at *my* own volition and choice, but since being outranked by my son was my in-laws' and my wife's detestable design, I promptly then left the business shortly thereafter, and much to my in-laws' chagrin, I cheerfully and spitefully worked for a competing car agency, which soon quadrupled its new car sales' volume because of my stellar salesmanship input and my sense of strategic organization.

My incensed wife wanted to abandon and divorce me for openly betraying her sacred family's present and future designs. At the time I was content because my contributions were finally being recognized by my new employer and ironically, I was being substantially rewarded by the rival automobile dealership that had intelligently hired my capable services.

Now in retrospect, I'm convinced *this* is why my mind had become in turmoil. Chaos on the job while working for my psychotic in-laws had converted into unceasing conflict at home between my sharp-tongued wife and myself.' "Our eldest son is more *blood* than you are!" she perpetually yelled and rankled. "That's why my parents favor him over you! And *our* son and I both know exactly what side our bread is buttered on! Now I want *you* to come back and work for my parents or else I'm going to file for divorce! You're a public embarrassment to the whole family, and every hair salon and barbershop in town is gossiping about you and us right now!"

That's precisely when I stopped being affectionate in any way and soon reflexively crawled into my protective shell as if I was a turtle during hibernation. My former good heart suddenly turned vindictive and unforgiving. I was developing a mean spiteful grudge that slowly penetrated every fiber, every cell, every molecule and every atom in my whole body. My new-found cold calculating heart naturally next contemplated revenge.

The new car agency that had employed my valuable services used me and profited from my special talents for the next seven smooth-sailing years. Then, jealous of my popularity among *their* established customers, the envious greedy owners abruptly fired me without any advance notice or reasonable cause for dismissal. I was depressed, despondent and on the verge of committing a violent crime as retribution for *their* unwarranted elimination of me from their then-thriving enterprise, which obviously I had fully engineered and developed. I even seriously contemplated burning *their* automobile showroom and service department to the ground in a giant arson-generated conflagration.

In 1986, I had invested in a novelty distribution company of my own while using the few dollars I had amassed in my meager savings account. My partner was an elderly man that could not lift a package because of a recent heart attack, so it was my responsibility to perform all of the packing of goods and the delivery of those products in the New Jersey, Pennsylvania and Delaware Tri-State area. But I was happy and relatively satisfied while engaged in that *independent* enterprise.

My in-laws made it their business to become friendly with my new-found business partner, and within two years, the scurrilous family dictators bought-out his majority stake in the then-flourishing operation. I was livid when I had learned that I was again indirectly working for and answerable to my exploitative in-laws, and also to my rambunctious opinionated estranged wife. I was now both the subject and the object of the fancies and caprices of those three maniacal control freaks. The indignity associated with that new circumstance mercilessly haunted my tender and abused psyche for the next several years.

That's precisely when I began eagerly consuming *Snickers* bars to achieve temporary escapism from the wicked humiliating hellish reality that I had to then experience and endure under *their* relentless dominion.

Saturday, November 1, 2003

Thank God *Halloween* 2003 has come and passed. I abhor that ghoulish morbid holiday. Now I can think more objectively and rationally without having to worry about being harassed by errant witches, itinerant vampires, zombies, clownish ghosts and villainous fake monsters.

My falsified diary reads like palatable propaganda that I've cunningly devised to both proclaim and to justify my "emotional rehabilitation." My main personal goal is to facilitate my eventual release from *this* horrid state asylum. I'm cleverly authoring *that second aforementioned record* to show the State of New Jersey how I'm cooperatively adjusting to and preparing for a return to the challenging rigors and nuances of modern American civilization. Can I ever be more cunningly sagacious?

But the whole explicit truth of my excruciating incarceration situation is solely represented in *this* most revealing and truthful addition to *"My* Journal." And so for authenticity purposes, I now feel compelled to voluntarily make another valid entry to this singular autobiography.

In June of a certain year which I can't now remember or specifically identify, my wife and I had visited our youngest son's home up in Paramus, New Jersey. Several blocks before reaching *his* house my all-too-curious wife spotted a yard sale and she implored me to stop so that the witch could browse all of the unwanted and undesirable cellar, attic and garage junk being on lawn display. She purchased (without even consulting me) a circular gilded gold-framed mirror (designated for my new computer room), which I then immediately objected owning.

The following day, my spouse hung the atrocious-looking mirror in my oldest son's former bedroom. I detested the lousy thing, mostly because my wife had selected it, and then naturally, because the stubborn-minded hag obstinately overruled me by hanging the unwanted hideous object inside *my* private sanctuary. As a weird coincidence, the purchased garage sale item is identical to the cheap covered mirror that's currently hanging in my Ancora Mental Hospital room. In fact, I now firmly believe that the evil mirror in my room is the same one (or its evil twin) that had been carelessly bought by my wife at the Paramus yard sale.

I'm so relieved that I can now hide the evil object's existence with the room's available pillowcases and towels. My always-vigilant sixth sense can readily recognize the encroachment of evil immediately before the sinister demon ever makes its unannounced grotesque appearance. This is the only advantage I enjoy over Satan's accursed mechanisms. I hope that the State Hospital staff isn't monitoring me with bugging devices or a hidden television camera. Thank Heaven that the omnipotent State bureaucrats are too parsimonious and too ruefully feeble-minded to ever finance such a clever Orwellian "Big Brother mirror monitoring scheme!"

From my diligent research studies, I've concluded that Maslow's hierarchy of human needs completely ignores the existence of evil. At the base of the notorious psychology pyramid are biological needs such as food, water, oxygen and a satisfactory temperature range where all animals including mankind could comfortably flourish. And then above the physical needs' level shared by all creatures on this delicate vulnerable planet are certain security needs such as safety, a heated shelter to protect families from the harsh elements and finally, sufficient food supplies during emergencies.

And as one's positional existence ascends the Maslow matrix, supposedly humans next have assumed social needs, which translate into feeling trustful among others, having a sense of belonging to a group and also, the need for having self-esteem within the surrounding family and community. Above social needs are the all-important human ego and attendant cultural requirements. One must experience empowerment, confidence, pride and a sense of accomplishment in order to derive necessary fulfillment and happiness from contributing to society.

My wife and my mother-in-law deliberately thwarted my social and ego needs and thus violated the relevant principles and teachings of Maslow's Theory. *They* dually strove to limit my success and my well-being by virtue of their premeditated stifling of my personal growth and development. But I had valiantly defeated their ignoble *psychological* initiatives. I brilliantly attained self-actualization on my own in spite of them, and also, basically just to spite them.

But *that* foreboding evil golden-framed mirror has perverted and sabotaged my self-actualization with *its* overpowering malignant influence. I need two tasty *Snickers* bars right now!

Saturday, November 8, 2003

I vividly recall that several peculiar habits my wife had developed began irritating me. She started wearing red nail polish. In the past my mate had only worn transparent plain polish that accentuated the natural beauty of her nails and skin. But that's precisely my point! Before we were married, she never painted or colored her nails, and the two of us were always compatible in that regard. Then suddenly she intentionally defied my wishes and my protests by coloring her finger and toenails in that obnoxious fiery red tone that nearly sent my mind over the edge.

A woman with red fingernails reminds me of a female panther or lion after it has made a vicious kill with the victim's blood oozing from its savage claws. That's the horrible image my sensitive mind conjures-up every time I see a woman with long red-painted fingernails, just like the red nails on prostitutes that sit at the end stools (during the warm summer months) at boardwalk open bars. Such a perverted hideous sight invariably turns my stomach sour!

Another deviant practice my wife had been doing also annoyed my highly focused concentration. She began traipsing around the house barefooted. I have always professed that the feet are the ugliest part of the human anatomy. I myself always wear socks whenever my shoes have been removed to cover my most ugly body parts.

And my bossy wife always had horrible-looking feet featuring grotesque hammertoes, and her second toes were longer than her big toes in the Sicilian fashion. I requested that she stop bothering my mind and cease tormenting my delicate psyche with her painted fingernails and atrocious-looking bare-feet with those despicable painted toes, but she persisted in pushing the envelope. Conflict was inevitable and events were rapidly ascending to a culmination. That's exactly where and when the evil wall mirror traumatically comes into play.

Saturday, November 15, 2003

One Sunday, while my wife was out grocery shopping, I stared into the hideous computer room wall mirror that my demanding wife had purchased at the Paramus yard sale. As I admired my clean-shaven countenance, my immediate thoughts centered on revving-up my computer and then randomly surfing the *Internet*. Amazingly a series of black words appeared upon the looking glass, and a rather strange message ominously warned, "Don't use your computer Tuesday night." Then the printed imperative language slowly faded and next vanished from the haunted mirror, just as mysteriously as it had instantly appeared.

Two days had passed and my mind had dismissed the mirror aberration I had witnessed as an "optical illusion or bizarre hallucination." Much to my total dismay, I was cruising along the *Internet* looking-up American writers on various search engines when a freak storm enveloped the South Jersey vicinity. A wicked bolt of lightning collided with the telephone pole outside *my* room and my computer's modem was instantaneously disabled because of the intense power surge. Then I sincerely wished that I had obediently heeded the awesome mirror's most prophetic "Tuesday night" words.

On the following Thursday morning, the fascinating soothsaying mirror signaled me in a similar writing to avoid the house's interior steps and to be especially careful when either ascending or descending the stairs. Late that afternoon I was in a hurry to deposit money into my bank checking account to cover impending utility and insurance bills. I quickly scampered-down the flight of steps while tucking my bank deposit slip into my wallet and then my right foot slipped, and consequently, I found myself awkwardly tumbling-head-first down the last seven steps.

My puffed-up left ankle had been severely double-sprained from the accident and I agonized for five full minutes on the foyer floor while attempting to stand. I managed to drive to the local bank and negotiate my business from my car, and next I intelligently motored to the family physician's office to obtain a painkiller prescription for my pharmacist to prepare. I really needed to alleviate the intense throbbing inside my injured extremely swollen left ankle.

As the next few weekdays passed, I was beginning to dread the circular golden-framed evil mirror hanging from the windowless wall inside my personal study. But several days later I was getting around without the assistance of crutches, since my ankle's swelling had considerably diminished. "Be sure to apply ice and not heat!" my doctor had recommended, and his sound advice had soon worked like a lucky charm.

After again entering the computer room, I then realized that I still had to obtain a new modem to install to replace the one that had been damaged beyond repair during the severe electrical storm. I glanced into the frightful supernatural mirror and before I could formulate an appropriate question to ask it, the independent-minded arcane object printed a new queer communication on its reflected surface. "Kill your wife and your meddling bossy mother-in-law or be killed!"

'Mirror, I was going to ask you who were my worst enemies, but now you've very adroitly answered that crucial riddle for me,' I thought while my hands suddenly trembled and my legs shuddered. I was appalled and my mind was in shock for a moment at the mirror's onerous communication as my numb brain finally absorbed the impact of the explicit words that had been communicated in a very imperative, almost military command manner. 'How best should I fulfill the mirror's statement?' I instinctively thought.

224

The didactic "evil order" was then incredibly erased upon the looking glass's surface, and next a new alarming sentence appeared, instructing me on precisely how I should perform the dastardly deed.

'Of course!' I readily acknowledged. 'How simple and impersonal yet so effective! Just as I' would like to have done it a thousand times before!'

Saturday, November 22, 2003

It's almost the *Thanksgiving* holidays here at inhospitable Ancora State Hospital, and pumpkin, pilgrim, cranberry and various turkey decorations are festooned and featured all over the walls and halls. I must confess that this felicitous scenario is hardly the most conducive atmosphere for recollecting how I ingenuously (with a bold suggestion from the heinously evil mirror) performed the dual murders. Psychiatrists know all about the "power of suggestion" and now so do I.

My wife and I had gotten back together for a temporary reconciliation, much to my mother-in-law's chagrin. I felt that the evil mirror's command was my predetermined absolute destiny and that I had no alternative other than to comply with its macabre instruction or die myself. Notice how sagaciously, how prudently I then completed the deceitful-but-necessary felony.

Every Saturday morning my mother-in-law invaded my sacred property to brainwash and lecture my naïve wife, who always later became aggressive and shrew-like towards me upon her mother's departure. I secretly planned the following Saturday morning to be the most efficacious time to satisfactorily enact the omnipotent mirror's definitive will. My scheme would be quick, bloodless, impersonal and very efficient. I would complete my dual felonies while the egotistical women were, as usual, preoccupied prattling away on my den's burgundy leather couch and matching love seat.

'My automobile has dual exhaust pipes,' I coyly recollected and considered. So exercising my mental versatility, I shrewdly opened the garage door while coming home from the local convenience store, my errand being to buy a newspaper and a giant *Snickers* bar. Instead of pulling directly into the garage, I coyly backed my vehicle inside. I smartly shut-off the ignition and removed from the trunk a plastic hose that had a bit larger circumference than my left exhaust pipe had. I then placed the plastic tube over the exhaust pipe and next channeled the other end into a heating and air conditioning duct's vent. I next opened the door leading from the garage to the laundry room to allow odorless carbon monoxide fumes to enter the house via a second lethal route.

I brilliantly turned-on my car's ignition and permitted the automobile to idle. Then I pressed my automatic door button and escaped the garage and its poisonous engine emissions. Finally, I nonchalantly strolled-out to the mailbox to check if the postman had delivered the usual bills and junk mail from Saturday's box stop. I cheerfully waved to my neighbor across the street, nimbly crossed the highway and then casually chatted with him for fifteen minutes about sports, national news and local gossip.

At last, I left my talkative neighbor's benign illustrious company and then garnered sufficient courage to trek back across the busy highway to the rear of my home and soon, my eyes anxiously peered into the den's side window. My pupils detected two figures slumped-over, one on the burgundy couch and the other upon the matching loveseat. Thanks to my splendid ingenuity, the lawn sale mirror's supernatural decree had been slyly and loyally implemented.

Using a pocket key, I entered the house via the laundry room door, opened the window and then furtively ambled into the garage, shut off my car's ignition, and next removed the plastic pipe from the exhaust and slyly hid it in the cellar. Then I opened the automatic garage door, fired-up my vehicle's engine, backed my automobile out, turned it around in my driveway and lastly, intelligently re-parked the reliable car in its proper place.

I next ambled into the interior of my home, opened six windows, found the portable telephone and very coolly and meticulously dialed *911,* gladly summoning the local authorities to my country residence. The skeptical police did not believe my firm argument that I had accidentally asphyxiated the two dominant women. "Why did you lower the garage door with the car's engine still running?" the chief investigator sternly interrogated. "Why did you lower the door and then cross the street to talk with a friendly neighbor?" the second patrolman wanted to know.

"I demand to talk to a lawyer before I answer any of your outrageous preposterous questions!" I vehemently exclaimed. 'I no longer have to contend with my wife's or her mother's sarcastic quips!' I thankfully imagined.

The militant town cops arrested me under suspicion of murder and eight months later my case went to trial. The rest is all documented in my personal confidential police record and in my top-secret psychiatric files, but the real truth exists in *this* true and factual secret chronicle I've carefully authored.

Now I cringe every time I ever glance at the identical round mirror with the golden trim that's hanging on my hospital room's wall. I feel that I must continuously keep the 'demonic agent of evil' covered with varicolored pillowcases and towels so that I won't have to ever read *its* dreadful diabolical messages. My greatest fear is that *this* sinister twin mirror is just as satanic and just as evil as the one still hanging on the windowless sidewall inside my home's upstairs computer room. I'm quite adamant and fearful about this dual mirror similarity and would swear by it on any *Bible*! What an abominable curse the two wretched twin mirrors actually are!"

Now can you appreciate why I keep the repulsive twin object covered day and night on my hospital room wall? Who knows what its disgusting future commands might be? And exactly what do the mentally deficient hospital doctors know about demonic mirrors that can write accursed messages?

I am not insane as my idiotic assigned psychiatrist claims. He knows nothing about evil because he has no morality or any functional ethical value system to judge sin by. All the bureaucratic parasite knows is stupid useless psychology and nothing more!

"The Curator"

I am certain of one distinct undeniable truth. My wife had unexpectedly died five years ago on my birthday, October 6th. The past five years I have been both miserable and inconsolable, especially during the gray-sky cold winter months. A husband does not sufficiently realize the anguish that accompanies loneliness until it is experienced firsthand.

My mind now lacks curiosity, zest, desire and motivation. My heart all-too-well knows emptiness, despair, desperation and futility. My soul now comprehends the significance of mourning, melancholy, devastation and damnation. Eternity practices no pity. I no longer have mortal incentives nor do I care to pursue those mundane activities.

My libido no longer craves biological pleasures. Presently the only sensation I endure is a prolonged torturous mental agony. This abnormal perception leads my thinking to suspect that I had recently coincidentally died on my wife's birthday, July 21st. I cannot scientifically prove or validate this particular assumption, but my encumbered mental awareness continually reinforces it. This extraordinary burdensome mental existence that I presently suffer totally defies traditional scientific cause-effect explanation. But undoubtedly my eye's mind sees colors, shapes, and certain objects in an arcane, warped dimension that nonetheless contradicts most everything that my former human identity as Dennis Collier had once fathomed and fully understood. But still the disgusting phenomenon I witness is all-too-baffling and bewildering to lucidly and effectively communicate.

Although blurry and vague, my sense of sight still remains functioning, but I no longer hear sounds and suspect that I am at least partially deaf. I have tried speaking and shouting, but my ears are now completely obsolete and no longer possess any noticeable auditory perception. Even my olfactory senses have lost their capabilities (as I write these difficult words), and I no longer smell or taste anything. I long for just smelling even a putrid malodorous waste dump or even a vile stench like the release of hydrogen sulfide gas. But those formerly terrible, unpleasant, distinguishing sense discriminations are indeed now alien to my new obscure existence and are but distant memories.

My confounded intelligence believes that I am confined and trapped inside a specially designated post-life private museum that is decorated with tarnished mirrors and paintings that continually remind me of specific negative events from my human past. My honesty must now confess and attest that I never require rest or sleep but instead, my pallid two-dimensional form incessantly wanders through designated passageways, halls and corridors that exhibit various murals depicting people, places and things from my former earthly existence. I speculate that this repeated patrolling activity I endure represents a Purgatory of sorts, a specially designed holding area for me to explore until my nagging grief finally eliminates all of the blemishes from my imperfect immortal soul. At least *that* is a theory that my troubled mind entertains.

After meandering around without the benefit of any watch, clock or timepiece to measure seconds, minutes or hours, eventually I always arrive at a bed (in fact a replica of my own past bedroom's king-size bed) at the end of a now-familiar dreary corridor. Then I enter under the covers and observe that my hands, arms and feet are still two-dimensional as if they are appearing on a television or movie screen. I no longer breathe, taste, swallow or have ordinary mortal physical stimulation. I have no knowledge of how long I sleep, for there are no windows to allow the warmth of sunlight or the eeriness of moonlight to penetrate into my irritating environment of captivity. This redundant ritual has my mind both frustrated and extremely bored.

Then invariably, I proceed to close my eyes, and without recollecting any particular dreams or haunting nightmares, I later pretend to wake-up, rise from the bed and next enter a bathroom that was not there before I had involuntarily entered the bedchamber. The sink and toilet do not work and I have no need for their unnecessary functions.

A vexing dull light not generated from any detectable source is present everywhere in this inexplicable place that my awareness currently occupies. I have counted nine hundred bed slumbers so I presume that I have been dead for approximately a three-year duration. This mathematical conjecture of mine might be erroneous, but it is based on earthly realities that no longer affect my current bizarre state of inexplicable suspended animation.

After entering the bathroom that is a facsimile to the one adjacent to my former home's master bedroom, I habitually look into the mirror but observe no image of facial features. The medicine cabinet's side panels do not open and also the vanity drawers below the sink appear to be facades that have no viable access or purpose. The faucet in the marble basin is inoperable and seems to be there simply for design. Invariably, the bathroom door slams shut and locks, and then I must exit the enclosure via a side door that directly leads to an upstairs corridor reminiscent of the one that had existed in my former two-story Hammonton, New Jersey colonial house.

As I amble forward, soon the familiar hallway fades and blends into a maze of corridors that eventually form a weird labyrinth with an uneven stone floor, the dingy passage leading to sixteen separate chambers, each of which I hypothesize corresponds to an hour of time (not including the eight hours I believe I spend in bed).

Upon searching through the sixteenth chamber on every journey through the perplexing maze, I finally re-discover my bed and then feel predisposed to slumber, even though my body (or lack thereof) has no apparent fatigue. This strange process is repeated daily (or what I imagine *is* daily) without evidence of any definitive purposeful rhyme or reason. The tedious repetition is naturally interpreted by myself' as a preordained requirement that I must obey. At least that is how my psyche processes it all. But my fragile mind feels inadequate without its attendant libido and its instinctive need to survive. Since I believe I am already dead, I have nothing to fear except my undefined eternal fate.

A dull artificial light is weakly emitted from various sconces attached at what I estimate are fifty-foot-intervals in the sidewalls of each of the sixteen sinister winding corridors. The now-familiar wall paintings I am able to distinguish depict people from my non-illustrious past, my grandparents, my parents, my relatives, my friends, my wife, my three children and my former acquaintances. But upon closer scrutiny, the portrayed figures simply look-like or are similar to those people I once knew, loved and even despised, and the color portraits are not identical likenesses of the aforementioned individuals.

But the sixteenth monotonous curving hallway (that always intimately leads to my secluded bed) is quite different than its counterparts. It contains paintings pertaining to me and me alone. Each work of art exhibited indicates an exact duplication of myself and is not a mere representation as is the case with the other individuals appearing in the other-fifteen-corridor presentations. I sorrow every time I analyze every portrait of me in the sixteenth gallery, since in each one, I am graphically depicted performing some sinful, improper, unethical or insincere act.

One deplorable canvas portrays my gorgeous secretary and me flirting at a bar after work, and I have found *that* memory to be particularly irritating and distressing so I grieve each time I encounter and inadvertently glance upon it. And my former greediness along with my notorious materialistic nature are also accurately chronicled in numerous drab oil renditions. This final monotonous serpentine-shaped chamber I repeatedly progress through (before retiring to an unneeded sleep) is the reason why I theorize that I am now a hostage to some sort of posthumous soul-purification detention. The sixteenth chamber I have appropriately labeled "The Atonement/Redemption Terminal."

* * * * * * * * * * * *

I later noticed one rather peculiar aspect associated with "The Atonement/Redemption Terminal," and that singular feature is a certain incredible mirror hanging on the right-side wall. In its center is a three-dimensional pen amazingly floating around a *3-D* diary that is remarkably suspended in space inside the fantastic 'looking glass.' Yesterday (or what I think was yesterday) I had performed an interesting experiment. My right hand carefully reached inside the mirror and was able to adroitly grab and remove the pen and accompanying journal, and much to my great satisfaction, I was then able to jot-down (with my two-dimensional left hand) some random impressions and observations into the leather-bound book.

After completing my assiduous penmanship enterprise, I meticulously returned the pen and diary inside the "magical mirror" where the two objects again appeared defying gravity by independently "floating in space," and upon journeying through the now-familiar corridor the next cycle around, I was exuberant upon observing that my previous day's notes had not been erased from the readily-available record book. I now have comprehensively documented an autobiographical chronicle of my daily routine employing usage of the utilitarian pen and diary.

My sense of reason has also noticed one strange recurring manifestation. Sometimes when I gaze into a hall mirror (in this haunted hell that I am helplessly incarcerated in), I see my deceased wife's face in the background, and when I turn my head for a better examination of the wall painting behind me, I have bizarrely discovered that only the back of her body is visible as if she had turned in the opposite direction upon my perceptive detection of her presence. This astonishing oddity of motion has been observed perhaps several hundred times, but the shadowy image of my wife does provide me with a degree of solace and security.

Being alone inside this perpetual desolation is indeed very disconcerting and quite frustrating, and I wish so much to be able to share and commiserate my pathetic existence with my former spouse. Having to be alone without the company of someone else is both stressful and accursed. And some weird instinct tells me that Joanne too is lonely, despondent and depressed and that she sincerely seeks my

232

company, yet she does not know how to break through the spell or barrier that marginally separates our overlapping afterlife paths as they are presently discerned in the wall mirrors and corresponding paintings that reflect her rather nebulous image.

'Rene Descartes is renowned for stating, 'I think; therefore, I am!' I often recollect and consider. 'But I presently do believe that 'I feel, hurt and sorrow, therefore I am!' I reckoned and qualified as I jot these ineffective words down in my black journal. 'My emotional and painful penance is adequate proof of my post-mortal existence,' I aptly concluded. 'Yes, pain truly is verification of reality!'

I believe that my wife is also concurrently haplessly wandering and roaming around in her own maze of corridors and that occasionally, our separate journeys coincide and temporarily share common space and eternal time, while we're briefly being united by ominous wall mirrors and accompanying obscure hanging paintings. If my creative analysis is truly the case, then Joanne and I are doomed to an apathetic world of surreal shadows and bleak shapes that all resemble grotesque hallucinations.

I insist that my mind's eye sees her inside my paintings and mirrors, and I strongly suspect that she also sees my mirage inside hers for fleeting moments where our mirrors are mounted back-to-back, but we only see the posteriors of each other's body upon turning around from the mirrors to the adjacent wall's dimly lit paintings. At least this queer theory seems somewhat plausible at the moment as I doggedly analyze my conception of this most twisted macabre Hell (or Purgatory).

But as I anxiously scribble-down these weak words (I don't know why I am rushing, for I sense I have all the time I need in this dim dismal world), I do believe that my wife's restless soul and her gray two-dimensional figure have evasively trekked into another passageway, and Joanne has again abandoned the area that our restive spirits had momentarily mutually occupied. I now suppose that my former spouse is industriously searching for me in one of her paintings, but why we suddenly depart without feasible reason is an enigma that presently eludes accepted logic and certainly defies ordinary explanation.

But truly, I must persevere to solve the mystery of this very daunting riddle that is rapidly eroding my flaccid confidence and is slowly gnawing-away at my feeble sense of purpose. But why Joanne and I pass like ships in the night and then disappear back into our dual repugnant realities remains (in my troubled mind) a challenging unanswered riddle.

Just a brief time-span (or interval) ago, something rather bizarre happened to supplement my erratic comprehension of this gloomy boring (now-almost-nondescript) environment. While peering into a dull mirror in the thirteenth corridor, I detected my wife standing next to me in a common painting that features a Spanish pueblo. I decided that I would not turn around because I desired staring at my wife's distant dull reflection in the mirror, oddly hanging before my mind's eye and not disappearing.

Joanne enthusiastically beckoned and vigorously waved to me, and simultaneously I did likewise to her, and so I determined that we could communicate indirectly by signaling and by utilizing pantomime. I attempted yelling and calling and noticed Joanne duplicating my futile endeavors, but our joint efforts were to no avail with neither of us having voices to express ourselves. Although joyed at seeing my wife, conversely, my fragile soul soon became saturated with disappointment and melancholy.

And next a rather fascinating thing occurred. As I stared into the enchanted mirror, I fathomed that Joanne was no longer standing beside me in the Spanish pueblo painting behind me, but instead, was then represented posing between two Japanese dancers that I immediately recognized as the ones displayed in an imported master bedroom wall painting that we had purchased on a *Y2K* vacation to Tokyo. And when I abruptly turned-around to confirm my unique sighting, I instantly perceived that my wife's back was then facing me in the Oriental painting while she no longer was standing beside me in the picture.

'Those two wall paintings are from *our* former bedroom,' I nostalgically remembered. 'I wonder if I appear in the same pair of wall ornaments in Joanne's corridor as she has physically been exhibited in mine. If only we could effectively reunite,' I regretted, 'then we could rely on each other for mental security and for emotional support in this mind-boggling dual condemnation. Being absolutely alone is without argument a very devastating and anguishing experience. I now feel abundantly remorseful for all of my past transgressors and genuinely pray that I will someday escape my repulsive abhorrent ongoing museum dilemma.'

I tried identifying certain predictable patterns and similar circumstances but was unsuccessful in my desperate deliberations. No rational connection existed between the sixteen puzzling corridors and the mirrors and paintings associated with each one. Sometimes the Pueblo painting was hung in passageway three and other times it was displayed in corridors seven or fourteen. The Japanese female dancers were sometimes evident next to the Spanish village, but most of the

234

time, the presentations were alongside other representations or hanging on remote walls all by themselves.

Reality and art borrowed from my past had somehow merged into a new artistic dimension that imaginatively blended specific settings and visitations with certain identifiable people, and there was no satisfactory rationale to account for the diverse phenomena to which I am exposed, other than the basic central fact that both Joanne and I were (and are) now dead.

I really miss physical sensations and now am cognizant of how I had neglected appreciating them when I had been alive. Even breathing was quite wonderful, and I now feel guilty not previously immensely enjoying each and every rhythmical respiration. The only feelings that my mind now interpret are gloomy ones that accentuate and reflect fear, boredom, penitence, anxiety, pessimism, cynicism and general negativity. This heavy grief that my intellect carries around is a terrible psychological burden that significantly hinders my former Jeffersonian concept of the "pursuit of happiness."

And I even miss my own nakedness. A gray tunic is what I wear (against my will) and I am rather perturbed at my two-dimensional garb every time I view my eerie apparel in a shadowy mirror. And even the fires in the wall sconces emit a peculiar light devoid of warmth and radiance. 'If only I could have the sensation of burning my hand with a match or even momentarily incinerating my entire body,' I often imagine. 'But unfortunately, I surmise that my human form could only die once. Apparently, all suffering in this new hellish-like uncanny dimension apparently must be emotional and not physical.'

One salient thing is quite certain: this is not a perverted illusion or hallucination that I am unfortunately experiencing. My facial image seen countless times in the myriad dusty mirrors is ashen and pallid. My heart yearns for vibrancy, youth, motivation, commitment and achievement. I only wish that Satan or his wicked henchmen would show-up and relentlessly harass me, but my shallow whim goes without fulfillment, for even *that* tantalizing stretch of imagination has up-to-now evaded my dreadful predicament.

And my only direction to amble is forward as if I am a mechanical robot obeying an electronic command, for several times I have initiated moving in the opposite direction, but my flimsy legs failed to honor my mind's intention. That salient fact verifies my assumption that I have partially surrendered my free will and that my volition can exercise only a very limited capacity to exercise voluntary thought. I don't seem to have the ability to act against the powerful invisible will that envelops my weakened spirit.

But past human affiliations haunt my every restless-yet-repetitious step, and I fully understand that I must incessantly walk the sixteen corridors of solitary confinement until my undeclared punishment terminates, whenever *that* obscure occurrence should eventually materialize.

And poor Joanne must be locked into a similar aggravating perpetual sentence, a sentence that has never been officially announced by any positive or negative Divine Authority. 'I must somehow use the floating pen and stationary diary to connect with my wife and miraculously break through these perverted barriers that have divided our mutual fates,' I often wish and reason.

And a rash of memories persistently surface that grossly annoy and dramatically strafe my' mental stability, and those recollections cause me to contemplate the foolish enterprise of suicide while I fully ascertain that such an activity constitutes folly in that I am indubitably already dead. Minutes, hours, weeks, months, years and decades are now not only transparent concepts *here*, but also mere abstractions that have lost their import and relevance.

'If only a Minotaur or Chimera would appear and eliminate me in a wild violent frenzy,' my mind fancies and my' hand writes. Nothingness would actually constitute progress and would be a much-desired movement away from this terrible cruel mental suffering. 'If only I could erase the past and reclaim my lost innocence I endure,' I frequently conjecture. 'Then I could focus on achieving what the Almighty believes is my original purpose in life. But there must be some constructive solution to my miserable wretched repetitious lamentations. Am I atoning for my sins in some sort of cyclic moral purging? How can I better decipher what's really happening to me? Am I being recycled like common trash?'

One thought undeniably dominates my addled thinking. 'I'm glad that I haven't earned the permanency of Hell,' I often imagine with great relief. 'Even though time seems to have no standard value or real measurement in this dusky, musky unenviable Purgatory I've mysteriously entered, I do gain some consolation in acknowledging that I may still merit eternal salvation after the Last Judgment finally commences. But when and where that grand adventure will begin, I have no inkling, whatsoever. Until then, I must remain vigilant, observant and receptive. Ignorance and sullenness might just lead to a drastic *rank demotion* in this dreadful afterlife,' I occasionally worry. 'What the hell is going on here?' I often wonder and regret.

Another incoherent realization bothers me. Joanne and I had sold our colonial home a year before her death, yet many of the mirrors and paintings I scrutinize in the sixteen corridors are reproductions of the ones that had adorned various walls of *our* former house. But occasionally some vestiges of objects in our smaller condominium (*our* most recent residence) are evident in random mirrors and paintings that mystically alternate and rearrange their befuddling reflections each time I make a scheduled circuit of the sixteen formerly extraordinary galleries.

I sometimes wonder if I am an insane mental patient haphazardly staggering about a distorted asylum or whether I have rejected all semblances of mental health with this absurd and reprehensible recurring grandiose delusion I encounter over and over again.

'Perhaps I am being tested,' I distrustfully evaluated and recorded in my black leather journal. 'Maybe my conscience is being assessed to discover its many weaknesses. Nevertheless, I must practice fortitude and prove my worth despite an absence of logic to account for my unfortunate dire circumstances evident throughout this grotesque Hades. I sincerely hope that this wonderful pen never runs out of ink and that the black diary keeps adding more blank pages!'

My still-curious mind has made another strange observation. Sometimes my oldest son's countenance is visible at different times in several separate mirrors. Since I presume Joseph now lives in my former condominium (he had been willed it in my estate's distribution), maybe I can accidentally connect with him because Joe is still living in my former residence where I had passed away. Since Joanne is also deceased, I therefore suppose that I cannot directly communicate with my better half because of *our* recently acquired dual Purgatory statuses. 'I'll try communicating with Joseph at the first opportunity,' I have recorded in my reliable black journal. 'I must not procrastinate in doing that!'

And how I crave performing simple commonplace functions such as eating, drinking, sweating, hearing, smelling, sneezing, scratching and even urinating. If only I could live another day I would cherish each and every second and each and every blink of my eyes. And oh how I fondly recall the rapturous splendor of glorious radiant sunshine, of majestic cloudless blue skies and of cheerful chirping birds flying overhead! Even placid moonlight would be a welcomed departure from my very despicable lackluster grueling fate.

An odd aspect of my imagination persistently disrupts my mental continuity. 'If this non-spirited spiritual odyssey were a capitalistic business, it would be a rather expensive boondoggle leading to absolute bankruptcy since these lengthy sixteen corridors would have cost a fortune to construct and maintain, and if most every dead soul suspended in its own limbo state has to have one of these costly 'white elephant labyrinths,' then the afterlife must be practically bankrupt and consequently running out of actual 'death space' and building materials.' But I always immediately dismiss *that* annoying vexation from my mind because I fear that my unsavory situation might become worse or perhaps extended, both by my selfish skepticism and by my very obvious ornery insolence, which in my mediocre cynical past had been weighty encumbrances that my dispassionate heart dragged around like a very heavy anchor.

And much of my deviant maverick character is prolifically revealed in each different tableau represented in the sixteen galleries of egregiously haunting paintings and mirrors. 'This continuous purification process is rather thorough and tedious,' I recently had written in the black leather diary, which along with the suspended pen seem to be the only items in this perplexing nightmare that have any accompanying *3-D* permanency.

'Every committed mortal and venial sin, every indiscretion, every discourtesy and every aberrant behavior of my former life is being systematically resurrected for my guilty awareness to seriously ponder, and I am hoping for some remarkable catharsis to suddenly transpire in order for me to somehow magically escape and finally exit this most aggravating vexation.'

Recently, only the more major violations from my past have been featured in the horrendous sixteenth corridor. This recorded fact hopefully suggests that perhaps my moral reprimand is about to be alleviated or possibly even expire. A rewarding ascension into a more favorable surrounding would be most propitious and indeed, genuinely welcomed. My naïve reverie conjures-up a blinking neon sign with an arrow stating: 'St. Peter and the Pearly Gates A Half Mile Ahead.' I fully recognize that I must gradually merit my independence from this confusing captivity and then somehow joyfully reunite with Joanne in a more desirable, more highly illuminated and more spiritually comforting place.

I cannot accurately calibrate or even estimate the exact duration of my 'solitary confinement' because I dare not document the necessary arithmetic in my black leather diary out of fear of accidentally precipitating potential malignant repercussions. And subsequently, my vexed mind apprehensively cancels-out *that* skeptical mathematical negativism every time the notion surfaces, this being done in order to avoid prolonging my exceptional 'hostage situation.'

And so I obediently trudge along the meandering hallways without expressing (here thinking) complaint, grievance or objection, intensely believing all the while that my disciplined compliance will ultimately result in some wonderful benign achievement. 'I must mot become complaisant with or defiant of my dreadful situation!' I continually remind myself.

My still-active mind often wonders if my 'personal Purgatory' is geographically located below the Earth's surface or whether I inhabit another realm somewhere else in the extensive galaxy. But then I habitually rationalize that my wife's abominable entrapment seems to have paralleled mine in her meandering about inside the adjoining parallel corridors, and I have determined that Joanne has at least as many or even more sins blemishing her soul in that I assume she has been cruelly interned in her coincidental limbo five years longer than I have been imprisoned in mine.

My sense of truthfulness should indicate that there is nothing morbid or morose about my present tenure in this overwhelming recurrent destiny. On the contrary, once I had adjusted to the continuous dark shadows and to the familiarly structured eight-foot-wide lurid labyrinths, my sole nemesis has been unrelenting boredom. And the aforementioned pen and diary are my only true symbols of sanity, my tools to interpret my confusing surroundings and my only real hope to successfully acclimate to this bizarre world's plenteous mysteries.

Fear no longer dwells in my heart, and general apathy is presently governing my lazy thought processes. And suicide (as I have alluded) is inconceivable since I profess that I am already dead even though I can't ever remember expiring. I have determined that I must've passed on in my deep sleep, and I can only fantasize that I possess the necessary wherewithal to lethargically endure this most lackluster penance predicament.

Redundancy is the essential theme of this detestable realm. Now I truly value the variety I had once ignored as a living mortal. The only new stimuli that I witness are the ever-changing impressions apparent in the ebony-framed wall paintings and the assortment of mirrors that monotonously bounce the dull artificial light being somehow generated from the macabre-looking wall sconces, which incidentally contain no oil or kerosene. My heart prays that Joanne has also adapted to her complementary maze and that she has valiantly conquered her apprehensions, for my wife had always been frightened of darkness and was indeed throughout our marriage a very light sleeper.

And thank goodness my faithful pen does not run-out of marvelous fluid. It seems to be supernaturally supplied with an endless quantity of black ink stored within its diminutive size. The thick diary has many pages and I dare not begin numerically labeling them, as I've already alluded, out of fear of additional persecution or some arbitrary retaliatory extension of my current penalty being invoked. Yet, my explicit descriptions have been accurate and my narrative comprehensively and concisely written.

I trust that Joanne is busy compiling comparable observations within *her* facsimile journal, presuming that she too has been graciously provided one along with an indispensable pen. 'If only our eternal paths could cross,' I constantly write. 'That spectacular event would make my heart abound with pure ecstasy. Until then I must remain steadfast in my quest to unravel the essence of this distorted-yet-monotonous actuality.'

'Ah, there's my bed again, all made with fresh clean sheets even though I had left it disheveled upon my last departure,' I considered after evacuating the drudgery of the now-routine sixteenth corridor. 'I shall feign sleep despite the fact that my body needs no particular replenishing or repair. This two-dimensional incarceration is far less demanding and requires little or no energy to sustain or need when I perform my daily corridors' trek. Perhaps tomorrow will bring much-needed information to enable me to unscramble this obnoxious inevitability to which I've been assigned without a fair trial or hearing. Until then, I must aspire to figure-out this drab place's particulars and bring cerebral illumination to explain these diabolical and non-inspiring doldrums to which I am confined. I must unravel this complex riddle!'

* * * * * * * * * * *

After my arrival into (and subsequent general acceptance of) this ugly Purgatory, I automatically assessed that this ungodly place was like a colossal-sized deck of cards being reshuffled over and over again with every successive exploration, and I imagined that thousands of sundry mirrors and paintings were being randomly repositioned and then shrewdly changed on each sixteen-corridor rotation, all performed simply to harass my judgment and to erode my confidence. All along my seemingly irreversible journey, my spirit has felt alienated while being a prisoner inside this grotesquely gnarled afterlife, but during one particular expedition inside the seventh corridor my steady advancement confronted what must be certainly described as an enlightening and defining moment. The revolutionary breakthrough occurred when I was momentarily shocked at witnessing a lurid-looking specter sitting erect and stationary in a never-before-observed porch wicker chair. The sullen-faced apparition appeared phlegmatically waiting to greet me.

The two-dimensional grim-faced creature (manifestation?) had a pair of wings attached to its back and upon fathoming that it was a cheerless woebegone angel, I immediately wondered how I should initiate a conversation without possessing any voice. The perturbed messenger instinctively understood my dilemma and my intentions and casually-but-skillfully proceeded to utilize an uncanny form of mental telepathy. Soon my great awe converted into natural curiosity, and I was absolutely intrigued about my new 'guest' and shortly thereafter, a rather ethereal exchange of ideas ensued.

'Hello Dennis Collier,' the dignified-but-peevish courier began in a rather formal mental salutation. 'Please do not be alarmed by my gruesome presence. My celestial name is Simon and I'm your designated temporary guardian angel. I'm officially here to provide you with some relevant guidance and reassurance.'

Naturally, I was still a degree dumbfounded, and then awkwardly attempted regaining my composure and next engaging in civilized mental communication. But my mind was so out-of-kilter and so much in disarray that I had difficulty organizing my thought patterns and then gearing them to intelligently express my abundant concerns. Still Simon patiently waited for me to conquer my very evident apprehensions and finally I was able to offer a basic inquiry.

I started my investigation by using an interrogative sentence. 'Is this some sort of Purgatory I'm trapped in?' I mentally related. 'Am I being held here until my immortal soul is eventually purified?'

'What you suspect Dennis Collier is actually true,' Simon perfunctorily declared through a very perceptible strong brainwave transmission. 'Why don't you ask what you don't know rather than waste your effort on what you probably already have learned? And please Dennis,' my awesome visitor qualified, 'only one question at a time. I don't like souls that are too nervous and too inquisitive!'

I paused to fully harness my cerebral dynamics, which were finally beginning to settle-down into a more relaxed comfort zone. 'How could this place exist with the world's population somewhere in the neighborhood of six billion people? I mean,' I moronically mentally qualified and explained, 'several million people must probably die every year in the United States alone, and it seems rather impractical to maintain millions upon millions of sixteen corridor labyrinths in this rather deformed afterlife for each and every one of them,' I diplomatically mentally conveyed and argued.

'You've always been fascinated by irrelevant trivia,' Simon quite effectively reprimanded. 'But to address your very minute point Dennis, it stands to reason that only Christians have guardian angels, and only a small percentage of devout Christians must be assigned a fate similar to yours, Mr. Collier. Now *that* impeccable logic instantly eliminates over nine tenths of the world's deceased, now doesn't it?' the impressive creature mentally transmitted. 'And in fact, most of our guests from the *Medieval Ages* have already advanced out of here so for all practical purposes, we then reuse our networked labyrinths to accommodate our influx of incoming occupants. I mean to communicate that since Hell is overcrowded with resident souls, this place can be easily operated. Does *that* accounting now sound fairly reasonable to you?'

I figured that I should urgently change the subject of discussion rather than risk being administered the wrath of a potentially volatile and unstable supernatural being. 'I must use discretion,' I concluded while finally discerning that Simon was capable of monitoring even my most secret meditations. 'Will I ever be reunited with my wife?' I inquired while showing my heavenly companion a degree of good judgment and good conscience. 'Permit me to rephrase my question Simon. What must I do to make contact with Joanne?'

'You must first complete the diary you have begun and then deliver it to your son Joseph,' Simon deftly beamed to my very focused sense of awareness. 'Then you and your wife will be happily reunited. But first Dennis, it is imperative that you convey your story to your oldest son. You are an author by trade, aren't you?' my austere grim-faced visitor rankled. 'Finishing the journal should be relatively easy for you!'

'Why yes I am!' I hastily admitted without actually exhaling or moving my lips. 'But how can I possibly convey the contents of the diary to my oldest son if he and I occupy entirely different dimensions? I mean, I do see Joseph from time to time in several wall paintings and in the corresponding mirrors, but we cannot exchange words nor can we share the same physical environment,' I strenuously maintained and objected. 'This serious problem projects itself as a nasty conundrum without any plausible method of resolution, at least that's how the issue frames itself in my bewildered and beleaguered mind.'

'What kind of a craven man are you, or should I say *were* you?' Simon indignantly admonished and chided. 'Are you so lazy and so listless that you want *me* to execute your elementary task for you? I'll be kind enough to leave a special magic marker in the diary mirror along with the permanent floating pen, and then perhaps eventually you'll be able to figure-out how to accomplish your prescribed mission. Your son Joseph will then deliver the diary's essence to your editor, Marilyn Jenkins, who will ambitiously publish an original novella outlining your monotonous episode here in the afterlife. Have I made myself clear?'

'After I solve the challenge of physically presenting the diary account to Joseph,' I defensively answered, 'then how will I be able to access Joanne trapped inside another parallel passageway? Please inform me of exactly how to enact *that* rather formidable inconvenience!' I defiantly mentally demanded.

'Dennis Collier, you are the unrivaled curator of your own petty life history museum,' Simon cryptically and firmly stated, 'and you will eventually solve how to correspond with your son and how to effectively meet and converse with your wife. Are you vainly endeavoring to make me become hostile toward you? You seem to be quite petulant and sarcastic for only being a mere mortal's spirit! I can be an extremely fierce adversary, you know! Do you wish to challenge my indomitable force?'

'No Simon, I don't have any wish to incur your anger or suffer your wrath in any way,' I anxiously apologized, for I felt quite inferior to my muscular winged visitor's massive ten-foot-tall physical prowess. 'Honestly, I was merely seeking additional helpful information, that's my entire motive!' I neurotically added. 'Now when will I have the honor of seeing you again?'

'You have too many ridiculous questions stored in your feeble mental repertoire, but since Dennis Collier you're fundamentally a hapless-but-earnest struggling individual,' Simon elucidated with a small hardly discernible snicker on his visage, 'I'll again visit you after you get the diary's text delivered to Joseph. But I must remind you that your first responsibility is to completely finish the journal. You may include my visitation as the culminating event of you final passages if you wish to incorporate this meeting.'

I thanked my laconic riddle-speaking guardian angel for his solicited non-genial cooperation. Then I decided to end our brief conference with another friendly question. 'How do you manage to spend time with all of your clients?' I more cordially inquired. 'How many customers must you service?'

My heavenly guest genuinely smiled for the first time and then mentally articulated, 'You my dear Dennis have a linear perception of the afterlife and should not judge it by exercising your finite mundane mortal understandings about the true magnitude of this paradoxical world. Earthly time is meaningless here in ubiquitous eternity,' the fearsome angel stubbornly postulated, 'and I can budget my patrons according to a very flexible scheduling arrangement by bouncing around in a multilayer abstract time-zone existence, a paradigm which supersedes and transcends your narrow, limited perspective of the *Universe*. Now if you'll forgive me Dennis Collier,' Simon requested in an agitated tone of voice, 'I must be off to perform another more drastic and urgent duty.'

And upon uttering those prophetic words, the flat, gray, giant apparition vanished into oblivion as I stood there transfixed, admiring his great fading excellence blending into the solid granite corridor wall. And so I dedicated my flawed mind to locating the described magic marker, but my first obligation was to continue authoring the contents of the black journal using the extraordinary services of the floating ballpoint pen.

I soon found my wondrous writing utensil, accompanying black diary and the new versatile magic marker, all three items inside the familiar sixteenth corridor mirror enclosure. Then I diligently labored authoring my journal as specifically prescribed by Simon, an occupation that I almost religiously enacted one cogent sentence at a time. All the while I exhausted my imagination constructing methodologies as to how to successfully deliver the lengthy journal's text to Joseph. My unsettled mind was in a vast quandary, and I despaired that my debacle was without any accessible answer.

Fortuitously, on one particular occasion, I casually scrutinized a mirror halfway through the third downward slanted gallery and coincidentally observed Joseph closely looking into my former condominium's medicine chest mirror while shaving. Immediately a thought flashed through my intellect, and realizing that the great inventor Leonardo Da Vinci had once employed mirror writing to encrypt his notations, I became inspired to duplicate *his* sage use of disguised communication.

Using my left index finger, I very deliberately and audaciously scribbled the simple message "Hi Joe! This is Dad!" jotted upside-down and backwards on my side of the steamed-up mirror. My son's lather-laden face reflected a terribly stunned expression as Joseph instantaneously stepped back from the mirror with his mouth agape. Then beneath those initial words I put an addendum, "Will write more the next time! Dad!"

Later, I unnecessarily rested on my bed and meditated about how each alphabet letter was to be intelligently configured in the exact art of mirror writing. And upon rising from the hard mattress, I retrieved my black journal along with the utilitarian magic marker and again accosted and surprised Joseph preoccupied in the shaving mirror, which doubled as my contemporary window to the real three-dimensional world I once knew.

Slowly-but-surely, I meticulously jotted-down in mirror writing (with the magic marker) the preface to my diary, which my fascinated son soon copied down word-for-word in a school spiral composition notebook. This disciplined activity ensued for countless days (perhaps years) until the thick diary's unnumbered pages had been totally transferred, and my son had persistently-copied down every detail of my fantastic autobiographical tome. Despite my great intensity and effervescence, I could only transcribe one paragraph per session because of the spatial size restrictions of the allotted mirror-writing surface, which I used to habitually erase the upside-down and backwards paragraph left over from the day before.

Upon persevering and finishing my astounding feat, I proudly signed my name upside-down and backwards, and amazingly Joseph confirmed his reception of my volume of sentences and paragraphs by returning his acknowledgment to me in Da Vinci-style mirror writing, which now appeared to my perception as normal printing on my side of the time-word portal:

This is absolutely incredible Dad! Glad you're not permanently deceased. I'll get this fantastic work to Marilyn Jenkins right away! Thanks a million!

Love always,
Joseph

My spirit instantly felt jubilation and my buoyed soul bathed in tranquility. 'I anticipate I'll soon receive another visit from my austere mentor Simon,' my mind synthesized. 'I have no alternative other than trusting his character and dare not suspect that he's trying to trick or provoke me into accidentally committing myself to an extended stay here in this nonsensical wicked Purgatory. I must however exercise self-discipline and be cautious with Simon because he's my only link to ever being able to evacuate from this horrid inhumane posthumous detention facility,' my adamant value system mentally editorialized. 'I must be very careful with every thought and strive to be virtuous or else my unheralded future reward might be placed in dire jeopardy. I can't afford appearing too arrogant, haughty or hypocritical. I wonder if Simon is actually an omniscient supernatural being? Oh well!' I gleefully pondered. 'Pretty soon I'll be judged and my fate will be more pronounced and better defined than it is right now. Eureka! That's precisely it! *Judgment Day* hasn't happened yet!' my mind and spirit joyfully concluded in simulated exasperation. 'The opportunity for eternal salvation is still at hand!'

During the culmination of my truly insane rumination, Simon's enormous pallid supernatural form again appeared in my midst. Confidently I instigated a rather erudite telepathic conversation with my returning itinerant guest. 'I presume you know that I have satisfactorily communicated the contents of my black journal to my son Joseph,' I mentally stated to my designated protector.

'Yes, and I must admit Dennis Collier, your accomplishment was quite meritorious and noteworthy for a mere novice,' Simon sternly congratulated. 'Your next more difficult project is to reunite with Joanne,' the melancholy winged angel revealed and reminded. 'Many other ambitious candidates have faltered in similar quests and have encountered imminent defeat while pursuing the second more intricate phase of the standard procedure. So Dennis,' Simon didactically lectured, 'don't show excessive emotion until you determine the secret of reuniting with your wife,' the winged specimen austerely warned. 'The Powers That Be don't look kindly upon egotistical preposterous mortal dunces that recklessly engage in unwarranted premature excessive celebration!' the guardian messenger confidentially disclosed. 'So wipe that exaggerated smirk off your ashen face right now and forget all about being presumptuous!' Simon menacingly threatened.

I loyally followed Simon's severe command but was unprepared for the death ambassador's next unorthodox maneuver. As my mind merrily reviewed my wonderful diary-transmission-achievement, the helpful angel instantly transformed from a benign magnificent apparition into a horrid red-skinned demon, just to symbolize his defiance of my tendency for conceit. The frightening hideous beast loudly cackled in mockery of my general impotency and then deftly disappeared into and then through the solid dark granite wall.

My sensibilities were so disheveled and my nerves so frayed that my two-dimensional form staggered around for a moment in a condition that could only be described as complete emotional trauma. My non-beating heart was appalled beyond belief with the blatant treachery I had just witnessed.

'Was Simon a vile fantasy hoax?' I neurotically wondered. 'Was he maliciously insulting my finite intellectual capacity? Will I ever interrogate the awesome angel again? Is he a ruthless devil deviously masquerading as a benevolent angel?'

* * * * * * * * * * * *

During one particular journey through the sixteenth lengthy hallway, I made a rather keen observation. The very useful magic marker and the trustworthy ballpoint pen were no longer displayed alongside the black suspended journal inside the lucky 'Giving Mirror.' I nervously retrieved the black journal and very thoroughly and conscientiously read the entire text in desperation, over and over again as verification and validation of the series of events that the diary so meticulously contained and disclosed.

In my past I had always demonstrated a propensity for having too much pride, and I feared that *that* negative attribute would diminish my chance for eventually evolving out of my 'Museum Curator Punishment.' 'My main objective must be inventing a means of reuniting with Joanne, but such an aspiration seemed beyond my problem-solving-ability-level.

The prudent transmission of the diary's text to Joseph was an elementary assignment compared to my present perplexing undertaking,' I reluctantly assessed. 'Sometimes the most monstrous labor has a rather simplistic answer. I'll just pretend that I'm Simon and harness all of my innate wisdom. Then my latent sense of creativity will eventually crack this stark riddle that's now persistently pestering my sanity.'

My dismal spirit wandered through the sixteen sinister slanted corridors and then I again reclined in the strange-but-familiar remote bed. 'How many carpenters were needed to build this impractical series of idiotic chambers?' I critically and cynically pondered. 'Since it's designed to morally rehabilitate one person at a time, this impractical edifice has to be one outrageously senseless poor investment in time and capital! But financial concerns are merely only important in my old reality and perhaps are significantly non-applicable in this new paradoxical environment,' I pensively and pessimistically reasoned. 'Why hasn't my grumpy counselor Simon returned here to either again tantalize or reward me? Is my guardian angel my helpful mentor or is he actually my' callous tormentor? In short, is my mentor also my tormentor?'

While meandering through the thirteenth corridor on my next circuitous routine occasion, I had a premonition that Joanne would appear on the opposite side of a rectangular mirror situated towards the end of the weirdly contoured dark passageway. My hunch was verified upon seeing her sad face reflected in a side wall mirror, and when I pivoted my ghostly form in her direction, I again noticed that her back was to me in the across-the-hall painting, which had as its background the pine barren forest located directly behind my former Hammonton,

New Jersey condominium. Then my vacillating erratic spirit was instilled with a sudden splendid inspiration.

'My pale shade-like body is two dimensional just like Simon's immense form is,' I lucidly deducted and reasoned. 'Why can't I simply imitate my elusive guardian angel and be absorbed like osmosis right through this supposedly solid black granite wall? The *3-D* physical barriers I have assumed to be dense hard boundaries might only be illusions, yes, only minor trivial mental obstacles, mere semblances from a former world and a former familiar life. I must test this theory before I lose my courage and my desire to act.'

Without any further hesitation, I bravely proceeded to awkwardly step into and then sensationally filter right through the black rock partition while clumsily mimicking what Simon had previously and so adroitly demonstrated. Much to my utter satisfaction, my courageous experiment was a fabulous success, and Joanne was absolutely aghast at visualizing my sudden appearance popping-up inside her formerly secluded dingy chamber.

Instantaneously we embraced, but our frail spirits synthesized and then amazingly meshed, and we simultaneously passed right through each other, since we both lacked (to put it in scientific physics terminology) mass and density.

'Dennis, how did you ever manage to break through the wall?' Joanne mentally inquired in an emotional tone of wave-like vibrations. 'I thought I'd never see your full face up close again.'

'I didn't exactly break through the wall,' I stubbornly mentally corrected. 'I passed through it just like a chemical or hormone entering or exiting a body cell does. I think that anyone isolated in this intriguing holding area Hell, including you Joanne, could easily do the exact same thing I had done. I now believe that the mirrors and wall portraits in this God-forsaken moral prison are like time/space portals to enter and exit other dimensions, along with some of the walls also, like the *illusion* I had just passed through!"

'Do you mean that I believed I had no escape and therefore in my mind I was restricted by these crazy corridors, weird mirrors, artificial rock walls and baffling paintings?' my wife marveled in pure astonishment. 'Is that what you're now suggesting?'

'Joanne, we *are* two-dimensional specters and everything else in this terrible nightmare happens *to appear* three dimensional,' I excitedly clarified. 'That makes it easy for either you or me to transform like magic from one passageway into another. We don't really need any time/space portal to perform *that* mobility. We simply can project our flat forms right into and through our targeted *3-D* illusion zone,' I enthusiastically divulged. 'It's all quite natural in this grotesque environment and there's very little mysticism about it once you develop the audacity and the knack.'

'You appeared just like Lucretius often came and went,' my wife contributed.

'Who is Lucretius?' I jealously countered. 'Was there another male in your life?'

'Oh, I'm so sorry Dennis!' Joanne nervously exclaimed. 'Lucretius is *my* guardian angel who visited me quite regularly. But he never mentioned what you have just claimed about *our* ability to penetrate through solid matter at will, even though supposedly in our minds we had surrendered our free wills upon dying.'

'Yes, our mobility in this oddball museum was being constrained by our understanding of the way three-dimensional space and time had operated in our former world,' my mental transmission spontaneously keenly shared. 'We have no three-dimensional limitations Joanne because all those *3-D* material items existed as physical objects to be avoided in our former Earth reality. Now I think that I somewhat comprehend the science-defying magnitude of it all.'

'It all does seem plausible my jealous handsome husband, now that you've broken it down into simple basic terms,' my wife mentally conceded. 'Yes Dennis, it does seem feasible now!'

'And I'll bet that I never had to complete the black journal to qualify to enter your domain and then eventually return back into a mortal human being!' I mentally stated to my spouse. 'That whole step was probably unnecessary for me to complete. A devious ruse or trick being played on me! A definite canard!'

'What black journal are you referring to?' my bewildered spouse asked through a strong mental signal. 'I can't recall any sort of black journal!'

'I promise I'll tell you all about it later!' I candidly returned. 'It does get a little complicated.'

My wife mentally confided that she wished that we could make amends for all of our past indiscretions and be able to return to our former living mortal selves. A full-length mirror had been situated suspended on a black plastered wall inside Joanne's thirteenth coincidental corridor that incidentally had before bordered mine. A sudden refreshing and imparting divine knowledge entered my being, a most definite cosmic-like inspiration. I then telepathically communicated my latest brainstorm to my still-in-awe spouse.

'The painting reflected behind us in this full-length mirror shows a young man and woman holding hands while strolling through a pine tree woods,' I thought and transmitted. 'Joanne, we'll rush and leap into the mirror together and if my wild theory is correct, we'll both wind-up back in our world where we can alter our behaviors and live good decent loving lives with enviable reputations for being both generous and charitable. This is a chance for us to redeem our besmirched characters and eradicate the deep embedded stains and blemishes from our immortal souls.'

My wife and I joined hands and then energetically dashed and jumped into the time portal and we immediately converted into standard three-dimensional human beings. We next mutually tripped over a fallen timber and clumsily fell to the ground, finally laughing and rolling around in prickly pine-cones.

"I can feel your warm hand!" Joanne shouted in a very discernible happy human female voice. "We're real people again living on the Earth, living back here in our New Jersey condominium situated right next to the pine-barrens forest! Yes Dennis, we're real flesh and blood mortals again!"

"And you're beautiful and you're flesh and blood alive again, looking almost just like the day I first saw you passing-by in the high school's main lobby!" my voice yelled. "Our fondest dreams have come true Joanne! Maybe we can relive our first date. Do you remember?"

"Yes!" my wife giddily recollected and exclaimed. "We went to a matinee movie on Market Street in Philadelphia and then we walked through..."

"The Philadelphia Museum of Art!" I eagerly finished her declarative sentence. "Now that we're three-dimensional mortals again Joanne, we have a terrific chance to change everything negative in our lives. And believe me Hon," I sincerely emphasized, "trust me when I solemnly say that a museum is definitely the last place I ever want to visit again."

"And I remember you once joking on an early date that you wanted to pursue being a curator after you graduated from college!" my wife appropriately laughed. "How absurdly ironic it all seems! You', a museum curator!"

"The Alien Minority"

While growing-up, I had originally believed that my character had been formed by a combination of three powerful influences: the Ten Commandments along with the Golden Rule, Greek thinking, which translates roughly into "Be all that you can be; challenge the status quo; strive for perfection and excellence," and thirdly Jeffersonian Democratic thinking, outlined and defined in the Bill of Rights of the United States Constitution. In my impressionable teen years I was aware of my need to be respected as an individual and to always reciprocate courtesy, but I also realized that I was vastly different than most other people in my immediate environment.

When I became cognizant that there was a distinct difference between "my character" and my "personality" my mind recognized that my genetics compelled me to instinctively gravitate toward and gradually embrace the three already cited aspects (or concepts) that coincidentally developed my character. After analyzing my basic uniqueness my heart and mind afforded me insights into identifying the traits of my personality that were reflected in my behavior, and around the age of 21 my psyche finally comprehended that I was a dye-in-the-wool alien, a human with humanoid thoughts and values, which incidentally incorporated Moses, Socrates, Plato and Thomas Jefferson's contributions to civilization and to history.

Aliens inhabiting Earth tend to naturally gravitate towards the "helping professions." If we aren't teachers, scientists or nurses then we're bound to be firefighters, policemen or doctors. Earth Aliens are builders and not destroyers; our culture is pure-hearted and not diabolical and we're also honest citizens without being criminals involved in illegal activities. Aliens believe that there's a "touch of the Divine" that acts as a moral compass and helps govern our consciences. I suppose that this "out-of-this-world alien business" requires some fundamental logical explanation so here it is.

Aliens on Earth have been biologically programmed to appear during troublesome periods of world history. Our genes and chromosomes have been designed by our visiting space ancestors to be released at various timed-intervals that make our appearances on this planet inconspicuous to common ordinary earthlings. The whole genetically sophisticated process had been deliberately formulated to purify the Earth's population along with the weak minds of its Non-Alien dwellers. Now I'll provide the characteristics that are emblematic of genetically engineered "Earth Aliens."

Earth Aliens have narrowly escaped death on more than one occasion and these "close encounters" are necessary "Wake-up calls" that allow us to fathom the "Urgency of our mission." These near-death-events validate us to ourselves and allow us to eventually identify others of our species. When I was five months old in February of 1943, I required a tonsillectomy, which at the time happened to be an extremely dangerous and life-threatening surgical procedure during the WWII era. My chance of surviving the operation was only thirty percent, but if I hadn't undergone the surgery in Baltimore then I most certainly would have died in infancy. Remarkably I pulled through and came out of it against very formidable odds. Later in life I understood that I was quite different than the seventy percent of the United States citizens that would have died from infection or perhaps from the risky operation.

The Catholic Church has sacraments that are practiced so that the congregation members could unify and ultimately strengthen parishioners' faith. Around the age of puberty Confirmation is given to teenage boys and girls to "awaken them" to the importance of leading exemplary lives so that they could earn eternal happiness as a just reward. Biologically programmed Earth Aliens (as teenagers) usually "awaken" and confront death and manage to escape their ordeals, thus making them aware that they are different than "the congregational flock adolescents" that the Bishop and the Pastor (remember, the designation "Pastor" means "shepherd") must initiate into either manhood or womanhood. Yes, regular earthlings need to be constantly preached to, disciplined and reminded of their religious duties and civic responsibilities (both to themselves and to their fellow man). Conversely Earth Aliens soon realize (after their traumatic near-death experiences) that they don't need Popes, Cardinals, Archbishops, Bishops, Monsignors and Priests to show them the path of moral wisdom. We automatically are knowledgeable of the righteous path of wisdom and of honor not only in thought but also in deed, and we instinctively practice the preacher's important precepts without having to be constantly reminded of our temporal existence on this sometimes, diabolical planet.

When I was fourteen years of age, I had narrowly escaped drowning. It was January of '56 in Levittown, Pennsylvania. A friend and I were ice skating on the Delaware Canal with him pretending to be the goalie and with me hitting a hockey puck (with an improvised stick) at a makeshift goal we had constructed out of lumber scraps and a very old fishing net. Suddenly I fell through the ice into eight-foot-deep-water. Before I perceived exactly what had happened, I was under the surface and all that I could recall at the time was seeing everything peaceful and tranquil, with me seemingly suspended in emerald green water. I must have been suffering hypothermia and shock because the underwater canal reeds and algae all seemed enchanting when my ice skates finally had made contact with the canal's bottom. Fortunately, I surfaced directly into the hole into which I had plunged. My goalie friend was lying flat on the cracking ice and he vigorously tugged my half-frozen body out of my "near-death" dilemma. That near-tragedy represented my young teen supplement to the Sacrament of Confirmation. It was my personal "wake-up call" that I had to explore my "assigned mission in life."

Fate and coincidence ordinarily and amazingly schedule other reminders of his or her "role obligation" in an Earth Alien's participation in history-in-the-making. These significant events reinforce the esoteric principle of "Who we really are!" In 1970 I was parked at a gas station pump getting my tank filled when an inattentive driver rapidly backed his car out of a garage bay without even looking into his rear-view mirror. A terrible collision resulted and it was a miracle that neither his nor my automobile had caught fire. Another time in 1990 I had fallen asleep late one night while driving east on the Atlantic City Expressway. A fly landed on my nose and I instantly awoke just in time to turn my steering wheel and swerve back into the right-hand-lane and out of the path of a car I had nearly sideswiped. To this day I believe that the fly that saved my life was "no accident."

I've had three other "near-death" experiences that I consider signals from "the Universe" instructing me not to deviate from the "building of character" teachings of Moses, Socrates and Thomas Jefferson. One such incident had me rolling off my parents' house's roof (while installing a TV aerial) and then having my back safely landing in a soft evergreen bush rather than smashing into the hard ground. That "destined situation" was a radical wake-up call for me to get my life together and to get my mind on task and focused in order to accomplish certain constructive goals. If I had horizontally plunged from the roof to the ground I might right-this-minute be either dead or paralyzed.

Earth Aliens have active protectors that many Catholic priests and Protestant ministers believe and preach are "guardian angels." These anonymous protectors assist us Earth Aliens through arduous times, through family members' deaths, through devastating natural catastrophes, and the moral benefactors insulate us from horrors like drowning and auto' accidents. By salvaging us from almost certain doom these guardian angels are reviewing for our benefit that our general purpose for inhabiting the Earth is to advance the human condition by advocating peace, harmony, justice, truth, beauty and good spirit. Earth Aliens are not particularly religious but we are indeed specifically beings possessing abundant "Alien inspired spirituality."

I estimate that Earth Aliens constitute a mere three percent of the world's population. Certainly, and arguably all of our great scientists, philosophers, teachers, authors, leaders and inventors have been inspired by the need they felt to "stay the course" regardless of opposition generated by less cerebral Non-Alien Earthlings. We special Earth Aliens tend to have high IQs, and our breed features such notable people as Albert Einstein, Thomas Edison, Marie Curie, George Washington, Abraham Lincoln, Plato, Aristotle, Miguel Cervantes and William Shakespeare. Earth Aliens show-up (and make their presence known on this planet) usually during times of crisis where action, leadership, moral clarity and sage discretion must be exercised to neutralize public indecision and/or confusion.

It is good that only a three-percent minority of the Earth's population are Earth Aliens. If all of this planet's inhabitants were of superior intelligence and of a creative nature everyone would be attempting to out-create and out-invent the other and such reckless competition would surely lead to inevitable conflict among tenacious rivals. Oftentimes when a great Earth Alien emerges, his or her ideas are rejected by the mediocre masses. Some EAs like Galileo might have to face adversity in the form of an Inquisition and others like Socrates might be put to death for "corrupting the minds of others." It usually takes the more belligerent and barbarian Earthlings a hundred years to decipher and learn that threatening, persecuting and executing EAs' represents the ultimate in human ignorance.

Most EAs don't like the limelight and actually shun and despise it. Only out of necessity will one become a President or a great General to verify and implement the axiom, "Crisis determines the great man!" And for the most part Earth Aliens indubitably are unselfish helpers thoroughly dedicated to constructively expanding and exploring the perimeters and parameters of culture. EAs practice a brand of "Reverse Transcendentalism" where (as opposed to false Emersonian philosophy) reason triumphantly supersedes and trumps emotion. Non-Aliens tend to be biologically oriented nondescript hedonistic humans that are principally governed and driven by primitive selfish feelings.

Generally speaking, Earth Aliens are not affectionate. We don't like perpetually hugging and kissing one another or our spouses or relatives. We instinctively know that we like most people and we have a sixth sense that can detect a potential evil person's sinister motives. EAs don't equate love with affection; we believe that love is a transcendent

254

abstract quality represented in honor, respect, courtesy, kindness, caring, helping, courage, justice, beauty and fairness. For example, Earth Aliens believe that the Commandment "Honor Thy Father and Thy Mother" literally means just that without perpetual phony hugging and sloppy kissing dominating family relationships.

EAs would make terrible political candidates going from town to town insincerely kissing and hugging babies just to selfishly accumulate votes. The erudite members of my species fully understand that any citizen/individual has tremendous difficulty governing himself' or herself without pretending to be capable of governing thousands of people by holding a public office. We diligently attempt to execute our illustrious aforementioned abstract virtues every day of the year so we don't really place a greater value on anniversaries, birthdays, Father's Day, Mother's Day, wedding-dates, Christmas, Thanksgiving, Fourth of July and Easter. To EAs every day is equally as important as any other twenty-four-hour period and our vital missions are essentially needed all twelve months on the calendar.

Here's precisely what showing affection (between Non-Alien humans) does and fosters. It stifles children's growth and spiritual maturity. Affectionate children tend to be raised thinking that they are the center of the Universe and they often evolve into arrogant egotistical brats. Children exposed to too much affection tend to fear competition and are intimidated by free enterprise, the essential tools that (in America and the rest of the Free World) can contribute to amassing wealth and developing moral strength and an ethical character. Affectionate children are too dependent on their doting and compromising parents. You don't teach a child a good example when the parents themselves act like four-year-old children and constantly hug and kiss their over-protected offspring. This is why spoiled children often lack self-discipline and long-term commitment to complete difficult goals and achieve full independence and "the pursuit of happiness" as prescribed by Thomas Jefferson. Affection between parents and children basically stifles the child's initiative to experiment and discover, and the continuous bonding makes the child helplessly dependent on its parents. Affectionate children are quite used to instant gratification and they don't possess the wherewithal to study, grow, sacrifice, struggle and demonstrate the capacity and the perseverance necessary to elevate themselves above mediocrity through continuous industry, application, persistence and self-discipline. Affectionate children don't have the propensity to understand and distinguish that they are part of a "Universal Soul" and that EAs are very unique and rather extraordinary global inhabitants.

Indeed, in a biological sense kissing promotes the sharing of billions of germs from one person to another, and it astounds hybrid EAs that most Non-Alien people prefer doing it when science has discovered that there are five times as many germs and bacteria in a person's mouth than in that same person's rectum. And since monkeys always feel that they need to groom, touch, hug and embrace one another for security, then that bad habit is genuine proof that ninety-seven percent of the Earth's inhabitants require continual bonding to feel safe while the three-percent EAs find other more creative things to do with their limited tenure in this imperfect world. The general Non-Alien population is a product of Darwin's Theory of Evolution while the mentally superior three-percent EAs are the requisite Missing Links responsible for most of the creativity and progress evident throughout the ages.

Basically, EAs are intellectually affectionate and not physically demonstrative about expressing their feelings. We don't have to kiss someone for that person to know that we strongly like and admire him or her. Over the eons EAs have evolved from other self-motivated space traveling ancestors and benefactors residing on distant planets and conversely, the Earth's ninety-seven percent general public can trace their origin back to prehistoric chimpanzees and apes. This simple explanatory principle of the minority "Intellectual Earth Aliens" and the corresponding majority "Simian-origin Earth Non-Aliens" has confounded Earth scientists for over a century now. Cerebral EAs think more objectively and demonstrate more creativity than feel-oriented subjective Non-Aliens do.

A popular Seals and Croft '70s song has the lyrics "We are stardust, we are golden!" I honestly believe that those wonderful words express both the essence and the function of being a complex Earth Alien. We love challenges and adventure, even if our endeavors pertain to making imminent enemies or opponents. EAs are "genetically blessed" with enough fortitude, perseverance, tenacity, ingenuity and spiritual strength to crusade for virtue in order to triumph over wickedness during any prospective formidable adversity, ranging from nuclear war to economic depression.

EAs' don't savor loud raucous parties and we absolutely loathe Mardi Gras and New Year's Day celebrations when obnoxious Non-Alien Earthlings pursue their absurd folly, which in truth is reminiscent of Moses climbing Mt. Sinai with all of the Israelites deviating from the Ten Commandments' wise teachings and acting like inebriated out-of-control juvenile delinquents on the plain below. Rap music, boisterous parades, large crowds at football games and big audiences at

256

rock concerts are all repugnant to our value systems and those kinds of disturbing occurrences invariably bring out the baser emotions of regular Non-Alien Earthlings.

EAs generally abhor tattoos and body piercing and assess those "grotesque externalizations" as being examples of primitive and anachronistic body desecration and mutilation. Our more judicious "three-percent species" realizes that a person's mind and achievements are what distinguishes him or her from the remainder of society and not gaudy tattoos and earrings through the tongue or cheek being indicative of "individuality." And oh yes, most EAs prefer to be altruistic left-handed creative folks to deliberately separate us from our Darwinian Earth-generated right-handed counterparts. Regrettably throughout history left-handed EAs have been unjustly persecuted by envious and jealous right-handers that fear our' potential and envy our unselfish pursuit of excellence. Motivated by fear, the traditional Non-Alien Earthling wants to reject the truths that we mercifully offer and they keep attempting to discredit, punish, control and manipulate us less greedy EAs.

Our breed wholeheartedly supports the institution of marriage as a privilege enjoyed between a husband and a wife whose indispensable mission is to "guide" our children through the myriad dangers and pitfalls associated with everyday life. EAs feel a natural compulsion to be monogamous and we will devotedly live with that one mate and make every effort to avoid marital arguments while continuously pursuing compatibility. And if our husband or wife (usually a regular Earthling) dies we seldom remarry out of respect to the person we had (nurtured and) shared our wedding vows with.

EAs are sometimes criticized as being "domineering" and "tyrannical," but this is only because we candidly believe that the human body should be maintained naturally. An EA male's wife might insist on wearing red or purple fingernail polish but since the husband admires "natural beauty," just plain glossy clear nail polish is tolerable as an alternative. Red lipstick on a woman is all right because it enhances the natural color of a woman's lips and therefore does not project any outward artificiality, which obviously connotes phoniness. And EAs truly think that the feet are the most ugly parts of the human body and we generally insist that our spouses wear shoes or socks at all times (except on the beach) to conceal those hideous-looking toes and leg and ankle appendages.

In conclusion, although EAs are not formal religious churchgoers (in the orthodox sense) we have much more faith than those "sheep" that must listen to a Pastor once a week to fortify their vulnerable hearts and consciences. EAs on the other hand have sufficient faith in our very pertinent Earth mission, which is to morally purify ever-developing Non-Alien human intelligence and to directly influence those aberrant individuals to walk the "Avenue of Righteousness." We have little apprehension of death or about dying, and EAs don't preoccupy our inquisitive minds with perpetually contemplating such triviality. If and when we die our superior species lucidly discerns that we're just involved in another inconvenient transit on the way to a new assignment somewhere else within the enormous Milky Way Galaxy, or to somewhere else inside the infinite Universe.

Yes, EAs are worthy candidates for reincarnation and Non-Aliens are earmarked for and doomed to permanent death if condemned to Hell. In the final analysis Earth Aliens have souls of fire and Non-Aliens have souls of clay. We have a spark of the Divine dwelling within our relentless spirits. And I firmly believe that when I die I'll be spiritually reincarnated into another humanoid body (and this phenomenon will happen redundantly) until my soul is finally pure enough to reach Cosmic Nirvana (Heaven).

But to the ninety-seven percent primate-to-man Non-Alien Earth dwellers, death will mean either permanent Hell or temporary Purgatory, the latter being enforced with the clay-souled recipient, who if lucky, will reappear as another lackluster ninety-seven percent personage on this humdrum planet or as a miraculous transformation into an EA on another world with a bona fide opportunity to legitimately attain Heaven (Nirvana).

"The Victim"

I opened my eyes and everything I discerned appeared nebulous and hazy. My mind was dizzily vacillating-around in suspended animation and my perception of my immediate environment was definitely distorted and quite convoluted. My only recollections were florescent lights behind translucent ceiling panels and what my addled brain vaguely recognized as an I.V. bag suspended from a portable stand. A gentle female voice assured me that I was safe and resting. My disarrayed thoughts were still in a swirling quandary, my encumbered brain desperately attempting to interpret my surroundings more lucidly. "Where am I?" I asked the figure dressed in white standing above my lower horizontal position.

"You're in a private room at Kessler Memorial Hospital, Hammonton, New Jersey," the attending nurse informed. My eyes then scanned the room to further validate the woman's bland statement. "You've just come out of unconsciousness. You've been in that coma-like condition for six hours now. Besides having a nasty bump on your head," the benign nurse proceeded to explain, "you've sustained a number of minor injuries ranging from superficial skin lacerations to a badly dislocated shoulder. But the Emergency Room doctor said you would pull through and so you have. But you must certainly be in pain."

I repeatedly blinked my eyelids endeavoring to clear some of the mental images that were cluttering and impeding my inquisitive mind. "Well then nurse, who am I?" I desperately wanted to know. "I can't seem to remember who I am."

"We're still trying to determine that!" the sympathetic caregiver informed me. "That's why two gentlemen are here to ask you some basic questions. Dr. Kalani has given approval for them to discuss certain matters with you. You must be an American because you're here in New Jersey speaking English with a local accent!"

The sympathetic nurse stepped out of the room and two men, one in plainclothes and the other wearing a police uniform entered from the adjacent hallway. Immediately the tall detective introduced himself along with then identifying his austere-looking colleague. My erratic thought processes were still intensively laboring to distinguish the true nature of my entire medical situation. My disheveled mind required more pertinent data to evaluate.

"Hello," the man in the business suit began. "I'm Detective Pete Reynolds from the Winslow Township Police Department and this is

Sergeant Tony Dunsmore from the Williamstown Police. We're here to ask you a few questions. Dr. Kalini told us that your physical condition is strong enough to endure a brief interrogation. If you cooperate," the grim-faced detective elaborated, "we'll be able to piece missing parts of the puzzle together and then have some solid answers about the circumstances relative to your recent injuries, and also about establishing your identity. Everything' is a bit sketchy at the moment since you had no I.D. or wallet on you when you had been rushed to the hospital."

"Our departments are also working closely with the Hammonton Police and all information we obtain will then be shared with them," Sergeant Dunsmore added. "In your sleep you kept mysteriously mumbling the words 'weed spray!' Sir, does 'weed spray' have any particular importance to you? We couldn't directly determine its exact significance!"

"No," I emphatically replied with excruciating pain being felt in my injured right shoulder. "I can't seem to associate that specific reference to anything right now. And I can't see how weed spray could land me in a hospital bed other than the fact that it's poisonous if swallowed. Have I been poisoned with toxic chemicals too besides having my right shoulder in a harness?"

"No Sir," Detective Reynolds assured me. "But I believe we have to go back to square one to ascertain certain facts. Tell Sergeant Dunsmore and me what you recall about getting that massive lump on top of your skull. Were you in a fight? Did more than one person assault you?"

My brain was still a little fuzzy with general ideas expanding and contracting like the colorful elements viewed inside a kaleidoscope. Then finally one thought settled and materialized in my head like eddying dust collapsing onto a wet pavement. I was finally capable of communicating something meaningful to the investigators that my recollection deemed relevant. "I remember waking-up lying on the side of a road," I related. "My head hurt really bad just above my right eye. An old bicycle was right there on the ground next to me and it had a flat tire with a broken front rim. My first impression was that I had been riding the bike and then got clipped by a passing vehicle in a hit and run accident," I candidly expressed as my right shoulder again badly throbbed. "But after feeling my aching head I then realized that I was not wearing a safety helmet. And then everything went blank again."

"I see," Detective Pete Reynolds said as the cop hastily scribbled-down some vital words onto his notepad. "Do you remember checking for your wallet before you passed-out? You didn't have any credentials on your possession so that's why we have no *I.D.* for you."

"No Sir," I respectfully returned, shaking my head in disappointment. "My sole concerns were the severe ache in my head and getting someone to help me. Everything else was a big senseless blur at that moment. Maybe some relative or friend will show-up here to identify me, I had thought."

"Can you describe the road where you had been dropped-off?" Sergeant Dunsmore asked. "For example, was it a dual highway, a farm road, an avenue?"

"There were woods on both sides, that I'm pretty sure of," I recalled and shared. "And the telephone poles appeared different than usual with larger wires, and I remember that there was a road-level wooden bridge to my left. And oh yes," I recalled and verbalized, "incidentally, it was a two-lane country road with plenty of garbage strewn all along, and also plenty of trash in the woods. The trees were mostly of the evergreen variety. Yes, that's correct; mostly evergreens," I reiterated with a degree of certainty.

"You've just described the Winslow-Williamstown Road," Detective Pete Reynolds of the Winslow Township Police Force verified. "It has two lanes, woods on either-side, a wooden bridge and a brook that separates Winslow Township from Williamstown Borough. The tall thick telephone poles on that road are of the high-tension line variety. And litter is often tossed into the woods and the debris can be seen strewn all along the rural highway. But we don't yet know whether or not you were riding a bicycle before suffering your nasty trauma! Are you in any way familiar with Winslow-Williamstown Road?"

"No Sir," I reluctantly answered. "Never heard of it. Is it near Hanf Avenue?"

"Where's Hanf Avenue?" Sergeant Dunsmore chimed-in. "I'm familiar with Winslow Township, Williamstown and the Hammonton area and there's no Hanf Avenue anywhere in those three South Jersey municipalities. We'll have to run a thorough computer check and locate Hanf Avenue. That search might help us figure-out exactly who you are since you had no wallet or *I.D.* on you when you were admitted into Kessler Hospital. How do you spell Hanf?"

"H-a-n-f!" I articulated from what was left of my somewhat disintegrated memory. "Yes, H-a-n-f! And how did I get here in New Jersey?"

"What state do you live in?" the Winslow Township detective inquired. "If we can learn *that* essential detail," Pete Reynolds declared, "it would make our job a lot easier and also will assist you in putting together your *I.D.*"

"I can't seem to remember," I honestly acknowledged. "But my street address is 8507 Hanf Avenue. Maybe I'm sufferin' from temporary....."

"Amnesia," the Williamstown Sergeant competently completed my statement. "That often happens after receiving a wicked blow on the head like you had. Did you snap out of your stupor after going unconscious along the road's shoulder? I mean to say, what happened next?"

"Well Officer, I staggered to my feet and my head was really pulsating like crazy as if it was goin' to explode. I was very groggy, to say the least," I replied in a frustrated tone of voice from my hospital bed. "I think I walked about a hundred feet or so and passed the wooden bridge I've already told you about. Suddenly a dark red car stopped and offered me a ride. Naturally I got inside."

"How many people were in the red car?" Detective Reynolds asked.

"Three," I promptly answered. "The driver and a passenger in the front and another man seated in the rear."

"What nationality were these three men, or was it a mixed ethnic group?" Sergeant Dunsmore queried.

"They all spoke what seemed to be Spanish and they looked like Mexicans," I visualized and uttered. "Yes Sergeant, I'm almost sure they were Mexican farm workers by their dress, their complexions and their spoken language."

"What make or what kind of dark red automobile was it that picked you up?" the Winslow Township Detective asked. "A *Toyota Camry*, a *Dodge Intrepid*? A *Pontiac Grand AM*?"

"I didn't get a good look at the car so I can't really say," I sincerely indicated, still a trifle bewildered. "It had good air-conditioning though, that I can tell you! And the car was definitely red with black interior."

"Where were you' taken?" the Winslow Township investigator questioned. "I mean, our report indicates that you had been dropped-off here in front of the Emergency Ward at Kessler Hospital!" Detective Pete Reynolds informed me. "You were discovered lying on the pavement by an outpatient and the woman immediately summoned a security guard. After you had been taken inside the building, the security guard immediately contacted the Hammonton Police," the very capable detective further contributed. "Captain Martinez is waiting downstairs and the three of us are going to coordinate all of our information and develop a few possible scenarios to finally explain how you received your injuries. Captain Martinez has already interviewed Dr. Kalani and Mrs. Hutchins, your nurse, and they've provided us with everything you've been mumbling while you were unconscious. After our conference we'll get back to you. I must admit that this is indeed a very fascinating case."

"Thank you," I solemnly said with an element of gratitude. "I'm very weak now and need to shut my eyes. Please get back to me with an update when I'm more rested!"

* * * * * * * * * * * *

The following afternoon I was visited by Detective Pete Reynolds of the Winslow Police Department, Sergeant Tony Dunsmore of the Williamstown Police and Captain Jerry Martinez of the Hammonton Police Force. It seemed logical to me that since my disappearance and travels had occurred in three separate political jurisdictions that naturally three simultaneous investigations were being jointly and cooperatively conducted.

"Good morning Mr. Robert Berkheimer of 8507 Hanf Avenue, Baltimore Maryland, Zip Code 21236," Detective Reynolds greeted me with a broad smile. "May I have the pleasure of introducing you to Captain Jerry Martinez of the Hammonton Police."

"Hello," I automatically and cordially responded. "Glad to make your acquaintance. Now Officers, I do remember that my name is Robert Berkheimer and my wife's name is Mary. If my memory serves me correctly, I had come to New Jersey to visit my second cousin John Wiessner who lives on...."

"The White Horse Pike, *Route 30*," Captain Martinez capably finished my incomplete sentence. "699 North White Horse Pike to be exact. Your second cousin is a retired English teacher that lives in a light gray two-story colonial house with dark blue shutters and matching dark blue garage doors. There's a wide u-shaped driveway in the front of his home."

"Yes, now I recall," I stammered as my fragile mind gradually exited its prolonged stupor. "Cousin John and I were going to attend a *Phillies-Baltimore Orioles* game, which I guess I missed because I'm here recuperating in the hospital. He's an avid *Phillies* fan and I'm an ardent *Orioles'* rooter. Cousin John had two box seat tickets at *Citizens Bank Park*. His wife Joanne and their children were spending the week in Ocean City, New Jersey at a rented beach house. I arrived early in the area," I continued my lengthy narrative, "and Cousin John was busy mowing his lawn and asked me a favor. He asked if I could drive to the local Hammonton *Wal-Mart* and buy him a quart of...."

"Concentrated weed spray," an animated Sergeant Dunsmore injected into the jigsaw-puzzle discussion. "*Round-Up* was the particular product's name, I do believe. But anyway Robert," the Williamstown cop continued, "after your cousin gave you directions to the local *Wal-Mart* store you made the purchase and when you left the place...."

"You were accosted by six Mexican farm workers that were planning to kidnap you and steal your fine car," Captain Martinez deductively informed me. "During the scuffle that ensued you were hit over the head with a blackjack and were knocked unconscious. The Mexicans were idly hanging-out there at the Hammonton *Wal-Mart* because they had just gotten-off work early from a blueberry farm. They clobbered you over the head and then recklessly tossed your limp body into the back of the white van and then others in their party stole your dark red..."

"*Nissan Maxima!*" I realized and exclaimed with apparent disgust. "Actually, the car's official color is merlot. Hey, I just comprehended something awesome. After I was dropped-off by the white van in the woods, the other Mexicans that had taken my' keys and had stolen my treasured vehicle in the *Wal-Mart* parking lot stopped and picked me up in my own merlot *Maxima*. And that business about the damaged bicycle lying beside the road...."

"Was just a crazy weird coincidence Mr. Berkheimer, a crazy weird coincidence that made you think that you might've been riding the object prior to going unconscious along the roadway," Sergeant Dunsmore very intelligently communicated. "The bike was just a discarded piece of litter along the roadway. And when your cousin got done mowing his acre property three hours later, he waited another two hours and then got nervous and finally reported you as missing to the Hammonton Police."

"Unfortunately, your' pilfered *Maxima* has not been found," Detective Reynolds piped-in. "But the Mexicans in the white van feared that you were not regaining consciousness so they then abandoned their ruthless kidnapping plan. It's amazing that most of these summer migrant laborers have their own cell phones so what *we* think happened next was that the Hispanics in the white van called their amigos in your merlot-colored *Maxima*. Your six abductors were afraid that you might die, and they decided to drive you to the nearest hospital and inconspicuously drop you off. They were smart enough to know that auto' theft is a much lesser crime than murder and that their chances of getting caught and convicted were much greater for committing a homicide than for engaging in grand theft and selling your highly coveted *Maxima* to a Philly' chop shop. Unfortunately," Detective Pete Reynolds persuasively concluded, "these transient farm workers have a knack for finding nefarious American citizens willing to collaborate in illicit business deals with them. That's at the moment what we think has happened in regard to your missing *Maxima*."

"I really loved that car with a passion!" I attested with a saddened heart. "But the honest-to-God truth is that most people value life over property. The 2002 *Maxima'* is fully insured and can be easily replaced. My life can't be! Thank the Lord that my brutal captors got cold feet and had the decency to deposit me in front of the Emergency Room!"

"The funny part about this entire episode is that you never realized that you had been beaten a second time and then dropped-off by the side of the Winslow-Williamstown Road by the Mexicans in the white van, which immediately took off," Sergeant Dunsmore emphasized with a wry smile accentuating his chubby facial features. "Several minutes later when you revived near the secluded woods on Winslow-Williamstown Road, you were apprehended and captured by the second wave of alleged criminals riding in *your* fancy merlot *Nissan Maxima*. And if you didn't pass-out and go unconscious for the third time after you were forced into your own red vehicle, for the purpose of being kidnapped for ransom and...."

Just then Cousin John Wiessner stepped into my hospital room to pay me a kind visit. "Heard you had quite a spine-tingling adventure this morning Bob," my blood relative on my father's side sarcastically announced and laughed. "That's the last time I'm ever going to ask you to do a favor or run an easy errand. I had no idea that I was putting your fragile life in jeopardy in these dangerous parts. From all of this insane misadventure of yours, I've learned that even performing a casual errand for someone at the neighborhood *Wal-Mart* could result in a life-threatening situation!"

"You said it Cousin John!" I concurred while feeling a degree of embarrassment for what had happened. "Nowadays a person isn't even safe livin' inside the main gold vault at *Fort Knox*."

"You said a mouthful!" Captain Martinez chuckled and supplemented. "The next time Mr. Berkheimer you have to perform a favor for someone around *this* town, kindly hire the Hammonton Unit of the *New* Jersey *National Guard* to protect you. And for added security you might want to take along two dozen well-trained *Secret Service* agents too!" the amused cop exaggerated as if he was doing stand-up comedy. All four thoroughly entertained visitors laughed indulgently at my unfortunate expense. But then Cousin John had something else pertinent to relate that added more accumulative mortification to my humiliation.

"Cousin Bob," my zany relative seriously addressed me with a stern expression on his sun-tanned countenance, "the *Phillies* won the baseball game against your beloved *Orioles*, 5-3. But more importantly Bob, I want to know where's my' weed spray? How could you' be so unreliable as to have misplaced it?"

Cousin John was literally and effectively adding insult to my aggravating and agonizing injuries. "It's either in the back of the Mexicans' white van or concealed somewhere inside my precious missing-in-action *Nissan Maxima*," I sorrowfully lamented and reported. "That regrettable occasion happens to be the last time I'm ever goin' to voluntarily do *you* a personal favor anywhere, including Baltimore! I feel much more comfortable, safe and less flustered ridin' around metropolitan Baltimore City than I do drivin' around rural South Jersey!"

"The three police authorities hearing *our* harmless quarrelsome exchange broke-out into a boisterous roar as if Cousin John and I were two famous veteran comedians engaging in and debating humorous on-stage banter.

"The Second Civil War"

I, House of Representatives member Andrew Roberts of New Jersey's First Congressional District, am in total shock as I anxiously write these desperate words onto my computer keyboard, words that feverishly describe the latest incident in the ongoing unofficially labeled *Second American Civil War*. My harrowed mind is presently organizing the details of the latest savage hostility that has been perpetuated upon a high-ranking advocate of the Nationalist Republican Party by certain anonymous heartless saboteurs belonging to the Enviro-Peacenik wing of the Liberal Democratic Coalition.

This most recent devastating brazen violence will only intensify in magnitude as acts of destruction and political assassinations are soon-to-be countered with swift and definite justice administered by the United States military and the American judicial system. But to ensure my safety, I must first reunite with my wife and then go into isolation. I strongly suspect that right this minute my name is on many homegrown fanatics' short lists.

Our all-too-tolerant American *democracy* has allowed the ruthless Socialist-minded Enviro-Peaceniks to go entirely too far while endeavoring to propagate their ultra-radical ideology. A true Republic has laws that are respected, appreciated and enforced. That is why throughout history republics have lasted for thousands of years and democracies have experienced short-lived durations. Our Founding Fathers back in 1776 knew this "longevity principle" very well and preferred depicting the United States as a *republic* and not as a *democracy*, the latter allusion being a synonym for anarchy when "liberal liberty" is permitted to simultaneously flourish and be fully practiced to the extreme.

The crazed "Global Warming and Save the Planet" ideologues randomly intimidate ordinary citizens in urban and suburban areas by shouting derogatory insults at old men innocently wearing leather jackets and at sophisticated civilized women discriminately wearing warm mink coats. The disgusting ultra-liberal thugs vandalize (and sometimes even destroy) national monuments, and the vile barbaric instigators deliberately cause widespread social disorganization by attacking and bombing U.S. Navy and Coast Guard ships at sea. At present no law-abiding citizen is safe from their' relentless treachery. The rabid proponents of the very dangerous "Cause-oriented Philosophy" also contribute to national instability by promoting chaos and rebellion at every given opportunity, regardless of time, place or circumstance.

Specifically, the most dangerous factions of the Liberal Democratic Coalition, which includes the fanatical Enviro-Peaceniks, the Pro-Choice (Pro-Death by Abortion) lunatic fringe, the inflexible Gay Marriage Community and the multitude of Anti-Oil-Drilling zealots have irresponsibly brought the United States of America into a grave period of domestic turmoil. The obstinate vociferous rebels have callously and cunningly pitted brother against brother, sister against sister and in many cases, generation against generation. What individual in his or her right mind would have ever contemplated the notion that undeterred grassroots' anarchists would be able to make the greatest nation in the history of civilization totter and decay right before *our* very eyes? The United States of America is ripe for a Nazi-like dictator to ascend to power and systematically purge this great land of its current banal proclivities!

Let me clarify matters for academic posterity to accurately assess. Yesterday, July 4th, 2076 our glorious nation proudly celebrated its tri-centennial. I was privileged to patriotically honor the very special anniversary in Atlantic City, New Jersey. I had been an invited guest, visiting Senator Clinton S. Byron's penthouse suite atop the Hilton Hotel situated at the south end of the world-famous boardwalk. I had always relished *his* company and *his* hospitality.

The hallmark "National Birthday Event" was accompanied by a spectacular aviation show enacted over the *Atlantic*. The marvelous display of air superiority featured crackerjack Airy Force, Navy, National Guard and Marine Corps' pilots. My revered friend Senator Byron was in an especially festive mood as he stared out at the "wild blue yonder" and enthusiastically evaluated the prowess of the United States' enviable air power.

"You know Andrew, today I feel as proud as a preening peacock," the distinguished gentleman began his narrative. "Those new stealth bombers and jet fighters performing their intricate aerial acrobatics are truly magnificent! And their extraordinary capabilities are second to none," Senator Byron supplemented in a powerful tone of voice. "I mean, where would the world be today without the existence of the United States of America, and where would the United States of America be without the U.S. military?"

"Yes Clint, I thoroughly agree," I instinctively concurred. "Freedom does have its merits! Our *democratic* free-society's scientists and engineers have masterminded a superb quantum leap in stealth applications with their deployment of our new 'Mandrake Technology.'

268

The public is getting its first glimpse of our mighty aircrafts' fantastic new ability to disappear, not only on enemy radar screens but also to vanish visually to the human eye. Quite a remarkable accomplishment, I must confess! Presto-change-o! Now you see the jets overhead, now you don't!" I euphorically exclaimed. "And just like magic, it all happens at the push of a button! Such mind-boggling advancements could only happen in a free enterprise type of economic structure!"

My garrulous friend felt inspired to expound on my statements. "But frankly Andy, I fear that our advanced science can't stop the internal erosion that's egregiously plaguing our great country," Senator Byron answered with a stern expression immediately appearing on his previous jovial countenance. "If America is to ever fall from being the greatest nation in the history of this planet," he theorized and emphasized, "it'll be because of diabolical domestic insurrection performed by the mindless masses and not because of any wicked foreign invasion. I think that Rome, Egypt and Ancient Greece are sufficient historical verifications of my all-too-truthful political science hypothesis! I say it's time for *our* counter-revolution to be hatched!"

"You're of course directly referring to the widespread acts of destruction done by the clandestine cowards belonging to the Enviro-Peacenik movement, aren't you?" I confidently asked. "Certainly Senator, those secretive villains are at best genuine hypocrites, spearheading, organizing and committing wanton acts of aggression against innocent citizens and against the government, all without provocation!" I sincerely stated. "And the domestic terrorists have the unmitigated audacity to call themselves 'Peaceniks' while they maliciously execute their detestable demolitions upon selected targets. And there for a long while *we* had thought that the Islamic jihadists were our most lethal enemies!"

"Yes Andy, your conclusion is absolutely correct!" Senator Byron vociferated. "And I plan to make *that* specific point when I address the state Nationalist Republican delegation tonight in Meeting Room A over at Harrah's Casino/Hotel," the Senior Senator from New Jersey reminded me. "Unfortunately, by necessity, over the years I've become quite an expert on the troubling subject of domestic terrorism. And as far as the dastardly Enviro-Peacenik scoundrels are concerned," the tall stocky baldheaded lawmaker said, "they're a modern-day offshoot of the..."

"Of the insidious PETA and Greenpeace nutcases that had endangered American civilization at the turn of the last century," I intelligently finished the famed statesman's articulation.

"Now really Andy, those ancient maniacs that you' had just mentioned were the precursors of *these* diabolical contemporary Peaceniks," Senator Byron acknowledged. "The warped-minded psychopaths set the tone for the cultural warfare that we're now encountering from coast-to-coast! Those obstinate nihilists are indeed a menace to society, let alone a threat to national security! Their violent activities are detrimental to the welfare of our *Republic*! There aren't enough psychiatrists' couches in the whole-wide-world to accommodate half of them!"

"Yes Clint," I readily confirmed as I stared down at the throngs of shore visitors milling around the boardwalk. "But the Enviro-Peaceniks are much more formidable than PETA and Greenpeace ever were back at the turn of the millennium. They've successfully established an underground network that's intentionally disrupting communications, commerce, transportation and the free movement of goods, services and people anywhere from Maine to California," I expressed to my longtime mentor. "Even Alaska, Hawaii, Puerto Rico and Guantanamo Bay, Cuba aren't immune from *their* vile destructive tendencies!"

"Fools and Idiots!" florid-faced Senator Clinton S. Byron evaluated and exclaimed as his eyes peered down from his tinted windows to also scrutinize the massive crowds enjoying the stellar military aerial 4th of July exhibition. "The same problems persist today as those that had flourished back in the year 2010. And all across the nation," my close friend expounded, "those all-too-numerous Idealistic Dolts are adamantly demonstrating against our American oil companies drilling on the Atlantic Continental Shelf and in Alaska while foreign Muslim nations antagonistic to the USA are allowed universal access to our oceans' abundant petroleum deposits. What an international travesty our 'Protect the Environment Movement' has become!"

My views on the 'sensitive topic' were identical to the Senator's. "Their positions are not only totally ridiculous! In a more serious vein, those 'Global Warming Lunatics' are a definite threat to the economic stability of America!" I wholeheartedly agreed with my fellow legislator. "The Naïve Ecological Imbeciles believe that oil rig platforms contribute to ocean pollution when geologic surveys clearly indicate that the bulk of ocean pollution originates from cracks and fissures under the sea releasing abundant amounts of leaked crude. Yes Clint, as you know, oilrig platforms contribute only 1% of ocean and gulf' pollution while sixty-three percent of the environmental damage is actually done by Mother Nature unto herself! Is *that* geologic fact revealing or what?"

A moment's pause interrupted our intense dialogue as Senator Byron re-lit his expensive Cuban cigar and then after extinguishing his match, vigorously puffed away. "You know Andy," Clinton exhaled and elaborated, "let me' tell you how hypocritical the Enviro-Peaceniks really are. Take that wonderful boardwalk down there for instance. Last winter it was supposed to be re-surfaced with excellent hardwood from Brazil but then the militant conservation-minded 'Save-the-Planet' Knuckleheads vehemently protested the use of durable South American lumber planks," the famous politician insisted. "The demented ideologues twisted logic was that they wanted to protect what they've characterized as the 'delicate pristine tropical rain forest.' Well Andy, it's now quite commonly known that..."

"That plants and trees give off oxygen that we human's breathe," I enthusiastically finished the noble orator's thought, "and humans then breathe in oxygen and exhale carbon dioxide, which vegetation naturally breathes in to help conduct photosynthesis. Yes, simple vegetable food making! It's all part of a scientific cycle that's repeated over and over again!"

"But then to the contrary Andy, the absurd Enviro-Peaceniks don't give one iota's hoot about trees from Oregon and Washington State being cut down to provide the necessary new boardwalk lumber!" Clint very conscientiously informed me. "They're more concerned about forests in Brazil than about those in Oregon and Washington State! And furthermore, My Good Friend," the renowned politician continued, "I refuse to give our overseas industrial adversaries any competitive advantage over the United States. Indeed, China and India are still the biggest environmental polluters in the world besides the Earth's ocean floors spewing tons of petroleum all over the planet, and China and India never signed the Kyoto Agreement, and since we've vowed to not endorse *that* silly contract until those two rogue nations have done so," the honorable Senator elucidated, "we've therefore received the animosity of every radical fringe group in America! If anything's ever been unwarranted and unmerited Andy," Senator Byron prattled, "it's *us* dedicated Congressmen being wrongfully attacked for being 'non-progressive' and 'too conservative' to suit the needs of the dysfunctional Environmentalists and the clownish Pacifists!"

Senator Byron and I then mutually acknowledged that the quixotic American Socialist Union, the Neo-Marxists, the Enviro-Peaceniks and the Liberal Democratic Coalition were all allied against *us* when advancing their relentless "Save-the-World" and "Global Warming" agendas while inadvertently allying themselves with the avowed international enemies of the United States. The Senator and I both recognized that "our fanciful-but-determined internal foes" desired for the world (including our staunchest opponents) to become "one big happy tribal family" governed under the aegis of the corrupt and incompetent *United Nations* at the expense and demise of that bastion of freedom, the USA. We eagerly admitted that our great country had to purge itself of the decadent reformists that "with impunity threaten our highly coveted prosperity along with our mortal existence."

"These Dangerous Rebellious Factions want chaos to reign supreme throughout the land," I answered and gladly shared with my Congressional colleague. "The radicals have what you've so aptly and accurately described as 'the Victim/Slave Mentality,' for surely Clint," I deliberately emphasized and commiserated, "when a plurality of Americans happens to think like *they* do, then they'll either become victims of, or slaves to, Islamic Fascism or to Communist Ideology, just like the populations of Europe had succumbed to the perils of Nazi tyranny prior to *World War II*! If anything is to be avoided at all cost, it's surrendering to Environmental tyranny!"

I then thought about how every ten-to-fifteen thousand years the Earth undergoes an Ice Age and how mankind' really has to fear an approaching condition of 'Global Cooling' and not 'Global Warming,' but then I refrained from injecting *that* salient concept, not wanting to prolong the conversation on the subject and thus further aggravating my illustrious associate. 'We're due for another Ice Age soon and ironically, this business of much-needed Global Warning is actually preventing the inevitable onslaught of Global Cooling!' I creatively imagined.

"Indeed Andy!" the loquacious Senior Senator from New Jersey commented before again exhaling a quantity of noxious smoke in my direction and then reflexively peering-down at the congested boardwalk. "The Enviro-Peaceniks want the United States to become exactly like the European nations have been ever since the atrocities of *World War II*. The warped Dissidents wish for America to become weak, lame, submissive and cooperative, ready to show subordination to a power-hungry New World Order and then willfully surrender to terrorists and to the nefarious schemes of oil rich ascending Islamic nations!" my Washington DC colleague attested. "Yes indeed, I do believe that the 'World Government Zealots' feel guilty that *this* great nation is the un-rivaled leader of the world, not to mention the un-rivaled leader of the free world. The gullible rebels want places like Jordan, Iran and Libya to be our equal! I promise that *that* will never happen on my watch! On my word," Senator Clinton S. Byron eloquently pledged with obvious conviction as he again gazed down

272

and examined the heavy boardwalk traffic, "I'll not waver in my opposition to the demands of these treacherous vermin that infect every community in our great Republic! Yes Andy, I vow these words with my life! As they' say up in New Hampshire, 'Live free or die'!"

* * * * * * * * * * * *

This morning, July 5th, Senator Byron and I, after enjoying delicious "Room Service breakfasts," had a brief conversation inside his Hilton Casino/Hotel penthouse. We were planning to meet at our scheduled appointment later that afternoon at Senator Thomas Norris' home on St. Louis Avenue in Ocean City, Maryland. Our clandestine intent was to form secret National Guard commando groups to infiltrate various Enviro-Peacenik cells throughout the contiguous United States. My patriotic associate was very congenial in his demeanor.

"Well Andrew," the eminent statesman said after we had formulated and comprehensively reviewed our grand design, "are you sure you don't want to accompany me down to Ocean City on my state-of-the-art yacht? *Lady Liberty's* docked just north of here at Gardner's Basin Marina over near Brigantine. I guarantee you', it'll be a most pleasurable excursion south to Ocean City! You might even get a little fishing in too if you'd wish!"

"No thank you Senator," I honestly answered. "I'll meet you at four this afternoon at Senator Norris' place after you dock your yacht at Captain Bill Bunting's Marina. We'll discuss our most recent strategies with Tom at the original Phillip's Restaurant on 21st and Philadelphia Avenue this evening at 5. I think that our' conscientious Congressional comrade will readily endorse our, how should I say', *our* more recently established aggressive objectives. Senator Norris is just as fed-up as we are with incidents of violence that have been proliferating all across this great land. These intolerable left-wing rebels must be swiftly and harshly dealt with if our *Republic* is to thrive and survive into the next century!"

"Oh yes Andy! Phillip's Restaurant!" Senator Byron stated and then smiled as if overcome with nostalgia. "The tiffany lamps suspended from the ceilings are quite beautiful! And as you well know, we now have three wonderful Phillip's restaurants right here in Atlantic City! The dynamic chain is a model example of American capitalism done right! Tonight, the three of us will drink a toast to free enterprise!"

"Yes!" I eagerly agreed and confirmed. "And I must confess that I really enjoy the seventeen-mile ferry ride across the bay from Cape May to Lewes, Delaware. On each mini-voyage my spirit is pacified.

The short sea excursion is quite relaxing and the hour and fifteen-minute crossing gets my mind off of the more pressing issues of our time," I amiably justified. "The trip's always a welcomed respite from the rigors that presently confront decision-makers in organized government. The ferry ride tends to rejuvenate me!"

"Confidentially, I'd like to build a bridge from Cape May to Lewes," Clint intimated before yawning, "but I'm afraid that those overzealous Enviro-Peacenik anarchists would label the whole project 'Pork Barrel Spending' and then dynamite the structure just for spite because the money wasn't being spent on the poor or on protecting the environment."

I pensively contemplated the Senator's remark for a moment. "Jesus said it best when he told Judas that His silver pieces spent on oil for the purpose of anointment should not be wasted on the poor because there will be poor always!" I remembered and uttered to my confederate. "Yes Clint, there comes a time when money should be earmarked for vital improvements that are needed to benefit the general welfare! But these brainwashed left-wing reformers don't have a clue when it comes to comprehending the big picture. Our biggest enemy is ignorance, that is, ignorance practiced by cause-based ideologues!"

"Well spoken!" Senator Byron commended while patting me on the back and then reactively chuckling to show his newfound happy disposition. "You're quite convincing and persuasive when you want to be! I'll wager a hundred thousand dollars that in the near future you'll be the next Speaker of the House!" Senator Byron expressed and laughed. "I trust we'll both have pleasant *Delaware Bay* crossings and I'll see you Andy at Captain Bill Bunting's Marina at Talbot Street and the bay around 4 p.m. this afternoon. Now bon voyage!"

I departed Atlantic City by automobile at nine this morning, which would allow me sufficient time to catch the 10:30 ferry out of Cape May. After exiting the *Atlantic City Expressway* at 7-S, I reckoned that the thirty-five-mile drive south along the scenic *Garden State Parkway* would be a very refreshing endeavor.

'I'll motor past Ocean City, New Jersey, Sea Isle City, Avalon, Stone Harbor, Wildwood and Wildwood Crest,' I imagined as my vehicle wove in and out of heavy southbound summer traffic. 'And it's too bad I don't have the time to drive through Cape May,' I sentimentally thought. 'The Victorian mansions and bed and breakfast lodges are simply stunning to behold. Oh well,' I reckoned, 'I'll just have to make a visit to the historic town at a later date. But the Lobster House on the channel is a terrific tourist destination for anyone who prefers eating fabulous crabmeat, delectable shrimp and succulent

274

broiled lobster tails. It's without a doubt one of my wife's favorite dining places! There's the ferry entrance up ahead!'

I drove my vehicle into the large asphalt parking area, paid my toll and then following the policeman's direction, steered my automobile onto the aforementioned Cape May-Lewes Ferry at 10:15. 'I'll throw some popcorn to the scavenging seagulls that always follow the boat and before I know it I'll be in Delaware heading south along the coast between Rehoboth Beach and Ocean City, Maryland,' I mused. Then my anxious mind considered a rather cynical thought. 'I hope I don't encounter any belligerent Peaceniks along the way! Those bizarre lunatics could easily ruin a good day and make me regret I had ever woken up.'

While standing on the ferry's portside deck, midway across *Delaware Bay* my ever-vigilant eyes spotted Senator Byron's sleek yacht in the distance, the vessel on a course paralleling the good ship *New Jersey's* familiar seventeen-mile route. I figured that my good-hearted friend would soon appear on deck and wave to me, but what transpired next was perhaps the most horrifying and horrendous spectacle that my pupils have ever witnessed.

Two *Coast Guard* boats out of Cape May were escorting Clint's expensive yacht *Lady Liberty* across the *Delaware Bay* when quite coincidentally off in the distance another gleaming vessel appeared. Immediately my distrustful nature sensed that danger was imminent. My ever-suspicious mind imagined that heinous Enviro-Peaceniks were about to cause mayhem and destruction.

Almost instantaneously three giant whales propelled out of the water, their huge bodies apparently on a collision course with the two *Coast Guard* ships and the ill-fated *Lady Liberty*. My throat choked-up as my lungs gasped for more air. 'Oh my God! I've seen porpoises swimming in this bay but never whales!' I frightfully realized. 'This is the evil work of the Enviro-Peaceniks! Now I understand exactly what's happening before my very eyes!' my mind hypothesized. 'Those destructionists have trained the three sea behemoths to conduct *their* brutal sabotage! Those immense whales are going to crush the three boats just like Moby Dick had made shambles out of Captain Ahab's *Pequod* in Herman Melville's classic novel!'

The series of horrible impacts that followed were both loud and distressful. After the three violent collisions had occurred, the Peaceniks' 'gleaming fishing boat' then bombarded *that* section of the placid bay with "Chum Bombs," the bloody fish parts being specifically designated to attract ocean and bay predators from all directions. In minutes teams of hungry sharks swam around consuming any and all edible items including frenetic sailors and Senator Byron, all frantically churning their arms and hysterically screaming amidst the wild in-progress feeding frenzy.

Soon human blood mingled with the slimy fish remains as the voracious sharks continued their biological preoccupation, biting and swallowing their terrorized victims. A minute later all was quiet upon the tranquil red debris-strewn sea. The only sounds that then dominated the fresh morning air were the shrieks and yells of appalled and delirious passengers and crew standing aboard the *New Jersey*.

'In the past Greenpeace radicals were merely obstructionists,' I rationalized as the emotions known as fear and awe governed my instincts, 'but now these wretched Enviro-Peaceniks are devout accomplished assassins hell-bent on destroying both Christian culture and institutionalized civilization.'

The heartless activists are no longer vocal pacifist demonstrators demanding change. Their grandiose goal is to send the entire United States of America topsy-turvy while attempting to create a 'New World Order' based on the perpetuation of *their* evil philosophy. 'If only *their*' reprehensible movement would fall subject to Divine Intervention!' I futilely prayed. 'But now it is virtually impossible to ignore their incessant intimidation! There're entirely too many of the itinerant subversives roaming around North America for the police, the FBI and the military to arrest and interrogate! Law enforcement is completely overwhelmed!'

Then my troubled mind considered other wholly palpable thoughts and observations. 'I've read in top secret government documents where the on-a-mission Peaceniks have trained deadly animals to help perform their dirty work,' I recollected. 'The creatures are taught by means of reward and punishment to attack and kill targeted human victims, particularly vulnerable and prominent Nationalist Republicans! This is indeed a most ugly day in the history of the United States of America! God rest your immortal soul Clint!' I solemnly and tearfully prayed as I gazed upon the crimson-colored water below. 'Senator Byron was *dead right* in his argument that America was engaged in a *Second Civil War* with a multitude of repulsive criminal guerrilla/thugs professing to believe in just causes. I must admit, my spirit and my will have both been broken!' I reflected as my automobile finally descended the ferry exit ramp into Lewes, Delaware.

I pressed my car's '3-D telescreen' button and listened intently to the "Latest Breaking News." My eyes noticed a grim-faced commentator sadly reporting that the President had just been attacked and killed by two hungry tigers that had been set free by "activist handlers" at the San Diego Zoo. It is also suspected that a high-ranking zoo-employee/conspirator sympathetic to the Enviro-Peacenik cause had instigated the "assassination-by-animal crime" in a similar manner to how Senator Clinton S. Byron had met his unfortunate *Delaware Bay* demise.

Another TV anchorman then appeared on the screen and interrupted the first announcer's remarks with equally terrible news, informing his TV audience that the Vice-President had just been assassinated by Peaceniks while attending a world peace conference in Anchorage, Alaska. "Although initial reports are sketchy," the news person informed, "poisonous darts from a primitive blowgun tainted with snake venom are believed to have been responsible for the death of *our* Second-in-Command."

Feeling quite melancholy and despondent, I pulled my vehicle over to the shoulder of the highway and quickly turned on my laptop computer. The Associated Press flashed an online bulletin stating that a pack of vicious wolves had killed the Speaker of the House and his family (along with three Secret Service agents) while the group had been hiking in the desert outside Las Vegas, Nevada. My mind was in a quandary as my distraught soul sunk further into a state of depression.

'All these regrettable events have the markings of demented Enviro-Peacenik terrorists!' I plausibly deducted. 'And the unscrupulous methods that have been employed are very consistent with the tactics utilized by ruthless left-wing fringe radicals in quest of power!'

Then my active mind drifted towards reviewing other relevant ideas swirling around inside my head. 'My life is now in jeopardy and my reputation will soon be permanently sullied when other important facts are made public!' I lamented. 'I must seriously consider how I am to escape from this terrible dilemma! Oh God! What can I do?'

My brain was full of fleeting ideas that suddenly seemed connected and related. 'Why couldn't my son be like my friends Bill and Fran Burns' boy Billy over in Stone Harbor?' I wondered as I drove south along the coast between Rehoboth Beach and Fenwick Island, Delaware. 'Billy had bought Bradley's Sub Shop and then developed the mediocre business into a popular seashore landmark! And now he's expanded his original operation and owns two other sub shops. The young man has proven his worth in the American free enterprise system!'

And finally, the pigeons came home to roost when my agonized mind focused on the identities of certain other young people besides successful Billy Burns. 'My obnoxious son and Senator Byron's disobedient daughter are engaged to be married, but I've learned from classified intelligence reports that the two lovebirds are active officers in the New Jersey Enviro-Peacenik Movement. They've deviously collaborated to spite and besmirch their parents' good names and outstanding characters. My son and the Senator's daughter have both been defiant of adult authority in addition to being guilty of jeopardizing the nation's security! Robert and Beth are pernicious traitors to their families and also to their country!' I determined.

My mind quickly became more resolute, my thoughts more lucid. 'I must insist that the insolent offenders be hunted-down and then be swiftly brought to justice! They'll no longer be shielded from federal prosecution and conviction because of who they are and what their fathers do for a living! Throw parental love out the window! This business of social revolution now thoroughly transcends the strength of family ties!'

But in reality, I have no desire to experience a similar fate to that which befell Senator Byron along with the other cruelly eliminated government officials. My family name has been shamed and disgraced by the misdeeds of my son and of my prospective daughter-in-law. And yes, call me a craven coward if you must, but I'm also a pragmatic realist when it comes to the art of survival. Since I am (in the final analysis) next in line to become the Speaker of the House, I plan to resign my Congressional seat effective immediately in order to avoid being systematically executed by certain fringe elements of our thoroughly out-of-kilter American society. I no longer wish to be a dignified public figure legislating the present and the future amidst all of the epidemic havoc and chaotic turbulence that happens to be spreading like wildfire throughout the entire United States of America. The fact is that I have no stomach for the diabolical present or for the unpredictable future.

I plan to submit this sincere declaration of resignation to my attorney. Then, there will be documented evidence of my explicit intentions in the event that militant Enviro-Peaceniks happen to maliciously assassinate me in the meantime.

Congressman Andrew Roberts
First Congressional District of New Jersey
July 5, 2076

"The Music Portal"

Up until four months ago I had regarded my very ordinary life as being a dismal failure. My mediocre occupation ever since I was fresh out of high school has been that of a dissatisfied shoe salesman at Brock Shoes Outlet in Berlin, New Jersey. For thirty-one miserable years I would loyally commute each working day from my French Street home in nearby Hammonton, a flourishing agricultural community located twelve miles east of Berlin and also conveniently situated midway between vacation destination Atlantic City and bustling Philadelphia, Pennsylvania, the distances being thirty miles in either direction from my house to the East Coast gambling Mecca and to Benjamin Franklin's City of Brotherly Love.

The principal factor that I do remember about my former employment was that I absolutely loathed being a common shoe salesman, feigning cheerfulness daily, having to look at some very ugly feet over the course of the last three-plus decades, and unfortunately having to smell some horrible stenches emanating from the toes of people who apparently neglected taking frequent baths and showers and who evidently had little regard for the psychological needs of a disgruntled oxfords, loafers and sandals' salesman who never seemed to have the desired exact size and the precise color on the Brock Shoes Outlet's stockroom shelves.

And my family life (or lack thereof) also had immensely contributed to my chronic emotionally depressed condition. My materialistic wife Virginia had left me seven years ago for a more prosperous man, a prominent Hammonton blueberry farmer owning (through inheritance) a highly lucrative, five hundred-acre-plantation on Middle Road. And to add to my quandary, my three children have disowned me, preferring to side with their now rich mother who continuously and generously dotes on them and helps the avaricious siblings with their high-cost college tuitions, with their monthly car payments and with their often-solicited recreation money.

Yes, all was utter despair in my lackluster financial existence, with my only real joy being the bad habit of blowing most of my spare money in various Atlantic City casinos. In time, *that* wretched addictive activity had become almost an uncontrollable obsession. Bally's Casino, Harrah's Hotel, the Showboat, Caesar's World, the Trump Taj Mahal, the Trump Marina, the Trump Plaza, Resorts International, the Borgata, the Claridge and the Hilton all provided my need for greed with basic gambling venue/entertainment while simultaneously confirming to my fragile psyche that I was a born loser and was surely destined to die as one.

But then last July 16th, 2008 (on a Wednesday if my undependable memory serves me correctly), I had attended the annual carnival feast of Our Lady of Mt. Carmel at the fair grounds on Third Street across from St. Joseph Catholic Church. Although I'm not the most congenial or convivial person in the world, I've always been a religious fellow and somewhat superstitious too, if I may mention *that* ancillary fact.

After attending the morning Mass that commemorates the festival, I sanctimoniously lit a candle next to the Hammonton church's altar and tabernacle. Then after stepping outside the building, I faithfully pinned a hundred-dollar bill on the statue of Our Lady of Mt. Carmel in the traditional Italian noon street procession that immediately followed the sacred church observances.

Later that afternoon, I indulged in swallowing-down two pepper and sausage sandwiches at the Assumption Concession Stand that had been erected in the St. Joseph Church asphalt parking lot to accommodate hungry feast-day patrons. Everything occurring on that particular July 16th day seemed normal, copacetic and consistent with my overall nondescript life.

Exactly one week later on Wednesday, July 23rd, the all-too-familiar brown UPS delivery truck pulled into my French Street driveway at 5:30 p.m. After exchanging a few casual pleasantries with the likeable driver, I carried my compact package into the house, a small carton weighing about two-to-three pounds. My curious eyes keenly noticed that the shipping address had been mysteriously labeled "Freiburg, Germany."

'This must be some mistake or error, or perhaps it's even a weird practical joke being played on me,' I initially considered. 'I don't know anybody that lives in Germany, let alone residing in a remote place like Freiburg. The town sounds pretty rural. True, my cleaning lady is from Germany and the janitor over at the elementary school is too, but outside of those two nice acquaintances,' I presumed and speculated, 'I have no other connections or associations with *that* particular European country.'

Before opening the unexpected brown-wrapped ordinary-looking package, I rechecked the mailing address to ascertain that the always-reliable UPS man had made an accurate drop-off. Feeling satisfied that my' assiduous inspection of the item's exterior had been completed, I ventured over to my den's book shelf and pulled-out *Encyclopedia G*. After leafing through the thick book's pages, my intensive research eventually located the "Population Distribution" map of Germany.

After admiring impressive color photographs of the Rhine River Valley and of the architectural wonder known as Hohenzollen Castle, my cursory 'information investigation' discovered that Freiburg, Germany was located in the vicinity of the Bavarian Black Forest.

After completing my research, I eagerly tore away the package's outer brown paper covering and then meticulously opened the small carton, making certain not to damage the contents inside. Much to my curious surprise and wonder, a small computer-like instrument, comparable to a Blackberry hand-held device, had been neatly tucked inside, enveloped in wrinkled-up German language newspaper pages. With my fascination running wild, my eyes closely examined and then really scrutinized the very intriguing item of interest, its purpose at that specific moment representing an enigma to me.

'Let's see,' I pensively analyzed, attempting to objectively keep my volatile emotions in harness. 'I must not allow my heart to interfere with my mind's goal here. Here's a folded-up instructions' leaflet,' I astutely observed, 'and wow, by coincidence it's written in English too! I don't even have to consult the German-to-English dictionary on the *Internet* for an interpretation. All there is on the facing of this peculiar device is one 'On' and one 'Off' switch along with a standard liquid display readout at the top!'

Then I carefully read the directions to the remarkable "Music Portal Product," and all along my mind was unusually captivated with its new-found interest, the extraordinary object instantly manifesting itself as a unique source of personal wonder.

"Use this very special mechanism only in a dire emergency where your life might be in danger or in jeopardy. There are twelve relevant songs programmed into this very sensitive device, the purpose of each tune you'll be able to accurately hypothesize after your full usage of the 'Music Portal'."

Then I read a more vivid description. "The first ten songs will pertain to your ability to deal with unsavory people that might be endangering your physical well-being while the final two musical arrangements will be pertinent to your much-needed growth as an individual, helping you achieve mortal self-actualization and therefore affecting *you* to ultimately finding a genuine reason for directly participating in the efficacious development of your psychological/spiritual self-fulfillment."

I then finished comprehending the remainder of the given instructions. "It is strongly advised that you implement and use this wonderful gift wisely. Simply plug the accompanying earphones into the device, and when threatened, use the first ten tunes to eliminate your immediate problem. And then upon developing the necessary courage to overcome your ten adversities, responsibly activate the final two songs at your own volition and during the transition, courageously commence discovering your purpose-driven life."

Your sympathetic Freiburg friends

My re-energized thought processes contemplated the intricate invention's possible significance in relation to my monotonous dejected life. I truly wanted to avoid any potential discrepancies concerning the successful operation of the Music Portal while my fertile imagination considered what would actually happen upon my intentional activation of the 'very handsome-looking foreign made computer.' My captivated mind still being somewhat befuddled, I very deliberately thrice re-read the very explicit directions on how to effectively optimize my ownership of the newly acquired electronic object. It didn't take me too long to perceptively figure out the magical power associated with the exceptional miniature apparatus that I had by good fortune obtained via standard UPS delivery.

On Monday morning, July 21st I had to honor a scheduled 10:00 a.m. doctor's appointment at *Thomas Jefferson University Hospital*, Philadelphia. I drove my blue *Nissan Altima* from Hammonton to the Lindenwold High Speed Line Terminal just west of Berlin, purchased my round-trip ticket from the lady cashier and soon boarded the nine o'clock train into Philly'.

My scheduled appointment (and routine medical checkup) went smoothly and I was very happy with my heart doctor's favorable report. I exited the brick-façade 1600 Walnut Street Building and very warily strolled the several blocks east and then south to the Port Authority Subway Station at 10th and Locust. Without any warning, four young city punks wielding switchblade knives accosted me at the base of the otherwise empty subterranean station's steps.

Startled as I was, luckily, I was holding the Music Portal Device in my right hand while wearing the accompanying attached earphones. Instinctively I entered my survival/self-preservation behavioral mode. I forcefully pressed the "On" button and my auditory senses heard the 1974 ABBA hit "Waterloo" being played through my earphones. Instantly the four unsavory city thugs disappeared into oblivion, the fantastic event occurring as if they had never occupied that particular time and space. It was then and there that I superficially grasped the specific functionality of the most incredible Music Portal Device.

'I wonder if those four villainous creeps are actually right now at the Battle of Waterloo with Wellington's or with Napoleon's troops, or perhaps instead they've been marvelously conveyed to a 1970s ABBA concert,' I conjectured and assessed. 'In my opinion those future criminals need all of the history lessons they can get. Could it be that the Music Portal is indeed some phenomenal kind of sophisticated geography and time travel piece of equipment? Whatever the circumstances,' I thought with relief as my eastbound train approached the underground station platform, 'I'm really glad to have the amazing thing in my possession!' And after I boarded the train I reckoned, 'And I was never really a big ABBA and disco fan, always preferring to listen to classic rock and roll back in the flashy bell-bottom jeans, Strobe lights and polyester clothes' '70s era!' I mused and then chuckled as tunnel lights flickered on and off and metallic wheels screeched around a bend outside the train car.

After finally getting off the partially-filled High Speed Line train at Lindenwold, I slowly trekked a good distance to my trusty car, which was parked around a quarter of a mile away in the far corner of the massive lot. As I grabbed for the front door handle of my *Altima*, an armed robber (that was hiding behind an adjacent vehicle) suddenly appeared and demanded that I hand over my wallet. Being inspired after my former musical success in the Locust Street Subway Station, my right thumb adroitly hit the contraption's contact button and instantaneously, the shocked and petrified lowlife vanished into thin air. Simultaneously my ears discerned the familiar rhythm and beat of Jan and Dean's catchy 1964 car song, "The Little Old Lady from Pasadena."

'Could it be that the wicked nasty-tempered robber has been inexplicably transported to Pasadena, California?' I asked myself. 'If so, I hope he stays there and gets to see the next *Rose Bowl Game*! And if he's meandering around Pasadena right this second, is he in the year 1964 or is he still in 2008? Oh well,' I concluded and shrugged my shoulders, 'that scar-faced fellow would be better off taking-up committing home burglaries instead of attempting bold-faced armed parking lot robbery as a chosen profession. In retrospect,' my mind reviewed, 'it's pretty hard for *him* to get teleported to a remote Golden State destination when nobody's there inside the place to operate a facsimile Music Portal mechanism to send *him* back here to Lindenwold! Maybe the relocated idiot will get to visit and tour 'Surf City' too while he's fully enjoying his unanticipated surprise West Coast jaunt!'

On Saturday morning, I did my usual grocery shopping at the nearby Wal-Mart and ShopRite stores and then after unpacking and putting away my new food products in the refrigerator, inside the freezer and into various respective cupboards, I changed out of my blue denim jeans, donned my jogging outfit and drove my *Nissan* down the White Horse Pike to somnolent Oak Grove Cemetery. I had once checked the mileage on my car's odometer, and if I traverse the entire graveyard's asphalt surface twice, my diligent labor would result in a very beneficial cardio-vascular-friendly three-mile hike. Of course, my *Altima* was parked in its regular shaded location beneath a canopy of three tall oak trees, and I felt especially secure walking around inside the old cemetery carrying my Music Portal while performing my habitual weekend exercise routine.

As I was circling the caretaker's maintenance building situated in the center of the cemetery, six motorcycle villains drove their gleaming machines inside the graveyard to pay their respects to a recently deceased gang member. Seeing me innocently pacing in their direction, the tough-looking bikers all perceived me as being an easy target, first for blatant intimidation, and second for larceny. The Harleys speedily rumbled up to me, the riders thinking that I was unprepared to defend myself against their aggressive demands and against their spontaneously planned molestation. But I was fully ready to deal with any of their antagonism and prospective havoc.

"Okay, let's make this little encounter short and sweet!" the very arrogant head honcho belligerently declared in a gruff tone of voice. "Now Pal, just hand over your wallet and I'll gladly confiscate all your cash. Don't worry though!" the disgusting black-hearted maniac clarified. "We ain't all that bad! You'll get to keep your credit cards, your driver's license and all of your' other personal ID! It's a lot better to be a live victim than a dead hero, that's what the hell I always say! Ha, ha, ha!"

The five other formidable-looking bikers all indulgently laughed at their leader's threatening comments and then mockingly applauded my apparent situational futility. Before any additional harassment could ensue from any of their lips, I nonchalantly touched the "On" button, and without any sign of hesitation or delay, the Music Portal played the melody and lyrics to the 1959 hit tune "Kansas City" by Wilbert Harrison. And before I could even begin to say '*Dick Clark's American Bandstand*,' the six nefarious derelicts that had been ridiculing me were miraculously erased from my presence, either swiftly being sent on their way to Kansas City, Missouri or to Kansas City, Kansas.

'I hope those desperate degenerates have enough dough to buy themselves some delicious Black Angus steaks,' I amused myself with a reflexive smile. 'Maybe they'll somehow be converted into bunkhouse cowboys working for a living on a sprawling dude ranch. I think that the flat-lands of the American Midwest would be a welcome change in scenery for those societal parasites when compared to the all-too-predictable South Jersey pine barren forest landscape that *they* no doubt have constantly abused in the past! Oh well, what could possibly happen next?'

The first Sunday in August, I was driving south to Vineland to have a delicious lunch at Esposito's Maplewood III Restaurant because I really think *that* establishment has the best tomato sauce and Italian pasta anywhere in South Jersey. After paying my moderate bill and leaving a generous tip, I sauntered out of the popular eatery and then hopped into my car, which much to my annoyance, failed to start. Upon opening the hood to diagnose the cause of the electrical problem, I recognized (much to my frustration) that the automobile's battery had been stolen. I angrily got out my cell phone and anxiously began dialing "Local Information" to obtain the name of the nearest road service that would dispatch a mechanic out to Delsea Drive to replace the vital missing part.

Suddenly, three mean-looking Mexicans emerged out of nowhere, violently opened my car door and then signaled for me to exit my vehicle. I ceased my cell phone dialing and gestured to the triumvirate of wise guys that I was going to obediently follow their command.

I gingerly lifted up my Music Portal from the passenger-side front bucket seat and slowly inserted the corresponding earphones into their appropriate auditory positions. My index finger methodically made contact with the "On" button, and before I could blink an eyelid or even fabricate a wink, the three dumbfounded desperados vaporized into the separate spaces that they had been occupying, their astonishing disappearances all occurring in unison with the very identifiable sound of Marty Robbins' 1960 number "El Paso" being wonderfully discernible to my ears.

'Oh well,' I reflected and weighed with a huge sigh of relief, 'the song selection could've been 'Tijuana Taxi' by Herb Alpert and the Tijuana Brass or maybe even Ritchie Valens' terrific version of 'La Bamba' or perhaps even the good old-fashioned favorite 'The Mexican Hat Dance!' Those three missing-in-action Hispanic jerks were probably the same dastardly rogues that had stolen my car battery! Now they're probably already trying to get to the *Rio Grande* to come back to New Jersey and get even with little old *me*, their chief antagonist!'

I finally got my blue *Altima* operational again late that Sunday afternoon. On Tuesday after work, I checked my refrigerator and noticed that I was completely out of beer. The *Phillies* were playing an important baseball game on television that evening so I decided to drive over to Canal's Discount Liquor Store on Broadway and *Route 30* and conveniently purchase a cold six-pack of *Coors Light*.

A desperate-looking fellow quickly entered the crowded store while I was checking out my beverage acquisition at the main cash register. The on-a-mission psycho' immediately pulled out a handgun and boldly announced that a holdup was in progress. Naturally I inserted the designated earphones and matter-of-factly hit the Music Portal's "On" button.

My ears instantly heard Elton John singing his 1975 smash hit "Philadelphia Freedom" and I assumed that the *Quaker City* was the audacious petty thief's appointed destination. 'The *Philadelphia Freedoms* were once a pro' tennis squad back in the long-gone 1970s and Elton John had written and dedicated the upbeat song to one of his closest friends, team captain Billie Jean King!' my non-photographic memory recollected. Then my very active mind conjured-up some additional spontaneous reactions.

'I hope that the criminal nutcase winds-up inside the 10th and Locust Street subway station and gets mugged by equally diabolical street hoods from the 'hood!' I creatively conceived and joked. 'One thing's for darned sure. Metropolitan crime is gradually trickling out of the urban areas and insidiously infecting the suburbs! If it weren't for this tremendous Music Portal Device,' I realized, 'I'd already be dead at least five times over!'

When I finally returned to my modest French Street residence, my rowdy immature neighbors were haughtily entertaining some of their very boisterous piney hunter friends at a "disturbing the peace" backyard picnic. The raucous intoxicated rednecks apparently were quite disenchanted with my audacity because I had called the police to break-up several other clamorous next-door warm weather parties, one on *Memorial Day* and the other on the 4th *of July*. I was busy putting my lawnmower inside my outdoor utility building when all twenty-four inebriated revelers (that had been attending the loud backyard barbecue) trespassed onto my property and then insolently began badgering me with a barrage of disparaging insults.

"Look!" I diplomatically answered. "My ears are very sensitive! I don't like excessive noise and I don't relish the shooting-off of loud fireworks. Let's have some moderate behavior here! Why don't you kind folks just learn to be a little more civil and respect other peoples' rights! Then we could get along like good neighbors and not have this type of unnecessary cultural conflict all the time!"

"You're goin' to get the beatin' of your life!" my bellicose under-the-influence twenty-two-year-old neighbor/nemesis predicted. "Now I'm challengin' you in front of all of these witnesses here to act like a man and let's see how tough ya' really are when your very survival is at stake!" the incensed psychopath yelled as he angrily clenched his fists. The other defiant barbarians (assembled on my back lawn) shouted a bevy of brazen cheers and jeers in response to the offensive knucklehead's sarcastic comments.

Without wasting a second of precious time, I suavely activated the invaluable Music Portal and my ears eagerly listened to Glen Campbell singing his 1969 hit "The Wichita Lineman." The twenty-four baneful delinquents magically dissolved into thin air with not a trace or a vestige of anyone or anything (in their possession) remaining behind.

'Those drunken Jersey hillbillies frequently terrorize the Wharton Tract woods up on *Route 206* and the ruffians hang-out at the infamous Pic-A-Lilli Inn,' I remember thinking. 'They all belong to a deer club that just uses hunting season as an excuse to get drunk, to cause a ruckus and to commit perpetual gluttony. Maybe while they're trekking around out in Wichita, Kansas,' I mentally humored myself, 'perhaps those two dozen un-illustrious scoundrels will introduce themselves to the six obnoxious cemetery bikers that I had very conveniently teleported out to Kansas City while the talented Wilbert Harrison was singing his mantra-like verses!'

At that psychologically rewarding moment of proud triumph, I must confess that I was feeling rather superhuman and omnipotent. It did dawn on my awareness that the wonderful Music Portal Device must contain some revolutionary proprietary technology that if "the science" ever became available to the general public and then be universally used, the plethora of "magical music devices" would have everyone sending everyone else into different times and/or into different places, thus contributing to mass societal chaos and ultimately, possibly causing the end of civilization itself. 'Not everyone can be trusted possessing such a powerful device!' I academically surmised. 'Evil people cannot have access to such a marvelous disciplinary tool! I mustn't share the secret of this wondrous thing with anyone!'

Two more notable incidents had occurred later in August. Being totally bored with my less-than-mediocre shoe salesman job, I had driven forty miles from Hammonton up to *Six Flags Great Adventure* amusement park in Jackson the fourth Saturday in August for some leisurely diversion and to pursue a much-needed attitude adjustment.

'In terms of its structure, this Music Portal appears to be just another typical I-pod,' I remember thinking as I paid my hefty park admission fee. 'Whoever owns the patent to this electronic gizmo will certainly make an unbelievable fortune!'

Three drunken New Yorkers with heavy Brooklyn accents attempted to instigate a fight with me inside a crowded park men's room. Without uttering any derogatory expletives or counter accusations, I confidently hit the readily available 'transportation switch' and upon me hearing the introduction to Freddy "Boom-Boom" Cannon's 1962 top seller "Palisades Park," the trio of punks promptly vanished from my midst.

'Palisades Park was torn down years ago,' I later recalled as I chewed on a hot dog near the Batman Roller Coaster Thrill Ride. 'So, if the three alcoholics were not time-travel-teleported back to 1962, then they're probably walking around Palisades Park, New Jersey right now in 2008 wondering what the heck had happened to them. The three tipsy bully maniacs more-than-likely now think that they've somehow been the victims of a mass hallucination!'

On Sunday morning, I needed some relaxing diversion in my life so I attached my twenty-four-foot-long boat trailer to my 1997 red Ford 150 truck and towed the "Sea Daze" to a launching slip at a Sweetwater marina. A forklift operator soon lowered and then deposited my boat into the *Mullica River*. An hour later my small Sea Daze was anchored in shallow water and I was quietly fishing in the vicinity of Crowley's Landing when three destructive wise-guy teenagers appeared on the riverbank and started cursing and throwing large stones at me. I activated my Music Portal and my ears heard the refrains of the "Bristol Stomp," a lively 1961 classic tune sung by the Dovells. 'Well,' I philosophically mused, 'those three despicable adolescents are probably now wandering on the banks of the *Delaware* in Bristol, Pennsylvania instead of bothering the daylights out of me here on the *Mullica!*' I logically concluded. 'Serves the roguish hooligans right! Maybe their little excursion into Bucks County, Pennsylvania will teach the discourteous instigators some much-needed manners!'

The second Saturday in September I felt an urge to drive thirty miles east to Atlantic City, stroll the world-famous boardwalk, buy some tasty salt water taffy, smell the fresh ocean air and blow five hundred hard-earned dollars at Caesar's World Casino. I parked my blue *Altima* on Pacific Avenue and while peacefully walking towards the A.C. Boardwalk I was accosted by a mugger who stopped me on Missouri Avenue to falsely ask directions to the *Steel Pier*.

Without thinking twice, Pattie Page's 1957 calming rendition of "Old Cape Cod" sent the annoying thug off to either Hyannisport or Provincetown on the famous Massachusetts peninsula. 'Maybe that vile fellow will be exposed to some New England culture, or more-than-likely he'll be manhandled by police and arrested for trespassing onto the Kennedy Compound,' I thought and laughed. Then my devil-may-care disposition changed to a more solid serious mode. 'The Music Portal's instructions indicated that I would have ten danger uses and then two additional personal growth uses,' I mulled over in my mind. 'That gives me just one more opportunity to dispose of harmful evil-minded individuals!'

Later that Saturday afternoon, my gambling habit was rewarded when I hit a three-thousand-dollar jackpot on a Caesar's World nickel slot machine. While mentally reveling in a jovial mood, I drove from Atlantic City and stopped in at Tony's Bar on *Route 322*, the Black Horse Pike, to down some hard liquor shots and watch the featured go-go doll dance around a brass pole situated near the bar. The girl's boyfriend (who was also her pimp) tried soliciting me for a three hundred dollar hit, and feeling threatened by his obvious gruff demeanor, I sent the saucy fellow down to Southern hillbilly country when my ears heard the unique guitar riff to Lynyrd Skynyrd's 1974 smash hit "Sweet Home Alabama."

'Well,' I steadfastly thought, 'this last tenth episode has exhausted all of my Music Portal opportunities. October 6th is my birthday. I think I'll begin exploring my personal growth segment then. If my brain remembers the exact instructions,' I paused before I gulped down a second shot of 100 Proof *Southern Comfort*, 'I only have two future chances to reach self-actualization. I wonder what side of Nirvana *that's* on? Oh well, instant karma or no instant karma, I think I'll order another jigger of whiskey and then hit the road before the bartender and the go-go dancer finally notice that the pushy pimp is missing-in-action.'

The attractive go-go-dancer with Rockette-type legs approached me and asked if I had seen a "Tall, handsome muscular brown-eyed young man with a dimple in the center of his chin!"

"I think he's away applying to the *University of Alabama*!" I cleverly answered the voluptuous well-built scantily clad blonde. "Yes, I think he had mentioned something about being a freshman and drowning in the Crimson Tide!" I jested.

The knockout well-endowed girl just stared at me with her mouth agape as if I was an unstable mental patient that had just escaped from the nearby Ancora State Hospital high-security psycho' ward.

* * * * * * * * * * * *

I had reserved a non-smoking room for October 6th at Caesar's World Casino/Hotel so that I could quietly and privately celebrate my birthday. Since I had earned a Harrah's Diamond Card, I often enjoyed the benefits of food and room comp' privileges at the corporation's four Atlantic City properties: Harrah's, the Showboat, Bally's Casino and Caesar's World.

Inside the confines of my seventh-floor suite, I felt motivated to take the time to again closely examine the amazing Music Portal Device. And then feeling a sudden compulsion to further explore the dimensions of my own "Self-actualization," I gathered my wits and courage and gently pressed the "On" button. Immediately I heard the harmonious Olivia-Newton-John song "Xanadu" and my suddenly disheveled mind found myself in a dazzling nightclub with several-hundred roller blade showoffs (along with equally skilled roller skaters) effortlessly whizzing by and all around me.

'Xanadu was definitely a weird movie about a romantic person's fondest dream of a romantic Utopia!' I thought as adroit roller skaters rushed by my stationary roller rink presence in all different directions. Then my overwhelmed brain found the wherewithal to recall a theory that I had once studied in a college psychology course. 'Maybe to reach my own special Utopia I have to explore my twelfth and final song and see how I can ascend to the very top of Maslow's Law of Human Hierarchal Development! Yes,' I decided, 'now I'm beginning to understand this rather puzzling phenomenon! Self-actualization should exist on a higher plateau than biological needs and *it* should also transcend emotional gratification too! *Its* awesome fruition should be the perfect culmination of all mortal enterprise, *its* manifestation represented in the full maturity of the human spirit, and in *my* case, *my* full emotional and mental maturity!'

After pressing the mechanism's "On" button for the twelfth time, my ears heard a familiar instrumental song which at first, my memory couldn't recall the melody's title. But in the meantime, my fantastic Music Portal Device had magically transported me to a beautiful mountainous pine forest environment. Then my dizzy mind finally recognized the title of the rhythmic song, "A Walk in the Black Forest" by Horst Jankowski. 'Of course!' I jubilantly thought as I intensely gazed upon my stunning new-found surroundings. 'The houses on that hill over there and the architecture of those buildings in the town down in the valley are German in nature! I'll bet I've arrived near Freiburg!'

I hastened along a narrow dirt path until all out of breath I reached a remote monastery retreat. I stubbornly rapped upon the large wooden door and was reluctantly greeted by a monk who spoke English with a thick accent. Father Sebastian escorted me inside the medieval-looking stone edifice and after we were sitting in two hard wooden chairs that occupied a corner of his crudely furnished office, we discussed how I had been successfully "recruited" into the select ranks of "Music Portal assemblers."

"How will I be able to achieve self-actualization?" I inquisitively asked my laconic pious sponsor. "I understand that *that's* the principal reason why I've been guided and conducted here."

"You'll have plenty of time for introspection while doing your required daily *Bible* reading," Father Sebastian aptly and curtly replied. "You'll become most inspired reading essential assigned passages, especially those moral lessons organized throughout the New Testament. That daily regimen will indeed accelerate your moral growth!"

My cynical side soon surfaced and its ego-based ugliness momentarily dominated my cerebral activity. My skeptical "outside world thinking" was not synchronized to my new self-examination reality. 'Father Sebastian and his fellow priests are isolated up here on this remote mountain and their narrow minds are trapped inside separate religious cartons!' I suspiciously conjectured. 'These holier-than-thou morons, or should I say 'these sanctimonious religious zealots', are quite ostensibly incapable of thinking outside the box!' I negatively and critically thought.

"You'll gradually learn self-discipline and after mastering that," Father Sebastian un-eloquently elaborated in an emotionless tone of voice, "you'll eventually rise above your propensity to vaguely communicate pessimistic ideas and also, at *that* juncture in time, you'll then finally conquer your affinity for being too liberally disingenuous!"

"Well then Father, what will be my assigned responsibilities here at this remote monastery?"

"First of all, you'll only be allowed to speak in sentences of ten words or less when sitting with others on our staff during our three regular daily meals, which are generally the only times that trivial conversation is tolerated," the no-nonsense priest informed me. "And starting first thing tomorrow morning, you'll be learning how to make Swiss cuckoo clocks and then also you'll be acquiring the art and science of beer brewing along with some preliminary exposure to botanical gardening, and after excelling in those basic mundane trades," the austere abbot continued his sermonizing, "we'll assign you at *our* discretion to help build sophisticated Music Portals that will be sent to psychologically depressed people all over this imperfect planet. But you'll be an expert at only one phase of the manufacturing process and will never know how to fully assemble a functioning Music Portal entirely on your own skill, and if I may add, no schematic of the entire design will ever be shown to you. Now then," Sebastian sternly stressed, "I'm a very busy man. Do you have any more curious questions?"

"Yes Father, will I ever be permitted to leave this cold all-stone monastery?" I inquired.

"After seven years of indentured labor, you'll be allowed to travel within a hundred fifty-mile radius of this rather insular retreat," Sebastian objectively related to his new subordinate. "Once you prove your worth through self-discipline and once you demonstrate an enviable work ethic, you'll be able to travel all around what is known as Baden-Wurttemberg and if your enlightened *spirit* moves you, you'll eventually even be able to visit the Rhine River Valley and tour Hohenzollen Castle, which as you know Cinderella's *Disneyland* and *Disney World* castles were modeled after. You could even visit Munich and engage in an inspirational Octoberfest or two! But first, you must start at square one!"

Right after that initial mind-opening interview with Father Sebastian, my cerebrum realized one very salient concept. My mind and body had been transported in geographic space to Freiburg, Germany but according to the hanging calendar in the abbot's office, the date was still October 6th, 2008. Based on my utterly illuminating experience here in this solitary-confinement-like large monastery, *that* sage date observation simply means that all of the people that I had teleported (when I had felt threatened during the ten confrontations involving the Music Portal Device) probably also had been transported in space to new locations mentioned in the various song titles, but probably not dispatched into other times or into other distinct historical eras.

I'm finally becoming acclimated to (and actually now enjoying) the stringent agenda associated with my daily secluded monastic way of life, the discipline of which I strongly believe has been helping me elevate my former inferior self-esteem and deficient confidence levels. I'm happy to report in this strange-but-factual humble autobiography that I'm learning some rudimentary German words and phrases and now can almost fully interpret what the sagacious priests and my fellow resident craftsmen are saying in abbreviated sentences at meals and during morning Vespers. Most importantly, I've now become accustomed to abhorring and rejecting the traditional lavish lifestyles that are greedily pursued in the baneful outside materialistic world by mostly self-centered humans.

I've been diligently making Swiss cuckoo clocks and conscientiously practicing basic beer brewing and botanical gardening for two glorious months now, and my ever-growing *spirit* is enthusiastically awaiting my eventual assignment and transfer to the highly prestigious Music Portal Assembly Workshop Wing. I truly wish to help other moral and good-hearted depressed people all over the world and give them hope for self-actualization by rescuing them through "music geographic transfers" when they happen to discover themselves being in harm's way. That genesis phase of "melancholy relocation displacement," as I now fathom it, is the primary stage of "*Spiritual* Self-actualization."

In retrospect, as I author these final very realistic words, the package that I had anonymously received from Freiburg via UPS is now fully comprehensible and its ultimate implementation makes perfect sense. I can't wait to make my significant contribution to the moral stability of civilization by helping to manufacture new innovative and sensational "next generation Music Portals" at my designated workstation, and then, in the process, attain great satisfaction by having the finished products of my extensive labor delivered to deserving-but-despondent human beings all over this dangerous-but-wonderful world.

"Like Clockwork"

My spirit has been petrified ever since I had experienced what my senses have perceived as a supernatural phenomenon! My consciousness has never been as paranoid in my entire life as it is right this very minute. After I regain a degree of confidence, I plan to seek professional counseling to help my desperate soul grapple with my current unbearable mental predicament. Let me explain the entire dilemma in detail. I promise to be completely thorough in rendering my accurate description of certain events that seemingly defy scientific explanation.

During my very smooth and comfortable United Airlines cross-country flight from Philadelphia to Los Angeles International Airport, my alert mind could not stop thinking about the one-year anniversary of my twin brother Richard Sullivan's unexpected cardiac arrest death on April 14th, 2008. Richard had been an extremely successful lawyer back in Hammonton, New Jersey and both his devoted wife Karen and myself' greatly miss his companionship. Besides my wife Susan, Rich had been my trusted confidante, friend, loyal supporter and expert financial adviser. My only brother's keen insight into evolving stock market trends was uncanny, and his shrewd decisions about often-speculative investments were accurate at least eighty percent of the times he had shared his terrific Wall Street recommendations with me.

While flying in the vicinity of Denver, my ever-anxious mind gradually refocused on my important purpose for making my three-thousand-mile week-long transcontinental excursion. 'Enough of this' sentimental fantasizing! I'm the regional manager for new product sales of a mid-sized clothing manufacturer and am presently in transit to meet-up with reliable West Coast distributors in L.A., Carlsbad, San Diego and Palm Springs before successfully completing my business odyssey back to good old familiar Hammonton,' I quite practically remembered. 'The truth hurts but Rich is regrettably gone from this Earth and I still must concentrate my full energy on coordinating sales and making an above-average- living! Now I must discard my terrible melancholy and get excited about showing off the company's new line of inventory to prospective buyers and store distributors. I gotta' convert negative emotion into positive drive!'

After the huge jet gracefully landed at LAX, I exited the lengthy concourse and then patiently waited for my luggage at Carousel #2 and upon finally retrieving my two suitcases, as is my responsible habit, I instinctively removed my cell phone from my pants' pocket and called my wife to inform Susan that I had indeed arrived in Los Angeles in one piece without being confronted with any perplexing obstacles or difficulties.

The previous week I had made arrangements to rent a *Ford Taurus* from Hertz and after picking-up the vehicle drove in the direction of the downtown Marriott Hotel located at 333 Figueroa Street, a distance of around seventeen miles northeast of L.A. International. Along the city's all-too-congested main traffic arteries my restless brain contemplated my future trip down scenic coastal U.S. 101 through Oceanside to beautiful Carlsbad, and after meeting with three corporate sales reps' as scheduled, then continuing on further south to my favorite place on the entire planet, majestic La Jolla, California.

'I can almost taste my sumptuous seafood meal at the Crab Catcher Restaurant on Prospect Street and I know I'll find it very relaxing strolling along tranquil Coast Boulevard and observing the idle seals casually basking on ocean rocks without a worry or a care,' I mused as I proceeded onward toward my accommodations' destination. 'Then I'll slowly get back to reality and the monotonous routine of motivating others to sell the company's new fall and winter merchandise lines. If it weren't for Susan and the kids,' I gratefully acknowledged, 'I think I'd be so depressed about Rich's death that I would seriously consider prematurely joining him in the hereafter! Holy Heaven!' I seriously evaluated. 'How preposterously evil! What in the world am I thinking? Since the name printed on my birth certificate reads Carl Sullivan, my often-fanciful mind has deliberately played with the words 'Carl's bad,' which is impishly toying with the identity of the coastal California city Carlsbad.'

At that particular moment, my all-too-suspect cerebral activity became more rational as I reflexively stopped for a sudden red light on Figueroa. 'I'll have to squeeze-in the San Diego Zoo, Old Town and the magnificent Hotel Del Coronado while meandering around San Diego,' I imagined and reckoned. 'I suppose I'm rather tired after the stress of traveling coast-to-coast. I'll park my car, check-in at the main desk, get to my reserved room and next take a hot shower to revitalize my senses. Then after a room service meal,' I speculated, 'I'll watch an hour or so of television and later call Susan around 7 p.m. It'll be ten o'clock back in Jersey and my wife will have put our staying-over grandchildren Joey and Debbie to sleep by then so actually, *we* could both enjoy some much-needed mutually beneficial adult conversation. Being away from home for seven days does have its therapeutic value! But in the final analysis,' I aptly concluded, 'it's always good to get back to your wife and family!'

I managed to check into Room 414 without any difficulty and wholeheartedly gave the courteous and affable bellhop a five-dollar tip for carrying my heavy luggage from the lobby to the elevator and next onward down the hallway to my temporary living quarters. After showering and then enjoying a delicious steak and mashed potatoes room service dinner, I decided to divert my attention to some popular television viewing.

As I conveniently channel surfed, I stopped my perusal upon incidentally landing on a re-run of a classic '50s Ed Sullivan Show featuring the premiere TV appearance of Elvis Presley. 'I was a mere ten years old at the time of *this* extraordinary performance,' I fondly recollected. 'Yes, Elvis's hip gyrations earned him the reputation and nickname of 'Elvis the Pelvis' and after his initial sensational appearance, thereafter Presley had to be seen on television screens from the waist up because of bitter outcries from incensed moral protesters, mostly church reverends and Catholic school nuns and priests,' I considered. 'My, how morality has vastly changed since the nostalgic 1950s!'

Soon, my astute mental activities associated other salient facts relevant to Elvis's first national network gig. 'Ed Sullivan had been in a bad auto accident and had been hospitalized and *that* evening actor Charles Laughton had been designated the substitute MC,' I observed from my random memory knowledge. 'Although the landmark show had originated in New York, Elvis was wiggling around on stage in Los Angeles at the time singing his hits Love Me Tender, Don't Be Cruel, Hound Dog and Ready Teddy with the Jordanaires providing background harmony. A record TV audience of sixty million Americans watched the show. It truly was one of the most spectacular events of the '50s decade.'

The next thing I knew, a negative thought entered my fine-tuned thinking as I rested under the covers in the soft king-size bed. 'Gee, Elvis Presley and Charles Laughton are both dead along with my twin brother. And I definitely remember that Richard was faithfully sitting there on the living room sofa alongside me and *our* parents, the four of us enthusiastically watching *this* particular entertainment show way back on the memorable date, September 9th, 1956! Oh, if only Richard and I could be somehow reunited, yes, brought together for only a brief moment!'

Fully reclined in the bed with my head propped-up with soft pillows, I became highly-frustrated and frightened with my twin brother reunion contemplation so I abruptly switched channels during an annoying commercial break. 'What a remarkable coincidence!' I amazingly recognized upon noticing the new cable offering. 'A black and white documentary film featuring the life of the late 19th century heavyweight gloved boxing champion John L. Sullivan, the first athlete to earn over a million dollars. First Ed Sullivan, now John L., the fighter's biography all-being witnessed by me, the usually unflappable and unfazed Carl Sullivan. The invincible puncher is traveling coast-to-coast arrogantly challenging all comers to brawl in a ring for a handsome five-hundred-dollar prize. Oh my God!' I quickly realized. 'John L. Sullivan is dead too, just like Ed Sullivan and my sibling Rich Sullivan!'

I swiftly grabbed the TV remote control in disgust and then very forcefully again changed the cable channel. My astonished eyes and mind couldn't appreciatively comprehend the next visual sequence, a graphic scene from the award-winning movie "The Miracle Worker." Anne Sullivan was devotedly teaching a blind and death Helen Keller how to communicate by establishing code language with her fingers on the blind girl's palm. The revolutionary breakthrough was occurring with Helen's unique understanding of the word "water" when I rapidly and promptly shut-off the aforementioned room television.

'What a bizarre series of events!' I reasoned. 'Ed Sullivan, John L. Sullivan, Anne Sullivan and my brother Richard Sullivan are all deceased! Am I the next one to bite the bullet?' I grievously wondered as sweat beads began cascading down from my forehead. 'Am I the next target in the Grim Reaper's shooting gallery? As a rule, I'm not generally superstitious but *these* weird hotel room coincidences are too inexplicable and too exceptional for me to fathom! I really have to close my eyes and get some essential sleep before I become a total basket case! An hour-long catnap will do my psyche good!'

* * * * * * * * * * * *

My deep slumber was rudely interrupted at 9:15 p.m. with the loud ringing of my cell phone. As a steadfast rule, I can only remember a pleasant dream or a reprehensible nightmare if I happen to wake-up in the middle of one. I fumbled with my communications' device and awkwardly answered the call. My ears were truly surprised to hear the exaggerated-but-worried voice of my normally calm sister-in-law, Karen Sullivan. She sounded hysterical, almost delirious.

"Karen, you appear to be alarmed, your sentences are almost frantic! What's disturbing you?" I began as my brain revved-up to normal speed. "Are you under some extreme duress?"

"Carl, I just have to talk to you. I'm at my wits' end!" Karen gasped and replied, almost out of breath. "Do you know that beautiful marble clock on my living room mantel?" she rhetorically continued. "You know, the one situated next to the large picture of my late husband."

"Yes," I stated, wiping the excess sleep away from my left eye. "Susan and I have an identical clock on *our* mantel that's right next to an identical picture of Richard. If my memory still serves me, the two facsimile Florentine clocks were expensive souvenirs given to Rich and me' after Uncle Jim had visited Italy fifteen years ago," I related. "The pair of handsome-looking made-in-Tuscany items were carefully packaged, neatly gift-wrapped and then specially shipped to the States."

"Well Carl," Karen declared with a heightened degree of exclamation, "the clock above my fireplace chimed twelve times exactly at midnight. As you're quite aware, it's been broken for over two years now. Because of my own negligence, I've never gotten it repaired despite all my good intentions. But Carl, the mystery of the unanticipated chiming has scared the living daylights out of me. You're sensitive enough to know exactly how I feel. I'm scared to death to go back to my bedroom."

"Did Tommy and Billy wake up during the chiming?" I inquired for lack of a better question to ask.

"No, fortunately *my* grand-kids had slept right through the rather strange ordeal. I mean to say Carl, the gorgeous clock is an electric one but its cord and plug had been disconnected from the wall socket behind it ever since it had ceased functioning. As you know, I seldom drink beer or alcohol but I'm so nervous that I intend to take a full shot of *Southern Comfort* after I get off the phone speaking with you."

"Please don't do anything drastic!" I diplomatically cautioned. "Are you sure someone isn't playing a mean prank on you? If they are, it certainly isn't very funny! Tomorrow morning, check your living room for a hidden tape recorder."

"Look Carl, I called you to achieve some emotional security, not to encounter some oddball guessing game on your part," Karen effectively reprimanded. "But truthfully, now that I've informed you of the unusual event, I sort of feel a little better. It always pays to express anxiety. It helps clear the mind."

"Get some rest Karen!" I sagely advised. "Broken electric clocks can't tell time or chime, especially when they're not getting any juice from a power outlet. Now then, be sure to take it easy and gulp down a second shot of *Southern Comfort* for me. That seems to be the perfect remedy to quell your temporarily neurotic condition. As long as the clock has stopped its bothersome chiming, you have nothing to worry about. But don't be too dumbfounded if you find out that your visiting grand-kids are naughtily playing a peculiar sadistic joke on you!"

"Okay Carl, thanks for your solicited reassurance," Richard's former wife sincerely conveyed. "I had felt a trifle fidgety so I figured that although it's after midnight here in Hammonton, it's just a quarter after nine out there in L.A. That's what is so remarkable about these modern cell phones. I can reach anyone day or night no matter where they happen to be."

"Yes, they're a distinct advantage over obsolete land-lines in that respect," I concurred. "Now get back to sleep and although it's no easy task, forget all about your apparent paranormal adventure. I pledge I'll call you back tomorrow morning to see if everything is all right!"

"Thanks again Carl! You're just as compassionate and caring as Richard was! Good night and please have a prosperous business trip out West!" Click.

After closing the lid on my cell phone, I pensively thought about Karen's fantastic clock experience and then was finally able to reassemble the various elements of my incredible nightmare that her phone call had trespassed into. 'Oh my word!' I concluded with awe. 'I had been dreaming that Richard and I were Union soldiers during the siege of Fort Sumter, the first battle of the *Civil War*. A powerful cannon ball sent us flying right out of our battle station, and the intense explosion propelled us all the way to Fort Moultrie on nearby Sullivan's Island on the other side of Charleston Harbor. Richard and I weakly staggered to our feet, both of us suffering from shock and bleeding from non-fatal wounds. Richard wrapped his right arm around my shoulder and we began trekking north toward what is now the Isle of Palms when we oddly encountered ashen-faced ghostly likenesses of Ed Sullivan, John L. Sullivan and Anne Sullivan, all refugee anachronisms wandering around *that* particular sector of Sullivan's Island. Yes indeed,' I considered, 'the subconscious mind certainly has the extraordinary propensity of playing imaginative tricks on one's mental health!'

I strolled over to my smaller suitcase, removed a pint of bourbon from its interior and lustily guzzled down several ounces of the delicious warm whiskey. Then I covetously approached my laptop computer to perform some preliminary investigation into the historic Confederate attack on Fort Sumter. The revelations that my dedicated discovery uncovered on Google Search Engine were both fascinating and mind-boggling.

'First of all, I had never heard of either the Isle of Palms or Fort Moultrie,' I incredulously realized. 'And according to these vivid color illustrations on my computer screen, the blue uniforms worn in my nightmare by Richard and me were indeed quite authentic and genuine-looking. And Pierre Beauregard, the Confederate general portrayed on the *Internet*, gave the orders to launch an all-out two-day assault on Major Robert Anderson and his Union Garrison defending Fort Sumter. On April 14, 1961,' I read from my trusty computer screen, 'and then the Northern troops reluctantly evacuated Fort Sumter, thus assuring a confidence-building Confederate victory. Hundreds of Charleston residents watched the ongoing conflict from the porches of mansions situated along the city's waterfront battery. And furthermore,' I marveled and comprehended, 'this entire set of circumstances is a bothersome enigma. I've never set foot in the city of Charleston, South Carolina, and I personally never desire doing so for the remainder of my life!'

Then a startling and intriguing coincidence momentarily held my mind hostage. I quickly imbibed another healthy swig of sweet bourbon from my glass bottle to provide my faltering mental state with adequate false courage. "April 12-14th, the Battle of Fort Sumter," I uttered to no one but the lavender sidewall of the well-appointed suite. "Today is April 14th, the one-year anniversary of Richard's death! According to my atrocious nightmare, I could be the next candidate to be escorted directly inside the Eternal Hotel! And yes, astoundingly, the numbers on my hotel room suspiciously match the dates of the Battle of Fort Sumter and of Richard's devastating death, 4/14. There isn't enough bourbon in this small bottle to satisfy me!"

I immediately closed my laptop, swallowed-down another mouthful of liquor and then gingerly slid my body into bed. I stubbornly refused to watch any more television out of fear of harvesting additional nightmares from my surfing cable selections, preferring as a much-warranted alternative to shut-off the room's table lamp and to then again journey into the fabled Sandman's Domain. Soon I was dozing-off, trying hard to discard recent unnerving academic disclosures about my haunting relationships with certain television programs, with departed-from-this-earth people having the last name of Sullivan, with famous Fort Sumter and with my deceased twin brother's demise. 'The *Civil War!*' I recall thinking and analyzing. 'What a horrendous oxymoron! What a malicious injustice to logical nomenclature! How in God's Name could any damned war ever be 'civil'?'

* * * * * * * * * * * *

My subsequent venture into dreamland was not a fortuitous mental voyage because it was an ugly repetition of the formerly depicted Fort Sumter disaster with Richard and myself being mutually blasted all the way to Fort Moultrie on Sullivan's Island where we again had our ironic and implausible rendezvous with Ed, John L. and Anne Sullivan. I recollected the same eerie aspects to my reoccurring nightmare because my characteristic deep slumber had been disrupted by a second disturbing call, this time from my very upset spouse. My right hand again wildly searched in the dark for my cell phone while my left appendage tried locating the side table's light switch. After several seconds of frenetic desperation, dual successes were finally achieved. A very familiar voice on the other end of the line initiated the conversation.

"Carl, I just had to call you!" my wife Susan fearfully exclaimed. "Do you know the marble clock on the living room mantel that Uncle Jim had purchased for us in Italy?"

"Susan," I answered as I clumsily flicked on the side table lamp to its 150watt setting. "I had meant to tell you. That mantel clock isn't working. I had noticed that the cord in the back had been slightly spliced since its plug had been placed into the back wall electrical socket at almost a right angle. I guess that over the years' regular wear-and-tear have taken their toll. I had thought that the bent cord might be dangerous so I had disconnected the clock before the potentially hazardous electrical wire caused a house fire. Better safe than sorry, that's what I've always believed."

"Yes Carl, I'm aware of exactly what you had done," Susan confirmed in a rather confused state of mind, "but something very outlandish happened at midnight. The clock had chimed twelve times, which as you know is absolutely impossible without its cord being attached to the rear wall receptacle! To tell you the truth, my nerves are even more frayed than the bent wire in the back of the marble mantel clock is!"

"I know it's really late back in Hammonton, but has Karen been in touch with you within the last half hour?" I honestly interrogated. "A similar mysterious occurrence had happened to our sister-in-law around midnight involving her previously broken mantel clock, which as you know is the twin to ours. You don't suppose that in some uncanny way that Richard is attempting…."

"To communicate with us!" Susan finished my impromptu theorizing in an appalled and nervous tone of voice. "Carl, I'm frightfully rattled. My mind's in big disarray! I wish that you were home here on Eagle Drive and not three thousand miles away at the

Downtown L.A. Marriott. Please come back as soon as you can. Can't you cut your trip short a day or two? I'm very jittery and I feel rather nauseous!"

"I suppose I can get out of the Palm Springs meeting later this week if I declare that an unforeseen family emergency has developed. Tell me Susan, did the grandchildren hear the chiming?" I curiously asked. "I've always argued that they watch too many ghost and horror movies as it is."

"No, I haven't heard a peep out of either Joey or Debbie all night long," my wife stated. "They're both exhausted from helping me clean-out the pool and then getting the lawn furniture out of the cellar this afternoon. Our annual Memorial Day weekend backyard barbecue is only six weeks away."

"Well Sue, I suggest you take a few of my heavy-duty sleeping pills from our bathroom medicine cabinet and please get some shut-eye," I recommended. "Karen told me that she planned to settle her nerves with a jigger or two of good old-fashioned *Southern Comfort*. At any rate, get in touch with our sister-in-law early tomorrow morning. Apparently, now you both have something in common. Like I had mentioned to Karen," I paused to collect and separate my fleeting thoughts, "I suspect that someone is playing a not-too-amusing prank on you both. That's the only feasible explanation I can offer. It's all totally beyond reason! But who in tar-nation could the dastardly culprit or instigators be?"

"I just don't know Carl," my very concerned wife replied, the tone of her delivery evidently returning to its normal decibel level. "As you often tell the children, when you think you've seen and heard everything, that's when the ordinary course of events mutate and then totally surprise you."

"Take those two sleeping pills and call me in the morning," I said, sounding a little too much like the stereotypical family physician. "I need to get some up-to-now evasive sleep myself to be mentally prepared for tomorrow morning's important power-point presentation. Some of my biggest sales reps' will be attending the conference downstairs in Meeting Room B. I can't allow strange events back in South Jersey to interfere with my informative slide show. In spite of the economic recession," I emphasized, "I gotta' be fully ready to motivate the buyers to purchase the company's fall and winter apparel lines."

"Okay Carl, you've very competently eased my anxiety," Susan assured. "Pardon the expression, but knock 'em dead tomorrow morning with your persuasive style. Call me around noon eastern time and I'll give you an update on the clock mystery once my erratic mind

is back to an even keel. The grand-kids will be glad to learn that you'll
be coming home a day or two earlier than had been expected. By then
the pool should be ready to be christened for the summer!"

"You take care Susan. Love ya' more than words can express."
Click.

'The strange episodes that Susan and Karen had perceived were
parallel conundrums,' I judged as my vagabond mind imagined words
that Sherlock Holmes might have uttered to Dr. Watson on numerous
occasions. 'But these dual puzzles are far from being elementary in
both scope and nature! Oh well,' I rationalized, 'it's time for some sleep
barring me being surreptitiously hexed and vexed by any additional
intruding nightmares!'

* * * * * * * * * * * *

Because of the influential teachings of my former ultra-liberal
Philosophy, Cultural Anthropology and Contemporary Sociology
college professors, I've never in my adult life been a superstitious or a
religious person. My contrary "practical disposition" never placed
much credence in the occult, in magic, in alchemy or in the arcane. My
ordinary approach to the notion of "paranormal" has always been to
regard such "remote phenomena" as being childish, insane and
basically naïve science fiction.

My skeptical heart along with my very cynical attitude in reference
to the off-the-wall stories related by both Susan and Karen were
together predisposed and inclined to make my interpretations both
biased and dubious. I realized that I needed to have my own 'physical
manifestation' occur to fully convince my 'objective scientifically-
oriented mind' to penetrate through its 'thick Doubting Thomas shell.'
Quite succinctly, I needed to be re-educated and converted back into
my superstitious pre-college thinking mode.

Before I fell fast asleep, my erratic brain mulled-over the notion
that only a personal 'out-of-this-world' aberration directed exclusively
toward *me* would be sufficient cause to affect any specific trepidation
that I might in the future feel. When it boiled-down to honoring
superstition, my obstinate core character was beyond the shadow of a
doubt that of a confirmed apostate.

As my tired mind sank into Sigmund Freud's favorite realm, the
same *Civil War* nightmare persisted in dominating my subconscious
psyche' as I was generally aware of my tossing and turning during the
initial stage of my stressful sleep. According to the recently established
pattern, Richard and I had been exploded out of Fort Sumter and we

304

were then violently rocketed across the harbor to the vicinity of Fort Moultrie. Upon rising to our feet, my injured brother and I were again meeting up with Ed, John L. and Anne Sullivan on the extreme tip of Sullivan's Island.

My senses were awakened from my irksome slumber by the sound of Uncle Jim's voice warning me that it was positively imperative for me to regain consciousness or else risk being escorted into the afterlife. My trembling hand managed to flick on the table lamp, thus illuminating Room 414. My strong instinct was to do all that I could to avoid the total permanency of eternal death. I felt that I had to endure and survive for the sake of Susan, my son Stephen and my two grandchildren.

Upon opening my eyes, my pupils were horrified to witness the pallid two-dimensional transparent form of Uncle James Garrison, whose frightening countenance bore an extremely lugubrious expression. Observed from my eyes' bedside perspective, Uncle Jim repeatedly was pointing toward the room's bureau and wall mirror situated directly across the suite.

Throughout the very perplexing frozen-in-time scenario, I dared not move a muscle, feeling almost paralyzed while lying perfectly still under the bed covers. Then amazingly, the visiting specter moved sideways without taking any apparent steps, instantly being absorbed into the locked door and ultimately vanishing out into the fourth-floor corridor. My senses were completely befuddled. All of a sudden my throat, esophagus and stomach all felt rather queasy and momentarily, I did feel an urge to regurgitate. I was wholly petrified.

My baffled mind felt rather feeble and my afflicted spirit was not sufficiently prepared to cope with the next sequence of unbelievable events. Upon the empty bureau there gradually appeared a color photograph of my twin brother, the impressive picture being a duplicate of the ones adorning both Karen's and my fireplace mantels back in New Jersey.

Several seconds later, a marble Florentine clock appeared next to the all-too-familiar color photograph. I turned and lifted my wristwatch from the side table to corroborate the time, just as the mystical clock stationed upon the mahogany bureau began chiming twelve times. When I set my watch down upon the lamp table, I hesitantly moved my head and eyes towards the bureau and the slightly elevated wall mirror. Slowly-but-surely the remarkable clock and accompanying picture simultaneously disappeared.

All throughout the frightful experience I had never felt that my life had been in jeopardy from an 'invisible world existential threat', but being a spectator to the anomaly, my vulnerable spirit had been both affected and intimidated. I nervously exited my bed, paced over to my suitcase, removed my precious pint of bourbon and avariciously chugged down the remaining three ounces. I cravenly hopped back into bed, and the next reality I remembered was being awakened by a requested courtesy call from the hotel's main desk at precisely 7 a.m. With the advent of daylight came the hope of continued mortal existence.

Over the course of the next five days, my normally abundant appetite for food had greatly diminished, and much to my utter dismay, I possessed no desire to visit the fabulous Crab Catcher Restaurant on Prospect Street in scenic La Jolla. In fact, I haven't eaten at any New Jersey seafood restaurant since my return from California six months ago. I seem to have altogether lost my desire to consume delectable crabs, lobsters, clams, oysters and scallops. Susan now affectionately calls me "a landlubber!"

Upon shortening my rigorous California business trip by two whole days and then after joyfully returning to 135 Eagle Drive in rural Hammonton, New Jersey, I've never felt any special need to divulge the grotesque supernatural 'weird phantom experience' that my senses had perceived at the L.A. Downtown Marriott to either Susan or Karen. My heart now knows what terror is and I find its mere contemplation to be both alien and excessively repulsive.

I've learned from recent Internet research reading that living twins often have telepathic ability, but my eerie West Coast communication with my dead brother was indeed way beyond

standard reasoning. Sometimes a recurrent nightmare reviewing my L.A. hotel room haunting occurs, savagely torturing my fragile psyche. At least once a week I'll awaken from my deep slumber, shivering and trembling. Susan insists that I discuss my dilemma with either my priest or my psychiatrist, but I stubbornly dismiss her sympathetic advice as being "unnecessary."

Just last month I had meticulously labeled the separate ownerships of the two Florentine mantel clocks, took them to a local electrician's shop and had new cords and accompanying wall plugs professionally installed. The splendid mechanisms have worked quite well ever since the essential repairs had been accomplished and I gladly paid the shop's proprietor the handsome sum of three hundred dollars for his invaluable skill and service.

Indeed, in this final contemplation of the bizarre chronology of the triple marble clock events, some matters demand that their inexplicable essence never be shared or further discussed with others, including my wife, my sister-in-law, my priest and my psychiatrist. But quite confidentially, I secretly promised my conscience that I would never again stay as a welcomed guest at the L.A. Downtown Marriott Hotel. As the immortal bard William Shakespeare had once aptly written, "All's Well That Ends Well!" That is, until the next traumatic nightmare violently interrupts and destroys my precious sleep.

"A Second Chance"

Ever since I became an acne-faced teenager back in the mid-1950s, I have always loved fast automobiles, especially ones with chrome-plated flat-head engines. When my family had lived in Bucks County, Pennsylvania from 1953-'59, my tough-guy friends and I would often hitchhike to the Langhorne Speedway on *Route 1* just above Fairless Hills and pay the dollar grandstand admission we had been diligently saving-up for just to sit in the bleachers and watch exciting motorcycle and stock car races. Then my family moved to Hammonton, New Jersey where my addiction to excessive speed persisted right into my junior and senior high school years.

And when I was old enough to drive my father's '55 green and white Chevy, I did surrender to temptation and drag race it on at least a dozen occasions, nearly smashing-up the old jalopy during four separate dangerous racing situations. Because of obstinate pride during those foolish escapades, I never fully comprehended that I had been recklessly putting my own life and the well-being of others in jeopardy.

I must admit that my lust for highway adventure has been radically reformed within the last year and I no longer value what I had once held in great esteem. Please allow me to review what has impacted my conscience (besides contemporary crazed psychos practicing road rage), and what has ultimately demonstrated to me that I really and truly do possess an immortal soul.

This present-time existence that *we* believe is ephemeral is but a "temporary platform dimension." Once the threshold of *our* current reality is fully breached, one's consciousness enters a higher dimension absolutely devoid of physical wants and needs. Based on my recent flirtation with death, I know that there is much veracity in the propitious notion that Divine Law easily transcends man's societal laws in addition to man's scientific laws. But I mustn't get too far ahead of my rather incredible narrative.

This great transformation of mine from "maniacal pride" to "sagacious mental and emotional tranquility" all started with me purchasing a magnificent white 2008 *Infiniti* sedan. But I must confess that when my grandchildren Dan and Karly are riding with me in their car seats, I instinctively abandoned my desire to speed, and subsequently, I drove defensively and cautiously in a conscious effort to protect them from injury and I kept the children safe from aggressive dangerous motorists like myself.

My wife Joanne and I have always enjoyed taking our two hyperactive grandchildren on driving trips, especially when Dan and Karly got commendable grades on their school report cards. Yes, I've always used the "reward excursions" as an incentive for the grand-kids to excel in their academic studies.

Two years ago, the four of us had traveled down to Disney World in Orlando and the year before, when both children had made their school honor roll, our itinerary had taken us to four different amusement parks in a two-week summer period: Kings Dominion in Virginia, Busch Gardens, also in Virginia, Dorney Park in Allentown, Pennsylvania and then finally winding-up our "East Coast odyssey" at popular Six Flags Great Adventure in Jackson, New Jersey.

Of course, Joanne and I justified all of the roller coaster and fun house rides by balancing-out the amusement activities with educational stops at the Smithsonian Institute in Washington, at Thomas Jefferson's Virginia home Monticello, at Luray Caverns on Skyline Drive, at Harper's Ferry snuggled in a corner of West Virginia, at Gettysburg and finally at Philadelphia's Independence Hall. Since I've always loved to drive, my cooperative wife voluntarily surrendered *that* important responsibility to me, and my body was always the one sitting behind the wheel and piloting the *Infiniti*.

Before June 15, 2009, without my wife and grand-kids riding in the car, my love affair with speed and automobiles continued unabated. Up until that dramatic life changing date, I had been a moody, materialistic, egocentric, money-motivated, Hubris-oriented, capitalistic, power hungry (and generally) introverted individual. All of *those* detrimental "personal cancerous attitudes" have been excised from my spirit as I finally realized that those derelict and selfish pursuits were not essential in *this* transitory life and are totally irrelevant in relation to "the finish line" that we (as a mindless race) are all heading towards.

But is there another (less survival-oriented) mysterious dimension beyond our physical deaths in this life? Yes, there certainly is! Is there a spiritual dimension beyond *this* human existence? The answer to *that* philosophical inquiry is indeed *yes*. All I know with certainty is that there *is* a next existence after our individual abbreviated performances on the stage of this transient world. Yes, another dimension, more of a spiritual than a physical nature, does exist after the final grains of sand fall inside our individual hourglasses.

* * * * * * * * * * * *

In 2002, I had purchased a brand-new red fully equipped Nissan Maxima and Joanne and I traveled together on many trips. One was up to the Balsams Resort in Dixville Notch, New Hampshire to admire the gorgeous autumn New England White Mountains' foliage, another trip was up to gawk at scenic Niagara Falls, a third one to tranquil Cape Cod and Boston and a fourth one to Baltimore's Inner Harbor and then touring historic Ft. McHenry. As I've already mentioned, I love to drive, but when alone, unfortunately, I *had* an uncontrollable propensity of throwing caution to the wind and then reflexively pressing my right foot hard on the accelerator.

Early morning on June 15th, 2009 I was craving sampling the first blueberries of the eight-week-long New Jersey harvest season. I dialed and called Atlantic Blueberry Company, the world's largest cultivated blueberry plantation and spoke with the always-courteous office manager Loretta Armstrong.

"Yes, we're picking the first crop today, the Duke variety," Mrs. Armstrong informed me, immediately recognizing my voice since I had in the past been a field manager for the company for eighteen hot summers. "As you know, there're what we call 'the leaders' and they'll be mostly large berries. We'll save you a flat but the wholesale market's bringing twenty-five dollars per twelve pints today so that's what we'll have to charge you. We're selling each loose pint for three dollars retail to our regular customers."

"No big problem!" I politely answered. "Price is not an issue after going eleven months without eating fresh sweet blueberries. I've read in magazine articles that blueberries are about the healthiest food a person can buy."

"That's not just industry propaganda!" Loretta laughed. "It's all true, 'true blue' as you know we like to say here at Atlantic! When are you stopping by?"

"In about an hour!" I replied, already keenly anticipating the savory fresh fruit flavor. "Yes, in an hour," I reiterated.

"Okay, I'll have a flat set aside for you, but don't worry. I promise that we won't run out. We plan to pick and pack around ten thousand crates today!"

After speaking with the very pleasant Atlantic Blueberry Company employee, I drank down the rest of my morning coffee, stepped upstairs, washed my face and shaved, combed the scant hair on my partially bald-head and told Joanne all about my fresh fruit destination. Next, I eagerly opened the garage door by remote control, anxiously hopped into my white *Infiniti*, backed-out slowly and then closed the automatic portal, which leads from the garage into the house's laundry room.

Five minutes later, I was on the outskirts of Hammonton and motoring south on serpentine-curved Atlantic County #559, better known to local residents as Weymouth Road, the two-lane highway upon which Atlantic Blueberry Company maintains nine hundred of its fourteen hundred fresh fruit acres.

I neglected to honor the vital statistics' data that most automobile accidents occur within a three-mile radius of a person's home. I could not resist the thrill and challenge of driving a powerful *Infiniti* around sharp turns on a very familiar bending road. I remember passing by Sunshine Vegetable Farm and then by Macrie Brothers Blueberry Company before ascending the *Route 559* overpass above the summer-busy *Atlantic City Expressway*.

I had gradually accelerated to a speed of sixty miles an hour, negotiating a challenging wicked curve, when an in-a-hurry eighteen-wheel tractor-trailer refrigeration rig was coming from the direction of Atlantic Blueberry and the roaring metallic monster was rounding the same curve heading north. The driver's front wheels crossed the double yellow lines and I frantically attempted swerving to the right, but to no avail. My *Infiniti* collided with (and soon caromed off) the loaded tractor-trailer, skidded off the highway and then zoomed across the narrow shoulder, smashing into a non-yielding telephone pole, which instantly brought my now-demolished new vehicle and me to an abrupt halt. To the best of my knowledge and memory, I had been momentarily knocked unconscious.

My eyes opened and managed to see several feet beyond the inflated airbag and to my right I was certain that I vaguely noticed my Father (who had passed away in September of 1974) sitting in the crumpled-up passenger side, a stern frown showing on his pallid gray two-dimensional countenance. Then much to my mounting consternation, my Father's pale stone face turned into that of a ghostly-looking supernatural personage who, to this very day, I do believe *was* and *is* my Guardian Angel.

'You've again demonstrated contempt for others as well as for your own safe existence,' the being mentally communicated without moving his lips or ever introducing himself to me.

'I know that I've been *gravely* injured!' I mentally answered, unaware at that moment of my terrible unintentional pun. 'I don't want to die, not now anyway! I have too much to live for!' I pleaded as my mind considered Joanne, my three grown sons and my exuberant grandchildren Dan and Karly.

'You might be beyond the level of self-redemption!' the mystical being mentally answered. 'You've never learned from near death omens in the past. Yes, you've never learned from treacherous situations and from close-call warnings where you had luckily escaped head-on collisions and near sideswipes, all of which had incidentally occurred rather frequently. You had always erroneously thought that you were invincible!'

Even though the brilliantly illuminated vastly intelligent flat form sitting beside me had no white feathery wings protruding from his back or any accompanying halo floating above his head, at *that* moment I was too frightened to request or question his true identity. 'Please give me another chance to pursue goodness!' I humbly begged as if I was an ancient suppliant in the *Old Testament Bible* or a feeble mendicant in Homer's *Iliad*. 'I now realize how wrong I've been in my past and wish to make amends for my gross wrongdoings. Can't I atone for my misdeeds? I promise you that I'll lead a dignified reformed life! I won't be negligent! I'll fulfill *your* every expectation!'

'Well then, I guess I could make a minor exception in this instance,' the glowing being telepathically stated. 'There's a remote-but-distinct possibility that your present perilous circumstance can be ameliorated. Tell you what I'm going to do, but if you fail the test you're soon to be given,' the superhuman being austerely stipulated, 'then you'll surely die, and consequently, your ultimate fate will be resolved by the supreme judgment of the Heavenly Hierarchy.'

'I think my left leg is broken and that my left lung has collapsed,' my faltering brain transmitted. 'And I fear I'm losing too much blood and that I've sustained a terrible concussion that might result in permanent brain damage. I think I'd rather die than live as a dependent human vegetable!'

'That's all quite reversible,' my spooky other-world companion mentally commented. 'Don't panic! Try to harness your escalating dread!' the specter encouraged. 'If it affords you any comfort, *my* will can control such simple mundane factors as broken arms and excessive loss of blood!'

'What do you want me to do?' my weary waning consciousness mentally communicated. 'What test are you speaking of, er, I mean what sort of test were you *thinking* of?'

'The task you'll be assigned to perform will be satisfactorily defined, for you see,' the sublime apparition attested and expounded, 'the concept of time in *this* awkward border state dimension that you've *accidentally* entered into can be either expanded or contracted, and therefore, it is not bound by any earthly clock or watch,' the erudite being on the front passenger side austerely explained. 'An hour, a day or a month could easily be condensed into a mere second's lapsing, so have no fear that your heart and body will expire before your prescribed project is completed. These unreliable measurements of time, namely minutes, hours, days, weeks, months, years, decades, centuries, millennia, well, they're all just arbitrary standards of expression that mere mortal men have developed over the ages, all based on the rotation of your planet and the revolution of the Earth around the sun.'

'And exactly what *project* must I do?' my weakened mind asked. 'I'm not strong enough to endure anything too strenuous!'

'First you must successfully tell me every car along with its color that you've owned since graduating from high school,' the Guardian Angel explicitly demanded. 'Recite all fifteen vehicles in chronological order!'

'Well now,' I nervously expressed to the extraordinary stone-faced supernatural being, 'after I had cracked the engine block in my father's '55 Chevy....'

'I warn you, don't use grammatically-inferior slang references!' the Guardian Angel sternly chastised. 'Say the word *Chevrolet* instead of the illegitimate terminology Chevy!'

'Sorry, Kind Spirit,' I sincerely apologized for my ridiculous impulsiveness. 'After I had cracked the engine in my father's Chevrolet,' I carefully mentally enunciated, 'my first car out of high school was my Dad's white 1961 Chevrolet Impala with a black stripe along both sides. I had been given that nifty auto' for graduating in June of 1965 from Glassboro State Teachers College, which incidentally now is Rowan University.'

'Even though time is not of the essence,' the awesome being mentally declared, 'please refrain in your narrative from engaging in descriptive over-elaboration.'

'Most sorry!' I again genuinely apologized. 'Much to my Father's chagrin, in 1966 I traded in the white Chevrolet Impala for a 1967 green British Triumph Spitfire convertible sports car that I loved driving down *Route 559* thirty miles all the way to the college bars in Somers Point, because across the bay, Ocean City, New Jersey has always been a dry town where beer, wine and liquor are frowned upon because that town had a very strict religious origin and....'

'Stop your very annoying rambling! I've already warned you about being too vociferous!' the aggravated Angel again insisted without talking. 'Try being a tad less loquacious when amateurishly employing your lackluster nomenclature!'

'Certainly!' I immediately compromised, my immortal soul's destiny weighing in the balance. 'In 1969 Joanne and I got married and her pop had given us a 1969 green Pontiac LeMans as a wedding gift. Next I believe....'

'You can't believe!' the Angel peevishly reprimanded. 'You must cite your testimony as fact and clearly communicate in concise mental declarative sentences!'

'Okay,' I consented and concurred. 'In 1972 I had purchased a used 1970 yellow Volkswagen convertible from Greg DeCicco, a teaching colleague of mine. And then for car number five, I had bought a green Pontiac station wagon from Frank Celona, and in 1980 I had traded the green wagon in for a brand-new blue Pontiac wagon from the same Bellevue Avenue dealer. And in 1983, I had also obtained a brown Pontiac Bonneville from Frank Celona because Joanne and I needed a second car to shuttle our two eldest sons around Hammonton pre-schools during our free preparation periods and during our forty-five-minute school lunch periods. According to my count,' I accurately estimated, 'that makes seven cars out of the necessary fifteen.'

'Your memory is more than adequate!' the mentally formidable Guardian Angel complimented me. 'Seven automobiles down and eight more to go!'

'Numbers eight and nine I had bought together as used cars from a dealer in Ocean City, that is Ocean City, New Jersey and not Ocean City, Maryland,' I lucidly clarified. 'The first car was a 1986 red Oldsmobile Toronado and the second was a two-tone brown 1986 Buick Riviera. I had exclusively owned Buick sedans from there on out except when I began preferring to drive Nissan products in the early 2000s.'

'You'll have to be less vague and more specific!' the Angel incisively chided. 'Now that's nine cars that you've recollected and only six more to go.'

'Well, in 1992 I had leased a white Buick Park Avenue from a dealer over in Hurfville just below Glassboro and then in 1996 my four-year lease had expired so then I proudly rented a luxurious 1996 cranberry-colored Park Avenue from the same dealership, Arnold Buick. And I liked *that* car with all its wonderful loaded accessories so much,' I continued mentally transmitting with my extensive automobile litany, 'that then I leased a 2000 metallic powder blue Buick LeSabre. That's twelve down and...'

'And only three to go!' my all-too-patient Heavenly companion mentally replied. 'Let's see if you could make it to the magic finish line without stumbling or defeating yourself.'

'Well now, we're into recent history, which is far easier for me to remember,' I responded with an increased level of confidence. 'In 2002 I decided to switch from General Motors to Nissan products. My first Nissan sports car was a nifty merlot-colored 2002 Maxima. Then in 2006 I had leased a white Maxima with rear wheel drive, but when Nissan returned to manufacturing front wheel drive cars again, I then switched to the motor company's *Infiniti* division over in Turnersville and now have a white *Infiniti*, which apparently I've just totally demolished.'

'Excellent concentration and marvelous presentation!' my immortal gray-faced companion congratulated without ever smiling. 'You've remarkably passed the first qualification. I had wrongly figured that by now I'd be transporting your blemished soul to the overcrowded and bureaucratic 'Spirit Holding and Deployment Area'!'

'Thank goodness my memory didn't fail me!' I expressed with a degree of relief. 'What's the second phase to *this* test that you had mentioned earlier?'

'Ever since you were a young man, you've liked to speed and race your various cars,' the grim-faced Angel recalled and stated. 'Your new task is that you have to race in a hundred-mile-long dangerous demolition derby against the fourteen other cars that you have owned! Are the instructions clear and simple?'

'As clear as a ton of wet mud on an already dirty windshield!' I nastily answered. 'And as simple as Einstein's Theory of Relativity mathematically expressed in reverse!'

* * * * * * * * * * * *

I don't know if I had endured an out-of-body experience during the crisis but the next thing I knew, I was sitting in my undamaged white *Infiniti* in a pack of my fourteen other former cars and waiting for the starter's flag to descend. I immediately recognized that the fifteen automobiles were stationed inside Dover Downs, a large auto-racing stadium and grounds in Dover, Delaware, which I comprehended with amazement, except that the massive grandstands were conspicuously empty. As the engines were started at the public address announcer's command, I impatiently waited for the demolition derby event to commence. My dread intensified when I noticed that all of my rivals' cars had dark-tinted windows and windshields and so, I was unable to observe the faces or forms of any of my determined opponents.

The grueling race designed for the continuation of my human life began and the first three competitive laps were without incident. Then

316

my *Infiniti* careened off of the '59 white Impala, which then rear-ended the red Toronado, with both vehicles smashing into a very solid retaining barrier. Then the driver of the blue Pontiac station wagon sideswiped me on the right rear side and I zipped across the track and knocked the green Pontiac wagon into the infield. I accurately sensed that the other crazed drivers all were keenly focused on specifically eliminating me rather than endeavoring to eradicate or dispose of each other.

The intense competition was very harrowing and nerve-racking, but all throughout the major obstacles I tenaciously persevered. I remember that the yellow Volkswagen convertible was sent rolling over and over into a pit after it had bounced-off my left front wheel's fender. I intrepidly endured all of the hazardous chaos, wanting desperately to continue living my mortal earthly existence.

Apparently, my aggressive driving habits had enabled me to prevail throughout that devastating nightmare, if indeed it was a nightmare. At the end of the surreal ordeal, all I can nebulously remember is that I had just beaten the merlot 2002 Nissan across the finish line, just before the familiar checkered flag was being slowly waved by a grotesque-looking cadaver.

The next sounds my diminished senses could recollect were the sirens of the Hammonton Rescue Squad ambulance along with a dispatched police car approaching from the south. Incredibly, I woke-up in the emergency room of Atlanticare inside Hammonton's Kessler Memorial Hospital. The doctors and the nurses were positively astounded that I had survived the terrible Weymouth Road collision without a minor scratch anywhere on my body. And I was extremely relieved to learn that the tractor-trailer driver had also escaped injury and that his cargo of delicious blueberries had been completely salvaged.

* * * * * * * * * * * *

The Hammonton Police's investigating officer was extremely puzzled by the unusual condition of my white *Infiniti*. The tractor-trailer cab that I had collided with on Weymouth Road was lavender in color but the many paint scrape marks among the dents and mangled metal on my much-maligned *Infiniti* were green, red, dark blue, yellow, powder blue, merlot and brown.

My Sicilian wife was relieved that I had not perished in the horrible accident and that I had not suffered irreparable injury to any part of my sixty-seven-year-old anatomy. A week after the near-tragedy Joanne and I had a minor argument in front of her father's mausoleum inside Oak Grove Cemetery. My mercurial-tempered spouse just doesn't appreciate my newly reformed and optimistic personality/character attributes.

"No Joanne, I refuse to spray and kill those meandering ants residing inside your father's geranium pot. My new motto is 'Live and let live'!"

"Don't be absurd!" my irked Sicilian spouse countered. "They're mere ants scooting around we're talking about, not people! I think you're turning into a devout Hindu or something like that. That tiny ant that's scurrying around down there on the bricks is not going to evolve into a Sacred Cow and then come back in a future life reincarnated as a human being!" Joanne loudly maintained. "Don't you get it? This is the United States of America we're living in! Primitive caste systems are only found in foreign distant places like India!"

A second incident validating my psychological and spiritual transformation happened just this morning. I had been reaching on top of the kitchen hutch for my basket of various vitamins and minerals when a sleeping moth was suddenly disturbed and the aroused bug instantly emerged from between the plastic bottles and then flew directly into my right eye. Ordinarily I would have searched for the downstairs fly swatter and would have violently sent the flitting moth directly into insect oblivion.

Instead of killing the small living creature, I slowly opened one of the kitchen's Andersen crank windows, lifted and removed the accompanying screen and then gently ushered the frenetic flying creation out of the house to peacefully enjoy its wonderful freedom.

'God, am I making the most out of my *new lease* on life and I don't even have to obtain a bank loan to further explore it,' I considered and then smiled. 'I'm no longer hedonistic, materialistic and egocentric, but now my most earnest objective in life is to constantly seek requiem and solace. I think I'll have some corn flakes generously sprinkled with delectable fresh blueberries for breakfast. The short berry season only lasts for eight weeks so I ought to swallow-down the luscious fruit while it's still plenteously available for local consumption.'

Then another random thought occurred to my permanently rejuvenated enthusiastic mind. 'I not only have a new lease on life but I also have learned from the guys at the Hammonton Auto Repair Shop that my white 2008 *Infiniti* can be made to look like it's brand new again. I guess I've gotten a *second chance* to participate in life's mysterious raffle, thanks to the glorious intercession of my anonymous-but-trusted extremely benign Guardian Angel!'

318

"Lost Identity"

My distraught mind's hollow memories gradually began coming together like myriad floating pieces converging into a lucid kaleidoscope pattern. But despite my noble mental effort, I still was not remotely cognizant of either my first or my last name.

"Well now Patient X," Dr. Anthony Thornwell solemnly addressed me as I was worriedly lying prone in my hard-mattress hospital bed, "after very tedious and thorough research, the four professionals gathered here have finally figured-out your true identity."

"Well then, who am I?" I politely asked the stern-mannered hospital physician. "I'm anxious to re-learn my name, even if it is simply John Doe."

"I believe *we* ought to gradually reveal that particular information to you as the delicate situation warrants," the truth-oriented doctor emphatically stated. "Let's first recap a few major items. The date today is Friday, February 22nd, 2013, and you're now resting comfortably in Room 307 of Mountain View Hospital, 3100 Tenaya Way, Las Vegas, Nevada. But before we get too involved in any actual detailed conversation," the medical man imperatively insisted, "let me briefly introduce you to these three other special people assembled inside your private room."

"Okay Doctor," I sincerely replied. "I'm sure that everyone present is here to help me discover who I am, or who I was. I hope I can remember everyone's name. My concentration is not one hundred percent at the moment!"

"This is Dr. Ivan Long to my immediate right," Dr. Thornwell calmly explained. "Dr. Long is a renowned psychiatrist with an international reputation and was instrumental in assisting us in painstakingly finding-out your identity. And to my left is Nurse Sierra Pierce, and standing next to her is Detective Thomas Manville of the Las Vegas Police Department."

"Was I the victim of a crime?" I promptly asked without any hesitation. "I think I remember being attacked and my head still aches! Yes, it all was abrupt and violent!"

"We'll comprehensively summarize *that* particular aspect of your predicament in a few minutes," Dr. Thornwell promised with a forced grin. "But first Nurse Pierce will review from her notes several extraordinary remarks and phrases that you had made during your sleep periods extending over the past six days. In the interim, perhaps you can recall some germane situations and clarify a few remote issues for us. We've documented just about everything in our files and might need to consult the accumulative data to analyze future amnesia cases," the doctor elaborated, "and I trust that we' can depend on your full and voluntary cooperation in constructively aiding our hospital study!"

"Yes, Doctor Thornwell," I courteously answered, vertically nodding my head. "As long as I get to find-out my name, recall why I am in Las Vegas and fathom exactly what had happened to me, I'll gladly give you any information I can."

"Thank you!" Dr. Ivan Long piped-up and stated as the conscientious psychiatrist jotted-down some supposedly relevant notes onto his hand-held pad. "As for *my* singular component in your case study, I've evaluated your individual circumstances and have concluded that the entire scope and sequence of vast time intervals happen to be most interesting, very intriguing to say the least."

The no-nonsense police officer next felt obligated to speak. "On Saturday afternoon, February 16th you were casually walking east in the direction of the Vegas Strip," Detective Thomas Manville contributed to the discussion, "but then you were wickedly assaulted from behind and knocked unconscious. An ambulance arrived and the paramedics administered immediate first responder assistance, eventually rendering your vital signs healthy enough to then transport you over here to the Mountain View Emergency Ward."

"What was the basic motivation for someone wanting to viciously clobber me?" I instantly asked. "Was the villain out to steal my' wallet? Was it mischief suddenly changed into malice? Do you know who had molested me?"

"Four young punks were swiftly following and targeting you without your knowledge," Detective Manville divulged. "Apparently three of them had convinced the fourth juvenile thug to play his version of the disturbing Knockout Game on you. After you were slugged on the right side of your skull," the officer informed, "you fell to the pavement, the second hard impact giving you a severe concussion. The four thrill-seeking creeps quickly realized that you had a wallet filled with cash and then the young rogues nefariously pilfered it. A moment later a senior citizen Good Samaritan was driving by and used his cell phone to call for help."

"Were the four irresponsible juvenile delinquents ever apprehended by the cops?" I wondered and verbally inquired. "I think I need to know *that* essential information so that I could have some much-needed closure to my current dilemma, having knowledge that justice is being served."

"Yes, but we'll provide you with that important background a little later," Detective Manville confided. "Now I'll defer to Nurse Pierce who will disclose what she had heard you mumbling and uttering during your bizarre deep sleep episodes."

"Your first sleep comments spoken on Sunday morning had to do with you toiling in a dimly lit salt mine, and your anxious voice was orally hoping that you could establish a better way of life somewhere else," Dr. Thornwell interrupted, asserting his ranking hospital authority and also austerely contributing to the dialogue while simultaneously trumping Nurse Sierra Pierce. "Now with the first stage salt mine scenario out of the way, I'll turn the remainder of the patient interview over to my competent Registered Nurse colleague."

Nurse Sierra Pierce then shared with her hospital room audience that I had been announcing from my sleep that I had been receiving Holy Communion in a strange foreign church with gruesome-looking three-dimensional figures of a crucified bleeding Christ being represented, the morbid-in-appearance spectacles being either statues or similar objects that were extending-out from the dark church's dull beige walls.

"I vaguely recollect those frightening images you've just described," I verbally responded, all the while attempting to comprehend various hazy thoughts originating deep inside my nebulous mind. "The visions do dwell and haunt my subconscious, and truthfully, I find the shocking manifestations to be rather reprehensible!"

Sierra Pierce then resumed her rather perplexing monologue. "And then on Monday evening you had been having another traumatic experience, this time being engaged in fighting a wild forest fire that was terribly devastating a country lumber camp," the garrulous Registered Nurse stated. "And again, later on that same Monday night, you were frightfully depicting yourself' witnessing a horrible mass cemetery burial somewhere in a large city ghetto. And then on Tuesday afternoon while heavily snoozing," the talkative R.N. continued her prattle, "you were writhing-about in your bed, yelling that you were feeling nauseous, and then you almost began vomiting from claiming to be affected from a bout of overwhelming sea sickness!"

"Yes Nurse, I do vaguely recall those very disgusting events you've just communicated, but as to their precise time and place," I paused to reflect further on the elusive subject matter, "I can't clearly determine the exact times and specific places. I wish that my sense of remembering things could be more vivid."

"But on Tuesday evening after dosing-off," Nurse Pierce proceeded with her unusual narrative, "you were laboring hard in a brewery, rolling and stacking barrels inside the company warehouse. Again the time setting and exact place of occupation were drastically missing from your fairly graphic verbal account."

"I wish I could be more helpful," I humbly apologized from my confined horizontal position upon the bed. "All that you're telling me now is somewhat meaningful in a small way, but precisely how it is significant to my life, well, that important aspect completely evades my general awareness!"

"And on Wednesday during an extended afternoon siesta," the hospital nurse continued her explicit recitation, "you were totally preoccupied in your sleep constructing a certain bridge spanning across a river, and in the meantime, having a stream of rifle bullets being shot at you as you speedily worked. And finally," Nurse Pierce summed-up her well-prepared report, "you kept repeating the strange words 'The Blue Heron', but being stymied, we couldn't decipher whether you were referring to a restaurant, to a bar, to a motel or perhaps to a golf course, any of which might be directly related to *that* specific phrase."

"I had found the Blue Heron allusion to be especially curious and fascinating," Dr. Ivan Long short-circuited the dedicated female nurse's speech. "In fact, those three words compelled me to develop a rather unique hypothesis, my evolving theory founded on the assumption that *you* had remarkably spoken about all of those eight aforementioned-but-disconnected events in a concise chronological order."

The reticent police official again felt a need to make a material comment. "But perhaps the biggest mystery of all Sir was your redundant reciting of the numbers 9783 over and over again," grim-faced Detective Manville declared. "At the outset, we were baffled and couldn't interpret whether the four digits pertained to a landline or cell phone number, to an obscure street address, or if they signified some enigmatic license plate, or whatever else. But in the end," the laconic Nevada police detective maintained, "those four muttered numbers 9783 became an absolutely vital clue in discovering who *you* really are and why *you* happened to be visiting Las Vegas."

* * * * * * * * * * * *

The pondering psychiatrist then honored his need to inject his exclusive observations into the hospital room conference. Dr. Ivan Long expressed that the assigned team had to mutually perform some "serious reverse engineering" in order to ascertain my given birth certificate appellations. The distinguished mind doctor disclosed that my mentioning of intensively working in a colossal salt mine immediately guided his mind to focus on an area of Southern Poland.

"It was sort of like me finding a Rosetta stone! I once visited the famous Wieliczka Salt Mine not too far from Krakow," the psyche examiner confidentially related. "Indeed, the incomparable mines had been constructed in the 13th Century and over the years had produced mainly common table salt. I had recently read in a geographic magazine where the massive underground facility had closed in 2007, but when they were still in operation, the famous mines featured a beautiful illuminated Cathedral Room along with three impressive side chapels and dozens of saint statues carved out of salt."

Before I could mentally synchronize any elements of Dr. Long's lucid revelation (since my addled psyche was encountering foggy memories swirling around inside), Dr. Thornwell's sanctimonious voice filled the void as the egocentric staff surgeon pontificated about me dreaming of the foreign country church where the gruesome figures of an anguishing Christ were on exhibit.

"We believe that the alluded to church you had indicated in your sleep is named Ecce Homo, which is a popular shrine located in Calvaruso, Sicily; and the unique structure had been built four-hundred years ago," the chief medical doctor orally conveyed. "Your paternal grandfather had received his First Holy Communion there, and we immediately speculated that your recollection of the powerful family story you had probably heard many times in your youth had caused your subconscious mumbling about it."

"And then the four of us collaborated and collectively conjectured that the colossal forest fire you were imagining and subconsciously witnessing was also a tale from your fraternal Polish grandfather's side of the family," Nurse Sierra Pierce aptly vocalized. "Our research found that your father had been born in Posen, just outside of Alpena, Michigan. Your grandfather, whom you had never known, had owned a logging camp, and ambitious Adalbert Wisniewski had leased hundreds of acres of forest land for timbering from the federal government. According to your younger brother's testimony over the phone," the R.N. elucidated, "in the early 1900s a huge conflagration had destroyed all of your grandfather's investment, and without owning any property insurance, your paternal ancestor had died a broken man a year later, and his remains are buried in a Posen Cemetery."

My befuddled cerebrum was attempting to contemplate and organize into a logical pattern this temporarily concealed pertinent family history when loquacious Dr. Thornwell further added to my puzzlement. "And *your* graphic citing of a mass city burial was again connected with your father's side of the family, most of whom had moved from Michigan to Baltimore around 1910. Then in 1918, just toward the end of World War I, your Polish grandmother had died in East Baltimore, a poorer section of the city. An extremely contagious flu epidemic had broken-out all over East Coast America in general and also in that section of Maryland in particular. The deadly strain was called 'the Blue Death'. Over 3,000 Baltimore residents had become afflicted and had ultimately perished from the lethal outbreak. City undertakers were immensely overwhelmed with the excessive body count, and as a stark necessity, a morbid mass grave had been dug in a local cemetery to accommodate all of the stricken corpses. Your grandmother Hedwig Wisniewski was unfortunately among the deceased in the mass cemetery burial."

"I now see the three Polish links on my father's side represented between the salt mine, the forest fire and the mass city burial," I acknowledged, "and yes, I do recall visiting Baltimore relatives with my parents back in the '50s, some residing on Foster Avenue and others on Conklin. And I suppose that the Sicily shrine comes from my mother's side. Now I believe I remember something! My maternal grandfather had emigrated from Sicily to Ellis Island in 1910. Later he settled in Philadelphia where other uncles and cousins had been residing, and yes, my Italian grandfather served as an orderly at Walter Reed Hospital during World War I, and thereafter, later moved to New Jersey to open a fruit and produce farm market."

"Yes indeed," Dr. Long concurred with my accurate commentary. "Your grandfather had gotten very sick on the rough cattle boat ride from Sicily to New York and according to your wife's recent account over the telephone, Antonio Giacobbe never attempted to learn how to swim or even ever stepped into a lake, river or swimming pool after experiencing *that* negative traumatic ocean crossing."

"And as a young man your father John once worked in a brewery in Baltimore, Maryland, which rapidly went bankrupt during the 1920s' Prohibition era," Dr. Thornwell enlightened my awakening memory. "Your original family surname was Wisniewski, but since Germans were better rooted in America in the early 1900s than were natives of Polish descent, your Aunt Marie had wisely changed your family name to...."

"To the German title Wiessner from the Polish surname Wisniewski!" I excitedly exclaimed. "Yes, now I remember everything almost as clear as crystal! My father would often tell me that both he and I had been named after an old Baltimore Brewery, the John F.

Wiessner Brewery on Gay St.! That's why my birth name is John Wiessner!"

"And your father was in the Army during World War II, serving in France, in Germany, in Luxembourg and in Holland," Dr. Thornwell embellished. "And your father…."

"Had been constructing a vital pontoon bridge across the Rhine River," I recollected and enthusiastically uttered to my four visitors, "and the urgent construction project was being done because that vile monster Adolph Hitler had ordered all bridges across the strategic river to be destroyed in order to impede the advancement of American troops. Dad had often told me that snipers were firing shots at him and his soldier buddies as they hastily rushed to assemble the pontoons together."

"Yes," agreed Dr. Ivan Long with a smile quickly appearing upon his formerly stoic countenance. "Your name is indeed John Wiessner. It seems that your vulnerable amnesia-laden mind had been dealing with your identity loss in a rather vicarious way, bringing certain stories from your family past to your mind's surface in an effort to finally recall who and what you have been and who and what you are! And the blue heron facet concerns…"

"Concerns a beautiful blue heron flying low across the Jersey highway near my home and then being clipped on the left wing by a speeding tractor trailer," I rightly answered, capably finishing the psychiatrist's statement. "The wounded bird managed to land upon the bank of a nearby pond, which had been its original destination. That perturbing incident happened the day before I had flown United Airways from Philadelphia to Las Vegas. My wife and I attempted to rescue the injured heron, but after several failed attempts, we called the county animal control, whose personnel came onto the scene right away and captured the hurt bird with a large net and then took the creature away in their white county van for possible rehabilitation."

* * * * * * * * * * * *

Detective Thomas Manville believed it was his turn to offer valuable anecdotal details to supplement the eight separate clue components. The policeman soon shared his present law enforcement activity regarding the "most current Knockout Game assault case." Naturally the plain-clothes officer's firm baritone voice methodically commanded everyone's attention.

"Mr. Wiessner, you had flown into McCarron International Airport on a direct United Airways flight from Philly', arriving in town at approximately noon on Saturday, February 16th. While here in Vegas, you were staying at your sister and brother-in-law's condo' located just several blocks from the Strip." The policeman then referred to his trusty notepad for clarification. "Their names are...."

"Stephen and Anne Hill," I said, finishing the stumped detective's declarative sentence. "And now I remember! The lock on the condo's door was much like one on a car entry, a combination of four numbers to be pressed on an outside hall wall pad, 9783."

"Do you remember why you were visiting Las Vegas?" Detective Manville interrogated. "I'm sure you do recollect if you think hard about it! And by the way, 'hard' does not mean 'hardly'!"

"My second son John Paul has a very stressful and sometimes excruciating hearing impairment," I answered. "When he was nineteen, someone else at an outdoor party lit a fire-cracker that exploded several inches from his right ear. Since then, John Paul suffers from hyperacusis, which is a condition far worse than tinnitus. Hyperacusis means that my son's ears are oversensitive to distinct noises and to high-frequency sounds like motorcycles, police car and ambulance sirens, and they're even hurt by small ice cubes plunking into a glass. The problem's far more debilitating than the more common ringing in the ears that's associated with tinnitus!"

"Okay John," plainclothesman Thomas Manville replied in a more personal manner, "but why were you in Vegas?"

"Well Sir, my sister and brother-in-law have made quite a decent living out of buying and flipping houses, especially ones located in warm climate resort areas like Vegas," I responded, inadvertently circumnavigating the fundamental question. "Of course, they've also done house flipping in Phoenix, but first got started in Palm Springs and then later in South Padre Island, Texas. Now they're spending a week gallivanting around down in Cape Coral, Florida, eagerly exploring for a new business venture."

"But John," Detective Manville patiently reiterated, "tell us why you've come to Vegas without readily deviating and explaining why Anne and Stephen Hill have temporarily left Sin City for a week!"

"I came here searching for a small quiet-type business for my son John Paul, so I had been planning on attending the 2013 Franchise Exposition at the MGM Grand up on the Strip. The show was slated to happen for four days starting Sunday, February 17th! It seems that my good intentions have been rudely sabotaged by some young street hoods bent on playing the dreaded Knockout Game on me!"

Detective Manville next plausibly outlined how my sister and my wife were key principals in assisting the Vegas cops with the successful resolution of my legal case. Both ladies had endeavored many times to call me on my already stolen cell phone, but when no one answered by Wednesday, February 20th, both women became suspicious and intelligently notified the Las Vegas Police.

"And how did you manage to collar the punk teenagers?" I curiously asked. "The kid that knocked me onto Weird Street ought to take-up professional boxing! Maybe the local junior college offers a course in Assassination!"

"Well Mr. Wiessner, your wife and sister have verified and defined the eight peculiar stories you had been mumbling in your sleep," chimed-in Dr. Ivan Long. "Their valued input gave us a better perception of your general mental condition, both conscious and subconscious."

Detective Manville was ready with a feasible explanation about the young goons' fate. "The idiots that stole your wallet and cell phone tried using your VISA Card at a nearby Bank of America ATM, but the inept fools didn't realize that you had a debit card and not a credit card, so when the machine demanded the four-digit pin number, the four imbeciles panicked and ran away. Of course, their faces had been captured on the bank's exterior surveillance cameras."

"And what about my heisted cell phone and how about my pilfered wallet?" I requested knowing. "Have they been recovered? I had brought along a thousand bucks in gambling cash, you know!"

"Yes John, your wallet has been repossessed," the Las Vegas investigator communicated, "but your money stash has been spent by the brazen thieves on drugs and also on a 60-inch flat screen TV. As for your cell phone," Detective Manville indulgently laughed, "it's been recovered, fully intact. The dumb fools had answered your number after your wife and sister had given it to us. After calling them, we instantaneously knew the GPS coordinates of the punk robbers, who were soon arrested patronizing a local crack house."

A moment of silence was succeeded by me vociferating a random speculation that had popped into my mind. "Well Folks, the Franchise Expo' is over, so I guess that my excursion out here to Vegas has evidently been a miserable failure!"

"Not exactly John!" Dr. Thornwell replied with a rare degree of emotion in his voice. "Here's my brother's business card! He's an ear doctor specializing in the treatment of hyperacusis. And his office is not far from your New Jersey home, located right smack in downtown Manhattan! I'm confident that Dr. Mark Thornwell will be able to help your son John Paul with his truly unenviable ear malady!"

"Rich Man, Poor Soul"

Sunday July 27th to Wednesday July 29th of 2014 my wife and I accompanied our grandson Dan and his eleven-year-old cousin Nick on a brief vacation excursion down to Ocean City, Maryland. The overall trip is rather scenic: Hammonton, New Jersey to the Garden State Parkway via the congested Atlantic City Expressway, and then motoring thirty-eight miles south to the Cape May-Lewes Ferry.

The hour and twenty-minute ride across tranquil Delaware Bay to Lewes was quite refreshing. And a short time-span later *that* nautical transit was followed by a pleasurable forty-five minute drive past Rehoboth Beach, Delaware and then short jaunts through Dewey Beach, picturesque Delaware Seashore Park, Bethany Beach, South Bethany and next Fenwick Island and amazingly, soon I was driving rather carefree into fabulous Ocean City, Maryland, a ten mile commercial stretch comprised of fantastic restaurants, modern shopping centers, condominiums, bars, motels, hotels and abundant popular amusement areas.

The summer trip's destination was a rather sentimental and nostalgic one for me, for from 1967 to 1981, I had co-owned the Dealers Choice Amusement Arcade under the Atlantic Hotel on the Ocean City Boardwalk. Joanne and I were excited to see what new businesses had been established in the general vicinity of our old summer haunts. We had booked reservations for connecting rooms on the fifth floor of the Quality Inn, 16th Street and the Boardwalk, twenty-one blocks north of my former place of commerce.

The first two days were spent with the four of us casually strolling along the crowded boardwalk, eating Thrashers French fries, consuming Dough Roller Pizza and also munching-on Candy Kitchen chocolates and Fishers Caramel Popcorn. Some random window shopping and buying seashore souvenirs were patiently accomplished in order to take home and distribute the purchased items to receptive family members. Of course, Dan and Nick enjoyed finding their way out of Trimpers Mirror Maze and taking a four-minute wooden carriage journey through the tourist-favorite Haunted House.

"Another arcade had occupied our former poker game store under the Atlantic," I reminded Joanne. "But now there's a retail sweatshirt and tee-shirt shop in the same location called 'Em Are Ducks."

"Why such a silly name?" my wife asked.

"Because that's the way local hunters talk down here on the Delmarva Peninsula," I clarified. "Instead of the mallard shooters pronouncing 'Them Are Ducks', in a totally grammatically incorrect manner they proudly say in local slang: 'Em Are Ducks'!"

After eating a hardy breakfast at the downstairs Quality Inn restaurant on our final day, the New Jersey group checked-out of the hotel at ten-thirty a.m., and honoring an impulsive whim, I decided to visit nearby Berlin, Maryland before heading north to exhaust the remainder of the afternoon in nearby Rehoboth Beach. On the main road leading into the town, my keen eyes spotted Ned's Nook, an oddball retail establishment that featured a wide variety of assorted junk, weird antiques and strange novelties dating back to the non-glorious Civil War era. Remembering that I would occasionally visit Ned's Nook to escape the hustle and bustle of the O.C. Boardwalk in the 1970s, I slowly pulled my silver Nissan Maxima into the almost-empty gray-stone parking lot.

"This place looks like an indoor junkyard," complained Dan from the back seat. "It has stuff that people back in Hammonton put-out for garbage collection. We could get most of this lousy junk for free at the Hammonton dump!"

"Let's go back to the boardwalk," Nick stubbornly insisted. "I wanna' go through the Haunted House and the Mirror Maze again! In fact, I think that this creepy place is much scarier than the Haunted House could ever be!"

"I used to come here when I had the store in Ocean City, just to get away from all of the loud noise and honky-tonk activity," I diplomatically explained. "Guys, I promise we'll be out of here in a half an hour. Then we'll drive up to Rehoboth Beach where I also had co-owned a beach and tee-shirt shop in the 1970s and early 80s. You two rascals can spend the entire afternoon eating hamburgers at Five Guys and playing arcade games at my expense. What do you two kids have to say about that?"

"It's a deal!" automatically agreed Dan. "I wanna' win a nice prize to take home. I hope they have some neat handcuffs like the ones that Nick won yesterday at Marty's Playland!"

"It's worth nothing being bored at this dump!" Nick concluded and concurred. "Don't buy any rotten hamburgers in there' Uncle John! They'll probably be over a hundred years old! You might get food poisoning and have to have your stomach pumped!"

Inside the dark and dreary tin-roof building I first cautiously admired an old RCA Radio cabinet, next a 1950s Muntz TV model followed by a rusty Kelvinator refrigerator, and then my wandering eyes scrutinized a large Flying-A Pegasus insignia along with several out-of-date greasy Esso and Sinclair gas station signs. While nonchalantly perusing the vast array of obsolete junk on display at Ned's Nook, my attention was instinctively drawn to a heavily dusty bookshelf where certain ancient-looking volumes were vertically exhibited. I reached-up my right hand and soon gingerly latched-onto an archaic-looking, tattered-but-impressive copy of 17th Century English poet John Milton's classic work *Paradise Lost* and being highly bemused, I curiously read the faded print that was fairly evident upon the back cover.

"This epic poem contains over ten thousand lines of verse written *in medias res* with the essential story background being revealed later. The text entails an angelic war being fought over absolute control of Heaven, Adam and Eve's fateful adventures in the Garden of Eden, the rise of Satan as a potent evil force in human events, the allusion to a futuristic Son of God appearance upon the Earth, a description of God the Father, a profile of the Archangel Raphael, who had been swiftly dispatched to Eden to warn Adam and Eve of Lucifer's imminent encroachment, and finally, this book presents a graphic depiction of mighty Michael the Archangel, God's most trusty lieutenant who had seriously wounded pernicious Satan during the aforementioned prehistoric, supernatural Angelic Wars."

'I always wanted to read this remarkable book when I was a public-school teacher,' I honestly admitted to myself. 'But I was always too busy preparing specialized lessons on Twain, Poe, O. Henry, Jack London, Shakespeare, Washington Irving and Sir Arthur Conan Doyle to ever get around to reading *Paradise Lost* in my thirty-four-year English teacher career. Now that I'm retired from education, here's my chance to finally make-up for lost leisure time!'

I politely asked the elderly clerk standing behind the grimy counter the price of the antiquated piece of merchandise, and after momentarily examining the object, he specifically quoted, "Nine dollars and seventy-five cents."

Without any hesitation, and indeed recognizing the existence of a true bargain, I hastily reached into my pocket and handed the wrinkle-faced gent a crisp ten-dollar bill. The gray-bearded fellow shakily inserted the flimsy-looking book into a brown paper bag, gave me my quarter change, thanked me for my acquisition and then stepped five paces to his right to attend to the particular needs of another enraptured customer.

Being rather happy with my belated obtainment of *Paradise Lost*, my understanding wife and I benevolently escorted totally bored Dan and argumentative Nick back to the silver Maxima, and soon the dynamic entourage commenced our northern advance to placid

Rehoboth Beach, Delaware, where we would relax and stay before eventually rendezvousing with the 4:30 Ferry from historic Lewes back to Victorian Cape May, New Jersey. Everything in the world seemed pleasantly normal up to then. My mind and heart were in complete harmony with the entire Universe. But I had no idea what John Milton's sensational masterpiece had in store for me.

* * * * * * * * * * * *

For thirty-four years I had been a dedicated New Jersey public school English teacher, and for sixteen of those same years an ambitious summertime businessman and an aspiring novelist and short story writer. I suspect that much truth exists in the speculated proposition that authors are tortured souls, possibly either struggling with self-inflicted masochistic tendencies or with recurring sadistic impulses prevalent in their neurotic nature. I've often wished that I could live my adult life over again, using my accumulative knowledge and experience of the future to avoid certain mistakes and bad investments I had regrettably made in my earlier years.

On Saturday morning, August 1st I predictably awoke as usual at 5 a.m. and quietly exited the shadowy master bedroom. Joanne had been spending the weekend relaxing down the shore in a rented home in Ocean City, New Jersey. I slowly paced down the rose-carpeted hall and very deliberately entered the upstairs computer room, turned on the wall switch to the overhead light, carefully shut the door out of force of habit, opened my desk drawer and then warily removed the tarnished Ned's Nook copy of John Milton's *Paradise Lost*.

I perceptively noticed the dull-looking publisher's page, which explicitly featured the date of publication, April 24th, 1784, London, England. I prudently turned the book's first leaf, observing that the opposite side was blank. But then my fascinated pupils observed certain typed words suddenly appearing in beautiful italics, the stunning new language all being magically represented in the form of a rather incredibly bold announcement:

By Heaven's decree, your extraordinary wish shall be granted in order for you to achieve your individual Paradise Lost. Lie-down upon this room's spare sofa and fall fast asleep. When you wake-up, you'll be age eighteen again, living with your' family. You shall live your life over from August 1st 1960 to August 1st, 2014, changing important wrong decisions you had made into dramatic positive results. You will have this exceptional *privilege once and once only, so optimistically avail yourself of this divine opportunity.*

Sincerely,

John Milton

Michael the Archangel

Astonishingly, the brief printed missive soon mystically vanished from the given space just as mysteriously as it had spectacularly appeared, leaving behind the formerly recognizable blank page. Being stunned and shocked from that most recent phenomenon, I meticulously placed the now-closed book back into the top desk drawer and anxiously pondered exactly what had just transpired.

Obeying the recently provided "blank page" instructions, I arose and promptly shut the overhead light switch, advanced my feet to the now-relevant side sofa, sat down, reclined my body, put my addled head on the soft pillow, closed my eyes and then gradually dozed-off. When I awoke, much to my utter disbelief, I was again eighteen years old and living with my parents and younger sister and brother in the small stone house situated next to Pete's Farm Market, the newly purchased family business.

Initially, it was an awkward, difficult adjustment for me, being a hormone-driven teenager again and having to abide by strict parental rules and regulations, but realizing that I had very special knowledge of future events, I immediately determined that I should make the most of my "most peculiar second chance predicament."

In April of 1959, my family had moved from Levittown, Pennsylvania to Elm, New Jersey, located in Camden County, just west of Hammonton in Atlantic County. In June of 1959, I had been invited to a Levittown birthday party given by a pretty girl I had once dated, Carol Zella. As I traveled *Route 206* south towards Hammonton after leaving my old flame's shindig, I saw that the two-lane highway was dark, quiet and deserted. I had mischievously buried the speedometer on Dad's '55 Chevy all the way from Atsion Lake to Hammonton, a distance of seven straight monotonous miles. Everything seemed copasetic until I had approached the traffic light at the intersection of *206* and *Route 30,* the *White Horse Pike.*

As I waited for the green light to appear, I noticed a large cloud of hot steam billowing-out from the Chevy's exhaust pipe. In my exuberance to experience intense speed I had inadvertently broken the six cylinder's head gasket, and engine water had leaked into the crankcase, causing a dense jet of white steam to be emitted. I had recklessly cracked the motor block and had stupidly damaged the engine's camshaft. My wild joyride had resulted in a considerable unexpected expense for Pop, who did not savor the overall damage one iota.

Although Dad was not Robert Young, he often had to show me that *Father Knows Best*. Pop was a good judge of character, believed in punishment for misdeeds, and he also had me easily figured-out as if I was a primary school simple addition problem. I was forbidden to drive his repaired '55 Chevy out of Hammonton for an entire year. But now, during my second time around as a teenager, I adroitly skirted conflict with my dad by dutifully honoring the 50 mile an hour *Route 206* speed limit from Atsion Lake to Hammonton.

Without a doubt my original senior year in high school I had neglectfully clowned-around and antagonized my self-righteous Trigonometry instructor, Mr. Andrews, who at the end of the term felt inclined to fail me, compelling me to attend summer school in a town fifteen miles east of Edgewood Regional High School. But on my second tour of duty as a high school senior, I suddenly became serious about obtaining a decent grade and so I became committed to conscientiously applying myself in learning the very complicated sine, cosine, tangent and cotangent Trigonometry functions. Much to my immense satisfaction, I had earned the respectable grade of B, and my genuine effort had skillfully evaded the necessity of attending the ever-dreaded summer school assignment.

Because I had then wisely passed Trigonometry, I could now be admitted into Glassboro State Teachers College. In my previous teen evolution, I had to stay out of higher education for an entire year, so after the family farm market closed in late October, my father had used his foreman's influence at his location of employment, Martin and Quade Company in Norristown, Pennsylvania, where against my obstinate will, I punctually became an apprentice welder of stainless-steel tube products, a job that I had formerly detested with a nasty passion. Fortunately, by showing emotional maturity and academic perseverance this fortuitous second time around, and by exerting myself and passing Trig, I no longer had wasted a full year of my life breathing-in toxic and obnoxious welding fumes.

On April 24th, 1966, Joanne and I were married at St. Joseph Church, Third Street, Hammonton, New Jersey. I was in my second year of teaching and my wife was about to graduate from Glassboro State College with an Elementary School teaching degree. I never had too much peace of mind working that first summer for my mercurial-tempered Sicilian father-in-law, who incidentally owned a reputable four hundred acre very successful peach and apple farm, so in my new alternate existence, I had intelligently traveled down to Ocean City, Maryland a year earlier than I had done the first time around while giddily riding upon the ever-revolving Wheel of Life. A fellow teacher/friend needed a competent and trustworthy assistant manager to help him run Dealers Choice Arcade, so naturally I had perfectly and luckily fit the basic job description.

The following winter, I had used my hard-earned savings and borrowed additional funds to invest in a partnership for Dealers Choice, an operation which consisted of thirty-poker machines, fifteen situated on either side of the store. A seated player would drop a dime into a side slot and five wheels would automatically rapidly rotate. Then the given player would press five red buttons on the machine's console and eventually develop a recognizable poker hand with actual playing cards indicated upon the five stopped wheels. Jacks or better would be worth ten cents towards prizes and merchandise, two pair twenty cents, three of a kind fifty cents, a straight seventy-five cents, a flush a dollar, four of a kind two dollars, a straight flush five dollars and finally, a royal flush would command Choice of the House, a noteworthy twenty-five-dollar prize.

Around two hundred different gift items ranging from ten cents to twenty-five-dollar stuffed animals, kitchen blenders and cooking skillets were on shelf display, and the interested clientele could accumulate coupons, add them together and upon finishing their boardwalk entertainment, trade the collected cash value tickets in for exhibited "plush" and "high-line" household appliances.

But several years later I quickly learned how the all-powerful Internal Revenue Service could absolutely crush an industrious boardwalk businessman's enthusiasm. Everything was functioning just fine until mid-July of 1976 when a pair of black-suited IRS agents sauntered into the Dealers Choice Arcade and stridently maintained that my thirty poker machines were "gaming devices" and not mere ordinary "amusement devices."

"These are not casino slot gaming machines with timers simultaneously halting the five wheels," I futilely argued. "They are common *amusement devices* approved by the State of Maryland, by the County and by the Town, which have all granted me licenses to legally operate. If they were *gaming devices* as you maintain, I would be violating my state, county and town *'game of skill'* licenses."

I next had my loyal manager demonstrate how he could use skill to register four aces and then a royal flush in spades on the five rectangular windows on one of the poker machine devices. The first unimpressed IRS agent declared, "He's a shill! The average person coming in here can't do that!"

The second IRS official then austerely stated, "You are hereby being assessed a hundred and fifty dollars per machine. How many years have you been in business here?"

"Ten years since 1967," I innocently and naively answered.

"Then your total fine liability will be in the neighborhood of forty-five thousand bucks," the first federal man cited with a broad grin, "and adding in associated interest and penalties of a decade-long non-compliance, your grand total owed Uncle Sam ought to be in the vicinity of seventy-five thousand smackers."

"And what if I don't pay you right away?" I shockingly asked. "What's the punishment under those circumstances?"

"Then we'll have to administer what we call 'a jeopardy seizure' of all your in-house machines and related property; we'll next padlock your doors and that drastic action will certainly make your landlord very unhappy with an empty closed store situated right in the middle of his busy block!"

In my second chance to redeem my former erratic economic life, thanks to the miraculous intercession of Mr. John Milton and the wondrous Archangel Michael, in the fall of 1975 my financially encumbered partner and I eagerly sold Dealers Choice to a Salisbury, Maryland amusement tycoon, and obviously the IRS investigation became *his* growing problem the following July. I then used half of the vital proceeds from the sale to invest in a very profitable boardwalk pretzel and lemonade concession, and the remainder of the sum was infused into a thriving hot dog and hamburger stand along with a majority stake in a well-patronized local bar, and soon I was making much more money with my new boardwalk enterprises in the altered version of 1976 than I had been earning before in 1976 when the rather distressful IRS Dealers Choice intrusion had occurred.

During that same time period, I still operated my Rehoboth Beach boardwalk tee-shirt store where decals were heat-transferred by machines onto summer apparel, and so thanks to my cherished copy of *Paradise Lost,* I had deftly evaded financial disaster and was in the process of adroitly amassing an envious Merrill Lynch stock portfolio in the interim.

During the spring of 1979 in my first tour of duty, several of my former Dealers Choice managers and I had opened an amusement arcade on Missouri Avenue and the Boardwalk, Atlantic City, New Jersey. In the fall of 1981, we were notified by our mercenary landlords that our lease had been ruled null and void because the whole block had been recently sold to Caesar's World Incorporated for the construction of a magnificent boardwalk casino.

However, in my new second 1979 reality, I never invested in the prospective Atlantic City arcade enterprise, instead using the original seed money to purchase Microsoft and Apple Computer stocks, which ultimately transformed into a terrific economic bonanza. My two partners and I also gambled our combined resources and acquired an old fleabag hotel on Pacific Avenue, which we gladly sold two years later to a huge casino syndicate for a considerable capital gain. That outstanding good fortune was soon parlayed into joint ownership of a prosperous Atlantic City Marina Bar, which effectively churned a handsome yearly dividend that subsequently allowed me in the 1990s to buy a rather decent amount of quality Google and Amazon.com stock.

In 1987, my loving grandmother had died, leaving me thirty-thousand dollars in her will. In my first mortal reality, I had foolishly invested the new-found money into an upstart computer company, which abruptly went bankrupt in 1991. In my second chance at Wall Street redemption, I sagaciously utilized the windfall inheritance to obtain a handsome chunk of Comcast Cable stock, which to my personal satisfaction, then greatly appreciated in value over the course of the next economically volatile decade.

In 1993 I originally had made a forty-thousand-dollar gain in an upstart biotech company, but then brainlessly lost the easy-found dough that had been plowed into the stock of a suddenly defunct North Jersey appliance store distributor. In my second opportunity that had been beneficially granted me by *Paradise Lost,* the formerly dissipated money was healthily put to excellent advantage in my possession of more Apple and Google stock, which naturally over the past two decades has tremendously and marvelously enhanced my personal wealth.

And because of my superb knowledge of history, I cleverly sold all of my stock market acquisitions just prior to the "anticipated stock market crash of 2008", and a full year later, purchased fifty thousand shares of Ford Motor Company at three dollars apiece, which today are worth a staggering seventeen dollars each. In my substitute 2014 scenario, I've now presently taken a mild risk and have invested half of my Ford proceeds into Yahoo and SoftBank Corporation, which together own fifty-one percent of a massive Chinese Internet juggernaut named Alibaba.

All the while during the lengthy enactment of my robust second series' financial escapades, I have been coyly using some of my sustained monetary resources to bolster my fledgling writing career, self-publishing various books in hardcover, in paperback and into familiar Kindle and Nook e-book formats. I'm hoping that this new minimum-risk entrepreneurial endeavor will sometime in the future translate into handsome inheritances for my devoted wife, my three sons and my four grandchildren.

Finally, looking back in retrospect, in 1968, during my alternate voyage through adulthood, I had diligently earned a Master's Degree in Guidance Counseling, so consequently, I engaged teenagers in one-to-one office conferences, and I didn't have to emotionally endure a thirty-four year teaching career being exposed to a plethora of defiant, insolent and recalcitrant public school "students" like I had encountered and suffered my first time around while wildly riding the extremely formidable educational career carousel.

* * * * * * * * * * * *

During my second tenure on this stellar planet, I recollected having certain ankle and knee sprains accidentally sustained in 1997-'98, which I then discreetly eliminated from my human experiences. And in late February of 2014, I had had my first routine colonostomy done, which revealed a large polyp present in my ascending colon. On March 8th I had gotten the benign growth removed along with eight inches of large intestine at Virtua Hospital, but later on my second trip around, I had the first colonostomy completed in 2005, and as a result of my judicious judgment and insight, I had cunningly bypassed the painful surgery along with the accompanying uncomfortable 2014 four-day hospital recovery.

On Sunday, July 27th to Wednesday July 29th of 2014 I again drove Joanne, Dan and Nick down to Ocean City, Maryland via the Cape May-Lewes Ferry, just as I had done fifty-four years before. On Wednesday after breakfast at the Quality Inn we traveled to Ned's Nook in Berlin, Maryland. Inside the dilapidated store I immediately found the all-too-familiar dusty bookshelf, and my on-a-mission awareness instantly noticed that a copy of John Milton's *Paradise Lost* was not there occupying any physical space. Instead, I observed an ancient representation of *Dante's Inferno,* but feeling despicably craven at that oddly stark moment, I dared not even examine it.

On August 1st 2014, I awoke for the second time; much more-discerning and wealthy than I had exited my slumber the first time around. Contrary to my previous mortal existence, my spouse now believes that I am a true stock market genius and that I'm not the pathetic loser that her gruff father had imagined me to be back in tumultuous 1965. Joanne and the rest of my merry family were safely away that particular Friday, vacationing at the splendid beach house I had purchased three years ago on 17th and the boardwalk, in pleasant Ocean City, New Jersey.

But my consciousness was aware that it was again August 1st. After fearfully and reluctantly stepping into the upstairs computer room, I hesitated before opening the top desk drawer, which I recollected had contained the sensational copy *of Paradise Lost*, the wonderful book that I had intended to finally read and fully appreciate.

I nervously opened the archaic masterpiece, turned the initial leaf and next intensely glanced at the dull-looking publication page, which then instantly transformed into a full blank. Suddenly, much to my mounting consternation, a distinct other-world statement slowly appeared in medieval-style italics' script and then several moments thereafter, the message eerily vanished into infinite oblivion. The incomparable dual synergies of the book's famous author along with the eternal talent of the omnipotent Archangel Michael were extraordinarily startling to say the least.

Well now, rich Jay Dubya, do the elementary math' and you'll arrive at the only possible conclusion. By Heaven's mandate, you had originally almost reached seventy-two years of age in 2014, and then your mediocre being was supernaturally transported back to 1960 to again live and rearrange your disheveled and haphazard financial and physical life. That unique opportunity has afforded you the expressed ability to make myriad shrewd business transactions. Now Sir, it is almost the appropriate time for your stained soul to finally make its necessary amends.

According to St. Peter's records, you are nearly seventy-two years old, and quite frankly, there isn't too much sand left inside your biological hourglass. In the final analysis, our accurate and infallible records clearly show that you will have to spend fifty-four monotonous Earth years quietly meditating your numerous faults languishing inside the vast confines of obscure Purgatory, the needed contemplations will be especially performed by your restive and secluded spirit. The specific punishment will be enacted for you to penitently atone for your nefarious propensity of blatantly and relentlessly practicing excessive and egotistical human greed.

May Almighty Merciful God save your poor lackluster soul,

John Milton

Archangel Michael

"It's in the Cards"

Up until most recently, I've never even superficially believed in Numerology, the oddball conjecture that a definite relationship exists between a particular number and a personal earthly event. I had always considered the primitive practice of Numerology to be casually classified and conveniently filed-away inside a remote desk drawer along with such other weird pseudo-sciences such as Astrology, Tarot Cards, Palm Reading, Zodiac Horoscopes and Medieval Alchemy.

My skeptical, cynical mind always had regarded the doubting hypothesis that no special "Divine Plan" exists and that unique situations and certain experiences happen to human beings because of the dominant Three C's: Chance, Circumstance and Coincidence. 'Placing credence in Providence, in Angels and in Archaic Religious Faith is fundamentally based on 'mystical superstition' along with a sprinkling of dreamful human desire in order to satisfy mankind's abundant hopes, fears, and dreads in addition to our peculiar species' myriad greedy ambitions,' I had often reckoned. In terms of "Numerology", throughout the years I have unmistakably been a professed apostate.

Predictably, being an insomniac, I had awakened quite early on Monday, October 6th, 2014. Joanne would be sleeping until 9 as was my wife's established habit, so I figured I would amble down the upstairs' hall into the comfortable computer room, which also served as my "territorial man cave," the area having a flat screen television and an overused DVR disc player. 'It's not my birthday, because my one and only *birthday* was October 6th, 1942,' I remember musing as I nonchalantly switched-on the room's overhead light. 'Today's actually my *birth date*!'

I was a trifle peeved that chilly autumnal morning since two days prior on Saturday, October 4th I had received in the mail an unwelcomed notice for Petit Jury Duty, the setting being thirty miles east in Atlantic City, with my required court-house appearance scheduled for Tuesday, November 18th.

'I've been called for Jury Duty six times in the last eighteen years and have never once been selected from a pool of one hundred registered voters who were commanded to show-up,' I very negatively pondered. 'And the court wants me to park my car in a high-rise garage on New York Avenue and then walk three long blocks through unsavory urban neighborhoods to Bacharach and Atlantic Avenues. I could be maliciously mugged in broad daylight while merely attempting to patriotically fulfill my civic duty! Thank goodness I won't be summoned again. In three years I'll be seventy-five and my old age will have evolved me out of the jury system!'

Then my annoyed mind reflected upon the frustrating matter a bit more. 'The last time I had to sit there in the court chamber for four hours while nit-picking lawyers on both sides found fault with and rejected prospective jurors, the fussy attorneys looking for twelve unbiased candidates. Meanwhile during the lengthy fiasco, I had to sit quietly in the 'cattle corral audience' knowing full-well that I could not possibly qualify because I had been acquainted with the trial's plaintiff, a relative of my wife' cousin, and besides that fact, I socially knew the judge and his wife, and finally, four years ago I had also had a traffic accident at the exact same intersection which was on the court docket currently under intense dispute with the defendant, whose lawyer's barrister father had once represented me in another complicated legal case that had been conducted way back in the 1970s!'

Feeling rather aggravated from excessive emotional duress, I quickly determined that I should activate my reliable computer and promptly ascend above my mounting indignation by scrupulously viewing the world's massive relevant problems, which obviously would eclipse and dwarf my own grievance associated with my upcoming Petit Jury Duty assignment. While my desktop Dell was loading (and with my challenged cerebrum in quest of some palpable emotional consolation) I mentally reviewed some of my mediocre life's highlights so that my slightly beleaguered mind could smoothly shift into a more positive, benign attitude.

'It's great being retired after enduring a besieged high school and middle school English teacher career for 34 years,' I rationally assessed. 'And then from 1967 to 1881, I had owned Dealers Choice Amusement Arcade on the boardwalk in Ocean City, Maryland, and also during the summer months from 1974-'81, I also had operated the New Horizon Gift and Beach Shop on the Rehoboth Beach, Delaware Boardwalk. And after eventually retiring from business, for eighteen summers I had been the field manager for Atlantic Blueberry Company, the largest cultivated blueberry farm in the world with thriving divisions in Hammonton and in Mays Landing, New Jersey.'

Just as my computer was developing a screen and displaying my all-too-familiar "Home Page", my alert senses were suddenly startled when my printer was somehow self-activated, since obviously the device was acting unilaterally without any specific command being initiated by myself. I was indeed very curious about *that* unexplained, totally bizarre irregularity.

Much to my surprise and befuddlement, a printed letter was being generated, which I swiftly removed from the underneath tray, and my general interest was soon quite astonished to comprehend that the message had originated from my Uncle Henry Mason, who had died of a massive heart attack in Baltimore, Maryland in July of 2014.

My eyes incredulously read the strange missive that apparently had been freshly authored and electronically sent, although no Google logo or Yahoo emblem or standard characteristic time of day identification had been evident anywhere on the extraordinarily transmitted document. The arcane communication read as follows:

Dear Nephew John,

This is your late Uncle Henry writing to you, and yes, I am permanently dead along with my wife, your Aunt Rachel, who as you know had died on September 18th, 2014. Thanks for loyally attending our Baltimore funerals.

Now John, in order for me to secure a better place in the afterlife, I need you to comply with honoring this one urgent request. As you are aware, I truly loved playing poker with my Highlandtown friends down in my club basement on Foster Avenue in East Baltimore. Now here's precisely what I need for you to do. Find a straight deck of fifty-two cards. Yes, it is ironic that there are coincidentally 52 weeks in a year.

Now then John: it's necessary that you ascribe numerical values to each level using the accompanying sequence and numerical weight for each set:

Four Aces	1 point each
Four Deuces	2 points each
Four 3's	3 points each
Four 4's	4 points each
Four 5's	5 points each
Four 6's	6 points each
Four 7's	7 points each
Four 8's	8 points each
Four 9's	9 points each
Four 10's	10 points each
Four Jacks	11 points each
Four Queens	12 points each
Four Kings	13 points each

Now Nephew, add-up the sum of the numbers, each to be multiplied by the *four*. For example, Four Jacks will be forty-four and Four Queens will be equivalent to forty-eight. When you add-up all 13 multiplied numbers, then simply write your recorded total on this paper in the remaining allotted space. Don't forget to add-in "1" at the end for good measure to allow for the small differential in the Earth's elliptical orbit! And in summary, kindly disregard the false notion that the number 13 is superstitiously feared by neurotic mortals as being an unlucky stereotype.

I clumsily reached for my hand calculator located upon a side table and carefully and industriously added-up the appropriate numbers: 4, 8, 12, 16, 20, 24, 28, 32, 36, 40, 44, 48, 52 and finally "1". Next I double-checked my answer to ascertain that my first calculation had been correct. I then apprehensively heeded my deceased uncle's explicit instructions by cautiously jotting-down the number 365 on the bottom of the printed sheet of paper.

'Yes John, how coincidental!' the affirmative words amazingly appeared directly below my 365 number. 'There are 52 cards in a straight poker deck, 52 weeks in a year, and as you've accurately verified, 365 days in a year. John, the interpretation of this ethereal experiment is that *you* have exactly one more year to live!'

I immediately comprehended right after the worrisome typed words had instantaneously materialized upon the formerly blank area. 'As Heaven is my witness, you will undeniably die on your *birth date*, October 6th, 2015!'

The extremely shocking final paragraph remained in existence for ten short seconds or so. Then the disturbing prophetic statement faded and next mysteriously and entirely vanished from the 'other-world' frightening letter. The only discernible language that was then evident upon the otherwise blank white printer-paper was my hand-written number '365.'

I sat motionless at my computer desk with my flashing, itinerant thoughts being burdened with complete awe, my addled brain endeavoring to logically evaluate the supernatural encounter in which I had just inadvertently participated. 'I won't disclose this unnerving encounter with Joanne,' I decided. 'This whole crazy scenario is absolutely worse than me claiming to have been abducted by cannibalistic space aliens. My wife's liable to have me permanently committed to nearby Ancora State Mental Hospital.'

* * * * * * * * * * * *

My bleary eyes were now focused upon the two decks of cards I had gingerly removed from the "man cave's" bottom desk drawer: the already examined straight poker deck and the other one being a seldom-used pinochle pack. I sat almost-petrified in my gray leather captain's chair, my confused psyche still-stunned by the disappearing nomenclature that had seemingly evaporated from Uncle Henry Mason's 'dire letter of prognostication.' Random stored ideas liberally swarmed-around inside my rattled consciousness.

'Aunt Rachel loved playing pinochle with her lady friends in the club basement of the always-popular Foster Avenue home,' I sentimentally recollected. 'All the neighbors were really proud of their front white marble steps leading into the well-maintained row-houses, the steps being a matter of joy that were diligently washed regularly by the homeowners several times a week.

'And when my family drove down to East Baltimore from New Jersey in the 1950s and '60s to visit Uncle Henry and Aunt Rachel, if the weather was accommodating, we all would merrily walk five blocks across Fleet Street (which paralleled Foster Avenue) to famous Haussner's Restaurant at 3244 Eastern Avenue,' I fondly recalled. 'The place had delicious food and especially featured a totally spectacular hundred-item art and statue collection. Enthralled diners would sit and eat their wonderful meals while strategically positioned among the various wall and floor treasures, the appreciative patrons seemingly consuming perfectly delectable meals at tables and booths cleverly situated inside what seemed to be a very fabulous art museum.'

Then, like a hostile foreign invader, a rather disturbing numerical consideration dramatically haunted my nostalgic remembrance. 'I've read on the Internet where Haussner's had opened in 1926 just before the Great Depression. The prestigious eatery had prospered as an ongoing enterprise for 76 years, and finally Haussner's closed (ironically and coincidentally) for good on Wednesday, October 6th, 1999, exactly on *my* 57th birth date,' I considered. 'And the fantastic art collection on exhibit was later successfully sold by Sotheby's Auctions of New York City for a remarkable ten million dollars.'

During my melancholy meditation my stressed thought processes were still engaged in contemplating a serious quandary. My somber introspection was soon interrupted when 'the phenomenal occult computer printer' again implausibly self-activated, and very conspicuously, the 'demonized machine' began systematically producing a second piece of startling 'Afterlife Correspondence', but this time the eerie source was being delivered by my father's recently deceased sister, Aunt Rachel Mason.

Dear Nephew,

Thank you for taking the time traveling to East Baltimore to attend my viewing and funeral. It was certainly kind for you to remember me since our families have drifted apart after your father's unexpected death in September of 1974. Now John, I truly need your help so that Uncle Henry and I can mutually ascend to a higher eternal echelon, so to speak.

As you can recall, I positively loved playing pinochle with my closest Foster Avenue neighbors who incidentally almost-daily frequented the family club basement. Now John, here is an easy numerical problem you must solve while utilizing a standard pinochle deck of 48 cards.

First, multiple the given number of cards (8) of each value or kind with the number appearing on each separate card of diamonds, hearts, spades and clubs. For example, multiply 8 X 9 and then 8 X 10 and then after you are through working with all six represented denominations, add the sum of the acquired numbers together to arrive at the desired answer. Please remember that each card will have two copies (2 nine of spades, two nine of clubs, etc.).

    8 cards of 9's (equals 9 each)
    8 cards of 10's (equals 10 each)
    8 cards of Jacks (equals 11 each)
    8 cards of Queens (equals 12 each)
    8 cards of Kings (equals 13 each)
    8 cards of Aces (equals 14 each)

John, when you have finished with your elementary arithmetic total, write-down on the bottom space of this paper your' grand total.

Worried about being smitten with some evil, omnipotent, supernatural punishment or potentially dangerous consequence, I obediently performed the rudimentary methodology described in Aunt

Rachel's ominous directions. 8 times 9 is 72, 8 times 10 is 80, 8 times 11 is 88, 8 X 12 is 96, 8 times 13 is 104 and finally, 8 X 14 amounts to 112.

Then after twice anxiously adding together the sums of 72, 80, 88, 96, 104 and 112, I very slowly and quite deliberately wrote the number 552 on the prescribed open area.

'What does the obscure number 552 mean?' I curiously wondered. 'Of what significance is it to anything?'

My random speculation was immediately rewarded and enlightened. The printer again self-activated, resulting in a series of new words enigmatically appearing on a newly printed page.

Congratulations John. Your mathematics happens to be impeccable! If you'll recall, on August 16th, 1977, the same day that Elvis Presley had died, your Uncle Ed and Aunt Jenny were killed in a horrible automobile accident in Virginia while driving to their river home on the Potomac. As you know, your Uncle Ed Garrison had owned several prominent fur stores on Grace Street in Richmond when mink coats and stoles were the fashion vogue, several decades before the emergence of P.E.T.A.

Anyway John, your Uncle Henry and I had visited Ed and Jenny in their Richmond mansion the week before the terrible car/tractor-trailer head-on collision. Your other uncle informed Uncle Henry and me that he was planning to include you in his will, which already had listed *us* as the chief beneficiaries, that is, after your father's sister, your Aunt Jenny Garrison's death.

Since your Aunt Jenny had unfortunately also died in the horrid highway accident, my husband and I had become the exclusive beneficiaries in your Uncle Ed's will. In effect John, we had cheated you out of your intended inheritance, which has over the years accumulated to the respectable sum of $552,000.00.

Please have the distinct courtesy to forgive your Uncle Henry and me for wickedly swindling the 552 thousand dollars from you. Naturally, we have to now make requisite amends to adequately atone for our avaricious, conniving, immoral selfishness.

Your Uncle Henry and I have also just communicated *this* important information with our sons Robert and William, who will within the next week transfer two checks, one each from their individual UBS Account Management stock portfolios totally in the amount of 552 thousand dollars to fully satisfy *our* guilty debt to you.

Again John, please forgive us for the mortal sin that your penitent Uncle Henry and I are conscientiously working to erase from our immortal souls.

Sincerely,

Aunt Rachel Mason

* * * * * * * * * * * *

No sooner had I thoroughly read and fathomed those rather incredible words that sensationally, everything observable magically and astoundingly disappeared from the three sheets of computer paper with the exception of the number 365 on sheet #1 and the number 552 scribbled upon sheet #2. Momentarily, my perplexed mind was rapidly drowning in a state of temporary paralysis. A minute later I was finally able to think more objectively and then effectively recognize all aspects of reality much more perceptively.

Now, feeling inspired, I was able to competently piece and tether together the several remaining jigsaw puzzle elements to this fully intriguing Numerology conundrum.

Aunt Jenny had been first married to Uncle Jim Shire, who had suffered with cancer and had passed-away at a young age in 1954. The couple had one son, my cousin Melvin, who had become a heroic B-17 bombardier during World War II. After surviving many perilous missions over Germany, upon returning to Baltimore, Melvin had experienced a severe mental breakdown, and in 1956 the decorated military veteran died from a variety of emotional and physical maladies. Thus, disconsolate Aunt Jenny married Uncle Ed Garrison five years later, but the Richmond, Virginia pair never had any children that would ever become prospective heirs.

As for myself, I definitely could have used the five hundred and fifty-two thousand dollars back in 1977, but Joanne and I now have more-than-enough income in 2014 to live comfortable lives from our combined pensions, social security checks and assorted stock and property investments.

I've presently determined that I'll place the anticipated five hundred and fifty-two-thousand-dollar bonanza in separate trusts for my three deserving sons. I've vowed that I'll never tell my spouse about the substantial October 6th, 2014 windfall and how it had ultimately been obtained because I don't want Joanne to learn (while I'm still breathing) that I had had several actively nefarious characters in my family whom my innocent wife had always considered (Uncle Henry and Aunt Rachel) as being eccentric-but-reputable individuals.

And as far as my remaining one-year tenure upon this wonderful Earth is concerned, I plan to live life to the hilt as long as my health warrants. Next month I'll be treating Joanne to a much-discussed vacation to Taormina, Sicily where we will eagerly visit the nearby mountain towns of Gesso and Calvaruso, the geographic origins of *our* maternal grandparents before our' ambitious ancestors had emigrated to America via Ellis Island in the early 1900s. If (as the esoteric poker deck had secretly divulged) I have only one more year to live, I indeed intend to make the coming duration the most memorable and glorious 365 days possible.

NON-FICTION

"Life on the Blueberry Farm"

Being a New Jersey public school teacher for thirty-four years meant that I had to find summer employment to supplement my mediocre yearly income. Since schoolteachers are "contracted" employees, they're not eligible to collect unemployment benefits during their ten-week unpaid summer vacations. And in fact teachers don't receive paid vacations or paid holidays at all since they're contracted to work a hundred and eighty school days! My former job predicament allowed me to find and explore many different alternative occupations during the summertime that I wouldn't have ordinarily dabbled-in if I had been employed in a profession that demanded a twelve-month-commitment and a corresponding twelve-month-remuneration schedule.

In the summers of 1965 through 1967 I had worked on my father-in-law's four-hundred-acre fruit and vegetable farm on the White Horse Pike (*Route 30*) in Elm just outside Hammonton, New Jersey. I drove a forklift, loaded tractor-trailers, spent many hours in the packinghouse's cold storage and generally helped manage the growing, harvesting and shipment of peaches, nectarines, apples, sugar plums, zucchini squash, corn, peppers and tomatoes, for those were the principal crops raised on White Horse Farm. My father-in-law was a tough Sicilian taskmaster, and we often didn't see eye-to-eye in regard to personnel management and also in regard to our colliding philosophies pertaining to regular day-to-day operations. Our dueling perspectives were quite often at very different ends of the thought spectrum.

From 1968 to 1981 I had co-owned and operated Dealers Choice, an amusement arcade doing summer business under the Atlantic Hotel at 410 South Boardwalk in Ocean City, Maryland. People (mostly tourists with money to burn) would come into the establishment and play poker machines that were activated upon the dropping of dimes into slots, and if the players obtained hands of "Jacks or Better," the customers received coupons of different values depending on whether the hand was a pair, two pair, three of a kind, a straight, a flush, a full house, four of a kind or a fabulous straight flush. If a rare Royal Flush occurred, the player was entitled to "Choice of the House," which constituted the top-value-prizes ranging from a giant stuffed animal to a blender, a roaster oven, a desk radio or perhaps an electric frying skillet. The boardwalk arcade also featured "money pushing games" like Flip-A-Winna', Splash Down and Pot of Gold where the player would insert a dime or a quarter and moving walls or shovels would push the inserted coin against a pile of similar coins. The object of the "Money Pushing Games" was to force coins to accumulate and then fall down a chute. Let's say if seven loose hanging coins fell and plummeted down the appropriate opening, seven tokens would be won and would then be dispensed into the winning tray compartment situated below where the player was standing. Each token was equal in value to a ten-cent coupon won on the poker machines, thus making the coupons and the tokens wholly compatible in terms of monetary exchange for displayed prizes.

From 1972 to 1981, I had also co-owned the New Horizon Gift Shop on the boardwalk in Rehoboth Beach, Delaware where the enterprise specialized in applying decals to tee shirts using special heat transfer machines. And for four summers I had also been a partner in an arcade business called Wheel and Deal on the Atlantic City Boardwalk near Missouri Avenue that was very similar to the Ocean City, Maryland operation. Wheel and Deal lasted until legalized gambling was passed in order to salvage the famous-but-declining New Jersey resort. My two partners and I lost our lease as competition for boardwalk space heated-up and when prospective casinos began buying-up strategic real estate all over the *Queen of Resorts*. So from 1977 to 1981 I had been frantically hopping back and forth like a neurotic jackrabbit from New Jersey to Delaware to Maryland riding the *Cape May-Lewes Ferry,* delivering and shuttling around store merchandise for the three independent summer operations.

In the sweltering summers of 1982 and '83, I returned to White Horse Farm to give the place (and my obstinate Sicilian father-in-law) a second chance of having a compatible business relationship, but the aging man stubbornly refused to relinquish any authority so I again bolted from that Hammonton, New Jersey business and began managing an almost defunct farm market a mile west down *Route 30*. Much to my father-in-law's chagrin, in three short summers Pastore Orchards Farm Market had been miraculously transformed into the busiest and best retail produce outlet on the busy highway.

From 1987 to 2004, I diligently worked the hot summers as a field manager for Atlantic Blueberry Company, the largest cultivated blueberry farm in the world. The farm, owned by the Galletta Brothers and Sons, actually consisted of two pretty massive plantations. The main farm called the Weymouth Division was located just southeast of Hammonton on Atlantic County Route 559 and was comprised of eight hundred and fifty acres growing the luscious blue fruit, and eight miles away on *Route 322* (the Black Horse Pike), the Mays Landing Division of Atlantic Blueberry sported five-hundred and fifty acres. All the berries harvested on the smaller New Jersey farm were transported by large company leased trucks from the Mays Landing plantation to the Weymouth Farm to be packed and then shipped via tractor-trailers all over continental United States and Canada.

Atlantic Blueberry was a massive operation growing anywhere from twelve to fifteen million pounds of the blue fruit (depending on seasonal crop volume) in what constituted an eight-week harvest season. The biggest problem with blueberries is that the crop is very labor intensive. A hundred men could operate a fourteen-hundred-acre peach farm but a fourteen-hundred-acre blueberry operation required anywhere from fifteen hundred to two thousand pickers a day during the height of the season. It was impossible for the owners of Atlantic Blueberry Company to house that many workers on their two properties.

The Weymouth Road camp accommodated three hundred Mexicans, a hundred of whom worked inside the packinghouse and in the bulk-house located next door, while the remaining two hundred men picked with the "Home Gang," which was supervised by brothers Mike and George Estrada, Puerto Ricans that had started as pickers back in the '60s and who had eventually been promoted to lower management positions. Mike and George each have small houses situated on Farm #1 and they and their families live rent-free as permanent year-round employees. And the smaller Mays Landing camp houses approximately two hundred and fifty men, all of whom' pick berries on that very scenic plantation. Juan Lopez (Lopey) and Ephraim Torres, long-time Puerto Rican employees, had the chore of overseeing the "Home Crew" and the prodigious harvests at the Mays Landing Division.

Because the combined farms only housed a total of four hundred and fifty pickers in their respective camps, Atlantic Blueberry had to contract with "Day Haul" crew-leaders that could provide additional daily farm labor. Modesto Flores (a mild-mannered long-time Puerto Rican employee) and I managed the "Day Haul" pickers at Plantation #1, and I was the Weymouth Road farm's liaison to the "outside crew-leaders" and in the process, had authority over *their* respective gangs.

In the mid-1980s the outside gangs were mostly Oriental with pickers (commuting from Philadelphia in vans and Farm Labor Transport buses) of Laotian, Cambodian and Vietnamese origins, all possessing "green cards" showing that they were "legal resident aliens." The Oriental crew-leaders had hard-to-remember names like Bunyan Yang, Lu Vang, Vang Kusanni, Inxay Pathatogong, Chia Lin, Muoa Lo, Khammy Pathong and Yang Lo. One black gang at the Mays

Landing Farm still remained from the 1950s and it was commandeered by a woman crew-leader, Frances Dantzler, also respectfully called "Miss Frances" by her obedient underlings.

But in the mid-1970s area Puerto Ricans that had started-out working on the local South Jersey peach and blueberry farms had found employment and more lucrative paying occupations in other industries and *that* job migration left a giant agricultural workforce vacuum that needed to be filled.

Soon an abundance of Mexican crew-leaders and their followers began appearing in the early 1990s and these new groups rapidly replaced the Oriental gangs that had previously fulfilled the farms' extensive labor needs. The Laotians, the Cambodians and the Vietnamese pickers had been sponsored into the USA by their crew-leaders, who in effect practiced a modern type of indenture system. The employees loyally toiled for their crew-leaders for seven or so years and then migrated to and assimilated into performing various factory jobs, construction work, laboring in fish canneries, engaging in lawn care services and toiling in tree and plant nurseries. Most of the Oriental blueberry pickers had traveled early each morning in "Farm Labor Transport" buses and in vans thirty miles from Philadelphia to begin work on the many Hammonton area New Jersey blueberry farms at 6 a.m.

The Mexican crew-leaders that replaced the Orientals in the 1990s had names like Hermann Castro, Juan Bravo, Mario Valesquez, Francisco Fuentes, Tomas Agguire, Margarito Gonzalez, Marco Rodriquez, Carlos Lopez, Olegario Garcia and Marco Sanchez. Most of the Mexican pickers now come to Atlantic Blueberry on yellow school buses hired by the company to transport them up to the Weymouth and Mays Landing farms from Bridgeton and from Vineland, New Jersey, communities where most of the Mexican pickers temporarily reside during the summer harvest season. This recent development is a win-win situation for all parties involved. The farm benefits because the workers now arrive safely to work on state inspected school buses that have the proper insurance coverage. The school bus company benefits because their drivers now have summer employment and so the bus owners can generate additional revenue when area schools are not in session. The "outside Day Haul" crew-leaders like having the new school bus transportation method because they save the expense of having their own "Farm Labor Transport" buses that in the past had required costly gas, maintenance, high insurance and also annual inspection expenses.

356

My responsibilities at Atlantic Blueberry were manifold and the farm owners had amusingly dubbed me "the Director of Documentation." Each "Day Haul" picker had to fill-out a federal I-9 Form (Immigration Paper) showing and proving that he or she was legally eligible to work in the United States. Many of the older Orientals and Mexicans were illiterate and could not read or write so the crew-leaders would fill-out the I-9 for the picker and I would check the forms to make sure that the information was correct before approving and collecting them to be photo-copied in the main office. For example, a social security number on the I-9 would have to have nine numbers and an alien green card cited as an official credential (birth certificate record) contained either eight or nine digits. For pickers that *were* U.S. citizens, a bona fide state driver's license and a valid school I.D. or a recently updated voter registration card or a government-issued welfare card had to also be presented along with a social security card for me to check.

The federal I-9 forms were a real challenge to keep track of because pickers would often get on different yellow school buses and travel to different South Jersey farms and work for other crew-leaders from day to day, so the daily work force was continually changing. The Weymouth Farm would have anywhere from between five hundred and a thousand "Day Haul" pickers show-up at the south-end dirt parking lot every morning, and the Mays Landing Farm would have anywhere between three and eight hundred prospective day workers waiting in line at the front gate to hook-up with a crew-leader and then be admitted onto the property at 6 a.m. A crew-leader would usually have anywhere from fifty to one-hundred-and-fifty workers that he or she would bring (or have transported) every morning to Atlantic Blueberry.

Another farm duty I had besides keeping track of the ever-challenging I-9 forms was monitoring and collecting daily pay slips. Every "Day Haul" picker was paid cash by his boss (the subcontracted crew-leader) at the end of the work day in the farm's parking lot. At the end of each afternoon every crew-leader had to fill-out a pay slip contract (on color-coded triplicate forms) for each worker with the worker's name, social security number, home address, date, hours worked, time in and time out, units picked and total daily wage jotted-down. The white copy went to the field worker, the yellow copy to the farm's main office and the pink copy was kept by the crew-leader. The following morning or afternoon I would drive my company assigned pickup truck to the crew-leaders' assigned fields (Atlantic Blueberry Company had over a hundred and twenty separate fields) and check each worker's yellow form (provided to me by the crew-leader) to ascertain that everyone had made more than minimum wage the day before. Then, I would drop-off the obtained crew-leaders' yellow copies to the farm's main office on Weymouth Road, *County Route 559* for Farm #1 or to the Mays Landing Division Farm office located off of *Route 322.*

Checking each Day Haul worker's yellow pay slip was necessary because the pickers were all paid by piecework or "units picked" and not by hourly minimum wage (the "home gang pickers" that lived in the camps on the two farms were paid weekly by Atlantic Blueberry checks). The piecework system was good for all parties concerned because it provided incentive for the Day Haul workers to fill flats fast since they were not paid by the hour and thus, they could make much more than minimum wage if they hustled (around forty-two dollars for an eight-hour work day would have been the minimum wage daily salary). Most pickers earned between fifty and a hundred dollars a day on piecework, being able to fill thirty-three 12-pint trays to make a hundred dollars. Some conscientious swift-handed pickers earned over a hundred and thirty dollars a day.

Each picker was distributed a plastic picking basket attached to a cord, which the field worker was required to wear around his or her waist. Usually, two full picking baskets would constitute a "full red picking tray," which was equivalent to a "flat" of twelve pints when brought to the packing house by one of the crew-leader's drivers. When two red picking trays were completed, the picker would carry the "two flats" to the crew-leader's company owned field truck and then the worker was given a ticket for each flat by the driver. Each "movie ticket" (with the crew-leader's color code and name printed on it) represented 'one flat' picked, and the worker was later paid three dollars and twenty-five cents for each tray filled. The farm would pay the crew-leaders three seventy-five for each 12-pint tray picked, so each "gang master" made on-the-average fifty cents a tray, with some of the bigger crews during the height of the season picking over two thousand flats a day for their ambitious crew boss.

The crew-leaders were also accountable for maintaining quality control in their assigned fields. The blueberries on their trucks destined for the packinghouse had to be hard and not green or black. Each flat when brought to the field truck had to be inspected by the driver and/or by his loader to make sure the fruit was acceptable to later take to the packinghouse. After *that* quality standard had been met, a picking ticket for each red tray was then handed to the worker, who would redeem his or her total tickets at the end of the day for cash in the dirt parking lot, the earned money (according to New Jersey Labor Law) being strictly disseminated by the employee's crew-leader.

The farm provided each "outside Day Haul crew-leader" with two box trucks. The crew-leaders' two drivers would circle their fields until four skids of forty-nine trays on each had been loaded onto one of the two assigned farm trucks. Then the berries were carefully driven to the packinghouse where each skid would be picked-up by forklift operators and separately put on a scale for weighing. If the weight did not conform to a specified reading standard, then the crew-leader would be "docked" (deducted) trays from his percentage of making fifty cents a tray, so the workers were constantly reminded to pick hard berries and to sufficiently fill their red trays so that their bosses made a decent profit.

At the packinghouse, each skid was labeled with the crew-leader's name, Field Number and Blueberry Variety, and then the berries were transported and temporarily held in the farm's cold storage, which for blueberries had to be maintained at forty-two degrees (conversely a peach farm's cold storage would be set for thirty-two degrees). When the packinghouse production crew was ready to pack the berries from the cold storage, a forklift driver would transport the skid of forty-nine red trays (neatly stacked seven flats by seven high) to one of ten conveyor belts on production lines. Next each red tray was carefully dumped onto a slow-moving conveyor belt.

Four sorters on each working line would take out the soft berries and the green and black ones to again ensure quality control. A weighing device would then insert the exact number of berries to make a standard satisfactory weight for each filled plastic pint. Another machine would then automatically close each lid on each plastic pint. Next the pints were trafficked to one of ten rotary tables at the end of each packing line, and finally, the finished product was hand-inserted into a handsome company shipping box neatly containing twelve pints each. The flats were then neatly stacked on skids and immediately loaded onto tractor-trailer refrigeration trucks to be shipped and transported all over continental United States and to various destinations in Canada.

When the berries arrive from the field to the packinghouse's unloading dock and accepted in terms of weight for each skid, the busy packinghouse manager gives the crew-leader's driver a yellow receipt for four skids (usually 196 red tray flats). Late in the afternoon the crew-leader takes all of his "yellow slips" to the farm's main office where a secretary adds-up all the receipts and then issues a farm check to the crew-leader. The field boss then goes to either the Hammonton or

Mays Landing bank and cashes the farm check, getting the necessary cash to pay his or her people paper money at the end of the day in the farm parking lot. Of course, the following morning or afternoon, I would visit each crew-leader in his assigned field and check for any errors and then collect the yellow copies of the pickers' previous workday hand-written contracts.

Another important duty I had as a blueberry farm field manager was filling-out and checking working papers for children between the ages of twelve and sixteen that had shown-up on the farms each morning as part of a crew. These kids were sorted-out each morning and not allowed to pick until proof of proper work-eligible documentation had been obtained. Even if Asian kids had Pennsylvania working papers or if Mexican children had working papers from another state, those substantiating documents were not valid in New Jersey. I had to make sure that each new arrival had an authentic birth certificate or alien card along with a social security card and an available parent to sign the official working paper form. Then I would transport the kids to either Hammonton High School for the Weymouth Farm or to Oakcrest High School for the Mays Landing Farm to get their credentials officially certified. Since the schools' main offices weren't open on weekends, kids that came with working papers completed and registered with the farm on Saturday or Sunday could not go into the fields to pick. And kids under the age of twelve were ineligible to perform labor for wages and were not allowed to work at all and had to remain in the parking lot until quitting time.

I also drove a bus for the Weymouth Farm. Modesto Flores and his son Willie (the farm's parking lot guard) would have each crew-leader line his or her people up in single file at 6 a.m. each morning and four buses would transfer each "gang" to their designated picking fields. First the "Home Gang" had to be transported from the camp to their field, and I would assist Mike Estrada driving his bus accompanied by my bus, good old faithful "Number 74." After the two hundred or so home crew pickers were efficiently deployed to their assigned field, I then drove white Bus Number 74 to the dirt parking lot where I joined the other three buses in transporting the eight hundred or so "Day Haul" pickers to their respective fields. A crew could not go into a field without its crew-leader present or a state registered crew-leader's agent wearing an appropriate state-issued badge. Usually, I would make six or seven bus excursions into the various fields each morning.

The crew-leader would assign two pickers to each row in a particular field. The two workers would stand on either side of the row and together pick each bush thoroughly. When a crew had finished picking a field, I ("Unit 13") would be called on my radio and I would quickly transport the workers from (let's say) Field #14 to Field #48, which might be over a mile away. Then at the end of the work day I would again drive white Bus Number 74 around the distant fields and pick-up tired workers at various waiting stations near irrigation pumps on the main gravel roads and then courteously return them' to the large dirt parking lot where they would eventually be paid cash by their bosses.

Ordinarily, each field was picked three times by hand at eight-day intervals. These are the berries that are sorted and packed in the packinghouse and then sold to the "fresh market" grocery and chain stores. After the third handpicking by the crews, large farm machines are deployed to do the fourth picking. The machine-picked berries are generally smaller and of lesser quality and they are taken to the farm's bulk house where the fruit is graded by hand sorters and then frozen and packed in either ten or twenty-pound boxes (for the better grade) or in fifty-gallon steel drums for the lesser grade "machine fourth picking fruit." The frozen machine-picked blueberries are ordinarily sold to large food processors and subsequently used for mass-produced pies, muffins and jams.

My final responsibility (as the Atlantic Blueberry Company field manager in charge of crew-leaders) was to represent them if they received citations for alleged violations from Inspectors from the New Jersey Department of Labor. Citations received might involve an under-aged child working in the field, a child found in the fields between the ages of twelve and sixteen without working papers, a pay slip discovered with a stated salary that did not conform with minimum wage laws, or a crew-leader without a badged agent in his field or with inadequate insurance on a privately owned van taking workers to the farm. Usually, the *New Jersey state inspectors* would visit each farm three times a summer and also, twice each summer they would stop the yellow school buses carrying workers to or from the farms at certain checkpoints on the area highways to look for specific violations. Conversely, *the federal labor inspectors* would check the workers' I-9 Forms along with other requirements (including field portable toilets and sanitary facilities) and would visit the two farms once each summer.

A crew-leader's day might have some significant downsides too. On rainy days the people could not work in the fields and all must go home disappointed without earning any pay. Sometimes it rains at noon and the workers only make a half-day's wages. But some gang bosses manage to compensate for their rainy-day losses by running food businesses that sell meals to their workers from their own food trucks and wagons that were constantly roaming around, especially out in the remote fields.

The Weymouth Road Farm's parking lot at the end of the day seemed like a combination of a carnival food bizarre and an amateur sporting event in progress. Tomas Agguire's wife and brother and Francisco Fuentes' wife would sell tacos and burritos from their enclosed food trucks, Ricky's Tacos and Franco's Tacos respectively. Other relatives of crew-leaders would set-up shop and vend food, chicken, cold soda, snacks and clothes from various homemade stalls or improvised benches and tables set-up along the dirt parking lot's perimeter.

In the meantime, children would play impromptu games of touch football and soccer in the center of the huge dirt parking lot until the crew-leaders finally arrived from the banks with their cash payrolls. Then everyone would quit their preoccupations and get in line to receive their daily wages.

In 2004 (my last year at Atlantic Blueberry), the Weymouth Farm had an empty field next to the parking lot seeded, and management installed soccer nets to allow for crews to compete against each other in friendly rivalry. And a baseball field still existed on the Weymouth plantation where Puerto Ricans from visiting Farm #2 would play softball (and sometimes hardball) against its rival Farm #1 home field opponents.

* * * * * * * * * * * *

I had witnessed and experienced some rather amusing and crazy things during my eighteen-year-tenure at Atlantic Blueberry Company. One July morning in the mid-1970s a black man and woman pulled-up to Field 29 on Weymouth Road where a Mexican crew was picking. The gentleman asked me if any black crews were on the farm.

"No!" I politely answered. "The only black crew belongs to Frances Dantzler over at the May Landing Division. Her pickers call her Miss Frances."

"What's your name?" the man requested.

"John!" I stated. "I'm the field manager in charge of crew-leaders here!" I proudly added. "Tell Miss Frances I said 'hi'."

"Well John, could you give me directions to the other farm you mentioned?" the concerned fellow asked. "This woman really wants to work."

I provided accurate directions to the Black Horse Pike Farm and later that afternoon when I arrived there to pick-up the yellow pay slips, Miss Frances, a *Bible*-toting chapter and verse quoter and a notorious stern crew disciplinarian, accosted me at the guard's gate, which was situated between the farm's dirt parking lot and the rest of the sprawling plantation.

"John, what's the big idea of you sending that woman over here to my field this mornin'?" Miss Frances demanded.

"The man she was with asked me if I knew of any black crews working and yours was the only one," I innocently and defensively replied, "so naturally I explained to the guy how to get to the Mays Landing Farm."

"Well John, for your information that black man was a lousy pimp and the lady that wanted work was a sinning prostitute!" Miss Frances chastised. "The next time someone wants to work for me please call Lopez on the radio so that I can meet that person at the parking lot gate. I'm a faithful churchwoman John! I'm sure you know that! I don't tolerate no guff, drinking, drugs or sex in my field from anyone! Ya' hear what I'm sayin'!"

"Yes Miss Frances!" I answered with embarrassment and regret evident in my tone of voice and showing all over my crimson-colored face.

Once I was driving a Federal Inspector around the enormous Weymouth Farm to show him that portable bathrooms had been specifically placed next to all fields being picked that day. No sooner had I finished boasting to the examiner how organized and efficient the farm was, that is, having six portable toilets on six different wagons that Modesto Flores would frequently move around the mammoth plantation to accommodate the workers in new fields being picked. Soon the Federal Inspector and I observed something that rendered itself as being rather humiliating, at least to me. An old Mexican was washing his arms and face splashing murky water onto himself' from an irrigation canal while a companion was urinating into the same canal only three feet from the first farm laborer.

"That's a serious violation!" the Inspector yelled as the federal official began intensively jotting-down notes thoroughly describing the reprehensible incident.

"But both men are only ten feet away from the portable toilets!" I angrily hollered back in defense of Atlantic Blueberry's reputable integrity. "It's not *our* fault if these uneducated workers don't have or use common sense!"

"Regardless John!" the angry Inspector maintained in an austere tone of voice. "All your workers must be advised of the law and how it applies to them. That's why *we* require portable sanitary facilities with sinks and toilets stationed in the fields. And no worker can be more than a quarter of a mile away from the portable facilities or it's a serious violation!"

"Those two men were only ten feet away from the portable bathroom!" I vigorously argued. "How can the farm be responsible for individual irresponsible behavior?"

"That's for you, Modesto and the Galletta family to figure out!" the incensed Inspector shot back. "I won't give the farm a citation this time but I assure you next time I will! A warning letter will definitely be issued however!"

Another time I got into a heated argument with a young New Jersey State Inspector in a field at the Mays Landing Farm. The over-aggressive labor law examiner had found fault with a Cambodian kid's working papers and brought the matter to my attention.

"The school principal did not sign on the line at the bottom!" the overly conscientious callow-minded inspector insisted. "The kid has an invalid working paper."

"Look!" I imperatively snapped back, demonstrating a degree of hostility. "There are two kinds of working papers. The first kind is for kids from ages twelve to sixteen that pick berries out in the field. The second kind like the one you have in your hand is for kids sixteen to eighteen that work near machinery, like any teenager working up in the packinghouse. Obviously, the school made a mistake by issuing the wrong working paper to this boy. He needed to be given the field working paper that does not require the principal's signature and not the packinghouse working paper that does for sixteen-to-eighteen-year-old kids."

The young state inspector became quite perturbed that I knew something about his job description that he didn't. He pointed to his New Jersey Department of Labor badge hanging around his neck, which looked exactly like a regular policeman's shield. "I'm the authority out here in this field!" he boisterously and sanctimoniously hollered in my face. "And I know exactly what I'm doing!"

'This guy is trying to *badger* me!' I sarcastically concluded. As the incensed inspector was busily writing out the (crew-leader's) citation (for having a kid with an incomplete working paper), a nasty fistfight broke-out around fifty feet away. Two Cambodian roughnecks began brawling and then wildly thrashing-around while throwing punches at each other in nearby blueberry bushes.

"Aren't you going to break-up the fight?" I yelled at the already rattled state inspector. "Now's the time to use your badge and exercise your' authority!"

"That's your job and not mine!" the perplexed young fellow volleyed back. "You're supposed to be the field boss here!"

I shook my head in disgust and called over the radio for emergency backup. Lopez showed-up with six burly Puerto Rican associates and thanks to stellar farm security, order finally was restored and civil behavior once again prevailed.

On another very interesting occasion, I was driving past "the Aqueduct" (also called "the Artesian Well") that fed water into the Weymouth Farm's main "grand canal." Laotian young men had killed a twenty-foot-long black snake and were standing on opposite sides of a smaller irrigation ditch using the dead serpent as a rope in a weird game of tug-of-war. Suddenly four vernal Laotians on the losing side of the deceased snake lost their equilibrium and then plunged into the shallow-water irrigation ditch below.

Another time I had come across a group of Cambodians that were roasting a small animal on a makeshift rotisserie in Field #29. Out of sheer curiosity I decided to stop my truck and chat with them for a moment.

"What's that you're cooking?" I casually asked. "Looks pretty delicious!"

"Raccoon!" a young Cambodian answered. "Want some?"

"Not really!" I laughed in total disbelief as I suddenly lost my appetite. "Where did you get it?"

"Up on the highway!" a second kid replied while pointing out to Weymouth Road. "Probably run over by a truck!"

"That animal might have rabies," I warned the two pickers. "Be careful! You are what you eat! Rabies is dangerous!"

"What's that?" the first Cambodian kid asked.

"It's a really bad disease!" I cautioned. "Make sure you roast that animal really good before you decide to eat it!"

Then one day in July of 2000 I received a call on my radio from Modesto Flores to drive out to Field #39 (Blue Crop variety) and transport a Cambodian to the dirt parking lot.

"Is he sick?" I inquired over the radio.

"No Juan," Modesto answered. "Willie just called me over the radio and said that the guy ya' gotta' take to the gate is the owner of a car that just turned over in the parking lot."

"How did it turn over?" I inquired. "is the car some kind of acrobat?"

"According to Willie, the driver had borrowed the car from the guy you're taking from Field 39," Modesto explained. "The guy was drunk and my son Willie wouldn't let him drive the car into the fields, which isn't allowed anyway! And then to harass Willie, the crazy guy started drivin' the car in wild circles real fast and then hit some soft sand and turned over! Serves him' right!"

"Does the guy I'm gonna' take to the parking lot know any English?" I asked.

"No!" Modesto yelled into his radio receiver. "And don't try tellin' him anything either! We're gonna' kick them both off the farm as soon as I get down to the parking lot myself!"

I picked-up the puzzled owner of the aforementioned car along with a friend and taxied them one mile down main elevated gravel roads to the dirt parking lot. During the lengthy ride the two Cambodians were conversing with each other in their native tongue and I could tell by their expressions and by their gestures that they were wondering what the present in-progress excursion was all about. A funny thing happened on the way to the parking lot (sic, forum). When we finally reached our destination, the owner of the white *Toyota* automobile noticed his vehicle resting upside-down in the white sand, and much to my astonishment, the owner loudly yelled at the top of his lungs, "What the hell! Oh shit!" 'At least he knows five words of English!' I thought with a smile decorating my facial features.

When I first began working at Atlantic Blueberry in 1986, I was basically unfamiliar with the various fields and their immediate environments. High reeds, weeds and grass grew between certain fields and several times I assumed that roads continued from one field to another and then suddenly (on at least six occasions) I found my pickup plunging into small canals or into irrigation ditches. Then I would call Modesto on Farm #1 or Lopez (Lopey) on Farm #2 over the radio to come by and drag me out of my entrapment using sturdy chains as towlines attached to their four-wheel drive trucks.

But one time in the early eighties I had a really close call. I confidently and nonchalantly drove my empty bus #74 up Puerto Rican Avenue (local farm reference) on Farm #1 to "the Columbian Highway" (another local farm jargon term) that wended through a narrow-woods. The dirt and gravel trail led to seven distant and remote blueberry fields (located above Creek Road) that bordered on the *Atlantic City Expressway*. I had been directed to help Mike Estrada deliver the "Home Gang" to Field Number 14 (The Funny Field). Two buses doing the job could make the transportation of two hundred men a lot easier with fewer trips back and forth for the genial Home Gang foreman.

At the end of "the Columbian Highway" was a wicked right-angle curve that only a very skilled bus driver could negotiate. I cautiously and slowly approached "Deadman's Curve" in my white #74 bus and after getting halfway around the bend, I feared that I had not sufficiently cut the angle. I panicked and then gingerly backed-up, not realizing that my right front wheel was passing over soft sand. The bus began sliding to the right and I feared that my vehicle was going to topple over into the large canal below. Luckily the bus stopped its slide down the rugged treacherous slope, but then the front door couldn't be opened because it had become embedded in sand. Furthermore, the bus's hood and engine had tilted sideways and motor oil had leaked-out and gotten onto the hot engine, causing fire and smoke to escape. "I'm trapped inside!" I yelled to Mike and George Estrada over the radio.

I attempted squeezing my body out one of the side windows of the old refurbished school bus, but my frame was too big and bulky. I tried escaping out the back door, but it was rusty and would not open. Meanwhile, smoke billowed and fire raged-out from the bus's very hot motor. Then I remembered that there was an ax under the driver's seat and I was about to smash my way out of the back door when an alert Mexican managed to open the hood and throw handfuls of sand inside, thus effectively smothering the engine fire. A farm front-end-loader was summoned and it dragged the bus out of its precarious entrapment. Once back on level ground I finally was able to open the door and personally thank my rescuers. 'Thank heaven that the bus wasn't jammed with fifty screaming hysterical Mexicans!' I solemnly thought.

In the summer of '99, a tremendous-sized septic truck came rumbling onto Farm #1 to empty and service the several dozen portable toilets strategically stationed between various fields being picked. Apparently, the in-a-hurry driver was behind schedule and the fellow was speeding (in the monster vehicle) down the parking lot entrance road, which was elevated eight feet or so above parallel canals that existed alongside the hard gravel raised thoroughfare. All of a sudden, the immense truck's right front wheel hit a soft spot and before the speeding driver could steer the out-of-control "Honey Wagon" in the opposite direction, the vehicle's great weight made it skid and then wildly flip sideways down into the right-side canal. I was the first responder on the scene and I stopped my vehicle on the gravel road, fearing that the septic truck driver had been killed, seriously injured or perhaps was unconscious.

"Hey, are you okay?" I yelled down into the canal. "Please answer me!" No response was forthcoming so I figured I should radio for help. After a third holler I noticed a hand and then a body slowing emerging from the driver's side of the cab, which was partially submerged in water (so to my imagination the fellow appeared to be exiting from a submarine hatch). The disoriented-but-unscathed driver climbed sideways out of the vehicle's open window and a half hour later two large farm bulldozer operators collaborated to extricate the massive septic truck from the brackish-water canal. Luckily (for the truck's navigator on that particular morning) the ditch was not filled to its seven-foot-deep capacity.

On the Fourth of July in 2002, Modesto Flores summoned me over the radio to come to Field Number 23 (Duke Variety) in a hurry and to bring several large sheets of cardboard and a blanket from the office "on the double." I immediately sped my truck towards the packinghouse to acquire the demanded materials.

"What's wrong?" I nervously asked into my radio. "What's going on Mo?"

"A Mexican lady is having a baby and you and me are gonna' be the doctors until an ambulance arrives!" Modesto screamed into his radio in a panic-oriented voice.

I rushed to the office, obtained the requested blanket, threw two sheets of cardboard onto the back of my company truck and frenetically raced out to Field Number 23. Dr. Modesto was in the process of delivering the baby and its head was already sticking-out of the woman's womb. I laid the cardboard down and handed Modesto the blue blanket.

"Quick John!" Modesto ordered as I gazed in amazement at the spectacle before me. "Go out on Weymouth Road in front of the packinghouse and wave-down the ambulance that's been called. Have them follow you to this field pronto!"

I did as had been instructed, and when the Hamilton Township emergency paramedics arrived, I dutifully led them from the main office to the scene of confusion. When the rescue squad unit's vehicle came to a halt, I noticed that the baby had already been delivered by Dr. Modesto' and that the male infant was being cuddled in its mother's arms with the umbilical cord still attached. The woman and her newborn were immediately conducted to a nearby hospital to receive professional medical care.

'Thank God there weren't any major complications!' I thought. "Modesto, I believe you've just performed a minor miracle!"

* * * * * * * * * * * *

My daily routines with Atlantic Blueberry Company were conducted from mid-June to August 1, the length of the main blueberry harvest. The company raised over twenty varieties of berries with Dukes, Bluetteas and Blue Crop being the most popular and abundant varieties. Many of the varieties were developed on Farm #1 under the supervision of the Agricultural Department of *Rutgers University*, New Brunswick. In fact the Duke variety name originated from Arthur "Duke" Galletta," one of Atlantic Blueberry's founders. The large sweet Dukes had replaced the early-season Weymouth and Collins varieties that were popular and prevalent in the 1950s, '60s and early '70s. The last variety of the season was the Elliotts, a tart berry used mostly for making pies and jellies. The Elliotts were handpicked a second time around August 10th and then machine-picked a third and a final fourth time thereafter.

My workday started at around 5:30 a.m. and lasted until 5:30 p.m. seven days a week for eight action-packed consecutive weeks. I only had off when it rained since the pickers couldn't work in the fields, which in total amounted to around six days each summer. And I drove my white company truck between the two farms and through dirt fields with dusty roads putting on an average of eighty miles on the odometer each and every day.

The crews of various nationalities had to be kept in separate fields far apart from each other in order to avoid conflicts. The Laotians didn't mix too well with the Vietnamese, who also had problems with the Cambodians. And the Mexicans didn't get along too well with the Guatemalans, and several times while driving around randomly "troubleshooting," I had to send-out a "Mayday" for help to break-up altercations that would instantly flare-up between nationality groups. In a matter of five minutes twenty farm trucks would converge on the scene of alarm to calm matters down.

Two crew-leaders that absolutely hated each other were Laotians Inxay Pathatogong and Khammy Pathong, who both claimed to speak ten languages including Chinese, English and Cambodian. Inxay (pronounced "In-sigh") claimed to be a tank gunner in Laos during the time of the *Vietnam War* and Khammy (pronounced Ka-my) claimed that Inxay was nothing more than a flunky foot soldier and jeep driver working for *him* when Pathong had been a respectable prestigious lofty Captain in the Laotian Army.

I tended to believe Khammy's version of *their* Southeast Asian relationship because I knew that Inxay had started-out at Atlantic

Blueberry as a field driver and loader for Khammy and then after gaining field experience, the maverick demonstrated his propensity for free enterprise and started his own crew and became a "gang leader" on his own initiative. That background (for all intent and purpose) explains the tremendous rift and fundamental animosity existing between the two strong-minded individuals.

Both Khammy and Inxay always wore paramilitary clothing and heavy combat boots and had gold-framed front teeth showing in their mouths. The two carried knives concealed inside sheaths that dangled from their thick-banded waist belts. And with the strange farm environments having plenty of canals, ditches, high reeds, thousands of blueberry bushes and accompanying military jets flying overhead from the nearby Pomona National Guard Air Base (located right next to *Atlantic City Airport*) practicing flight maneuvers above and around Atlantic Blueberry (with all of the Oriental and Mexican pickers peering-up at the A-10 Warthog jets), the immense place actually at times seemed like a foreign country to me.

The Galletta family made sure that they had assigned Inxay to Farm #1 and Khammy to the *Route 322* Mays Landing Division to keep the two dedicated enemies eight miles apart from one another. Inxay would often hop-up on the back of a pickup truck in Farm #1's dirt parking lot and violently yell-out instructions to his scared workers in his native language as if he were Pol Pot or a formidable Asian military general laying-out battle plans to *his* hundred intimidated troops grouped below and all around him. But Khammy once told me that *he* had worked closely with the *CIA* in Laos during the *Vietnam War* and that Inxay had never had the opportunity or the courage to shoot or kill anyone.

"Did you ever kill anyone?" I respectfully and warily asked Khammy.

"Yes John, I kill many, many people!" Khammy tersely answered.

"Did you shoot them with a rifle or pistol?" I sincerely inquired.

"No!" Khammy curtly replied. "I kill at least a hundred people with my knife!" the maniac indicated as he removed his sharp weapon from his belt sheath and boldly exhibited it to me. "I cut their throat like this!" the fanatic exclaimed as he gestured menacingly while realistically wielding his knife.

"Okay Khammy, I do believe you!" I remarked with great apprehension and feigned admiration. "Now you're peacefully living in the United States of America so please put your knife away."

Khammy had at least twenty-five red-bandanna Bloods working in his crew, which consisted mostly of a South Philly' Oriental street gang whose tattooed members looked both fearsome and gruesome. One day at around 5 p.m. a New Jersey State Trooper followed a gang member off of *Route 322* into Farm #2's parking lot with his patrol car's overhead red lights flashing. No sooner did the trooper come to a halt when twenty or so Blood' Cambodians surrounded his patrol vehicle and the thugs began throwing cherry bombs and firecrackers onto and underneath the cop's car. The young trooper panicked and called for backup units, and in a matter of three minutes at least twenty State Trooper and Hamilton Township Police cars converged on the parking lot, and the responding officers by sheer numbers managed to successfully quell the disturbance.

One day vindictive Khammy surprisingly showed-up on Farm #1 and drove out to Inxay's field, removed a rifle from his truck's cab and hostilely began shooting at his prime Laotian foe. Inxay instinctively fled for cover inside a field of tall blueberry bushes and then sprinted into a nearby woods. The State Labor Inspectors had heard about the bizarre assault incident and issued five citations to Khammy citing the sensational rifle confrontation along with four other more minor already-outstanding labor-related violations that the wily Laotian crew-leader had committed and accumulated.

"Look Frank," I told the New Jersey Chief Labor Inspector before Khammy's hearing inside *his* partitioned office in the State of New Jersey's Hammonton Labor Building, "this crazy guy Khammy is not wrapped too tight. Don't trigger him off or else he might have a flashback to Laos during the *Vietnam War* and then become volatile and uncontrollable! In fact," I elaborated, "Khammy confided to me that he had personally slit at least a hundred people's throats back in Laos and had mercilessly killed them without showing any conscience or remorse!"

"Look John," the overconfident Chief Inspector calmly answered, "he's in the United States now and the rule of law prevails here. And besides," the Chief Inspector bragged, "I myself was in the *U.S. Army* and I know exactly how to defend myself if it becomes necessary!"

The scheduled hearing commenced in a rather orthodox placid manner for the first ten minutes, but when Khammy learned that the State of New Jersey was going to fine him five hundred dollars and also revoke his Crew-leader's License, the dysfunctional Laotian felt threatened and was instantaneously provoked to take action. Khammy stood-up and much to the Chief Inspector's astonishment and consternation, the lunatic removed his sharp knife from his belt sheath and then almost spontaneously lunged at the extremely alarmed Chief Inspector, who reacted by fleeing the room as if he were a rattled rabbit (while I stupidly and foolishly wrapped my arms around Khammy's shoulders to prevent him from pursuing after his newly-declared adversary).

But in the final analysis, I must confess that Khammy maintained excellent discipline over his crew of Bloods, who all feared him worse than they feared either a hundred' Los Angeles or South Philly' blue bandanna Crips or policemen. His pickers always sent quality berries to the loading dock, and the intimidating Laotian's pay slips were always done correctly with hardly ever an error to be found. Khammy was organized and meticulous and I must confess that the awesome Laotian conducted his field operations as if his assigned turf was a sophisticated military staging area, but the State of New Jersey and its nit-picking Labor Department Inspectors viewed the dangerous and unpredictable cold-eyed surreptitious Pathong as if he were an *FBI* "Most Wanted Criminal." Nevertheless, Khammy was always regarded by everyone associated with the farm who knew him as being a very dangerous mercurial-tempered individual.

In the winter of 2001, Khammy Pathong and three henchmen slipped into a Philadelphia factory where Inxay was managing a work crew and the culprit maliciously jumped his avowed rival, wantonly beating Pathatogong up badly. Police warrants were issued for Khammy's arrest, and the last I have heard of him, the itinerant maverick is reported to be a fugitive from justice hiding-out in either Alabama or Mississippi operating a flourishing fish store. The following summer Inxay (with his characteristic volatile temper) had a disagreement with one of the owners of Atlantic Blueberry Company and the temperamental easily-triggered crew-leader was promptly dismissed from the farm's employ. Rumor has it that the Laotian now is the proprietor of an Oriental food store in West Philadelphia and his somewhat reputable new business caters to former Laotian, Thai, Vietnamese and Cambodian Jersey blueberry pickers. I presume (with a relative degree of certainty) that on-the-lam Khammy Pathong is not one of Inxay Pathatogong's current steady grocery store customers.

"Growing-up in Hammonton"

I was born (not hatched as some acquaintances might believe) in 1942 at the Swenson Home on Horton Street on the north side of the railroad tracks in Hammonton, New Jersey. The town had no hospital back then so many other Hammontonians that were not delivered by midwives were also naturally born (or born naturally) at the Swenson Home on the "proper side of the tracks."

On December 7, 1941 Pearl Harbor had been attacked. *World War II* was in progress in the European and in the Pacific Theaters (where the war was playing). My father had volunteered his service after the Pearl Harbor sneak attack and was away training at U.S. military camps and later after 1943 had been stationed in France and in Germany during my early childhood. When Dad returned from the terrible conflict, he opened a small gas station/repair' shop next to the family's modest white bungalow, which was situated beside my mother's parents' Hammonton business, Square Deal Farm Market on *Route 30*, the White Horse Pike.

Grand-pop Tony had pioneered the farm market trade on that busy highway, which at the time was the major summer tourist link between Philadelphia and Atlantic City. Gramps would often drive me around South Jersey in his black stake-body truck to various fruit and vegetable farmers, where he would purchase corn, peaches, apples, blueberries, cucumbers, peppers, zucchini squash, tomatoes and other locally grown produce. Several times he even brought me to Dock Street in Philadelphia, which at the time was the area's major fresh food distribution center.

Antonio Giacobbe was a Sicilian immigrant who had come over to America via Ellis Island and settled with former Old-World Messina, Sicily relatives near Ninth Street in Philadelphia. Gramps started out in the American free enterprise system by vending fruit and vegetables from a pushcart around the Italian Market on Ninth Street. In a few years he earned enough money to invest in a five-acre tract on the White Horse Pike in Hammonton.

Italian immigrants were not too well received by the firmly entrenched and established English Hammonton WASPs. A year after my grandparents erected Square Deal Market during the mid-1930s' Depression, an influential farm family of British descent was determined to knock them out of business by building a similar farm market right next to Square Deal. When a customer would stop his or her automobile between the two properties, Grandma Annie would rush over and nail the fresh fruit shopper before the competition had a chance to react to the prospective customer's arrival.

Eventually, Antonio Giacobbe prevailed and proudly bought the other market from his chief rival. My Sicilian grandparents on my mother's side had overcome 1930s WASP discrimination through hard work and personal determination. Perseverance was a good lesson I had learned at an early age. It has as much to do with human economic' survival as persistence has to do with human success.

Grandma Annie Giacobbe also had a difficult childhood. She had come from a very poor Sicilian family that lived beyond the end of Pine Road in an area known as Sandy Crossways. She had to wear her father's discarded tattered shoes with holes in the soles to school and was often mocked by the other children fortunate enough to have wealthier parents and better shoes. Young Annie vowed to elevate herself above poverty. She always remembered the emotional scars she had suffered in her impoverished childhood. After marrying Grandpa Tony, my grandmother gained self-esteem by running Square Deal Farm Market with steadfast precision and a terrific Old World work ethic.

Kindergarten was not mandatory back in 1948. I remember entering first grade at St. Joseph School on Third Street in downtown Hammonton. I managed to master the fundamentals of reading and writing in four years of schooling, and when Grandpa Tony took me to buy fruit and other produce I soon realized at a young age that I knew how to read and write and that he didn't. Grandpa would ask me on our excursions around South Jersey to read the various billboards and signs that dotted *Route 206, Route 54, Route 322* and *Route 30* and I would gladly oblige. All Gramps had mastered was how to scribble two letters, his initials "A.G.," which he used to certify his approval on sales receipts that verified his wholesale purchases.

No matter where Grandpa would drive me, he would always reiterate his reason for moving to New Jersey. The fat, bald-headed man knew very little English and repeated at least ten times to and ten times from our given destination, "Giovanni, there's too much true-bulla in Pencil-bania!" he would repeat in between smoking his huge *El Producto* cigar, before coughing like a tuberculosis victim. Then Grandpa Tony would again ask me the identification of words that puzzled him on various highway billboards. But Gramps knew his mathematics without the need of a pencil, eraser or adding machine. He could calculate and subtract figures in his head and would tell amazed commission house men the exact total of his purchases to the penny that took *them* minutes to figure out.

When I was six years old in 1948 Mom and Aunt Frances took me one Saturday night to The Rivoli Theater on Bellevue Avenue in downtown Hammonton to see the Otto Preminger film *Forever Amber*, starring Cornell Wilde and Linda Darnell. The movie had a very spectacular fire scene and at six years of age, I thought that the whole theater was engulfed in the inferno that was being shown up on the big screen. I panicked and started screaming my lungs out until Mom removed me from my seat, walked me to the foyer and soothed my alarm by buying some much-needed popcorn and soda.

The *Philadelphia Phillies* had won the National League Pennant in 1950 and I recall how psyched-up I was watching them on a small screen black and white TV play in the *World Series* against the *New York Yankees*. Joe DiMaggio hit the winning home run in game two and then the *Yankees* cruised to a four-game sweep in spite of inspirational play by *Phillies'* center-fielder Richie Ashburn, my boyhood hero.

During the summer months Gramps would take me north on *206* to Indian Mills where he would daily buy two thousand ears of freshly "pulled" Jersey corn. Then he would bury me up to my chest with corn' ears as I sat in a back *corn*er of his black Chevy stake-body truck. I got a thrill waving to surprised motorists and their passengers passing us going south toward Hammonton on *206*.

Grandpa Tony often took me in his large black truck to the Hammonton Auction Block where he would buy fruit and vegetables to resell at his farm market. Post *WWII* Hammonton was an agricultural town of around ten thousand inhabitants with a large Italian immigrant population and most of the farmers wore caps, flannel shirts, gray wool vested sweaters, baggy pants and had mustaches. Some older Sicilian farmers even still brought their crops to the auction "block" in horse drawn wagons. The local growers would line up their trucks and wagons in four lanes that passed through the "auction block." Lots were drawn to see which line would go through "the block" first, second, third and fourth. Commission produce brokers and independent buyers like Grandpa would bid on items after being shown "sample packages" of the fruit and vegetables up for sale.

Downtown Hammonton hadn't changed much since the late 1940s. Dad was away in Europe going up against Hitler's minions so Mom would take me onto Bellevue Avenue every Friday night to do shopping. During the daytime Monday to Saturday, she would faithfully wait for the daily mail to see if a letter from France or from Germany was forthcoming. Many American kids grew-up in the mid-'40s without fathers (that were in the military) around to give them guidance and discipline. So, like many other young boys during that decade, I was more exposed to female nurturing than to male naturing.

The small town's early claims to fame were having Presidential candidate Teddy Roosevelt's campaign train arrive for a whistle stop speech and having noted anthropologist Margaret Mead living on Fairview Avenue during her younger days where she studied the cultural adaptations of Italian immigrants. Another important event in the town's history was when acclaimed virtuoso John Philip Sousa and his famous touring band gave a sit-down concert for local citizens at the Hammonton Lake Pavilion.

I remember that late '40s and early '50s Bellevue Avenue was crowded with enthusiastic shoppers. There were soda fountains all over the main street. Every drug store, five and ten and luncheonette had one. I recall Vega's Drugs on the corner of Third and Bellevue, Godfrey's Drug Store at Bellevue and Egg Harbor Road, Kern's Drugs at 2nd and Bellevue, J.J. Newberry's and Joanne's Restaurant on the main drag all having splendid soda fountains.

Grandpa Tony spoiled me rotten by taking a young J.W. to see the dependable four a.m. freight train rumble past the intersection of Fairview Avenue and Egg Harbor Road; situated next to Vet's Bakery. My biological clock would wake me up at 3:30 in the morning and then I would bawl and throw a tantrum until Grandpa put me in his black stake-body truck and transported me to the *Pennsylvania Railroad* tracks to see the steam locomotive, the tankers and boxcars and finally the caboose.

When Dad returned from fighting the Nazis overseas, he opened his small gas station/repair shop next to the little white bungalow, which was adjacent to Square Deal Farm Market. One day after supper Dad sent me on an errand. I had to fetch a bill of sale from his office desk inside the garage. I left the building closing the garage door very hard, and the descending object smashed down on my left foot, crushing my big toe. I was afraid to tell Pop of the catastrophe but since the pain was so excruciating, I finally had to divulge my self-inflicted injury.

Dad, who had seen all kinds of dead mutilated corpses in Nazi Germany, was horrified. He rushed me to Dr. Frazier Elliott's Office on Packard Street, two blocks from the center of Hammonton. Dr. Elliott was a remarkable man who inspected my ugly wound without batting an eyelash. Then he administered a needle and proceeded to cut the entire toenail off my big toe as if he were casually peeling a potato. Even at age ten I had to admire the fine dedicated small-town doctor who settled me down, allayed my fears and kept his cool under very dire circumstances.

Saturday afternoons the Rivoli Theater at Bellevue and Third (across the street from Vega's Drugs) had matinee movies. I still vividly recollect seeing *King Kong, Mighty Joe Young, The Beast from 20,000 Fathoms, The Creature from the Black Lagoon,* and *The Day the Earth Stood Still* at the downtown movie house with St. Joseph School friends. The theater boasted an ornate ceiling with crystal chandeliers that made it a showplace for the proud small town in the '40s and early '50s.

Most '50s businesses were little mom and pop operations like Rescignio's candy store across Third Street from St. Joseph School and like Miller's Family Department Store on Bellevue Avenue. Then, highway custard stands began replacing main street soda fountains and malls started sprouting up knocking places like Miller's Department Store and Rescignio's Candy out of business. Finally, in the early '60s the popularity of a new medium, television led to the demise of the glorious Rivoli Theater.

In the early fifties, Grandpa Tony would take me over to the Sons of Italy Garibaldi Lodge on North Third Street and park me on a barstool to drink all of the *Cokes* and eat all of the pretzels and potato chips I wanted. Gramps would then play an Italian fingers game with some old cronies, and if Grandpa had had a dispute with Grandma Annie, he was determined to win the fingers game. Then Gramps would become the Capa or Boss and appoint a Lieutenant. Everyone else who had lost in the fingers' game would have to watch Grandpa drink-down eleven beers on the table (paid for by the losers) and then appoint his lucky Lieutenant to drink the twelfth.

Many Saturday nights Grandpa Tony would arrive back home drunk and then tripped and stumbled in the dark over living room furniture on his way upstairs to bed. Later in life his bad case of diabetes had been compounded, which eventually led to wheelchair confinement. His excessive drinking and need to be the "beer Capa" and the nasty-looking bruises on his legs didn't help his physical condition any.

Downtown Hammonton in the early '50s was very similar to the way Bellevue Avenue appeared in the '40s. On Friday and Saturday Nights the Hammonton High School kids hung out on their side of town in front of Vega's Drugs and Augie's Sub Shop and Hamburger Paradise and across the street the St. Joseph High teens usually congregated in front of the Rivoli Theater. Bellevue Avenue acted as sort of a demilitarized zone separating the two rival factions. The Ramrodders greaser gang hung out in front of the Central Café on Egg Harbor Road three blocks away.

Certain business establishments were neutral territory where all three teen groups would share space. Those businesses were the Gem Burger Bar on Central Avenue, a block west of Hammonton High School, and DiDonato's Bowling Alleys and Royale Crown Custard Stand on the White Horse Pike on the Atlantic City side of Hammonton.

When I turned nine, I became a friend of David Parkwell, whose family had a Farm and Garden Center across the White Horse Pike from Square Deal Market. David was two years older than I was, and I admired his mischievous nature.

"Slow John" DiAngelo was an elderly grower that owned ground behind Grand-pop Tony's five acres of peach and apple orchards. Several times I pretended that I had been naughtily picking (stealing) cucumbers in "Slow John's" field when the gimpy farmer was riding down a sandy road on his old *John Deere* tractor. This would infuriate the partially lame old grower. He would halt his tractor, leap off and then awkwardly chase me across twenty or so rows of cucumbers until I safely gained shelter in a nearby' woods.

While "Slow John" pursued his elusive nemesis (who had also been wearing a Halloween Dracula mask), Dave Parkwell would exit a clump of trees from the opposite side of the field, alongside the dirt road. Then he would hop onto the *John Deere* and drive it along farm roads through pepper and tomato fields until he parked the piece of machinery a mile or so away.

Dave and I would then reunite at my parents' snack bar located inside of Square Deal Market, and we would celebrate our dual mischief with "Electrocuted Hot Dogs" and bottles of *Ma's Old Fashion Root Beer*. Then I would furtively show Dave the neat Dracula mask I intended to wear next Halloween.

Dave convinced me to join the Hammonton Little League, which had the distinction of winning the 1949 Little League World Championship. He was the star of our team, DiDonato's Bowling. I played an occasional second base or left field.

In one particular night game, a big kid named Rollie Cantrobone hit a towering fly ball to left field. I backed-up to the green wooden fence, held my glove up toward the blinding lights, and then defensively searched the night sky for the obscure baseball. A small miracle happened. The baseball plopped down into my glove as I shielded my face to protect it from the descending white object. The fans on both sides of the field erupted in a boisterous cheer in recognition of my fantastic accidental accomplishment.

378

I had a great time making and having friends at St. Joseph School on North Third Street. During recess we played marbles on the hardtop playground, and yo-yos were prized possessions, too. I invented the baseball card game known as "three-way matchies." Two close friends and I would simultaneously flip to the ground baseball cards with the images of major league players on the front and their' performance statistics on the other side. The owner of the odd-sided flip would win "the jackpot." If two cards showed their backsides, then the player that owned the face-up card would be declared the winner. My buddies and I spent hours of leisure school recess time perfecting and demonstrating our marble, yo-yo and "matchies" skills.

I remember when I was ten that all the Catholic school kids from grades three to twelve had to attend an assembly at the Rivoli Theater. We all walked by grade level classes from the Catholic school two blocks east to the movie house on the corner of Bellevue Avenue and Third Street. All that week the St. Joseph School Fillipini nuns and Pallottine priests had been talking about heavenly visitations from the Blessed Virgin Mary, angels and saints while hyping the new religious movie *Our Lady of Fatima*. The cinema presentation was an awesome experience to a ten-year-old kid. The film must have had a profound impact on my vulnerable subconscious. It probably also sparked my fertile imagination.

Sometimes I would sleep the night in the spare bedroom upstairs in my grandparents' red brick home, which was situated behind Square Deal Farm Market. A statue of St. Anne (the Virgin Mary's mother) dressed in a macabre black robe rested atop the brown mahogany bureau next to the bed. The statue's stern face was always peering down at me and I always had to go to sleep turning my body and my head in the opposite direction. St. Anne's hands held black rosary beads, suggesting that she was praying for the soul of the bed's occupant lying beneath her presence.

Every 16th of July the town of Hammonton celebrates the Feast of Our Lady of Mount Carmel with a large traveling carnival and an Old-World religious street procession. Statues of Jesus, Mary, Joseph and saints from St. Joseph Church are mounted on carts with drapes covering their frames and wheels and escorted by the faithful through the major streets of the community and then back to the Third Street church. Clusters of donations in the form of five, ten, twenty, fifty and hundred-dollar bills were hung from and adorned the statues. In the years after *WWII* fifty thousand visitors would attend the 16th of July Mount Carmel Festival. The pilgrims were mostly Italian immigrants or first-generation offspring.

Grandma Annie Giacobbe gave me a five-dollar bill to have pinned onto the statue of Our Lady of Mount Carmel. My grandparents did not trust banks because many had collapsed during the Depression, so they stashed cash in the mattress of an old bed stored in the brick house's attic. I discovered the cache (of cash) and stole five dollars from the attic mattress. I had received five dollars spending money from my parents and I also had in my pocket the *Abe Lincoln* my grandmother had given me' to have pinned on the Our Lady of Mount Carmel procession statue in addition to five dollars I had been saving for the carnival.

I met some friends at the carnival grounds, and the four of us bought popcorn, soda, pizza and cotton candy. Then we addictively played different games of chance and tried out various amusement rides. Before I knew it I had exhausted all the money in my possession including the five dollars I was supposed to have pinned on the Blessed Mother's statue.

"Did you pin the money on Our Lady's statue?" my grandmother asked.

"Yes," I lied, "and the man said 'Thank you'."

"Good boy," Grandma complimented. "Marie, I think your son is goin' to grow up and become a priest. He's such a *bona, belle* boy!"

That night I slept in the spare bedroom of the red brick house. As my guilty mind approached the drowsy state that usually comes before actual sleeping, I turned my head and thought I saw St. Anne's statue kneeling beside the bed, praying for my wandering straying soul. "You must return the ten dollars you have stolen," she commanded, "or else your soul will burn in hell!"

The next morning, I didn't know what to do. I entered the small white bungalow and saw my father's wallet on the kitchen table. While dad was in the bathroom shaving, I opened his wallet that contained only ten-dollar bills and removed one. That night mom told me I had to sleep in the red brick house because she and dad were going out to dinner.

I was tossing and turning in bed from the guilt of my third misdeed involving Dad's wallet. I had planned to go over to David Parkwell's parents' Farm and Garden business the following morning and have my pal change the ten-dollar bill into two fives, which I would then surreptitiously plant into the stuffed attic mattress since it contained mostly five-dollar bills.

As I feared, I opened my eyes around midnight and St. Anne was again kneeling beside the bed. "You've been a sinful boy again," the statue said to me while sobbing and weeping. "I don't want to see you burn in hell for all eternity!" I turned my face and when I looked back, the statue was no longer on the floor beside my bed. It was again stationed up on the mahogany bureau.

My vernal heart and conscience were both in the same miserable quandary. How would I get twenty dollars to repay my debts to the Blessed Mother and to Dad? I prayed to St. Anne for a solution to my heartfelt dilemma. I was in for the surprise of my young life!

The next morning Steve Van Buren, an all-pro football player for the *Philadelphia Eagles* stopped at Square Deal Market to acquire some tomatoes, corn, blueberries and peaches on his way to the Jersey shore. I immediately recognized the famous sports' celebrity from *Eagle'* television football games and from sports' news clips I had seen at the Rivoli Theater.

I almost swallowed my tongue when Steve Van Buren and his wife approached the little candy/soda/hot dog concession where I had been standing behind the counter. They ordered *Pepsi-Colas* and hot dogs, which I began to prepare on the "Hot Dog Electrocutor." Then the football star and I struck up a casual conversation.

"Do you know who I am?" he casually asked while his wife chuckled in the background.

"I think you're Steve Van Buren, my very favorite football player!" I exclaimed.

"You're absolutely right," the tough athlete remarked. "Would it be all right if I signed and gave you an autographed picture? I have some in my car."

"Can I have one for my friend David Parkwell too?" I begged.

"Why sure, no problem," Van Buren returned. "I'll be right back with two of 'em."

I graciously and thankfully received the two unexpected gifts. I was thrilled to death to obtain them' from the *Eagle'* great.

After Steve Van Buren gathered his produce and then drove off with his pretty wife another farm market patron made his way to the concession stand.

"Wasn't that Steve Van Buren?" the man asked.

"Sure was," I answered.

"He's the best fullback in all professional football," the man elaborated. "I'll give ya' twenty bucks for one of those signed pictures. What do ya' say?"

"Okay," I said, "but this is a big sacrifice," recalling a synonym I had learned for the word *bunt* in baseball.

"I'll cherish this picture for the rest of my life," the fellow commented. "I'll even have it framed."

That afternoon my father again was shaving. I sneaked into the bungalow's bigger bedroom, found his wallet on the bureau and replaced "the ten-dollar loan" I had borrowed. Then the next time I was in church I put five dollars in the collection basket. And finally I replaced the five dollars I had pilfered from the attic mattress.

'Thank you, St. Anne!' I respectfully acknowledged as I rolled my appreciative blue eyes toward the ceiling. 'Now I'm off the hook!' And that's how David Parkwell never got his autographed Steve Van Buren photo' (which *he* never knew about).

My parents had purchased their first television in early 1953. I was forced to sit down for a "lesson in history" and watch the boring Queen Elizabeth Coronation in network black and white. Even at ten years of age I hated royal pomp and ritual. The ceremony went on for hours and hours. I thought to myself that the mere act of placing a crown on somebody's head (even a *Head* of State) should require no longer than fifteen-seconds. So even at age ten, I had already been exhibiting symptoms of cynicism towards the artificiality of "stupid" adult traditions.

In March of '54, I received some bad news. Dad explained that the family would be moving away from Hammonton, New Jersey to a newly constructed community, Levittown, Pennsylvania. "Levittown is closer to Norristown than Hammonton is," Dad explained. "Uncle Frank got me a good job as a stainless-steel fabricator at his company, Martin and Quade. It's an opportunity for advancement."

Before 1954 my life was rather nondescript. At age ten I was satisfied and content doing simple basic chores around Square Deal Farm Market. I felt threatened having to abandon the security of playing Little League for DiDonato's Bowling and of leaving the familiar halls and rooms of St. Joseph School.

I had turned eleven in the spring of '54 when my family made the move to 50 Daffodil Lane in the Dogwood Hollow section of Levittown, Pennsylvania. My sister Annie was six and my younger brother Skip was an infant. I was rather melancholy for having to break away from all I had known and valued as a youngster growing-up in an Italian agricultural community. I was extremely apprehensive about what to expect in my new social environment. At age ten I had concluded that some things in life just were not fair.

"Dogwood Hollow: 1954-'55"

New schools, changing environments, new towns and different friends can all be traumatic experiences for any kid struggling through maturation. From fifth grade through high school graduation, I had attended six different schools and so like a Darwinian chameleon, I had learned to adapt to new situations as second nature. I had discovered plenty about human "social survival," which can sometimes be just as treacherous as battling for physical dominance in the animal kingdom.

Before 1954 my early youth was rather nondescript. At age ten I recall helping-out with chores at my grandparents' farm market on *Route 30* in Hammonton, New Jersey, playing *Little League* baseball for DiDonato's Bowling, and being very sad leaving childhood friends at St. Joseph School.

I had just turned eleven in 1954 when my family moved out of New Jersey to 50 Daffodil Lane in the Dogwood Hollow section of Levittown, Pennsylvania. My sister Annie was six and my younger brother Skip was an infant.

My parents became friendly with Jack and Stella Burns, who looked almost identical to Fred and Ethel Mertz on the popular *I Love Lucy Show*. The Burns' lived next door to Sal Palermo, his wife Carmella and their beautiful daughter, Angie. Mom and Dad would return home from the Burns' in the spring of '54 and report tales of yelling, cursing, bullying and general mayhem originating at 66 Daffodil Lane, the Palermo domicile, where Dad thought "the local Mafia" resided.

Levittown was designed to be a "middle-class community" but more specifically it was a "white middle-class community." Caucasian families moved there in quest of a better way of life free from the rampant social disorganization that existed in eastern U.S. cities. Levittown was an innovative experiment in suburban living where shopping centers, houses, highways, schools and recreation areas were engineered to mix together like a kitchen recipe to form a tranquil, harmonious physical environment. All in all it seemed like a great place to live.

In 1954, human interaction was stratified and compartmentalized in Levittown. The place was exclusively "white." I would come in contact with some black kids at St. Mark's School over in Bristol but most of them lived several miles away in that town and few blacks belonged to my Catholic faith. Blacks mostly interacted with blacks and whites stayed mostly with whites, and that brand of racial segregation was explained to young people as "separate but equal" by their parents.

"Ethnic and religious segregation" as well as racial separation was quite evident. The Kalens, who were Jewish, lived across the street from us on Daffodil Lane, and their neighbors, who were Irish and Scottish, wouldn't allow *their* kids to play with the Hebrew children. To avert neighborhood conflict Dad allowed Annie to play with the Kalen children on Monday, Wednesday and Friday and she was permitted to interact with the Irish and Scottish kids on the other four days of the week.

Divisions along nationality and Christian religious lines also existed. Protestants did not marry Catholics and Irish Catholics did not marry Italian Catholics, and Baptists did not marry Presbyterians, and Christians did not marry Jews, and Occidentals did not marry Orientals.

So, to me looking back, Levittown, Pennsylvania was like a giant Bingo card with horizontal and vertical lines drawn in orderly rows to demarcate race, religion, culture, nationality and a person's economic status. Levittown reflected the rigid norms and standards of America that had been established by the predominance of White Anglo-Saxon Protestantism.

Before I could even talk about a girl the elders wanted to know about her family's economic level, their religion, their nationality, her father's employment and the ancestral tree. People were imprisoned in rigid general classifications. At least that is the way I recollect American society as being constructed in the 1950s.

I don't remember too much about 1954 except that Mom would faithfully watch the *Arthur Godfrey Show* and Betty Furness would always say, "You can be sure if it's *Westinghouse*," and if I was well behaved, I was allowed to stay up and watch *The Tonight Show* with Steve Allen. Everyone was afraid of someone calling him or her "a Communist." And an American adult's greatest dread was to be called a "Communist" or "a Communist Sympathizer" on national TV by Senator Joseph McCarthy of Wisconsin.

Twenty-nine million American households had television sets in the mid-fifties, or about sixty percent of the national population. The new media was already anchoring itself as a powerful force in the marketing of products and in the forging of a new set of contemporary values to challenge the practices supported by WASP America.

In 1954 the Cold War was mounting between the United States and Russia and on the domestic scene, racial segregation in public schools was being challenged in the judicial system, with rulings outlawing the practice of "separate but equal schools" in certain parts of the United States.

Jackie Robinson had recently broken the baseball color barrier with the *Brooklyn Dodgers*, and Little Richard, Fats Domino and Chuck Berry were about to do the same thing in the music world. The stage was set for massive and sweeping changes and Levittown was like a vast social test tube, ready to undergo cultural experimentation, upheaval and evolution.

In '54, at age eleven, like most starry-eyed boys, my aspiration was to become a professional baseball player. I loved athletics: baseball, football, basketball and running. In *Little League* I played second base for Meenan Oil and the coach was grooming me to be a pitcher for the team in 1955.

I was thrilled with Willie Mays' over-the-head catch off the bat of Cleveland's Vic Wertz at the Polo Grounds and being a National League fan, I was elated when the *New York Giants* beat the *Indians* four games to zip in the '54 *World Series*. That was done in spite of Cleveland's awesome pitching staff that included Bob Lemon, Bob Feller, Mike Garcia and Early Wynn.

I was greatly influenced by long distance runner Roger Bannister who had broken the four-minute-mile with a time of 3:58.8. The circumference of Dogwood Drive was approximately a mile long so I would imitate Roger Bannister's feat by dashing and sprinting as fast as my legs would carry me. If I could have improved my training methods and my conditioning, I might have been able to shave some time off of eight minutes and fifty-three seconds, my fastest lap.

The modest home at 50 Daffodil Lane cost Dad $10,000, a considerable sum in 1954. As a rule I use the "ten times principle" because most goods, items, products and services are at least ten times as expensive today as they were in the 1950s.

Deliverymen were always faithfully prowling the Daffodil Lane neighborhood. Milk was mostly brought to the door in glass bottles. We got ours from *Harbison's Dairies*, which competed with *Abbotts Dairy*. I remember what a dramatic change it was when *Harbison's* orange juice was suddenly packaged in a waxed carton as opposed to the standard glass bottle, and I recall how reluctant Mom was to try the new product.

And then there was the *Bond Bread* man, and the fruit and vegetable hucksters, and the three ice cream trucks that competed for business, *O'Boyle's, Jack and Jill* and *Good Humor*, all claiming to sell the best flavors in their mixtures.

When I think of the year 1955 my memory suddenly becomes more acute. I began to really enjoy music and when "Rock Around the Clock" hit the air-waves, that' song by Bill Haley and the Comets became the new national anthem for young people. The lyrics said it all, a new generation with boundless energy, capable of partying all night, going far beyond the normal limits of fun. There was also a trace of rebellion in the song's words that was more than rhythm, that in fact was a statement of youth exploding out of *our* David Nelson stereotype and revealing to the world, "This is what we're really made of!"

"Rock Around the Clock" was without a doubt my generation's version of Patrick Henry's "Give me liberty or give me death!" It was also my generation's *Declaration of Independence* to the adult world, saying "We the Teens of the United States," and my generation's *Bill of Rights* and *United States Constitution* all compacted into one refrain, "We're gonna' rock, rock, rock till the broad daylight." Bill Haley and the Comets, a little-known Country and Western band from Chester, Pennsylvania performed summer gigs down at the Jersey Shore. But the group accomplished something magical when they bridged the gap between white country and western music and black rhythm and blues. Their hit song gained national attention in '55 when it was used as the theme for the motion picture *Blackboard Jungle* and it opened the floodgates for Elvis, Chuck Berry, Buddy Holly, Little Richard and the other founding fathers of rock and roll.

In the summer of '55, dances for teens in our area of Levittown were held in the outdoor basketball court, which was located in back of the Olympic-sized Brook Swimming Pool in the recreation area between the Farmbrook, Stonybrook and Greenbrook sections. I wore my standard attire of pegged pants with saddle stitching down each side and of course flaps on the back pockets were in vogue. A plain cotton short-sleeved shirt was worn and penny loafers and white socks completed the ensemble.

In 1955, I had a flattop haircut that was symbolic of being a jock as opposed to the James Dean greaser look of sideburns, long hair smeared with *Vaseline*, and engineer boots with rolled-up dungarees. And tough guys wore either a white or a black tee shirt, depending on whether one was a "good tuff greaser" or a "bad-ass greaser."

Other songs in 1955 were played on the radio like: "Moments To Remember" by the Four Lads, "The Yellow Rose of Texas" by Mitch Miller and his orchestra, "Love is a Many Splendored Thing" by the Four Aces, "Mr. Sandman" by the Chordettes and "Autumn Leaves" by Roger Williams. Although I spent time listening to those other artists, "Rock Around the Clock" was the song that captured my imagination, stirred my soul, activated my spirits and made me think about evolving into a greaser.

What Bill Haley had done to my ears, James Dean and *Rebel without a Cause* had done to my eyes and it was the synthesis of those two magnificent cultural forces that affected my choice to "switch" from an avid jock into a prospective greaser.

When I was twelve, Mom took me to see *The Wizard of Oz* and a month later I painfully struggled through her favorite movie, *Gone with the Wind*, because Mom had almost memorized Margaret Mitchell's lengthy novel, which she had read so many times. And after I became really friendly with Carnie we saw Walt Disney's *Twenty Thousand Leagues under the Sea* seven times, which was five less than we had seen *Rebel without a Cause*. Almost my entire allowance was spent on movies and theater popcorn.

Smoking was regarded as a glamorous activity in '55. Mom and Dad each smoked over a pack of cigarettes a day. Dad smoked *Pall Mall* and Mom puffed on the shorter *Lucky Strikes*. It's amazing that I don't presently have lung cancer from all of the passive smoking I had experienced.

One-time Dad drove us down to Baltimore to visit relatives and when we stopped at a traffic light on *Route 40,* the *Pulaski Highway,* I looked over to another kid, just like myself, traveling with *his* parents. The kid was enveloped in smoke and I was trapped in a thick cloud of tar and nicotine, and I truly sympathized with my unidentified colleague as we both endured our dense environments. I waved to the poor kid and he waved back in tacit acknowledgment of our mutual situations.

On the return trip from Baltimore, I tried an experiment. I lit up a cigarette in the back seat and I signaled to Annie to remain quiet. I smoked the entire *Chesterfield* down to the bottom without my parents ever knowing, because the '55 Chevy was so saturated with fumes that my additional puffs spiraling upward went completely undetected. It was then that I seriously contemplated becoming a greaser.

The *Philadelphia Athletics* had left Connie Mack Stadium, moving to Kansas City, Missouri in 1955. My pal Tinker liked the *A's* and he and I got into countless arguments as to which was the better team, the *A's* or the *Phillies*, and which league was better, the *American* or the *National.*

Some of my friends thought that Bobby Shantz was a better pitcher than Robin Roberts, and that Gus Zernial was a better cleanup hitter than Del Ennis, and that Ferris Fain was a better first baseman on the *A's* than Eddie Waitkus had been on the 1950 *Whiz Kids.* Tinker did make a concession when it came to center fielders. The *Phillies'* Richie

Ashburn was easily the winner, hands down. Richie Ashburn was my baseball idol and hero.

I fondly recall the 1950s. The *Korean War* had ended, prosperity was flourishing, Suburbia was expanding, and with the *G.I. Bill* war veterans like my father were able to obtain low interest loans to purchase homes.

White families had evacuated the crowded cities in pursuit of a higher standard of living, cleaner air, better shopping centers, escape from urban crime, and most particularly, a brighter future for the baby boomer generation.

The '50s decade was a less complicated era than the present computer age. Interaction between human beings was direct and personal. There were no ATM Machines, no *Xerox* machines, no fax machines', no telephone answering devices', no cell phones, no compact discs, no video games, no personal computers, no databases, no *911*, and no cable television. Strangely enough my greaser gang "the Diablos" lived perfectly well without *McDonald's, Burger Kings, Pizza Huts, Denny's, Taco Bells, IHops* or *Boston Markets*. All we needed were places like our hangouts the Feed Bag and the Dairy DeLite to satisfy our lust for food.

Most stores and restaurants back then were mom and pop operations or were family run, like Luigi and Domenic managing the Feed Bag and Hal Irving overseeing Hal's Talk of the Town Delicatessen, where I was employed "under the table" at age thirteen as a teen kitchen laborer.

The '50s decade was a much simpler and less chaotic period before the deluge of giant franchises, corporate conglomerates and the perils of an impersonal Megalopolis. And we got along pretty well with only one public telephone company serving our needs.

I nostalgically cherish that very special time before Rap Music, before the Eagles, before Fleetwood Mac, before the Doors, before the Beach Boys, before ABBA, before the Rolling Stones, before the Supremes, before the Temptations, and yes, even before the Beatles.

Roller blades and skateboards were unheard of in Levittown, Pennsylvania in the '50s era. Hula-hoops, Davy Crockett coonskin hats, poodle skirts, saddle shoes, and black and white sneakers were "cool." Pegged pants, hangouts, saddle stitching, *Edsels*, white bucks, penny-loafers, pedal pushers, sock hops, and *American Bandstand* were "boss." Passion pits, "submarine races," DA haircuts and multi-zipper black leather jackets were "not square." And finally 3-D glasses, the jitterbug, and "cruisin" around the main drag in a sleek convertible were the "in things" to do.

There were friendly greetings like "Boogety-boogety-boogety-shoo" and "Ootie-ootie." There were fifteen-cent hamburgers, the Salk vaccine had been developed, roll-on deodorant was invented, *Disneyland* had opened in California and the *Hand Jive* had become a new dance sensation. And '50s teenagers were not haunted by the twin specters of drugs and AIDS. The '50s decade was a very special time for guys and gals to grow up', to share friendships, to fall in love and to experience life. The only real perils were neighborhood greaser gangs looking for vulnerable kids to pick on.

The a.m. dial dominated the radio waves, and in the Philadelphia metropolitan area, the "in" station was WIBG, Wibbage Radio' 99. The biggest name DJ was Joe Niagara, whose "Niagara Calls in Philly" was a battle cry for great rhythm and lyrics about to be spun. Later there was Hy Lit, another popular WIBG disc jockey whose immortal refrain "Hyski-O-Roonie-McVouty-O-Zoot" captivated the hearts of millions of teen fans. Other great radio personalities like Jerry Blavat, the "Geator with the Heater," also known as "The Boss with the Hot Sauce," soon would also appear.

Every once in a while, my friends and I would tune in Cousin Brucie out of New York, or Alan Freed, a DJ transplant from Cleveland to Manhattan. Freed had coined the term "Rock and Roll" as a code name for "black rhythm and blues." But for the most part Philly' was where it was at, and "Wibbage" gave us Levittown kids our daily diet of Bill Haley and the Comets, Buddy Holly and the Crickets and Jerry Lee Lewis.

Many of my friends and I despised "cover versions" of black rhythm and blues performed by such lily-white artists as Pat Boone. We didn't mind Pat Boone's original "white" melodies like "Love Letters In the Sand" and "April Love" but when he did "white cover versions" of Fats Domino's "Ain't That A Shame" and Little Richard's "Tutti-Frutti," the nice guy with the "white bucks" turned the "Dogwood Hollow guys" off from the first note.

Yesterday, I was riding through downtown Hammonton, New Jersey and my car stereo picked up the familiar baritone of a Philly' DJ, "Let's take a walk down Memory Lane." "Born Too Late" by the Poni-Tails was played and I felt a degree of remorse for all of those twenty-first century kids who were not interacting with their peers, sitting in their bedrooms playing video games on their computers, living a lonely isolated existence, and having machines as their best friends.

Today "virtual reality" allows kids to function in an artificial environment but back in the '50s, we had "actual reality" where we experienced firsthand thrills and chills, not through a machine or floppy disc but through minute-to-minute, face-to-face contact with other human beings. I'm so glad that I had the opportunity to grow up during the nifty fifties.

"Little League Baseball"

Kids' baseball is a really great American tradition. Fathers can relate to their children who play *Little League* because male adults remember the experience as something vital that taught them life-skills and socialization during *their* youth. *Little League* is as American as apple pie and now the rest of the world is finally wonderfully acclimated to enjoying everything American including baseball. That particular American sports' heritage was very special to me while growing-up in the 1950s and I will always have many fond recollections of *Little League Baseball.*

Even an institution as wonderful as *Little League* has its vocal critics. Some carpers complain that the sport emphasizes competition too much and that the lesser skilled kids sitting on the bench ought to get more playing time. Other grievers cite that the risk of injury is all-too-real.

I wholeheartedly believe that *Little League* is a terrific "coming of age" American growth experience. It teaches kids organizational skills, division of labor, cooperation and competition. By organization I mean nine kids have to function like one unit harmoniously working under one main coach. In division of labor those same nine kids must efficiently perform different tasks and responsibilities. The players must cooperate with each other in order to defeat the opposing team in fair and square competition. Dual Motors versus Kiwanis is actually a small-scale version of *Apple* going up against *IBM* or of *General Motors* taking on *Ford.* That's what makes *Little League* so uniquely American and why the inherent rivalries in sports help to perpetuate this country's unparalleled "free enterprise" value system.

For those critics who claim and insist that *LL* is dangerous, I should remind them that there is danger and risk everywhere. If every young boy or girl lived in a protective bubble, no kids would ever interact. Each one would be floating around in a separate vacuum. Those squeaky-gear *LL* critics should not cross streets, should not walk down crowded aisles in *Wal-Mart* having merchandise stacked up to the ceiling and should not mow their lawns or drive to Wildwood or Cape May on summer vacations because something threatening might unexpectedly happen.

Dangers exist and loom all around us and in *Little League* competition, injuries predominantly happen *by accident* and they are not deliberately or maliciously inflicted. I guess that's one particular reason I absolutely love *Little League Baseball.* I have always been quite fascinated by physical danger and by intense competition, especially in sports.

In 1953, I had played Hammonton *Little League* ball for the town *team DiDonato's Bowling*. My coach was Mr. Reid, and his son Bruce was also the shortstop on the team. Bruce's older brother Frank would come to the practices and help his dad work with the players and ironically, Frank's son Scott wound-up working for me in my boardwalk arcade in Ocean City, Maryland two decades later. From my own life experience, there's no doubt in my mind that *LL* promotes an appreciation of the American free-enterprise economic system. It made me love the thrill of competition on the field and later in my adult life in my business enterprises.

I remember how thrilled I was in '53 as a ten-year-old getting my first hit, a bunt single. I also recall playing in a game when an older kid on the Hammonton Dual Motors team hit a towering fly ball to me in left field. I anxiously backed up to the fence, looked up above the lights into the night sky, closed my eyes, and miraculously, the white ball plopped into my glove as my knees were clattering. I opened my lids when I heard the fans on both sides of the field cheering my stellar achievement. That adventure was a real confidence builder I could have never found living in a protective bubble.

In '53, I still recollect kids still leaving their mitts on the field between innings. I still think about the thrill of playing night baseball at Hammonton (New Jersey) Lake Park just like the *Phillies* and the *A's* had done under the lights at *Shibe Park* (later Connie Mack Stadium) and how terrific it felt proudly playing ball in a league that had won the coveted *Little League World Championship* just four years earlier in 1949.

The following year, my family moved to Levittown, Pennsylvania where I had to make new friends and find a new baseball team on which to play. I was assigned to Meenan Oil in the spring of '54, and there were so many kids out for each position that I was becoming discouraged. I had to beat out eight rivals to be the starting second baseman. The intense "competition" brought out the best in me and with sheer determination I eventually won the starting job. I played for Coach Siegel, who like Coach Reid back in Hammonton derived satisfaction from working with kids. Both men (and most adults associated with *Little League*) were (and are) good concerned citizens volunteering their time and effort to help youngsters accomplish and grow.

In 1955, my good friend Mike Hunter and I were selected from Meenan Oil to play on the Levittown National League All-Star Team.

We went up against our bitter rivals, the American League squad and with an element of luck won the game. After another victory, my National League All-Star Team encountered Morrisville, which had two kids that stood six-feet-three. One was Dick Hart (who later in life was a lineman for the *Philadelphia Eagles*) and the other Tommy Kaczor, who was Morrisville's main pitcher. Both kids were very intimidating. It was a close contest but then in the fifth inning Hart hit a ball so high to the centerfielder that when it came down, it split the webbing in Jerry Friedrich's glove. Hart was already on third base when the ball finally hit the ground and then he trotted home with the go ahead run.

I was devastated because I believed that Levittown National had a better overall team. But then Morrisville went on to win the *Little League World Championship* at Williamsport, and I listened to every one of their games on the radio. I got to admit that I became a loyal Morrisville fan that summer of '55 after being very disappointed from being defeated by them.

So, in conclusion, I suppose that possibly the best things *Little League* experience teaches kids are how to handle failure and how to show good sportsmanship after being defeated. And then in 1960 I was elated when Levittown, Pa. went on to win the highly coveted *Little League World Series.*

And coincidentally, I came from a league (Hammonton, NJ) that had won the *Little League World Championship* in '49, played against an excellent Morrisville, Pennsylvania team that won it all in '55, and cheered for the old Levittown, PA (American) League squad that won it all in '60. Those three unforgettable fond memories will always remain with me as long as I shall live, and in 1954-'60, the remarkable events could only happen in America.

"Wacky College Professors"

I certainly had a cross section of diverse professor personalities during my four-year teacher college preparation. Some were austere and pompous, while others were liberal charlatans and many of them were eccentric in his or her unique way. Most of my college professors certainly didn't appear as members of mainstream America.

After registering in the college's main building with its "Majestic Golden Dome," I noticed that only the professors' last names were provided on my weekly schedule so unless one knew a particular instructor by appearance, the freshman didn't know whether the teacher was a man or a woman.

A good former high school friend of mine attending the college had almost the same class schedule as I had. The first day of fall semester I had inadvertently left my schedule home in the rush of excitement to drive my father's blue pickup truck twenty miles southwest to the picturesque college campus. I managed to remember the time and place of my first 8 a.m. class and waved to my friend Tim Amoro sitting on the opposite side of the classroom. After the dismissal bell for "The Fundamentals of School Organization," I met my friend and started up a conversation.

"Where's the next class Tim?" I asked. "I left my schedule at home on my bedroom desk."

"English," my acquaintance answered.

I remembered that English was *my* second class of the day also. "Your schedule was almost identical to mine," I stated, "so I'll just tag along if you don't mind."

After seating ourselves in the crowded second period classroom, the professor took roll from his master list. I felt rather uneasy when I recognized that my name had not been called. I raised my hand after the distinguished mustached professor asked, "Is everyone present and accounted for?"

"Are you Professor Sankin?" I innocently inquired. "My name was not called!"

The class then broke out in raucous hysteria. The abashed male professor's thick eyebrows slanted down at almost forty-five-degree angles expressing his displeasure with my inquiry. "My good fellow," the chagrined sage began, "I certainly am not Professor Sankin. I am Professor Stevens. I happen to be a man the last time I checked. Professor Sankin happens to be a member of the opposite gender. Since you are not supposed to be in this room," Professor Stevens rankled, "I strongly suggest that it would be in everybody's best interest if you proceed immediately to Room 217!"

Boisterous laughter could be discerned as Professor Stevens terminated his deriding and stern dissertation. I recall thinking at the time that I wished some faster mode of transportation would be available other than that provided by my two lower appendages. I rushed out of Room 212 red-faced, slightly humiliated and almost sweating bullets.

I finally located Professor Sankin's class down the second-floor corridor and unfortunately my belated entrance interrupted her introductory lecture. The class remained hush as the austere elderly woman taciturnly surveyed the rude intruder's body from head to toe. The no-nonsense matronly gray-haired lady motioned for me to occupy the last remaining desk next to the window overlooking the main building's scenic "campus green."

Professor Sankin had the distinct habit of carefully enunciating every syllable of every word. Her small oval-shaped mouth exposed her very active tongue continuously lubricating a *Lifesaver* wedged underneath it. The old dame had a warty face that would make any non-blind frog leap with terror. Her voice was either shrill or squawky depending on her articulation and when Professor Sankin hit a high pitch, a clanging burglar alarm would have seemed more melodious and appealing to the ears.

While managing to get mostly B's and C's on Professor Sankin's labyrinth-length *objective* tests, I was baffled by the professor's harsh criticism of my writing style. She *subjectively* described my compositions as being too "wordy" and too "flowery" using "too many adjectives and adverbs," and I was assured of a D or an F on every essay and theme that I submitted, no matter how meticulously each one had been organized.

'I know I have some writing and language arts' talent,' I thought. 'Creative writing and journalism are my strong suits. Professor Sankin is trying to stifle my aspiration to become an author. She's deliberately breaking my testicles in this lousy Fundamentals of Communications' 101 class!' I concluded.

Professor Sankin's attacks on my themes were comparable to how the *U.S. Marine Corps* trains' its soldiers. First the recruit is harshly broken down to demoralize his confidence, and then he is built up according to standards practiced by the drill instructor. My creativity had to be sacrificed to allow for the rebuilding of my mastery of basic writing mechanics.

Coincidentally, the girls in the freshman English class were all receiving B's and C's on their compositions while all of the frustrated male peons were *earning* D's and F's. In fact it was the two freshman' year D's I had *earned* from Professor Sankin first and second semesters that compelled me to switch my college major from Teacher of English to Junior High School Teacher.

'Professor Sankin isn't the first teacher trying to destroy my future with her dumb little dictatorial power game!' I thought. 'Somehow I'm going to graduate from this place and defy both Mr. Andrews (my high school trigonometry instructor) and Professor Sankin!'

I mentally thanked Miss Sankin for introducing me to the unwritten rules of *student* survival on the perilous college frontier:

1. Never challenge the professor (even though he or she' insists that he or she likes it).

2. Be courteous (falsely if necessary) and nice to the professor (color your nose brown).

3. Pretend to copy down everything the professor utters (for he or she speaks a rare English dialect known as gospel).

4. Ask questions that compliment (not complement) the prof's knowledge. Don't make the professor think of more than he or she actually wants to contemplate.

5. Avoid using the pronouns *I, me,* and *my* when asking a question (be humble, submissive and *subordinate* at all times).

In addition to the above classroom commandments, I soon discovered that other secondary understandings would enable me to "play the game" and get better grades (while I exploited the "*subjective* factor" in teacher evaluation).

1. Work or study with other students in the class and always be cooperative (learn to kiss-up and flatter the teacher and be genial to his or her favorite students).

2. Buy the college outline series to the course (authored by the professor) at the campus bookstore and make sure the professor observes you reading his or her "companion book" to the course.

3. Cheat whenever necessary or when it is expedient.

During my freshman year, in keeping with a Human Behavior and Development course requirement, I was assigned to visit a nearby elementary school and observe a "single unique *student*" (translation: discipline problem) and copy down every disruptive thing he or she did in the class. Then I had to write a case study term paper on what I had noted and attempt to explain the *child's* aberrant behavior and propose solutions demonstrating how I would rectify the misbehaviors if I were the *child's* teacher. "Choose a candidate whose deportment slightly deviates from the norm!" our erudite professor instructed.

I believed that such a selection would add color and variety to my report and make it more intriguing to compile. It was really hard choosing a targeted *student* since half the members of the class demonstrated a definite affinity for naughtiness. Three times a week for an entire semester I watched fiendish public-school *students* perform their' repertoire of juvenile pranks and recorded the teacher's very apparent frustration for lack of an antidote to remedy the erratic idiotic antics.

The elementary school *children* were showing off to me by chewing gum, passing notes, being defiant and insolent to adult authority, name-calling, blaming each other for unruliness and squealing on one another instead of listening to the directions of the perplexed teacher. This was my first insight into classroom dynamics as an independent observer assessing the many behavioral adversities that seriously blight the modern American education process.

'Instead of we must understand the *child*,' I thought, 'the philosophy of education should be 'the *child* must understand'!' Teachers are often the prey of merciless adolescent predators that are protected by law, the school system's philosophy and the general society. The only defense the teacher has against young anarchists is "educational psychology," which is as effective as trying to down a charging rhinoceros with an empty water pistol.

'Education should be based on what a *child* needs to know and not on what a *child's* needs are, which vary from kid to kid and are not specifically identified!' I concluded. 'Serious consequences should await the *child* that refuses to understand and respect adult authority in a school building.'

First Period Gym Class was probably my favorite freshman curricular activity. Coach Holmes seemed to fancy me because my personality stood out like a sore thumb and my overall lack of athletic coordination managed to always capture his keen attention.

I usually showed up during roll call several minutes tardy from the locker room. In late September I had not yet obtained my brown and yellow college gym suit and instead wore my old *Edgewood High* green and white outfit to class. When I finally bought a brown and yellow gym uniform and wore it to class Coach Holmes had my gym locker secretly opened, removed my green and white shirt and trunks and directed the class to leave the gym and assemble outside on an athletic field.

The imaginative coach ignited my high school uniform with a cigarette lighter and the class began to chant in response to the ritual "Up in smoke! Up in smoke!" The other freshmen sounded as if they were members of a primitive jungle tribe worshiping and extolling arson. Their dissonant medley then transformed into a ceremonial dance and the fellows hopped and skipped around my smoldering forest green *Edgewood High* gym apparel. Little incidents like the tribal dance, towel fights in the shower room and the overall congenial looseness of Coach Holmes' informal gym class made it my favorite curricular freshman enterprise.

Looking back on my college preparation, I envision an asylum of wacky liberal and eccentric professors trying to rearrange my mind. Mr. Rolphs taught sociology and anthropology. He was a restless neurotic speaker who oscillated from one side of the classroom to the other as if he was a person with diarrhea seeking entry into an already occupied lavatory stall. Professor Rolphs' speeches were saturated with vitriolic condemnations of traditional institutions and their' failure to solve the country's many domestic dilemmas. Rolphs made 'Blame America first' a common understanding forty years before the motto became popular on radio talk shows.

Most of Professor Rolphs lessons would envelop arguments questioning the existence of God, the limitations of our breast-oriented civilization, and the myriad inadequacies of *our* evil materialistic keeping-up-with-the-Jonses' culture. Rolphs and his vituperations wouldn't last a marking period in the average American public high school, but a liberal dissident endorsing a quasi-Communist ideology could easily thrive on most college campuses as a beneficial and a meritorious professor that promotes freedom of thought and freedom of speech.

I witnessed a half-dozen virtuous girls at various times storm out of Rolphs sociology class weeping after engaging in a bitter emotional debate with the professor over the virginity of Mary or the divine nature of Christ. Although Rolphs repetitiously indicated that his sole purpose was to stimulate open-mindedness, it was plainly obvious that his podium provided a convenient soapbox where the professor could (at liberty) perpetuate the doctrines of Marx, Engels, Lenin, Stalin and Rolphs.

I concluded in early 1962 that many frustrated thespians, actors and scriptwriters masqueraded as college professors under the guise of "academic freedom." The liberal lecturers experimented with *their* uninspiring rhetoric and used it on their captive audiences and as in the case of Professor Rolphs, many professors thoroughly enjoyed playing the role of "Devil's Advocate" while probing the minds and eroding away the traditional values of their insulted and/or fascinated listeners.

As long as *academic freedom* is the benchmark of liberal arts college courses professors feel quite comfortable incorporating *their* own radical liberal views and creeds into each lecture to challenge conventional (traditional) wisdom. And the majority of college *students* going through a rebellion against adult authority in their own personal lives find the bizarre and the extraordinaire "new forum approach" fascinating. The learners associate *bizarre* and *extraordinaire* with freedom of speech and with individual expression guaranteed under the auspices of the *First Amendment* to the *Constitution*. Any blitzkrieg of traditional moral or religious values is categorized as "intellectual investigation," and therefore those professorial assaults are tolerated by *students*, condoned by colleges and universities and perpetuated by professors.

So, when someone like Professor Rolphs gets his or her jollies by blasting the maternal instincts of motherhood or the infallibility of the Pope, he or she is only executing his or her job description. The exposure to radical left-wing ideas will surely introduce *his* or her *students* to a vista of new perspectives that will undoubtedly widen their horizons and make them think and behave like avowed atheists and like loyal contemporary Communists and Socialists.

Dr. Peaferm was a strange Economics professor that appeared to be more interested in his private stock portfolio than in the balance of international trade, the guns-versus-butter debate, inflation or the rising cost-of-living index. His drowsy monotone (even during his most enthusiastic oral presentation) eventually sent the most avid *students* on one-way excursions to Slumberland. Dr. Peaferm's boring lecture method could never cut it in a public high school but a fellow of his unremarkable caliber could easily flourish in a college classroom environment.

The highlight of Peaferm's Economics seminar was a coed that Bob Abrams (a fraternity friend) had labeled and code-named Tokyo Rose. Bob and I would sit in Peaferm's crowded lecture hall and watch Tokyo Rose systematically squeeze the pus out of her facial and neck pimples.

This daily ritual would make us revel because it added a new dimension to an otherwise very dull and dismal class.

In a way though, Dr. Peaferm's style was different and unique. Peaferm had no axes to grind or dragons to slay as Rolphs and Sankin had. Peaferm was more interested in *Standard and Poors* than he was in raising the standard of the poor by sharing and redistributing the limited wealth and resources of the average middle-class American. Despite his nauseating mediocrity Peaferm's course was refreshing in the sense that he wasn't riding a white charger looking for the *Holy Grail* or crusading for the downfall of selfish capitalism while simultaneously championing the pursuit of reconstructing and redistributing the world's wealth.

And then there was Dr. Su, a petite Chinese lady who dressed in 1962 as if *WWI* was still in progress. Dr. Su's class was titled Teaching Methods I, but it would have been more appropriately identified as The Evils of Mao Tse-tung. Dr. Su spoke with a heavy Oriental accent', despised Red Chinese Communism with a passion and she always mispronounced my last name Wiener (as in hot dog) instead of Wiessner.

One day, before class a friend (during a moment of jocularity) scribbled on the front blackboard, "Do not erase-Dr. Wiener." Before I had a chance to remove the prosaic verse, Professor Su entered the room. She automatically grabbed an eraser and then momentarily hesitated as she somberly studied the message scrawled upon the black slate. She then innocently prattled, "Ah so, class! Dr. Wiener say I should not erase board, so I just lecture today and not write notes with chalk for you to copy." The class slipped into a minor state of pandemonium in response to her shallow perception and reaction to my friend's juvenile prank.

On another occasion I had cut Dr. Su's class to engage in an impromptu softball game on the baseball diamond adjacent to her corner second-floor classroom. Dr. Su stepped to the back of the room to open a window and observed me gallivanting on the baseball field below. "Wiener!" she imperatively bellowed. "You come up here this instant to my class!"

Although I had distinctly heard her piercing soprano voice, I ignored the diminutive lady professor's command pretending not to hear the dictum. Dr. Su re-evaluated her impetuosity and exclaimed to the already hysterical class, "Maybe that isn't Wiener down there after all!" A thunderous burst of laughter blared down to the baseball field from the upstairs corner classroom window.

Dr. Attleburg taught the subject of Mental Health and had a gruff-looking square face that qualified her to enter and win any ferocious dog show as a female pit bull. Her wrinkled countenance was a portrait of emotional anguish and her tainted breath exuded an odor akin to a dried-up Manhattan. Her anomalous lectures sounded very much like humdrum epistles from the lips of a peevish tavern patron about to fall off of her bar-stool.

Dayton, a black *student* in Dr. Attleburg's nondescript seminar, sat in the fifth seat in the row to my right next to the sidewall. Dayton worked nights on the back of a garbage truck, was extremely fatigued during the day and would always lean his body against the wall and fall asleep during the climax of Dr. Attleburg's dissertation. During one particular lecture the lady professor was elaborating about the need for love, forgiveness and sympathy in *our* interpersonal relationships as if she was giving an examination of conscience testimony at an Alcoholics Anonymous meeting. I then quite mischievously removed and opened a safety pin from my pocket and next quite methodically pierced the sleeping Dayton's pants and leg with it.

Dayton howled as his reflexive reaction to instant pain sent both him' and his desk crashing onto the polished wooden floor. Dr. Attleburg continued her lazy lecture as if nothing at all had happened. I wondered how such a numb person could be an authority on the manifold operations of the human mind after she had been completely oblivious to reality transpiring in her midst. But people of her ilk thrive in education, especially at the college level. They draw *lush* salaries and help pollute the educational canal by supporting the advancement of non-learning.

Dr. Attleburg's favorite maxim was "There's a big difference between teaching thirty years and teaching one year thirty times!" The most lamentable aspect of her oratory was that Dr. Attleburg had been uttering the impressive proverb ever since her initial year of professoring.

Speech with Dr. Lane was another class I had to attend. On the first meeting of the September session of my junior year, I sedately sat in my desk awaiting the instructor's arrival. An older gentleman I had presumed was pursuing a teaching degree sat next to me. The self-proclaimed *Korean War* veteran initiated a conversation. I soon discovered that he was very critical of the speech professor who was to teach *our* course. The elderly man used the terms "lousy" and "hideous" in his depiction of Dr. Lane.

I explained that I hardly knew anything about Dr. Lane except that the speech teacher's behavior was rumored being "a bit on the eccentric side." Five minutes elapsed and then the distinguished-looking *Korean War* veteran sitting next to me arose and announced to the class that *he* was the inimitable Dr. Lane.

On the class's second session, Dr. Lane made what he considered to be "a spectacular entrance." The nutcase had scaled the tall oak tree that had grown parallel to the main campus building, crawled out onto a sturdy limb and then clumsily swung his frame inside an opened second floor window.

Dr. Lane's interpretation of the meaning of the word *creativity* was doing something excessively peculiar or something unexpectedly sensational. His mannerisms were predictably unpredictable and one could only expect the unexpected from him. However, even climbing through opened second floor windows, standing and lecturing from atop the teacher's desk and shouting slanderous obscenities for no reason at all soon became tedious and unimpressive after becoming accustomed to their constant enactments.

Professor Flank taught History and Issues in United States Government. His lectures were as dull as an eight-inch-thick razor blade. Flank reveled in discussing American social disorganization, world chaos and the general frailness of the culturally retarded human species. Somehow, his "Blame America first" quips always seemed devoid of integrity, sincerity, honor and courage.

One winter day, while delivering a vitriolic critique on American imperialistic military/economic institutions, Dr. Flank's nose began bleeding. Feeling the slight trickle, the critical professor dabbed his nostrils with a handkerchief, but the flow of scarlet became even more profuse.

Flank glanced down in horror at the quantity of blood in his handkerchief, and feeling exceedingly frightened and embarrassed, his face turned as white as a lily. The professor swiftly canceled the remainder of the pathetic lesson, dismissed the class and hastily departed the scene looking as if he was a wounded infantryman searching for the nearest Florence Nightingale.

Professor O'Connor was a very outspoken man that thought his essential destiny in life was to expose the numerous faults and weaknesses of our corrupt American social structure. The intellectual establishment (college deans) regarded O'Connor's attacks on U.S. institutions as productive and scholarly as long as the axe-to-grind crusader lectured his way through issues like American racial prejudice and evil capitalistic exploitation both on the domestic scene and abroad.

But Professor O'Connor began skating on thin ice when *his* research investigations revealed instances of homosexuality among other notable members of the college faculty. Although he was one of the *students'* favorite professors O'Connor soon became the object of detestation (of his envenomed colleagues on the faculty). In an incredibly short time, Professor O'Connor earned the disfavor of the college administration that suddenly abhorred *his* inquiries into his fellow instructors' bedfellows' habits rather than focusing his attention upon what was diabolically wrong with America.

O'Connor's bold muckraking and whistle blowing activities drew newspaper attention to the local college campus, thus casting a dusky pall that immediately eclipsed all of the favorable publicity that the school's deans so sanctimoniously had labored to build. O' Connor's flirtations with attempting to right all wrongs (including social injustices and sexual perversions) became an uncontrollable obsession and the maverick professor did not heed the admonitions of the school's executives about what *he* had deemed immoral on the college campus. O'Connor was no longer an outspoken iconoclast! He was now perceived as a threat to the college!

Professor O'Connor could best be described as a combination of Upton Sinclair and *Don Quixote* and he appeared quite oblivious to the hatchet of doom being held over his head. His obsessive determination to expose all evil ruined his career. O'Connor was denied tenure, not because of his incompetence but because his mouth had oracled bad publicity about the school.

It was perfectly all right for O'Connor to subvert and indict the *United States of America,* but when he made it too personal by demonizing the college's good reputation then he was abruptly dismissed from academic service. The image of the school was much more important than the necessary criticisms prolifically directed at corrupt America.

Professor McIntire was an English prof' and a scholarly expert on William Shakespeare's work and life. McIntire relished several of my literary contributions that appeared in the campus newspaper and in the school's literary magazine. The fellow was a jolly sort of man who seemed to be knowledgeable and conversant in almost every subject. McIntire was rumored to be a "gay instructor" and to listen to his unique speech patterns, which featured a distinct effeminate twinge, I had good reason to place credence in the hearsay. On one occasion inside the *Student Union,* Dr. McIntire politely invited me over to his abode for cocktails to discuss *romance* in British literature, but I took a rain check when he intimated that only the two of us would be "romanticizing."

In all fairness to my college education, I had several dozen other dedicated professors that contributed positively to my professional development. To them, I will be eternally grateful. But decades later, the professors I have just described somehow seem to stand out in my mind for several very obvious reasons. The most discernible explanation is that instructors of their kind still populate virtually every college and university faculty in America. But Miss Sankin's skeleton is probably spinning around and gyrating in her grave with her "D Average" mediocre talent-less *student* evolving into an author of sorts.

"Reminiscing College Days"

The lucky *thirteen*-mile April 1, 2004 drive from Hammonton to Glassboro, New Jersey was pleasant and almost inspirational. As my merlot-colored *Nissan Maxima* passed through downtown Williamstown and onto *Route 322*, I pondered the four years I had spent at *Glassboro State College* preparing to become an idealistic New Jersey public school teacher, a difficult career which I had diligently pursued for thirty-four years until my very happy retirement in June of 1999.

But many important fragments of my past have been erased by circumstances beyond my control, further adding to my general quandary that often hypothesizes whether those four incredible years between ages nineteen and twenty-three had really occurred or not, for my entire life has been dangerously lived "on the cusp." Let me explain the basis for my current rumination.

I had attended Bishop Egan High in Levittown, Pennsylvania from 1957-'59 but now the former parochial school is boarded up and its identity no longer exists. And then in 1960 I managed to finally evolve out of Edgewood Regional High School in Atco, New Jersey, but the name of that institution is now Winslow Township High School. And consistent with *that* strange coincidence of my educational past being eradicated, the *Glassboro State Teachers College* of 1965 I had known and often reflect upon has now been transformed into *Rowan University*.

But for some remote inexplicable reason, I seldom revisited my former *Glassboro State* Alma Mater, but now I felt driven by a strong compulsion to re-connect with my past escapades. Perhaps it was pure nostalgia, or maybe I was motivated by fanciful memories that still haunted my delicate psyche, or perhaps my impulse to visit Glassboro was a desperate measure to recapture the essence of my youth. 'April is symbolic of the rebirth of nature and plant life in the *Northern*

Hemisphere,' I rationally considered, 'and just like daffodils sprouting out of the ground and deciduous trees miraculously forming new green spring foliage, my soul too is being rejuvenated this *April Fools' Day* by the wonderful annual spring regeneration.'

Upon crossing two-lane *Delsea Drive*, which also masquerades as *Route 47*, I ambitiously entered the small college town. I figured I would tour some exclusive sites to determine if any of my old haunts were still around and viably functioning. My eyes instantly recognized that Mazzeo's Bar and Lounge on High Street on my right was now the Study Hall Coffee House, a defunct boarded-up business that obviously had seen more prosperous times. Across the street and a block west was the former splendid Glassboro Movie Theater, now a mere empty bankrupt business with a huge "For Sale" sign hung in its ancient window, but back in 1964 the cinema was the site of a raucous fraternity shindig. That particular violation along with other high-jinks almost got my Greek brothers and me expelled from the school of higher learning for the final time, our fifth ultimatum from the college's beleaguered administration.

Joe's Sub Shop further down on High Street now had the creative appellation Little Beef's Hoagie Shop, a true indication that nothing is really permanent in this ephemeral life in an ever-changing world. I recalled that the Glassboro Police Station had formerly occupied the space behind the town bank situated at the central intersection of High and Main Streets, but now I observed that a new police building occupies the corner opposite the prestigious financial institution. The town's gendarmes had moved a fantastic hundred feet away from the address where I had known them to operate and practice their brand of law enforcement back in the early '60s.

I felt my heart pound a little more robustly when I stopped my vehicle to study the upstairs rooms of 38 South Main Street, where my roommates and I had hibernated for three fabulous coming-of-age years. Our sophomore-to-senior residence was located right next to a funeral home, which no longer exists as a family business. 38 South Main now appeared old with its light green siding fading as a result of four decades of wear and tear and exposure to Mother Nature's indiscriminate cruelty, but nevertheless the aging house still represented the space I had shared, a little smaller than I appropriately remembered it being as my "home away from home" from September of 1964 to June of '65.

Back in the early-to-mid '60s Seedy's Bar was a popular hangout for my unauthorized non-sanctioned off-campus fraternity, the Lambda Phi Sigmas, a social group of Greek wannabes' more interested in

406

chugging *Budweiser* and hustling pretty girls than becoming engrossed in the actual pursuit of academic excellence. Ironically Seedy's suds and sandwich hangout was just down the street from St. Bridget's Catholic Church, which predictably held its Sunday services on Church Street. But now the site where Seedy's was situated back in 1965 is presently a barren vacant lot.

I slowly navigated my *Maxima* west down Oakwood Avenue, which I had often used as a back approach to the rustic and still handsome college campus, and while passing over the familiar railroad tracks I noticed the old Glassboro Train Station and Depot, empty, boarded up and depressingly decrepit-looking. That ramshackle edifice also brought back several sentimental memories that I'll never forget as long as Alzheimer's disease doesn't completely evaporate my recollections. But the dilapidated condition of the once vibrant train station made my heart feel melancholy and had my sixty-two-year-old body suddenly feeling worn out and tired too, for both the train station and I had seen better days.

I took Whitney Avenue past #501, Hollybush, the *Glassboro State College* President's residence back in 1965, but today the structure proudly stands as a historic building dedicated to commemorate the famous 1967 *Summit Meeting* between President Lyndon Baines Johnson and the U.S.S.R. Premier Alexei B. Kosygin, which coincidentally had transpired on the *Glassboro State College Campus,* and the great international conference remains today the venerable Jersey sandstone college mansion's greatest claim to fame.

My vehicle made a right on *322* wanting to view the historic Franklin House, which was an inn dating back to the aristocratic fox-hunting days of the early 1790s, but I was disappointed in discovering that the building had been renovated and converted into the Landmark Americana Tap, Grill and Liquor Mart. Across from the former Franklin House was State Street, which formed a Y two blocks down at New Street where Academy Street began. So being a little sad and disappointed at the Franklin House's demise, I turned around in the Landmark Americana's parking lot and returned west on *322*, which now divides the old campus from the new building additions, most of which have been constructed since my graduation in '65.

Only *Bosshart Hall, Winans Dining Hall* and the *Esbjornson Gymnasium* were situated on the north side of *322* my senior year, but now a grand *Student Union Building, Robinson Hall, Mimosa Hall, Rowan Hall, Wilson Hall,* the new *Savitz Library* along with six massive co-ed dormitories have been added to the north *322* campus scenario. *Winans Cafeteria* has been renovated and ingeniously converted into *Winans College Bookstore,* and so the *Glassboro State College* campus (now *Rowan University*) like the rest of the universities on the planet continues its new growth and its unique chameleon retooling of older facilities.

Glassboro's residential streets west of *Rowan University* (*Glassboro State*) attempt to confirm and promote a college-town atmosphere theme. Girard Road parallels the railroad tracks that happen to form the campus's western perimeter, and the remembrance of *our* Lambda Phi Sigma initiation along the railroad tracks immediately surfaced from my subconscious and managed to rekindle my flagging spirit. Princeton, Pennsylvania, Columbia, Yale, Harvard and Lehigh Roads horizontally followed in succession to the west after Girard, and then Georgetown, Dickinson, Villanova and Swarthmore Roads run vertically west forming a characteristic lattice pattern with the aforementioned west-layered streets, which traditionally have housed many off-campus students from back in the '60s up to the present time.

University Road is the main residential thoroughfare that parallels Dickinson and Villanova in the well-conceived interlacing pattern. Many of the University Road homes that I had considered mansions back in the '60s now appear in need of repair and rather mediocre in appearance. But it was not University Road's stately oak and elm trees nor the architectural grandeur of its aging palaces that prompted me to nostalgically desire re-exploring the remainder of the serene boulevard.

At the very end of the avenue was Peaks Horse Apple and Peach Farm', which is now fenced in and designated off limits to strangers. But despite the three prominent "No Trespassing" signs, I felt a need to exit my *Maxima* and traverse down a familiar rural trail a hundred feet into the woods where I intended to re-discover a shallow stream. I rushed along the still-secluded path, now tangled in dense brush until I came to the "Sacred Oak," majestically towering above me and deeply rooted amidst the woods' briars, thick brambles and wild vegetation.

The old severed "Tarzan jungle vine" still dangled from around the still-dignified oak's third revered limb and the fallen-but-decomposing elm tree footbridge still spanned over the fifteen-foot-wide brook that remains today a rather imposing sight, but absolutely ravaged by time, rotted through its decayed bark and trunk and in its present flimsy condition, totally incapable of holding a sixty-two-year-old male of average weight. 'That's the third of nine major memorable scenes I want to see besides the railroad tracks and 38 South Main,' I evaluated. 'The fourth through seventh items of interest are on the old-side of the college campus and the eighth and ninth can be found two miles south of Glassboro in rural Aura.'

I then carefully ambled back to my *Nissan'*, gingerly entered the vehicle, cautiously backed up, turned around and drove the mile-distance to the still-attractive countryside campus. 'I wish I had phoned a classmate fellow graduate friend of mine to accompany me on this ramble,' I thought. 'My Buddy Tim Amoro would relish this nostalgia as much as I am fondly recalling it right now.'

I halted my auto in the makeshift parking lot owned by the Pennsylvania Railroad. 'It's safe during the daytime,' I reckoned while recalling that once I was taking a graduate night course at the college, arrived at the campus a bit behind schedule, hastily parked my wife's green *Pontiac* in the same lot and returned from class finding the car's battery stolen. 'My brother-in-law was not too keen on driving from Hammonton to Glassboro with a replacement battery in the middle of a wicked January snowstorm,' I recollected with a naughty grin.

Although it was an early spring day, fallen leaves cushioned my steps to the old campus buildings I wished to observe. The bright golden dome still formed a cupola above the main academic building erected in 1923, then *College Hall* up until '65 but now renamed *Bunce Hall* after a revered college dean. I stopped to marvel at the majestic spectacle as students less impressed with its essential existence chatted and rushed to their next scheduled classes.

I detoured to where the Student Co-op snack bar used to be, a unique 1960s malt-shop carryover from the previous less hostile '50s decade. The mammoth *Student Union* across *Route 322* had replaced the Co-op (and its attendant lounges in nearby *Memorial Hall*) as the campus nerve center, and the entire *Memorial Hall* complex was now a suite of specialized offices being utilized for student organizations, clubs, the *Whit* newspaper, the *Avant Literary Magazine*, and for individual student counseling.

I passed by several groups of garrulous preoccupied students, oblivious to my intense scrutiny of their taken-for-granted physical environment. The walkers were laughing and exchanging gossip en route to their next destinations. Four decades before I had shared their youthful vim and vigor, their enterprise, their great expectations for individual accomplishments and their vision for a more peaceful world, along with *their* rosy hopes and dreams for prosperous futures, but then I felt myself' being quite out of place standing there, a realist and modern-day cynic among those that were still vulnerable to professors' unbridled entreaties and idealistic optimisms. Forty years separated their same enterprise from mine (as a student trekking down that same well-worn asphalt path), and my skeptical mind appreciated and rehashed the salient fact that I did not have to relive those forty years from 1965 to 2004 over again.

I next casually strolled to the old magnificent dorm' Quadrangle consisting of *Laurel Hall* and *Oak Hall*, originally constructed parallel to each other in the 1920s to accommodate the women attending the two-year "Normal School" to earn teaching certification, and to the far end of *that* most beautiful sector of the scenic campus was *Linden Hall*, built in the late 1950s to complement the more distinguished twin dormitories. *Oak Hall* was just a short saunter from Hollybush, where several asphalt paths lead to *Evergreen Hall*, where Joanne (my future wife) once cheerfully resided. And next to *Evergreen* is *Mullica Hall*, a men's dormitory back in '65.

My eyes peered across *Route 322* at the numerous building additions supplementing what I had known in '65, and the edifices now stretched all the way to Carpenter Street, which in my senior year seemed to be in another county. Behind the new dormitories and brick-faced academic buildings are numerous parking lots, tennis courts, softball, hockey, la-crosse and soccer fields, intramural fields, and finally the rather outstanding *Rowan University Football Stadium.*

I cut back across the area next to *Memorial Hall* and jaunted through a nice clean pristine-looking park that was once a student parking lot for "commuters." *Hawthorn Hall* was now altered into an administrative office building and no longer was the men's dorm' I had recalled from '65. The *Campus School*, where many of my colleagues had completed their Student Teaching and fundamental Practicum experiences was now called *Bozarth Hall*, named after another college dean of my era. Next to the former *Campus School* was the old baseball field where Ralph Crenshaw and I used to broadcast the games for *WGLS-FM*, the college radio station, which was now housed in *Bozarth Hall* and no longer was situated above the old *Savitz Library* building (now an administrative building) on the entrance oval next to what is now *Bunce Hall.*

I stood gazing at "*College Hall*" for a full minute on the pitcher's mound as the April 1st wind swirled dust and the remains of the autumn leaves about my black leather shoes. Forty-five years had elapsed since I had played gym-class soccer for Coach Holmes on that same verdant field, and only the passage of time separated my present memories from those past happy experiences that had occurred in that exact same place.

'Now that I've seen the railroad tracks, the vine, the elm tree bridge and the creek, the *College Hall Golden Dome*, the *Quadrangle*, the former Co-op, and *Evergreen Hall* there's only two more essential memories to see on my *April Fool Day Glassboro State* excursion,' I pondered as I slowly stepped around the corner of *Bunce Hall* (College Hall) to the oval drive before it, now blocked off to local traffic. Arriving at my parked automobile in the dirt and stone railroad parking lot, I decided to motor south two miles to Aura to complete my day's personal itinerary.

I anxiously drove through downtown Glassboro on High to Main Street, looked left and smiled upon seeing that all-too-familiar Angelo's Diner was still in business, and then traveled south until Main became *Gloucester County Road 533*. Soon I crossed the railroad tracks a mile from the college town and then crossed *County 610*. Another mile or so on *County 533* I arrived at good old *Gloucester County Road 608*. After turning left, my right foot stepped more heavily on the accelerator as I wondered whether or not my fraternity's old original Lambda Phi Sigma party place was still standing.

I halted my *Nissan* to obtain a closer inspection of the structure that I had been so anxious to see. Yes, there it now stood, painted red, but still in the exact shape I had remembered it being. The ultimate objective of my Hammonton-to-Glassboro excursion was Steve "Hoppy" Cassidy's chicken coop, but in 1962 the commonplace building had been imaginatively converted to a swinging college student attraction, the infamous Lambda Phi Sigma fraternity house.

On the way back to *Delsea Drive* following *County 608* I passed by another landmark from my past, the picturesque *Academy Street Lake* in the rural town of Clayton. Feeling satisfied and renewed from my morning excursion, I then motored back to Hammonton.

"School Assemblies"

The Teachers Handbook prepared by the school administration explicitly states, "All school assemblies are scheduled by the main office and the meetings constitute an integral part of the total school program. Assemblies provide opportunities for the *cultural* and *intellectual* growth of *students* and they contribute significantly to the development of school spirit and school morale."

I have attended in the neighborhood of three hundred school assembles in my thirty-four-year teaching career ranging from pep' assemblies and science demonstrations to boring lectures, spelling bees and popular "G-Rated" movies shown before major holidays to "Keep the lid on."

Recently the tone of assembly subjects has turned from *cultural* and *intellectual* to *bleak* and almost *macabre* themes such as drugs, teen pregnancies and question and answer sessions with convicted prisoners with the convicts showing up on stage (with prison guards) in their official orange uniforms. However, several extraordinary assemblies that I had the misfortune of attending stand out in my mind.

Once I had the displeasure of attending a junior-high school assembly in the high school auditorium. A circus clown wearing oversized shoes walked onto the front stage from behind the curtain and began doing magic tricks that were about as complicated as a basal reader. The *students* became quite restive and soon were hooting and shouting like a pack of vitriolic hyenas.

It is embarrassing to have to stand during the entire assembly and play Gestapo when the teacher himself' wished he had an old vaudeville cane to yank the idiot off the stage. 'A profit-minded huckster could amass a small fortune vending soft rotten tomatoes for the *children* to hurl at the zany entertainer,' I thought. That particular assembly definitely contributed to the "cultural and intellectual growth of the *students*."

The intellectually gifted *student* is often stifled spending thirteen years in a public school system that promoted *democracy in education* within the comprehensive high school. Ben Locanta was a gifted *child* whose public-school preparation was about as useful as a bamboo paperweight during a tornado. The gifted *student* possessed admirable resourcefulness.

Whenever the school videotape machine went haywire or whenever the intercom went amuck, Ben was summoned to the office before any outside repairman was contacted. The young genius's knowledge of physics, electricity and chemistry was praiseworthy indeed. Regrettably Ben Locanta was so advanced that his mental needs were sadly neglected by the school curriculum. In the early '70s the high school had no modus operandi to effectively deal with the exceptionally talented *student*.

Usually in high school education the intellectually precocious *child* gets the short end of the stick since the entire system is geared to raising the mentally downtrodden up to "academic mediocrity." When schools have *students* like Ben Locanta, that is when they' need the "laboratory approach to learning," "independent study" and "the *student*-oriented curriculum."

As it is according to the mandates of *democratic education*, those three splendid programs apply to the masses and not exclusively to the gifted *student*. Ben was the *child* that really needed to explore, create, invent, discover, synthesize and push his intelligence to the max'. But in American education *those* marvelous terms were and still are harnessed mostly to *students* that didn't (and don't) know a Bunsen burner from a Franklin stove and who' don't care to know.

One afternoon, an opera company visited the school to give two assembly performances for the *student* body. Ben Locanta assisted the troupe with the stage arrangements, stationing the props', positioning and focusing the spotlights and overheads, and operating the backstage electrical controls.

One of the more-cocky thespians traveling with the opera production bent down to adjust a spotlight that would be shining on him during the first scene. The light had been turned on for only a minute and Ben cautioned the fellow, "You'd better not touch that right now or your hands will get scorched!"

The middle-aged fellow, who was wearing a medieval costume with leotards, felt more than slightly chagrined at being admonished by a young high school *student*. The actor snorted back to Ben "I've been in show business all my life!" he boasted. "Do you think I'm some kind of greenhorn when it comes to simple high school stage lighting!"

The enraged actor/baritone bent down and grabbed the spotlight with both hands, and then an instant expression of agony beamed from his facial features. The fellow howled so loudly that I thought he was going to turn himself inside out and the heat from his sizzling hands almost triggered the school's fire alarm. Ben was gracious enough to escort the anguishing singer/actor down to the nurse's office where his seriously blistered fingers were professionally bandaged.

The assembly opera program did commence an hour later and the distressed fellow with the gauze around his hands didn't even have to wear white gloves. "That guy was punished by fate for being so nasty to Ben," history teacher Bob Gordon confided to me. "He deserved to get roasted because the nurse told me he's about as sociable as the Abominable Snowman."

That same year I was the adviser to the high school's chapter of the *National Honor Society*. Ben Locanta was president of the *NHS* and as usual, the week before the induction assembly the entire ceremony program was rehearsed. This was in the early '70s during the *Vietnam War* era, and most of the male *students* in the school had long hair, sideburns, mustaches and wore bell-bottom' denim-jeans. I soon found out that there was a degree of rebelliousness and anti-war sentiments even among the school's most honorable *students*.

Towards the end of the *NHS* induction assembly there was always a segment where the *students* broke away from formal decorum and did a "Have You Heard" routine where high school gossip was done between two *students* over two separate microphones. Of course, Ben and another *NHS* officer stepped over the line and announced that *students* with certain initials were having casual sex with *students* with certain other initials. Before the principal could run onto the stage and terminate the assembly the *NHS* officers gave the familiar '70s peace sign and all of the *students* in attendance stood up, cheered and gave reciprocal peace signs to their honorary academic leaders on the stage.

"That assembly was a disgrace to this school!" the principal screamed at me in his office.

"Look, *we* rehearsed the whole program last week and none of that sex stuff at the end was in the rehearsal!" I defended myself by yelling back. "Those *students* inserted that dialogue at the end without my knowledge or permission!"

"You're through as *NHS* adviser!" the head honcho bellowed. "And this disgrace will definitely go into your personal folder!" he added.

And so that's the way it often goes in American education. Botch up either unintentionally or deliberately and by a stroke of luck the teacher is suddenly and fortuitously freed of an important responsibility like being *NHS* adviser.

At another school assembly the faculty and *students* were honored to have an inspirational guest speaker whom John Rizzotte had heard address the local Kiwanis Club. The driver education teacher was very impressed with the hard life and tough approach of the self-made businessman so he convinced the administration to schedule the fellow to be an assembly speaker.

The assembly was slated for eighth period, the final time slot of the school day. John Rizzotte introduced the self-made man and a distinct hush followed by light applause filled the six-hundred-seat chamber. The fellow approached the podium and then began speaking didactically into the microphone. The man's "talking down to his audience" style completely turned off his youthful listeners after the first three minutes of his biographical presentation.

At first, I felt a degree of compassion for the silver-haired Pericles. I got up from my seat like a dozen other teachers and patrolled the aisles chastising snickering wise guys. But then the speaker used an excessive amount of *selfish* personal pronouns like *I, me, my, myself* and *mine.*

The *students* were becoming more neurotic, impolite, obnoxious and unruly as the man's rigid speech continued. Again, I rebuked several young punks by saying, "This fellow is a self-made millionaire. He has gone from rags to riches!" I clearly lectured. "Maybe you can learn something from him about success by paying this man the respect he deserves!"

But most of the *students* (who were used to being entertained at assemblies and not *lectured* to) were as interested in Horatio Alger stories as they were in quadratic equations. The elderly gent then sanctimoniously spoke with a heavy Polish accent about the need for patriotism, nationalism, free enterprise and loyalty to flag and country. By then nine-tenths of the *children* in the jam-packed audience were becoming quite antsy. The undercurrent of muffled *student* conversations could be heard throughout the auditorium when the entire assembly became less and less receptive to the self-made Polish immigrant millionaire's speech. Civil peace was rapidly reaching the danger level.

'This guy is completely turning these spoiled *students* off!' I thought. 'What was John Rizzotte possibly thinking when he invited this man to speak? What works great at the Kiwanis Club might bomb when immature *students* are asked to sit still and listen for forty-five minutes!'

The end of the period arrived on the clock and the dismissal bell finally sounded. But the self-appointed Polish Demosthenes at the podium microphone disregarded the bell and kept on addressing the totally bored *students*. The guy just wouldn't shut up!

The assistant principal and John Rizzotte motioned and waved their hands for the man to finish his presentation but the undaunted speaker simply waved back responding to what he thought was a supportive salutation and kept talking to his lost audience.

The old fellow then sensed the restlessness that existed in the auditorium so he demonstrated his dexterity. The former circus acrobat did three consecutive cartwheels on the stage for the benefit of his audience. The *students* then went crazy and gave the old gentleman a standing mock round-of-applause as the principal, vice principal and John Rizzotte first gesticulated with their hands and then wildly and frantically signaled with both arms for the *students* to be seated so that an orderly dismissal could be initiated.

The hapless old gent started speaking again since he interpreted the *students'* reaction as a relishing of his work-ethic philosophy. Ben Locanta came out on stage with a plaque to present to the speaker to terminate the bizarre assembly program. By then the school day was over by a full ten minutes and all of the bus routes to the elementary school were already messed up and off schedule.

The now-enthusiastic *students* again swiftly stood up after the brief plaque presentation and the assembled *children* gave the oblivious speaker a second mock ovation. The old man left the school five minutes later thinking that his talk had been well' received and he told John Rizzotte on his way out of the building's front entrance that he "has faith in the future of America based on the fine *students* in your high school."

At another daft assembly just before the *Easter* holiday break, the *students* were slated to view an hour and a half Hollywood motion picture entitled *A Man Called Horse.* The *children* silently filed into the auditorium by homerooms, sat in their prearranged seating sections, the lights were dimmed and the projector began flickering the film's frames upon the stage's white screen.

The movie's opening scenes was a real eye-catcher. Richard Harris had been stripped of his attire and was running naked through prairie grasslands while being chased by a virulent Indian tribe. Any teacher seated in the auditorium could hear a pin drop. The silent *students* were amazed that their high school (a bastion of Victorian middle-class morality) auditorium would suddenly be converted into a bawdy X-rated movie house.

The abashed school czars scurried to the back of the auditorium and had the head of the *student* audiovisual crew (now a prominent town councilman) place a flimsy piece of cardboard in front of the projector lens every time a bare pair of buttocks flashed onto the white screen. The unhappy *students* booed, jeered and chanted every time their innocent eyes were denied the opportunity to view what they considered carnal pleasure.

A later scene in the film *A Man Called Horse* was one of the goriest and most gruesome spectacles I had ever seen in a movie. The pursued cowpoke (Richard Harris) had been captured by the Indians and was about to be accepted as a leader in the tribe after winning the clan's approval by demonstrating extraordinary bravery. His acceptance as honorary chief was accompanied by a most bizarre and sadistic Indian' initiation rite.

Two gaping incisions were made into the paleface's chest, one into each *breast* (if this were a woman being initiated into the tribe then obviously the audiovisual crew would have to cover the projector lens with the piece of cardboard as commanded by the nervous school principal standing nearby). Two meat hooks were tethered to ropes that had been suspended from a rafter and then the hooks were inserted inside Richard Harris's chest.

The white man' honorary chief was next hoisted up into the air, hanging and suspended in a vertical position from the ropes with the inserted meat hooks being on either side of his sternum. The actor's body was then spun around so fast that, as his form assumed a horizontal plane, the honorary white chief resembled a gyroscope whirling around.

The scene was so hideous that even the most daring pugnacious *students* had to turn their heads on lower their eyes. Not even the worst behaved *students* that were always *suspended* themselves' could watch the climax to the ugly Indian initiation exhibition.

But the entire *A Man Called Horse* movie assembly was quite indicative of our Neo-Victorian American Puritanical society. It's all right to show bloodshed, murder, death, suicide, homicide and shootings, so gore and violence are generally regarded as acceptable and almost commendable. But to show a man's buttocks, a woman's breast or a pubic hair required a rectangular piece of cardboard in front of the movie projector's lens. The elite *student* audiovisual crew however was able to focus the forbidden images on their side of the piece of cardboard and had a few visual treats all to their own.

The week after *Easter* break, I saw Mr. Bill W., the assembly program adviser in the hall. "What happened with the administration after you showed that movie before the Easter break?" I asked.

"I was really chewed out!" the adviser confessed. "I guess they'll now get somebody else to order and show the films."

"Don't feel bad!" I empathized. "I was fired as *NHS* adviser after the honor *students* pulled a fast one on me and changed the ending of the assembly."

"Good, you can have my former job as assembly film organizer!" my colleague joked. "If the boss doesn't formally fire me I'll quit!"

"No thanks," I replied. "I think I'd rather go into alligator mud-wrestling or wild elephant training!"

Another pretty interesting assembly was of the school spirit-pep' variety type and this one particular event happened in the late 1990s. The middle school *football team* ran out onto the school gymnasium *basketball court*. The last *student* football player carried a manikin's faceless head with a woman's wig on top. He was enacting an imitation of a famous and popular *World Wrestling Federation* professional wrestler at the time, Al Snow. Just like *WWF* fans had done on television many times in response to the appearance of the manikin's head, the energized *students* in the gallery wildly chanted, "We want head! We want head!"

The next morning, the beleaguered principal called the *student* that had held the manikin's head down to the office and the *child* claimed that he was unaware that the chant "We want head!" involved any sexual connotation. "And besides if it did," the *student* argued to the principal, "the kids in the stands were yelling the dirty words and not me! I was only holding the fake head up in the air!"

The clever *student* got away with murder conducting his little "inappropriate" charade and received only two days of Office Detention for causing widespread chaos and instigating the ultimate in bad taste during a school spirit pep' assembly.

And finally, schools also have quasi-assemblies where films are shown on rainy days to fill the second half of a forty-five-minute lunch period. I usually stepped into the main office just before lunch duty and asked the principal what films might be available to show to the eighth graders in the auditorium after they had eaten their lunches in the cafeteria.

"Here, try this one!" the busy principal confidently suggested. "It came from the county film library."

"*Code Blue!*" I exclaimed with surprise. "Have you screened or previewed it to make sure it's safe to show to eighth graders?"

"I just told you it came from the county film library," the school executive insisted, "so it's probably something like *Blue Hawaii* or something like that!"

"Okay, you're the boss!" I sarcastically complimented and then left the main office to set up the film for viewing.

The *students* were expertly transferred from the cafeteria to the auditorium and after settling down, I dimmed the lights while the other teacher on duty started up the projector. Neither Joe Sacci nor I had realized at the time that *Code Blue* was hospital terminology for "Emergency Operating Room."

The first bloody scene showed a man with a bashed-up head being assiduously stitched-up by a very skilled surgeon. The second scene showed a huge Afro-American woman giving birth. The corpulent lady's legs were wide open and all of her femininity was right there for the absolutely captivated audience of fourteen-year-olds to inspect and evaluate.

The other teacher on duty and I rushed to the projector to shut the questionable film off when suddenly the hospital scene shifted to two unconscious automobile accident victims in need of immediate surgery being wheeled on gurneys into the very busy emergency area operating suite. The scene continued and showed the men being attended to and resuscitated by qualified and competent hospital nurses and doctors.

Then suddenly the medical film shifted back to the black Afro-American woman giving birth to her second and third babies. Joe Sacci and I made a beeline to the film projector and shut it off just as the second part of the lunch period came to an end. A deluge of boos generated from the disappointed *students* engulfed my embarrassed colleague and myself.

"I think I'll stay home after living through *that* fiasco," my friend related. "I need a mental health day!"

"Me too Joe!" I concurred. "There's bound to be a ton of parent flack after this farce, that's for sure!"

The next day was Friday and Joe Sacci and I both took a "mental health" or "stay alive" day off from school. The following Monday we both showed up and were amazed to find out that not one irate parent phone call had been received in the main office about multiple birth scenes shown in the second half of the previous Thursday's eighth grade lunch period.

"The High School Faculty"

Tim Carley and Bob Gordon were close friends and almost inseparable amigos on the high school faculty. Tim taught both U.S. and Ancient History courses in a room that had been originally designed as part of a larger family living classroom. A toilet that was once in the family living room had been partitioned off and soon became a part of Tim's social studies' office. An entrance door to the office and toilet separated the porcelain fixture from Tim's history classroom.

The availability of the toilet proved very *commod*ious to Tim. Whenever a *student* with weak kidneys asked the history teacher if he or she could visit the lavatory Tim would open the door to *his* office and say, "Sure! Use the facilities right in here!" The history mentor would then proudly open the door to his *office* exposing the glistening hopper to the view of the appreciative class.

The *student* seeking relief would consider the thought of embarr*ass*ing noises emanating from *the office* into the classroom and then become discouraged from attempting to conveniently answer nature's call. Tim Carley was seldom plagued with continuous annoying *student* requests to leave the room and use the bathroom facilities.

One day, when Tim was enlightening his second period World Civilizations advanced *students* on the brilliant attainments of the ancient Mesopotamian culture, a temporary classroom silence was created when everyone in the room heard a distinct gurgling reverberation. All heads turned left as the office door opened and then out stepped the unabashed Bob Gordon. He casually waved a cute salutation to Tim and *his* World Civilizations class, acting totally nonchalant about the impropriety of *his* "unprofessional toilet flushing conduct." Tim Carley's face turned redder than a beet as the mixed class snickered and chuckled for a full five minutes.

On another memorable occasion, Tim Carley and Bob Gordon were chaperones on the senior class Washington Trip. The two teachers supervised rooms and randomly searched *student* luggage for booze that might have illegally been smuggled into the motel. After confiscating six pints of alcohol in true Eliot Ness fashion Bob and Tim generously re-distributed their plunder to the ten faculty chaperones on duty as a well' deserved "Washington Trip fringe benefit." And so the grateful teachers had a small all-night party at the expense of some irascible-minded *students* trying to pull a fast one.

On that same Washington Trip, Tim and Bob had a photo taken of them sitting with a manikin of Lyndon B. Johnson at a District of Columbia wax museum. A mock newspaper headline along with the photo' was published at a novelty store and it read, "Local Teachers Confer with President Johnson." The front page of the mock newspaper was conspicuously hung on a central bulletin board in the main high school corridor. The unique piece of journalism lingered there for two whole months without it ever being noticed or scrutinized by *students* changing classes. Then I decided to bring the unique newspaper item to a talkative *student's* attention and it wasn't long before the thumb' tacked poster became one of the featured points of *student* interest while *they* were passing and then stopping to gander at the newspaper headline spectacle between classes.

Bob Gordon was notorious for playing pranks at teacher parties. Once while Mr. Gordon was attending a rollicking Friday night affair hosted by math' teacher Jim Kyle, Bob tested the alcoholic capacity of seven fish swimming about in Jim's aquarium. When no one was looking, Mr. Gordon poured a large quantity of vodka into the fish tank to scientifically study how the intoxicant would influence the swimming patterns of the victimized marine-life.

The next morning the teacher that had thrown the big shindig the night before discovered his seven fish floating on top of the water instead of in it. The following Monday at school I consoled the depressed party host by saying, "Well Jim, I guess there isn't too much validity to the statement *he drinks like a fish*! I believe someone with unscrupulous intentions must have poured vodka or gin into your aquarium! What a way to get *tanked*!"

"Thanks a lot!" the despondent teacher disgustedly answered. "Your kindness *underwhelms* me!"

At another wild faculty party given by Jim Kyle, Bob Gordon raided the bathroom medicine chest. He secretly confiscated our host's razor blades leaving only one behind, which the trickster mercilessly warped out of shape and then somehow managed to insert the twisted shaving blade into Jim Kyle's razor. On Monday morning the aggravated teacher that had just lost seven aquarium fish the week before showed up at school with a face that appeared as if it had been shaven by a power lawnmower.

"Well, there Jim, at least you don't have a five o'clock shadow! Anyway, that was a great happening at your place Sunday night!" I commented as I stared at the nicks and gashes that gutted Mr. Kyle's countenance.

"Somebody else is gonna' throw the next damned teacher party," Jim glumly answered. "I've just about had it hosting this damned unappreciative faculty!"

Bob Gordon always had a prank or two up his sleeve. The main corridor of the high school had two attractive planters attached to a wall with neatly arranged displays of artificial plants and flowers inside them. Bob surreptitiously noticed that certain overhead spotlights ideally beamed shafts of light directly into the flower-boxes.

In January of '68, early each morning Mr. Bob Gordon would clandestinely deposit several pounds of dirt into the flower-boxes before any administrators were in the building. After two weeks passed Bob was ready to initiate phase two of his devious scheme. He planted pumpkin and sunflower seeds into the freshly transferred soil. Several weeks' later *student* passers-by stopped and incredulously peered at the remarkable planter, which had a splendid array of real natural vegetation and then huge vines growing above the dwarfed synthetic greenery.

In conjunction with the late '60s ecology fad, Bob Gordon and Ron LeFey took two conservation-minded biology classes on a school-sponsored three-day camping trip to a lake located twenty miles from the high school. Tim Carley and I drove out to the lake the second night to see how the contemporary Thoreaus were doing. When we arrived at our destination larking *students* were chasing each other through the briars while others were already paired off and passionately necking under tall pine trees. Tim noticed a mixed group' of *children* dash into the woods and the errant *students* immediately vanished to avoid the detection of the two old-fashioned newly arrived conservative visitors.

"I hope those *students* don't eat any poisonous mushrooms!" Tim exclaimed after witnessing the sudden exodus into the forest.

"I think the *students* are more interested in basic biological pursuits than in honest intellectual ecological inquiry!" I replied.

About the only souls in the immediate environment that Tim and I could locate were Bob Gordon and Ron LeFey, the organizers of the frolicking nature study junket. The curfew was supposed to be ten' o clock, but the dials of my trusty *Timex* accurately read 11:30.

"The *students* are really infected with the pioneering spirit now," I jested to Bob and Ron as Tim laughed his rear end off. "What happened to the Conestoga wagons?" I joked as I watched silhouettes darting in and out of the distant foliage.

"It looks like a screwed-up primitive Sadie Hawkins Day with a surplus of Little Abners and Daisy Mays," Tim Carley added while still laughing. "But it's about equal the number of boys chasing after girls and the number of girls chasing boys!"

Bob Gordon was more optimistic than we were and attributed the excessive chaos we were witnessing to something else. "Guys, it's just the first time these *students* have had any freedom on their own," he generalized. "They simply don't know how to act when not under their parents' domination!"

"I'm glad I'm only a social studies teacher and don't have to teach *wild life*!" Tim amusingly interrupted his favorite faculty pal.

"Actually, these sensational *student* shenanigans do look a little Saturnalian to the, pardon the expression, to the *naked* eye!" I calmly stated to the two embarrassed and slightly chagrined chaperones.

With two reinforcements from the high school faculty on hand, Bob and Ron (with the assistance of Tim and myself') rounded up the revelers and herded them back into their respective gender-separated designated cabins.

But before the *students* had been officially returned to their particular corrals Bob Gordon had taken the time to smear butter on all the bunk bed sheets in the four *student* cabins of the kids that had been assigned to *his* custody. After his *students* tramped into their cabins for the night devilish Bob sternly entered each logged building and reprimanded his underlings a cabin at a time for their aberrant conduct cavorting around in the pine-barrens forest. "I didn't appreciate your Pan-like goofing off one bit!" he yelled out in relation to the *students'* wild gamboling. "Now get to bed in a hurry and I don't want to hear one peep outa' any of ya' for the rest of the night!" he vehemently snarled.

The *students* under Bob's care washed up and when they slid under their bed-covers, a low chatter could be discerned outside the cabins as the victimized *students* accused each other of skullduggery. Bob Gordon pretended to be angry after hearing the recriminations being volleyed back and forth. He opened the cabin door and rebuked the chatterers, "What's wrong with you imbeciles!" he boomed. "I just yelled at ya' for foolin' around in the woods! Don't you kids have any sense of shame?" Bob screamed at his doubly startled prodigies.

When Bob left the third cabin after hollering at his *students* Tim Carley said, "Well Bob, I'm sure glad to see that you know how to *butter up* your advanced learners!"

"You leave little *margarine* for error!" I added referring to the butter *spread* in the bed sheets.

"Those obnoxious kids will blame each other all night long and never suspect that Mr. Gordon would play such a dastardly prank!" Ron LeFey laughed.

"Yeah, it's almost like Smokey the Bear moonlighting as an arsonist or George Washington turning turncoat for the redcoats!" the amused sophomore history teacher stated. "Somebody's got to get back at these kids for all the crap they pull on us!" Bob Gordon summarized. "So, I've deputized myself a one-man vigilante committee!"

Being an accomplished prankster sometimes has its pitfalls as Bob Gordon once found out. Every *Halloween* the sophomore social studies' teacher would unexpectedly dart into a classroom where I would be permanent subbing and Mr. Gordon would be wearing a dreadful-looking Dracula mask. The unexpected intrusion would startle the wits out of even the most bored *students*.

I thought that Bob's *Halloween* caper was amusing so I always kept a Frankenstein mask in the desk of the room where I was instructing. And towards the end of October when the *students* would be busy taking a test or doing a worksheet, I would get the mask out of the desk and hide it under my sport jacket. Then I would put the mask over my face in the back of the room and walk around until the first *student* (usually a female) would see me, become frightened and then let out a shrill shriek. So when Bob Gordon would unexpectedly enter the same classroom a day later wearing the grotesque Dracula mask the *students* believed that the entire faculty was going off the deep end.

The laws of karma however have a way of boomeranging when one' least expects a negative consequence to happen. One *Halloween* afternoon Bob Gordon was driving his red *Volkswagen* home from the high school. The sophomore social studies teacher had the bad habit of attempting to scare adults he knew with his hideous Dracula mask (besides startling his *students*).

Bob's red *Volkswagen* was approaching a very friendly school-crossing guard that always enjoyed waving greetings at motorists and exchanging pleasantries with pedestrians. When the red foreign car neared the woman traffic director Mr. Gordon donned his frightening mask.

As the red *Volkswagen* slowly passed by the pleasant crossing-guard Bob let out a ferocious growl that immediately stunned the woman. However, as Bob removed his mask to reveal his true identity to the shocked guard his small vehicle was still advancing forward keeping pace with the slow-moving road traffic. A town garbage truck turned the intersection corner and Bob's red *Volkswagen* plowed into it as Gordon was exposing his true identity to the amiable crossing-guard.

The total damage amounted to four-hundred-dollars and ironically, the next day at school Mr. Gordon told everyone in the faculty room that his costly impractical joke turned out to be a "smashing success."

Jim Kyle wanted to get even with Bob Gordon for drowning *his* seven tropical fish and for warping his only remaining razor blade. Bob was a big citizen-band-radio operator and would talk incessantly over his *CB* with big-rig truckers and other radio-talking enthusiasts.

Tim Carley, Jim Kyle and I pulled up in front of Bob's condominium with a walkie-talkie that was electronically set to communicate with Bob's *CB*. We sat in Tim's car and Jim disguised his voice with a handkerchief while conversing with Bob. But Mr. Gordon was slightly paranoid and thought that other *CB*ers and the *FCC* might be monitoring his transmissions so *he* practiced keeping all his conversations over the airwaves clean and free of foul language.

Jim's walkie-talkie in the car could send and receive to Bob's *CB* in his condo', but no one else could hear Jim's transmissions except Gordon on *his* receiver. All other *CBs* were out of range and could only hear Bob Gordon speaking, but talking to no one that (apparently) was communicating back.

"Well Bob," Jim said over his walkie-talkie, "how the hell are ya'!"

"Hey, who is this anyway?" Bob barked into his *CB* microphone. "Watch your language!"

"I've been listening to your bullshit over the *CB* for years," Jim indicted, "and everyone I know thinks you're totally full of crap. Why don't ya' just piss off and leave everybody the hell alone!"

"Hey, what's your handle?" Bob demanded to his entire *CB* audience. "Who are you?"

"Do I sound like a pot? I don't need a damned handle! And I don't like talkin' to stupid assholes," Jim enunciated into the speaker through his handkerchief while Tim and I were biting our tongues to avoid splitting our guts. "I thought you had balls Gordon! You're probably even friggin' scared of the damned *FCC!*"

"You can lose your license talking foul language like that!" Bob yelled to everyone out there operating a *CB* on or near his popular frequency. "Stop with the obscene language already!"

The three of us sat in Tim Carley's car and laughed our rear ends off as we watched Bob Gordon's silhouette pacing back and forth in front of his sheer drapes. After a few minutes other *CB*ers were calling Bob and asking him why he had been talking to himself. Tim backed his auto' up and after we left the condominiums' asphalt driveway the navigator put his headlights on and drove Jim and me to the nearest

tavern to enjoy some great conversation, a few really good roast-beef'
sandwiches and several cold mugs of tasty brew.

A guidance counselor with curly hair named Mark Singleton looked just like a junior *student* Ken Tomasini. So every time Mark would come into the faculty lounge and sit in a chair Bob Gordon would sit down right next to the guidance counselor and say to me, "Hey J.W., do you know a *student* named Ken Tomasini!"

I knew that Bob was actually referring to the physical similarity between Mark Singleton and Ken Tomasini, but Mark thought that Mr. Gordon was simply engaging in *his* typical zany frivolity.

"No Bob," I would say with a stoical look on my face, "tell me more about this *student* Ken Tomasini!"

Bob Gordon would always talk about imaginary places whose names *he* would creatively make up. "Well, J.W., for your information Ken Tomasini has been accepted at the Driftwood Naval Academy up in East Squirrelsneck, Pennsylvania." Then Bob Gordon turned to Singleton and said to the look-alike guidance counselor, "Say Mark, do you know a kid named Ken Tomasini!"

"No, I don't!" Mark honestly answered while holding a morning newspaper in front of his face. "I'm in charge of all the *students* whose last names range from A to G!"

"Oh, okay!" Bob solemnly answered. "I meant to tell ya' that Ken Tomasini's been accepted at the Driftwood Naval Academy up in Squirrelsneck, Pennsylvania!"

"Ya' don't say!" Mark Singleton reflexively replied.

I was holding back laughing so hard that I thought my kidneys were both going to burst. I got up from my chair and made a beeline for the Men's Lavatory just in time to make it to the urinal.

Dean Miles was an affable general science and environmental science teacher on the high school faculty. Miles possessed an abundance of trust in his *students* and was always optimistic with the glass being half-full all of the time instead of always half' empty. Mr. Miles strongly believed in a permissive classroom atmosphere where *students* could ramble around from experiment to experiment giving their input and advice to their comrades. "*Student* freedom is necessary for kids to grow up becoming mature thinkers and eventually realizing their own potential and also achieving their own destinies," Dean once preached to me in the faculty room.

"That approach works with small classes with honor *students*," I answered, "but I don't think it would be too practical trying it with unmotivated general *students*. Say Dean, what college department are you in charge of anyway?"

A narrow creek ran parallel to the high school property and the recent ecology trend in late '60s education promoted the preservation of the natural environment. Dean Miles ambitiously organized a *student* cleanup program that would purge the stream of litter and debris. Assisted by a crew of conscientious select science *students*, Miles and his loyal disciples diligently converted the half-mile-long murky creek and its bramble banks into an attractive brook-like setting.

"Do you now see what a team of motivated *students* can accomplish?" Dean Miles informed me at lunchtime in the faculty room. "All I had to do was establish the goal and then set *them* free to attain it any way they wanted!"

"I don't trust human nature quite as much as you do," I suspiciously maintained. "Over the summer the stream will again become polluted with litter despite the fact that your environmental *students* have wonderfully cleaned up the place three times each week."

"I'm even having trash barrels installed every hundred feet to cut down on the random litter!" Mr. Miles related.

Three days later before school some of the more humanitarian *students* had transported six full-barrel-waste cans from the sides of the creek and then maliciously hurled the metal cylinders loaded with debris into the formerly pristine stream.

Tim Carley and I parked our cars in the teachers' lot between the high school and the creek and then walked over to talk with Dean Miles, who suddenly appeared quite disillusioned. The metal trash receptacles were bobbing up and down in the water. I suggested to Mr. Miles, "Maybe the *students* are studying Virginia Woolf's *Stream of Consciousness* literary technique in senior English."

"Yeah Dean," Tim Carley pitched in. "The *students* might be integrating English with ecology!" he offered. "Whoever did this to *your* stream has really gotten *into the swim of things*, wouldn't you say?"

Dean Miles did not savor Tim's remarks or my comment very much. The stealthy *student* vandalism triggered off a good deal of faculty banter that Mr. Dean Miles had to suffer. Poor Mr. Miles had to endure incessant jesting from his peers about *his* major twentieth century contribution to American education, "The Barrel-Stream Concept of Learning and Talking Trash!"

Tim Carley had a reputation for being a fair-but-tough history teacher that did not tolerate *student* dereliction. One fine morning he stepped from his home to his car to find several gallons of paint splattered on the hood and trunk. By coincidence the history instructor had failed several *students* the previous marking period and Tim

428

interpreted that the ugly vandalism had been deliberately targeted at him. The school administration didn't want to get involved in the case because the destruction had not occurred on school property. So Mr. Carley had a good idea who had performed the acts but the suspected perpetrators had influential parents and relatives in the community and also connections with school board members.

Miss Presti was another victim of *student* retribution. The English instructor had made the mistake of not locking her car in the B-Wing parking lot. When she returned to the parking lot after school, she found a dozen egg yolks staining the upholstery of her new sedan. Another time Miss Presti was having nighttime conferences with concerned parents on Teacher/Parent Conference Night. When she returned to her car after thirty exhausting ten-minute conferences all four tires on her auto' were deflated. Destructive *students* ought to find more constructive ways to *air* their opinions and frustrations.

John Taylor taught math' and had the displeasure of walking out to the parking lot after school one Wednesday only to find a gaping hole in his car's rear window. Another time John's auto' wouldn't start because a number of wires in his engine had been mysteriously disconnected and severed.

Phil Tweston was a well-mannered man that demanded strict self-discipline from his *students*. The *students* mischievously called him "Stone Face" after some of Phil's literature classes had read Nathaniel Hawthorne's classic tale "The Great Stone Face."

One Saturday night Phil was sitting in his living room with his wife when the town rescue squad burst into his house with a stretcher and respiratory apparatus. The paramedics were very seriously responding to a crank phone call about an emergency heart attack victim at Phil's residence. After the incident Mr. Tweston confided that "Someone should never live in the town in which he or she teaches." Phil along with other teachers also frequently complained about anonymous phone calls at all hours in the morning. And this was in the early '70s before American society became even more dysfunctional than it is today.

All-too-serious Jack DeCicco was really revered by other faculty members mostly because he had taught most of them or at least one of their parents through rough times during the '40s and '50s. The French and Spanish instructor was a carryover from the past who' had instructed his foreign language *students* on the same staff as veteran teachers Bill Catello and Charles B. Sipley. I always enjoyed listening to Jack DeCicco's stories that focused on the past.

One time, Jack related that he was on his way home from teaching at the old high school in the 1940s when he was stopped on the highway by state policemen and told to get out of his car and help firefighters combat a raging forest fire.

"Didn't you have a choice in the matter?" I asked Jack. "I don't think that today the state police could get away with making someone involuntarily do something against his will!"

"Back in those days it was part of a citizen's civic responsibility to chip in and help whenever requested to do so by someone in authority!" Jack respectfully replied. "And that's the way it was in the old days! People respected and obeyed authority and gladly assumed responsibility when asked to help out!"

I always regarded Jack as a noble and distinguished man and it was sad that he was close to retirement in 1968. He still possessed a great fervency for his foreign language subjects and for the art of teaching. But unfortunately for Mr. DeCicco in 1968, times were changing and *students* were changing too with the *Vietnam War* protest movement gaining momentum. In addition to being gray-haired and elderly in appearance Jack was short in stature and a trifle bulging around his waist.

When Jack was assigned to the doom of cafeteria mass study hall patrol, several of the more fiendish male demons hibernating in the mass educational study hall wasteland showed little homage for either age or decency. They would deliberately call Jack "meatball" and "old geezer" whenever he walked by the *students'* tables.

When I was assigned to permanent sub' on cafeteria mass study hall duty with Jack, I would shudder upon hearing the ugly adolescent disrespect being mumbled and muttered in *his* direction. The man had dedicated his entire adult life to the education of youth and some of those audacious imbeciles in the mass cafeteria study hall (around eighty kids) were brazenly ridiculing the fine teacher that had devoted *his* entire professional energy to *student* betterment.

I had to control myself and show cool self-restraint because my first instinct was to grab one or two of the juvenile fools and bash their skulls against the cafeteria's tan-painted cinder-block walls.

Either Jack or I would eventually escort two or three of the impudent clowns down to the vice-principal's office and write out Discipline Referral Cards on the uncivilized renegades. The punks would then receive two or three days of Office Detention and of course some unfortunate teachers would have to be punished after school sitting in the atonement room for forty-five minutes with them.

Jack DeCicco despised both cafeteria duty and the mass study halls because he only wanted to teach good kids in French and Spanish classes of fifteen or so *students*. He even requested an extra teaching period to avoid the horrendous "mass duty periods" and the administration finally granted Jack's wish the last two years of his teaching career.

Jack once told me something during a teacher lunch period that has stuck in my mind. "Years ago the teachers didn't have community respect back in the '40s and the '50s," he began, "but at least the *kids* respected *us*. They saw the value of education while their parents mostly worked with their hands in local factories and resented teachers since they thought *we* never got our hands dirty," Mr. DeCicco noted. "Today teachers neither have community respect nor *student* respect either! That's the big difference between 1948 and 1968!"

Jack then told me that even in the "old days" a teacher's life was never peaches and cream. He had been assigned *to volunteer* and collect gate money for high school football games without pay as part of *his* professional *duty* as a teacher. Cash wasn't too readily available in the late '30s and early '40s. And when Jack first started teaching, the board of education paid him and his colleagues in *script*, which was a promise of salary that was honored by town pharmacists, barbers, doctors, retail stores and other businesses and services during the tough times before and during *World War II.*

Mrs. Finnian was another teacher on the high school faculty who was ready to retire. Her starting salary was $1,200.00 and was paid in *script*, a board of education "I owe you!" as she called it. To secure a teaching position in the system, Mrs. Finnian had to orally agree to purchase a new automobile from a school board member that also coincidentally owned a local retail car dealership. The acquisition had cost Mrs. Finnian an entire year's salary, but that's the way educational politics worked in small towns during and right after the 1930s' *Great Depression.*

In 1968, Mrs. Finnian had failed several *students* second marking period in Math' and in Algebra. Upon entering her B-Wing class- room between the changing of classes, the elderly woman noticed that her grade book and her attendance record book had been pilfered. And upon going to the teacher parking lot after school Mrs. Finnian's car would not start. It was soon towed to a town garage and the mechanics found a mixture of sand and sugar in the gas line.

The administration did not want to get the town police involved because of the bad publicity a police report would generate in local newspapers. So, Mrs. Finnian had to quietly absorb the expense for the damage to her car's engine herself' and re-do her roll book and her attendance record journal for the reticent-but-authoritative administration.

European *students* that immigrated to America were amazed at the amount of irreverence directed toward teachers by rebellious and obnoxious kids that had grown up in this country. Bill Catello summed it all up rather nicely. "J.W.", he said, "we can thank the community for the remnants of teacher serfdom that we now experience daily, and we can thank educational psychology for the disrespect *we* get from *students.* The rules of the game have changed since when I started out in this *profession,*" Bill articulated. "Teachers must respect and must be courteous to all kids but all kids don't have to reciprocate! It's no longer a level playing field!"

Over the past forty years, school authority has been transferred from teachers to school *specialists* like principals, vice-principals and guidance counselors. The teacher is still a *generalist* as he or she was back in the 1930s. But now teachers are the vulnerable prey of certain nasty *students,* of certain irate parents of nasty *students,* of cloud-nine college professors, of amateur school board members and of bungling/public-relations-minded school administrators. Some may consider my position on this matter as being "cynical or unprofessional," but I maintain that teachers (in the taxpayers' eyes) have never been professional people during the last century.

The daily activities associated with being permanent 'subs' were a formidable challenge to both Bill Catello and me. We both preferred the euphemism "special assignment teacher," only because it sounded more professional than the appellation "permanent substitute" did. Bill was getting weaker with each passing day so he decided to call it quits and retire before cancer made him "die on the job" as he put it. In June of 1970 the frugal-minded board of education and the administration agreed to eliminate two of the four permanent substitute positions in the school district. "One from the elementary school and one from the high school *must* go!" the principal told me.

I saw the writing on the wall that soon, all four high school permanent sub' teaching positions would be eliminated. 'It was a real innovation of this school system having four certified teachers as subs and now it's being junked for the sake of saving taxpayers' dollars!' I realized and concluded.

I also finally surmised that teachers were regarded as expendable entities regardless of one's worth to the system, one's personal dedication or one's total contributions. The administration and the board of education believed that replacing any teacher was as easy as removing a dead light bulb and then twisting a replacement in the temporarily empty electrical socket. 'No matter how a person looks at it, in the end the teacher will get *screwed* (or unscrewed),' I concluded.

"The MEATs"

The teachers on the high school faculty felt a great deal of anxiety and stress from always having to be perfect role models and knowing that at any time a parent or a *student* or a *student* conspiracy could fabricate some outlandish lie and get an instructor suspended. The men teachers had our own fraternity, which met (usually at bars) several times a year both in our town and out of our community. The MEATs was our unprofessional organization, and the acronym stood for "Men's Epicurean Association of Teachers." The MEATs was a convenient safety valve where the male faculty members could let off steam and the bizarre social organization was a terrific escape mechanism from the rigors of teaching.

The acronym MEATs had nothing to do with the local teachers' association, the *New Jersey Educational Association* or the *NEA*. The loosely configured "teachers' fraternity" was an appropriate emotional outlet because it afforded the men teachers a chance to have male bonding, to commiserate with one another and also to get away from the mental anguish associated with educational pressure. Our beer and venison bashes unveiled our hidden carnivorous natures and gave us a way of basically thinking and behaving like primitive *Neanderthal Men*. Some of the guys on the high school faculty were accomplished hunters so boar, deer and bear meat were often on the dinner menu.

In 1972-'73, I was President of the MEATs and conducted the general meetings. I was also the vice-president of the district's teachers' association at the time and the one thing I didn't like about the MEATs was the fact that the school administrators had helped found the organization before I had commenced my teaching career in September of 1965. I had always been suspicious of school administrators "in the organization" fearing that their' motive for membership was a means of intelligence gathering about male faculty members. Some town school board members didn't exactly savor *my* opposition to their directives during teacher contract negotiations and I really didn't need any principal or superintendent spouting off about how I had acted "unprofessionally" at the MEATs' unprofessional dinner meetings.

New male teachers in the district had to be accepted into *our* social rank by initiation. The men teachers all recognized that we needed such an ignoble organization to temporarily lose our identities, get plastered and behave unprofessionally just like the community attitudes had always perceived us as being and doing.

Each prospective first year teacher was given a topic for a "ten-minute formal induction speech" that had to be presented to the group of eighty-or-so educators in attendance at the first of two annual MEATs' feasts. Each new male teacher had a sponsor, who would lead the candidate from the restaurant's bar area to the secretive meeting room. The Board of Directors and Officers had carefully constructed and distributed speech assignments for the novices' final acceptance into the prestigious brotherhood. Here is a typical speech topic for a junior high school English teacher.

"Your subject is as follows: An intensive dissertation on the relevancy of subjects and predicates (as opposed to nouns and verbs) in this age of technological transformation and cultural upheaval."

A social studies teacher might be given the subject: "The need for non-tenure teachers to get directly involved in national and local social and educational controversial issues."

A science teacher might draw the speech premise: "The necessity of permissiveness in an unstructured high school laboratory classroom to teach *students* independence, responsibility, rebellion and anarchy."

A new high school literature teacher might have the speech topic: "The significance of the development of thespian and lesbian appreciation in education ranging from the gay nineties to the modern gay community."

Each new male teacher received a letter of invitation outlining his prescribed oratory. Here was the official cover letter sent to all candidates.

"The MEATs speech committee, after contemplative investigation has agreed upon the subject appearing at the bottom of this page as the most applicable to your ten-minute formal presentation to our noble organization.

"Your monologue must not exceed fifteen minutes nor should it constitute a mere nine-minute rhetorical utterance. All fledglings seeking membership into this esteemed organization should pay particular attention to your poise, dignity, confidence and mastery of content during your presentation along with other pertinent ramifications. We suggest that you practice as

Demosthenes had done by putting pebbles in your mouth to improve your elocution and your enunciation.

"You will be addressing knowledgeable professionals having eminent and distinguished reputations. Our organization is comprised mostly of dedicated educators that have proven themselves worthy of the title of public-school teacher. Be prepared to defend awkward intellectual positions that you might inadvertently propose or maintain, and above all else, don't act like an arrogant asshole. Your social acceptance into our most reputable association depends almost exclusively on your competency at defending your generalizations and hypotheses on your assigned topic. Be prepared to answer questions advanced by the MEATs' Officers and by the Board of Directors after you deliver your speech. Any hint of frivolity on your part will not be tolerated and might result in you being ostracized from the faculty."

An incoming Spanish teacher was given this speech topic. "You are to present a provocative comparison and contrast report on the structural analysis, etymology and evolution of frequently used Spanish and English expletives and exclamatory obscene nomenclature. Your fundamental focus should be on past history, current trends, phonetic patterns and tonal accents as opposed to traditional English and Spanish vernacular.

"Also, Gentlemen, come to the meeting prepared to attack and critique all new innovations in the teaching of Spanish in the curriculum that have surfaced in the last twenty years. Finally, you should include in your presentation a justification of the need to teach Spanish to *students* in a community that espouses a WASPish Anglo-Saxon tradition and heritage."

The greenhorn teachers literally spent hours of honest research and mirror-practice perfecting their dissertations. At the initiation meeting each candidate's sponsor (at twenty-minute intervals) escorted *his* novice instructor from the bar into the stone-silent general meeting/banquet room. After the department area sponsor introduced the novice to the assembled MEATs' conclave, the newcomer to the district would initiate his lecture.

Naturally, all MEATs' members would politely sit attentively and pensively listen to the novice's articulation for the first five minutes.

But then the MEATs' members would begin talking among themselves' while the new teacher was struggling through his oral presentation. Soon everyone seated in the room was ignoring the standing speaker's sincere words.

As the stunned newcomer labored on with his oration intermittent burps and belches and also occasional loud farting interrupted *his* sentences. Despite the chafing distractions most of the shocked neophytes would persevere on until the conclusion of *their* discourses. Then heckling and jeering would ensue and several of the more muscular MEATs' members would rise from their chairs, grab the new candidate and threaten to pulverize the pledge, much to the elation of the membership.

Once the MEATs even had two local uniformed policemen enter the meeting during a speech presentation with a barking German shepherd baring sharp fangs and the cops then put the candidate in handcuffs, made a pretend arrest and finally the serious-looking patrolmen conducted the shocked rejected speech giver out of the smoky meeting room.

After a speech was finally delivered the rookie was shown a large hypodermic needle, which the President had earlier told "the candidate" would be used to inject a potent stimulant into *his* buttocks. He was also shown a large club and had been told that the awesome weapon would be used against him if *he* did not fully cooperate and give a professional presentation. The pledge would then be blindfolded and instructed to bend over holding the seat of a restaurant chair. He would then be stuck in the buttocks with a safety pin, which the anxious pledge naturally suspected was the giant hypodermic needle.

Next came the highlight of the MEATs' initiation ceremony. Bob Gordon and Tim Carley poured red food coloring onto a feminine sanitary napkin and then placed the wet fabric into the blindfolded pledge's mouth. Jack DeCicco (the smallest MEAT member) next lifted and held the aforementioned giant club above *his* head. The blindfolded candidate was told to again bend over.

As the assembled male teachers all yelled "One, two,..." sweat beads would be cascading down the pledge's forehead during the extended hesitation. On the count of "three," Jack then slammed the huge shillelagh against the leather seat of another chair other than the one the anxious blindfolded candidate had been gripping.

Usually, the most laughter was derived when the newcomer was instructed to "take the blindfold off and also remove the *handkerchief* out of your mouth." The staggered first-year teacher would incredulously gape at the red-stained feminine napkin being held in the

436

palm of his hand. The newly accepted fully initiated teacher would then join his colleagues in harassing the next incoming prospect, who would soon be escorted into the room by *his* department sponsor.

As President of the MEATs, I had the distinct honor and the unenviable task of controlling the avid half-inebriated beer guzzlers while attempting to preside over the meetings. My concluding remarks to the membership had been designed to make absolutely no sense at all. It was well' received and went like this:

My fellow processionals:

I would like to extonate to you', my trulifinated colleagues the salutrified experience it has been for me to be enulbed as el presidente of this trankanimous organization. This sobravenous group behoones me to be very podulent and pedistic about our civic troduncidies.

While you dang hornts and you cubinators have been blitumated in *men*struation, I have been sedunting about the future mentronals of tomorrow, which will certainly allutinate our present circumcisions.

With such a relantrified faculty, ajending in consulfinating challenges, I am confident that the hermotudes of our civilization will certainly be donafied.

The ventrunal nature between teacher and *student* couldn't be more robundant and reperdidified. It can almost be vernificated that without being fully kakrinated into our produngeous society the citizens of tomorrow might be doomed to being ad-hutinrotted. I thank the MEATs for your gruntudinous attention and I hope I have merited your metronical conjuence.

I'll never forget the time I organized a Saturday noontime spring MEATs' fishing expedition to a salt-river-inlet that was fed by the *Atlantic Ocean*. The fellows showed up en masse, many of them not knowing a fishing rod from a lightning rod. After the six dozen of us consumed gallons of homemade Dago' wine and cases of *Budweiser* along with other potent intoxicants, the male teachers were more prepared to lampoon than to harpoon.

Several of *our* aberrant fishing lines became entangled with those of three more skilled and serious-minded fishermen that frequented the isolated beach every day. Then one of the more extroverted MEATs' members demonstrated his casting prowess and suddenly his line intersected with those of the three serious regular anglers right after they had spent fifteen minutes unscrambling their lines from the first major entanglement. After *they* finished unwinding and unraveling the incredible knots the three disgruntled fishermen evacuated the sandy beach and left the MEATs stranded there to contend with each other's obnoxious high jinks. The MEATs continued our merriment, drank some more intoxicants, and a few of us even danced around on the hot sand to accordion music provided by one of our newest inductees, which incidentally scared every fish within a five-mile radius far out to sea.

The MEATs' activities provided the men teachers the opportunity to abandon the tensions associated with the demanding role of being school teachers and gave us a license to act imperfectly and unprofessionally in secluded places far from our base of employment. It was a way for us to have some connection with the manner in which "regular civilian people" enjoyed themselves.

I recall a minor vendetta brewing between two members of the MEATs' fraternal order. Many of the fellows took sides in the friendly quarrel, which soon escalated into intense one-upmanship between the two competing camps.

Cars in the school parking lots were found stuffed with crinkled-up papers, which at first some instructors suspected had been done by naughty *students*. Bob Gordon was getting long-distance phone calls to buy swampland Florida real estate and defunct alligator farms. Tim Carley received inquiries at his home phone over falsified newspaper want ads published in *his* name advertising to sell "pedigree dogs', thoroughbred horses and collectible skunks."

The escapade expanded and more faculty members were soon affected by the imaginative pranks. I was summoned by a secretary over the intercom to the main office to answer a phone call before my lunch period. A man from Colorado wanted to sell me a bulldozer and a steam shovel and became rather angry when I informed the long-distance caller that *we* were being "innocent victims in a mass practical joke." Joe Sacci (a music teacher) woke up one morning and found over a hundred dead blackbirds and sparrows strewn all over his front lawn.

But the issuance of junk mail was perhaps the biggest craze. Men teachers were scanning every available magazine and newspaper and clipping out coupons guaranteeing free information on any product "with no obligation." Then *we* would print another staff' member's name and address in the information blanks instead of our own.

Some days I would go to my teacher mailbox and discover forty pieces of junk mail and then go home and find forty more waiting for me in my driveway mailbox. And the problem was growing to monster-proportions because all our names were being placed on other mailing lists all the time.

Teachers were getting mail addressed to crazy names like Sir Loin' Kyle and Missed Her Carley. And the junk mail was coming from unknown hamburger franchises, from taxidermy schools, from locksmith institutes of higher learning and from butchering academies. Jack DeCicco (a diminutive man) received at least five "Big and Tall Men's Catalogs" every week. Ron LeFey drove home from school one fine afternoon and found that a "test-drive camper" had been left in his driveway for a "free week's trial demonstration." And three years after the height of the junk mail deluge I was still receiving vestiges of the wild male faculty members' royal caper.

John Rizzotte was a personable driver education teacher. John and I were appointed by the MEATs' executive committee to go to a local slaughterhouse and pick up a hog for the next annual end-of-year pig roast. John and I were standing in the meat house's receiving area and talking about what kind of hog we would be getting when a trap door opened behind Rizzotte and a tremendous pork belly (slit down the middle) came rolling upside down toward us on a chain rotary.

The fresh out-of-the-freezer recently severed pig was speeding directly toward Rizzotte. John turned around, saw the suspended animal heading his way and let out a scream that scared the heck out of me. The gigantic moving pig had blood oozing out of its nostrils and had just been carved open by skilled butchers.

At the end-of-year pig roast Zeke Shullmon, a junior high science teacher entertained the assembled MEATs. Zeke showed us images from a slide projector of past MEATs' banquets with certain members vomiting in toilet bowls or having simulated sex with a rubberized woman dummy used in health classes to demonstrate artificial respiration. That particular meeting was perhaps the most raucous one ever for our illustrious organization.

The high school vice-principal tied one on good that afternoon. First, he mixed the salad by putting all of the chopped-up lettuce, radishes, pickles, green peppers and onions into a new clean waist-high trashcan. Then he liberally poured a gallon of oil and a gallon of vinegar into the mix, put the trashcan lid down onto the container, lifted the metal can upside-down over his head and blended all of the delicious salad ingredients together. Actually, that was the best salad I had ever tasted.

Next, the feeling-no-pain vice-principal put the decapitated pig's head on his own crown and stuck bones in his nose and mouth, looking very much like a cannibal out of *Robinson Crusoe*. The school administrator and I soon got into a heated argument over "teachers' rights" and "educational philosophy" and the school executive stood up and wildly took a swing at me. I ducked down and his fist penetrated a wall of the club we had rented for the *MEATs'* party. The fellows then moved a piano over from an adjacent wall to cover up the hole that had recently been formed.

The following Monday morning the high school principal called me into his office. I thought I was going to be interrogated about the hole in the clubhouse wall incident. Instead, the principal was upset that I was violating the school's teacher dress code by wearing a '70s leisure suit with an open collar and no tie.

"I want to see you wearing a tie to school," the very straight-laced principal (who was not at the most recent *MEATs'* feast) insisted.

"Leisure suits are now in style," I argued, "and ties aren't worn with them. Check any men's fashion catalog to see what I mean."

"I still want *you* to wear a tie at all times," the principal rankled. "I have nothing against leisure suits, but if you want to wear one then you must wear a tie too!"

"Ties strangulate blood circulation to the brain," I replied. "Do you want me to suffer a massive stroke?"

"Wear ties!" he maintained. "If you don't, you'll be regarded and treated as being *insubordinate*!"

"Ties *are* symbols of *subordination*!" I fired back. "And besides, the women teachers don't have to wear ties when *they* wear suits! It's gender discrimination against male teachers!" I shouted. "Yes, that's what you're advocating with this stupid tie thing! You're playing a silly power game, that's all you're doing!"

"Wear ties!" the principal yelled as his face turned red. "*Wear ties* I said!" he repeated in a maniacal tone of voice.

"I can only wear one tie at a time," I laughed in response to *his* crazy and animated anger.

"Why are you so stubborn!" he challenged. "Why can't you' just wear a tie as a favor to me' instead of being so obstinate!"

"Do you see this gold necklace?" I exclaimed to the uptight principal while pointing to an expensive piece of jewelry hanging down from my neck. "This golden necklace cost as much as fifty ties, so the next time *you* see me wearing a leisure suit with this golden necklace around my throat just pretend you're looking at me wearing fifty ties!"

"Very well then, you can leave now!" the principal ordered. "I only wish that you were more cooperative!"

"You mean more subordinate!" I answered as I rose from my chair and then left *his* comfortable beautifully decorated office.

The *MEATs* to the male teachers was like a twice a year *New Year's Eve* party where everyone (except the high school principal) could deviate from stiff rigid "professional behavior," discard our inflexible public' image and then explore the suppressed *Mr. Hydes* that dwelled deep inside of us. Over the years our membership has gotten older and has mellowed. The members from the early 1970s are mostly now married, have wives and families or are retired or dead. The '70s *MEATs*' camaraderie has lost much of its former momentum, zaniness and spunk, and by 2003 it is but a faint memory of a happy bygone era.

Short-in-stature rather amiable John Magliari had been inducted as a new member into the *MEATs*. But I remember John (who was actually shorter than Jack DeCicco) from the first day of school in September of '69. I was in the main office seeing if any teacher had been absent when Magliari entered to put a check next to his name on the teacher attendance sheet.

"Are you an administrator?" John asked seeing that I was hanging around in the main office.

Before I had a chance to answer or even introduce myself as a permanent sub', the principal came out of his office and said, "Mr. Magliari, I'd like to talk with you a minute!"

That early September day I had little to do and was becoming bored. No teachers were absent so Bill Catello and I walked around the building and gave teachers on cafeteria or on study hall duty fifteen-minute breaks to freshen up or to use the facilities. When I stepped into an A-Wing classroom, I was about to formally introduce myself to John Magliari but he beat me to the punch.

"Oh, you administration!" he exclaimed in his broken Argentine Spanish accent. "Just sit in back of room and observe my lesson if you'd like!"

I stepped to the back of the room, watched John's entire lesson and then told him *he* had done a "satisfactory and almost excellent job." He thanked me for my compliment and still thinking that I was an administrator, John invited me (the permanent sub') to come in anytime I needed to write up an official lesson observation report.

A month later, Bob Gordon told John Magliari that he had heard that the principal was going to observe the jittery teacher the next period, which was only five minutes away. "You'd better use the bathroom now. I know I would if I were you!" Bob told the recently hired English-As-A-Second-Language teacher.

"That's a very good idea!" the new *ESL* teacher acknowledged.

After John Magliari entered the Men's Room (which was really part of the faculty lounge), Bob Gordon, Tim Carley and I slid the *Coke* machine from a side area to the lavatory door, which needed to open outwards for someone to exit.

After John had finished doing his bathroom business, he attempted to open the bathroom door but couldn't because of the huge heavy obstacle in the way. He began pounding on the door and screaming and begging, "I need to keep my job! Let me out of here! I have to be observed by the principal!" John was screaming.

I had the next period off so I walked down to the A-Wing to get John's next class settled. Two minutes later Bob and Tim moved the heavy *Coke* machine back to where it belonged. Magliari rushed out of the Men's Room and sprinted like a wild man down the C-Wing to the A-Wing. He entered the classroom and was very relieved to see no principal seated in the rear. Then he thanked me for "watching my class!" John did not realize that I had been one of the conspirators and perpetrators who had blocked the Men's Room door with the bulky soda machine.

The following fall, I organized a little MEATs' hunting trip to a small game preserve not far from Gettysburg, Pennsylvania. Bob Gordon was a skilled taxidermist' who promised to stuff any animal that one of us might bag. John Magliari came along on the hunting expedition, and my brother-in-law was a guest member of the hunting excursion.

I had shot a white ram on the expedition, which Bob Gordon later mounted onto a large plaque that now hangs from a wall in my den. My brother-in-law was on the other side of a hill. He fired several shots from his rifle, and before John Magliari or I knew what was happening, a wild boar with sharp tusks came snorting over the crest heading right towards Magliari and me.

John and I dropped our rifles, dashed to the nearest tree and then started scaling the oak as fast as we could. The ferocious wounded beast slammed its head into the base of the oak, nearly knocking John and me off our limbs. When the MEATs' hunting trip had ended, I had shot the ram, my brother-in-law had killed the boar, Bob Gordon had gotten a deer head trophy and John Magliari had killed three blackbirds while frantically shooting at a wild turkey.

I had always liked John Magliari. He often came over to my home along with math' teachers Jim Smythe and John Senna and we played cards in my carpeted basement and enjoyed more than a few beers together. John would even accompany me down to Ocean City, Maryland on April weekends and help me set up the arcade prizes at 410 South Boardwalk.

Being an *ESL* teacher, John Magliari always had small classes with around *ten* or less *students* in each one. Then the administration assigned the shy young man cafeteria duty and a difficult study hall loaded with eighth grade hellions that John had trouble disciplining. "I can't control those crazy kids!" John openly cried one evening at my house. "In Argentina the *students* always respected the *teachers*. Here the kids try crucifying me every day!"

John went to the administration and asked for small classes to teach rather than be abused in the cafeteria or having rolled-up paper balls hitting him in the back of the head when he was facing the opposite direction in the hard-to-handle eighth grade *study hall*. John Magliari was never re-assigned and subsequently went into a deep state of depression. "Learn how to keep the lid on!" he was told. "You're a teacher and you have to be able to control *students* in all situations! You have to earn their respect!" was *his* advice received from the administration.

John's unfortunate fate was chronicled in the local newspaper with a headline: "Local Teacher Shot to Death". The article described John and it included his exemplary teaching record. Administrators that had been interviewed stated that his work was most satisfactory. The newspaper never reported the truth that John Magliari had shot and killed himself because he was despondent about not knowing how to cope with or even how to control the malicious, discipline-problemed, non-*ESL students* he had encountered both in the cafeteria and in the very challenging eighth grade study hall.

* * * * * * * * * * * *

The breaking-up of the MEATs came soon after John Maglieri's suicide. Several months' later four male teachers and I decided to escape dismal reality and journey thirty miles east to the Aquarius Strip Tease Club in Camden, New Jersey. We were enjoying ourselves immensely until the third stripper paraded from behind a red curtain onto the dark catwalk.

"My God!" I whispered. "That's Maria C. I had taught her in eighth grade seven years ago!"

"And her younger sister is now in eighth grade!" the MEATs member sitting next to me verified. "This is dangerous shit! Really serious shit!"

All six of us slinked-down inside our tawdry cloth seats and hid our faces with either our baseball caps or our hands. After that close encounter of the first kind, all of us present at the Aquarius Club determined that it was indeed time for us to act professional both inside and outside our South Jersey community.

"The End of a Teaching Career"

Up until 1995 I had worked for administrators that were all older than I was. After 1995 my employment was under the dominion of less experienced superiors' that were somewhat intimidated by the veteran teachers on the middle school staff. I got the impression that the new generation of school executives wanted a faculty that was loyal to them and the school administrators were a trifle defensive when dealing with instructors that were in the school system thirty years before the new power elite had made their appearances.

I knew that the end of my teaching career was near when teaching methods gradually changed to sociological activity-oriented classrooms as opposed to the academic structured teacher-guided teacher-centered approach. Hostile parent conferences increased in frequency from around four a year to eight. I had taught over four thousand *students* in thirty-four years and I began thinking that I should go out while I was still on top of my game and remarkably still had most of my marbles.

I was not getting along too well with my supervisor and the vice-principal, who both were my junior by around two decades. The supervisor would always be putting *Mickey Mouse* memos' in my mailbox and I would correct all of the grammar and spelling errors (and there were many) and then return them. The vice-principal was catering to hostile parents and acting like their surrogate representative against teachers rather than deflecting the overprotective meddlers into oblivion where *they* rightfully belonged. I instinctively knew that the new school leadership wanted the old faculty to go and have teachers that *they* had hired and who' were beholding to *them*.

And most of my old buddies had retired from the *profession* including Bob Gordon, Tim Carley, Ron LeFey, Phil Tweston, Jim Kyle, Larry DeLancy and Rob Renbeck. Dean Miles had moved to another district in Pennsylvania, Tim Amoro had become a principal in another New Jersey' town, Ron Carputis was now a curriculum coordinator in my district, Joe Sacci was now a school supervisor and John Rizzo had gone into the oil business. Charlie Southard, John Magliari, Mrs. Finnian, Jack DeCicco and Bill Catello had all died.

Mack Fascito had wanted me to retire with him in June of '99 but I was hesitant. As the school year progressed, I soon became more and more interested in the prospect of living to see retirement.

"Mack, I want to stay around for one more year and retire in 2000," I said. "It's a nice round figure!"

"What difference does it make?" Mack maintained. "All the old guys are gone. The administration and your supervisor are gonna' make life miserable for you and besides, the board of education is offering a buyout for our sick days. How many have you accumulated?"

"Over two hundred and fifty!" I proudly answered.

"That means you're eligible for the maximum buyout!" Mack persuasively indicated. "I think the time has come!"

"I think you're right!" I agreed. "The principal told me that the accumulated sick day' buyout would be only a one-year-deal. Take it or leave it! The window closes on September 1st!"

I still kept my summer employment as a field manager at Atlantic Blueberry Company, the world's largest cultivated blueberry farm. I figured that since my wife was still teaching that I would try substituting two or three days a week starting in September of '99 to keep my mind and spirit active.

Substitute teaching was not exactly a royal cup of tea. And local school districts were only paying substitutes seventy dollars a day. 'Gee, if I work for a hundred and eighty days as a sub',' I thought, 'I can make a whopping twelve-thousand-six-hundred-dollars! The average cleaning lady makes more than seventy-dollars-a-day cash without deductions!' I mused. 'If it weren't for my pension and my sick day' buyout I would be eligible for food stamps!'

Substitute teachers really have their hands full when taking on an assignment. *Students'* eyes light up when they suddenly realize that the regular teacher is absent. The *children* have their own glossary of words to describe that festive realization: "Party!" "Kill!" and "Fun Time!" are some of the vernacular that *students* use while their eyes widen as if they are a pride of lions spotting a fat, wounded water buffalo the minute they see a substitute.

Substitutes encounter interesting experiences such as chalk in eraser grooves, tacks or chewing gum wads on the teacher's desk chair and *students* changing their seats to see if the sub' is smart enough to read a seating chart to relocate the *children* where they belong. *Students* will volunteer misinformation about where the regular teacher had left off in the textbook and will try to leave the room at every possible opportunity to make a phone call, visit the lavatory or take a stroll to the nurse's office. A hard day of substituting could wind-up being about as rewarding as a day touring the New York' sewer system.

"I would have to substitute one whole week to stay in a decent New York hotel for one night with meals included!" I told my wife.

"Grin and bear it!" she answered. "A day of substituting at least pays the television cable bill!"

446

"Yes, but that's not including any premium channels or a digital box!" I elaborated.

One of my first substituting assignments was at a neighboring district's elementary school. The principal told me that I was to be in charge of only one male *student* that had In-School Suspension.

"How old is the boy?" I inquired.

"Five years old! A kindergarten kid!" the administrator answered.

"What did this *child* do to warrant In-School Suspension?" I inquisitively asked.

"He became angry and kicked a male teacher in the testicles during cafeteria period," the principal replied. "I know you have plenty of experience and can easily handle the *child*!"

The kid cried and protested for an hour and a half in the detention office so I took him to the cafeteria and bought him plenty of snacks. After that "reward" I bent the rules, became his friend and we played *Bingo*, checkers and card games' until the 3: 15 dismissal bell finally rang.

Any time a substitute comes into contact with a hundred and thirty *students* in an eight-period day, that instructor is bound to have conflict with at least one. I was subbing at the local high school in March of 2000. After taking attendance, I was ten minutes into the lesson when a *student* stood up and started walking out the room.   "Where are you going?" I asked him.

"Oh, I'm not a *student* in this class!" he answered. "This is my lunch period so I thought I'd just sit in and see how *you* were doing!"

"Enjoy your lunch!" I responded with a smile. I registered in my mind what the anonymous sixteen-year-old junior droll *child* looked like. Every time that same *student* was in a class where I was subbing, I would ask him, "Shouldn't you be in lunch now? The first time I had you in a Spanish II' class you were *out to lunch*!" The boy would always blush at my allusion and then slouch down in his desk in sheer admiration every time I mentioned those wonderful words as a reminder to him that I had not yet passed senility.

Another time at the high school, I had entered a remedial mathematics classroom and all the *students* were milling around. "Please sit down so that I can take attendance and get the math' lesson started!" I implored the twenty-six seemingly uncooperative and disenchanted *students*.

Everyone abided by my' request with the exception of one haughty senior girl. "Mrs. Warner lets us walk around and talk to each other all the time!" she arrogantly insisted. "Why do I have to listen to you?"

"Because Mrs. Warner isn't here today and I am!" I answered. "Now just sit down so that things can start in an orderly organized manner!"

"You're mean! Do ya' know that?" the girl accused while still not sitting down.

"Look!" I exclaimed. "I think you're being very uncooperative under the circumstances! I don't think that asking you to sit down is too much of a demand!" I added. "Why do you suppose these desks are in the classroom? Waiting for termites to devour them?"

"I've had about enough of your rude shit!" the girl yelled. "You're an asshole!" the distraught girl screamed as she bolted out of the classroom honoring *flight* in the notorious "fight or flight" mindset.

No *student* in the class would tell me who the nasty girl was so I quickly took roll and figured it out for myself. I buzzed the office and reported the girl as being *AWOL*.

"Oh, she's sitting in the office waiting to see the principal or vice-principal right now!" the main office secretary replied over the intercom. "I believe she's complaining about *you*! Send down a Discipline Referral Card on the *student* after *you* have time to write one up!"

I assigned the day's math' lesson and then I wrote up the aforementioned discipline card. A girl' friend of the defiant young miss (now seated in the office) raised her hand and requested to go to the lavatory.

"Okay, I'll write you out a pass as soon as I finish with this discipline card," I promised.

"I have to go right now because I'm having my period and I gotta' get a rag' from the nurse!" the girl snottily replied.

"Look, I promise you you'll be out of here in just another minute!" I answered as I jotted down the final information describing the first classroom' incident with the other girl. "Please try to have a little patience and extend to me some basic respect and courtesy!"

"Fuck you!" the girl squealed as she insolently walked out of the classroom without a hall pass. "Asshole!" she yelled out into the otherwise empty corridor.

I had remembered the second girl's name because I had taught her when she used to be a respectful eighth grader three years before. I wrote down the second incident on the back of the Discipline Card and reported the second girl as also being *AWOL* from the math' class.

The office secretary called the classroom over the intercom. "Mr. Wiessner, the new school policy is that two *students* can't be listed on the same Discipline Referral Card," the voice specified. "You'll have to present two separate cards to the office for each of the incidents with the two different girls!"

I spent the balance of the period re-doing the first card and then writing up the second regrettable repulsive event. The class had become silent and cooperative once the remaining *students* realized that the substitute was not afraid to assert some authority and send *students* down to the vice-principal's office.

After the class was dismissed at the ringing of the bell, I had a teacher lunch period so I had time to then drop off the two discipline cards in the main office. As I was entering the main office, I observed two policemen dragging a girl I had never seen before out of the vice-principal's office.

When I got to the teacher's lounge to eat my brown-bagged lunch and to enjoy a *Coke* I asked the other faculty members at the table if anyone knew what had happened with the girl being taken into custody by the police.

"Oh," a social studies teacher said, "she had called Mr. Jackson an *asshole* because she didn't like the way he had graded her essay question on a test!"

"So regular teachers receive that kind of back-talk just like substitutes do!" I laughed.

"Yes, Jackson wrote her up," the female social studies teacher continued, "and the vice-principal told the *student* to go to In-School Suspension because she had accumulated a whole series of violations, but the girl refused to budge from the chair in *his* office!"

"And then the vice-principal called the police?" I asked.

"Yes, I was in the main office at the time," another teacher seated at the lunch table politely interrupted. "The assistant-principal told the girl that if she didn't get up and go to In-School Suspension that she would be trespassing in his office! The girl was stubborn and refused to get up so the cops hustled her out of the building while she was screaming like a maniac!"

"You don't know how lucky you are being retired!" the first teacher added. "I wish I were *you* right now!" she honestly congratulated my thirty-four-year career.

I glanced around the crowded high school faculty room and noticed only one familiar face that I had known from the past. I felt like *Rip Van Winkle* must have when he had returned to his native village after sleeping for twenty years in the *Catskill Mountains*. All of *his* old chums and cronies were gone from the village.

I walked to the men's room and noticed that one thing hadn't changed in the last thirty years. The same *Coke* machine that Bob

Gordon, Tim Carley and I had moved to trap John Magliari in the teachers' lounge's men's room was still situated in the exact same spot.

On my way to instruct the next class, I noticed a destructive-minded *student* walking down the crowded C-Wing corridor breaking four balloons in a row with his long fingernails. The decorations along with crepe paper were festooning the hallways because the high school football team was to play a major opponent later that week in an important league game.

'Let another teacher notice and report the balloon breakings!' I thought. 'I've already written out two too many discipline cards today! Give me a break!' I pleaded as my eyes rolled up to briefly view the C-corridor's ceiling panels.

Twenty feet ahead down the corridor Mr. Joe Wilkins intercepted the *student* breaking the balloons and started escorting the young violator to the main office for a ride on the familiar discipline carousel.

Eighth period study hall was an absolute nightmare that afternoon. I was alone and in charge of fifty restive but lethargic *students* that just wanted to fool around and talk. I separated them into sets of two at various cafeteria tables despite their protesting. Two girls and a boy refused to break up and move to another table. Finally, they did and the young ladies then tried grossing me out.

"Hey man, did you ever have sex on a washing machine when it was runnin'?" the first girl asked me.

"That's too personal of a question," I answered. "Now please move to another table or I'll have to write you up."

"Once I had sex with my boyfriend in the back of a church while a service was going on!" the second young lady disrespectfully informed me.

"Look young lady, there are at least three ambitious *students* in this mass study hall that want to do some work!" I reprimanded. "Now please show more consideration for them. Not everyone wants to hear about your lackluster personal life. There's more to living than a mere biological existence!"

One of the girls and the boy then got-up and moved to another table. On my next rotation of the cafeteria mass study hall, I stopped at the table to where the two *students* had switched. "Say Mr. Wiessner, did you know that Peggy and I like to have sex together with Greg here!" Jenn guiltlessly and shamelessly stated. "We like threesomes!"

"Maybe by the time all three of you mature into normal adults," I calmly said, "you'll finally realize that you all also have hearts', minds and souls besides just simply having physical bodies!"

My comment appeared to have an impact because all three *students* actually opened books and began reading. I glanced out the cafeteria's back windows and saw the board of education president, the principal and the superintendent sitting at a picnic table eating barbecued meat. 'I wonder if any of them have any clue as to what has been going on for nearly forty-five minutes in this cafeteria mass study hall only fifty feet away?' I wondered.

I was happy that no further incidents happened in that eighth period cafeteria mass study hall. I thought about how cafeteria study hall *students* back in 1975 had mocked Jack DeCicco by calling him "Meatball!" and I quickly realized that things had not really changed that much in the past quarter-century. The only thing was that I was the new elderly Jack DeCicco on patrol. When I checked out at the office the principal asked me, "Did you have a good day Mr. Wiessner?"

"The best!" I falsely replied. "It was without a doubt the absolute best!"

"Glad to hear everything went smoothly for you!" he cutely answered.

As I left the building and proceeded to my car in the A-Wing parking lot, a red-haired *student* exited the high school and yelled, "Fuck this shit hole!" at the top of his lungs.

'I can relate to that!' I thought as I entered my automobile. 'This has been my worst day of subbing so far. Now where's the nearest bar? I think I need a double *Southern Comfort* on the rocks right away! I'll dedicate my first double shot to the memory of Jack DeCicco!'

In June of 2000, I received a phone call from the new middle school principal (my old middle school principal was now the new high school chief executive and the old high school vice-principal was now the new middle school head honcho).

"Say *John*," he enthusiastically began, "how would you like your old English teaching job back from September to *Thanksgiving*? Mrs. Grasi will be out on maternity' leave and I figured I would give you the nod."

"Okay," I replied. "I think I could handle that assignment. It sure beats regular subbing in certain subject' areas I'm not that familiar with!"

When I had left my position as the major eighth grade English teacher in June of '99, I had a hundred and ten *students* scattered over six class periods. Now my attendance roster read a hundred and thirty-five *students* condensed into the same six classes. Special needs *students* requiring individualized attention had been *mainstreamed* into the regular academic English classes.

Five of the classes had twenty-seven *students* each. The *children* generally were quite immature and many of them were outright obnoxious. 'This is going to be a very challenging assignment!' I thought on the first day of school. 'It's a good thing this stint will be over in less than ninety days! I hope my heart holds out!'

I didn't win too much favor with the new school administrators when this substitute replacement' English teacher criticized and slammed the basic unfairness of the *GEPA* writing test to eighth graders' parents on Open House Night.

And then the new middle school vice-principal was my' old supervisor whose frequent handwritten memos' used to receive my critical grammar and spelling corrections. Trouble was about to explode because the new Educational Aristocracy at the middle school embraced everything that *this manuscript* has been attacking from page one.

The vice-principal was acting like a surrogate representative of aggressive overprotective concerned parents that thought I was being too stringent and severe with their *children*. Just about every day a memo' would be in my mailbox that Mr. or Mrs. so-and-so was complaining about something "insensitive and sarcastic" I had said to their son or daughter in class or about me being too harsh in grading his or her *child's* compositions.

In mid-November the vice-principal came up to the second floor to briefly discuss a parental concern with me' between seventh and eighth' periods. I had just had a challenging session with the seventh period general English *students*, a class of twenty-seven *students* comparable in many ways to the old 8-6ers.

A seventh period *student* seated in the back of the first row next to the teacher's desk hadn't done homework or class work for the entire marking period. I was standing in front of the room at the lectern when the child stretched out his arms and loudly yawned as I was addressing the abominable seventh period' class. The fatigued *student* had inadvertently knocked the set of metal bookends off the teacher's desk onto the floor.

"Would you please pick up the metal bookends from the floor and place them back on the teacher's desk?" I politely asked.

"No!" the *student* adamantly replied and then put his head down on the desk feigning sleeping.

"Look, if *I* had accidentally knocked the bookends on the floor and then asked *you* to pick them up," I said, "I could then understand your refusal. But *you* have knocked them on the floor. Why don't *you* simply pick them up?"

452

"Stop buggin' me man!" the *student* nastily replied. "Get off my damned case!"

When the vice-principal accosted me out in the hallway, I told the school administrator that I would be writing out a discipline card on the defiant *student* that had refused to put the metal bookends back on the teacher' desk.

"Okay Mr. Wiessner, but I'm really here to tell you that Mrs. Larson had called and thinks you shouldn't have embarrassed her son by reprimanding him so harshly in front of his peers!" the paranoid school' administrator related.

"Well, I handled the situation just the way I always have in the past," I said. "I've never backed down to any *student* and I don't think I've going to start at this stage of the game!"

"Try being a little more sensitive!" the vice-principal suggested. "The times are changing!"

"Look!" I replied. "The classes *are changing* from seventh to eighth period, and if you haven't noticed, I've got to get back to my primary responsibilities."

When I re-entered the upstairs classroom, I immediately noticed that the roll and grade book had been stolen from the lectern in the front of the room. While the vice-principal had been distracting me about a parental grievance some *student* in the seventh period class had pilfered the teacher' records and I had a good hunch that it was the same *student* that refused to pick up the metal bookends off of the floor. I immediately buzzed the office and requested that the vice-principal come back up to the classroom.

I explained what had happened and the vice-principal said that the major suspects would be interviewed the next day.

"Interviewed?" I asked. "Valuable teacher records, school property has been taken and *you* want to *interview* the suspects tomorrow? Get the police over here right now and have them *interrogate* the *students* and let's crack this mystery wide open today!"

'I'll *interview* the *students* first thing tomorrow morning," the politically correct vice-principal related. "I can't keep them after school and have them' miss their buses unless they've been given a full day's notice! It's school policy in the *Student* Handbook!"

On Thursday morning, I was on early morning bus duty when the on-a-mission vice-principal approached me. "*Mr. Wiessner*, it is the administration's position that if the grade book can't be found that you'll have to prepare a new book with the grades in it for when Mrs. Grasi returns after *Thanksgiving!*"

"Well, I'm just a substitute teacher' fill-in and I'm not going to do it!" I answered. "The first marking period' grades had already been submitted to the guidance office two days before the grade and roll' book had been stolen from the lectern!"

"I think you're being quite difficult!" the vice-principal admonished. "Didn't *you* take the time to make a copy of all the grades in the grade book?" the school executive indicted.

"Look," I angrily replied, "in my thirty-four years of teaching I have never had a grade book stolen! And I only remember it happening once to Mrs. Finnian back in the early 1970s at the high school when I was teaching there!" I emphasized. "A *student* has committed a punishable *crime* by stealing school records and *you* want to reward that *student* by having *me* rewrite the grade book!"

The vice-principal realized that I couldn't be coerced into re-doing the roll and grade' book, which was an impossible task because all of the first marking period individual test, homework and writing grades for the hundred and thirty-five *students* were missing. Later that day I telephoned Mrs. Grasi about the theft and she agreed to make up a fresh roll and grade book starting with the second marking period.

On Friday morning, I was in the office during my *PPSA* picking up my paycheck. I had just signed out to leave the building to drive to the bank and deposit my hard-earned wages into my checking account.

"Mr. Wiessner," the vice-principal said, "I'd like to see you in my office!"

"Well, I'm on my way to the bank right now so why not make it later!" I answered while thinking that I never wanted to see or hear the vice-principal again ever in this life or in the next one.

Two periods later was my teacher lunch break. The vice-principal entered the teacher's room and said, "Mr. Wiessner, I want to see you in my office right now!"

"Does it involve the roll and grade book?" I asked.

"Yes!" the vice-principal testily replied.

"Has it been returned?" I queried.

"No!" was the terse response.

"Do you want to see me about a parent calling?" I questioned.

"Yes, now come to my office immediately!" the school official inflexibly demanded.

"Well then," I said, "the school has a definite procedure that the parent must follow. Have the parent call the Guidance Office and schedule a conference! Let the parent be inconvenienced by having to come in and complain about something instead of using the telephone and having *you* do his or her dirty work!" I suggested. "A parent has

454

never to my knowledge called the school to arrange a conference to praise me! No, that has never happened in thirty-four years! This parent wants to have a hostile conference! And in two days I'm outa' here!"

The vice-principal felt that I was being *insubordinate* and also a bad example in front of other younger teachers having lunch in the faculty room. One could easily hear a pin drop at the end of our heated disagreement. The school executive left the faculty room virtually in tears.

Five minutes later, I marched upstairs to set up the *VCR* for a film I would be showing the following period. The principal entered the classroom and slammed the door behind him in anger.

"*Mr. Wiessner*, this is one of the hardest things I've ever had to do," he anxiously but firmly stated, "but I'm going to have to ask you to leave the building because you have been *insubordinate* to the vice-principal."

"But I only have two more days until *Thanksgiving* break!" I replied. "Why don't you just let me finish my assignment *we* had agreed upon?"

"Sorry, but I can't tolerate teachers being *insubordinate* to administrators!" the principal declared. "You must leave the building immediately!"

"Well, I just want you to know that I told the vice-principal off because I don't think that school administrators should be the surrogates of overprotective parents!" I succinctly stated.

I knew that I had not signed a contract but had only made a verbal agreement with the principal to teach until the *Thanksgiving* holidays. I left the school building where I had taught for twenty-seven of my thirty-four years in a stupor. I had been exiled for being *insubordinate* to administrative discretion while the vice-principal was acting as an undesired parent' surrogate. 'Evicted from the school system I had worked with all my heart to *professionally* represent for thirty-four years!' I pondered.

I was happy that I had not surrendered my convictions and my principles right up to the end. When I explained to my wife what had happened, she said that she was not-at-all surprised at the outcome and sounded pleasantly optimistic about the future. "The administration wanted you out because they believed you were influencing the younger teachers by setting a bad example!" my wife intelligently concluded. "You were a definite threat to their authority! You've always been sort of a rebel!"

"Joanne," I said, "I'm just sick and tired of hearing bells ring all day long. The school bells ring seventeen times a day. Times that by a hundred and eighty days a year and that comes to over three thousand times a year," I indicated. "Multiple three thousand times a year by thirty-four years and I've listened to bells blast over a hundred and five thousand times in my career. No wonder why *you* say I'm deaf!"

"And that's not counting the fifty thousand times you also heard bells ring between classes as a *student* before you ever became a teacher!" my wife impressively elaborated. "And don't forget the over seven hundred fire alarms you've listened to!" my wife reminded. "Look at the positive side," my spouse suggested. "You've taught over four thousand *students* in your educational career!"

The principal and the vice-principal taught the six eighth grade classes the last two days before *Thanksgiving* break. My mother's cleaning woman's daughter was in one of the Accelerated English classes and related that the administrators had told the *students* that Mr. Wiessner had taken sick and could not teach them the last two days before the four-day-holiday' vacation.

'They lied to the kids!' I considered. 'Education is not really about academics, or teaching, or learning or knowing right from wrong. It is just a big American power game where administrative might makes administrative right!' I sadly concluded.

"Maybe *you* can begin that writing career you've always dreamed of doing!" my wife recommended and consoled.

"You're right Joanne, my pension is safe and secure and now that I'm no longer a teacher," I added, "I can actually be an ordinary citizen with genuine freedom of expression and other remarkable *Constitutional* rights! I might even produce several PG-13 type books with graphic content!"

I knew that I had written sixteen manuscripts from 1974-1999 while I had been an instructor and this book *So Ya' Wanna' Be A Teacher* has become the sixteenth work.

"You're absolutely right!" I reiterated and agreed with my wife. "Teaching is over in my life and it's time for a new career! There *is* life after teaching!" I laughed. "Thanks to the principal and the vice-principal now I finally have a good ending for book number sixteen! No more teacher serfdom!"

"At last, you've come to your senses!" Joanne answered with a smile. "Writing should be much more relaxing than teaching was. It's time for someone else to step up and fill your big shoes!"

"Darwin, Einstein and John Dewey"

On the average, democracies usually last for up to two hundred and fifty years. That historical pattern gives the United States of America around three more decades until we're put on artificial life support, *our* systemic malady principally caused by moral decay, by legal and political corruption and by widespread economic inefficiency. Yes, ever since WWI we've created a grotesque-looking Ponzi pyramid,

In another thirty years, government spending will drastically exceed GNP (Gross National Production), seventy percent of the burgeoning American population will not be paying federal income taxes, and also, more money will be going out of Social Security and out of Medicare than entering into those specific government program safety nets. At present, our U.S. total federal, state and local government expenditure is 39% of GNP, when 20% is the most desirable percentage ratio in order to fully assure national economic stability.

What obscure factors besides government waste and federal and state over-regulation will ultimately accelerate the demise of the USA? It is this writer's contention that the decline of America will be attributable to an extension of the philosophies and teachings of three currently venerated individuals: Charles Darwin, Albert Einstein and John Dewey.

Back in the early 1900s, Charles Darwin's Theory of Evolution was not exclusively confined to the scientific realm. Instead, Evolution's basic premise of continuous change (along with an expanding spiral progressively developing) bled over into such social disciplines as political science, psychology, the law and most dramatically, American education. Nothing in today's reality (not even God) is "absolute." Everything constantly changes and mutates into something else! Is not "change" the watchword of our time in American history?

Karl Marx and Vladimir Lenin were indeed highly influenced with the notion of Darwin's Evolution. Those two political intellectuals reasoned that in ancient times mankind had Aristocracies (warlords, city-state rulers and local despots). Eventually the existence of Aristocracy melded into Monarchy with one king controlling all activity within a certain region or country. And then in 1776, rebellion against King George III's tyranny resulted in the Revolutionary War, and with great inspiration, a fantastic rebirth combining Greek Athenian Democracy and the concept of the Roman Republic's law and order gradually integrated into what is now the United States of America.

Marx and Lenin (being affected by Darwinian Theory), believed that Democracy would surely evolve into Socialism and Lenin's successor, Joseph Stalin, theorized that Bolshevik Socialism should predictably evolve into another predestined disaster, Soviet Russian Communism. Just think of the millions of innocent victims that had (and have) died under the aegis of inflexible iron-fisted Communist doctrine!

Isn't it a marvelous miracle that the USA (along with its free enterprise and free market capitalist system) has over the course of the last century proven Marx, Lenin and Stalin to be total political frauds? And yet, with the obvious fact that Soviet Socialism and militant Communism have both miserably failed as evidenced with the crumbling of the Berlin Wall, ironically, the USA today is rapidly moving in the direction of Socialism to attempt solving its proliferating domestic woes.

But don't despair! There is still time for economic salvation once Americans come to their senses. If everyone in the U.S. took responsibility for their own lives and pulled their own weight in this land of abundant opportunity and free public-school education, then government could wisely shrink-down to twenty percent of GNP from its current 39% level and our REPUBLIC (respect for law and order) could be effectively preserved and future financial disaster could be strategically averted. But first things first: For *our* time-honored traditions (Christmas, Thanksgiving, Easter, Fourth of July, etc.) and for our all-important historical heritage to adequately survive, political *evolution*, societal flux and class warfare must be removed from American culture.

Yes, Americans are truly living in the closest thing to a Utopia that can be manifested by man on this good Earth. When Judas Iscariot challenged Jesus, "Why do you spend *our* money on expensive oils when the money could be spent on the poor?" Jesus simply and succinctly answered, "Judas, there will be poor always!"

But unlike almost any other culture on this planet, the United States affords all its citizens the opportunity to take risks, to succeed (or to fail), and to engage in freedom of speech, freedom of the press, freedom of religion and finally, "individual opportunity" along with freedom of education to advance and to become upwardly mobile, all of these wonderful "liberties" based on individual initiative, individual determination, individual motivation and individual perseverance.

Let's examine history. The only real success at democracy (following a revolution) had occurred after July Fourth, 1776 in Philadelphia's Independence Hall, and then over a decade of extremely

458

difficult growing pains, regional rebellions and full-blown arguments over the tenets of the Articles of Confederation had ensued, but finally, the U.S. Constitution had been drafted and signed in 1787, with the "democratic" Bill of Rights being completely ratified in 1795, nearly twenty years after the famous Declaration of Independence had been authored and proclaimed. All of *that'* exhaustive and dangerous establishment of American democracy (the Republic) required nearly two decades of great sacrifice to complete.

Now look at what had happened in France after the French Revolution: Anarchy, a Reign of Terror and the tyranny of Napoleon came to be. What about the Bolshevik Revolution of 1917? Socialism eventually evolving into Communism? Remember the film Dr. Zhivago? The good humanitarian doctor returns to Moscow after the "People's Revolution" and finds his house occupied by a rabble of belligerent dissidents that threaten to evict Zhivago from his own property if he doesn't abide by *their* mob-rule control.

And what about the infamous Nazi Revolution in pre-WWII Germany and the accompanying Fascist Revolt in Italy? How did Hitler and Mussolini ever improve their countries without thoroughly devastating Germany, Europe and Italy in the end? And how about the recent Iranian Revolution against the Shah? How did *that* historical phenomenon work out for the still-dominated and exploited natives of Iran?

And how could *we* be naïve and gullible enough to assume that good things are now going to happen in Egypt, Libya, Algeria and Syria *after* their bloody "Revolutions!" More theocratic Mullahs sponsored by the radical Islamic/Muslim Brotherhoods perhaps! How about a little Middle-East separation of "Mosque and State" like we have a fundamental division of "church and state" right here in America!

And what about Albert Einstein's colossal impact on American culture? With the Theory of Relativity came the unique notion that everything in society is "relative": nothing anywhere in America (save death and taxes) is *absolute,* permanent and fixed. And so now we have such things as the Bill of Rights to the Constitution coming into conflict with widely-recognized traditional American family values. The First Ten Amendments (under the guise of freedom of speech and freedom of expression) are now insidiously undermining the Ten Commandments handed-down to Moses on Mt. Sinai.

Take this rather disturbing gay rights marriage issue for example in regard to what Einstein's relativity has mutated into. Remember: today everything is evolving and must be 'Relative" and not "Absolute"

(God's Ten Stone Tablet Laws). Two iconic Commandments are: "Honor Thy Father and Thy Mother" and "Thou Shall not covet thy neighbor's wife!"

Just think about *those* two Commandments for a second. The principal purpose of heterosexual (man-woman) marriage is to biologically conceive children and then to nurture them through mature parenting skills. The very vocal gay and lesbian political activists want gays to get married, to adopt children and then to have loving families.

Now someone please explain *this* paradoxical situation to me. How could an adopted child with gay "parents" know who the mother is if two males are his or her parents? If two lesbians are his or her parents, which one is the father according to the very explicit Commandment: "Honor Thy Father and Thy Mother?" And if two gay married men are living next door, according to the Ninth Commandment, which one is "thy neighbor's wife" to be coveted?

Under recent gay rights' laws, the idea of certain "sins" against God has been totally eradicated and "sin" is now basically obsolete and "relative." And needless to say, a woman's right to choose or to have an "Abortion" too violates the Stone Tablets' ABSOLUTE Commandments because a conceived child is sinfully *killed,* "Thou Shall Not Kill," and has no opportunity whatsoever to ever honor either a mother or a father. And indeed, if the very vocal in-your-face abortion rights activists had been themselves *aborted* before birth by a "Right to Choose" mother, we would not be having any legal wrangles with the whole lot of them at present. Was Sodom and Gomorrah a Biblical myth or could it soon again be happening right here in America? I'll let *you* be the judge of that!

Finally, John Dewey is the "father of modern-day American public-school education." Dewey was a sociologist, a psychologist in addition to being an educator, and his "Revolutionary" classroom theories had been drastically influenced by Charles Darwin's Theory of Evolution and by Albert Einstein's Theory of Relativity. John Dewey was undeniably a confirmed Socialist, and most of our contemporary public school teaching methods and practices are based on the socialistic idea of "sharing" in a "community (commune) classroom" atmosphere.

Dewey espoused the idea that "children learn by doing," and I often wonder if *this* particular theory of his pertains to the literal teaching of sex education inside the classroom, for without a doubt, the rampant implementation of sex education seems to be quite pervasive among brazen and *in*discriminate young teenagers in numerous environments outside the classroom.

460

Socialism in our public schools is stealthily taught under the guise of ever-evolving "democratic education." American free enterprise in the form of student classroom *competition* is de-emphasized by modern educational psychology. *Individual* academic achievement is often discouraged in deference to group (class) accomplishment. Soon there will be no honored valedictorians or salutatorians at high school or college graduations because being "outstanding" or being "excellent" automatically makes the other lower-ability *students* in attendance look publicly bad and makes *them* feel inferior in comparison.

In order for *it* to be successful, mediocrity must be both promoted and maintained in John Dewey's anemic academic performance system, so when public school teachers put kids into classroom "groups," the students that want to succeed wind-up doing the bulk of the "group's work" so that *they* could get decent grades while the less-motivated (and socially deprived) freeloaders get by with almost the same recognition given by the teacher, and if you further examine our current American economic welfare system, the productive members of society are encumbered with carrying the weight of the un-motivated adult masses on *their* backs.

When I had my first "Educational Classroom Methods" course in college, during the initial session the professor stated, "Every child has an innate desire to learn." During the second day of the seminar, the same professor declared, "You must motivate the students at the start of every lesson." These separate contradictory comments greatly puzzled me and raised a large red flag in my mind. 'Why do I have to motivate "students" at the start of each lesson when they're all supposed to have an innate desire to learn?' I speculated. 'There's something inherently wrong with this convoluted ambivalent picture!' I conjectured.

And so, classrooms all over the American landscape are slowly-but-surely evolving into miniature European-style socialistic "nanny states," both tolerating and promoting academic mediocrity to guarantee the continuation of John Dewey's counter-productive Socialist Education System.

Dewey's egregious educational quagmire and his' associated quixotic child psychology enforcement has, over the decades, negatively led to child-centered families and to child-centered classrooms. Parents have been demoted in the home and teachers have essentially been demoted in the classroom and are now labeled in academic jargon as "educational facilitators." Free enterprise (student class and subject competition) has been conveniently junked to accommodate John Dewey's lunacy in regard to socialistic "class democratic" education. But forget the euphemisms! Students that aspire to academic excellence are wickedly stifled from doing so by Dewey-centered classroom mandates, those ambitious kids being falsely labeled as being "arrogant," "self-centered," "selfish" and "uncaring" about the "group."

As sure as the existence of precious oxygen, we do have plenty of lackluster students hibernating and vegetating inside "group-dominated classrooms," idealistically wanting to change the world for the better, but those sedentary, callow, well-intentioned sorry souls lack the skill and the talent to successfully attain their dreams of a better America. It is only when *our* students learn to pursue their own self-actualization and to introspectively explore their own individuality through dedication and through ambition that *those* presently victimized young people will learn to mature (not evolve) into responsible adults, contributing to society and distinguishing themselves through community service, charity, compassion and a noteworthy career.

The main idea of this article is this: Utopia can never occur on a national scale; Utopia can only be attained in an ambitious person's individual life.

But first off, American education must reject John Dewey's detrimental "socialistic group-sharing" system and in keeping with competitive free enterprise capitalistic democracy, everyone attending public school must drop this "group-sharing nonsense" and modify their behavior to confidently believe in themselves. Is there any wonder why many astute parents elect to ignore lackluster public school education and send their children to private and to parochial schools?

While growing-up in New Jersey and Pennsylvania, my' father had taught me several cherished principles that to this very day still govern my life. Be self-reliant and try helping others who are *temporarily* having bad luck, and then there was Dad's favorite bit of advice, "The world doesn't owe you a living so learn to distinguish yourself! Show some passion about achieving your personal dreams and goals!"

Americans must have both "the dream" and "the drive," but unfortunately, many of us lack *that* second vital and more necessary quality: that is, a deliberate plan to achieve "the dream" through strong labor and relentless desire. Yes, twenty-three-thousand or so dollars might now be the standard "Poverty Level" for a family of four, but if a motivated person living in the U.S. makes 50 thousand dollars and pays income tax on salary, property tax for a house, state income tax, state sales tax, gas tax, federal withholding tax, etc., then money-wise, he or she is as good as being on welfare too while simultaneously having the burden of working for a living to support a family!

And for those cynical critics out there that will insist that I am guilty of discrimination, they are ABSOLUTELY right! I do possess discriminating tastes and values! I do discriminate against laziness! Throughout history, right has always discriminated against wrong, good has always discriminated against evil and morality has always discriminated against immorality; otherwise, in stark contrast, there would be no distinct difference between the two polarized entities, namely, good and evil, the two diametrically-opposed forces blending eventually into the same existence and also into the same definition, just as radical left-wing rights' activists want to legitimize and finalize!

So, in the final analysis, thanks to Charles Darwin and Albert Einstein's theories as catastrophically interpreted by the disillusioned Socialist John Dewey, our present dysfunctional American public school educational system, our litigious-oriented legal system and our corrupt political system (along with our ever-evolving and ever-relative morality) are entirely convoluted and presently without clarity or focus, and consequently, the United States of America is soon on the verge of entering a very perilous self-destruct mode!

"Wall Street Protesters"

Government cannot create wealth. It can only consume wealth through taxation. Only the industrious private sector can create wealth and genuine prosperity. When Americans sober-up and finally recognize *this* basic economic truth, then capitalism will once again be honestly revered and not falsely vilified.

I maintain that the Occupy Wall Street protesters conducting lengthy rallies across the USA (and across the world) just don't understand and appreciate the United States of America, the greatest force for good that this Earth has ever known.

I suppose to begin with, I have a little trouble with the profoundly un-American operative word "Occupy." True "Democratic" protesters don't stubbornly "Occupy" anything that isn't their own personal property in the first place. They compliantly apply for a permit to publicly address their various grievances, demonstrate their major points of view between the reasonable hours of nine a.m. to five p.m., and then after conducting their peaceful demonstration, the bona fide protesters go home. Isn't extended loitering still against the law?

Whenever I ponder the terminology "Occupy", I think of Adolph Hitler and his crazed Nazis "Occupying" France, Holland, Belgium, Austria and Poland. My traditional mind contemplates someone actually taking and using something that is unlawfully his or hers. Genuine demonstrators don't "Occupy" anything. They peacefully make their public statement and then use the "democratic" method of the Election Day ballot box to actively change society to conform to their perspective's immediate goals and objectives.

When I further think of the suspect word "Occupy", my mind instantly contemplates a stark scene from the movie *Dr. Zhivago*. Zhivago returns home to Moscow after serving his country at the Russian WWI front. Meanwhile, the 1917 Bolshevik Revolution has occurred and Zhivago finds his formerly beautiful home "Occupied" by fifty irate dissidents. The Bolshevik "protesters/occupiers" tell Zhivago that he would be allowed to stay in his former home if he abides by *their* inflexible rules and if he gratefully pays for *their* food and for *their* basic daily necessities.

If the New York Wall Street protesters had their druthers, they would first take over Zuccotti Park, ultimately handicap Wall Street, next destroy "greedy" American Capitalism and then swiftly replace its "corruption" with a voracious, exploitative and even more corrupt European-style nanny state.

But please don't expect productive and retired American adults and through-the-mill senior citizens to voluntarily provide for the abundant needs of mostly vocal young people, adamantly demanding privileges and "economic justice" (Socialism) that the all-too-vocal demonstrators have not legitimately and rightfully earned on their own effort.

Perhaps I can't satisfactorily identify with the mostly eighteen-year-old to twenty-four-year-old Wall Street protesters because I have diligently worked my rear-end off for over forty-two years at all sorts of jobs, and have over that long span managed to borrow money and then faithfully repay it after taking several entrepreneurial risks owning and operating various business enterprises.

Not to sound too religious and too old-fashioned, the Wall Street protesters don't fully comprehend the Protestant Work Ethic. They quit too easily and lack the confidence and the fortitude to succeed. They don't like challenges or obstacles. They seem to despise competition and free enterprise. They interpret their "selfish" needs as being more important than (and positively above) the needs of self-reliant "selfish" Americans laboring and providing for their families, day in and day out. They appear to be saying, "The world owes me a living!"

When I was eight years old, I worked for my grandparents, who had a small concession stand inside their farm market. Work was consistently emphasized to me by my parents and grandparents when I was expected to ambitiously dip ice cream, fetch sodas, sell candy bars and electrocute hot dogs for prospective customers. Yes, I confess that in my formative years I had been exploited by my parents and by my maternal grandparents. I always had to work before I ever was allowed to play. Work and self-sacrifice for the good of the family always trumped and preceded the concept of "self-indulgence" and play.

When I was thirteen in the mid-1950s, my family lived in Levittown, Pa. My father was a stainless-steel fabricator whose company laid him off during one of several terrible economic recessions that had occurred during that explosive decade.

I had to find a way to earn my suddenly lost weekly "allowance." My dad lent me 25 dollars to purchase a daily newspaper route, which I soon paid off and then expanded from 75 customers to 125 within a year. I managed to make 10 dollars a week at my first adventure into free market capitalism. Ten dollars a week was a considerable sum for a thirteen-year-old kid back in the 1950s, equivalent to around 100 dollars a week in today's inflated money nomenclature.

But I could not keep all of my ten dollars a week. Half of my earnings had to be given to the family, twenty-five percent was used for my acquisition of shoes and school clothing and the remaining twenty-five percent I could use for my own "selfish" teenage pleasures. That's how I originally learned about the mechanics of "American Capitalism."

In high school, I worked in the back room of a delicatessen three nights a week and on weekends, spending plenty of time making sandwiches and peeling potatoes. After graduating from a New Jersey high school in 1960, my dad got me a year's employment as a welder where he worked in Norristown, Pa. I decided I didn't like breathing in nasty gas fumes all day long, so the next year I attended a teachers' college in Southern New Jersey.

And my parents, through their own individual sacrifices, had saved enough money over the years to pay for my advanced education. I too have learned from their example and had saved sufficient cash to pay for my' three sons' educations, two at *Rutgers* and one at *Rowan University.* I just can't fathom how many of today's nanny-state "entitlement-oriented" college students are several hundred thousand dollars in debt and feel "entitled" to something when they had the option of attending inexpensive community colleges and rather minimally extravagant state colleges.

And yes, capitalism certainly does involve taking risks. I had borrowed money to start-up businesses on the Ocean City, Maryland, Rehoboth Beach, Delaware and Atlantic City, New Jersey boardwalks, worked fourteen-hour days for sixteen summers from Memorial Day to Labor Day and managed to frugally save sufficient money to pay for my home and educate my three sons. But if it weren't for me having the initiative, freedom and the opportunity to voluntarily engage in free-enterprise risk-oriented American Capitalism, I could have never successfully achieved *those* particular family and parental obligations.

And yes, I had worked for 34 years as a public-school teacher, so I definitely understand both the private sector business world and the public sector government world as well. My wife also worked for 31 years as a teacher in another school district to help me pay monthly household debts, so I really have trouble understanding a 21-year-old complaining about how rough it is for him or her to find employment or to pay for his or her college education.

And I didn't get the position of English teacher I had desired right away. For the first three years of my career I was a sixth grade all-subjects teacher and the next two years I patiently was the permanent substitute at the local high school before I finally earned my English teacher status. If "instant gratification" were my watchwords in the mid-1960s, then I might have become a disgruntled 60s hippie protester comparable to the current frustrated Wall Street protesters that happen to prevail today.

What disturbs me most about the misguided Wall Street protesters (and their' movement in general) is that it is basically an economic socialistic "re-distribute the wealth" scheme where the advocates claim to represent the 99% of Americans who vehemently resent the 1% millionaires and billionaires. Well, I too am not in the top 1% income bracket, and these garrulous Wall Street protesters do not speak for me in any way, shape or form.

And for those insistent Wall Street objectors who have no employment and have accumulated massive advanced education tuition debts, the participants never explored the option of enlisting in the U.S. military, which would pay towards a college education after the young adult volunteers contribute several years of their lives loyally serving and preserving the security of the United States of America.

But regrettably, the mercurial Wall Street protesters don't appreciate the hand that feeds them, obviously the benign provider being American Capitalism. Free enterprise is the indispensable engine that affords economic stability to American democracy. If you only want "Democracy," then move to Iraq or Afghanistan. If you desire true "Democratic freedom" founded on solid "free market" economic principles, then live in and learn to contribute to the prosperity of the United States of America. Think about it for a moment. What would the world be like today if the United States of America (or American Capitalism) never happened?

When the Wall Street protesters profess that they desire to dismantle American Capitalism, those dissidents are actually vowing to destroy their own dreams of personal success and the goal of ever achieving personal economic prosperity. Talk about biting the hand that feeds them. Capitalism has created more wealth than any other economic system in the history of the world, including Marxism, Socialism and Communism. How's that 1959 social experiment going down there in Cuba, Fidel?

And capitalism has made America the envy of the world. But what other nation has freed so many millions of people in other countries and liberated them from cruel tyranny, from crazed dictators and from widespread oppression? What other political/economic system provides more for its citizens than American capitalism does? One thing is for sure. Being poor in America is like being upper middle class in foreign places such as Uganda, Indonesia, Libya and Syria.

But here's exactly what the Wall Street protesters fail to understand about the merits of American Capitalism. Wall Street (and the large banking and insurance companies) by itself did not cause the present economic recession. And if the protesters really want to take their animosity about the recent financial meltdown crisis out on the right people, they should be vigorously marching in front of the White House and in front of the Capitol Building in Washington DC to forcefully express their twisted anti-money anti-capitalism sentiments.

I think that the Wall Street protesters inadvertently practice a warped inverted value system that idealistically espouses various abstract amalgamated causes. They worry about disadvantaged people living in Africa, about curing the international AIDS epidemic, about the salvation of the endangered world environment, about egregious corporate Wall Street greed while the very provocative demonstrators simultaneously are conspiring against the perils and evils of American Capitalism.

On the other hand, people like myself' believe in self-reliance and the pursuit of individual success in a challenging and fluid-free, market-free-enterprise economic structure model. In my own value system, I first want to "greedily" advance and help myself, then assist my family, then support my relatives followed by my community population, then performing charity for constructive national and international organizations, and after all of that is eventually responded to, finally I want to consider aiding the poor people of Africa and the shrinking rain forests of South America.

I humbly value the fact that I live in a stable, organized community, and quite frankly, *we* are proud and independent folks that don't need or wish for any community organizers and political activists around to *disorganize* my town so that *they* can reconstruct and re-organize the community according to *their* ultra-liberal activist economic and assumed legal justice standards.

But in reality, the Wall Street protesters just don't comprehend Wall Street and the myriad attendant benefits of American Capitalism, which argumentatively represent the only true hopes (the private sector) of getting this grand nation out of the current encumbering recession. Although the *public sector* performs an invaluable service to society, teachers, police officers and firemen basically consume wealth; they effectively don't produce wealth like the *private sector* Wall Street corporations do.

And policemen, teachers and firemen (along with most contributing adults) have pension plans and/or 401 K's that generate and accumulate wealth by investing in high grade stocks, bonds and mutual funds, all invaluable pillars of American "greed" and capitalism that the Wall Street protesters totally and explicitly abhor. And may I add that most

American corporations are wisely structured "democratically" in that the stockholders have the opportunity to vote on company policies and consequently, also decide executive salaries and compensations.

How many of the boisterous Wall Street protesters realize that the major banks that had been saved by the federal government have all repaid their TARP loans while in the process, the U. S. Government has made hundreds of millions on interest money paid on those same government loans when stock options, bonds and preferred stock had been finally redeemed?

How many Wall Street protesters realize that the bank bailouts were done to principally save Europe's fragile nanny-state economies from collapsing? AIG, Bank of America, Wells Fargo, Goldman and Citi Bank all have Gordian-knot types of entanglements inside the colossal global economy!

And how many Wall Street protesters realize that the U.S. Government coerced Wells Fargo into swallowing down Wachovia, which was in danger of defaulting on its mortgage loans, and the Feds also were engaged in forcing Bank of America to choke on dangerous Countrywide Inc. mortgages and also obtaining Merrill Lynch on the verge of tanking, *that* coincidentally grossly mismanaged in-jeopardy company also going belly-up? That's the main reason why Wells Fargo and Bank of America needed concurrent TARP assistance!

Republican George W. Bush was asleep at the wheel when he didn't observe that Freddie Mac and Fannie Mae were egregiously giving frivolous home mortgages with little or no collateral being offered by the buyers. Truly, everyone who is *not* credit-worthy does *not* deserve living in a home (forgive the double negative). That's why we have public housing apartments.

Now enter Chris Dodd and Barney Frank, both Democratic politicians overseeing wasteful government regulated institutions Freddie Mac and Fannie Mae. Low interest adjustable rates were quickly and generously offered to credit-unworthy mortgage recipients, and when the adjustable rates rose from three and a half percent interest to seven and a half percent, soon the mortgages and mounting debts became much greater than the houses' true value. Millions of unnecessary national foreclosures (since credit-worthiness precautions had not been originally defined and observed) soon became inevitable realities.

But perhaps the biggest travesty of all was when the large banks were told by the government that they also would have to offer low interest adjustable rates to credit-unworthy home buyers (just like Freddie Mac and Fannie Mae were doing) or else the Fed would cut down on issuing paper and electronic money to the B. of A., to Citi and to Wells Fargo.

The big banks reluctantly went along with the flimsy mortgage-lending Ponzi scheme, so to protect themselves, they quickly bundled the bad loans into complex derivatives, sold the derivatives to smaller investment companies, and when the housing bubble burst, the government determined that the banks were still responsible for the bundled derivatives when the smaller firms that assumed the bundled debts went insolvent. And so, *this* salient fact is why the Wall Street protesters ought to be demonstrating outside the Freddie Mac and Fannie Mae corporate offices, outside the Capitol and outside the White House, and not blaming the complicated mess specifically on Wall Street.

And then there was Stan O'Neal, the CEO of Merrill Lynch who had received a departure bonus of 161.5 million dollars soon before Merrill Lynch tanked and had to be acquired (by government coercion) by Bank of America. And let's not forget the 12 executives at Freddie Mac and Fannie Mae (all government friends) who in 2009 had received 42 million in taxpayer money in the form of remuneration.

On the topic of excessive compensation from Freddie Mac and Fannie Mae, and also in regard to Stan O'Neal and Merrill Lynch, I'm in absolute agreement with the Wall Street protesters. And yes, I admit that "greed" is the root of all evil, but I insist that "money" is honestly the genesis of all good!

I wholeheartedly believe that if a corporation tanks, then the CEO deserves little or no bonus compensation. However, if a corporation is extremely profitable, then the executives should be rewarded at any reasonable level "democratically" determined and approved by the voting stockholders.

And in the final analysis, I suppose that what most greatly disturbs and disappoints me about these mediocre Occupy Wall Street rallies is the lack of American flags being proudly displayed. This obvious fact suggests that much of the Wall Street protest debacle consists of misguided, cause-oriented youth, and it is a motley array of anarchists, elements of nihilists, a mix of Socialists, Communists Environmentalists and U.S. Muslims, all being aggressively infiltrated and motivated by wily *public sector* union organizers, who are deviously mobilizing the angry demonstrators for the purpose of advancing *their* own unions' goals and agendas.

But what really hugely alarms me most about the Wall Street protests is that they have been inspired by the so-called Arab Spring phenomenon, a recent Mideast revolutionary upheaval which has no demonstrable "democratic track record," "democratic tradition" or "democratic history." What's next? Sharia Law replacing Constitutional Law? Social disorganization replacing community organization so that each defective American town and village will eventually require the services of far-left "community organizers?"

When I watch the vociferous Wall Street protesters on TV, I see a conglomerate of folks that don't believe in their own individual potentials, a group that wants to see the government play Robin Hood and take from me (and people like me) to re-distribute wealth for the sake of "economic justice," young people who would rather believe in elusive remote causes than in themselves and in American opportunity, a lot of grasshoppers desiring to extort money from Aesop's fabled industrious ants, and finally, last but not least, I see Hitler's minions "Occupying" Europe, and my wary mind still envisions that belligerent rabble of Bolsheviks commandeering and "Occupying" Dr. Zhivago's formerly beautiful Moscow home.

"Catty Cat Catching"

In the spring of 2005, a neighborhood mother cat gave birth to four adorable kittens. In May the mother cat brought her litter of four to my back yard to show them off and introduce the new brood to some friendly surroundings where future food and an accommodating environment would be provided. My wife named the four kittens Fluffy (an orange-furred critter with an attractive broad bushy tail), Midge (an orange and white striped animal), Calico (a patched offspring) and Smarty, a smarty-cat tabby that was always first to spot and eat available cat food conveniently placed outside in clear plastic bowls.

Joanne and I took immense pleasure in watching the four daily visitors grow and mature to where they were establishing their independence and developing different personality traits while playing and amusingly wrestling on the backyard grass, honing their individual hunting skills and at the same time creating a pecking order and instinctively determining dominance and subordination within the group. The quartet would entertain us by sparring one another around the black capped pipe that led to the septic tank, accidentally knocking the round lid off at least once a week, would advantageously jump and ambush each other at every opportunity and would chase squirrels and attempt to hijack birds whenever bored with each other's rambunctious company.

In August, Midge and Calico disappeared, presumably in search of "greener pastures" or more generous humans with unlimited cat food supplies. At least that supposition is what my wife and I had suspected.

"Perhaps Calico and Midge are following their innate drives and contemplating starting new families," I suggested to my wife. "Maybe we didn't feed them as often as they were demanding. I would feel guilty if I found one or both of their carcasses as road kill on the busy White Horse Pike!"

"Whatever will be will be!" Joanne answered sounding a lot like a contemporary Doris Day. "I think that Fluffy and Smarty will probably be our permanent local back yard residents. Although I'm no cat authority I do believe Fluffy to be a male and Smarty a soon-to-be-fertile female!"

"We won't have to buy as many twenty-five-pound bags of fish-flavored cat food at Wal-Mart," I stated. "Those four kittens were becoming mighty expensive with their discriminating gourmet culinary preferences! I'm sort of glad that our cat population has now diminished to two persistent beggars!"

"Yes, my frugal husband," Joanne concurred. "Now we're down to two bowls of leftovers and cat food instead of four. The absence of Midge and Calico has definitely allowed us to be more economical in the cat food acquisition department!"

But then in the spring of '06 Smarty gave birth to a liter of five and a mere month later brought her new obedient disciples over to our back lawn to be proudly exhibited. Joanne and I were immediately concerned about overpopulation regarding the new animal influx.

"I've decided I'm going to call the black one with the attractive brown markings Tiger," Joanne declared. "And the small gray and white striped one will have the name Tiny. And the aggressive solid gray kitten ought to be dubbed Knight and the pitch-black beauty will be referred to as Midnight. And the totally weak-looking little orange kitten should be...."

"Runt!" I confidently replied. "That poor creature seems to be partially blind and will have a difficult time surviving on its own. It's just the type of weak slow kitty that preying hawks look for to swoop down from the sky and capture!"

"But Runt is so cute standing in the middle of the plastic bowl and eating its kitty food!" my wife humorously noted. "I hope that Smarty protects it! The poor thing is too small and too slow to adequately fend for itself!"

Soon two additional strays joined the enclave and Joanne designated the two "freeloading guests" as Silver and Renegade. Now we had nine mooching cats hanging around our property and at nighttime taking residence in various flowerbeds and bushes situated around our house's perimeter. My wife cleverly used a play-on-words and genially referred to the thriving throng as "the whole *kitten*-kaboodle!"

"At least we won't have any mice pesterin' us!" I said putting a positive spin on our invasion dilemma. "We now have a decent rodent patrol!"

"This whole scenario is intolerable!" Joanne remarked and exclaimed. "Next year there'll be eighteen hungry cats and the following summer thirty-six! Something drastic has to be done or else we'll have to turn our mortgage over to Smarty and Fluffy!"

"Okay!" I admitted and agreed. "And now the venerable elder Gramps is coming around too! I presume that he's a patriarch in the clan because the others all lower their heads in submission each and every time *he* makes his regal grand appearance! Even Renegade shows Gramps exceptional respect!"

"I think that you and J.T. should catch the four youngsters and take them to an animal refuge," Joanne candidly recommended. "Perhaps the staff there can locate the kittens into people's homes! They're still young enough to be domesticated!"

"My brother Skip has a cage we can borrow!" I recollected and offered. "If our son and I can lure the kittens onto the side porch, then J.T. and I can deftly apprehend the little varmints! I had read in a magazine where a frightened wild cat can be tricked, cornered and taken into custody by throwing a towel on top of its head! I'll assign J.T. the task of performing that very complicated duty! Obviously, he's less likely to get a coronary than I am!"

"It's too bad that Runt no longer is coming around!" my devoted spouse indicated with an element of regret. "But still, Tiger, Tiny, Knight and Midnight should all prove to be formidable challenges to catch!"

"I wish there was a way to get the four into a *cat*atonic state!" I awkwardly joked. "That method would be a sure way to avoid any impending *cat*astrophe during the ongoing search-and-seizure operation!"

"You make a terrible stand-up comedian! It's amazing that you haven't been hit by any red-ripe juicy tomatoes in your lifetime!" Joanne mockingly jested. "On second thought, a few pounds of messy ketchup on your face might actually improve your overall appearance!"

Joanne contacted the Delaware Valley Animal Clinic over the telephone, a facility located thirty miles southwest of Hammonton in Mullica Hill, New Jersey. The courteous receptionist said that the clinic would take all four of the cantankerous kittens and promised to find caring keepers for them for a donation of fifteen dollars each. Reluctantly my wife and I acceded to those simple conditions to eliminate the proliferating and potentially unbearable "cat dilemma."

On a Wednesday morning in mid-October, J.T. and I planned to collar the four impetuous but still-gullible fast-growing kittens. After obtaining the aforementioned large cage from Skip, my son and I cunningly initiated our well-rehearsed deception. First, we strategically placed the heavy cage on the side screened-in porch. Then we placed several bowls of tempting cat food inside the enclosure and next opened the porch door to allow our targeted kittens to enter. Much to our surprise Smarty (the mother), Fluffy, and Silver stepped into the area followed by the four intended victims: Tiger, Tiny, Knight and Midnight. But only Tiger had the appetite to cautiously go inside the cage.

I swiftly and courageously closed the cage door and managed to quickly lock Tiger inside. The alarmed kitten freaked-out and leaped and jumped about inside, almost knocking itself unconscious from banging its head. A wild scramble ensued as Smarty, Fluffy and Silver darted around various chairs and obstacles on the side porch before finally exiting via the screen door. Joanne stepped onto the porch to inspect *our* progress but panic-stricken Tiny squeezed through the opening between the dining room door and its frame and escaped into our two-story colonial home. During the ongoing mayhem J.T. shut the porch screen door just after Midnight had escaped, leaving only scared-to-death Knight trapped on the cement floor with the still-frantic Tiger confined to its all-too-certain incarceration.

J.T. and I then entered the house, closed the dining room door and initiated our search to discover Tiny's hiding spot. My son observed the neurotic gray and white-striped kitten furtively lying under the dining room table and we simultaneously exclaimed, "There it is!" No sooner had that declaration been loudly articulated that the intimidated kitten scurried around the polished hardwood floor, spinning its wheels (paws) and unable to generate any needed traction. The small animal then bolted across the dining room and leaped up to clamber onto a serving tray. Next the ornery-but-nimble critter appeared to perform four consecutive chin-ups attempting to elevate its torso onto the expensive two and a half foot high serving tray. After realizing the futility of its endeavor, the frustrated two-toned kitten plummeted to the floor and then skittered behind a statue of a Roman maiden pouring water from a jug. And before either J.T. or I could throw a towel over the bewildered terrified kitty, it zipped across the room and soon totally evaded our scrutiny.

"Great!" I shouted in utter aggravation. "Now Tiny's hiding somewhere in the house! We have to search every nook and cranny as if this home is one of those infamous English muffins you see advertised on TV!"

"It could've rambled and scrambled off to anywhere!" J.T. inadvertently rhymed and added. "Let's search the entire place before Tiny makes a mess somewhere like under the sofa. Then I'll never hear the end of Mother's protesting!"

The three of us looked everywhere inside the dwelling. We peeked under every chair, beneath every table and behind every desk and television. The frantic expedition required a full forty-five minutes to complete but nevertheless our efforts were in vain. The wily gray and white kitten had the wherewithal not to make a sound as J.T. and I maneuvered furniture and used flashlights to examine underneath every bed and behind every end table.

"It's a good thing that Smarty didn't become too overprotective and attack in defense of her young!" I noted as I wiped sweat from my brow. "She was hissing when I chased her off the porch with the broom! That cat can be vicious!"

"I have an idea!" my wife constructively said. "Why don't you two heroes venture out onto the porch and retrieve Knight and put him in the cage with Tiger. In the meantime, everything will be sufficiently quiet in the house and perhaps I'll be able to hear Tiny whimpering for its mother."

Catching Knight on the side porch proved to be a Herculean task. J.T. seemed quite comical chasing the nervous kitten around the cement floor in all directions and throwing the towel and missing its head over and over again, looking like a crazy matador going amuck with his cape. Finally, Knight leaped up onto the side ledge and tried climbing up the screen, but then J.T. managed to hurl the blue towel over its head and next grasped the cat, the creature making my son fumble the loaded towel against his chest as if the round mass curled-up inside the towel was a slippery greased pigskin.

"What tremendous excitement! That combative kitten is a real *wild cat*!" I bellowed all out of breath from observing J.T.'s frenetic ordeal.

"Yeah Dad! Maybe it plans attending either Villanova or the University of Kentucky!" my son cynically panted. "I definitely need to be in better shape and intend to spend more time exercising at the gym! But thanks for helping me pursue and isolate this extremely evasive animal! That dependable broom you're holding sure came in handy as a persuasion device."

After J.T. gingerly inserted the disoriented Knight inside the cage to accompany Tiger, my wife abruptly opened the dining room door and anxiously announced, "Tiny's definitely hiding behind the dining room breakfront! I just heard it meowing after I had opened a can of tuna fish and placed it on the dining room floor!"

"Let's be as gentle as possible!" I related to J.T. "We don't want this furry creature arrest to be a harrowing experience for us and a traumatic one for poor Tiny."

"Maybe Mom can film the adventure and send it to *Animal Planet*!" my son laughed. "On second thought, maybe she should just destroy the evidence!"

The credenza/breakfront must have weighed over five hundred pounds but J.T. and I gradually maneuvered it back and forth until we budged the heavy object an additional foot away from the wall. The back panel was around three inches above the floor and it had allowed just enough room for Tiny to wriggle underneath. Soon the petrified kitten emerged from the crevice and reflexively tried making its desperate escape. It fiercely scampered upon the polished hardwood floor (next to the wall) in my direction and upon detecting my' illustrious presence, Tiny accomplished a full backward somersault in mid-air, thumped against the wall and then rapidly headed toward J.T.'s position. Two seconds later the acrobatic phenom performed a similar mid-air act of dexterity and next again proceeded fleeing toward me. Tiny remarkably launched itself to a knee-high level and its all-or-nothing lunge resulted in the animal being contained between my thick winter gloves.

The terrified kitten clawed and wiggled around and then temporarily eluded my grasp by wriggling free and then flipping itself around as I incompetently fumbled to regain its control. Tiny scratched away (at my heavy coat at greased-lightning speed) while simultaneously executing its super-impressive circus-like gyrations. Much to my relief J.T. was successful at putting his familiar blue towel over the animal's head, thus preventing it from engaging in any more hectic havoc. And then demonstrating marvelous precision, my son skillfully deposited Tiny into the cage so that the hard-to-catch kitten could be reunited with Tiger and Knight.

Accompanied by my wife and my son I drove the three stubborn prisoners to the Delaware Valley Animal Clinic over in Mullica Hill where we presented the brood along with the forty-five dollar contribution.

"I thought you had said that you had four kittens," the alert receptionist mentioned. "Where's the fourth little guy?"

"Midnight had shrewdly escaped our entrapment scheme!" I solemnly confessed. "If we ever catch the little savvy imp I promise to bring it right over!"

Upon completing our important mission and then arriving back in Hammonton, the three of us immediately spotted Smarty and Midnight prowling around in our backyard. We automatically explained to each other that the two wanderers were searching for the whereabouts of their beloved missing companions. But we humans were in for a rather shocking surprise.

Amazingly, three carefree itinerant kittens came ambling around the corner of our home's "Great Room" and the newly arrived trio appeared to be identical reproductions of recently conveyed Tiger, Knight and Tiny. 'Is this some sort of weird paranormal mirage or illusion?' I conjectured. And next a fourth kitten having jet-black fur made its backyard debut. 'How could this be? Midnight astoundingly has an identical twin!'

Then I perceptively noticed that long-lost Midge rounded the corner and appeared on the scene and I finally understood exactly what had happened. Midge was indeed a female and had returned home after giving birth to a litter that was almost a facsimile to Smarty's. And my wife and J.T. speculated (and subsequently believed) that amorous Gramps had proudly fathered both families. At least *their* theory did make some sense out of what at first had been a rather confusing riddle.

"The cycle's being repeated!" my wife moaned. "We'll have to collar the new ones while they're still naïve and easy to catch! "Apparently Skip's cage won't stay empty for long!"

A week later my wife, J.T. and I re-did our thirty-mile excursion to Mullica Hill but this time with "five furry inmates." J.T. humorously joked about how we had admirably completed our splendid roundup without ever being reported for animal cruelty to the local *SPCA*. All throughout the forty-five-minute trip the five imprisoned cats sat mum in Skip's huge cage resigned to their fate and feeling quite comfortable resting and traveling with their familiar companions. Upon returning to our Hammonton home J.T. had a pleasant surprise in store for Joanne and myself.

"Here's a little token to fondly remember our spectacular cat escapade!" J.T. said as he very deliberately handed me a sealed envelope.

"Can you give me a vague clue as to its contents?" I genuinely requested.

"Yes, just think of a series of poems written by T.S. Eliot!" our son (who was pursuing a Master's Degree in Creative Writing at *Rowan University*) uttered just to intentionally prolong the suspense.

I hastily opened the envelope and much to my elation discovered a rather appropriate gift. "Look Joanne! Tickets for two to see the play *Cats* now being presented at Philadelphia's Forrest Theater!"

"Fighting in Schools: Zero Tolerance"

The sacred Teachers Handbook states in regard to student discipline: "Since the success of a democratic nation relies on the ability of its citizens to exercise self-discipline, it is the purpose of the school to teach boys and girls our main objective, which is the philosophy of self-control." Everything looks good on paper where democratic education in the comprehensive school is concerned, but a tremendous Grand Canyon exists between educational theory and everyday public-school reality.

A core of seventy-five to a hundred nasty *students* are continuously disrupting the smooth operation of the average sized middle or high school and also suckering good kids into altercations and committing uncivilized behavior through peer pressure, intimidation, extortion and other sinister tactics. Those hundred young barbarians are as *self-disciplined* as a colony of wild baboons. Educational psychology, the law and ultra-liberal *democracy* in a comprehensive school protect those seventy-five to a hundred terrorists from much needed reprimand and police intervention.

The public schools are often dumping grounds for recalcitrant *students* that have been *expelled* from parochial schools and from private schools. The hands of school officials and teachers are tied when dealing with the "comes with the territory" riffraff so the standard approach is to tolerate their antics and attempt to rehabilitate them by being especially nice to the young thugs.

And then inequality in punishment when it is meted out in small community schools is a daily practice. Given the same offense the son of the village drunk is more likely to be suspended than the son of a prominent citizen is. The internal problems inside schools are often concealed, whitewashed and squashed while only the good tidings filter out into the newspapers. The only time bad news is published is when police reports are organized and available to journalists, so *that* is precisely why school public-relations-minded administrators are reluctant to call in the local cops.

I remember one year when I was teaching at the high school that one of the boys' lavatories was virtually demolished. The crime scene looked almost as bad as San Francisco after the great earthquake of 1906. Ceiling panels were reduced to what looked like shredded wheat, sinks had been yanked out of the wall and cherry bombs had rocked the commodes from their anchoring. The story of the vandalism had circulated around the community but since the police were not called in the destruction was only a rumor to the common taxpayer. Administrators want only the superlatives leaking out to the public and the chance of the total school picture being accurately portrayed in the mass media is very slim indeed.

I want to emphasize that I had taught in what is regarded as a model school district so I can't imagine what's going on in urban schools or in schools with bad reputations for violence and vandalism. One thing is for sure and that is fighting in any public high school with a *student* population of a thousand or more teenagers is as certain as death and taxes. But administrators regard student fighting as "business as usual" when the local police ought to be notified and come into the building and arrest the brawlers with assault charges being issued against the main perpetrator.

I once had the displeasure of intervening in a juicy brawl in the C-Wing corridor while I was on my way to cafeteria duty. One fairly large *student* had another in a headlock with his left arm while the lad's right fist was riveting off the other *child's* head and face like a jackhammer destroying an ancient sidewalk. The recipient of the brutal blows' cheeks looked like crushed hamburger meat with a thick layer of ketchup squirted on.

I used the ice hockey official's approach and waited thirty more seconds until the *student* that was hammering away finally became a degree fatigued. After I separated the wild combatants, I sent the bloodstained victim to the nurse's office for medical attention and then escorted the aggressor down to the main office where I had to write out Discipline Referral Cards on two antagonistic *students* I didn't even know.

That afternoon I encountered the principal in the main corridor. "Just look at these bloodstains splattered all over my sport coat from breaking up that vicious brawl this morning!" I complained. "Do you think that the board of education would defray the cleaner's expenses if I submit a voucher?"

"That's okay Mr. Wiessner," the principal jokingly responded. "The red stains almost blend right-in with the cranberry-colored jacket you're wearing."

At that particular moment I vowed to my conscience that I would disappear into the woodwork the next time I would observe a *student* fracas erupting. "That's just great!" I answered the high school administrator. "Tomorrow I definitely will be wearing my green leisure suit with no tie!"

A teacher might suspect that a *student* involved in a bloody altercation might be on drugs or maybe on alcohol. One time back in the mid-'70s three eighth graders arrived at my homeroom hung-over from a wedding reception they had attended the night before. I dispatched the trio down to the nurse's office for medical exams' and verification of my theory. The nurse (under administrative suggestion) diplomatically had the boys sent home for "headaches" and for "feeling ill," thus averting adverse publicity in the newspapers.

If certain *students* are on drugs (illegal or prescription), it is more difficult to prove than when they have imbibed alcohol. Hazy eyes might suggest narcotics usage and the teacher is reluctant to report evidence of drowsiness, hyperactivity, depression or nervous twitching to the nurse because many *students* show those same symptoms normally every day.

If a teacher is daring enough to send a *student* to the nurse on suspicion of drug usage, and if the instructor's observations prove to be false, then the possibility remains that a lethal libel suit might result claiming that the *child's* integrity had been maligned by a false allegation. The lawsuit might be filed against the teacher by the parents if the instructor had written a descriptive note to the nurse. That innocent teacher memo' could be used by the plaintiff's attorney as evidence against the instructor'.

Once in the early '80s (after an intense home high school football game with a cross-town rival), one of the more eminent *students* was screaming a collection of assorted profanities at the opposing team's players. An assistant coach on the home team yelled over to the *child* making the grotesque linguistics to stop in the interest of good sportsmanship.

The dastardly *student* resented being rebuked by the assistant coach in front of his equally obnoxious cohorts. The belligerent *student* then defied the coach by verbally bombarding *him* with a flurry of obscene idioms that are seldom heard in monasteries and convents. In seconds the assistant coach and the vile instigator wound-up on the ground hostilely flailing away at each other and thrashing around.

Coaches and players finally separated the two combatants. The *student's* eyes were rolling around like cherries and lemons in a slot machine's windows. The teachers on the faculty had long suspected for quite some time that the abusive *student* had been experimenting with drugs, but since his father was always quick to defend his son's bad deportment, no one was going to ever accuse the teenager of narcotics usage and then have to defend that daring position in court.

Daily cafeteria duty was without a doubt my greatest headache. Most high school teachers would prefer being trapped in an endless maze having a multitude of cul-de-sacs rather than being exposed to the cruel and unusual punishment known as the cafeteria. Just imagine two hundred and fifty howling adolescents bending spoons into goose eggs, tossing macaroni and *Jell-o* at each other and deliberately making messes to upset the teachers on duty. The poor head teacher's incantations over the microphone are ignored because the PA system is weak', the acoustics are bad and the microphone works every other time. Yet the teachers are responsible for an orderly dismissal.

I found that the best way to patrol the cafeteria was to revolve around the perimeter with my back to the walls facing the *students* at all times. When I was courageous enough to patrol the aisles between cloistered tables, then I constituted a convenient moving target for flying debris and miscellaneous (*missile*aneous) food chunks hurtling from behind toward my head and my back.

Sometimes my wife claimed she could tell the school menu that day by inspecting my sport jacket's fabric. She saw and identified pea smears, string bean stains and carrot splotches on different occasions that had added a new exquisite design to my school attire.

The cafeteria is a mass situation where fights are most likely to flare-up in a hurry. In 1971 before John Rizzotte and I could stave off a *student* altercation, one teenaged anarchist had hit the *student* sitting across the table with a sticky meat particle. The victim then escalated the stakes by picking-up a pickle slice and a handful of lemon meringue pie and hurled the food into the first *student's* face. The crusaders that were supposed to be good friends then leaped-up onto the cafeteria table and started flailing away. That was a hard fight for John Rizzotte, Tim Amoro and myself' to break up because the brawlers were standing above us on the table. Tim Amoro wound-up with his glasses being crushed and a broken nose to boot.

Whenever a cafeteria fight is triggered, a sudden dichotomy of *student* loyalties develops, and if the teachers aren't quick to intervene other *students* may enter the battle. A distinct occupational hazard indeed exists. The teachers have to focus their energies on immediately separating the first two junior (or maybe even senior) gladiators, yanking them down to the vice-principal's office and then dutifully returning right away to the "rectum of the school," its cafeteria.

In my younger days, I used to be more aggressive in stopping lunchroom altercations but after being involved in over two hundred and fifty different *student* fisticuffs over a span of thirty-four years I gradually became less assertive. And if the *student* that I despised more was getting the worse of it on the bottom while being pummeled, then I would make sure I got to the fight scene a little slower than I ordinarily would have.

In my school district, an effective cafeteria disciplinarian was usually awarded an asterisk next to his or her name on the cafeteria duty roster. The un-coveted star signified that the teacher with the asterisk was in charge of the cafeteria and responsible for keeping order during the raucous forty-five-minute lunch period.

The asterisk did not bring any additional monetary reward for me being assigned the official charge d' affaires. The only honor of being the possessor of the un-envied asterisk was having a defective microphone, of having a *student* audio-visual club (with the mechanical skills of the Marx Brothers) to repair the sound magnifier, and the distinction of being abused daily by the merciless juvenile mob. The asterisk certainly didn't qualify me to be a certified boxing referee.

Usually, the same teachers pulled cafeteria duty each year while the balance of the faculty members were assigned to easier study hall' situations. Several cafeteria-assigned teachers learned that when they had performed a mediocre job in the lunchroom, they had been re-assigned to "easier to cope with" study hall duties the following school year.

Administrators and school board' members often contended that teachers can command respect from *students* in the cafeteria, whereas, cafeteria aides cannot. Teachers are saddled with the ugly duty because the public believes that certified instructors know how to manage *students* in mass situations.

The truth of the matter is that there is little transfer of *student* respect from the classroom to the school cafeteria. The same *students* that love a teacher in English might emulsify the instructor in the cafeteria. Teachers seldom have serious trouble with *children* in their classrooms but in the cafeteria sometimes even the good kids go sour or bonkers. Instructors are continually getting into hassles with *students* over who threw the napkin on the floor, who left the tray on the table or who' threw his or her silverware into the food garbage can. Teachers suddenly have to become police investigators.

Daily cafeteria duty is one of the best ways to ensure acid indigestion. And then when the *students* finally return to their classrooms after lunch, oftentimes they must face a strung-out exasperated teacher that had spent a very hectic forty-five-minute interval in the cafeteria dungeon. The emotions known as anger and frustration are not faucets that are easily turned off. A teacher must be careful to not carry his or her petulance from the lunchroom into the classroom. Several times I had overly admonished *students* in the classroom immediately after cafeteria duty and then had to contend with parent-initiated hostile conferences.

In the early '70s, two brawny high school *students* were really hammering away at each other in the cafeteria. By the time John Rizzotte and I hustled to the battle scene boisterous *students* were shrieking and also scurrying to the battle to add an additional dash of pandemonium to the mounting crisis. John and I tried tugging the brawlers apart but they were interlocked in a clinch like two magnetized mastodons. By that time the cafeteria marathon fight scene sounded like a blend of the *Kentucky Derby's* homestretch and the climax to the Roman *Circus Maximus*. The teachers' inability to separate the grapplers added a dimension of slapstick comedy to the already exciting event.

The bigger *student* had the smaller one in a bear hug while the more diminutive *child* had his arms locked around the huskier kid's head and neck. I leaped upon the bigger kid and eventually managed to separate him from his opponent. The bigger *student* whirled around with the two-hundred-pound teacher attached to his back. I felt like I was a rodeo cowpuncher atop a berserk Brahma bull. The larger *student* (with me on his back) re-entered the fight with the smaller *child,* who had broken away from John Rizzotte's grasp. Siamese twins would have been easier to separate than those two battlers were. The other two hundred and fifty maniac spectators were clamorously cheering the zany scene that was crazily transpiring before their eyes. Thank goodness a rescue squad of five male teachers zoomed into the cafeteria from the nearby teacher's lounge or John and I would have lost what represented the *main event* of the day for the thoroughly delighted *students.*

In another cafeteria period, several enterprising *students* thought that they would evoke certain behavioral responses from the female teachers on duty. Two boys stripped the husk from a healthy-looking banana and in a gesture of inspiration they ingeniously stretched a prophylactic over the fruit, which was then placed perpen*dic*ularly on the lunch table for other *students* to *rubber*neck and admire. Perversions of that nature are designed to rattle or unnerve teachers, so the worst thing an instructor should do is act appalled. But if the bad cafeteria behavior is not handled properly, a heated argument between the teacher and the mischievous *students* might ensue and that's precisely what the *students* were attempting to instigate, an argument with a teacher over a stupid inappropriate behavior.

I took the wind out of the violators' sails by stating, "I didn't know that bananas were capable of contracting venereal diseases!" I had successfully stolen the boys' thunder and had reduced their queer impropriety to the level of "So what!" If one plans to last for thirty-four years in the educational field, minor occurrences like the banana/prophylactic incident should not ruffle a teacher's feathers.

Students' cutting into the cafeteria line could constitute a major daily challenge for lunchroom duty teachers. Many of today's *students* belong to a peculiar breed. Besides thinking that *Hamlet* is some sort of new breakfast sensation (like an omelette), many *children'* adhere to a unique relative morality where lying, cheating and stealing are acceptable modes of behavior. It might be easier to lasso a bucking bronco with a rubber band attached to a shoelace than to get the truth from an uncooperative *student*. Perhaps schools should teach more wisdom and less knowledge and more ethics and less irrelevant facts.

I remember noticing a husky lass slipping into an already formed cafeteria line. I thought that her action had been unfair to the other *students* so I told the young lady to have a seat and then get up to be served last. Although the girl heard my directive she acted as if I had been addressing her from a soundproof booth. I repeated my command more vigorously.

"Man, stop spittin' in my face!" she indignantly sneered at me.

"Sit down and then get in the back of the line!" I repeated.

"Fuck off bro'!" she snarled back, much to the amusement of her appreciative peers.

In the midst of a temper tantrum, I told the cafeteria brunhildas not to serve the girl when she came through the line. The *student* defied my authority by grabbing a platter of food and putting it on her serving tray and then she promptly proceeded to the cashier. I notified the office. The vice-principal was tied up with another discipline problem so the principal cruised into the cafeteria.

I explained the situation and the chief school executive told the bellicose girl, "Bring the tray back to the cashier because you didn't pay her!" the principal diplomatically commanded.

The hysterical girl arose from her cafeteria seat and sauntered back to the serving line carrying her red tray. The perturbed principal followed the *student* into the serving area to ascertain that the girl would return her tray and then take a seat before moving to the back of the food line as I had directed.

A verbal exchange then ensued between the defiant *student* and the principal. The angry girl threw food particles from her tray that instantly ornamented the school official's haberdashery. The administrator reached to apprehend the disrespectful girl and she took a wild swipe at his face. The female violator zipped out of the cafeteria and fled to a place of hiding.

The principal notified the police and the girl was found seated in a telephone booth in the main corridor, holding the door shut while calling home for advice and counsel. The principal and two policemen attempted wedging the door open as the young lady kept it shut with one hand while talking on the phone with the other. I casually dismissed the craziness by thinking, 'Our' great American *democratic* educational system is for all the *children* and it is not just for the elite college-bound *students*!'

In the mid-'80s, a juicy fight had broken-out inside the middle school cafetorium. Two boys were really doing damage to each other's faces. I separated the brawlers three times but then they continued their donnybrook. I became angry from the continuous fighting so I got the more aggressive *student,* flung him into the ice cream freezer, quickly put the lid on the refrigeration unit and then sat on top. The *student* inside was smashing the top from the frigid dark interior but could not move the covering with my body weight holding it down.

"Chill out!" I yelled to the trapped instigator inside the ice cream box.

A minute later, I opened the freezer. Several dozen ice cream sandwiches and chocolate pops had been destroyed during the bizarre fiasco. Another teacher on cafeteria duty then escorted the cooled-off violator to the main office while I enjoyed eating one of the lesser crushed chocolate-covered ice cream pops.

Another time I was in after-school Office Detention with a seventh-grade *student* that had told one of his teachers to "Fuck off!" The *student* had to write a sincere letter to the teacher apologizing for his misdemeanor so I was kind enough to depart from Office Detention policy (as prescribed by the administration) and allow the *child* to write the theme under my jurisdiction.

At the end of the Office Detention session I commented to the *student,* "I'm glad you used your time constructively!"

"Blow me asshole!" he nastily responded.

Sometimes it just doesn't pay to say anything at all (polite or otherwise) to a nasty *student.* "What did you say?" I politely requested to know.

"I said 'Eat me raw asshole'!" the manner-less individual replied.

The *student* was given three additional days of Office Detention for using profanity directed toward a teacher. A week later the *student* got into a nice bloody fight in the cafeteria while I was on duty. I broke the boxers up twice but they still were going at it. The *student* that had used the obscene references in Office Detention again began swinging at his adversary.

In a fit of anger, I un-gently grabbed the aggressor and pushed him through the cafeteria doors. The *student* had been broken open with blood cascading down his face and cheeks from his forehead.

"Go to the nurse's office right now!" I bellowed to the *student* bleeding profusely on the corridor floor.

"Fuck you!" The upset *child* yelled back as he got up onto his feet. Before I could utter another word the *child* darted out of the building, scurried across the avenue and entered the police department to cite me for corporal assault. Luckily the police chief returned the brawler to school jurisdiction, but I recently read in the newspapers of a similar episode in a Pennsylvania school where the police came to the school and then arrested the teacher for assaulting a *student*.

In another cafeteria fistfight involving two huge eight graders, I forcefully pushed the main aggressor against the closed entrance doors in an effort to separate the fierce combatants. The kid hit his head against the wooden frame and some blood was trickling-down from a cut on his forehead. I quickly instructed the pugnacious *student* (who incidentally loathed me because he was failing my English class) to immediately go to the nurse's office, after which I soon wrote-out a pass and then directed a better-behaved student to deliver the message to the nurse. The belligerent instigator, instead of going to the nurse, intentionally entered the downstairs bathroom and proceeded to repeatedly slam his head against a toilet stall, thus making his head bleed excessively. The insolent kid then stepped across the hall and told the nurse that I had caused the head wound during the brawl. However, the time of the pass I had written compared to the lad's appearance in the nurse's office was a five-minute interval. A half-hour later the janitor discovered fresh blood stained upon the bathroom stall wall, and thus I was exonerated by the school administration from the frivolous accusation of beating-up the defiant *student* in the school cafeteria.

* * * * * * * * * * * *

Fighting is not only limited to the cafeteria. Brawls erupt in the halls and in study halls too. A large study hall in the lunchroom can rival the treachery of cafeteria duty. On several occasions fistfights had broken out in the cafeteria study hall before I could arrive there' from my classroom on the other side of the building over three hundred feet away through crowded corridors. I have had as many as a hundred and fifty students crammed into a cafeteria mass study hall and out of that number only about fifty of them were genuinely studying. Study halls in public schools are generally vast educational wastelands that operate on maybe a forty-percent efficiency level. Teachers are constantly taking attendance, moving talkative students to specially isolated seats and correcting those infidels that are determined to violate the sanctity of the forced silence the teachers are trying to maintain. And one time during a study hall fight I was punched twice in the back by a craven spectator while I was breaking-up the fracas.

A fight may erupt in the halls while a teacher is casually en route to his or her next class. In 1999 two eighth grade girls liking the same boy got into a real fingernail hair-pulling cat-fight. I was exiting the main office with a hundred and forty worksheets in my hand that I had just Xeroxed. A short substitute teacher was already on the scene trying to intervene in the fracas but he was taking as much of a beating as the two combatants were. I dropped my papers on the corridor floor and assisted the substitute teacher in his grave enterprise. I yanked one of the girls off but she raised her feet and was savagely kicking away at the other cat-fighter. The student in my clutches then kicked the fire extinguisher attached to the wall and it tilted sideways, mixing its chemicals and then giving off a noxious spray. The corridor was immediately filled with choking students and the chemical vapors swirling in the air looked like a miniature atomic mushroom cloud. The vice-principal exited the office, lifted one of the combatants onto his right shoulder and carried her into the main office like Little Abner eloping with Daisy May on Sadie Hawkins Day.

I remember one instance where a school janitor attempted to break up a brawl between two pretty big *students* and the custodian wound-up in the hospital getting stitches and treatment for multiple lacerations for his benign intervention.

Finally, I recollect a really terrible girls' fight that had erupted outside on the asphalt playground between an eighth-grade *child* bully and a new seventh grade transfer *student*. When I arrived to the combat zone the two girls were really pummeling and mauling one another in what amounted to a vicious battle featuring wicked hair pulling and the violent scratching of faces and arms.

Charlie Southard (an affable math' teacher) and I separated the felines three times but the marathon battle ensued. It was one of the most difficult struggles I had ever dealt with and it took Charlie and me five full minutes to restore order among the shrieking *student* eyewitnesses.

Three weeks after that horrible ordeal, Charlie Southard died from a massive heart attack. I have often wondered if there had been any residual connection between the stress and strain of separating the two

490

girls in that terrible fight and the passing away of my good friend and colleague.

I really still consider it a minor miracle that I had managed to survive in public school teaching for thirty-four years. *Student* fighting comes with the total teaching package and it has nothing at all to do with either teaching or with learning.

But today's school fights are not always one-on-one with fist against jaw combat. Honor (one-on-one fighting) is now often abandoned. The "wolf pack mentality" is presently pervading many urban schools and *students* are now employing the herd attack practice in rural high schools as well. Four *children* will now fight maybe six *students*. Sometimes a *student* will be knocked to the ground outside the building or to the floor inside the edifice and five or six members of the assaulting wolf pack will stomp and trounce the ribs and face of the unfortunate recipient of *their* collective hostility.

If a *student* fight happens first thing in the morning, it could set the tone for and ruin a teacher's entire day. Fortunately for the already encumbered instructors most days are more tranquil than those dates that are tainted with wall-to-wall *student* conflicts. On those chaotic mind-boggling days (usually before extended holidays like *Thanksgiving, Christmas* and *Easter*) public school teaching could seem like the *Wild, Wild West*.

* * * * * * * * * * * * *

I firmly believe that all *students* between the ages of thirteen and eighteen should be required to spend six weeks of each summer vacation involved in community service. Such a program would develop a spirit of commitment and responsibility so that adolescents could realize from experience that there is more to life than the all-too-prevalent "Me first" attitude, which most egocentric teenagers of today assume and practice. A strong sense of purpose among juveniles could drastically reduce the number of *student* fights that currently take place. And administrators and boards of education should treat school fighting as serious assaults and batteries worthy of police investigation and not as business-as-usual events resulting in mere *student* detentions and suspensions.

Also, I think it would be beneficial to our great American society if each high school graduate be put on hold and have college (or work) delayed for two years so that every eighteen and nineteen-year-old could fulfill a societal contribution by either serving in the military or by assisting in their communities as voluntary helpers given assigned responsibilities and duties. Then perhaps our college dropout rates would be diminished when more mature, more disciplined and more ethically minded twenty-year-old freshman students enter those hallowed university halls to finally engage in serious academic pursuits.

"Being Gay Versus Being a Practicing Gay"

I am not frightened or scared of gays, and I do not suffer from homophobia. I believe it's more like "homo-dislike-ia" of homosexual behavior. Proponents of gay rights have their nasty habit of labeling anyone opposing gay behavior as being homophobic, and they expect me (or anyone like me) to feel guilty about my "discriminating." In my mind, there's a big difference between someone being gay and someone practicing gay behavior, which I personally find abhorrent and immoral.

Let me explain my position. Let's say that I own a restaurant. If two men come into my place of business, I don't know if they are gay or straight, so how could I possibly discriminate against them by not providing service? The same observation would hold true for two females sitting down at a table. If the two men or two ladies act like normal restaurant customers, even if the men show effeminate mannerisms or if the women seem to have masculine appearances, I cannot prove that they are "gay" and must cordially give them the benefit of the doubt.

Gay is okay! But there's a caveat here in my moral reasoning! Gay is okay if the gay person is celibate and engages in abstinence. In other words, I have no problem accepting gay folks if they are professed "gay virgins."

But if the two seated men (or women) begin holding hands incessantly and then lip-kissing for prolonged periods of time in "my restaurant," offending either my other patrons or myself, then I would definitely insist on evicting them. My conscience (moral compass) would determine that their practicing of "gay public behavior" is both inappropriate and unacceptable. Conversely, if the two men or two women were acting in more traditional restaurant etiquette, blending in with the crowd, then they would be more-than-welcome to dine in my establishment.

Now let's say that a photographer having strict Christian moral values is approached by a same-sex couple planning wedding pictures. The photographer automatically knows that the same-sex couple desires being "practicing gays" so he refuses them his services and hands them a business card of another photographer who would gladly accommodate their wedding day needs. But the same-sex couple does not honor the photographer's moral values and the adamant pair unreasonably threatens to sue him and destroy his business for wickedly violating their civil marital rights. I believe that such blatant discourtesy and inflexible disregard for another person's moral value system is both reprehensible and totally selfish, especially if the photographer had tried to peacefully resolve the issue by politely referring the vindictive same-sex couple to another more liberal-minded photographer. But in most cases, the two militant same-sex gays will attempt to destroy the photographer's livelihood simply for the purpose of stubbornly advancing their "immoral" agenda.

Let's say that a gay couple enters a bakery. The owner suspects that the pair happens to be gay but will gladly sell the twosome doughnuts, bagels, bread, cookies, Danish, cream puffs, eclairs, buns, rolls, muffins or even a birthday cake. But the intolerant gay couple wants the baker to cater their wedding and provide a reception cake, which is obvious code language for the duo being "practicing gays". The baker refuses, so a day later a vigilante mob of gay rights activists pickets the bakery in an effort to economically punish the Christian-oriented owner and consequently shut the business down.

As for my own personal behavior, I feel no need to publicly announce over and over my sexuality yelling-out the statement, "I am straight! I am straight!" Conversely, I can't lucidly fathom why it is so necessary for mostly "practicing gays" to repeatedly tell the world all about their unorthodox sexual orientation by shouting "I am gay! I am gay!" Who really cares?

Ask yourself several elementary questions to fully comprehend the absurdity of "same-sex marriage." "Was my grandfather a woman?" "Was my grandmother a man?" "Was my father a female?" "Was my mother a man?"

The gay and lesbian advocates are endeavoring to rewrite the dictionary, making opposites have the same definitions. These' obdurate social revisionists desire to create a 21st Century Tower of Babel where basic gender descriptions are virtually identical and where all differentiation pertinent to traditional male/female gender references are erased.

Years ago, a high school friend of mine came "out of the closet" and announced to his former classmates that he was a "homosexual" at the high school reunion. This old friend told me that he now is retired as a social worker and presently often performs nude "gay entertainment shows" up in western Canada.

My old friend came back to my town to visit his only living aunt, who immediately got in touch with me and related the news. I contacted the fellow and invited him to a restaurant nicely situated near a local river. My wife decided to tag along for a delicious meal.

During the dinner, I innocently asked my friend, "Tell me, how long have you' been officially declared gay?" Surprisingly, my benign inquiry sent my homosexual past acquaintance into a terrible verbal tirade. "Why do you call me gay?" he obnoxiously screamed out loud. "I'm not gay! I'm queer!" he boisterously ranted.

My wife and I were extremely embarrassed at his loud outburst occurring inside the crowded dining room. My old chum's unwarranted holler was indicative of "indecent gay public behavior," and if I were the establishment's manager or its owner, I would have either reprimanded my old pal or thrown him off the premises.

Even if a gay is a "practicing gay," it's okay with me as long as either he or she doesn't shout it in my face. I don't like wild and raucous gay parades, and I would never attend a raucous straight one, either. I contend that one's sexuality is private knowledge that is unfit for public consumption. If someone engages in homosexual conduct, I prefer that it be performed in a bedroom or in a hotel room, but please be sensitive to my "discriminating sensitivities" when out in public. Gays should exercise discretion and prudence when navigating around in public or in mixed company.

I suppose the principal reasons for my basic "homo-dislike-ia" are as follows:

Homosexuality goes against nature, or against the "natural order." Humans and animals reproduce through natural sexual intercourse. I have a problem with the "gay practice" promulgating that another man's rectum is an entrance and not the obvious exit that's been effectively designed by nature. Furthermore, let's assume that all animals were suddenly transformed into homosexuals. Cherish your dogs and your cats. Within twenty-five years, most animal species would cease to exist. And if all humans were homosexuals, then human existence would quite possibly disappear into oblivion after a century.

Oh yes, I know all about sperm and egg fertilization outside the womb and then having embryo implants inserted into the uterus. But don't we straight folks get it? Since practicing gays can't reproduce "naturally," adoption is the next logical and predictable step on their radical agenda.

Yes, I certainly know that married gays love each other very much, but how they practice their gay love (sodomy, etc.), well quite frankly, most religious-value-oriented people find the enactment of homosexual physical love to be egregiously offensive, repulsive and distasteful. And I just have to wonder how many same-sex marriage "adopted children" will grow-up being straight "traditional marriage" adults?

Yes, I suppose that Christian morality does "discriminate" against "the practice of gay behavior." Throughout recorded history, morality has always "discriminated" against immorality; good has "discriminated" against evil and moral right has "discriminated" against moral wrongdoing. The main objective of the uber-liberal left and of the gay rights activists is to cloud the prominent line between morality and immorality (under the surreptitious guise of Constitutional Rights), cleverly blurring the difference so much that soon it will be impossible to distinguish the contrast between "religious morality" and "legal immorality."

Forget all of the redundant, hackneyed legal arguments! Someone please explain to me exactly what is moral about homosexual-sexual activity? Or is gay the New Morality? In many cases, legalizing gay marriage is a government permission slip to immorally practice sodomy.

Much of this new 21st Century interpretation of the legal rights of gays (along with woman's rights' abortionists) can actually be attributed to the theories of two famous scientists, Charles Darwin (everything in animal life must evolve and change) and Albert Einstein (relativity). In effect, the Ten Amendments in the U.S. Bill of Rights are presently in direct conflict with the Old Testament's Ten Commandments.

Who can deny Albert Einstein's colossal impact on American culture? With the revolutionary Theory of Relativity came the unique notion that everything in society is "relative": yes indeed, nothing anywhere in America (save death and taxes) is absolute, is permanent or is fixed. And so now we have such things as the Bill of Rights to the Constitution coming into clashing conflict with widely-recognized traditional American family values.

The First Ten Amendments (under the guise of freedom of speech and freedom of expression) are now insidiously undermining the original Ten Commandments handed-down to Moses on Mt. Sinai, simply because now all truths (gay rights included) must be *relative* and not *absolute.*

Indeed, Darwin and Einstein have inadvertently affected the change in American values from absolute moral truths to relative values. This stunning societal switch happened when scientific thinking bled over into the social sciences in the early 1900s.

Take this rather disturbing gay rights marriage issue for example in regard to what Einstein's relativity has mutated into. Remember: everything today is rapidly evolving and must be "Relative" and not "Absolute" (for example, God's Ten Stone Tablet Laws). Two iconic

496

Commandments are: "Honor Thy Father and Thy Mother" and "Thou Shall not covet thy neighbor's wife!"

Just think about those two simple-but-sage Commandments for a second. The principal purpose of heterosexual (man-woman) marriage is to biologically conceive children and then to nurture them through mature parenting skills. The very vocal gay and lesbian political activists want gays to get married, to then adopt children and next to have loving families.

Now someone please explain this rather paradoxical situation to me. How could an adopted child with gay "parents" know who the mother is if two males are his or her parents? If two lesbians are his or her parents, which one is the father according to the very explicit Commandment: "Honor Thy Father and Thy Mother?" And if two gay married men are living next door, according to the Ninth Commandment, which one is "thy neighbor's wife" to be possibly sinfully coveted? Evidently, the sixth and the ninth Commandments are being blatantly violated by "practicing gays actively engaged in gay marriage."

Under the Charles Darwin "evolutionary pattern" and under Albert Einstein's politically correct "relativity law," which have both morphed into gay rights' laws, the idea of certain "sins" against God has been almost eradicated, and "sin" is now basically obsolete and simply a "relative" insignificant matter. In order for Biblical teaching to survive in this modern era, Ten Commandments' morality must gradually evolve into immorality, or else it is destined to perish when contradicted by perpetual "gay and freedom of choice immorality."

And needless to say, coincidentally, a woman's right to choose having an "Abortion" also very obviously violates the Stone Tablets' ABSOLUTE Commandments because a conceived child is sinfully killed, "Thou Shall Not Kill," and the fetus has no opportunity whatsoever to ever honor either a mother or a father, or for that matter, ever coveting a neighbor's wife.

And indeed, if the very vocal in-your-face abortion rights' activists/hypocrites had themselves been aborted before their sacred births by "Right to Choose" mothers, the conservative Christian community would not be having any legal wrangles with any of them at present.

Was Sodom and Gomorrah a Biblical myth or could it all soon again be happening right here in America? I'll let *you* be the judge of that! But still, acceptance of gays, lesbians and tolerating a woman's "right to choose" are currently being taught in our all-too-liberal socialistic public schools, thus affecting and influencing young impressionable minds, thanks partially to the impact of Darwin's Theory of Evolution and Albert Einstein's Theory of Relativity, both scientific principles ironically skewing American Constitutional Law and thus, changing former absolute tenets of morality as exhibited and taught for over two millenniums in the Bible's Ten Commandments.

No, I am not part of the invented left-wing propaganda nomenclature "homophobic." Instead, I am merely "dis-like-ia" of boisterous, bellicose, arrogant, obnoxious, egocentric, intolerant radicals who proudly practice sodomy and other gay and lesbian homosexual behavior. I mean, quite succinctly, does it totally defy standard definition and traditional explanation? What part of the precise dictionary word "immoral" do practicing gays not understand?

"Multicultural Education"

I had been named into "Who's Who Among American Teachers!" three times and two of those nominations have been by minority *students* (now Dean's List college achievers), one black and one Hispanic. Those *minority students* realized that *my* classroom standards were just as tough on them as they were on the majority Caucasian *students* and that I gave them no favoritism, slack or handicap for their minority-status ethnicity. I had always refused to "dumb down" the English curriculum (Grammar, Vocabulary, Literature, Writing Skills) to accommodate Accelerated English *students* that lacked motivation, desire, curiosity, cooperation, respect for teacher authority and a willingness to learn.

A year before I retired in 1999 my Middle School's English Department had a special curriculum meeting and the Administration and my Supervisor wanted to change and "modernize" the literature textbook program. The choice eventually narrowed down to two distinct textbook series (grades six-to-eight) and my school's nine English teachers voted on which company's series to incorporate into the school's English curriculum. Obviously administrative fiat (and pressure and trends from the State Department of Education) was more important than teacher *democratic* input and the English Department's overwhelmingly selected first choice was abruptly discarded because the other more "politically correct" literature textbook series from the administratively preferred company happened to have "more cultural diversity" and subsequently was more "multicultural."

For thirty-four years I had loved teaching imaginative literature featuring such accomplished authors including Edgar Allan Poe, Jack London, Alexander Dumas, Charles Dickens, H.G. Wells, Washington Irving, Jules Verne, Mark Twain, S.E. Hinton, George Eliot, Sir Arthur Conan Doyle, Victor Hugo, William Shakespeare, George Orwell, Kurt Vonnegut, O. Henry and James Thurber. Apparently, the fact that all of the aforementioned famous authors were "white" was a major problem because most of them had been effectively *excluded* in the newly acquired middle school literature texts. The old literature texts and program were too "white-oriented" and were not consistent with New Jersey and USA politically correct trends in "Multicultural Education."

The new eighth grade literature textbook featured on its cover a painting of Sam Adoquei's *Portrait of Rockney C.* A statement inside the text indicated that Sam Adoquei was born in the West African country of Ghana and that Adoquei was a contemporary artist that loved painting landscapes. Older literature textbooks might have featured on their covers works by Michelangelo, Rembrandt, Vincent van Gogh or Leonardo DaVinci but in this day and age those great contributing artists to *Western Civilization* have been demoted (in public schools) in deference to people like Sam Adoquei of Ghana, West Africa.

I must honestly admit that the new eighth grade administratively selected (and faculty overruled) literature textbook did have a token representation of established white authors. However the bulk of the contributors had names like Gloria Gonzalez (Cuban American), Luci Tapahonso (Navajo Indian), Yoshiko Uchida (Oriental American), Gwendolyn Brooks (Black American), Gary Soto (son of California migrant workers), William Saroyan (Armenian American), Maya Angelou (Black American), Diane Mei Lin Mark (Hawaiian American), Julio Noboa Polanco (bilingual poet), Judith Ortiz Cofer (Puerto Rican), Langston Hughes (Black American), Julia Alvarez (Hispanic), Ophelia Rivas (Mexican), Nereida Roman (Hispanic), Rudolfo A. Anaya (Mexican American), Esmerela Santiago (Puerto Rican), Wing Tex Lum (Chinese poet), Naomi Shihab Nye (Palestinian), Ved Mehta (from India), Paul Yee (American Chinese) and Li-Young Lee (Chinese).

There is no doubt in my mind that Multicultural Education is contributing to *socialistically* "dumbing down" American public schools. Many of the obscure "authors" being presented to American *students* in the name of "cultural diversity" have produced works that have weak vocabulary, shallow plots, lackluster characters, non-intellectual subject matter and demonstrably unsophisticated writing skills. Yet these minority *writers* (I wouldn't call all of them "authors") are presented to naïve and impressionable eighth graders as being valuable contributors to literature when *their* works pale in comparison to those of more traditional great *Western Civilization authors* that are presently being systematically removed from literature textbooks and gradually being replaced by (in most cases) obscure or lesser known "minority authors."

The same type of phenomenon is happening in middle and high school "History" classes' as is happening in Literature courses. When *Martin Luther King Day* was established as a National Holiday celebrated in January George Washington and Abraham Lincoln had to be diminished in stature to accommodate *MLK* on the school calendar. The traditional *Washington's Birthday* and *Lincoln's Birthday* were shrewdly consolidated into *"Presidents Day"* with "Washington and Lincoln's regular February birthdays being abandoned to allow room for *Martin Luther King Day* in January on the school calendar. And February (which used to almost exclusively belong to Washington and Lincoln) is now declared "Black American Month" in schools across the country. It is no wonder that American *children* now know more about Harriet Tubman, Crispus Attucks, Malcolm X, Jesse Jackson and George Washington Carver than they do about George Washington, Abraham Lincoln, Thomas Jefferson, Franklin D. Roosevelt and Dwight David Eisenhower. History (and literature) is being re-written by contemporary *re-visionists* that are attempting to diminish and discredit the accomplishments of white people and simultaneously magnifying the deeds and works of lesser-known minority figures.

One unique irony of all this Multicultural and curricular craziness is that teachers are now being held accountable for higher standardized test scores and "higher academic performance" when *their* curriculums are being systematically watered down and diluted to allow for the priority implementation of "Multicultural Education." Stories (by minority writers) in literature now have simple vocabulary and easy-to-understand (more simplistic) themes, characters and plots. Presently teachers are compelled to "teach down" to the *students'* level of achievement instead of challenging the kids seated in the desks to raise *their* level of performance up to the plateau of superior subject matter content being read and studied in the works of Poe, Twain, Shakespeare and Orwell. And this sort of insane farce is happening in public schools all over America.

Teachers are being coerced into propagating a system of American public-school education that is both designed and destined to fail. Teachers are not only accountable for teaching "weaker subject matter content" with low-academic challenge; they are also now held accountable to the State for *students* acquiring sufficient subject matter skills for the learners to pass state sponsored "*academic* standardized tests." Whatever happened to individual (*student*) responsibility?

"Multicultural Education" should not be eliminated from the curriculum but it should be diminished in influence to allow for a more accurate perspective of Literature and History to be presented to American school *children*. Crispus Attucks and Harriet Tubman should not supplant George Washington and Abraham Lincoln in February as equals sharing common historical prominence. And furthermore M.E. should be a part of regular traditional public-school history, literature, math' and science courses and not the entire curriculum in core subject areas.

And there's no way that Sam Adoquei is in the same league as Picasso or that Gloria Gonzalez and Yoshiko Uchida are the literary equivalents of Mark Twain and O. Henry. Our great American culture is being distorted and perverted enough by *MTV, VH-I* and by the *Comedy Channel* without ineffective social engineering and an excess of Multicultural Education polluting our American public school *students* and also our public schools already ambivalent academic standards.

I have been scrutinizing and studying Multicultural Education for four decades now and have heard too-many-times the lackluster educational jargon originating from college professors and from misguided advocates of M.E., and quite frankly those "elitist arguments" have become rather redundant, hackneyed and monotonous, and to think that I once wholeheartedly espoused those ethereal Multicultural Education principles as an idealistic teacher beginning my career back in September of 1965.

Despite the "Happy Face Image" that supporters of Multicultural Education are attempting to promote and propagandize, one distinct adjective comes to mind whenever I think about Multicultural Education and that particular word is "insidious." To the unsuspecting layman or college student "Diversity through M.E." is a nifty catch phrase that sounds awfully noble and pleasant to the ears upon hearing its utterance but the process is actually quite detrimental to the implementation of effective American education. I deliberately describe the scourge as *insidious* because over the past forty years M.E. has imperceptibly and very cunningly been introduced, advanced and perpetuated by its militant proponents without the American public realizing exactly how harmful, how treacherous and how detrimental the seemingly benign terminology appears to be.

Multicultural Education never clearly defines and identifies itself to the American public for what it really is. U.S. citizens automatically equate and associate M.E. with Bilingual Education and *ESL* (English as a Second Language), which the clever campaigners for M.E. never lucidly delineate and differentiate. Bilingual Education and *ESL* are indeed definite, positive, beneficial and necessary programs in our American public schools. Those two activities encourage and facilitate the cultural "Melting Pot" ideal whereby immigrant and certain minority *students* learn English and *ESL* and are hopefully successfully assimilated into regular grade-level classrooms after two-to-four years of exposure to a new language and a new culture.

But Multicultural Education is the complete opposite and inverse of Bilingual Education and *ESL*. Here's what Multicultural education really is: It is an attempt to manipulate history, English, literature, math' and science to make those subjects appear to *all students* in *all classrooms* that blacks, Hispanics and other minorities have contributed as much (if not more) to *Western Civilization* than Einstein, Jefferson, Washington, Thoreau, Shakespeare, Cervantes, Hugo, Twain, Newton, Steinbeck, Hemingway, Poe, Socrates, Plato, Aristotle, H.G. Wells, Arthur Conan Doyle, Abraham Lincoln and other noteworthy Caucasians have. Multicultural Education attempts to diminish the great "White" benefactors of the *Western World* while simultaneously elevating the works of obscure minorities to *their* plane. And the entire *student* body is exposed to and forced to suffer through this ruse in *their* various core curriculum textbooks and it's not just *ESL students* and Bilingual Education *children* being exposed to the ongoing brainwashing. And once the American public fully recognizes *that* important concept' separating M.E. from Bilingual Education and *ESL*, Multicultural Education will finally be satisfactorily challenged and ultimately rejected.

Although the Multicultural Education academic elitists claim to be "visionaries" they are in effect *revisionists*. Their impractical goal is to create a Utopian *future* by first rewriting the *past* and next changing the *present*. First relegate icons like Shakespeare, Cervantes, Jefferson and Newton and then give equal or greater stature to James Baldwin, Langston Hughes, Jesse Jackson and George Washington Carver. It is true that George Washington Carver remarkably found over three hundred applied uses for the peanut but the Multicultural Education activists want us to believe that the black scientist is just as important to American culture, science, technology and history as is Bill Gates and Thomas Edison. I don't think so!

This is not to say that minority inventors and authors are not to be studied in public schools. As a teacher I remember enjoying reading terrific biographies of Louis Armstrong, Harriet Tubman and Ralph Bunche with my literature classes but if Multicultural Education advocates had their way *that type* of minority-oriented reading should constitute the bulk of the literature, history, math' and science curriculums taught in our schools. And I truly admire the accomplishments of Colin Powell, Condie Rice and Clarence Thomas because they didn't need any cause, movement or national organization to inspire them to excellence. They (according to the American free enterprise tradition) reached down inside and motivated themselves "as individuals" to strive for greatness but many liberal socialistic Multiculturalists will call the three cited black achievers "Uncle Toms" since they have succeeded in the American competitive capitalistic culture on their own without a massive crusade or national "special interest agenda" advancing their *individual* attainments.

To get their way the M.E. elitists must shrewdly label and demonize traditional curriculum by calling it "Eurocentric," which automatically connotes a bad moniker. The long-range objective of the M.E. masterminds is to first condemn "Eurocentric" history, literature and science and then to systematically dismantle *"Western Civilization,"* which in reality is what the stereotype "Eurocentic" means.

I have eight elementary questions that pertain to significant developments in the history of mankind to ask the Multicultural elitists:

1) Where did the concept of *Democracy* begin? (Clue: the city is the capital of Greece)

2) Where did the *Renaissance* happen? (Clue: a country that has cities Florence, Rome and Venice)

3) Where did the *Age of Exploration and Discovery* begin? (Clue: cities like Genoa, Lisbon and London)

4) Where did the *Age of Enlightenment* have its roots? (Clue: Cities are found on rivers *Seine* and *Thames*)

5) Where did the *Protestant Reformation* take place? (Clue: Main players were Martin Luther of Germany and Henry the VIII of England)

6) Where did the *Industrial Revolution* get started? (Clue: a country that has cities named Manchester, Coventry, Sheffield, Leeds and New Castle)

7) Where did the *Atomic Age* happen? (Clue: the country has an eagle and an old chap named *Uncle Sam* as its symbols)

8) Where did the *Computer Age* have its origins? (Clue: corporations named *IBM, Microsoft, Intel* and *Apple* inspired it to happen).

The phenomenal freedoms that Americans enjoy today are outgrowths from the eight Eurocentric eras enumerated above. The concept of *Democracy* had originated in ancient Greece. The *Renaissance* liberated the human spirit and gave birth to cultural creativity. The *Age of Discovery* and *Exploration* sent men on great adventures to distant continents. The *Age of Enlightenment* swiftly led to the development of modern-day political philosophy. The *Protestant Reformation* loosened church authority and created an atmosphere where thinkers could contemplate and publish their works, where scientists could freely experiment and where inventors could create.

This newfound freedom of thought and expression eventually led to the development of Constitutional governments where the rights of citizens were protected under law. This fantastic newfound revolutionary *"Western Civilization"* liberty led to freedom of thought, which led to discovery, which led to technology, which led to progress and to our contemporary American (and European) way of life and high standards of living. But if the determined Multicultural Education zealots had their druthers the eight important eras of *Western Civilization* would be diminished and relegated because they are "Eurocentric" while the accomplishments of minorities will be elevated, given accolades and praised in our public schools, thus dooming our *students* to perpetual mediocrity.

Now knowing the above-mentioned salient facts, the majority of adult Americans would prefer having their *children* exposed to the same kind of "Eurocentric" education that *they* had received and understood as *"Western Civilization."* Every mature U.S. citizen with any scruples wishes to have the culture and history of America expertly transmitted to the younger generation, for that particular function is the central purpose of schools besides teaching *students* vital skills in reading, writing, speaking, mathematics, science and thinking. But if the adamant M.E. crusaders had their way teachers would have to pretend that *Western Civilization* never happened and that minorities were equally (if not more) responsible for the prosperity, economy and government that America presently maintains and enjoys.

The goal of Multiculturalists is to make every public-school *student* into a (tribal) member of a *UN* model "global village." This is why Multicultural Education is both un-American and unpatriotic. And those stubborn Multicultural Education advocates are very inflexible and quite obstinate too. They want you to believe that M.E. is a powerful new "science" and not a topic that should be comprehended as a "controversial issue" having an opposing point of view.

I had submitted a critique of M.E. to a college professor that maintains an "Essays on Multicultural Education" *Internet* website. The academic elitist refused to post my article on the basis that it was a prejudiced and biased view of Multicultural Education based on "stereotypes." Well now, isn't that a wicked contradiction! The M.E. proponents suddenly take on a "ban-the-essay censorship Fascist mentality" when someone who values *Western Civilization* dares to present an alternative position on *their* pet subject. And this is perhaps the greatest danger that will materialize should intellectual democratic elitist educators get their way: intolerance to other people's points of view and a blatant violation of *First Amendment* freedom of speech rights. And the irony of it all is that Multicultural Education is masked, marketed and sold as "democratic education." Such a canard is advertised as making American public-school *children* more aware of "diversity." I suppose *that* specific definition does not include *diverse* opinions or contrary philosophical positions about Multicultural Education.

Once the general public fathoms the true nature of the Multicultural Education fanatics' motives, I am convinced that the adherents and their movement will subsequently be soundly defeated. Their agenda (and they do have an agenda) is disguised as and masquerades as a necessary feature of "Educational Socialism," which conceals itself under the mantle of "Educational Democratic Equality for All." But if all *students* are *equal*, therefore no *student* could ever become more *academically* superior, more wealthy, more outstanding, more achievement-oriented, or more creative as long as he or she remains in a public school under the dominion of "Educational Socialism." In the Multicultural Education Universe there can be no Valedictorians or Salutatorians because that type of *academic* honor *discriminates* against the masses and makes the average *student* (minority or otherwise) feel inferior. "Just try and blend in with everyone else! Let's have a Melting Pot or giant salad!" is the watchword of the M.E. enthusiasts.

Educational Socialism and affiliated Multicultural Education are conveniently bolstered in classroom subjects with the implementation of a Neo-Industrial Education Factory-Oriented Classroom Model. As has been alluded to before, our American public schools are run like factories. Administrators and supervisors are the bosses, boards of education are the boards of directors, taxpayers are the stockholders, teachers are regarded as the employees in the system and the *students* are the products of a twelve-year-long manufacturing process. This educational factory model has been in existence for over a hundred years now and as long as it persists and as long as administrators are influenced by state-supported mandates like Multicultural Education, then mass mediocrity will in the final-analysis be the result. Schools are operated like factories and Multicultural Education will still guarantee a very nondescript product (the homogenized "salad-Melting Pot *students*" constituting the entire *student* body).

Now here's where and why I believe that Multicultural Education will ultimately be vanquished. Multicultural Education proponents are generally also Educational Socialists. In addition to desiring to dismantle *Western Civilization* (calling it "Eurocentric") they absolutely loathe capitalism, the indispensable economic engine of America. If it weren't for "free enterprise" (capitalism) and the economic security that the accumulation of personal wealth affords and provides then our great American democracy would be vulnerable to eroding, then decaying into civil unrest and gradually heading in the direction of anarchy. Think about it! Our *free* enterprise economy is what makes Americans truly *free* and the essential economic idea of "risk-reward" is hardly ever taught in our public schools because it involves free enterprise and individual achievement.

But Ivory Tower Educational Socialists think that "capitalism" and "competition" cause *students* to become selfish and greedy without *sharing* with others. They frown upon capitalism as being a negative influence because it engenders *students* becoming too egocentric and arrogant and therefore capable of being distinguished as achievement-oriented individuals from the rest of the group (their *student comrades*). In M.E. classrooms *students* are discouraged from thinking outside the box because then they would be an obvious danger to the system and a threat to the dominance of Educational Socialism. Blend in and be exactly like everyone else in the great *Melting Pot*. Be an average pepper, carrot or onion in the Giant American Salad. Don't aspire to accomplish more than your fellow *students* and never be exposed to the evils of capitalism and free enterprise. "Now let's eliminate grades so that everyone can think and be on the same level at all times because we're all *equal*." That is another immediate goal of these educational socialistic maniacs.

Capitalism (a wonderful concept of Eurocentric *Western Civilization*) is the great hope and foundation of any free and democratic society. Capitalism (Wall Street and Main Street) is what gives the *United States of America* its stability and security. Heaven forbid if our entrepreneurs and risk takers are ever silenced! They employ people', and these ambitious pioneers open new frontiers and establish new dynamic businesses and corporations. It's all quite simple and "Elementary, dear Watson!" as Sherlock Holmes often states. Without capitalism there would be no profits, no employees, no taxes being paid, no companies, no businesses, no government programs, no public schools, no colleges being financed and contributed to, and no wealth being created. Without capitalism the *United States'* flourishing economy would soon deteriorate and go the way of the *Soviet Union*.

Thank Heaven that free enterprise is still the most vibrant and productive force in America! But please remember: college professors in general are liberal-minded and many of them are elitists that despise free enterprise while advancing the causes of Educational Socialism and of Multicultural Education.

Instead of endorsing a hypothesis that postulates that America is a great Melting Pot where all public-school students are *equal* (the same) American Education needs to get on the right track and instruct its students, "If you want to achieve individual prosperity become a capitalist and not a factory or office worker. You have the potential to become an employer and not settle for just being an employee. Pursue excellence and work hard towards everything that you attempt or do and never simply settle for being just like everyone else in a cultural salad! Dig deep down inside yourself and produce more than your peers! Become an individual and don't be satisfied just being referred to as one!" But that inspiration will never happen on a broad scale as long as Educational Socialists (that hate American capitalism) and Multicultural Educationists (that resent "Eurocentric" history and literature) are at the academic helm and wielding tremendous influence over the fate of millions of American public-school *students*. "Ambition" is now an absolute dirty word in American education! It suggests that an aggressive self-motivated *child* will distinguish himself or herself from his or her fellow *students* and learn to grow and excel as an individual.

The elitist critics of free enterprise again use labeling to endeavor smearing and debunking capitalism, accusing the greedy method of being "trickle-down economics!" But will someone please explain to me how gravity could be successfully defied by having "trickle-up economics?" And I boldly venture to state that most Multicultural Education elitists are also Educational Socialists.

In conclusion, only free enterprise (and our *students'* awareness of and their belief in its greatness), a continuation of the teachings of *Western Civilization* and some sober realistic thinking will ensure the future of the *United States of America*. The public must first become aware that Multicultural Education is the problematic antithesis of this country's past glory. But as long as Multiculturalists are powerful elements performing their egregious harm inside American Educational Philosophy and Psychology, our public schools are destined and doomed to mediocrity.

There will be no future Multicultural Utopia produced by the Educational Aristocracy (college professors, school administrators, school supervisors, curriculum coordinators, and State-Mandated Programs) as the academic boyars would like us to believe. Multicultural Education isn't even a placebo let alone a civilization-saving elixir. Our only hopes for a prosperous future are Free

508

Enterprise (capitalism) and the preservation of *Western Civilization*, two extraordinary disciplines that the educational elite (in general) ignore, abhor and reject. Please remember that the opposite of the phrase "Cultural Unity" is the phrase "Multicultural Diversity."

And it was principally because of that "politically correct and multicultural" new literature textbook series that had been administratively imposed on my middle school's English Department that convinced me it would be expedient for John Wiessner to retire from the teaching profession after thirty-four years of dedicated classroom instruction.

"A Self-Analysis"

From my perspective, everyone has two basic psychological needs: a need to socialize with others of his/her species and secondly, a need to be alone by oneself. I, like most introverted writers and authors, much greater prefer the latter to the former. Confidentially, I totally enjoy being removed from social clutter for my self-motivated brain to quietly explore the development of new story plots and themes. When I'm preoccupied writing, my fleeting thoughts at that intense moment are just as indispensable as oxygen and food. To preface my personal observations, I maintain that an author's examination of conscience is both a meritorious and a healthy sort of worthwhile enterprise.

As a young boy attending the afternoon black and white cowboy movie matinees at the Rivoli Theater on Bellevue Avenue in downtown Hammonton, New Jersey, I quickly comprehended the valuable concept that is readily apparent in the nomenclature, "It is better to make dust than to eat it." In other words, I always admired either the Sheriff or the Marshal leading the on-a-mission posse and simultaneously felt sorry for the poor deputies having to eat the dust of the head guys up front chasing the dastardly outlaws across the cactus-laden wilderness. And oh yes, Rule #1 of being a nationally recognized author is that no one will take either you or your writing seriously until *you* first take you and your writing seriously.

When I was a New Jersey teacher of literature for thirty-four years, one of my favorite tales that I used to orally read with my classroom students was the mythological story of "Perseus." One fine day, the young Greek hero was curiously standing on a mountain cliff when the goddess Athena appeared, then approached him upon a floating cloud and imperatively asked, "Before I send you on a dangerous challenge to slay the formidable monster known as Medusa the Gorgon, I'd like for you Perseus to courageously answer this one simple question. 'Which would you rather have; a soul of clay or a soul of fire'?"

Perseus did not hesitate to answer the odd interrogative by intrepidly articulating, "A soul of fire, because most vain cowardly men commonly possess souls of clay. Dear goddess, pardon my audacity but I won't ever want to be greedy and weak like most other craven humans behave on this rather corrupt planet!"

And so, I wholeheartedly maintain that to be the proud-but-humble owner of "a soul of fire" happens to constitute the very essence of my literary philosophy. A mortal in quest of literary excellence must search for and find a viable writing voice to adequately complement his or her writing style, and then the aspiring author should avoid being timid and next boldly address any relevant issue that should enter his or her psyche.

While vacationing with our wives ten years ago on the West Coast, a professor friend and I stepped into a Palm Springs, California bar to savor a few cold drafts of beer. Being gregarious, we struck-up a conversation with two other elderly retired tourists, and the topic of discussion soon changed from "the pleasant weather" to the subject of "property." The two wealthy gray-haired gentlemen each bragged that they had owned houses in Florida and California, and each respective fellow extensively cherished his coveted lengthy stock portfolio. "What kind of properties do you own?" the first zealous capitalist bluntly asked me.

I pondered the conceited guy's direct inquiry and soon carefully replied, "Most of the property I own is 'Intellectual Property'." "I am the author of 52 copyrighted books, and every idea, every character, every plot scenario, every conflict, every aspect in the stories' constructions is owned exclusively by me. I honestly mean Guys," I paused and deliberately emphasized, "I do own my New Jersey home, I have some blue-chip stocks and bonds, and my wife and I have an acre of land in the Poconos along with several building lots in Florida, but believe me, the most priceless properties I value still are the intellectual properties I own that nicely exist in my fifty-two published books."

Naturally, my strange unexpected declaration made my new bar acquaintances pause and stare blankly at me with their dual mouths agape as my New Jersey pedagogue/companion giggled profusely and then anxiously proceeded to swallow-down another gulp of his delicious cold beer.

Eminent New England nineteenth century writer Ralph Waldo Emerson had imaginatively invented the now-obsolete "Theory of Transcendentalism", the romantic notion that Emotion should "transcend" Reason in order for a regular person to ultimately experience true satisfaction and complete fulfillment in life. On the contrary, I staunchly subscribe to the principle of what I describe as "Reverse Transcendentalism", or the requisite speculation that Reason should valiantly triumph and dominate over Emotion in a story presentation.

Yes indeed, it is true that one could have emotion demonstrated in the content of one's story, but the evolution of the plot along with the accompanying vital subplots ought to be both logical and plausible in construction for the captivated reader to easily grasp the tale's scope and sequence. The prescription for a terrific story is quite elementary

512

from my lifelong writing point of view. The appropriate literary formula to faithfully apply is this: Quality + Quantity + Author Discipline + Perseverance = Eventual Success. In the final analysis, *that* particular recipe has loyally worked for me.

Being a public-school English teacher for thirty-four years, I had been fully aware of distinguished educational psychologist Abraham Maslow's Theory of Hierarchal Needs, represented in a standard pyramid illustration. At the bottom of the isosceles matrix is any living creature's need for food, shelter and clothing (fur or other external protection). Then above those fundamental essentials is a definite need for basic socialization, recognition, love, acceptance "emotional security" and group or family approval.

And now, inside the triangle formation, we get into the more complicated and intricate "lower thinking skills," which along with important problem-solving ability, dramatically and intellectually separates mankind from the lower animals. Here's where I selectively believe the strict differentiation between writers and authors comes into stark focus.

I strongly insist that *authors* write fiction novels and fictional short stories, and on the other hand, *writers* systematically research and organize non-fiction books, term papers and newspaper and magazine narratives. Non-fiction writing (in its architectural format) involves the explicit use of general description. The whole process is akin to newspaper front page articles that are characterized by the creation of "a hook" introduction to gain the reader's instant attention. Next the non-fiction *journalist* accurately exploits the presentation of "Who? What? When? Where? How? and "Why?" in his' or her' newspaper article. And then to add a personal non-fiction touch, a few direct quotes are slickly thrown into the *writer's* process of front-page narrative construction in order to add a distinct degree of "human interest" to the initial exposition being adroitly fabricated and communicated.

On the periodical's Editorial Page, certain higher level thinking skills are evident with the deft utilization of Opinion, Interpretation and Analysis, three distinct thought synthesizes that are significantly emblematic of us mortal humans and which are not widely present anywhere in the lower animal world. College term reports and theses papers are very similar to a *writer* preparing a serious newspaper or magazine task. One must austerely employ lower-level thinking skills encompassing the methods of Research, Description, Interpretation, Analysis and possibly Opinion/Conclusion.

But conversely, *fiction authors* take their thinking dynamics to a higher level than non-fiction writers do. They perilously enter the lofty realms of Imagination, Creativity, Originality and Invention, thus attempting to fearlessly imitate the Glorious Creator. Renowned Abraham Maslow calls this highest level of thought ascension "Self-Actualization," and *this* coveted perch is the thinking plateau that authors audaciously pursue and that non-fiction writers dare not enter or tread.

Three areas of human classification represent the population of American academic organization ranging from lowly kindergarten up to the prominent university niche. It has been statistically established that around 75% of the people associated with American education are students, 22% are dedicated teachers, aides, librarians, instructors, administrators and professors, and the remaining 3% or so are the gifted creators and inventors of knowledge.

By consistently producing quality fiction as being an elevated dimension of accepted literature, authors are conscientiously competing for respectable inclusion into the revered 3% "creators and inventors" who are superbly contributing to the advancement of modern civilization.

Even though I consider Non-Fiction scribes as "Writers," and despite the fact that my literary efforts venture mostly into "Fiction," I insist that I am not yet an *author* in the same sense as Mark Twain, O. Henry, Jack London, Edgar Allan Poe or Nathaniel Hawthorne, but if people are reading and relishing my works a century from now, I will have then satisfactorily risen my accumulated literature up to international fame and therefore, my fictional works will have earned me the coveted designation of finally becoming an "Author."

A certain nebulous facet of fiction writing is the obscure enigmas of Creativity, Imagination, Invention and Originality. Exactly what are the defining characteristics of these often-elusive authorial phantoms? In reality, it's fairly easy to explain but rather difficult to fully fathom.

First of all, I realize that I first require a suitable outline to effectively arrange and present a well-structured story in a rational manner. What I'm about to disclose is my former secret method that predictably always had worked for me, and I hope I'm not precariously jinxing myself by hereby revealing its former surreptitious mechanics. The up-to-now reliable practice ordinarily determined how something inside my head mystically connects like an electrical extension cord into the Universe's master wall socket AC power plug.

Allow me to first sincerely divulge that I am not a particularly religious human being. Now in my home's computer room there are

514

three lamps (two identical table ones and the third light located upon a tall thin stand), which I mentally reference as 'the Father, the Son and the Holy Spirit'. Like a submissive suppliant, I reverently invoke each lamp individually to assist me in my writing endeavor, obediently reciting in a silent prayer, "Lamp of wisdom, lamp of light; please help me' to create a new story idea." Amazingly, this unique, mysterious and esoteric technique has always enabled me to become spontaneously erudite and capable of "Inventing" numerous outlines and subsequently, of scheming-up quite "Original" characters, settings, conflicts and noteworthy story patterns.

Essentially, I acknowledge that there are two types of Creativity: "Reactionary Creativity" and "Imaginative and Original Creativity". Reactionary Creativity is rather easy to perform. A good example is shown in the biography of L. Frank Baum, who was sitting as a restless patient inside a doctor's nondescript office. According to the legend, Baum was thinking about what should be the name of a fantasy land that would be the functional title to a new children's book he had been contemplating. Out of sheer boredom, L. Frank glanced over at the doctor's metallic filing cabinet of patients' information and then perceptively noticed two ordinary-looking drawers. The first compartment was labeled "A-N", and the bottom one remarkably read "O-Z." 'Oz!' Baum mentally exclaimed. "That's it! My new book has both a title and a very neat setting!'

Here are several instances of Reactionary Creativity from my own life's mundane adventures. While I had been authoring the novel *The Great Teen Fruit War*, I was driving my auto' on Fairview Avenue in downtown Hammonton when the railroad crossing gates began descending along with the objects' corresponding flashing red lights. Immediately I "Imagined" the Blueberry Gang kids tying two Peach Gang teens to the already descended gates as the extended passenger train speedily whizzed-by. When the gates eventually ascended (in the novel), the two Peach Gang kids were elevated to straight vertical positions, giving the victims the appearance of being primitively crucified to the all-astonished motorists encountering and passing-by the bizarre prank scene.

Another occasion of Reactionary Creativity was when my wife and I were vacationing in beautiful Taormina, Sicily. We were staying at the quaint Hotel Villa Schuller, which had a terrific penthouse lounge that allowed a fantastic view of distant Mt. Etna. I 'Imagined', 'Now I really have discovered the ending to my latest detective story. Terrorists are captured by the local Mafia. The U.S. government had hired the Mafia to perform the critical service and pays the awesome Messina and Palermo crime syndicate a handsome stipend to conveniently dispose of the diabolic villains. The Sicilian Mafia rents a huge helicopter, and then the notorious mobsters toss the alarmed handcuffed terrorists into the steaming lava crater of the gorgeous island's constantly active volcano.'

A third situation where Reactionary Creativity is identifiable was when I had ventured on an excursion through Bristol, Pennsylvania on my nostalgic way to Levittown, where my family had resided from 1953-'59. Immediately a worthy story title popped into my head "Doing Bristol," and then thanks to my knowledge of United States geography, I recollected that in addition to Bristol, Pennsylvania, there is a Bristol, Virginia, a Bristol, Connecticut, a Bristol, Tennessee, a Bristol, England and a Bristol Rhode Island. I 'Imagined' that the main character of the story would go to sleep in one Bristol (Pennsylvania) and then each night would surprisingly wake-up each morning in another Bristol until the protagonist gradually would wind-up back in a familiar motel in his original destination, Bristol, Pennsylvania.

Another form of Reactionary Creativity that I habitually employ is when I satirize or parody the serious works of acclaimed writers like William Shakespeare, Edgar Allan Poe, O. Henry, Mark Twain, Jack London and Nathaniel Hawthorne. This type of "Reactionary Creativity" comes easy to me because all I have to do is rewrite what already has been expertly organized as quality literature.

However, since "Original Creativity" is much harder to achieve than "Reactionary Creativity" happens to be, that's precisely where and when the three magical, admirable, aforementioned computer room lamps come into play. Quite candidly, I often seek (and obtain) inspiration originating from outside myself. As I've already indicated, the lamps (along with my special personal incantations of solicitation) were always a trilogy of fabulous charms for me to be able to accomplish my central authorial ambition. But I cannot guarantee (toward the end of my writing career) that my little treasured secret would magnificently work for everyone or anyone else.

Throughout my life, I've always been a rather persistent, stubborn, and obstinate individual, and coincidentally, the general thrust of my exerted energy was specifically to prove the venerable Albert Einstein wrong. Einstein is reputed to have confidently stated, "A stupid person keeps redundantly committing the same silly mistakes over and over again without ever obtaining any favorable results."

Well then, after I had written my first book *Enchanta,* the overall sales effect was absolutely negligible. After my thirtieth book, Einstein's genius was still essentially infallible with me having dismal sales' results from my frustrating labor. But after my forty-eighth book *Hawthorne: Hazed, Hooked, Hammered and Hijacked,* the popularity of my previous literary products suddenly began to proliferate. For the past fifteen years, I just felt totally compelled to prove Einstein's provocative declaration to be (in my extraordinary case) erroneous.

Since childhood, finding my environment rather lackluster and horribly mediocre, at every opportunity I've attempted to "think outside the box". But conversely, morally speaking, I've always tried my best to "believe inside the box". Sometimes I've discovered my subjective conscience to be at continuous war with my objective-oriented mind. At times, even to this very day, this ongoing mental struggle is a troubling disappointment to me, and the battle causes my intelligence to be plagued with both mental and emotional turbulence. In truth, many authors are hapless tortured souls of their own doing.

I conjecture that three elements have over the years formed my spirit's core philosophy. Sometimes the three items are compatible; sometimes the triple ingredients are combative adversaries. To be sure, I've always honored the ancient teachings of the Ten Commandments, especially adhering to the principal tenets "Thou shall not kill; Thou shall not steal; Honor thy father and mother; and Thou shall not covet thy neighbor's goods."

But then my thinking has also been influenced by Ancient Greek thought, an afflictive effect that encourages me to literally doubt almost anything and everything. The sterling expressions of Socrates, Plato, Aristotle and Aristophanes have suggested to me that I should chronically be cynical and mutually skeptical of most things, including religious history and the Bible's *Old Testament.*

And in retrospect, the third feature prevalent in my ambivalent personality, Jeffersonian thought, is thoroughly embodied in the Declaration of Independence and also in the Bill of Rights. This American "freedom of thought" perspective often puts my mind at odds with prevalent religious teachings and with their "absolute truths".

But in the final analysis, my moral compass (hammered into my vulnerable cerebrum for eleven years by various Catholic school nuns and priests) is usually victorious over Reason, the Commandments trumping both Greek Thought and the alluded-to Ten Amendments to the United States Constitution.

In conclusion, I generally try to behave in a humble/modest life style even though I'm relatively proud of my abundant stories and novels. But to authentically communicate with the outside world, I needed a nom de plume in a similar fashion that Samuel Langhorne Clemens needed to be Mark Twain, William Sydney Porter needed to be O. Henry and Mary Anne Evans needed to be George Eliot. Lacking full confidence writing as John Wiessner, I respectfully summoned the very necessary assistance of the magical "Trinity 3-Way Illumination Lamps" stationed in my upstairs computer room, and then in a sudden inspiration, my brain incredibly came-up with the all-too-obvious pseudonym "Jay Dubya," which is a genuine corruption of my very common "J.W." initials.

"The Liberals 3 Card Playing Deck"

The very vocal American left-wing political entity consists mostly of the ultra-liberal Main Street Media, Far-left Democrats, the archaic and self-patronizing NAACP, Black Lives Matter agitators, Radical Feminists, anarchistic Occupy Wall Street fanatics along with various militant Socialist and Communist affiliates. These various "Grievance Industry" factions are not playing the U.S. Game of Life with a full deck, their overly aggressive poker hands featuring three major playing cards: the Race Card, the Victim Card and the Slavery Card. And any fair-minded conservative traditionalist who challenges the validity of the repetitious 3 Liberal Playing Cards is automatically labeled a Racist, a Bigot, a Fascist or a Neo-Nazi.

The misguided Liberals erroneously think and believe that the United States is a "Democracy". But our colonial Founding Fathers created "a Republic," featuring a very just and reasonable Bill of Rights. *Individual* DEMOCRATIC rights are specifically outlined in the U.S. Constitution's First Ten Amendments, and these honorable covenants grant individual citizens an array of privileges ranging from Freedom of Speech to Freedom to Worship; from Freedom of the Press to Freedom to Bear Arms. The wisdom principle of "A Republic" (including the American Republic) is that *this* enduring form of government is primarily based on "the Rule of Law," and *our* American form of government also heavily relies on the preservation and continuation of the nation's culture and traditions for its survival. A "Democracy" tends to foment defiance of established Law, enacts opposition to "Old Morality", believes in the dismantling of time-honored traditions and finally, the Far-Left desires a quixotic "Revision of America's Culture and History".

Our very wise Founding Fathers aptly understood that historically, "Republics" last much longer than do "Democracies". For example, the Athenian Democracy lasted for only 186 years while the Roman Republic lasted for over five centuries, finally falling because of the same debilitating conditions that our current American Republic is detrimentally experiencing: Open Borders, Anarchy and Government Corruption. The Roman Empire had long been besieged with invading Visigoths, Vandals and Huns (Open Borders), barbaric tribes who later fought among themselves and then battled against the Roman Legions (Anarchy), while avaricious Roman Government Officials and Politicians bought votes from citizens by accepting bribes and simultaneously raiding the Empire's Treasury (Corruption). Yes,

History tends to repeat itself! The U.S. Republic is presently being negatively besieged and affected by Illegal Aliens (Open Borders), clashing Left-Wing and Right-Wing coalitions (Anarchy) and most obviously, modern-day avaricious Politicians (Corruption). These three present-day catalysts are the same malignant factors that had led to the gradual fall of the once-mighty Roman Republic.

Vociferous Far-Left liberals don't really pragmatically practice the U.S. Constitution and the Declaration of Independence, which the latter document advocates the promotion of INDIVIDUAL "Life, Liberty and the Pursuit of Happiness". Far-Left Liberals COLLECTIVELY believe in GROUP CAUSES rather than espousing the conviction of *each person* being directly responsible for his or her actions, which is what the U.S. Constitution and our Founding Fathers were all about: Citizen Responsibility balancing the deployment and enjoyment of abundant Citizen Rights! In essence, each INDIVUDUAL is a free-thinking Sovereign Human Being, a small model of our Sovereign Nation.

As has been already indicated, the Liberals myopic 3 Card Playing Deck redundantly advances the Race Card, the Victim Card and the Slavery Card. Liberals have a short-sighted perception of human history when they think that only blacks had been slaves. Let's journey back into the ugly past a thousand-years or so. Most anyone reading this essay more-than-likely had ancestors in the year 1,000 A.D. who were slaves, serfs, servants, chattels, vassals, peasants, indentured workers or poor sharecroppers. A millennium ago people (the masses) were stratified into virtual caste systems without any chance for any upward social mobility or "individual accomplishment". Humans were classified either in the wealthy 2% noble class or into the 98% exploited fiefdom servitude class.

Then on June 15, 1215 a political miracle began taking shape in Runnymede, England. King John (brother and successor to King Richard the Lion-hearted) was compelled by the threat of bankruptcy to sign the Magna Carta (Great Charter), which granted certain rights and privileges to Norman Barons, which over the next several centuries evolved and led to lower-class Saxons eventually obtaining their own *individual* right to own property and to *not* be dependent on wealthy Norman Nobles for security and protection in exchange for *their* grueling labor. Over the course of several-centuries, the English economic/political progress (began by the Magna Carta) slowly led to the Age of Exploration (Columbus, Magellan, etc.) and then the Age of Enlightenment (Voltaire, John Locke), the influential predecessors to the Age of the American and French Revolutions.

520

Beginning in 1776, our Founding Fathers finally freed the suppressed inhabitants of the original 13 colonies from the vile tyranny of King George III of England. The Revolutionary War along with the Declaration of Independence and the U.S. Constitution wonderfully granted colonial men the civil rights that elevated the general population from second-class subject-of-king status to citizens being able to have free enterprise, to participate in upward economic mobility, and to basically enjoy the benefits of both reward and profit through INDIVIDUAL initiative, thus allowing free members of the NEW REPUBLIC to engage in the unique experiment of American Capitalism.

What the Far-Left must fathom is that the White Man had to emancipate himself from British Monarchial Despotism in 1776 before the White Man could ever LIBERATE the black slaves from *their* plantation masters 70 or so years later. And yes, it was a Republican President named Abraham Lincoln who had authorized the Emancipation Proclamation, and yes, it was Southern Democrats who (after the Civil War) created the KKK to deliberately intimidate the recently freed slaves.

The Liberal Race/Victim/Slave Card peddlers don't have a monopoly when it comes to being discriminated against. For example, I never knew my Polish grandparents, descendants of Slavs (Slaves, Serfs and Peasants). My father's father had been a logger in upstate Michigan. A raging forest fire destroyed his camp, and not having any property insurance, my paternal grandfather was devastated after going bankrupt, and died shortly thereafter. No welfare safety net or food stamps existed in the early 1900s. My (also legal Ellis Island) Polish grandmother, who I had never known had later died from the horrendous influenza epidemic that flourished in East Coast cities from 1917-1919.

After my paternal grandfather's death, my father's family had moved from Michigan to Baltimore to be near Polish relatives. English and German people had settled in America decades before the Poles immigrated, so consequently, Poles had trouble getting work from the already established British and German employers. A nearby Baltimore business named the John F. Wiessner Brewery (later defunct in the 1920s because of Prohibition) affected the opportunity for my family surname to be changed from the Polish Wiesniewski to the German Wiessner so that my *discriminated against* father and his five sisters could more easily get factory jobs in Baltimore City.

My maternal Sicilian grandfather (who also legally came to America via Ellis Island) daily operated a fruit and vegetable pushcart on Ninth Street in Philadelphia. My maternal grandmother's family was so poor that she had to wear her father's old tattered and weatherworn shoes to school and was egregiously mocked and scorned by the other more fortunate children whose families were of better means. After my grandparents married, Grandpop Antonio diligently saved and finally had enough money to buy five acres of ground on Route 30 in Hammonton, New Jersey, where he and Grandmom Annie built a small roadside farm market. An established British farm family owned the adjacent property and proceeded to build a much larger farm market only 50 feet away from the one constructed by my grandparents, obviously in a strong effort to run "the Sicilians" out of business and out of town. After 3 years of intense competition, my maternal grandparents prevailed and were able to proudly buy the larger farm market from the disgruntled English farm family.

And then there was my wife's Sicilian father and uncle who in the early 1940s were shunned and ostracized from playing baseball and football by other area Italian kids because the two brothers happened to have a darker complexion. Like my maternal grandparents, my wife's father and uncle prevailed in a hostile social environment and eventually became very successful businessmen, not because of any COLLECTIVE POLITICAL CAUSE but because of their own INDIVIDUAL DETERMINATION to overcome discrimination. They refused to be *"victims"!*

In the early-to-mid 20th Century, America was a true "Melting Pot". The established immigration system worked because the new ethnic arrivals were predominantly from Europe, were of the Christian/Catholic/Jewish faiths, possessed and fervently practiced the Protestant Work Ethic, and were mostly Polish, Irish and Italian Caucasians who (overcoming difficulty) gradually blended-in with the already entrenched English and German early settlers.

But then occurring in 1965, Democrat President Lyndon Johnson implemented the Immigration and Nationality Act, which in 1968 soon morphed into the Hart-Celler Act, a law that changed the Immigration Quota System from being 90% White European newcomers and 10% People of Color to a reversal of 10% European and mostly new people from Africa, from the Middle East, from Central and South America and from Asia. That 1968 experimental "Melting Pot" is not working too well in the year 2018, and its unintended consequences are burgeoning our very beleaguered Welfare System, our schools and our prisons because many of these new clannish arrivals are not assimilating swiftly and smoothly into our American culture, principally because they have DIVERSE religions, languages, cultures and more relaxed "work ethics" carried-over from former dependency lifestyles in their previous countries. The current socialistic "Diversity Movement" is actually CULTURAL DISUNITY and WESTERN CIVILIZATION DILUTION in disguise.

The Democrats appear to relish putting new U.S. arrivals on Welfare and Food Stamps, thus insuring the Liberal Party of future votes in future elections. But honestly, Republicans also like having the new arrivals (especially from Central and South America) for cheap labor, and the GOP too shares the blame in this illegal immigration matter because these aforementioned migrant populations are a good source of higher company profits.

The Liberal Dems often criticize American Capitalism as being "Trickle-Down Economics", but someone please explain to me exactly how anti-economic-gravity "Trickle-Up Economics" is supposed to work? If the Democrats are so concerned about "Income Inequality", don't they realize that "Income Equality" in code language means "Socialism?" But Socialism (which had failed miserably in the now-extinct USSR) is the gospel of countless college professor demagogues, many of whom could never survive in the highly competitive "free PRIVATE-SECTOR markets of Wall Street and Main Street". I can still hear my father lecturing, "Son, if you listen to and advocate the indoctrinating words of your Liberal college professors, you'll never make more money than *they* do lecturing from their PUBLIC-SECTOR Ivory Towers!"

The only legitimate reason for foreigners to secretly cross U.S. borders is the need for them to escape Religious Persecution and Political Persecution in their native land. Natural disasters are also a legitimate reason to enter the U.S. without a VISA or PASSPORT. Economic Opportunity and Receiving Welfare are not bona-fide justifications for encroaching into the United States illegally, for most of the world's six billion "DREAMERS" would prefer living in the United States than in their current country. But as already stated, Democrats gladly welcome "Open Borders" because their existence almost guarantees more future Dem "DREAMER and CHAIN MIGRATION" voters at the ballot box.

The Far-Left elitists sanctimoniously claim to have the High Moral Ground, when actually their conceited High Morality is a bane of Immorality where the First Ten Amendments to the U.S. Constitution are being systematically utilized to dismantle the Ten Commandments handed-down to Moses on Mt. Sinai. Consider these circumstances:

Old Morality: Thou Shall Not Kill

New Left-Wing Morality: Have 2 million U.S. abortions annually.

Old Morality: Honor Thy Father & Mother

New Left-Wing Morality: Get rid of sexist terms Father & Mother.

Old Morality: Thou Shall Not Covet Thy Neighbor's Wife.

New Morals: Your neighbor's wife could be a male.

Old Morality: Thou Shall Not Commit Adultery.

New Morality: Let's have total sexual & homosexual liberation.

Old Morality: Thou Shall Not Steal.

New Morality: Make Government Politicians steal *for you* by more taxation.

Finally, President Trump has been greatly criticized for saying that "Both Sides were equally to blame at Charlottesville". True, the Alt-Right consisted of White Supremacists, White Nationalists, KKK Members, Neo-Nazis Ultra-Conservatives "and some good people". But conversely, the acrimonious Alt-Left doing battle at Charlottesville was composed of Antifa Anarchists, Black Lives Matter Insurgents, Occupation Wall Street Maniacs, Neo-Socialists, Neo-Communists and "some good people". Charlottesville was a classic 2017 version of WWII's Adolf Hitler versus Joseph Stalin, with both warring "Fascist" sides acting belligerently in an Anti-American fashion.

It's been eight generations since the terrible Civil War and the abolishment of Slavery. And as far as U.S. Blacks are concerned, I think that the aggregate minority incessantly calling themselves "Black Americans" and "Afro-Americans" fundamentally alienates their CAUSE from the remainder of our great society. When Blacks simply begin to call themselves "Americans", I firmly believe that a better harmony could be attained between Caucasians and Blacks.

Now imagine that your life is graphically represented as an isosceles triangle. At the apex is you; then immediately below is your spouse; then below you or him/her are your children; then below your offspring are your relatives, your community, your church and your charities; then below *that* level are the people around the world, and lastly at the bottom of the triangle, are climate change and the people

524

with AIDS around the globe. The Liberals want YOU and ME to invert or reverse *that* "Traditional Triangle" and have *us* concerned mostly about CAUSES such as climate change, the people around the world with AIDS, and at the bottom of the newly-established inverted triangle, the least important elements are *you* and *your spouse.* Liberals want you (and me) to sacrifice your (my) entire existence for everything else besides yourself (myself), for if you or I don't, you and I are labeled "greedy capitalists".

In conclusion, the Great American Experiment so adequately described in the Declaration of Independence and in the United States Constitution is primarily about the right of the INDIVIDUAL exploring his or her own potential in a highly competitive, risk-oriented Free Enterprise economy. On the other hand, Democrats and Socialists believe in SOCIAL CAUSES being the necessary agenda mechanisms to elevate various minority groups into more prosperous life stations through incessant dependency on government handouts, food stamps, redistribution of wealth and "free stuff welfare". Most Democrat voters don't fully realize that the free market/free enterprise PRIVATE SECTOR creates wealth and prosperity in America and that the GOVERNMENT PUBLIC SECTOR consumes wealth through excessive taxation and through inefficient redistribution of wealth. In the final analysis, it's the longtime struggle of the INDIVIDUAL PURSUIT OF HAPPINESS principle versus the COLLECTIVE Robin Hood REDISTRIBUTION OF WEALTH philosophy that are relentlessly engaged in chaotic, contemporary political warfare. In a nutshell, Democrats and Socialists desire to artificially and COLLECTIVELY manufacture a Bureaucratic UTOPIA. The LEFTIES don't truly comprehend that "UTOPIA" can only be achieved on an INDIVIDUAL basis through personal sacrifice and through determined perseverance, ultimately leading the pursuer to success.

In my lifetime, I had been an English teacher for 34 years, had been a field manager on the world's largest cultivated blueberry farm for 18 summers, had owned boardwalk businesses (after borrowing money from relatives and banks and taking financial risks) on the Ocean City, Maryland Boardwalk for 16 summers and on the Rehoboth Beach, Delaware Boardwalk for 8 summers and on the Atlantic City Boardwalk for 3 summers, and I have written and published 54 hardcover/paperback/e-books. If I was Black or if I had been a foreign-born "Person of Color" living in America, I believe that I would have likewise accomplished my goal of authoring 54 books. The specific manuscripts might not have been exactly the same content as the present ones, but with steadfast desire and INDIVIDUAL resolve, the

54 books would still have been written, even if Hillary Clinton would falsely claim that the government had written those particular 54 books for me.

And in summary, I profess that over the years I've been blessed by proudly exercising my own 3 Card Playing Deck, "INDIVIDUAL Life, Liberty and Pursuit of Happiness!"

About the Author

Jay Dubya is author' John Wiessner's pen name and also his initials (J.W.) John is a retired New Jersey public school English teacher and he had taught the subject for thirty-four years. John lives in southern New Jersey with wife Joanne and the couple has three grown sons. John is the creator of fifty-five published books.

Jay Dubya has written adult satires *Fractured Frazzled Folk Fables and Fairy Farces* and *FFFF and FF, Part II. Black Leather and Blue Denim, A '50s Novel* and its sequel, *The Great Teen Fruit War, A 1960' Novel* and *Frat' Brats, A '60s Novel* are adult-oriented literary endeavors constituting a trilogy.

Pieces of Eight, Pieces of Eight, Part II, Pieces of Eight Part III and *Pieces of Eight, Part IV* are short story/novella collections featuring science fiction, paranormal and humorous plots and themes. *Nine New Novellas* is the companion book to *Nine New Novellas, Part II, Nine New Novellas, Part III* and *Nine New Novellas, Part IV.* And *So Ya' Wanna' Be A Teacher* is a satirical autobiography describing the author's thirty-four-year educational career in American public schools.

Ron Coyote, Man of La Mangia is adult humor and the work is an imaginative satire/parody on Miguel Cervantes' Don Quixote, published in 1605. *Mauled Maimed Mangled Mutilated Mythology* is a work that satires twenty-one famous ancient tales. *The Wholly* Book *of Genesis* and *The Wholly Book of Exodus* are also adult satirical humor. *Thirteen Sick Tasteless Classics, Thirteen Sick Tasteless Classics, Part II, Thirteen Sick Tasteless Classics, Part III* and *Thirteen Sick Tasteless Classics, Part IV* are adult satirical rewrites of famous short fiction.

John has also authored a trilogy of young adult fantasy novels, *Enchanta, Pot of Gold* and *Space Bugs, Earth Invasion. The Eighteen Story Gingerbread House* is a new collection of eighteen diverse and creative children's stories.

Jay Dubya likes '50s rock and roll music and he also enjoys pop' songs by the Beach Boys', Fleetwood Mac, the Eagles, the Rolling Stones, ELO, John Mellencamp and by John Fogerty. When not writing or listening to music, Jay Dubya likes watching 76ers basketball and Phillies and Yankees television baseball games.

Author Biography

Born in Hammonton, NJ in 1942, John Wiessner had attended St. Joseph School up to and including Grade 5. After his family moved from Hammonton to Levittown, Pa in 1954, John attended St. Mark School in Bristol, Pa. for Grade 6, St. Michael the Archangel School in Levittown for Grades 7 and 8 and then Immaculate Conception School, Levittown, Pa. for Grade 9. Bishop Egan High School, Levittown Pa was John's educational base for Grades 10 and 11, and later in 1960, the aspiring author graduated from Edgewood Regional High, Tansboro, NJ. John then next attended Glassboro State College, where he was an announcer for the school's baseball games and also read the nightly news and sports over WGLS, GSC's radio station.

John Wiessner had been primarily an English teacher in the Hammonton Public School System for 34 years, specializing in the instruction of middle school language arts. Mr. Wiessner was quite active in the Hammonton Education Association, serving in the capacities of Vice-President, building representative and finally, teachers' head negotiator for 7 years. During his lengthy teaching career, John had been nominated into "Who's Who among American Teachers" three times. He also was quite active giving professional workshops at schools around South Jersey on the subjects of creative writing and the use of movie videos to motivate students to organize their classroom theme compositions.

John Wiessner was very active in community service, being a past President of the Hammonton Lions Club, where he also functioned for many years as the club's Tail-Twister, Vice-President and Liontamer. John had been named Hammonton Lion of the Year in 1979 and in 2009 received the prestigious Melvin Jones Fellow Award, the highest honor a Lion can receive from Lions International.

John also was a successful businessman, starting with being a Philadelphia Bulletin newspaper delivery boy for two years in the late 1950s in Levittown, Pennsylvania. After his family moved back to New Jersey in 1959, John worked at his grandparents and his parents' farm markets, Square Deal Farm (now Ron's Gardens in Hammonton) and Pete's Farm Market in Elm, respectively. He later managed his wife's parents' farm market, White Horse Farms in Elm for three summers.

Also, in a business capacity, for 16 summers starting in 1967 John Wiessner had co-owned Dealers Choice Amusement Arcade on the Ocean City, Maryland boardwalk and also co-owned the New Horizon Tee-Shirt Store for eight summers (1973-'81) on the Rehoboth Beach,

528

Delaware boardwalk. In addition, "Jay Dubya" was a co-owner of Wheel and Deal Amusement Arcade, Missouri Avenue and Boardwalk, Atlantic City. And then, for 18 summers beginning in 1986, John had been the Field Manager in charge of crew-leaders for Atlantic Blueberry Company (the world's largest cultivated blueberry farm), both the Weymouth and Mays Landing Divisions.

After retiring from teaching in 1999, writing under the pen name Jay Dubya (his initials), John Wiessner became the author of 55 books in the genre Action/Adventure Novels, Sci-Fi/Paranormal Story Collections, Adult Satire, Young Adult Fantasy Novels and Non-Fiction Books. His books exist in hardcover, in paperback and in popular Kindle and Nook e-book formats.